W9-AWX-683

Giants

Also by Jack Ansell

His Brother, The Bear
The Shermans of Mannerville
Jelly
Gospel: An American Success Story
Summer
Dynasty of Air

Giants

A Novel
by Jack Ansell

ARBOR HOUSE
New York

Copyright © 1975 by Jack Ansell

All rights reserved, including the right of reproduction in whole or in part in any form. Published in the United States by Arbor House Publishing Company, Inc., New York, and simultaneously in Canada by Clarke, Irwin & Co., Ltd.

Library of Congress Catalog Card Number: 75–11149

ISBN: 0–87795–111–X

Manufactured in the United States of America

Lyrics from "As Time Goes By" are reprinted with permission of Warner Bros. Music. Copyright © 1931 Harms, Inc. All rights reserved.

51896

In Loving Memory
Sadie Flimin Ansell

All characters in this novel, with the exception of those identifiable by name, are fictitious, and any resemblance to persons living or dead is purely accidental.

Contents

O! it is excellent
To have a giant's strength, but it is tyrannous
To use it like a giant.
                                    —William Shakespeare

One
A Day in the Present
Monday

1

THE DAY is perhaps too dreary, too inclement, for the old man to make the long, tiring trip into the city, particularly when he doesn't really need to. The rain is restless, relentless, a numbing parade across the roof of the car. The fog it pricks, perforates, is thick, incursive. The sharp winds, cold damp, are everywhere present—penetrating, if only in imagination, even the well-heated, specially reinforced interior of the new Cadillac. Ellen had pleaded with him not to make the drive. Even his driver, Big Long, had hesitated bringing the car around. But he has always done what he wanted, gone where he wanted. Simply being eighty-one, nearing -two, and only three weeks up from another crucial viral pneumonia, aren't likely candidates for a change of mind or style. Not, at any rate, for David Abrams, chairman of the board and chief executive officer of United Broadcasting Companies, Inc. Some men are born to go to their graves in lusty obstinacy.

He enjoys the drive in, weather or no. It gives him the opportunity to query Big Long on what he and Mrs. Big watched on television last night, what they liked, didn't like. Not all his division presidents, not all his battalions of vice presidents, not the Board of Directors or affiliate Board of Governors, not the lot of them put together carry quite the weight of Big and Mrs. Big.

"You catch the *Larry Lester Show*, Big? You see the new comedy show, *Hooray for Hilda*?" His voice, even raised several octaves against the driving rain, is hardly the voice of a failing old man. Its vigor, full and unstrained, is as natural to the morning as his minimally lined smile, the firm set of his shoulders, the positive islands of blond through the gray of his hair, itself remarkably vigorous for a man of his years.

3

Big, on the other hand, is a man of forty who looks eighty, mainly because the broad, thick face is practically a map of the deep-rutted Dakota country he grew up in. He waits now, clears his throat, and since he rarely smiles (it only deepens the rills and gulleys), simply, expressionlessly, says, finally, "Stank."

David's smile is large. He knows his man. "Both of them?" he says. "Or just Lester?"

"Just Lester," says Big. "That other crap I leave for the missus."

It is the light of David's morning. He leans forward with an agility that unsettles even Big. "And just what specifically did Lester do that rankled you?" he asks.

"Talked too goddern 'in,' that's what he did." Big makes a sound not unlike a Dakotan coyote in his throat. "There's a limit how far these clowns should go, chief. I mean, talkin' to Dean Martin and Debbie Reynolds about all that show-business crap, laughin' and clickin' his heels over stuff nobody ever heard of, much less gives a crap about, it's goddern insultin' to the intel'gent viewer."

Bingo! David sits back again, smile wider than ever; vindication of his own opinion the sweeter part of it. With the ways and means to do something about it—still. After all these years, these times.

He leans back even further, bringing forth a treasured (and forbidden) cigar. Thinking. Smiling. Chuckling to himself.

Brighter day already, by God.

2

A FEW MILES AWAY, to the west, on the Bronx River Parkway, his son and heir, president and chief operating officer of United Broadcasting Companies, is somewhat more attuned to the day. The gray of Robert Abrams' face is indistinguishable from the morning's.

He is often like this—pale, drawn. At forty-eight, Robert is an exceptionally handsome man; tall, imposing. Only the dour pallor, bolstered by no-nonsense eyes, renders him formidable. He, too, is being driven; by a young, rather cocky Irish chauffeur, behind the wheel of a 1938 Rolls, to whom he consciously, even self-righteously, doesn't speak.

Today is impossible. Not that yesterday, the day before were any great shakes. These two or three weeks in September, October, when the television networks premiere their new nighttime schedules, are always the most racking of the year. This year even more so: the big competitive circus is compounded threefold by an upcoming Board of Directors meeting at which Robert will try, once and for all, to retire his meddlesome father. Of course, the pallor may also be attributable to his third wife, Jean Marie, who just before he left the house in Scarsdale announced that she too, like the others, was divorcing him. Her crisp parting shot—"Maybe you can get it up for Jean-Paul Sartre!"—still rings like cracked bells in his ears.

He too, like his father, leans further back in his seat. Thinking. But definitely not smiling. Not on this, this really impossible day.

3

Two OTHER KEY EXECUTIVES of UBC are driving to New York this morning as well, these from Connecticut: Adrian Miller, the fifty-year-old president of the Broadcast Division, and Mark Banner, the thirty-nine-year-old president of the Television Network. Their limousine, a Lincoln Continental, is on the Connecticut Turnpike; they both live on Westport's Gold Coast. With them is Adrian's wife, Joslyn, daughter of the man who founded UBC with David Abrams back in 1926, Bernard Strauss, and who died before the television network aired. She's making the trip in to lunch with two of UBC's top stars, Larry Lester and Sharon Moore, both of whose shows are UBC staples, while they're interviewed by the noted critic and columnist Bryson Randolph; "to lend a bit of brass class," as her husband quipped (spuriously? cynically?) when they opened the door for Mark. She sits between them.

Tension does, too. The day—next ten days—is for both men a knotty extension of the angst that it is for Robert. And not only because of the premieres, crucial as they are; or even the inevitable confrontation over David Abrams' "retirement." But because the outcome of each, the dust-clearing of both, determines whether Mark Banner himself remains or "respectfully" resigns.

The journey is slow, lethargic, nerve-bending by the mile; traffic in the snail's-pace fog is devastating, a devastation, in fact, that is driving the driver, Joe Castellano, bananas. Only his favorite vehicular pastime compensates for it. A small wiry man with the sharpest ears in the business, he has been driving UBC brass for more than a decade, missing little, if anything, said or unsaid, in the sanctified back seat of his sleek charge. Today he is particularly attuned. The hyped-up conversation of the two royal VIPs—Sir Adrian and Sir Mark, as he likes to think of them—along with the unusual tight-lipped silence from the blonde, throaty, spreading and fiftyish woman between them will make fine telling to the other UBC drivers during the long hours of lolling around the cavernous UBC lobby, waiting for calls to take Sir Big here, Lord Big there, a Waldorf luncheon, a UN conference, JFK; a discreet cache of cunt at the Plaza. Yessir, some fine telling today!

"Yessir, some very big days ahead," says Adrian Miller. He looks straight ahead as he does in most conversations; particularly personal/professional conversations. His eyes are a luminous gray, almost the same color as his full head of hair. He is a young, very virile fifty. Larry Lester, UBC's star comedian, calls him broadcasting's Dorian Gray.

By contrast Mark Banner, though equally handsome in more understated tones, looks older. A youthful blondness, lightness, have not worn so well on him. He smiles a lot to belie it. "We'll take Monday, Tuesday and Friday by ten share points," he says, his voice still slightly flat—after all these years in the East—with the bland inflections of Kansas, Missouri.

Smiling.

"It's still Wednesday, that's the key," says Adrian, still staring dead ahead. It's said casually, conversationally, but it lands on Joe Castellano's spine. Joe knows that it sits larger between them than the broad —Wednesday. Because on that long-awaited night Mark Banner's big and ballsy brainchild, *The UBC Magazine of the Air,* will have its premiere—a weekly three-hour format containing everything from comedy to drama, music to news, which will lay an egg or a golden goose, take your pick. Joe Castellano is sweating.

Mark is too, but you'd never know it. He's an expert at smiling away the wetness of crotch and armpit. "'Wednesday's child is full of woe'?" he says. Laughs.

Adrian makes it all right again. "'To conceive extravagant hopes of the future is the common disposition of mankind.' *I'm* the original quoter, remember?"

"Who with any sense of self-preservation can forget?" says Mark. "Self-preservation being the color of brown."

Joe Castellano is beside himself.

4

MARK ISN'T.

Smiles and all, he burns.

Adrian Miller, who brought him back to UBC as program chief seven years ago—from a shadowy major studio stable in a shaky Hollywood—is the kind of friend and patron you can bless from the grave he digs you.

"I spoke with Bobby just before we left the house," he says.

"Oh?" says Mark.

"He wanted to know if we'd gotten the overnight SIA on the Lester show."

The overnight SIAs—A. C. Nielsen Simultaneous/Instantaneous Autometer twenty-four-hour national ratings—are the passion of the industry these days. Lives and fortunes, if not exactly made or broken by them, are invariably buoyed or tainted by them. The significance (and even "Hello" and "Goodbye" are not without significance in Adrian Miller's mouth) lies in the fact that he mentions them at all.

"Lester's ratings can hardly be considered indicative of new season sampling," Mark says, Missouri voice slower and flatter by the minute. Ashamed of himself in a way; if truth be known, he thinks the entire ratings system and structure are as unsound as they are dishonest. But this is hardly the time to broach it. "Lester's ratings can hardly be considered indicative of new season sampling"—it is the best he can do for the moment.

"Bobby thinks otherwise," says Adrian.

"And beware of Bobby's otherwises," says Joslyn, the first words she has uttered, and these punctuated by a thrust of her restless behind. It is this insistent movement of hers, in fact, that compounds as much as anything else the whole dimension of Mark's day: Vivian this morning before he left the house, pretending sleep to avoid his hand on her hip; his own sleepless night with *Magazine* a nightmare; having to drive in like this, the Millers practically on top of him; the company's whole limousine syndrome, in fact—Joslyn Miller's ass is merely the prism of all of it.

"How's the stewardship report coming? For the Board meeting."

Adrian fishing again? Mark smiles. The old Talleyrand quip comes to mind: "Friend? He would toss his friends in the river in order to fish them out."

"Fine," Mark replies, switching his weight (he hopes) imperceptibly; knowing full well the neighborly expanse is going to follow him. "Sales Promotion's doing a damn good job. Best in-house presentation we've ever had."

"Visually, you mean."

"Damn fine visuals."

"Visuals are the smallest part of it."

It is really too much. What in hell is the bastard trying to do? Particularly with Castellano's ears practically a microphone two inches from his mouth. Mark decides not even to acknowledge it. Besides which, protecting his thigh and hip from Joslyn's early-morning interest takes concentration enough.

He must do something about these morning drives. He really must. Even if it means selling the house, moving from Westport altogether. That is, if he survives long enough even to be thinking about it.

The rest of the drive is eternal. There's conversation, of course—Adrian's mainly, and a few one-liners from Joslyn. Impersonal things. The Congressional hearing next month on pay-cable TV, direst threat yet to commercial television. The government's umpteenth threat on the so-called permissiveness content of prime-time programming. The spectre of children's programming on the trouble horizon again, a Senate subcommittee primed for new kicks. The News Department's new *People* series. The Sports Department's pitch for professional soccer. An Autumn Love Apple Ball scheduled at the Fairfield County Hunt Club in October, of which Good Queen Butt Baiter here is chairperson. Mark hears, records, only fragments of it. His responses are brief, perfunctory. Somewhere between Joslyn Miller's behind and Joe Castellano's ears he is behind the wheel of his own Porsche, blowing down the Thruway—free of the Millers, the Lincoln, the sponge of a driver. . . .

This above all. Even if he were President of the United States instead of president of a television network, he'd still never get used to being driven; the *idea* of being driven. It demoralizes him. He is always demoralized when his hands are inactive. He takes great pride in his hands. They are big hands, full hands; hands made to hold things. Steering wheels, anything. Anything solid, anything a man can grip, hold onto.

Pressure.

"Whatever you've heard this morning you keep to yourself. Right, Joe?" Miller addresses Castellano familiarly, as they skid onto the East River Drive; as he addresses him, cautions him, every morning of their lives—and more often than not at this very same turn into the city.

Castellano's smile seeks his, Mark's, in the rear-view mirror. Mark has no recourse but to return it. He knows—better than most, perhaps—that for all their bad grammar and cheek, their conspiratorial insinuations, the drivers of his crazy world are just that: the *drivers*. And you are wise to kiss their royal butts. Even though—especially if—you're president of a television network.

5

THEY ARRIVE—Mark and Adrian, Robert and David Abrams—within minutes of each other.

The UBC lobby is brilliant with brass. The ground-floor receptionist, a dimpled and fading beauty, twitches, her excited breasts practically talking to each other. The uniformed guards and elevator starters posture and beam like good-behavior soldiers. The morning traffic of employees, visitors, messengers and tourists takes on—seems to take on—a brisker pace; a collective, self-conscious pace. Old Isaac Meyer, behind the counter of his lobby concession stand, preens as though he's been capitally blessed.

It's a circus of a lobby, actually. The great floor-to-ceiling windows are draped with bright green sequins symbolizing the old days—the radio days—when UBC was known as the Green Network, the Fun Network. The speckled green tiles of the floor, an imitation terrazzo, look even more counterfeit under wet sloshing feet. Luminous "show" banners are everywhere—Sharon Moore, Larry Lester and *Magazine* most prominent among them. Oversized peonies pack the space between windows, the corners. There are tongue-in-cheek names for them—the steel-and-concrete structures along midtown Sixth Avenue that house the four national networks: 30 Rock (NBC), Black Rock (CBS), Hard Rock (ABC) and Schlock Rock—UBC. David Abrams has always laughed it off; the public feels an affinity, an indelible closeness to Show Business, to the mystery and magic inside the building's fantasy-filled walls—that's all that matters. His son, Robert, has a minor coronary every time he enters it.

Discomfiture is plainly evident on his face this morning. Mark, observing him, and in spite of his own mood, is amused. Given his way, he thinks (and it could damn well be within days), Robert Abrams would turn Disneyland into Dismalland—Lord, he can practically see it: Edwardian mirrors with Wedgwood pilasters and gilded oak leaves, the "Southern" elegances with which his mother— David Abrams' first wife—had been so obsessed. Maybe even dark funereal drapes to shut out forever the nagging glare of the old Green, the old Fun, Network.

Amusement, however, gives way again to irritability as another inevitable morning ritual confronts him. The Elevator Pecking Game, he has come to call it, and no one—not even his wife, Vivian, in her more sympathetic times—knows how deeply he's offended. With any number of "up" elevators in four busy rows of them, to stand aside (even with Adrian, the Abramses; *especially* with Adrian, the Abramses), waiting for the special lift marked "Executive Personnel Only," while hundreds of employee eyes glare their understandable resentment and envy—some way to begin a day. And this morning, to compound it, the privileged echelon is joined by Fred Wiener, vice president in charge of Programming for the television network (not to mention the Old Man's adopted "grandson," Robert's "nephew"), and Gerald McAlister, corporate vice president in charge of Public Relations. Carl, the head dispatcher, grandly switches the mechanism from automatic to manual, lending personal escort to the prize catch.

Nothing unusual is said really; said or done. The exchange of greetings, the pleasantries, while hardly profuse (they never are when Robert Abrams' are among them), are polite enough. But Carl, Mark suspects, will have a wealth of material to dissect and dramatize when he gets back down to the lobby for the morning rap with the other dispatchers, the guards, the worldly-wise drivers. Except for David Abrams, who's long past hiding his amusement, nerve ends are as exposed as inadequate wiring.

Adrian's deference to the Old Man is the most conspicuous. Robert's self-conscious detachment runs a close second. David Abrams, keenly aware, turns to him—Mark—somewhere between floors twenty and thirty, and poking him playfully in the ribs says, "We're pleased as punch with you, you know. Ellen and me," causing the loudest silence in the eight-year history of the holy elevator.

Gerald McAlister gets off at thirty-two, Fred Wiener at thirty-six, and he, Mark, at forty. And while not ordinarily given to corporate fantasizing, he has a field day cramming thoughts into Robert Abrams' and Adrian Miller's and even the Old Man's heads as the inner-sanctum car speeds on to the forty-second floor.

6

As HAPPENS PRACTICALLY EVERY MORNING when he arrives at his offices —just as he's passing among his executive secretary and her two assistants in the large outer office appended to his own—the telephone rings. And David, youthful twinkle on his tongue as well as in his eyes, says, "The star of stage, screen, radio and television . . ." and sure enough, it is: his wife, Ellen.

David, shaking his head in pleasurable, familiar anticipation, takes the call on the phone of one of his assistant secretaries.

"David? You're all right? The drive in wasn't too much for you?"

" 'Damn, said the duchess as she reached for her cigar!' " Which he does, a Corona-Corona smuggled in from Cuba.

"I know exactly what you're doing," she says. "While you're quoting that old saw about the best first line of a short story ever written, if only there'd been a story to go with it, you're acually lighting up one of those damn things, which I needn't remind you Dr. Rosenberg specifically—"

"I love you, Star."

A laugh. A sigh.

"Do you, David?"

"Cross my heart."

"I'm silly calling like this, I know. It's just that this last bout you had . . ."

"I'm perfectly swell, really. Just swell. Ready for the day. Or some of it, anyway. I'll probably drive back midafternoon or so."

"I hope it's not as nerve-racking as I know it will be."

"The premieres, you mean?" He laughs. "I've already had a taste of it. In the elevator. You should see Bobby's face. Long and dour, you might say. And Adrian's. Inscrutable, like always."

"And Mark Banner's?"

"Hard to say. I suppose because it's harder on him than any of them. Whatever the cockamamie season brings."

"I wish him well," she says. "I wish him very well. He's my kind of people. I suppose Freddie's in too?"

"Wiener? Oh, yes. Not knowing which way to turn. I suppose spitting on your finger to test which way the wind's blowing is too old-fashioned these days. Might help him, though. Lord knows the wind can blow any which way in this business. The quicksilver business . . . that's what Bernie used to call it, remember?"

"Well, just make sure you don't stay there all day. And don't get too deep in the politics, not today. Promise?"

"You know something? A voice like that and I could make you a star. If I tried hard."

"I said, 'Promise?' "

"I said I love you. And goodbye."

"If you light that goddamn cigar . . ."

"See you around four, old love, old Star."

At which ring-off he fondly lights his Corona-Corona, affecting a quick soft-shoe and bow, to the delighted smiles of his ladies.

IF THE UBC LOBBY is a posthumous Barnum invention, credit the forty-second floor to the ghost of Louis B. Mayer. From the thick gold carpeting of its corridors to the paintings and tapestries on its pure white walls, it is the way Hollywood once envisioned New York. It is also a plush monument to the life and times of David Abrams, reflecting the reality as well as the legend of an extraordinary span, wholly appropriate to the last of the great entertainment czars.

There are only five offices on forty-two—David's, his son Robert's, his son's close friend Adrian Miller's, Paul DuBarry's (president in charge of all nonbroadcast activities) and Arthur Merck's (senior vice president and general counsel). And all of them, except perhaps Robert's, is almost a set from *Poor Little Rich Girl* or maybe *Executive Suite*. Robert's, while at first glance of the same fantasy-inspired genre, is modified by: an Italian marble coffee table from the estate of the late Count Ciano; a discreet teakwood escritoire reputedly owned and used in his later years by Thomas Mann; an intricately carved mahogany breakfront from his mother's old Shoreham Drive home in Atlanta. Even the desk, a contemporary expanse of steel, glass and brilliantly polished rosewood, long enough and wide enough to keep even intimates at their proper distance, seems nouveau in the presence of an Empire desk set reproduced from the original in the Josephine collection at Versailles.

Robert sits at the oversized desk this morning, with little appreciation of these treasured possessions; little appreciation, in fact, of any possessions at all as he labors through his morning-arrival ritual: a cursory but selective glance at the day's mail; a quick jotting of ideas and reminders on an "R.A."-embossed memo pad; a hurried swallow of two vitamin C tablets and one A with a half glass of iced water (one cube); an annoyed foray of fingers through alarmingly thinning hair, the well-kept fingernails of the other hand tapping impatiently on the desk; a tug at his tie, tightening it to discomfort—deliberately; a forceful adjustment of the everpresent handkerchief in the pocket of his jacket; an authoritative clearing of his throat; all with measured, if nervous, sips of steaming black coffee with chicory (his late mother's prescription for practically everything) served him by his senior executive secretary, Miss Lily Pinkerton, whose tall, mannish presence stands at corseted attention beside him.

Waiting his pleasure.

Or pain.

"We'll dictate later in the morning," he says, pushing the neat folder of mail aside; fingering for a long thoughtful second the embossed ROBERT SACKMAN ABRAMS on its elegant leather cover. "Any calls?"

"Only the dining room," says Miss Lily, "wanting to confirm your luncheon tomorrow with Mr. Miller and the senators." Her voice sounds typewriter-crisp, full of commas.

"You checked with the senators' offices?"

"They look forward."

"They damn well ought to."

Fingers again—restive, impatient; angry even; but almost loving on the capital R, capital S. The buzz of his intercom stills them. It's his father.

"Bobby?"

"Yes, father?"

"On the *Larry Lester Show*. It's getting too . . . esoteric. That *is* the word for it?"

"It's according to what you mean."

"You know damn well what I mean. Too showbizzy 'in.' Fruitcake 'in.' All right?"

"We'll . . . look into it, father."

"We? Who's we?"

"Adrian, of course. And Mark, Fred Wiener—"

"Yeah. Wiener. I might have known. His kind of 'dahling' crap all right. Not Mark's, that's for sure. I'll talk to Mark myself on it."

"Father . . . please. I've asked you a hundred times not to go directly to people, whoever they are. It . . . it only complicates things. I'm sure Adrian can get the point across to Mark without—"

"I'll talk to Mark."

Click. Robert's fingers resume their impatient activity, as he snaps to Miss Lily, "Have Adrian Miller come in here. Now. Immediately."

7

IN HIS OWN OFFICE—more on the order of David Abrams' than Robert's; nothing of sentiment mars its impersonal grandeur—Adrian Miller waits a calculated twelve minutes; no more, no less. He is the only one at UBC who can get away with it, and he knows it. He spends the time drinking coffee, smoking a cigarette, buffing his fingernails; also fantasizing about how he can get out of cocktails with his wife, Joslyn (who's in the city for shopping and the talent luncheon and will be changing clothes at the company apartment in the Bristol Hotel for dinner and the theatre with the James Mortimers of Chase Manhattan—he also sits as a senior member of UBC's Board of Directors), so he can spend the hour or so more peacefully being blown by Karen Green, UBC's leading lady on Daytime Television's highest-rated soap, *Love and Life*. He also indulges himself in visions of Bobby Abrams seething while he waits, an exercise that always makes the twelve minutes pass like two. Bobby, while surprisingly efficient as chief operating officer, can be an awful ass at times. Who better than he, Adrian, to apply the corrective ... ?

At the appointed hour he sets his most ingratiating smile and, sailing past one of his secretaries (a tempting bronze statue named Eve he's determined to crack, unwritten office rules or not), walks across the field of gold to his boss's and best friend's office.

Robert is the way he usually is.

"Why do you have to do this, Adrian? And don't tell me you were on long distance. I checked."

Adrian is all grin. "Come on, Bobby. You've got the planet by the balls. Stop dramatizing."

"I am not dramatizing. And it's not necessary for you to come bounding in here like a . . . a capuchin monkey—"

"I think you mean Cheshire cat."

"I know goddamn well *what* I think, *when* I think, *how* I think!"

"Yes, *sir*."

It's like this with them. Has been, ever since they were young men together—boys—in the army overseas. If large parts (chunks!) of Robert's earlier years are shadowy retreats to his consciousness, the weeks and months in a replacement depot outside Manila in the Philippines in 1945 are not. They are as much his burden today—his shame today—as they were through the actual hell of them. This morning, for some reason—Adrian's condescension, perhaps—they are festering more than ever.

"I am a corporal—and glad of it—in this miserable army because my big-shot father finally got it through his head that one phone call to one of his so-called friends in our nation's capital to use his fucking influence would have created in front of his wonderful chrome-and-gilt office a hara-kiri act by his own unbeloved son. . . ." Half-drunk in the Repple Depple Rag just off the post, pouring himself out to the only friend he'd made in the army (the only friend he'd had in his whole life, really), Staff Sergeant Adrian Miller of the adjutant general's staff, who talked with him about things like books and philosophy and life's mysteries and dreams . . . A dark night, dreary; moonless night. Dreamier, drunker, passed in haze; seen through haze. Taunted from a nearby table by guys from his barracks—big, brawling recruits—"Rich suck-ass Jew, laps up sergeant shit." Dragged from the sound of it by his strong-armed friend—strong-armed, strong-willed, alternately gentle and malevolent friend—finding himself at some time, in some space in the crazed drunk hours, in the arms of an Alabang whore named Lina in the first frenzied penetration of his nineteen years, coming to consciousness later—days and days later—in an army hospital in Manila, half dead from the reported beating by the animals from his barracks, having the will to live thanks only to the long, faithful, kind and cruel ministrations of his only friend, whose life from that time on would be so inseparable from his that . . .

Which the master, which the slave?
Which the noble, which the knave?

Lines scribbled in a hand almost unable to move during the long months of convalescence; that blessed, cursed time before the return to the States, before the meeting of Adrian with his cousin Joslyn, before his father's gratefulness to Adrian had led to a position with his UBC radio network, before the plunge into television, which Adrian had embraced like a lover, before . . .

No, not before. During. During those agonizing weeks, months, stretching into years, when that one night's orgasm might prove to be the only one he'd know, ever know . . . ?

"I promise thee, Zeus"—pompous invocation, perhaps, but somehow fitting. After all, having felt by age thirteen junked by father—junk network, junk wares, junk ex-girlfriend famous damn singer to humili-

ate his loving gentle mother—"that should the gods see fit for me to get up again, to live, I will not abandon, not ever, this friend you've seen fit to give me in my worst, my lowest time . . ."

That, too, in his fear, in those hours of delirium . . .

No, he has never forgotten it—nor at times ever quite forgiven it. This decidedly is one of those times.

"We have to be absolutely letter-perfect in this thing," he says, more than a trace of annoyance still edging his voice. "We can leave nothing to chance, nothing. And central to all of it is timing. *My* timing. When I want to see you I want to see you—*now*. When and if you become president of this so-called empire I don't think it reasonable to expect any less promptness and courtesy to the new chairman of the Board than you always manage to show father. I notice you're practically in his doorway before he even hangs up from buzzing you."

Adrian takes a white leather chair across from him, grins even more broadly, and lighting a Haitian cigar says, "Go fuck yourself, Bobby," billowy and aromatic as the sudden smoke.

Robert, who it is known hates cigar smoke, smiles; what passes for a smile. "You love to inflict pain, don't you, Adrian?" he says. "All the time telling yourself it's some kind of horseplay."

Adrian proffers smoke rings. "You were saying, Bobby?"

"I was saying—and no more games, Adrian—these are the crucial days. The Board must be absolutely—"

"We're seeing the Mortimers tonight. Dinner, theatre."

"Jim Mortimer's only a fraction of it. A large fraction, I'll grant you, but simply a shoring-up operation, to borrow from father's vernacular. And Stampler and Kastle would go along with him if he suggested a midnight swim across the Hudson. No, it's hardly Jim Mortimer I'm worried about."

Adrian simply shrugs. "If you mean Hal Borland, rest your balls. I'm lunching with him Thursday. At Twenty-one." Harold Borland is chairman of the Board of Silvertone Rubber and one of David Abrams' oldest and closest associates.

"Two martinis and sautéed frog legs do not constitute an overnight transformation," says Robert—so pompously that even he has to smile.

"Would you buy the old Miller charm?" says Adrian. "Not to mention logic, appeal to the most intimate of passions, namely the pocketbook, and perhaps a subtle, not insensitive, suggestion of blackmail?"

Robert's icy smile is unchanged. "You've always had candor, Adrian," he says. "Never honesty, but . . . candor." Smile collapses, entirely. "I want to hear nothing more. Borland controls three votes. That's all I know, all I need to know. How you manage it, the rest—"

"We may have three martinis."

Robert relaxes somewhat. At least, his restless hands are stilled.

"It's going to be a terrible week," he says. "So much riding on it." He looks up and away. "It may also be the beginning of the end for your bright protégé Mr. Banner," he says. "I presume I'll have the overnights by phone every morning?"

"Like clockwork," says Adrian.

"Like hell," says Robert. "Most of the rabbits do it in their pants when they pass me in the hall—boss's son, you know—much less having to talk for five minutes on the phone. Let them call you. *You* call *me*." Long sigh. "Terrible week. He looks well, doesn't he?"

"Who?"

"Father. He looks exceptionally well. You'd never know he'd been ill."

"Yes," says Adrian, his only inarticulate murmur of the morning.

"He's starting in again. The Lester show. Big Long representing thirty million television homes again. He says he's talking to Mark about it. Tell Mark to go through the motions of talking with Lester anyway."

"Your ball game," says Adrian, knowing well how eager his friend's fingers are to rake the smile off his face, if nothing else.

"I want a personal report from Banner at ten o'clock every morning," he says at Adrian's retreating back as he starts to leave, reaching in a drawer for one of his innumerable, often unnamable pills. "Every morning this week. Here in this office. Right here in this office." He looks off, fusses with his tie. "Lunch today at the Laurent?" he says quietly, abruptly. "I . . . I need to talk to you, goddamn it."

His friend and associate—and nemesis—pauses, the crinkly remains of his smile intact, by a genuine Louis XV commode near the door. "Sure, kid," he says. "Lunch at the Laurent." His exit is more expansive, if that is possible, than his entrance.

THE OBJECT of their discussion—at least part of it—sits at the oversized marble-top desk in his own office on forty, reviewing the day's mail and agenda with his senior secretary of long standing (she had been with him in the old UBC days, as well as in Hollywood during his stint with Metro, tramping back to New York with him when he returned to the network), who by now reads him like a well-thumbed copy of, say, *Tom Swift*. He is all business this morning, and therefore all knots inside: Edith Stewart (forty-five, full-chested, stylish, unpretty; sharp as a rapier) knows precisely the role she must play.

"As for the morning," she says, "it's everybody and his twin brother. All two-headed monsters, of course. But separating wheat from chaff like the indispensable doll I am, we can boil it down to these. Mr. Abrams—Abrams *père*—his office just called asking that you do everything you can to clear lunch today. In his office, not the dining room. I do envy you, sire. Mr. McAlister called, says he knows it's a bitch of a day—he didn't say 'bitch' actually, he said 'heck of,' the candy-ass—but could you possibly see your way clear to a few minutes around eleven. Says it's terribly. Yuch. Joe Warren at KXTL in Memphis wants you to call. Seems he's boiling over about the 'gawdam vilence' on the Saturday-night movie. And Bob Welch on the Coast says it's barely dawn out there and he hopes the hour gives you some idea of how urgent it is he talk to you. Oh, and Ed Lowry at McMahon and Peterson called. Said he won't talk to anyone except Mark Banner about his first-quarter budget. Usual. Who first, sire?"

Mark draws a quick graph in his mind. It's the way he always sorts out people and ideas. His mind, he sometimes thinks, is an endless roll of ruled paper. *Yellow* ruled paper, the way he feels today. Anyway, now—four lines, two columns. Column One: Name. Column Two: Importance.

Now . . .

The Old Man. Lunch. His office, no less. The rib punch in the elevator: *We're pleased as punch with you, you know. Ellen and me.* Of what help can I of all people be to him now? Of what harm can he be to me? Lunching privately! Well, no matter. The gods, even crippled ones, call, and you go, you run. You . . .

McAlister. Keeper of the precious Corporate Image. Rhetoric garbage. But he's Robert Abrams', Adrian Miller's boy; what can you do?

Joe Warren. Vice president and general manager of KXTL-TV in Memphis, a major primary affiliate. More importantly, Warren is one of the most influential of the Southern station people. But the call, violence on television being as perennial as *I Love Lucy* reruns, can wait.

Welch. Case of producer's nerves, probably. Second thoughts on which episode of the *Anna Layton Show* should kick it off. As if hanging around New York for six weeks while they tried to sell the damn thing weren't enough. Too many pep pills. He too can wait.

Ed Lowry. Sticky, that one. No more than a million, million and a half, in his television budget for St. Peter Aspirins for the whole quarter, and sitting on it like a virgin on sand. But he'll have to call him. McMahon has too many important clients.

"Tell you what," he says. "Have Barbara bring my coffee, get me Goldberg in Sales Planning, cancel my lunch date with Lee Godkin at United Artists—it *was* with Godkin, wasn't it?—and I'll call Lowry later. Deal?"

Edith smiles, writes "McAlister" by the "11:00" on his desk calendar in her neat round hand, and starts out. "You're due at the screening of that possible midseason replacement at four," she says at the door. "*Home Town*?"

"Yes. Did you want Steve Lilly there?"

"Better," he says. "And ask Maury Sherman in Research."

"I'll call him."

"Thanks. Oh, and Edith . . ." He grins up at the plain, intelligent face that has reflected his bidding through eleven years and five positions. "McAlister notwithstanding," he says, "it's going to be a bitch of a day."

9

WHEN SHE HAS GONE, Mark looks absently about the big, arresting, surprisingly spare office, his eyes coming to rest on a built-in color television set at the other end of it. His gaze is fixed. The lapse, however, lasts no more than a few seconds. In a way, it is like an hour's sleep. It happens several times a day. He sleeps little at night.

He is reaching for the morning's mail, which Edith has placed neatly to one side of the desk, when Barbara Ermeling, her assistant, comes in with his coffee. Mark steels himself for the inevitable ritual. It got started only weeks after the quiet, pale brunette (given, incongruously, to practically X-rated miniskirts) was transferred from UBC Sales Service to his personal staff. Each morning she brings his coffee, perfectly prepared—cream, no sugar—and placing it always to the right of him somehow positions herself so that his right elbow touches one of her small but insinuating breasts. The phenomenon lasts all of three seconds. Neither of them ever acknowledges it. He finds it somehow a pleasant relief—the uninvolving contrivance of it all. And considerably more inspiring than Joslyn Miller's ass.

This morning, of course, is no different. Three seconds. "See if Edith got Goldberg in Sales Planning," he says. Her "Yes, sir" is as crisp and unrevealing as it is every morning, but as he continues scanning the mail he has the distinct impression that she's lingering a moment too long. Like the wrong move of a performer in a well-rehearsed play, it disturbs him. He finally looks up inquiringly, but already her back is to him, and her buttocks, neatly turned, are almost reproving. His buzzer sounds.

"Yes, Edith?"

"Marv Goldberg's out of the building. Sid Newton's sending up a draft of your speech for Cincinnati next week. You well into your coffee?"

"Two sips."

"Fred Wiener's out here. Says it's urgent."

"When isn't it?"

"Send him in?"

"Send him in."

The vice president in charge of network programming is an impatient man. It shows in his eyes as well as his quick, acquisitive body. He is of medium height, medium weight—practically everything about him, in fact, is medium, however tall and imposing he looms in sacred elevators. His hair is dark, not too. His complexion as well would have to be called dark, although often during a day, such as now, he appears almost fair. Women find him particularly attractive. More than one has described his appeal vaguely as Jewish Good Looks. "But clean Jewish," Mark's wife, Vivian, said once. This inch, Mark sometimes thinks, is more than a mile. Miles more than a mile. In New York, anyway. At UBC.

"Well, Fred," he says, "good morning again. Sorry we couldn't chat more in the elevator. But brass being brass . . ."

Fred Wiener doesn't wait until he's finished. "Have you seen the overnight twenty-four market ratings, Mark?" Unsmiling, he pushes himself against the desk.

Mark nods. "Research called me at home."

"And you can *sit* there?"

"Why don't you?"

Wiener's eyes are wide. "Jesus! Our first premiere and the goddamn thing comes up with a twenty-seven share of audience. A lousy twenty-seven goddamn share! And crapped on by repeats, no less. Here . . ." He tosses a newspaper clipping on the desk. "Bryson Randolph's column this morning. Seen it?"

"Barbara hasn't brought the crow's nest in yet." Mark runs his eyes down the long first paragraph of a two-column feature headed "TV CRITIC AT LARGE: HOORAY FOR WHAT?"

UBC-TV premiered its new season last evening with a 30-minute situation comedy about a trailer-traveling female manager of a hill-

billy singer, something called "Hooray for Hilda." Undoubtedly the
show's producers and some of the network's VIPs said "Hooray" a few
times, or the silly thing would never have gotten past a script. It's
doubtful that anybody else who saw it said "Hooray." Even the twelve-
year-old mentality, which TV's most ardent critics use as the viewing
average, must have been insulted. The big question is whether this
fiasco of a kickoff is indicative of what's in store for us the rest of the
week. As of this writing, there's no way of knowing what kind of
sampling the show got (sampling is an industry term for a small
tune-in group that's supposedly representative of the viewing public
at large), but it's my guess that if the first three minutes of it was
considerable, the last twenty-seven minutes were a bust. Too early to tell,
of course, but one or two more atrocities like "Hilda" and Mark Banner
& Company could be in serious trouble. As it is, UBC—which began
slipping badly last year after several seasons as Number One or Two in
the ratings race—is entering the new season on pretty shaky ground.
Meanwhile,

Mark pushes it aside. "Looks like you'll have to take the fag to
lunch again," he says. This is by now a standard joke at UBC. Every so
often Bryson Randolph, considered by many the dean of television
critics, launches a full-scale attack on the network, which only a quiet
lunch or two with Fred Wiener seems to soften. This morning, however, Fred Wiener looks anything but amused.

"I'd laugh," he says, "except that laughing all the way to the grave
isn't quite my bag."

Mark leans back in his chair. "If one night and one show have you
this balled up," he says, "how the hell do you expect to get through
the rest of the week?"

Wiener practically falls onto the Swedish-modern sofa to the side
of the desk. "Come off it, Mark," he says. "This is Fred Wiener, remember? You've been in this business long enough to know what first
impressions mean. What looks like a brush fire can send a whole
goddamn forest up in smoke. And this time we can't even dust off
the old standby, 'If the critics rate it low, A. C. Nielsen rates it high.'
What was it you told the Board last month, Mark? 'Like it or not, we
rise or we fall by the numbers.' See? I can quote you verbatim."

"Well, your own dramatic performance isn't going to alter things,"
Mark says. "We all knew *Hilda* was a long shot in the first place. But
Adrian Miller wanted it and Selby Foods wanted it and we're committed to it. Thirteen weeks of it. So relax, pal, it's earlier than you
think. And speaking of coming off it . . . since when did one number
and one half-baked review determine a show's future? This is television, Freddie, not the Broadway theatre. And in the second place,

I don't think you came in here for a good old buddy-buddy commiseration. What's bugging you, Fred?"

Fred Wiener's eyes, if everywhere but on Mark before, are focused sharply on him now. "I had nothing to do with selecting that particular episode," he said. "For the first airing, I mean. *I* wanted the Nashville one, remember?"

"But bowed to my good judgment," says Mark. "How could I forget?"

"I just wanted it set straight."

Mark smiles. "Bob Abrams call you?"

"At home. I managed to make him think it was all of us—you, me, Steve, the studio, all of us. So this setting-the-record-straight is twixt thee and me. But I'll tell you something, Mark. Your good judgment was a little off this time, baby. Just a little fucking off."

Mark brings both elbows to the desk, his hands clasped firmly under his chin. "Out of the four they've shot," he says, "this one was the best. I thought so last week and I think so now. It was a matter of choosing between evils and I've never been one to let hindsight give me the hives."

Wiener stands up. "Well, it's done," he says. "I just hope it doesn't affect tonight. The newspaper ads are good, anyway. I'm glad you talked Adrian into full pages in the *Times* and *Post*. Jesus, I hope *Felony* goes through the roof. Christ knows it's a soft time period."

"Fred." Mark's head is cocked. "Why don't you go get a drink or a piece of tail or something? At this rate you won't last till Wednesday."

Wiener's tone is lighter. "Let's just hope that by Wednesday it won't be *our* ass," he says. At the door he pauses. "At least I'm open with you, Mark. I always have been. And Bob and the Old Man know it."

Mark nods. Open, he thinks. How long ago had he learned that when a man says he's open, that's when he has the most to conceal? And *our* ass, yet. When in hell had it ever been *our* ass?

"Take care, Fred," he says. "And calm down. By next Sunday we'll be roses."

"If you say so, Mark. If you say so." Adding casually, very casually, "Amen."

There is a curious vibration when he's gone. Mark knows it's the vibration of his own thoughts. The words come: Wiener's got to go. His family connections aside, he's got to go.

You've got to go, Freddie *boy* . . . Freddie *baby* . . .

His half-smile is thoughtful.

10

EDITH STEWART's is thoughtful, too. That she smiles at all when he passes her on his way out is in itself unusual, for Fred Wiener is not one of her favorite people. She has been wary of him for two years, ever since he came to UBC—and not just because his stepmother is the Old Man's daughter, Robert Abrams' sister, Mandy Jo. Edith, like Mark, has come up through the ranks, and the fact that Fred Wiener, who produced one moderately successful musical off-Broadway and one unsuccessful (and now forgotten) movie comedy, came to the medium green—and in such a key position—makes him, at least to Edith's mind, something of an interloper. Edith, as she freely admits, can't see beyond her nose; that is, beyond Mark Banner's.

She hasn't heard the conversation behind the apple-green door, except the brief "Amen" when it opened, but she knows instinctively what was said, or not said. The same nose she can't see beyond is doubly valuable to Mark, for in its protectiveness is the imbalance of a radar-equipped antenna, which catches whiffs of the rotten in Denmark, indeed the great globe itself, long before other nostrils are even alerted. They have faced downwind where Fred Wiener is concerned from the very beginning, and in her offhand way she has passed her caution on to Mark. This morning, however, there are more than a few faint whiffs; the office is positively suffocating with them. Which is why she smiles at him when he passes her. Instinct again. Fred Wiener is coming out from under the table.

But then so are a lot of things, she thinks. Her own restlessness the last few days—the sleeplessness at night—have gone beyond mere instinct; Lord knows beyond caution. And it isn't just last night's disaster, or Bryson Randolph's column this morning, or even Fred Wiener's sly "Amen" before he left. It's . . . Oh, Lord, she thinks, a whole profusion of things; a real alley of things. Things not really very real through all the unreal months just past—those hectic dreamlike months of doing, always doing, always going. Mark back and forth to the Coast with Fred Wiener every week, first to see the presentations of the various studios for series pilots, then the decisions, the mountains of scripts, the rewrites, the rejections, the go-aheads; the pilots themselves. The pilots: screening them, studying them, reveling in them, throwing up from them; and always the big question, the big thorn: Will it sell? Will it hit thirty share or above? Mark in and out with Steve Lilly in Sales until even time is farcical—the hurried conferences, the major clients, the crises, the victories too. And no hour free of the pressures from Abrams *fils*, from Adrian Miller, the outguessing of the other networks, the final schedule; above all, the schedule. *UBC can't afford even one under-thirty-share night. . . .*

The words are Adrian Miller's, but Edith hears them everywhere: in hasty good mornings, in lame good nights, in doubtful sleep. Only last week, Allen, her husband (an uncomplicated cemetery plot salesman, thank God), said, "I hope your Mark Banner walks off with a hundred share. Maybe then I'll get mine." She laughed—"When don't you get yours?"—but in truth she has carried the office home much too often this year; in itself more telling than she likes to think. In all the years with Mark, wherever he's led—radio, TV programming, the West Coast studios, UBC programming again, the network presidency itself —in all the years she has never doubted him. Lord knows she doesn't doubt him now. Mark Banner is one of the chosen ones, the rare, unerring, almost magic ones; it's in everything he says, everything he touches. Even Bryson Randolph had to admit it, just two seasons back. She can remember the column by heart. *Why is UBC far and away the nation's most popular network? You need look no further than Mark Banner. Call it by whatever name you will, this young programming giant is Television's modern messiah. He seems to know what the people want, perhaps even need, before the people themselves know it. While older heads reject practically everything that isn't formula—whatever that is—Mr. Banner breaks down walls as if they were made of paper. Certainly he has raised the standards of both daytime serials and children's programming, insisting on themes more attuned to today's youth in the former, more live-action "inspiration" themes in the latter. His influence has enlivened both newscasts and news documentaries, not to mention the beefing up of prime-time specials. As for prime-time entertainment series . . . well, the bulk of his program ideas may not be great, in any critical sense—many of them, in fact, are without real depth or distinction—but they're daring, and more often than not they work. What's more, they sell. Sponsors and public alike appear to be eating them up, and it looks as if the feast might just go on until the millennium.*

Where has it gone wrong? In only two years, where has it gone wrong? Oh, UBC still enjoys a parity with the other networks, but . . . It's one thing to smell out people, she thinks; even easier to smell out motives. But it's quite another to smell out influences. The sleek snake who just left, for example. Is he responsible for the fickle millions who change tastes the way they change socks? Certainly Mark has overridden Fred Wiener at every turn. And Steve Lilly in Sales. Is Lilly responsible? Did he overinfluence last year's schedule? Hasn't Sales always influenced practically every series on the air? Or Gerald Mc-Alister—Adrian Miller—even the Abramses themselves. Have they gotten too involved with the day-to-day life of the network? Surely Mark handles them with the precision of a past master. Or maybe all of them—all of them together. Have they spirited themselves through some crazy chemistry into sixty-eight million American homes, shouting, "You made him, now break him, all you have to do is turn a dial." Or Mark. Mark himself. Has Mark . . . ?

Edith pulls herself up short. Nose or no nose, she thinks, it is outrageous to let Fred Wiener get her back on the trip to nowhere. Briskly, she completes a call to Gerald McAlister's secretary—"Yes, Mr. Banner will be by at eleven"—and reaches resolutely for a file of FCC correspondence she started bringing up to date earlier in the morning.

"Barbara," she says, turning to ask her assistant if she's finished with the morning's newspaper clippings. But something in the way the girl looks at her makes her pause. It is a curious look, in a way almost fearful; but entreating, too. The look, Edith thinks, of a caged white mouse. It takes several seconds before the girl looks down at her work again, and Edith, with one too many thoughts, can get on with hers.

11

WHEN FRED WIENER is back in his own office on thirty-six, he says to his own secretary, Linda—a criminally beautiful redhead in her early twenties—"So who sought the lord and master in his absence?"

"Steve Lilly called," she says, not bothering to look up from her nails, which at the moment she is painting a lively silver.

"And?"

"He's having lunch on Wednesday with somebody named Rick Toliver from some agency or other. Said you'd know. Wants you to join them if you're free."

"Am I?"

"Um-hmm."

He laughs softly. "That's too bad. Because I'm afraid we'll have to wait for a bigger fish than Rick Toliver. Let Lilly lunch with him. I don't even return his phone calls." When the girl's expression doesn't change he says, less softly, "Ask Greer to come up. Right away." Joel Greer, in charge of Program Development, is with the rest of the Program Department on the eighteenth floor. The girl nods, reaching delicately for a pencil to dial with. Fred goes into his office and closes the door.

Wiener's Workshop, as his office is sometimes called, looks like anything but an office, much less a workshop. Richly appointed, with deep red carpeting even on the walls, it looks startlingly like the lobby of a miniature Viennese theatre. Imposing eighteenth-century furniture (except for several graceful Hepplewhite chairs) and great gold draperies give the room a heavy elegance that unsettles most visitors at the moment of entrance. It usually takes a few minutes before one realizes the most unusual feature of the office: It has no desk. A corner mahogany secretary conceals customary desk articles, and a glass-enclosed bookcase distributes television and theatre trade books among the bright jackets of popular novels. Small end tables provide the only writing surfaces.

Wiener loves the place. His ease in it is much in evidence when Joel Greer comes in. Legs crossed, he sits on one of the sofas reading (actually pretending to read) a new political history of Washington, which he has recently recommended to Mark and Bill Kelly of UBC News for a quasi-documentary series. He nods Greer to a chair opposite him while he finishes a page. It's a ploy, of course—his favorite —but it almost always works, creating certain unease, especially with subordinates. He doesn't particularly relish having to use it with Joel Greer, but a subordinate is a subordinate, however you slice him, and Greer simply waits patiently until he finally puts the book aside.

Wiener's smile is almost affectionate. The young man across from him is a not unpleasant, merely serious, young man, only three or four years younger than himself—twenty-nine, thirty, no more. What's more, he is considered by most agencies and producers to be one of the ablest program men in the industry. But it is neither his charm nor his talent that causes Fred Wiener to smile so generously. Joel Greer (few besides Wiener know it once was Griebsberg) is the one top man in the eastern program division personally brought in by David Abrams. It was a situation as bizarre as it was unprofessional, but the coup—at a not inconsiderable $58,000 a year—netted him, Wiener, two good right arms.

"How's it going?" he asks.

Joel Greer shrugs. "Nothing on the *Napoleon* script yet. You'd think Mallin could get a decent script out of somebody. One more delay and I'm recommending the whole project be shelved." *Napoleon* is a projected dramatic series for next season and Mallin an executive producer with Universal.

"You wouldn't hurt my feelings, baby." Fred laughs. "I never could see why Mark thinks a series about Napoleon would work. But I didn't get you up here to talk about five-foot heroes. I want you to do something for me."

"Oh?"

"I want you to find out, to the penny, if possible, just what the other networks spent on pilots this past year." He pauses briefly. This is the first time he has ever asked Greer to use his personal contacts at the other networks for anything other than routine business. He has to give it what he likes to call *entre-nous* impact. This means lowering his voice to a confidential whisper. "And I don't mean what they're budgeted at, Joel, or what they tell the FCC, or what goes into their stockholder reports. I mean what they *really* spent, what kind of deals they got with the studios, the works. Did they or didn't they get better deals than we got. And who did the dealing, particularly on the big ones. The program guy or the president. Frankly, I don't know whether it means a frigging thing, but I'd like to have it. Okay?"

Greer's face, always pensive, reveals little. "I'll see what I can do," he says.

"Good boy."

"Just don't ask me how I did it—*if* I do it." Standing, he looks deceptively tall. He is almost dangerously thin. "*Hilda* giving everybody hell?"

Fred does his best to keep it light. "Everybody except Mark Antony," he says. "You know. Ice outside, fire inside, he thinks he invented it. But then, even Antony got impassioned once or twice. Right?"

"Once or twice."

"Wait'll Thursday. If his Wednesday-night *Magazine* shit doesn't come off . . ."

"I'll be in most of the day if you need me, Fred."

Wiener's jaw clenches with the soft closing of the door. He doesn't need abrupt exits to tell him he's letting his bitterness get the better of his patience. Damn! Those juvenile jabs at Mark—even to Greer. He'll have to watch it. Mark is as omnipresent as air. Clients, studios, the talent—you never know. You could be holed up in Yucatan and there he'd be, grinning at you from some lousy fisherman's face, waiting for you to take that one drink too many, say that one word too many— Damn. If only the bastard . . .

Bastard! Sonofabitchingmotherfucking bastard! Jesus. If he could just let the words spill out on the room, just hear them; nothing more, just *hear* them! Spit them up, once and for all! Get the taste of them

out of his mouth! Get Mark Banner out of his throat! Christ knows
he's been there long enough.

Two years and two weeks, to be exact. Two years and two weeks
of an $85,000 in-name-only vacuum, where vice president in charge of
network programs is the laugh of the industry. Oh, sure, Mark Banner
is known to have his thumb in everybody's pie. Certainly he himself
wasn't unaware of it when Bob Abrams talked him into the job. But
here he was, two years and two weeks later, still little more than the
rest of the audience, still watching a one-man show. Mark doing everything. And not only with Programming. With Sales, with Advertising,
with Publicity . . . News, Daytime, everything. When you take a leak
it's as if Mark Banner has determined the color of your urine; even
that isn't your own at UBC. And then having the gall to tell the network's affiliates at their San Francisco meeting in June that if-this-
year's-schedule-is-as-successful-as-it-looks-like-it-will-be-then-much-of-
the-credit-goes-to-my-good-right-arm-here-Fred-Wiener.

Well—and here Fred paces the floor the way his jugular vein paces
his neck—well, those roses he expects by Sunday might just be roses
after all; nice fat cemetery roses. If things go right (he smiles wryly:
that is, if things go *wrong*), the week could damn well explode in
Mark's face. Oh, granted he's right about *Hilda,* and even *Felony* tonight. They're not the really big ifs. The big if comes Wednesday with
the *UBC Magazine of the Air.* This potpourri format, borrowed from
radio, has a single host for the entire evening, 8:00 to 11:00, with all
the known ingredients—musical-variety, action-adventure, drama, situation comedy, documentary—tossed into the pot. It's diametrically
opposed to the block-programming concept that made UBC number
one in the first place; the concept that once gave UBC's comedies and
action-adventures the edge, precisely because they were stacked to
sustain a mood. The bastard may claim to know the American viewer
better than the rest of the industry put together, but viewers resent—
haven't failures on the other networks proved it?—genuinely resent
being cut up into fragments too many times during an evening; not
having the luxury of a good long laugh or a good long cry. There's
nothing wrong with the block concept, regardless of the crap Mark's
fed Adrian Miller and "Uncle Bob." What's wrong are the programs *in*
the block; last year's, anyway. The programs the superior bastard has
fought him on all the way. Well, the whole Banner Theory (as the
press has tagged it)—that magazine programming would in time
create one-channel viewing over an entire evening, thereby making
full evenings, not just single time periods, the real competition—is
just about the costliest risk Mark Banner has ever taken. An eighth of
it is still unsold. Advertisers are playing wait-and-see like crazy. Well,

just let Wednesday night go down the drain and not even the Board of Directors (who worship Mark ad nauseam) or the Old Man, or even Bob (who halfway fears him because of it), will be easy pickings. In television you're as good as your last season, your last Nielsen, and if the bastard thinks he has troubles now . . .

"Just let your little old magazine concept burn like paper, Mr. Wonder Boy Banner, old Mark old baby, and see how much wonder there is then."

The words are loud and clear. He's somewhat startled to hear them, even more startled when he finds he can't stop.

"And all your right-arm crap won't mean a frigging thing, when you're a one-man show you're a one-man loser, don't think Bob Abrams and Adrian Miller don't know I've tried to fight you tooth and nail . . ."

When Linda sticks her head in the door—"D'you want something?" —he says, "No!" very sharply, and it's not unlike being found out in the bathroom, doing yourself. He has to settle down, that's all there is to it. There's too much to do, too much to think about. Too much at stake. Mark Banner's in trouble, you go from there.

He takes Valium from one of the end-table drawers, pours half a glass of water from a decanter on the sideboard, and as he's finishing it his private telephone rings. It rarely does. Only a chosen few know the number, and those who do—Mark, the Old Man, "Uncle Bob," Adrian Miller, Steve Lilly, McAlister—call it from outside only when they don't want to go through the switchboard. Inside, they use the intercom. His slow "Hello" is cautious.

"Fred?"

He's almost certain, yet . . .

"Fred, this is Vivian. Can you talk?"

"Of course."

"You're surprised."

"A little."

"I'm surprised at myself. I'm even more surprised at why I'm calling. I know I swore I never would but . . . Freddie, I have to come into the city today. Could we lunch?"

"Well, I'm not sure what . . ."

"Fred, don't."

"Well, you sound sober, anyway."

"I'm very sober. A friend of mine has an apartment at Six-ten Park. Fourteen B. She'll be away for the day. We can lunch there. I'll have something sent in."

"That private?"

"How else?"

"All right. Twelve-thirty?"

"One."

"One it is. I hope ..."

"No, *I* hope. Thank you, darling."

The click is deafening.

12

HANGING UP, Vivian Banner reaches for a cigarette, lights it slowly, surprised that her hands aren't shaking more than they are. She's in the upstairs bedroom she shares with Mark (*sometimes* shares with Mark) in their Westport home, which overlooks a small lake. It's a man-made lake, and on sunny mornings it glistens like cotton candy. From her window it looks as fragile as the spun confection, too; as fragile and as shimmeringly unreal. She has been looking out on it, off and on, for hours.

The bedroom, flaunting its expensiveness even in disorder, has not been cleaned. She has asked the maid to wait until after lunch. Nothing about the morning is very orderly, in fact. She especially. She is still in her nightgown, she hasn't reached once to push back her hair, she has—for the first time since she can remember—ignored a paddle-tennis date with Jean Marie Abrams at the club, and she has been drinking cold coffee for over an hour. Even more, she has just made a telephone call that was the most deliberate act she has probably ever committed.

Why—like most of the whys in her life—is incidental. It is more a question of Who. That she called a man, with only one purpose in mind, is—at least in her present state—endurable. That it was Fred Wiener is shattering.

She can remember ...

She remembers so little. A spring night—when? Three years ago? Four? Mark away—where? Washington? Los Angeles? Does it matter? Another planet. She had been to the David Abramses' in Mamaroneck for dinner. He was there with his stepmother (the Old Man's daughter, M. J.), a producer of sorts; full of theatre, full of himself. She didn't really like him. He was in the process of being divorced—his wife drank; narcotics; something—and he was unconscionably hard—no, soft—no, both at the same time; which oddly, though it repelled her, attracted her. And the wine was generous. It seemed so natural when Ellen Abrams asked him to drive her home, to Westport. . . .

She has never felt guilty, not the way she's wanted to. All these years it has seemed so remote, so . . . oh, gossamer, as though it were something that happened to her when she was a young girl, long before Mark. In a way she *was* a girl again, however knowingly she provoked the whole thing. Touching him while he drove, squirming shamelessly when he touched her; making only the feeblest move to stop him when he parked the car in a Southport wood; climbing into the back seat with him. Doing it in a *car*—not once but twice, without a word; not even the most elementary affection in their hands, just . . .

She has seen him again, of course, since he came to UBC: at dinners, official functions, there is no avoiding him. But no sign has ever passed between them, nothing that in the least suggests darkness; it's really as if it never happened at all. Yet this morning, waking, she felt— physically felt—the rough texture of his buttocks as her legs sought him, closed him in. . . .

A sob escapes her. Showering, she experiences it again (only this time in the fantasy they are standing up, and it is her hands, not her legs, that pinion him), so intensely that she dares not touch herself, even with a washcloth, in the areas where she has grown so sensitive; again, as if she were a girl, discovering for the first time the terrifying sensation of herself. . . .

The lovely sensation of herself. Dry, calm, seated before the massive mirror of her dressing-room wall, she looks no more than a girl—a tall, blonde, even willowy girl. The smoothness of her skin denies her thirty-seven years—years seen only in the corners of her eyes and mouth, and which cosmetics and concentration make short shrift of. She is applying the makeup now, relieved to be doing something; the morning has been too much. For a few moments, eyes riveted on herself, she actually forgets—at least, keeps at bay—what has brought her to it.

But then he's back, Mark, with the first brush stroke of her hair; as unrevealing, after fourteen years, as the day she married him. It had been exciting then, of course, simply watching him rise; simply sharing, however obliquely, the path of a meteor in a sky so starry it blotted out every light of the earth; simply being there, another plaque on his wall. *Vivian Seaworth, of the Oklahoma City Seaworths, awarded to Mark Banner of Kansas City and New York in recognition of . . .*

"It wasn't just the baby, Mark. Not just losing the baby. Neither of us could help that. No, my friend. It happened long before the baby. It happened the day you said, 'Bear with me, I've got this mountain of work ahead.' It happened the night you said, 'Good God, is that all you ever think of—sex?" It happened— Damn you, Mark, if you just . . ."

They aren't unusual, these morning talks to the mirror, but enough is enough. So she called Fred Wiener, whom Mark looks on as a bug. It doesn't mean anything has to happen. Does it? And if it does, so to hell with it. She's a woman, isn't she, a perfectly healthy woman who needs . . .

"A man, Mark. A man who has time to touch me, fuck me."

It pleases her to say it. She dresses quickly, and when Elke, her plump German maid, comes in to ask if she'll be lunching in, she says, "No, I've decided to go to the club after all. Tell Henry I'll take the Jaguar."

"*Und* dinner?" says the girl. "Vill you and Mr. Benner be to dinner?"

"I doubt Mr. Banner will be home," she says. "He'll call one way or the other, though. If I'm not here, just take the message."

"*Ja.*"

"And tell Emma to have something ready just in case. Lamb chops, I suppose. Yes, lamb chops. All right?"

"*Ja.*"

"It's an old American maxim, Elke. Roll with the punches. You've never heard it?"

"No, mom."

"I should be home around five."

It is 10:25. She feels like a schoolgirl.

13

It is 11:30 when Robert Abrams' third wife, Jean Marie, finally gives up any expectation of Vivian Banner's making it to the club. Her maid, the two times she called the house, said she'd left over an hour ago. So no bouncing little balls with Vibrant Viv this morning.

Which is just as well. They'd have gotten into another of their husband-Lord! exchanges—half-truths, half-lies, candor stretched just enough to preserve a semblance of intimacy, not quite so far as to topple even one of UBC's fragile little fucking houses of cards. An exchange that she, at least, decidedly doesn't need today. Today when she has decided—irrevocably, irrefuckingtrievably—to leave Robert Sackman Abrams as far behind as existing seas and continents can accommodate her. Besides which, she already has two bourbon manhattans under her belt—a new $175 rhinestone-studded belt from Bonwit's, which is only the beginning of what she'll take the sonofabitch for!—and which is just enough to give her the encouragement she needs to drive to Mamaroneck and the Old Man's old girl and let the whole thing . . .

She's a beauty, Jean Marie. A real beauty. Knows it. Thirty-four, looking a trim twenty-five, coal-black hair framing a warm smooth tan, voice a subtle if challenging reminder that she hails from Sea Island, Georgia, as she asks the parking attendant to bring her Mercedes to the canopied front entrance. She's the penultimate in good health and high spirit. The third Mrs. Robert Abrams in all her glory.

"And up his." She laughs as she drives through timid rain with brazen courage.

ELLEN ABRAMS has never been as fond of her daughter-in-law (by marriage) as her husband appears to be. But then, she wasn't exactly mesmerized by Brenda and Beverly, Robert's two earlier mistakes, either. One of America's foremost actresses, she is not overwhelmed by good acting.

"Then you're definitely leaving?" she asks again of her young visitor, not so much to establish certainty as to prolong it. With this adventuress (and it is the most charitable description Ellen can spare her for the moment)—unlike her shifty predecessors—she just may learn something that can be of value to David.

"Nothing will change my mind," says Jean Marie, the toss of her thick black hair, Ellen has to admit, a decided stunner.

"You realize, of course, how disturbed David will be?"

"Oh, I do, Ellen, I do. That's the most distressin' thing about it. Truly." Ermines and rubies wouldn't melt in her mouth.

"We had thought—we had hoped—that this time . . ."

"Yeah." Her smile, if not malicious, is decidedly mischievous. "You really don't know, do you?"

Ellen simply stares her down.

"Then it's time you did," her daughter-in-law says, eyes cast down just enough to placate modesty. "If the others couldn't bring themselves to tell you, then I must. He . . . he can't . . . he can't perform, Ellen."

The *you know* and *between us girls* coziness in her voice is an irritant, of course, but one Ellen manages gracefully to hide. "I see," she says—and for the first time she really does. Despite subtle hints, from Brenda at least, she has always assumed that Robert's temperament, his rather deadly moodiness, were the miscreants.

More to come.

"And I think you should know somethin' else too. Somethin' you may or may not have suspected. UBC's high and mighty heir is out to get your darlin' husband but good. I heard him talkin' with Adrian Miller on an extension the other night. They're goin' to try to get him through the Board of Directors. Get him good and out, that is."

Ellen, changing expression only slightly, sets down her cup. They are having tea in the spacious solarium of the Mamaroneck house, a room Ellen, soon after she and David were married, had appended to it. Its greenery and light, even on sullen days like this, are a blessing, especially when talk is as strained and desultory as it is today. In the ensuing silence, she is once again grateful for it.

The room perhaps, more than any other in the big ramshackle house, expresses her, the essence of her, in much the way the UBC building and executive offices in the city express her husband. Like her, it is both new and timeless—a long time being annexed but, once there, a presence that seems always to have been. As Ellen Curry, the UBC actress and songstress who became known as the First Lady of Radio, she had been David Abrams' lover from the early twenties on, through two marriages and the birth—and merciful death—of their illegitimate retarded child, becoming Mrs. Abrams only ten years ago, when his first wife, Arrabella, died. No one seeing her at his side, sitting with her in his house, could ever imagine her not having been there forever.

It is in this sense, this light, that she accepts and absorbs what Robert's third wife is revealing; quietly, almost pleasantly, while vindication stirs inside her: There is no one whom she feels more antipathy toward—and sympathy for—than David's son and heir.

Robert's resentment of her, of course, had begun as naturally, and as fervently, as his devotion to his mother, Arrabella. As a child he had a sense beyond his years, and if he never actually saw David and her together, alone at any rate, he had the imagination to create a kind of Medea/Jason/Glauce thing of it. The years had only magnified, exacerbated it. Perhaps its climax, if such a silent, sullen feeling can be said to have one, occurred during the war years, in particular at a concert she had scheduled at Fort Ord, California, toward the end of the war. Having refused a commission or special placement that his father, David, could so easily have gotten him, Robert had been drafted into the infantry while completing his freshman year at Princeton. He was stationed at Fort Ord when she, then at the top of her form as the First Lady of Radio, accepted the engagement. Knowing Robert's real identity, the camp commander asked him, as the son of United Broadcasting's famed David Abrams, to come forward and share the stage with the network's most prominent star. Whereupon Robert got up and marched woodenly, almost monarchically, from the open-air auditorium. Somehow the press got the story and for several weeks the incident sparked renewed speculation on the notorious "love nest" that Ellen and David had purportedly enjoyed in the thirties. The press also replowed the dirt of the homosexual murder of her first husband (a UBC Radio programmer and closet homosexual whom she'd married to protect David's marriage while she was pregnant with his child), along with David and Arrabella's separation and eventual reconciliation, as well as the sponsor cancelation of the *Ellen Curry Hour* and UBC's plunge to an all-time listenership low. That the show eventually was rescheduled, that David went back to Arrabella (whose UBC purse strings left him with almost no purse to dangle), that Robert himself came close to dying in a hospital in Manila, only aggravated further his vendetta. Even now, under the shade tree of years, there is at best a nervous accommodation. No matter how consciously, how earnestly, she tries.

But David is the one to think of, not his son. And it doesn't have to be spoken for her to know what this one, Robert's third wife, is saying; it has graced hundreds of UBC soap operas through the years. *I don't care how fond of me the Old Man is, I'll smear all of it through the tabloids, all of it. If I don't get everything I want, everything that's coming to me, the whole cruddy story will wind up in headlines in* the Daily News. *And I don't think you'd like that, any of you. Not after the headlines you and the Old Man made for yourselves back in '38, after the murder of your faggoty husband. . . .*

"When do you plan on leaving, dear?" she asks, turning back to her dazzling vistor with her famous smile.

14

IT IS ALMOST NOON when Mark finally makes it to Gerald McAlister's office. Nothing has been on schedule this morning. He wasn't planning on seeing Jack Stroud in Advertising, for example, or getting involved with Freeman & Smith, UBC's advertising agency, or having to spend so long on the Cincinnati speech that Sid Newton in Sales Planning is writing for him. Of all things, he wasn't planning on a lengthy phone conversation with the sanitarium in Boston where Vivian's mother, with acute hardening of the arteries, has been confined for a number of years. But she has taken a fever, and it is the standing rule that they always call him, never Vivian, when these things happen. The call made its dent in the morning. Not that the poor woman really means so much to him; it's simply that helplessness, isolation—in any form, for anyone—always disturbs him, affronts him. Just as talks with doctors always catapult shadows into substance, impersonality into personal drama. At any rate, he is in no mood for McAlister. But then when is he ever in the mood for McAlister?

Gerald McAlister, whose official title is Vice President in Charge of Corporate Affairs (still PR and Publicity, however you slice it; just as the network's "account executives" are simply salesmen, screw the label), is a short, dour man in his early fifties. He has been with UBC for at least three hundred years. Mark grants that in his time Gerald McAlister has made significant contributions to broadcasting (especially in the area of self-regulatory codes), but at UBC itself he has been little more than the eyes, ears, nose and throat of Adrian Miller and Robert Abrams. It's an irony of the trade, he thinks, that the man is still considered a leading industry spokesman, especially with the Washington crowd. He stands up when Mark comes in, and although they see each other nearly every day, in corridor or conference room, holds out his hand as though he, Mark, were an emissary from the White House.

"Ah, Mark. Glad you could drop around." His gravelly voice is a favorite target of amateur imitators.

Mark takes one of the two blue leather chairs in front of the desk. "Sorry I couldn't make it at eleven," he says. "One of those mornings."

"*Hilda?*"

"Who's that?"

The deadpan exchange has a disquieting effect. Gerald McAlister, if only because of the gruffness of his face, is also a humorless man.

"Well, the week's hardly begun," he says. "I told Bobby that this morning. You know how personally he feels everything."

Mark nods. "And you know what a false gauge the premieres are, Jerry. Premieres are good for little more than sampling. We should know that by now. Hits aren't made by overnight ratings, reviews or ulcers."

"Yes, it's all psychological."

Mark studies him without changing the rather bland expression he came in with. McAlister has a way of bringing a subject to a close with some truism or other. It's just difficult knowing which way to take him. His voice, like his face, has one plateau.

Swiveling, McAlister says now, slowly, "Mark, this is of course between us."

Mark nods again. It is always "between us" at UBC.

"Bob Abrams would have discussed it with you himself," he continues, "but he feels it's an area he shouldn't let himself get involved with."

So that's it, Mark thinks. When Robert Abrams doesn't want to get involved it means either (1) Jews or (2) blacks, or at the outside (3) a network star whose revelations to the press "invariably misquote me." Suddenly, and without a straw in the wind, Mark knows that this morning it is 2.

"Bob's had a couple of calls, Mark. One from the Coast, he won't say who, but he doesn't attach much importance to it. The other was from the NAACP here in New York, however. You know how sensitive Bob is to organizations. He was a little unprepared for it."

"Oh?"

"The drama switch on the Wednesday *Magazine* show, I mean. The one about blacks in a hospital ward *was* originally scheduled, wasn't it?"

"It was."

"Bad?"

"As social commentary? No. As drama? Yes. Probably the most inept thing Harold Lewisohn's ever done. If it's any comfort to you, Jerry, I believe I knew what I was doing."

"I don't doubt that for a second," McAlister says. "It's just . . . Bob wishes it hadn't been released to the press, Mark. The original scheduling, I mean."

"It shouldn't have been," says Mark. "It was tentative in the first place."

"Then why . . . ?"

"Why what, Jerry?"

They both know, and the parrying, Mark thinks, stinks to heaven. McAlister has come perilously close to a smile. "Wiener?"

Mark starts to say, "I was on my way to the Coast when he inadvertently . . ." but draws himself up sharply. Better to get past Wiener as quickly as possible, he thinks. McAlister holds no great love for him, but Abrams blood—even stepson Abrams blood—is Abrams blood, and Abrams blood is sacred. Besides, Wiener obviously isn't the reason he's sitting here.

"These things happen all the time, Jerry," he says. "We can't program for the press. Last Thursday alone I rescheduled three episodes for this first week. No more than par for the course."

"I know. It's just that this gets into the corporate—"

"Everything gets into the corporate," says Mark. "Sooner or later every move you make is corporate. But you know me well enough to know that when it comes to a choice between good television and good public relations, I'm going to say good television. That's what makes a network, Jerry. Like they say, the worst public relations is a bad show."

McAlister does something now that he rarely, if ever, does. He walks around the desk and puts his hand on Mark's shoulder. Mark isn't certain what it means—if anything—and he certainly has no intention of taking it to an analyst's couch. He only knows that he doesn't like being touched by this man, and a subtle shifting of his weight must have conveyed itself to McAlister, for the Vice President in Charge of Corporate Affairs removes his hand and says, even carelessly, "Frankly, I don't think anything's going to come of it. The NAACP's registered its protest—it was mild, considering—and we've alerted Arthur Merck in Legal. But the press might call and we ought to have some sort of statement ready."

"I'll prepare one," Mark said.

"Thank you."

Mark has no intention of leaving. It is obvious McAlister has something more on his mind. He's a deliberate man, and if for the most part he simply echoes Robert Abrams or Adrian Miller, he weighs his words with far more care. As considerately chosen as they now are, however, Mark is strangely unprepared for them.

"I have to ask you this, Mark. I think you'll understand why. Did Steve Lilly . . . did Steve exert any influence on this thing?"

Mark stiffens perceptibly. "Of course not," he snaps.

"But he . . . concurred?"

"Of course he concurred. Just as the sponsors concurred. If you think because Lilly's a Southerner . . ."

"Yes," said McAlister. "Lilly's a Southerner."

"And I'm from Kansas City. You know, Jerry, I'm a little surprised here. This isn't like you. Or Robert Abrams. Particularly since all three of his wives, if I'm not mistaken, have come from below the Line, so to speak. Not to mention his dear departed mother."

It is perhaps unwise, impertinent even, but McAlister simply brings a thin, cupped hand to his chin. "His name came up in the protest, Mark. Steve's not one to hide his magnolia blossoms under a bushel, you know." He turns back to his desk. "I have to operate under the premise that where there's smoke there's fire, Mark. It's my job. You tell me there isn't any, then there isn't any. That ends it as far as I'm concerned. And if your friend Bryson Randolph gets hold of it . . ."

"Wiener takes him to lunch."

They talk a few minutes more: the Randolph column this morning; Mark's impending speech to a regional affiliates' meeting in Cincinnati; another quick trip to the Coast, possibly even this week; a new golf tournament franchise McAlister is particularly interested in acquiring; the possibility that the President—the U.S. President, that is—might ask for time, prime time, in the next few days to speak on Congressional action on his new energy proposals. Mark endures them all mechanically. And when he does rise to leave, it is the same as when he came in, handshake and all. But unlike most partings from Gerald McAlister, this one has actually provoked thought:

He should have brought Miller and Robert Abrams into the thing, yes. At the very beginning, when he knew he'd have to switch episodes. God knows anything having to do with blacks on television these days is sticky.

But involving Robert Abrams and Adrian Miller would have meant McAlister, and Merck in Legal, and that endless round of memorandums and conferences that take you nowhere, drain you dry.

Besides:

It is *his* province, image or no image.

And routine, no more than routine.

Still . . .

Lilly. Why Lilly? Why all of a sudden Lilly? Granted, the man has a sugar-cane accent you couldn't cut with a machete, but he's always so careful in areas like this. Inordinately careful. Then how . . . ?

The real thing? A decoy? Fred Wiener?

Miller?

Miller *and* Fred Wiener?

Together?

And *had* Lilly influenced him? One of the show's sponsors, March & Hare Foods, *had* been concerned about the black segment, true. Usual isolated station clearance problem in the South as well. But that was before he scheduled it in the first place, weeks before. He scheduled over their objections then, it stood to reason that canceling it later had nothing to do with them. He honestly believed (he believes now)— and after long consideration—that the black drama was inferior to any of several they had in the can. Still, would he have made such a change last season—the season before—when first decisions were his trademark and no decision he made was up for question?

He looks at his watch. Twelve-forty already. His lunch date with the Old Man was for twelve-thirty. David Abrams is a maniac about time. Mark quickens his pace.

15

THE SUBJECT, or object, of Mark's conversation with Gerald McAlister is himself lunching in a private dining room of "21," where he and his eastern sales manager, Wolf Glover, are giving an easel-card presentation on a series of dramatic specials to several agency media buyers and account executives. It has been a long, convivial, three-martini lunch. The table has been cleared a half hour at least, they're on third cups of coffee, and the last of the brightly lettered easel cards is on display. It reads "NEW IMPACT FOR CONTINENTAL TIRES," and the concluding remarks that accompany it—"And that's about the size of it, gennulmen, Cont'nental's got a real blockbustuh heah"—are soft and sparing and, in their way, spellbinding.

Sitting down, Steve Lilly smiles ingenuously at the men across from him. He has performed well, and he knows it. It is reflected like cups running over in the eyes of his beholders—eyes in which he always sees himself the most clearly, the most munificently. *Steve Lilly*, they say—for reflections in eyes are articulate, and articulateness is his business—*Steve Lilly, they say, old Lilly there, one hell of a guy. Big, solid, good-looking fellow, little heavy maybe, but what the hell. Gives him humanity. Born salesman, Lilly, Chinaman's balls kind of salesman. Persuasive as sin, but sincere, real sincere. You can see it right off. Good breeding, too, aristocratic Southerner if there ever was one, UBC's damn lucky to have him. Knowledgeable, too, knows exactly what he's saying. For a one-time studio page, he holds his own with the best of them. Quotes A. C. Nielsen like a sonofabitch. Real easygoing fellow but there's strength there, Charlie. Goes all out for you, but don't try to screw him. Steve Lilly's not a man to be taken lightly. There's nothing solider on God's green earth than a good-natured Louisiana boy.*

As though to prove it, he folds his thick arms firmly on the table, pushes his weight into them, and drawls good-naturedly, "Any questions, gennulmen? Mac? Tom? Allen? How 'bout you, Marv?"

The last-named, a short young man in large horn-rimmed glasses, says, "I do have one question, Steve. About the commercials. You know how ape Continental goes over having a show's star do the commercials. What happens if you get Rod Marshall to do these specials? From all I hear, he's not particularly enamored of being a pitchman. He refused to do International Steel's things last year, didn't he?"

Steve beams expansively. "I reckon you might say I've preceded you heah, Marv. We've already talked to Rod, and he's ready, willin' and able. Specials like these don't grow on trees, you know. Rod likes his caviar and his pussy too much to quibble these days. Right, Tom?"

"That's what they say." The older man directly across from him nods, fingering his watch. "And if we don't get back to the office it just might mean a long cold winter of pork and beans. Good pitch, Steve. Your audience estimates are amazingly close to ours. I'm recommending it to the client."

It's a goddamn beautiful way to conclude a luncheon. Steve is bounty itself. It is well known that Continental Tires never goes against an agency recommendation. And these guys would never know how little hope he had when he walked in here. Even Mark had been skeptical when Joel Greer suggested the package. Not only did Rod Marshall's demands shoot production costs through the roof; Marshall himself is a boa constrictor to work with. The whole thing is decidedly a smasher. Well, Lilly's coming home with some rare bacon today. Six million beautiful bucks' worth, to be exact. Six million potatoes nobody else knew where to dig for. Even those friggin' Jews on the forty-second floor would be impressed with this one. Lord, he feels great.

He is also the only one in the room who hasn't been dulled by the martinis and steaks. Leaving, he clasps shoulders and steers elbows with the agility of a trained-to-be-tireless host. And outside, in the broiling afternoon sun, he is given the opportunity of a perfect exit line. One of the media people asks him, "Between us, Steve, whose brainchild was this? Wiener's?"

"Greer's," says Steve.

"You wouldn't snow me?"

"Is Lincoln a car?"

"Good. Not that it matters. Greer's just easier to work with. Maybe I'm prejudiced anyway. My wife and I know his wife, you know. Wiener's, I mean. *Ex-*wife, that is. She's never said why he humiliated her the way he did. All that crap about her drinking and sleeping around is just that, though. Crap."

Perfect cue. Lord, the best. "Well, I'll tell you, Allen. I got a sneakin' hunch she left him cause he wasn't doin' to her what he's been doin' to the UBC Television Network." It was an old line, but it worked every time. The parting in front of "21" is a corker.

After they've left, Wolf Glover—whose admiration of him is downright vulgar, it's so worshipful—says, "Fine show, Steve. Looks like you've sewed it up in one session. Really done your number on 'em. Can you make it with me to that meeting at J. Walter's? Here's a cab."

"I'll tell you what," says Steve. "Why don't you take this one by yourself, Wolfie? I've got a while yet before that screenin' with Mark. I need to take care of somethin' near heah. Okay?"

"Sure, Steve." The taxi pulls up. "See you later?"

"You better believe it."

Watching the cab until it rounds the corner at Fifth, Steve says to himself, You need another drink like a hole in the head, buddy; but he knows he'll have it. It's a craving he has after every sales presentation, successful or not. And preferably alone. Mike Manuche's, considerately, is just up the street.

The bar's still crowded, although it's three in the afternoon. Steve edges his way in and orders a double scotch on the rocks with a twist of lemon. It tastes sharp, needle-prick sharp, but then all his senses are blessed with sharpness today. He can see, hear, touch and smell with incredible acuteness, but even more he's a whetstone for those around him. His very presence seems to make them keener, too. He can sense it—no, damn it, he can *feel* it: it's stinging every nerve in his body. That old man there, the one who couldn't hold his head up a minute ago. Look at him. Moving it up a storm. That young kid next to him, the one who was staring dully into space when Steve came in. Look at him now. Eyes lit up with all kinds of plans and ideas, rarin' to go. That woman across the way, the one between those two bar lizards. Already she's sent pleasure through his groin, sweet as that first sting of scotch. Now suddenly she's laughing, wriggling on that stool like a garden worm. Boy, this is *one* day . . .

A smile crosses his face. All right, he's indulging himself, so who has a better right? Continental Tires—hell, they aren't even a tenth of it! If some people knew what he knew . . .

He finishes his drink, indulges himself spiritedly in another, and leaves an outrageously generous tip. On his way out he makes two phone calls. Both are brief. In the first one he simply says, "Six-thirty, same place," and hangs up. In the second one he speaks a moment longer: "I'll get a late train, honey. One of those damn evenin' agency things. Kiss the kids." All in all, they're pretty ordinary calls. Except of course that even an afternoon's indulgence notwithstanding, no ordinary fellow has made them.

16

OTHER LUNCHES are less successful.

At least on the surface they're less successful.

At the elegant Laurent on Fifty-sixth Street—over *potage Paulette*, a blanquette of boned pike with truffles, a rare *vin blanc*—Robert tells Adrian, manages almost inarticulately to tell Adrian, that his third wife is about to slam the gate.

"That's hardly unexpected." His old friend laughs; half laughs. "Maybe the fourth time out you'll find a cunt who can say 'you all' in the plural. From Philadelphia maybe. Or Boston. It's all plural as hell in Boston."

To which Robert responds with dark, narrowed eyes: "You're a great comfort, Adrian. Thirty years ago, when we first met—in the army, remember? The Philippines?—when you learned who I was, what I liked to read, to talk about, you quoted Wordsworth, if I recall. 'How nourished there through that long time, He knows who gave that love sublime.' It must be a rewarding feeling, not to have to suck ass any more. Not to *think* you have to suck ass any more. It's my cousin, don't forget—your lovely, oversexed, overbearing wife—who owns the stock. Or had you forgotten?"

Adrian's laughter, this time, is much more hearty. "Poor Bobby," he says. "They really do it to you, don't they, kid?"

"They?"

"Everybody."

Robert looks off, into the soft, measured din of the sumptuous room. "I'm sure father won't take it so lightly. He's pretty fond of Jean Marie."

Adrian's face, for a moment, appears to sober. "Same old trouble?" he says; gently even.

Robert shrugs, nods, avoids him still.

"So," says Adrian, grin back large and intact, lighting a Gauloise, the only cigarette he'd be caught dead smoking, "maybe all's not lost after all. You can always eat it to death, you know."

Robert reaches to his pocket for a pill. A bright, plump pink of a pill. And closes his eyes.

"The truffles," he says.

But despite the truffles, it's not a very inviting lunch. Not even when the exchange, as inevitably it must, gets back on the track—to the trials of UBC. And where Robert manages, even with Adrian, to be unmistakably, even impressively, Mr. President.

17

AT THE OAK ROOM of the Plaza, Joslyn Miller is faring no better, despite the fact that the interview with Larry Lester and Sharon Moore is both bright and engaging, and the trout amandine downright exquisite. The problem, of course, is Joslyn herself.

She's bored. To tears, to screams—bored. The idea of even being here (Adrian and his damned pampering of talent!) somehow borders on the ridiculous, smiling gaily or thoughtfully at each witticism or reflection (witticism or reflection, her ass! Goddamn phonies! Larry Lester with his $12,000 toupee, his everybody-who's-anybody drivel; Sharon Moore with her babydoll innocence, Miss Silicon Betty Boop of the decade—you can sit both of them in a crematorium as far as *she's* concerned), glancing approvingly now and then to the network's publicist, Tom Larkin (who, if he weren't so absurdly young, would stretch her fantasies to hell and back), nodding appreciatively every time the columnist Bryson Randolph gets one of his famous zingers in. Ridiculous! But when Adrian asks . . . when Adrian *demands* . . .

"Sure, I know. People won't believe that I like my work so much that it's not work. I mean, not *really* work. It's a golden rut maybe, but I enjoy it. I mean, people think it has to do with a lot of money and everything, but it doesn't, it truly doesn't. I mean, I just like doing my little opening night every week. That's why I like television so much. I mean, it keeps the old adrenalin going," Miss Boop is saying (*reciting*, to be more accurate; how many goddamn times has she played it?), and "Guys like me, we was born for teevee, you know? I mean, gettin' crime 'n violence off o' the streets and back in the home where it belongs," Mr. $12,000 Hairpiece is giggling (silly man would giggle the Lord's Prayer if you'd let him), and she is expiring by the minute. And having to be with those awful bores tonight, the Board of Directors' Mortimers of all people—it's too much, too geedee much! If only there were some . . .

And fat chance of that!

Adrian!

Adrian Goddamn Adrian!

If only . . .

And when for God's sake hasn't there been "If Only"? That silly couplet Robert wrote years ago, the one Adrian discovered when Bobby was so sick, and mimicked to her almost the first time she met him—*Who the master, who the slave;* fucking thing says as much about her as it does about Bobby. How many thousands of times, in those first days with him, did she tell herself that he was just a cock, just another cock, and how many thousands of those has she seen; at any rate fantasized over? And how many thousands of times has she told herself that with a mother who died in an insane asylum (knocked off her *own* mother, for God's sake!), with a stepmother (Ellen Curry, now Uncle David's wife) whose show-business stardom kept her away half the time, with a father whose devotion to UBC bordered on the near-maniacal—with all these and a penchant for every unmade bed she happened onto, isn't the prospect of some kind of permanence all she wanted from Adrian, needed from Adrian? And how many thousands of times has she known as surely as she knows her own breath that the UBC stock her father left her has as sweet an aroma for her husband as the most generous of her private parts? And thrown it in his face every chance she got? And how many thousands of times has she known in her heart (if she still has one, that is, after a thousand-year lifetime with Adrian)—known in her heart at even the smallest touch of him—that master-slave in her own damn psyche begs no question. No matter what she has done and with whom, through all the years, Adrian's power over her is as total as it is humiliating. Physically, emotionally, mentally, all: the power that he holds over Bobby, over so many people really—power, mystique, whatever Svengalian crap you call it by—that's the power he holds over her. However base. However degrading. That's the power he holds over her.

And Adrian, Jr. After all these years, Adrian, Jr. Not to mention that other thing. After all these years, that other thing. If he knew, had known. *Knows* . . .

Bastard.

Goddamn bastard.

If only . . .

Pity Bryson Randolph is what they say he is, she thinks. He *does* have an intriguing little bulge there.

Goddamn day.

18

IN DAVID ABRAMS' OFFICE, over a bland Yankee pot roast with potatoes and cauliflower, Mark is uncomfortable too. And not because the Old Man intimidates him; there is always something warm and reassuring in David Abrams' presence, a kind of feeling basically alien to his son and heir.

No. It's something else. Something largely unsaid, perhaps even unthought, but something positioning him, in a very real and chilling way, between the chairman of the board and his son the president; something just within reach and a thousand miles out of it.

The conversation itself is relaxed, pleasant actually. Mark has always liked David Abrams, been comfortable around him. And while their goals, their styles, certainly their broadcast philosophies, are practically a definition of polarity itself, they share the rewards of indefinable empathy. David, in fact, while he views the younger man as an idealist who has been inordinately lucky, sees him also as bold, healthily balanced, and honest. Mark senses this, respects it, responds to it. And rarely takes it too seriously. The Old Man, after all, has been critically ill, and even before that, for several years, took little active part in the day-to-day operation of the Broadcast Division. He simply enjoys talking about it, particularly in the last year or two, with Mark. Still, today . . .

"Then explain this to me, Mark." They've been discussing the vitality (or lack of it), the proliferation of "permissiveness," in situation comedy, a subject evolving somehow from the Old Man's request that he look personally into format changes of the *Larry Lester Show.* "Please explain this to me, son. If this so-called corny comedy—we called it 'wholesome comedy' in my day—if Ozzie and Harriet and Eve Arden and Ann Sothern, and yessir, even Lucille Ball, if this kind of broad is so hard to swallow, then what the hell tastes good any more?"

"Mary Tyler Moore?" says Mark. "Valerie Harper? Our own Sharon Moore?"

"Our own Sharon Moore. Oy! Even my wife, one of the great radio and television stars of all time, even my good Ellen, who practically invented the four-letter word, even Ellen practically throws up when I turn the set on."

Mark smiles. "The times, they are a-changin'," he says. "Not to mention the demographics. You can't forget all those bright young consumers out there. The eighteen-to-forty-nine's, remember? The key marketing group? Without some raunch—even watered-down raunch —from Sharon Moore, they might not make it through the night."

His sardonic tone is not lost on David. The Old Man cocks his head almost waggishly. "There are times, Mark," he says, "when despite all your 'with it' kind of wizardry, I think you're really, I mean deep down where it counts, pretty much on my side, kid."

"Side?" says Mark. "I don't believe I really think in terms of 'sides,' Mr. Abrams . . . David," remembering hastily that the Old Man insists on being called that by his "boys."

"There are sides," says David, and Robert Abrams hovers like the Frustrate Ghost over the stringy meat.

They go on talking, of course: generally, abstractedly, mainly now about the network's new five-year game plan for progressive gross revenue increase and additional primary affiliate markets, the new season per se touched upon only lightly, the Wednesday-night experiment—on which so much depends—mentioned only in passing; the upcoming Board of Directors meeting (of which rumors are thirsty and thick) mentioned not at all. Mark has almost convinced himself that his earlier discomfort was simply a case of nerves—that anything deeper, more complex than an old man's whim, an old man's wisfulness (particularly when the old man is on his last corporate leg), is paranoia at its fanciful best—when David Abrams smiles like some comical brontosaur resurrected as a lion, and with the last bite of a lumpy apple crumb cake says, "I'll tell you something, kid. While there's lots of small things we're several planets apart on, like my Ellen likes to say, there's one big, overriding star we got in common. We both got philosophies. Most people in this business, they don't have philosophies. They go their whole lives, touching, influencing millions of other lives, without ever once stopping to think of *direction*, real goals—and I don't mean profit centers—hell, we've all of us got that.

"But us—you and me—we got values. Values and philosophies, any way you hack it, as the goddamn kinky youngsters say these days. Me, I knew even before Bernie Strauss and I started the UBC Radio Network back there in 1924 what I wanted to do. I wanted to entertain— just that, entertain. A song, a laugh, give 'em a good night's sleep. A *good* something . . .

"You, well . . . you want to entertain too. Maybe not just entertain. Maybe *enlighten* while you entertain, maybe that's the word. But word or not, it's a philosophy. It's got philosophy. We care, you and me. About those millions of people out there. We differ, son, but we care. You get what I mean?"

He pauses, and Mark—flattered as he is—feels peculiarly like disarmed prey. The Old Man's eyes may be gentle, agingly weak; but they're still sharp, even hungry.

"There's one other of us in these premises who's got a philosophy, too, of course. That is, if you care to call plotting philosophy. Some cockamamie philosophy, huh?" And the Ghost, almost materialized now, manages to make mincemeat of the already soggy apple crumb cake.

Then this: "The Board of Directors like you, Mark. Most of them. Like you and respect you. And that does the old heart good. You don't bend with the wind. And there's a wind brewing out there that a man, if he didn't have his head about him, just might take to be a blizzard or something."

And that's all. Circles, uncertainties, spectres galore. Mark smiles pleasantly, and thanks him for lunch. And wishes to Christ he hadn't gotten up this morning.

19

LUNCH—THE THOUGHT of lunch—is the furthest thing from Vivian Banner's mind.

Likewise, UBC.

"No, I won't be taking it with me, you can send it out to Westport," Vivian tells the attractive salesgirl at the street-floor handbag counter of Saks. Then, fingering again the soft leather of the bag she's just purchased, and signing the sales slip, she leaves the store on the Forty-ninth Street side.

Several people, both men and women, turn to look at her as she comes out. This often happens, for she has been on best-dressed lists for years, but even she can never remember looking quite like this. Her dress is simple, actually—a pale-blue Indian silk, with shoes and bag to match; her hair is up and sweeping, but not extreme. Her makeup, while complete, has merely heightened a naturally unblemished complexion. Yet taken together, these simplicities are practically an enterprise, and today—accented as they are by an unconcealed excitement in her walk—eminently stunning. She smiles to herself as she steps into a cab.

She's more than an hour early, but she's planned it this way: the early trip in, leaving the car at a small garage on Sixty-third Street, taking a taxi to Fifth, shopping, another taxi to the apartment on Park; an hour or so to herself before he gets there. She finds it remarkable, even after the calculated act of calling him, that she's doing all of this with such elaborate deliberateness. She really feels quite uncomplicated.

The apartment house squats on its fashionable corner like an imperious, if dumpy, dowager. Vivian enters its comfortable old grayness (which a faded lavender-and-gold lobby does nothing to offend) with a quiet smile for the aging, rather starchy doorman.

"I'm Mrs. Banner," she says. "I'll be occupying Mrs. Graham's apartment for the afternoon."

"Yes, ma'am, she informed me." The old man nods, handing her a rather grotesque set of keys. "She asked me also to inform you that her maid was in earlier, and that lunch, if you desire it, is in the refrigerator."

"How nice," she says. "Thank you."

She hesitates at the elevator, wondering whether to tell him she's expecting a friend; then, deciding against it ("friend" is such a contrivance; Fred Wiener could be her brother for all he knew), announces "Fourteen" to an equally aging, drowsy attendant. It's an old elevator, and the journey seems endless.

The apartment, which her friend Marian Graham often describes as "dowdy but decent," is just that. Like Marian herself, Vivian thinks, setting her purse on a small table in the entrance hall. Both of them, woman and home, look about as Park Avenue as a West Side laundry, but then ten-or-so million dollars can make even horsehair sofas the latest thing. Marian has always had a fetish about unpretentiousness, even to the extent of a single day-maid. Vivian has known her, a spinster in her early forties (Graham Industrials, Daddy's Little Girl), for a number of years, and when she offered the apartment—"Whenever you're in the city, pet, whether I'm there or not"—it seemed such a perfect solution. Now she's not so sure. If several cuts above a cheap hotel room, it still has the psychological effect of one.

She makes a quick tour of the apartment. There are two bedrooms, two baths, a dining area and a kitchen, one as dismal as the other. The kitchen is a stale chocolate. The salad and cold cuts, anyway, look bright and fresh. There are also small parfaits in the refrigerator.

She is suddenly, almost contentiously, very nervous. The marvelous unconcern that enlivened her morning isn't quite at home in the dull, overstuffed rooms. She hasn't been planning on drinking (at least, not this early), but the vodka and vermouth on a tray-table in the living room (a really dreadful, oddly pretentious piece) is tempting. She mixes a vodka martini and sits back on the uncomfortable sofa.

And thinks about Mark. She hasn't thought about him for three hours. Not since she left the house. Actually, she isn't *really* thinking about him now; merely things that concern him: the upcoming network party Saturday night, a benefit performance of the new Hal Prince musical opening next week, the people he's written concerning a Mediterranean cruise she's thinking of taking with her sister from Des Moines; but she hasn't thought about *him*. Just as her rejection of him this morning—and how many other mornings, nights?—has yet to get up the nerve to enter her one-channel consciousness. Just as the baby, losing the baby, learning she'd never have another, refusing adamantly to adopt, to . . .

The baby.

Seeing him, holding him, even kissing him, yet unborn. It was almost as though, when she opened her eyes this morning, Mark had been . . . She makes another vodka martini.

It helps. Even if it doesn't erase them—the baby; Mark. Strange. That if she does have to think about them, why should she remember only . . .

It *was* lovely once, even the flakiest minute of it. Even when he was out of her arms almost before the final . . . No, that's a lie. It was cruel, degrading, dis . . . wasn't it? Not even the kindest fantasy could make it right, make it up to her. . . .

I'm *trying* to hate him, she thinks. For months, years . . . oh, God, how I've hated him! Now, when I need to most, when I need so desperately . . .

She really didn't mean to have a third martini. She's glad she does. By the time Fred Wiener arrives she has no need to hate Mark; she doesn't even think about him. Anything about him. And the apartment isn't nearly so depressing as she imagined.

"Depressing, isn't it?" he says, looking about the stuffy gloom of the living room.

She has forgotten, from time to time, how attractive he is; dark, yet light, like a small, swift animal stalking a campfire.

"It grows on you," she says, steadying herself against a chair. "Would you like me to draw the shades?"

"Not especially."

She looks irresolutely away. "I was having a vodka martini. What would you like?"

He shrugs. "The same, I suppose. I try to make one my limit during the day. Steve Lilly's the toper in our little family."

How odd, she thinks. Why would he allude this way to Steve Lilly? Particularly to her? And why the damn network—so deliberately, right off? She shakes her head clear. Tries to.

"Martini," she says; rather dumbly, numbly. Then, mixing it: "I hope you didn't have to cancel an important lunch."

"Just my broker. Pain-in-the-ass one at that."

"I see," she says. "Well, won't you . . . sit down?"

"Now, I'm glad you asked that." There's just the slightest condescension—no, tease—in his manner. She hands him the drink and sits across from him. Very nearly on the floor, the way she's flying.

"I suppose you're wondering why I . . . ?" She's delivering lines and she knows it.

"Passionately," he says.

"It must have left you curious. I . . ."

"I'm not sure 'curious' is the word."

"Oh." She lights a cigarette and puts a hand to her hair. "You're looking well, Fred. You've lost weight since I saw you. When was it, anyway? Oh . . . the party at the Plaza in June, for that actress, who is she?"

"Anna Layton."

"Yes, Anna Layton. A charming woman really. I liked her immediately, which is unusual for me. I don't think she spoke of herself once, not once, which is itself disarming."

"And it's dialogue like this that makes the *Anna Layton Show* such a healthy drawing-room comedy."

She surrenders the cigarette, in a single jerky grind, to a small porcelain dish, which is all Marian Graham has provided in the way of ashtrays. "You're a very clever man, Fred," she says. "Freddie."

"And you're very beautiful today, Vivian."

She flushes, or hopes she does. The martinis are more insidious than she thought. "Thank you," she says. "You know, this is the first time we've . . . No, that isn't true. I mean, it's the . . . No more martinis for this broad. And I really haven't asked you how you are. How . . . how are you, Fred?"

"I'm well. Well as you can expect. Bachelors only age on the outside, you know." Is it amused tolerance or indulgence in his smile? Suddenly she wishes with all her heart she hadn't done this. But no . . . no, that isn't quite true. She wishes . . .

"There's lunch," she says. "In the refrigerator. I mean, whenever you . . ."

"Why don't we get undressed, Vivian?"

Eyes hard, she smiles. "You had to say that, didn't you?"

"It was tempting." He laughs softly—too softly. "From the dialogue, I was reasonably certain the next line would be . . . let's see . . . 'Freddie, you make me feel so cheap' . . ."

"The word is 'expensive,'" she snaps. "As long as we're playing Scrabble."

"Hey, wait a minute"—hands protectively (playfully) across his face. "This wasn't my idea, you know. I honestly thought you never wanted to see me again. After all, with Mark . . . I mean I thought you'd blocked it from your mind."

"I thought I had, too."

"So whatever happens . . ."

"I wish to hell I hadn't called you."

His smile now is certain; treacherous even. "But you did. And I came. So all this chitchat . . ."

"Go, Fred," she says. "Would you please? Would you please just go?"

"I haven't the least intention of going."

"Then you could at least . . ." There's no help for it. A curious knowing crosses her face. "Freddie, touch me," she says, and reaches behind her to release the top of the paper-thin dress.

He is on the ridiculous sofa almost before the snap of the tiny clasp, and his hands do the rest.

"Good," he says—murmurs; he can be lovely, really—his mouth on hers, on her breast. It's been a long time. . . . She's forgotten how marvelously hard a breast, a nipple, can get under the persuasive gentleness of a man's greedy tongue.

"The guest bedroom," she whispers.

It is a more oppressive room than she'd remembered. Slipping all the way out of the dress (her resolute back to him, in time-honored dignity), she says, "I think I'll turn down the spread. I'll tell Marian I didn't feel well and needed . . ."

But he's behind her, all over her, pulling her to him, and she can feel his pressuring nakedness through the half-slip. He takes it from her and turns her around. Hard. She either cries or moans, she isn't certain which. "Jesus," he confides to her hair (reaching below to mesh them together), "you *are* beautiful. You have the body of a young girl."

It's almost comical. Beside him on the outrageously hard bed, cradling him, she says, "Fred, now, yes, now." But as he is still slipping into what he calls his "pajamas," the prophylactic splits ("I believe in the Pill like I believe in the FCC," he's fond of saying), and when he goes to get another from his trousers across the room, he catches his foot on a leg of the bed, diminishing his passion as much as it heightens his talent for expletives, and it takes a minute or two to gentle him back to an erection. But he's a strangely satisfying lover. The impatience that characterizes him in clothes (the very latest styles, of course) hardly describes him out of them, for—enduringly, controlled —his every movement is channeled to her demands. He seems endless, infinite. And when she cries out, "Now! All the way in, goddamn you, now, now!" he is so deep inside her she thinks her middle has exploded. Beneath him, still locked to him, as dizzy from the drinks as she is from exhaustion, she discovers a shattering thing: At this moment, at least, she isn't so much hating Mark as she is loving Fred Wiener. But it will pass, she thinks; it will have to. How could she ever have called him in the first place, his office no more than two hundred feet from Mark's . . . ?

"Darling bastard darling sonofabitch darling darling," she whispers, caressing his hard, wet neck.

WIENER FINDS the old-fashioned tub shower a little hard to adjust, but otherwise cool and welcome. He lets the large, stinging spray carry off his tenseness and perspiration, while he guards the taste of triumph on his tongue.

Son of a! Sweeter slice than he'd remembered, but that was the least of it. Damn, he was great. Prolonging it the way he did. Concentrating on water going up a hill, not coming down—an Oriental stratagem an Indonesian had described to him once, and it worked every time. But the best part—saying it with every stratagem, every stroke: *For you, Mark. For you, Mark. For you, baby. You, Mark.* It's all he can do not to laugh out loud.

There is a sobering thought, though. When the gods give gifts, you have to assume they are given for a purpose, not handed out like balloons at a children's fair. Not ordinary playthings, to stow in a closet, to become bored with; forget. Today was neither a toy nor an accident. The last time was both, a fool thing in a car, a few dark panting minutes that seemed illusion even then; later, an outright trick of the mind. But today, full daylight, a deliberate setup . . . The question is how to use it. He has some thinking to do.

Shutting off the shower, opening the curtain, starting to reach for a towel, he has a slight start. She stands in the doorway, still naked, a kittenish smile on her face. "You're not getting off that easy," she says.

"I'm not what?"

She keeps the towel from him. "I said you're not getting off that easy. Don't leave yet, Fred."

He feels himself responding. "Vivian, please. The towel."

She folds it across her breasts. "Not yet. Besides, we both have to use it. I couldn't possibly explain *two* towels to Marian."

"Vivian. I have appointments . . ." One for sure—I have to see Bob Abrams this afternoon. He'll be interested in how your husband . . .

She is staring now, and curiously. "You know, I've never *seen* a Jewish man like this. I mean . . . Oh, I don't know, I'm just . . ."

"You mean Mark's is what we used to call unclean meat?" He can't resist.

She turns her head sharply. "That was lousy of you. But then the whole thing's pretty lousy, isn't it?"

"More dialogue?" He laughs, snatching the towel.

With an impish swiftness (Christ, her moods change faster than any woman's he's ever known) she steps into the tub as he's about to step out of it, and before he can stop her the water's cascading over both of them. The towel is irretrievable.

"I'll have to think up a good excuse for Marian," she says hoarsely, pressing against him. Within seconds they're swaying, interlocked; helped along, no doubt, by the sting of the shower.

"*Fred, God. Freddie . . .*" It's a commanding litany in his ear.

Almost together they step from the tub to the worn bathroom carpet, where—sliding wetly beneath him—she takes him into her with fingers clawing at his buttocks, and this time he forgets protections, and the hard tiles beneath the carpeting, and the waters are all downhill.

"We left the shower on," she says dumbly when he pushes himself from her, and after a weary rinse shuts it off. She's still lying on the floor, on her stomach, but she doesn't look at him.

When he's dressed, and has made a hasty sandwich from the cold cuts in the refrigerator, he goes back into the living room, where she sits on the sofa in an outdated dressing gown. She's smoking, and her expression is strained.

"Will I see you again?"

"Do you want to?"

"Tomorrow, Fred? I could arrange . . ."

"No, not tomorrow. Soon, but not . . ."

"There's our place in the Hamptons. I haven't closed it yet."

"Vivian, look . . ."

"Bastard." Quicksilver again, she smiles; cryptically, foolishly. "Is it that men in broadcasting are all empty?" she says. "Or is it just the men *I* . . ."

"God," he says under his breath. "You wouldn't know the difference between empty and full."

She doesn't hear him.

Mark's on his way down. Fred Wiener's on his way up. Is that what I am, the kind of monster I am, is that what it all comes down to? Is that what all this erotic dreamlanding is all about? Is something strange, beautiful, mysterious simply the banal ravings of a bored housewife? The opportunistic plotting of a corporate cunt?

"Why does someone as really kind and generous as Mark make me want to die?" she asks aloud of the empty room. "And someone as cruel and filthy and self-centered as Fred Wiener make me want to live? Or at least make me feel alive? Answer me *that*."

After a while, exhausted as much from the self-demands she can't satisfy as she is from the strenuousness of lovemaking, she takes herself to the bar for another drink.

20

EARLY AFTERNOON is that compulsive talk time that has UBC telephone operators pulling their hair.

"HELLO, MARK. I was hoping you'd call."

"How are you, Larry? How'd the luncheon with Bryson Randolph go?"

"The usual. I'm still chaste."

"Good. How long will you be in town, Larry?"

"I leave tomorrow night. I'm doing a turn on your morning show at seven."

"I see. Tell you what. Drop in tomorrow about three. Some things I want to throw at you."

"Throw at me, Mark?"

"Some new format ideas. The *Larry Lester Show* isn't beyond new format ideas, is it?"

"Will Wiener be there?"

"I doubt it."

"Have you discussed any of this with Len on the Coast? He's still my producer, you know."

"Unnecessary at this point. We'll *entre-nous* it for the time being. All right?"

"Should I bring the old Roman armor I wore on the last show?"

"Just bring your old star-quality self, Larry. I may even ask for your autograph."

"Cock teaser!"

"Freddie?"

"Yes, Larry?"

"That son of a bitch Banner just called me. Wants to see me tomorrow. *Sans* you, old buddy. Some format ideas, he says. You have any idea what's eating him?"

"Well, there are some . . . Listen, Larry, I'll get back to you. All right? My call to London's coming through."

"You'd better, Freddie. You'd just sure as hell . . ."

"Sorry, Mr. Wiener. Mr. Banner's in a meeting right now. I'll tell him you . . ."

"Joel?"

"Yes, Fred?"

"Has Mark said anything to you about format changes on the Lester show?"

"No, no, he hasn't. Why? Is there anything I should . . . ?"

"Mr. Abrams, please. Fred Wiener calling. Bob?"

"Yes, Fred?"

"I wouldn't have called except I think there's something you should know. Banner's meeting with Larry Lester tomorrow on possible format changes on the show."

"Oh? Well, of course with you there . . ."

"I'm not invited."

"I see. What do you think he . . . ?"

"He had lunch with your father today. In the Old Man's office, I might add."

"I see. After all we've . . . *you've* done to bring some kind of sophistication to that show, we're back to the old song-and-dance routine. Is that it?"

"Well, of course at this point I don't . . ."

"You were right to call, Fred. We'll speak later."

"Calm down, Bob. The Old Man having Mark to lunch doesn't mean a thing. He likes him, that's all."

"Oh? And has it occurred to you that the Board of Directors happen to like Banner as well? He could program reruns of *Lassie* and they'd cheer him. I don't like it, Adrian."

"Bob, you're too prickly about all this. The Board's olés are for bottom lines. Not valentines."

"I said I don't like it, Adrian. How deaf can you be? I, Robert Abrams, president of the goddamn United Broadcasting Companies, Incorporated, do not, I repeat, *do not* . . ."

"Mac?"

"Ah, Adrian."

"You'll meet with Lilly?"

"Most discreetly."

"Good."

"Edith? It's Sue."

"Yes, dear?"

"Secret Agent X-O-two reporting."

"Go it, X-O-two."

"My divine boss, Mr. Gerald McAlister, has had me make reservations for two at Sweet's for dinner this evening."

"Oh? Who's the lucky girl? I mean guy."

"Steve Lilly."

"You're a pip, X-O-two."

"Thanks, Edith. I trust you'll be equally astute in letting me know the next time Bob Abrams or Adrian Miller takes a leak. Now, be a good

girl and get me Charlie Marx on the Coast. Then return the call to
Joe Warren at KXTL in Memphis. Then Steve Lilly."

"THAT YOU, Charles?"

"Barely."

"What's wrong?"

"Up all night again, Mark."

"The Godiva bit for *Magazine*?"

"Still editing, Mark. Jesus! At six-thirty this morning we still saw an
inch and a half of pubic hair."

"No wonder you couldn't sleep. But stay in there, pal."

"We're trying. Anything special you wanted, Mark?"

"Yes, there is, Charlie. I think I want to drop the Larry Lester
segment from next week's *Magazine*. Use the Milton Berle one instead."

"Ho-ho! Wiener know?"

"He will."

"Okay by me. You're the boss, Mark."

"I figure so, Charlie. Thanks, Charlie."

"JOE?"

"Greetings, Mark."

"Sorry I'm just getting back to you. Livelier Monday than usual, as
you can imagine."

"Sokay, boy, forget it. Besides, bad news can always wait a few
hours."

"Bad news?"

"Afraid so, Mark. I know this is one hell of a time to be pulling
this, two days before the premiere, but we're not going to clear the
last hour of *Magazine* here in Memphis. And it looks like Little Rock,
Jackson, Biloxi, Shreveport and Tyler, Texas, are going along with us.
And—I hope you're sittin' down, Mark—Atlanta too."

"The rape scene in the Tennessee Williams segment?"

"You guessed it. It's just carryin' things too far, Mark. I don't care
how many times the old slice-of-life routine is thrown at us."

"Joe, be reasonable. Our Standards and Practices people passed that
scene without blinking an eye. It's well within the NAB Code and you
know it."

"Screw NAB. It's Memphis I'm concerned with."

"I don't doubt that in the least, Joe. But am I hearing more than a
trace of the old parochial here? I mean, would this call have been

necessary if the lady in question had gotten it in Vermont instead of Mississippi?"

"I'm sure Bob Abrams would have loved to hear that remark, Mark. Loved hell out of it."

"Look, Joe, this is serious business. All we need is for the press to get hold of this—"

"Sorry, old buddy. They're gettin' it in about an hour. Joint statement from all five stations."

"You're a sweetheart, Joe. You know that? You're a real sweetheart."

"There's just got be a limit to how far we let you guys go, Mark. This country's not just New York and Los Angeles, you know. In between there's a lot of people and places, old buddy."

". . . ABOUT THE SIZE of it, Mark. Bob's quite disturbed about the Southern stations' not clearing. You know how he feels about the South. Atlanta particularly. He's in quite a snit, you might say."

"What are you getting at, Adrian?"

"Getting at? Why, nothing, Mark. I can't recall when I've been so direct, actually. I just think—that is, *we* just think—that Fred Wiener should be more . . . *present*, shall we say? He was against the scene in question from the beginning, I'm told. And you might take under advisement the fact that Larry Lester telephoned him the moment he'd hung up with you, and our boy didn't waste a precious second in getting to guess who. Enough said, Mark?"

"MARK?"

"Yes, sir?"

"Just wanted to tell you again how much I enjoyed our lunch, son. Before I leave for the day."

"Thank you, Mr. Abrams. Me too."

"Seems strange to be going home in midafternoon, but Ellen would have my old hide if I didn't. Rough day for you, Mark?"

"Nothing I can't handle."

"I believe that."

"Thank you, sir."

"It's a funny thing, Mark. You're the only man outside of my old partner Bernie Strauss—I wish you could have known him—the only man outside of Bernie I never completely saw eye to eye with, that I find I like getting along with. There are days and days ahead. Days and days. You're a good man, son."

"DID YOU EVER get Steve Lilly, Edith?"

"Sorry, sire. Haig and Haig is still out to lunch."

"TOM MITCHUM from Continental Tires on four. Do you want to take the call now or . . . Uh-uh. Mr. Abrams, Mr. Robert Abrams, wants you, Mr. Miller and Bill Kelly from News in his office now, pronto. Like haul ass. Need an upper, boss? I've got one in my purse."

"Can you make it a downer, Edith? Any more excitement today and I may run out and hug old ladies on the street."

It is a Robert of control and authority who faces a bewildered Adrian Miller, Mark Banner and Bill Kelly from his throne of a desk, hands remarkably stilled, voice challenging even the hint of disagreement. Insurrection of any nature, within the first ten seconds, is not only out of the question, it augurs instant death.

"I have made a decision," he begins. "A unilateral decision, you might say." His eyes capture all of them. "Regardless of ratings or critical reaction to this season's product, I want next year's schedule to reflect—I mean, overwhelmingly reflect—an emphasis on special, and I mean *special*, programming. For too long now, we've given a lot of lip service to it—all of us, all the networks—and if by the end of a season we've come up with even a half-dozen mediocre programs of some kind of quality or other, we're lucky as hell. So next year—I don't give a damn what the excuses—we are going to be out there in the forefront, and with product, not promise. I trust there is no misreading of this. On *anybody's* part."

There is as yet not even a reading, much less misreading, evidenced by the manner in which none of them seeks to look at the other.

"I have three specific projects in mind, to start us off," he says now. "The first two are in the dramatic area—Tolkien's *Lord of the Rings* and Thomas Mann's *Joseph and His Brothers*. Regardless of how many hours it takes to present them."

Here, Adrian, if only by force of habit, speaks out. "For God's sake, Bobby, we haven't even had a meeting with the financial people . . ."

And is stilled by a frozen glare from the president. "This time, the cart *does* come before the horse. I'll take care of the financial situation. As well as the Board. Anything else?"

"I'm not sure of their availability," Mark says. "The last I heard, CBS . . ."

"Just see that they're available," Robert says. "Anything else?"

Hardly.

"Then the third project—third *initial* project—is a joint news and programming effort to bring Will and Ariel Durant's *Story of Civiliza-*

tion to television. You can perhaps imagine the kind of documentary-dramatic form it could take—"

This time "Anything else?" would have been gratuitous.

"Then begin thinking about them, all three of them, and we'll meet again one week from today, with Fred Wiener present, I might add, at which time each of you will have a decent amount of material to contribute. And an enthusiasm, I trust."

And, as if an afterthought: "I plan to have a personal hand in these productions, regardless of whom we finally decide on to produce, write, direct. Keep that in mind too."

Mark, walking from the office, cannot help but be slowed by irony: to agree with the man's concept, his determination, with his obviously genuine intensity, while despising him with even more. It says as much about the industry as it does of himself, and he knows it.

In the corridor outside (Bill Kelly having remained behind to discuss live coverage of an upcoming presidential press conference), Adrian, taking Mark by the elbow, says, "Come on in my office a minute. I think we have something to discuss before this charade goes any further."

Mark smiles (he hopes sincerely). "Sorry, Adrian. I'm late for the *Home Town* screening."

"I see," says Adrian. "Well, I'm glad you have a meeting of one kind or another set up. If not, you'd probably have to invent one."

Mark has no intention of asking him what he means. There are enough games being played in this building today to keep F. A. O. Schwartz in business for the next ten years.

And it's a long journey between floors, from forty-two to thirty-five.

21

DUSK. Slivers of light on the circular driveway. The great Tudor house ominous in the deepening shadows. Door opens. Slowly. Girl appears. Dressed simply; skirt, blouse, light sweater. Stands for a moment on front steps. Wistful but resigned. Eyes down. "Goodbye. Goodbye, years." Walks quickly to car, revealed now in shadows; drives off. Slow dissolve to house, to upstairs window of house. Light on. Now off. Music up and under, out.

"Shit."

This unvarnished critique can have come from no one but Maury Sherman, UBC's blunt, even gross but somehow shrewd head of Audience Research. As the ceiling lights of the thirty-fifth-floor screening room come on and the screen goes dark, Mark looks around. He had forgotten Sherman was attending. The media chief, as seedy in dress as he is in speech (he always looks as if he's just been out-fitted by Montgomery Ward—ten years ago, Mark thinks), is sitting several rows back, alone; slumped indifferently in his seat like the maverick he is. The man hasn't the remotest conception—at least, intention—of tact, but Mark isn't about to treat his opinion of the *Home Town* pilot they've just seen with less than respect. Sherman has been with UBC since the early radio days, once even as general manager, and his reputation for cutting through all the fat—sparing only the lean—is well deserved. Probably no one else in the network—and that includes some of the way-out Hollywood crowd—holds quite the unique position Maury Sherman holds. He gets away, as they say, with murder; twice, three times; four. In a way he plays a kind of in-house devil's advocate, Mark realizes. And while he may rattle the sensibilities, nine times out of ten his advice is valid. Agencies and advertisers may shudder at the sight of him—they have for years—but the man is invaluable.

No one else in the room would have said it, Mark thinks, for all their "individualism." They'd either make a pretense of weighing the film's good points and bad—always, will it sell?—or else keep silent, which is precisely what they're doing now. Mark glances about him. It's difficult to tell just what their reactions to the hour-long pilot episode are; Maury Sherman has stopped them in their tracks. But one thing's sure: *They* aren't sure; that's the thing. None of them—Steve Lilly, Wiener, Joel Greer, Ashton Corey and Fred Dix (two other divisional program heads under Wiener), Marv Goldberg of Sales Planning—none of them can afford the balls of a Maury Sherman. They're young men, the new breed of men, "creative" men; they're ambitious men. Too much depends on their judgments for them to be too black-or-white too quickly. And before the president of the network has reacted first. All except Joel Greer, perhaps, Mark amends. In many ways, he likes to think, Greer reminds him of himself a few years back. Less salesman in him, maybe. But he has convictions. *Before* the fact, not after. And then again, perhaps—perhaps Steve Lilly . . .

And he himself is sitting here too long. He stands and stretches. "We'll discuss it at the Plans meeting tomorrow," he says. "I'll be interested in your reactions." He turns to Sherman. "Could you stop by the office a minute, Maury?"

"Sure."

"Thanks." Then to Steve Lilly, who sits next to him, and who obviously has had an even wetter luncheon than usual: "Walk me back, Steve. I want to hear about the Continental presentation."

In the canyon of corridor, Lilly buoyant beside him, he says, "Went well?"

"How'd you guess?"

"I didn't," he says. "Tom Mitchum at the agency called me. Said you made a splendid pitch. That was his adjective. Splendid. You may have to go to Akron with it, by the way. And they may want you to bring Rod Marshall along. If we can get him. Have Wiener talk to his agent about it. Just in case."

"Will do."

"Oh, and Steve . . . drop a memo to Sales Planning, Research, the Art Department. You know. Pat on the back. We haven't been doing enough of that lately."

"You bet."

They had reached the side corridor to his suite of offices. "I'm not sure anyone else could have pulled this off, Steve," he says. "Good work."

"Mark, you're beautiful."

There are several other things Mark had wanted to speak with him about. A stewardship report for P&G, the sloppy way Doug Johnson, UBC's Detroit sales manager, was handling General Motors. The party at the Waldorf Saturday to celebrate *Magazine* and the new season. But something in his walk, the sheer delight of the man— that special kind of triumph that comes so seldom, if at all—restrains him. That and . . .

And something in himself. Something . . . tired. Something that has been trying to push through to his consciousness all afternoon, ever since his conversation with McAlister, the lunch with the Old Man, the startling and still cryptic meeting with Robert Abrams, and which he hasn't allowed through, has consciously forbidden passage to, even during the screening, when his mind had journeyed cities and plains. "I'll talk to you later," he says; more abruptly than he wants to, than he likes.

He has hardly reached his office, and given a brief instruction to Edith, when Maury Sherman balls in. Unannounced, as usual.

"I know," he growls, "you want to know where the shit I come off calling a five-hundred-seventy-five-thousand-dollar pilot shit. What is it umpires say? I calls 'em as I sees 'em. And when I sees 'em shit, I calls 'em . . ."

Mark smiles. "Number one, I don't know where the shit you come off calling a five-hundred-*ninety*-five-thousand-dollar pilot shit," he says. "And number two, you're no umpire. Have a seat."

"I like you, Mark. I honest to shit like you."

"Use that word once more," Mark says, "and you're going out on your . . . behind."

Cackling, Sherman sits. "Shoot."

Mark's eyes are level. "Was it just the phony ending you objected to, Maury? The studio snowed us into it, I admit. The original script's ending was more provocative."

"It'll take more than an ending to save that one, Mark. And I'm a numbers man, not a Bryson Randolph."

"I asked for your opinion, didn't I?"

"Okay, you got it. It's dull, it's pretentious, it's insulting. It also stinks."

"That bad?"

"Twenty share. *Hilda's* a gold mine alongside it."

Mark lights a cigarette. "I'll tell you something, Maury. I asked for the budget for this pilot for one reason. Prestige. I know that's a dirty word these days, or even a hollow echo of Bob Abrams, but I happen to believe that quality drama isn't just a critic's cry in the wilderness. People are hungry for quality, Maury. They just don't know that they are. The human condition's not exclusively measured by share of audience, Maury."

"And you wouldn't have stuck your neck out on this turkey if you hadn't had Wilson's Drugs' interest in half of it. Right?"

Mark laughs, really for the first time all day. "You're damn right I wouldn't," he says. "But trying to cover your bets doesn't make them wrong, my friend. The idea comes first. That's what we're all about, should be . . ."

"Yeah," says Sherman. "That's what the Board of Directors tells itself every day. The idea, boys, that's what we're all about. Screw the ratings. Fuck the profits."

Mark laughs again. "You're letting your five thousand shares of common stock get to you, Maury."

"Seven thousand. And you'd made up your mind about *Home Town* halfway through it, Mark, script or no script. It disappointed hell out of you and you know it. You just wanted to pick my brain a little, right? Well, consider it picked."

In a mock gesture of defeat, Mark rises. There is probably no one in the network, in the whole damn industry, that he enjoys more than Maury Sherman. But it is already past five and he still has hours to go—the calls to the Coast, a five-thirty closed-circuit to the affiliates (they've scheduled them daily this week), another session with Newton on the Cincinnati speech at seven. "Picked?" he said. "Hardly touched."

Sherman, however, lingers a minute or so longer, and his gaze, while kindly, is firm. And as usual, his transition is direct and abrupt. "Mark, I'm a fucking fixture around this place, right? I'll be right where I am till I croak, or until the Old Man croaks, which ain't very bloody likely, as they say in France. Years ago, I actually had an eye on your chair, did you know that? But I learned early that a Jew— a *Jew* Jew like me, that is—can get just about every strategic position there is in this company—except sales chief and president. That's as certain as Bob Abrams' passel of pills." Getting to his feet, he makes a futile attempt to adjust his tie, which is stained with coffee, yesterday's lunch, and God knows how many years. "My old man has a saying, Mark. The Jews never crucified Christ, they just probably worried him to death. But worrying ain't crucifying, any way you slice it."

And leaving, a rumpled mess: "Keep an eye out for the goyim, kid. And that includes Bobby Son-of-the-Bitch-Goddess Abrams. And don't take any wooden cunts. They don't go so well with your human condition there." Grinning broadly. "No shit."

22

JOEL GREER leaves the screening room shortly after Mark and Steve Lilly, walking out with Ashton Corey as if they had something to discuss. He has nothing at all to discuss, but it's a reasonable out. He can tell by the way the others stay behind that Wiener is in the mood to hold court. Joel knows he can take anything today but Wiener's court.

He takes an elevator to the thirty-sixth floor, where Programming and Production are. It's five after five, and the noisy end-of-day ritual —that flurry of activity so swiftly born of fatigue—has begun. Soon they'll be pouring into the halls and elevators, the chattering hundreds from all the UBC floors; a swollen army on its benevolent overnight pass, rain and all, Joel reflects; and not daring to think of it that way. Ignoring it, he goes directly to his office (modest and nondescript in comparison with Wiener's), where he informs his secretary, an incredibly fragile young thing, that she can leave if she's finished the synopsis report on new scripts he prepared for Mark and Fred Wiener. He settles himself down for another script-reading session. He isn't meeting his wife, Janet, until six, at a cocktail lounge in the next block, and they aren't due at his mother's weekly family dinner until seven. Joel has to make every minute count these days. This is his frantic season, and when he isn't on the Coast talking scripts, he is here in New York reading them, most of them with an eye on next year's crop, but some projected as far as three years in advance. Leaving before six tonight is in itself uncommon. His is usually the last light on the floor.

With the half hour or so left him, however, he can't concentrate. The script (an uninspired espionage comedy) makes little sense. He has no need to ask himself why. *Why* is a single word, a single name. Wiener. He acquiesced to Wiener's subterfuge this morning, when in truth the subterfuge is his. He has no intention of securing information for Fred Wiener, even (assuming a Wiener ascendency) for a real crack at programming chief for himself.

He had known he wouldn't within seconds of being asked, but he had played loyal-and-obedient underling to the hilt. Thus he spends the half hour before meeting Janet (as he has spent most of the afternoon) in a mild state of self-denigration, and not only because of Wiener. There are the other scores, too, the old scores; the black guilts that only Janet has ever detected; the day he went along with his mother and brothers and gave up the name of Griebsberg, the day he gave up the novel he had only half completed, the day he walked through the doors of an advertising agency (where he started his career in television) and made a success of it. These twenty-lash crimes are always waiting in the wings, and—like his relationship with Fred Wiener—are really one and the same. *Joel, darling,* his mother pleading, like a bad line in a Yiddish satire, *your brother Sylvan's successful, your brother Albert's successful, your cousin Aaron* . . . It's ten to six before he knows it.

It's raining hard when he gets outside. Forgoing an umbrella, he half runs the block and a half to the High Life cocktail lounge just off Fifth, where Janet is to meet him for their traditional gibson before taxiing across town to Central Park West and his mother's. When he arrives, his face is chapped and damp, his fingers sticky when he touches it. Not quite leaning against the redwood bar, nor altogether sitting on one of its high leather stools, he feels rangier, more lumbering, much wetter than he is. But the awkwardness is swallowed by the relaxed bodies around him. Joel is a grave young man. His saving grace, he sometimes thinks, is that he knows it.

He glances at the clock on the far wall. Six-ten. He shifts weight. Frowns. Janet should have been here by this time. She's spent the afternoon shopping, he supposes; Monday, as she likes to call it, is her Bergdorf-Bonwit-Bendel day—a compensation, he often thinks, for the Monday evenings at his mother's. Janet so dreads them that years ago he had taken to meeting her here at the High Life before they went, hoping (admittedly, with small success) that the cocktail-hour banter would ease the tension she would invariably have spent the day building up. It is a day that always begins the same, whenever he isn't on the Coast: Janet distant in the early morning, grandly silent, untouchable by so much as a finger. Like a time to love and a time to talk, it has made its way into their lives; mutely established, mutually understood. And lately Richard has been uncommonly fretful when he comes to their bedroom to tell them good morning. His five-year-old son's moods are so perfectly attuned to his mother's that he behaves as if Janet sends him her dispositions by electrical impulse, hours in advance. And then, of course, *his* mother . . . Always the Monday-morning phone call, just before he leaves the house. The "little reminder" of dinner at seven; the perfunctory mention of Janet and Richard, as if she were merely inquiring after vaguely remembered friends.

Well, this is one Monday evening he can do without. He can almost see it through Janet's eyes: the careful politenesses, the predictable gestures, the relentless unity (was that Janet's phrase?), the guarded tongues; the one cocktail before dinner, the almost prescribed amount of peas one brings to his plate ("I think I took one too many tonight," Janet bragged on their way home last week), the so-dear reminiscences of Sylvan as a baby; the way Albert would stare at Janet when he thought she wasn't looking (Janet staring curiously back), his brother's eyes poor camouflage for the desire that strains his handsome face. And more: the little looks of pity and disbelief his mother gives to his sister, Sophie (her now-legendary question "But who on earth marries laundrymen, dear?" repeated in every silence); the after-dinner remembrances of Morris Griebsberg, their father, who was a good man in his way but who didn't live to savor the sweeter taste of Greer.

But damn it, no, it isn't like that at all. Not so warped and one-dimensional, the way Janet sees it. One night a week is precious little to give . . . isn't it? And how could Janet ever really understand? You had to *be* a Griebsberg (*Greer!*) to understand. It goes back so far, runs so long, so deep: the family. Forsake God and country, love and law, but not the family. Not the Griebsbergs, who by God made it to Greer.

Joel shakes his head, as though the motion itself will clear it of thought. He glances again at the clock. Six-twenty. It's always unsettling when Janet is late. But he has no sooner looked down again than she's there.

"I know, I know, I'm late as the devil, but the rain's impossible, the traffic's hideous, and it's a wonder I'm here at all. Gibson, please, dry. You look exhausted, Joel. Mean day, darling?"

"So-so," he says.

"Fred Wiener?"

"He's a psychotic."

"You're fully convinced?"

"I am."

"Then so am I. Forgive me?"

Joel smiles as she squeezes in beside him, slides onto the single stool—smiles, he knows, as he probably smiled the first time he ever saw her, seven years ago at an agency party at the Pierre when Charley Rubin, then his superior, introduced her (grudgingly) as "Janet Mintz from Great Barrington . . . a cousin of my wife," and she, inadvertently spilling champagne on his dinner jacket, breathed softly but unapologetically, as though it were the most natural thing on earth to spill champagne at an introduction, "Oh, wouldn't you know. Forgive me?" He said, and was surprised to discover how much he meant it, "I think I would forgive you just about anything," and smiled. The years have not changed the quiet seriousness of his smile any more than they have changed Janet Mintz. Her thick auburn hair may be shorter, thinner, her waist half an inch smaller (she diets with conviction), but the clear proud skin, the light swell of her breasts, the cautious advance of her slender legs (as if the very next step may be the decisive one)—these have lost none of their excitement. Even with the wet gray hood hugging her face (he finds her least attractive in headpieces of any kind) there is a radiance about her, a vitality that touches even the remotest parts of her with a nervelike precision. Away from her for more than the accustomed hours of a day he feels strangely gutted. Even to look seriously at another woman is intolerable to imagine, much less descend to—Monday mornings and all.

Janet has lifted her drink in a mock toast. "To my getting here at all," she says.

"Which means the rain's not the culprit," he says, knowing full well that it isn't.

She nods, the tip of her tongue resting lightly on the rim of her glass. Joel recognizes the pose immediately. It is a sister to the way she pauses during a meal, her tongue halting querulously at the edge of her fork, or the way she looks up from her corner desk in their bedroom, her tongue poised on the sharp tip of a pencil—involuntary signs that something is being unsaid. He touches her arm. In a moment, two, her eyes are level with his. "Joel," she says, "I almost didn't come. I was halfway home in a taxi."

"In a taxi? You were going back to the apartment? Why on earth—"

"Oh . . . a hundred reasons, I suppose, and none of them very clear. Instinctive me on the prowl again. Autumn days when it rains are portentous. Janet and her Mondays. Take your choice." Her tongue now holds a tiny cocktail onion as if it were a prisoner; or a lover. She laughs sharply. "Halfway home and I couldn't go through with it. I kept seeing you sitting here like Father Time. It was too much. If only you weren't so serious . . . so goddamn responsible . . . when I picture you."

Joel, in spite of himself, flushing—looks hastily away. Janet, he knows, draws some sort of comfort from raillery whenever she's tense or indecisive or bored, and although (with him, at least) it is gently chiding, even affectionate, he is always unprepared. He sometimes wonders if his occasional self-consciousness isn't Janet's best crutch. If there is even the suggestion of guilt in something she says or does (or doesn't say or doesn't do), it is set free by his own deep blush. Within seconds it is he who's guilty of something. Now, as if every stranger crowding the small bar has found him out, he clears his throat and lifts his face, guaranteeing not an earnest nor a disquieting thought. "Well," he says, blithely dismissing the poor start they seem to have got off to, "you're here and I'm happy. How much poorer am I?"

"Gorgeous cocktail dress at Altman's," she says. "And a really mad little hat at Bonwit's. For Helen Jacobson's tea next week." The Jacobsons are neighbors on Sutton Place South. "I promise not to let you see me in it," she adds.

"Thanks." Then, finishing his drink, he says (it sounds almost lame), "You'd better hurry it, honey. We're already late. Taxis must be scarce as hell in this rain."

Her gloved hand is on his. "Joel . . . Joel, wait." There is an unexpected urgency in her voice. "Joel, listen, I . . . I've had the oddest feeling all day. I know it sounds ridiculous . . . God knows your mother's dinners hardly change from one week to the next. But . . . Joel, let's not go. I know it must sound like the rankest heresy, but . . . for me, this once, let's *not* go. We're both dressed and Mrs. Kirschman will stay with Richard until twelve or so. Let's . . . let's eat at Chez Renée, just the two of us, maybe even see a play. Tickets aren't too difficult at the last minute, not this season anyway, and Helen says the new Papp thing is . . ."

He stares in disbelief. Whatever fantasy he or his brothers and sister entertain in anticipation of the Monday-night dinners, being absent is never one of them. "Janet, what in the world are you talking about?"

"Us," she says, and her eyes are wide. "I think I'm talking about us, Joel. Us . . . UBC . . . your mother . . . they're not so different, really. . . . I don't know. God knows I don't know. I've just had this ridiculous feeling all day, I . . . Joel, it would be so simple. We could say you're sick."

"Hardly," he says. "Nobody gets sick on Monday. Mother wouldn't allow it." He wonders if his bantering tone will ease the strange desperation in her face. And for an instant it *is* desperation he sees: her lips are pale with it. "Now come on, honey." He touches her shoulder. "One good long swallow." He pays the sallow, mostly indifferent bartender who has waited on them for almost three years and has yet to acknowledge them with more than a peremptory nod.

The moment's strain passes quickly. "I knew it was a fool's errand before I started it," Janet says lightly. "But don't rush me. I just got here, remember?"

"It's almost seven, Janet . . ."

"Ah, the witching hour. All right, Joel, don't get panicky. Tradition's blood won't be on your wife's hands. You know, sometimes I wish your name were still Griebsberg and you were still writing a novel. Even a bad novel."

"I'll bet you do. I know how much you love dresses off the racks at Korvette's."

"I don't understand you. I really don't understand you. If the network . . . television . . . oh, whatever it is. If it bothers you so much, why are you so good at it? Mark Banner told me himself you work like you were born to it."

"And what does your not wanting to go to mother's have to do with the UBC Television Network?"

"Oh, I don't know. Everything, probably. And probably I'm just being flaky, and was flaky before I ever heard the silly word. And you didn't answer my question."

"What question?"

"If it eats your heart out, why are you so good at it?"

"My job?"

"Your job."

"That's an indecent question."

"I wonder if you'd ever have finished that book in the first place."

"And *that's* indecent."

"I know. I love you, Joel."

"I know you do."

"Shall we?"

The rain has slackened. A little. They pause for a moment outside the High Life as though startled to find the air so fresh. It had been very muggy inside.

23

Not four blocks away, at the Bristol Hotel, in UBC's permanent suite for its big brass treasures (the Old Man's side-of-the-mouth euphemism for $200,000-a-year assholes—pet saying of his drinking days), Joslyn Miller applies a battalion of extravagant cosmetics to her sagging face and girds herself for her husband's inevitable pre-evening instructions. Which come as soon as he has completed his shave and shower.

"Now, this is the important thing," Adrian says, towel straining to stay attached to his expanding middle. "When the Old Man's name comes up—and either Jim or Sally Mortimer *will* bring it up, you can bet your ass on that—when his name does come up, you're to *cluck*. Sympathetically, of course, but cluck. Get it? Now try it."

"Oh, for God's sake," she says, laughing in spite of herself. "You get more paranoid every day. Cluck! You're too much. You really are."

He finds neither himself nor her very funny. If anything, the scowl he has showered with (one wholly rare, reserved generally for their moments alone) is deeper, more intense. "I said cluck," he says. And this time, despite a pancake makeup guaranteed to prevent it, she flushes.

"I do not cluck!"

Laughter again—this time his, and harsh. "Good! You just did. Just as you always have, dear heart. When it goes in or comes out, doesn't matter. You cluck."

"And you're a son of a bitch!" But there's little real force, even less conviction, in her outrage. After all these years it still lands at his feet, not his head. "And then after you've clucked—sympathetically—" he says, "you say something innocuous, like 'Poor darling. So many illnesses. And at his age . . . I guess he'll just never be the same.' And then bug off. I'll manage it from there." The discussion ended, as far as he's concerned, he lets the exhausted towel fall to the floor and reaches to the bed for his shorts.

But on deaf ears or not, she's determined. "It just happens to be my uncle we're talking about. My *blood* uncle, in case you've forgotten. Not that anyone as bloodless as you would understand." No response, of course, but on . . . on: "And the man who made you, for

God's sake. The man who made you as much a son as his own Bobby, for God's sake. God knows daddy, my own darling, darling daddy, saw through you from the very minute he met you, the very minute he ever laid eyes on you, *he* knew. Rotten, that's all it's ever been, all *you've* ever been. As if the Mortimers won't see through it, anybody with half a brain could see through it, the whole thing's . . . God! You and Bobby! You and your Bobby, you make me . . . God! If daddy could see! If only daddy could see . . . daddy or even my poor sainted mama could see . . ."

Adrian has his tie on, and properly Windsored, before he speaks again. "Just cluck," he says, and runs a finger or two along the crack of her behind, a message that has always, more than any other, gotten to her.

In the Bristol Bar, waiting for the Board of Directors Mortimers, she whispers over a double Margarita, straight up, "It's still *my* stock, you know, still in *my* name, you know," but it seems to have about as much impact as a TV test pattern. The real impact, his . . . promised later . . . later. That's all that matters. All that ever mattered. All that . . .

Mama? Please don't cry so, mama. Daddy only does it to you so he can have pretty little things like me. It's what people have to do, mama, what they have to do to each other, mama, else how could there ever be nice little babies like me? No, she never said it, never wanted to say it even; ever. Still, all her life she's thought it, thought maybe she's even said it. She was little more than an infant, not even walking well yet, when her mother screamed in the night, night after night, fighting her daddy's body as she fought everything else in her life—her own mother, Grandma Sarah; the beautiful apartment daddy surprised her with; the neighbors, daddy's friends; the radio network. Only Uncle David has been her bridge to reality; her true heart, her joy, her meaning. The rest a jungle or a desert, depending on the hour, the day, the year. Even she herself, "Sweet Baby Joslyn" in her crib—even she has been as unreal, as unwanted, as the rest. Only an infant, yes—but every second of it somehow still vivid as though her eyes have actually seen, ears actually heard, insides actually felt. Mama gone mad at last, last link to the world now severed. Daddy away on a trip (Washington, she learned later, negotiating still another of infant broadcasting's endless entanglements), only she in her crib and mama and Grandma Sarah in the living room, when somewhere out of nightmare (hers, Joslyn's, as likely as not; she has been given to them from the beginning), a screeching, scratching, slashing holocaust embracing them all. Then Grandma Sarah was crumpled like a rag doll in a corner, her neck broken, little body split open like a Seder chicken's. The radios in the living room, dining room, bedroom, the kitchen—daddy's precious short-wave receiving equipment in the study—smashed to the floor like so many silly broken dreams. Even her own crib slashed nearly to splinters. And blood. Blood, blood and blood. Mama sitting glassy-eyed, kitchen knife still in her hands, washed in blood. "Thank God you were too young to see it," her father, Bernie Strauss, and his partner, David Abrams, Uncle David, told her later, and often. But she did, she did. No matter what they say, how chemically, psychically impossible it is to remember, she does. *Does.* Just as she has heard, *seen* her crazy mother in dreams. *Don't you ever let nobody put that thing in you, you hear? Don't you ever let nobody even show it to you, you hear?*

"AND WHAT THE HELL does this infantile reminiscence have to do with my husband's cock?" she asks the mirror, putting the finishing touches to her face, ready now for the long hours ahead; thoughts of Adrian's touch in the early morning—however indifferent or perfunctory—the only thing that can get her through the night. But if the mirror answers her, as it is said to have done Snow White, she somehow finds the courage not to hear it.

24

ACROSS TOWN, in a back booth at Christy's—a small bar near her apartment on Ninth Avenue—Barbara Ermeling sits fingering a whiskey sour and nervously watching the door. She's wearing more makeup than she usually wears in the office, but under the bar's dim colored lights her pallor is unmistakable. It is the kind of pallor that many men go out of their skulls over, for it's both delicate and sensuous, suggesting both innocence and debauchery, and the dark hair that crowns it —the dark eyes that look out from it—compound the crime.

That's the way Barbara Ermeling thinks of herself—as a crime. Like now, for instance. The men at the bar, the ones in the other booths: all of them are staring, licking their lips, touching themselves, something. It has always been this way, as long as she can remember, as far back as Toledo, where she developed too early, and her tits were the talk of the seventh grade. And at all the places she worked before coming to UBC—the places she had to leave, one by one, because sooner or later somebody wouldn't be content with just looking.

And it would start, the things that always led to things, the things she couldn't—wouldn't—do. But she can still hold her head up (when she wants to), and proudly, too. For no man has ever penetrated her, not ever. Not one. Not with his . . . No man. Not one. Not even the one man she herself finally wants so awfully, so awfully she actually cries that she can't bring herself to let him. But she hasn't. She won't. Not even he. . . .

But *he* is here. He slides in across from her, drawls, "Hi," and taps her knee. She, from long habit, keeps her eyes lowered. "I wasn't sure you'd come," she says.

"Wasn't sure I'd come?" Steve Lilly laughs; a rich laugh; many heads turn toward him. "Lord, girl. I called you 'round three, didn't I?"

"You've called before and not shown up," she says.

"Well, I'm heah now."

"Yes."

She looks up. As always, she has to draw in her breath when she sees him. It seems incredible still that this big, beautiful, important human being has actually been born on a farm in some hick Louisiana town; even more, that he started at UBC as a page boy.

"I've missed you," she says.

Steve orders a scotch—God knows how many he had at lunch—settling into the booth with the kind of wide-eyed boyishness that has attracted her to him from the first. "It's been rough lately," he says. "Last-minute push. You know. You're not that far removed from Sales. Slavin' away for ol' Mark, I mean."

There's nothing at all suggestive (no, the word is *conspiratorial*) in the way he says it, but she feels her heart race nonetheless. He never mentions it, the terrible thing she's doing; not in so many words, anyway. It's always there, though. She's a spy. It sounds silly and melodramatic when you think of it like that, but it's true. She's a spy. She used to be a secretary in Sales Promotion, which was where she met him, and when Edith Stewart needed an assistant, he recommended her. At first it didn't hit her, he was so casual about his questions, but after a few times she understood. By then, of course, it was too late. She knows she'll tell him anything, anything he wants. For this. A few minutes like this. A few heartbreaking little minutes like this.

"How's it goin'?" he asks. He always asks, "How's it goin'?" Usually she replies, "All right, I guess"—something like that, something that will make him have to ask her what he wants to know; the things about Mr. Banner, like who he sees and how long they stay in his office or how long he's gone when he's in somebody else's office. Or if she's overheard anything, which so far she really hasn't. Tonight, however, it seems kind of silly, the game has gotten to be so . . . oh, predictable.

"He saw Mr. McAlister at eleven and he had lunch with Mr.

Abrams," she says. "Mr. Abrams senior that is. And a hush-hush meeting with Mr. Abrams junior. Lots of other people were in and out all day. We had a hectic day. And that telephone . . ."

"He *did* see McAlister, hunh? Where? His office? Banner's, I mean?"

"Mr. McAlister's."

"Hot damn. Good."

In his exhilaration he reaches out under the table and pats her leg; actually, her thigh. There's roughness in it—his hands are big and mysterious; but there's sweetness, too. Actually, she likes it.

"You're terrible," she says.

"Good again." He grins. She can tell he's been drinking before he came here, even beyond lunch. His grin is pink when he drinks.

"I really wasn't sure you'd come," she says again, she doesn't know why.

He looks as if he's going to burst or something. He's all over the booth as if his skin can't hold him. She's never seen him quite like this. "Jeet yet?" he asks.

He asks it every time they're together, though usually not this early. He asked it the first time he ever spoke to her. She was working late— it was a Tuesday, she'd never forget it—on the promotion report she was typing for him. He made her nervous at first, coming down to the sixteenth floor so often, pacing the way he did. But when she finished he said, "Jeet yet?"—just like that. She loved the way he said it—she still loves the way he says it. Some people think it's all affectation—the deep-South accent and all. She can't really imagine him without it.

"I'm not very hungry," she says.

He isn't either. He never is. He orders several more drinks (she nurses her second), and in an hour or so he touches her leg again.

Outside, in the thinning rain, she presses close to him, as if his nearness could blot out not only the petering rain but the ugly neighborhood.

"It gets uglier and uglier, doesn't it?" she says.

"What does?"

"This street." Her eyes sweep the seemingly endless brownness (it's never really gray, not even when it rains), a sameness of dull, dingy storefronts and crowded window displays that not even an occasional new pizza sign or new drugstore facade can relieve.

"Well," says Steve, "it may be a lousy neighborhood but you got yourself a nice apartment. So what the hell."

She sighs. "I don't know," she says. "I was thinking earlier, though, when I got off the subway. Do you know what made me fall in love with New York, when I first saw it? I know it sounds silly, but it was the drugstores on Madison and, oh, all over the East Side. You know. The ones that call themselves chemists and things like that. Now here

I am in a neighborhood where all the signs say 'Drugs.' Just like back in Toledo."

"Life's like that," he says.

She can tell he isn't listening, because all the time she's talking to him he's tucking a hand up under her breast, and humming something under his breath, and walking faster. She does so like to stroll, even when it rains. But he's always in such a hurry, he's such a wind.

The whiskey's affecting him, too. They almost bump into a man at the Forty-ninth Street corner, and he crosses the street against the light. It's dark, true, but his hands are really at her now, it's like she's a pillow being fluffed into shape. She's actually glad when they reach her building in the middle of the next block, where an obscure entranceway and a flight of stairs lead to her apartment, where it will be just the two of them. He actually lumbers up the stairs.

They're no sooner in the living room of her tiny apartment than they're in the bedroom. He's like a wild bird tonight. He's everywhere at once, it's like he has a hundred mouths; and she's somewhere in all of them (how did her clothes get off so soon?), kind of warm and wet on the hundred tongues, and breathing so hard it seems no breath at all. And her good bedspread, how could she have forgotten to turn it down? Now he's naked, too. His hardness against her leg is demanding.

"You promised," she manages to say. "Everything but . . . that. You promised, Steve."

"Sure," he says as his lips covers hers, and oh God his fingers in her like that, now two fingers, three, they're such big hands, so . . .

"No!" She pushes him back with the strength she can summon, and as he rolls to his back cursing she begins to cry.

"I can't," she mumbles, the tears blending with her perspiration, "you know I can't. I won't have a baby."

"Who the hell's talkin' about a baby? You take the Pill, don't you? Hell, you must have a diaphragm . . ."

"No! Oh, Lord, no! Women's lib or no women's lib, I . . ."

"Christ! I've got a rubber in my wallet here, wait a minute."

"No! Steve, understand . . ."

"Understand, my ass! That's the craziest, childishest . . ."

"Steve, you promised! You promised!"

He murmurs something else, deep under his breath, then suddenly he's boyish and affectionate again, kissing her breasts and her stomach and sweet yes her yes, and stroking her head, which is so dizzy and sweaty under his great warm arms. Now his mouth covers her ear. "Go down," he whispers.

She knows she will. It always ends this way. And for all his protests about the other, it's this he really wants; she divined that the first time she ever did it.

When it's over, and he's getting dressed, the oddest words come to her mind. *Presterilized . . . ultraviolet radiation . . . internal sterility . . . aseptic surgery . . . cortisone.* Then she remembers that a *Time* magazine, open at the "Medicine" section, had been lying near his buttocks, and she had just naturally read it, under the dim light from the night table, while she did it. Somehow that makes it shameful, when usually it isn't, and she doesn't know why.

Leaving, he asks (rather seriously, actually), "Mark Banner tried anything with you yet?"

"No," she says.

"Nothin'?"

"No."

"You'd tell me if he did?"

"I'd tell you."

"Hmmm." He brushes a strand of hair from her face. "Somethin' must be wrong with him."

She reaches for her dress, a yellow pile on the floor. It's a dotted Swiss, and every dot seems a contemptuous eye. "His mind's always on the network," she says.

"Whose ain't?" He laughs softly. "But a man's still a man, right?"

"I like him," she says.

"Yeah. He's a real likable fella."

She reaches for his arm. "Steve . . ." she starts to say, but then decides to say nothing, there's no way really to say it. Whatever it is she was thinking, which was muddled in the first place. It had to do with Mr. Banner, and how much she likes him, she supposes; but then she isn't exactly innocent about the thing. Steve's kiss good night is quick and sparing.

When he's gone, she goes into the bathroom, where she takes a long, cool shower, then shuffles to the small kitchen off the living room to boil water for a cup of tea. Hot and strong, it makes her feel better almost immediately. She still feels shame, of course, but her mind is filled with pleasant things, too. She's very thankful, actually—that Steve is going to be president of the network someday, and that in some way she's helping him to do it. It might seem so little, really, just being with him whenever he's horny or when he wants to know something about Mr. Banner or when he wants to just be away from his wife and kids, but there's really an awful lot to be grateful for. He doesn't have to screw her to be satisfied, and there aren't many men around like that. She adores him, too; that's the nice thing about it. And while she's never pressed him for anything—absolutely nothing— still he *did* furnish the apartment for her, he *did* do that. And someday there will be another apartment, larger and really much lovelier than this; she's sure of it.

She's almost happy when she goes into the living room—modest perhaps, but cozy—and turns on the television set to watch the eight-o'clock premiere of *Felony*.

25

MARK, ALONE in his office, is watching *Felony*, too. He's seen it a dozen times at least (this is the pilot episode, and he's personally screened it for several major clients), but an on-air premiere is always exciting. After all these years, this single event—this culmination of all the months of discussion, planning, and finally production, station clearance, sales—it's still the most satisfying moment on earth. And in the case of *Felony*, a rather comfortable one. He has little doubt the show will make it. The critics may howl, even punctuate their outrage with the old violence-on-television chestnut, especially during the so-called Family Viewing Hour—he himself may be slightly revolted by it—but it has tested well in secret theatre showings on the Coast, and it occupies a relatively "soft" time period—the competition's new situation comedies and Revolutionary War dramas, all of which have already premiered, look like lukewarm entries. Besides: It's a damn good format, even if Fred Wiener did initiate it. Its principal continuing characters—three brothers, all detective sergeants—contribute to a nice blend of high purpose and low comedy, a kind of hip-American Three Musketeers.

It's almost over. The last minutes of dialogue, which he knows practically by heart (there's a tongue-in-cheek quality here he hasn't really detected before, though), are racing to the fade-out when the telephone rings. He's been expecting it. It will be either Herb Mackin, UBC's legal counsel in Washington, reporting an early dinner meeting with one of the FCC commissioners to talk about the government's prime-time access ruling, or Shepherd Jaffee, v.p. in charge of programming on the West Coast, calling about a new daytime strip. Mark turns down the TV sound and picks up the receiver. It's Jaffee in Hollywood.

"Shep, how are you?"

"Well, Mark, doing well. I've set up a meeting at the studio Friday. Haven't been able to get Wiener."

"Morning?"

"Afternoon."

"I'll fly out Thursday night."

"Good. Wiener coming with you?"

"I'll be alone."

"Nobody from Daytime Programming?"

"I said alone."

"Yes, of course."

"Anything on a star?"

"They're talking to Sally Leeds."

"For the young girl?"

"Yes."

"She's a little old for it, isn't she?"

"Borderline. But a name. You know how rough it is getting a name for soaps, Mark."

"Don't be so defensive."

"What?"

"I said don't be so defensive."

"Well, I didn't mean . . ."

"Tell the studio we'll talk about it Friday. Right now I'm cool on Leeds. You can make that known."

"Well, certainly, Mark, I . . ."

"And set up an appointment with Bob Watkins at Gem Pictures. Looks like I can't avoid him. Cocktails Friday night."

"Yes, I've got it."

"And try to keep the trade press from knowing I'm in town. No interviews."

"I'll try."

"Fine. We'll see you Friday, Shep."

The final credits of *Felony* are just fading. *Produced by Caligula Productions in Association with the UBC Television Network.* Mark switches it off. His hand on the remote-control button is tense. This isn't like him at all. He'd been unnecessarily sharp with Jaffee, a good man and, as far as it went, a good friend. Looking back, he realizes there was an edge to his voice with Sid Newton too when they went over the Cincinnati speech earlier in the evening. And with Edith—yes, even with Edith—when she came in around seven to say good night. It's all very well to blame a day and a pace, but . . . It's there again, nagging at his consciousness, fretful that he won't let it through. The harsh ring of the phone again is a reprieve. He's actually grateful. Even if it is his private line and the voice on it an insinuation of private deceits.

"I thought I'd find you there. You're always there, aren't you, darling? Mark Banner. You can't say *he* doesn't work his ass off for the Abrams empire."

"Hello, Sharon. I heard you were in town."

"PR, no doubt."

"PR."

"Not to mention the fact that your number-one star is mentioned in every tabloid fucking gossip column in New York. Thanks for calling, sweet."

"How are you, Sharon?"

"Oh, Christ. Well, I'm just splendid, Mark. And how are you? Well, I trust. I mean, when weren't you well, Mark? And you can just go fuck a duck, Mark. And if you don't think Sharon Moore is important enough to warrant a phone call from the great fucking Mark Banner . . ."

"You're horny."

"You're damn right I'm horny! I'm furious! I'm miserable, darling. And I have two hours before I do the Long John Nebel radio show. Plaza, Suite Five-thirty. The same. *More* of the same. Fifteen minutes?"

"Not tonight, Sharon. Sorry. Tonight . . ."

"Fuck the duck, Mr. Banner!"

The click is almost as scornful as the lady scorned. For a moment —two—Mark feels a twinge of regret, remembered lust. But Sharon Moore tonight? No. Not tonight.

But why so cruel? At least he could have . . .

Know this, Mark. Success, particularly in a world as mercurial as television, is no more than a pimple on an elephant's ass. The elephant knows it's there, at least that something is there, but there's an awful lot of ass for an awful lot of pimples, and pimples are not as permanent as elephants.

Odd he remembers that. Meaningless drunken drivel from the farewell party in Hollywood, on the eve of his leaving to become program chief of UBC; not the remotest recollection of who said it, or why.

Odd.

Odder still that it should add so immeasurably to loss. Loss of *what?*

. . . for I believe, with all my heart, that no less than survival itself is at stake. And just as man, to survive, must find some new and rightful accommodation with his environment—some workable balance between his own resources and the resources of nature he depends on —so must we in communications, particularly in that awesome giant we call Television, so must we find a balance between our competitive needs and goals and our moral and ethical responsibilities. And while talk of such responsibilities may in some quarters be viewed as simply hollow rhetoric in a society already choking on it . . .

Page fourteen of the draft of his speech next week to the Ohio broadcasters in Cincinnati, and as his eye roams it, the loss (*what* loss?) seems larger still. Not to mention the fact that he has a couple of practical, *physical* decisions to make. Like whether to take a car from the company garage (where one is always held in reserve for him) and drive home—it's already after nine—or stay over at the Regency, since the Millers are occupying the Bristol suite.

As alternatives, neither is particularly attractive. If he drives home he won't arrive until midnight or after, and tomorrow's schedule is as unrelenting as today's, including a dinner party at G. B. Hare's (March & Hare Foods, he and Vivian have no choice) tomorrow evening. Too, Vivian may still be up. And that means the silences that are really more demoralizing than words—the unasked questions he can answer only with preoccupied smiles. On the other hand, if he stays in the city, he won't sleep. The need will come (why always when he sleeps over in New York, rarely so demanding in Los Angeles or Chicago?)—two, three in the morning—and he will end up calling one of the numbers, and when the girl arrives, then the same old fierce and muscular compulsion to drive it home and get her out, to be alone again with ideas, and finally, restoringly, sleep.

Perhaps Sharon Moore after all . . .

In the end he decides to drive home. It's always pleasant after a rain. He thinks more logically after a rain, behind a wheel. Methodically he gathers up papers he may want to scan on the drive in tomorrow, squares them neatly in his attaché case, calls the garage to have the car ready, goes to the private lavatory behind his desk where he urinates without philosophy (he's more himself now than he's been most of the day; *Lear* and *Hamlet* are decidedly not his meat), and locking his office and suite doors, takes an elevator to the subterranean garage.

Mario, the lone attendant, has a Buick waiting. He's a stout young man with a slight limp. "Saw *Felony* tonight, Mr. Banner," he says. "Looks like we got ourselves a winner."

We. Mark smiles. He forgets sometimes how many people are actually involved in UBC's fortunes. All the way down to a garage attendant—and beyond: the stockholders, too. All *we.* An employee number or a stock certificate and suddenly—*we.* On the fortieth, forty-second floors it's *I.*

"I think we do, Mario," he says. "Thank you."

"Have a good night, sir."

"Yeah. Same to you."

The air is fresh, the feel of the car right, the traffic negligible. He loves New York at night. He never sees it that he doesn't remember the sense of frustration he felt in Kansas City, and later in Los Angeles, where buildings and neon signs and even traffic lights seemed only carbon copies of the original. He regrets sometimes that he's taken the house in Westport. Except for an occasional round of golf on Saturdays (and Robert Abrams' peculiar emphasis on suburban living

—Westchester and Fairfield counties, that is— for his executives), the area means nothing. If Vivian weren't so adamant . . . He makes a mental note to see about taking an apartment in town.

It bursts through when he stops for a traffic light at Fifth and Ninety-second. It often happens like this, when for a minute or two he isn't thinking about the network. Nor does it happen in fragments, bits and pieces to be strung together, sequences to be sorted out into some kind of reasonable order. It comes instead, almost theatrically, as a total vision—the unities present and accounted for; the weeks and months, even years, a single moment in time; the truth (and with Mark, that means instinct) as unconditional as the savagery of dreams. There's even dialogue.

GERALD McALISTER: *I want him out.*

STEVE LILLY: *I'm your boy.*

The whys and hows will come later. *Why* McAlister, who has never approved the unprofessional way Lilly operates, has condescended to use him. *Why* Lilly, about whom even Bob Abrams and Adrian Miller have misgivings, can entertain the thought of an unknown quantity heading the network, when he, Mark, has been his protector —hell, mentor—from the very first (and God knows Lilly himself wouldn't be considered in the old thousand years). *Why* McAlister made the charge of prejudice against Steve this morning, when it's obviously (now, anyway) simply bait. *Why* he himself, with Edith's little needles, has been so busy looking at Wiener that he hasn't once really looked at Lilly. *Why* McAlister wants him out in the first place. *How* Maury Sherman detected it. *How* Adrian Miller figures in. *Why* the Old Man had him to lunch. *How* . . .

It's a long ride home to Westport.

26

AND TO SCARSDALE.

That he's driving home at all—*being driven* home at all—at such an inelegant hour is an assault on sensibility to Robert Abrams. But there's small help for it. When he called the house earlier, only to find Jean Marie out ("Just out, sir," the cryptic explanation of her maid, her suppressed tittering still in his ears), he knew he couldn't, wouldn't face dinner alone at his house, any more than he could face it at his father's, Ellen having called him in the late afternoon to suggest it, "since your little bride paid me a visit today." And the thought of eating alone in a restaurant, being seen eating alone in a restaurant —God! The food he had sent in from Mercurio's may have stuck in his throat, but it was better—infinitely better—than chewing on humiliation, as he phrased it to himself over veal Marsala, a light rosé, and some liver pills.

And he didn't watch *Felony,* even though he hasn't seen the final print version. Egregious piece of crap, any way you look at it. Even if it's profitable. Probably make Nielsen's top twenty as well. His father's and Mark Banner's idea of bread-and-butter product. God! No, he most definitely did not watch *Felony.* For a while he studied the latest sales reports from the radio network and owned stations, from the Leisure Time Activities operation, from the Theatre Division; the program development charts of the television network; an article in *Broadcasting* on the threat of pay television. But his mind is opaque, grasshopperish, concentration (his shining virtue) a virtual flop. Nor was his father's phone call on the private line antidotal.

"You should have come here like Ellen asked. You got troubles."

"I'm fine, really."

"I know. You got troubles."

"I said I'm fine. And you?"

"I got home early. Had a warm bath. Thought about putting it to your mother-in-law, but decided to wait a week or two. At my age and condition you got to be practical. I'm watching Felony *instead."*

"And?"

"I'll let you know when I've talked it over with Big Long in the morning."

"Really, father . . ."

"Really father. So? He's the American viewing public, ain't he? I reckon my kind of autometer's as accurate as any. At least it's done okay by me for fifty years. No, sixty. Make that sixty."

"You should be in bed."

"And do what still comes naturally? You want me dead? You watching the premieres too?"

"Hardly. I've seen them all a half-dozen times."

"On the big screens? Hell, son. Shows are a whole other ball game on the small screen. Seems to me you should have gotten hold of that difference by now."

"Nice talking to you, father. Get some rest."

"So what are you doing?"

"I'm having a bite. Going over some divisional reports."

"And hatching eggs?"

"I beg your pardon?"

"Who's due for the axe with this debacle—your kind of word, not mine."

"What debacle? What are you talking about?"

"The little cutie. Jean Marie. I've got a twenty-twenty memory, you know, son. When Brenda walked out on you it was old Saltzman in Engineering who got it. And poor Kessler in Personnel, wasn't it, I mean when Beverly ran off to Mexico with that Hollywood fruitcake."

"Good night, father."

"We have to talk about it sooner or later."

"There's nothing to talk about. Now just take your warm milk and honey . . ."

"Can't yet. Still a couple more Board members I have to speak to. Like guess what about. And maybe some old pals, too. Like Maury Sherman."

"Father, please. Haven't we already . . ."

"Poor Bobby. Poor little Bobby. Always such big, big problems."

The after-rain countryside is damp even to the eyes; he provides his own perspiration to cloud them. He squirms uneasily in the roomy back seat, edgily aware of the driver's (an ex-boxer) darting eyes, as much on him via the rear-view mirror as they are on the dark slick highway. The lone consolation for Robert is that this muscle-bound character doesn't try to involve him in conversation. Still, it's a relief of sorts, at least on a scale of one to ten, to turn onto the circular driveway of his large, fanatically authentic antebellum home.

Fanatic is the only word for it. Both in design and execution it is the sum, if not the spirit, of his mother's (*sainted* mother's) old family home (manse) in Atlanta, long since razed to accommodate a high-rise condominium. Robert's consolation (if in so great a loss there can be consolation) is that she never lived to see it. Much of the furnishings, her somber treasures, grace its carbon here in Scarsdale. Each of Robert's three wives has hated them.

His third most of all. And Jean Marie Abrams' contempt for them has never manifested itself more vigorously than on this particular night—her last—among them.

Robert stands in stony horror in the doorway of their bedroom suite. Strewn about the fine, delicate chairs, the filigreed rosewood night tables and bureaus, his mother's beloved chaise longue—open, half open, upside down, on their sides—are his wife's hundreds (they seem like hundreds) of cosmetic liquids and lotions, their dizzying colors and thicknesses devouring cloth and wood alike, almost as if all had been let loose in a slow-motion nightmare of conquest. Dresses and pants suits and nightgowns and sweaters and scarves and hats and pantyhose and shoes and chinchillas and minks and the latest ermine from Altman's—all crowd them, caress them, cheer them on.

Several half-packed pieces of luggage (delivered only last week from Bloomingdale's) cover both the queen-size beds.

The specially built thirty-two-inch color television set, sound turned down to a barely audible chatter—the *UBC Monday Night Movie* a flashing montage of horses and guns, leather and dust (John Wayne even in a 1973 release is good for at least a forty share)—the set commands and in its way caparisons it all. Jean Marie, naked and singing —some silly Beatles thing from the sixties—emerges like the original wood nymph from her dressing room.

Lo! Imagine cunt in all its seraglio fantasy, challenging and mocking in a single step. Steps. Robert stares with the glazed vision of one not quite certain whether he is awake or asleep, whether all about him is real, is actual, or only the continuation of strange, confused dreams. Her small breasts with their large roseate nipples, seeming oddly as she moves—half-dances—to expand and absorb much like the slow liquid of her endless bottles, are at once tantalizing and taunting, creating a rigidity in every part of his body—all, that is, save one. The crazed, hysterical one.

And the generous breadth of her underbelly, the subtle moisture of thighs, the way her eyes laugh and pity and sing their contempt . . .

"Hang tough," she says, pirouetting nimbly about, proffering her graceful buttocks for one last loving, choking look.

"He'll never be the man his father is."

"Wart, that's what he is. Old Dave must shit apples every time the kid opens his mouth."

"An empire, man, a real empire he's got. And God gives him a cunt for a son."

"Good thing his old lady holds the purse strings all right. Hate to think what David Abrams would do to the kid if she didn't."

"Makes you pause a little, don't it? Man like David Abrams with the world at his feet, and a pimple of a son on his ass."

"Funny goddamn thing, people. Take Bobby Abrams, now. Hates his old man's guts, and wishes every day of his life he had just one half of one ball in the old man's trousers."

"Must be hell, you know? Working your ass off to please him, the guy you resent most in the world. Having to prove yourself over and over again, carry your manhood around like they was Corona-Coronas . . ."

"Good thing the boy's got Adrian Miller around. God help UBC if he didn't."

"Hear another one of his wives is leaving him. Makes you wonder a little, don't it? Hell, more than a little."

Alone, in his downstairs study, looking out on a veranda so like his mother's in Atlanta it nearly cracks his heart, he manages—with the aid of an imported sherry and a mild Percodan—to plan lavishly dramatic exits for both his father and Mark Banner, to fantasize a prime-time television schedule devoted to such as Proust and Brecht and Henry James and Shakespeare, while waiting fitfully for Adrian Miller to call (as of course he will) to report on his evening with the Mortimers.

Adrian. Another one he'll have to start thinking long and hard about. Yes.

Hang tough.

27

"You DARLING! I swear, if you hadn't been home when I called I'd have climbed every wall in this fucking suite."

"I'm just naturally intuitive."

"Not to mention virile as ever. Are you on special prescription, pet?"

"Hardly, baby. It's the famous Sharon Moore ass. Hell, I get a boner on just watching you in rough cut in a screening room."

"You angel."

"In fact, Mark Banner and I compare longevity every third or fourth episode."

"You devil."

"He catch your act this trip? Or you his?"

"Is this really necessary, Freddie?"

"Maybe more necessary than you think."

"I see. Well, I'll tell you something, darling, your own innocence aside. I'd like to take this gorgeous thing of yours I'm having such fun with and ram it up Mr. Mark Banner's royal . . ."

"I was hoping you'd feel that way."

"And so you know. Now, may I resume?"

"You'd damn well better."

"You're really out for him, hunh?"

"You'd damn well better know it."

"And little Sharon, who just happens to be the UBC Network's bread and butter, just also happens to be little Freddie Wiener's new meal ticket?"

"As if you didn't know when you called."

"You bastard. Oh, well. Sigh. God only knows what I'll do when I've fucked my way through UBC. They're so stuffy at CBS."

It's not so bad, really, he thinks, lying beside her while she caresses him back to ten. He's exhausted, of course—Vivian Banner and Sharon Moore in the same day. But then when was Fred Wiener ever less than at peak? Besides: for all her rapier-quick wit (what she *imagines* to be rapier-quick wit), Sharon Moore is piggy as hell in the hay. And hay and a piggy nympho are precisely what the doctor ordered for tonight. What the good doctor (that is, his aims and aspirations; Christ, how delicious: right out of Mark Banner's last speech!)—what the good doctor ordered for tonight.

The smell of her is splendid. She may have been born on a farm and never passed the fifth grade and had her first cock before puberty, but she'd conquered, even in her first television triumphs, the art of camouflaging Iowa or Ohio or wherever it was with the most creative of Paris scents.

Particularly down below. And it is here—warm and breathy and breathless and thinking—that he knows (*intends*) that this superstar of the superseries *will* be his meal ticket, right to the presidency of UBC. She, and Vivian; not to mention Joel Greer; or the predestined disaster for Mark Banner on good old Wednesday night. And he'll enjoy it, really—that final confrontation. Christ, will he enjoy it: a kind of Brooks Brothers *High Noon*, a Gucci *Showdown at the UBC Corral*. A good old whopping, thumping, resounding meet . . .

"Darling? You're dwindling."

"I am? Well, we'll just have to do something about that, won't we?"

"Yes, pet, we will. And if not for this luscious flesh that's burning to consume you, then maybe the old college try for one Mark Fucking Banner."

28

FOUR OTHERS' evenings are somewhat less stimulating, more strained.

IN THEIR APARTMENT on Sutton Place South, Joel and Janet Greer are far from even the fantasy of wish-fulfillment. As always after Monday-night dinner at his mother's, their discomfort—physically—is considerably more urgent than their need to comfort (or even confront) one another.

"I'll get the bicarb," she says, tossing her coat onto a chair, switching on a Tiffany lamp that makes their small living room seem that much smaller, heading for the cubicle of a kitchen beyond.

Joel nods—he supposes; wonders why his stomach distress tonight is so severe. God knows it has been the usual Monday night. No one did anything, said anything (finally, probably even thought anything) that veered a hair's breadth from a score of Mondays. She was charming (his mother)—in her way, wasn't she always?—and nothing, except maybe asparagus instead of green peas, was different. Even Janet, after her plea at the High Life, settled in for the evening, meeting even his brother Sylvan's sly covetousness with smiles. No, nothing different. The Griebsberg-Greers at dinner with brave and admirable restraint. But it was there all the same. The loss of himself. Too self-important for now, but it amused him once to think of it that way. He doesn't get amused very often these days. He's climbing a thousand walls and he knows it. His stomach definitely isn't his own.

"Here."

Together they swallow it, the age-old bicarbonate of soda, while his eyes light on a sheaf of paper on the small desk in a corner. He doesn't need to read the top yellowing page to know what lies beneath it: *A Distant Lover: A Novel in Progress by Joel Griebsberg*—shattering what little the baking soda has accomplished.

"When did you drag that out?" he says.

"This morning. After you left." She stands beside him without moving.

"Why?"

She touches his arm. "Finish it, Joel."

"Easy to say, isn't it?" Now it's he who doesn't move.

"Leave that place, Joel. Leave that terrible place, baby."

His smile—an autumnal one for so young a man—seems the outer reflection of his stomach. "That's a decision that might easily be taken from me—"

BACK in their suite at the Bristol, closing the door softly behind him, Adrian Miller slaps his wife across the face. "Maybe that will remind you," he says. "The next time you slop up too much wine and mouth off about how 'UBC may just go to pot if anything ever happens to dear Uncle David.' Remember dear Uncle David handpicked me for this job. *I'm* what happens if anything ever happens. . . . And whooping it up for your dear old cousin Bobby every two or three minutes wasn't exactly the cutest act of your career either. Asshole!" And leaving her sobered, speechless, he stamps off into the bedroom to make his ritual nightly call to Robert.

WHILE TWO OTHERS, who basically detest each other, are exhibit A for "strange bedfellows."

Gerald McAlister, dining downtown at Sweet's with Steve Lilly (an Eyes Only meeting, arranged impulsively in midafternoon, for which Lilly has sobered considerably), brings the last of a trout amandine to his mouth, chews and swallows it gravely, and in his coarse, fretful voice (he himself finds it sonorous) says, "Let me quote you something, Steve."

He pauses briefly, just long enough to be profound, and when he resumes, his speech is slower, his pitch higher. Lectern-like: " 'Whether a man accepts from Fortune her spade, and will look downward and dig, or from Aspiration her axe and cord, and will scale the ice, the one and only success which it is his to command is to bring to his work a mighty heart.' " Another pause, briefer, voice normal again. "Justice Oliver Wendell Holmes said that. I believe it profoundly. It has guided me for most of my adult life. It is the reason—and I mean this—it is the reason you and I are sitting here right now."

Lilly's reaction, quick in coming, is as McAlister has anticipated: part bewilderment, part awe, and part salesman. This last he can dismiss, for it is simply assent by profession. The point is: several years back, in a sincere if unguarded moment that probably only he remembers, he said substantially the same thing to Mark Banner—and Mark Banner showed only contempt. Oh, not right out; Mark Banner is never right out. But he, Gerald McAlister, is nothing if not a perceptive man—in this he takes infinite pride—and he knew it was there—in the sudden shift of the man's weight, in the way he looked about the room, in the coolness with which he moved back to the business at hand.

Contempt. That was the key. The single overriding factor that no one else ever seemed really to perceive. The incident itself, the quotation (it is truly his favorite; he's used it numerous times in NAB convention speeches), are unimportant. But what they have revealed about the president of UBC-TV is not. McAlister has never forgotten it. More, it has sharpened his need (that is, duty) for observation. For how, he has asked himself (another quality he prides himself on: fairness, unqualified fairness), how can a man in such a position be contemptuous not only of those around him, but of the very medium —the *work*—itself? Well: he has long ago concluded (and guarded it brilliantly) that while Mark Banner in his day may have been impressive—yes, that's the word, *impressive*—the appalling truth is that he doesn't care.

Caring. The second key. Many to command but few to care. His blessed father told him that, those years ago in Providence, and he has remembered it faithfully; held it as sacred and dear as he has held Emerson and Holmes. Even in the commercial world of broadcasting it has guided principle to practice. The want of solid, responsible, genuinely Republican thinking in this industry makes him feel proud.

Ah, but why this justification, all over again? Hasn't he long since passed rationale? The man's a demagogue (more, Rooseveltian, which is unforgivable), and surely . . .

Lilly. He has let him be impressed in silence much too long. "Do you understand the significance of what I said?" he asks.

Steve Lilly's expression is as respectful as he has ever seen it. "I think I do," he says. "Yessir, Jerry, I admire that thought a lot."

Appraising this man he's always had very grave doubts about (and for the how manyth time?), McAlister thinks: Yes, he'll do, he's decidedly the one we want. He's personable, persuasive, which are basic, of course. He has an air of independence, even authority, which is good. But he knows how to rely on others, how to ask help in making decisions, which is essential. If he can just learn to control his prejudices. That's the one area Bob Abrams will need the most convincing on. But he *can* be convinced. After all, the boy's well-liked, he's got "executive" written all over him, and of course he's a gentile. A bona fide Dixie one at that. Robert Abrams has few overriding obsessions, but when it comes to the president of the television network, this is one of them. Wasp, at any cost. Yes, unquestionably, he's right for it. It's his brashness that bothers me, but that can be controlled, too. The boy's reasonable, he listens, and he can be . . .

Controlled? No, that's hardly what I mean. Still, it's necessary that Bob allow me a greater hand in the operation, Adrian Miller notwithstanding. This autonomy thing the Old Man makes such a show of is just what we have to set right. The television network cannot, I say cannot, be allowed to continue its independence at the price of corporate unity, the corporate image.

The unspoken speech falls from the speaker's stand—that is, his napkin falls from the table—and he is flushing intensely, no doubt of that. Clearing his throat (which plainly tickles—heavens, not another Indian-summer cold! His wife, Martha, bedridden these twenty years, will be plying him with all those witches' brews in her ghastly bedroom pharmacy), he says, "These moments don't come often in such a frenetic business as ours, do they, Steve? When we can contemplate ourselves, I mean . . . Look at where we've been, where we're going. . . ." He glances unseeingly about the crowded, noisy room. "And I think you'll be going far, as I believe I've intimated a time or two. Now . . . let me see . . . have we covered everything?"

They've covered a great deal in the two hours they've been here. Steve has recited (with proper humility at having to do so, but the good of the company, etc.) as much as he knows of Mark's activities, especially where Sales are concerned. He, McAlister, has advised him to get as close as possible to those key accounts Mark personally has wet-nursed for so long, and to start holding more Sales Department meetings when Mark is away from the city. They've discussed the remarkable absence of scandal in Mark's private life, which he, Mc-Alister, has asserted is all to the good, it serves no purpose to resort to cheap political tricks. They've talked about Wolf Glover, UBC's eastern sales manager, who Steve assured him would make a "damn fine sales director . . . someday. I mean, no need goin' outside for somebody . . ."

The waiter approaches them; they order coffee, no dessert. "Yes, I think we've said all we can . . . or should . . . at this time," McAlister says, his eyes fastened on the heavy silverware. "There's perhaps one other thing I should apprise you of, however." Again he pauses significantly. Unable, physically, to lower his voice to the confiding level, he nonetheless brings his head nearer to Steve's. "In tomorrow's *Variety* there'll be an item—the first of its breed, I believe—to the effect that Mr. Abrams—*fils*—and Mr. Banner are not seeing eye to eye these days. Oh, not a factual report, of course . . . a grapevine thing . . . which, of course, when I heard about it, I did my best to discourage, even squelch. They, uh, wouldn't disclose their source, but then, how could they? At any rate, Bobby and Mark will have to deny it vehemently. I've personally prepared Bob's statement, though he doesn't know it. I haven't told him about the item, no need upsetting him unduly. And I can't see bringing any other Public Relations people into it. See . . . well, what all this leads to, of course, is . . . well, once it starts . . ."

"And somebody like Bryson Randolph sees it?"

"Perhaps."

"Lord."

They finish their coffee, pay, and leave. Outside, the smell of fish is suffocating. The Fulton market is busy.

"We'll take separate cabs," says McAlister. "Even at this late hour, a drive together through midtown . . . Well, who knows?"

"Sure thing."

The thick air has him positively nauseated. "You take the first one. I know you have a heavy schedule tomorrow. Plus your sales meeting, ah?"

"Well, if it's all right . . ." Lilly holds out his hand. "Thanks, Jerry," he says. "Not only for taking me into your confidence, but . . . 'The one and only success that it's his to command' . . . Thanks, Jerry."

Watching the taxi pull away, McAlister thinks: Yes, I was right.

He'll do. *Have* to do. In spite of a shrinking, socially unsatisfying wife. I'll have to start the gradual buildup with Bob Abrams. Word here, one there. Of course, Miller must be gotten to also, he's really an incredible influence on him. And then there's . . .

Perhaps it's the heat, the smell, the heavy dinner—he's perspiring, something he hardly ever does—but for an instant, for once, he wishes he could just take off for the rest of the night—Yes, be unfaithful to poor Martha, even call Edward . . . But he knows he won't. If UBC is his shield, Martha is his cross: The responsible man forsakes neither. And it doesn't bother him so often any more—the abstinence. There is, and mercifully, UBC.

He starts to hail a cab at the corner, when out of rain-swollen shadows (a scene right out of *Felony*, for heaven's sake!) a swarthy, actually centaurian, Maury Sherman emerges, the twisted smile surely the devil's, the devil's own.

And the voice! "Give the kid a decent blow job, Mac?"

It's a long and painful ride through dark Manhattan.

29

THE SOUR-FACED, long-winded crud, Steve Lilly thinks. Boy! Imagine having to spend a weekend or something with a windbag like that. But—as an old colored fella down home used to say—you don't have to love 'em to sleep with 'em.

"Watch television much?" he leans forward to ask the driver, a thickset man whose license identification reads "Joseph Mussilli." Like the Old Man, he likes talking to cab drivers about television. They sometimes reveal what Nielsen never could.

"Yeh, some," the man replies, turning the corner at Canal.

"Tell me somethin', then. Which network—I mean, which channel—do you watch the most?"

"Who knows from channels? Me, I look at shows. If I wanna see it, yeh. If I don't wanna see it . . . Hey, you one of them poll takers?"

"Not I, old buddy. I'm with a television network."

"Yeh? Which one?"

"UBC."

"No crap? Now ain't that a coincidence. That's the station I look at all the time."

Steve grins. "You mean WUBC," he says.

"Huh?"

"WUBC. That's the New York outlet for the network. UBC's the network. You see, there's a network, then there's stations, and the network's what you might call the daddy of 'em, see? Or stepdaddy in some cases, dependin' on the market."

"Yeh?"

"Yeh."

They have quite an exchange, the man detailing the programs he likes and doesn't like (only about a fourth of which are UBC properties, "But you got great sports shows, man"), and Steve explaining the difference between networks and stations. "I sure enjoyed speaking with you, mister, you got a real interesting perfession," the man says when—after more than an hour or so of moving and talking, and not having to think about the significance of this triumphant day and night until he has done his duty by his wife, Beth, and is left alone in the living room (or somewhere) with a tall soothing scotch—they pull up in front of his house in Bronxville, a relatively modest but expensive Georgian brick.

BETH LILLY is a pretty woman, auburn and Melba peaches. But she wears it with neither confidence nor joy. Sometimes when you look at her you're struck by what has to be the most radiant of smiles, only to realize, when she starts to speak, how really impersonal it is.

She's a good wife and mother. That is, duty, responsibility—they're not simply words to her, they're the hours between waking and sleeping. She has few friends, even acquaintances, outside the tight family unit. Steve and their three children (Andrea, ten; Marietta, eight; Stephen Jr., five) are not only her walls, they're her windows on the world.

She is rarely known (knows herself) to be less than patient, self-sacrificing, kind. She is the timeless *macho*'s timeless ideal. And of course the single, potentially most dangerous helpmeet in Steve Lilly's corner. Her one, her abiding passion is a deep-rooted distaste for the kind of professionally social life her salesman husband lives in, an almost obsessive hatred of UBC itself.

Tonight, pretending sleep, fighting to keep her breathing even, she knows with absolute certainty that the television network is about to invade her private preserve even further. Rarely has she seen her husband so restive, so keyed up; twice already he has left her side to drink alone in the living room, to pace its length with the eager heaviness she has learned by heart. Something brews, she knows. Something she'll not—not ever—be up to. She'll let him down, she knows. Whatever it is, wherever he goes, she'll humiliate him. She knows.

"Honey."

Eyes closed, breath even; careful.

"Honey."

Still again.

"Honey."

Now.

"Oh. I'm sorry, Steve. I . . . I was asleep, I guess. Do you need something? Can I help?"

She sees him smiling, even in the dark.

"Just wanted to remind you not to bite your fingernails when you're sleepin'," he says.

And her heart goes out to him, her arms soon after.

30

VIVIAN IS DROWSY, but she isn't asleep. She's taken phenobarbital and gone to bed early. She had to. The day, Fred Wiener—she had to.

Limp, if not relaxed, her left cheek light on the softest hand that care and money can buy, she is murmuring to it. Not words exactly, just the shells of words; sounds uttered without thought or meaning. In the way of drowsiness, she is thinking in pictures rather than words, and the pictures themselves—if intense—are vague. Earlier, before taking the pill, she'd been remembering a day in Kansas City, shortly after they'd become engaged, when Mark took her to meet his father. It was toward the end of the day, and all of them were weary—of themselves, of the dingy apartment; Mark had gone outside for a few minutes—when Charles Banner took her hand and said, "I'm sure Mark loves you, my dear. I only hope he lets you love him. He never let his mother, rest her. Me either, for that matter, though I don't think he'd ever admit it. He just . . . respected us, you see. Mark has a highly developed sense of respect. Try your damnedest, will you?" Now, however, in the gray graphics of half-sleep, it is Mark, not his father, who is taking her hand and talking, and about *his* son, *his* son she carries, and she is cold and then terribly warm and, needing suddenly to touch instead of always being touched, is reaching only to cover his hand, only it isn't his hand at all and she's *alone,* and weeping, and there are shadows, and something dead. . . .

She turns to her other side, which revives her somewhat. She's nearly awake when Mark climbs the stairs and goes to his room, adjoining hers on the left. Her breath quickens, but she lies very still when she hears him pacing near the door. His steps are large and bearish. In spite of the pill, she feels every part of herself responding, and she knows he'll come in, knows that in his need (so telling in his walk) he will come, that in minutes she will feel him, even perhaps hold him; banishing Fred Wiener to wherever Fred Wieners are banished. . . .

But he doesn't come. Minutes pass (hours), her hands are cramped and clammy, her mouth dry with the taste of the pill; of her own perversity, desire. She'll be damned if she'll tell him Maury Sherman called. That it's important. Damned if she'll even think about UBC.

"Damn you, Mark," she whispers, biting the pillow and praying for sleep.

And knowing it won't come. Knowing that there is something terribly wrong with her, viciously wrong with her; that wanting Mark still, even as she burns for Fred Wiener, is as sick as it is crazy, inexplicable. But knowing, too, in some other part of her, that it is she who should go to him, she who should fall on her knees to him—he is in trouble, terrible trouble, and she knows it. A disaster on Wednesday night and it could all be over—and whatever else she might lie to herself about, find excuses for herself about, being the wife of the president of a television network is not one of them. She *likes* being the wife of a television network president, she *likes* being catered to, she *likes* having her ass kissed. For all the mess she's making of her life, she *likes* it; maybe she even *lives* for it.

She won't be dragged down with him, she won't! Even if it means forcing herself to tie up with Fred Wiener, if he were to be the one . . . ?

No. No! That isn't in the script. It *can't* be in the script. It just isn't her, it's not her nature, it's against everything she ever thought about herself, *knew* about herself. Everything she ever planned, dreamed . . . for their lost child that had once been inside her . . .

Wrong with her. Something terribly wrong with her. Too many drinks today, too many . . .

Reaching to the drawer of her night table, she swallows two more of the pills, knowing even as she does that they'll be little more than placebos, that there's no hope for her tonight, no sleep for her tonight.

Tonight. No sleep tonight.

THERE'S LITTLE SLEEP for Mark, either. But it isn't desire for Vivian—for any woman—that keeps him awake half the night, animal-alert and hard. It's anger. Not righteous anger or even tortuous anger, but the kind he always functions best in: a clear, deliberate, pragmatic anger, where mind and will are together. It's a complex feeling, but from its complexities, sooner or later, he draws resolve.

He falls asleep around three. It is a dreamless sleep. Except perhaps for that second or two before sleep when reality, no matter its clarity, is unavoidably dreamlike, when he has a vision of Maury Sherman—shadowy and gnomish and uncharacteristically well dressed—standing at a pulpit and cackling, "Now come on, kid—what's all this shit about the human condition?"

31

IN THE HOUSE on Cold Creek Drive at the eastern edge of Mamaroneck, there is fitful sleeping and waking as well. A dangerous situation for David Abrams—as Ellen has been told by his doctors in no uncertain instruction—who needs a full, uninterrupted night's rest.

Lying beside him now in these snails' morning hours, she reminds him of it for the third time at least, in a voice as rich and vibrant as the first time she heard it, in a speakeasy called Ragatto's over a half century ago. "David, David, my darling, you're insane. You *know* you need sleep. Take one of the pills Dr. Rosenberg sent you, please, dear, you must."

Sighing, he takes her hand and says, "You know something, Star?" Fifty-odd years later and he still calls her Star, still sends sparklers through her breasts every time he does. "I'll tell you something, Star. I'm like Churchill right now. I'll fight 'em on the beaches, in the streets, from ditches, from rooftops . . ."

She has to laugh. "Can it hold for a few hours, darling? The sleep will do you wonders. Dr. Rosenberg's pills might even make hand-to-hand combat heroic again. Sleep, David." But he's full awake and, on an elbow, full of himself; three-in-the-morning memory of himself. "Ellen . . . Star. Listen. This thing with the Board, it's not sewed up by a mile. Bobby may have some stock, and his buddies the muscle, but I've still got some loyalty in there. You heard what three of them said tonight when I phoned. That I not only *was* UBC, I *am* UBC . . . am and damn well will be. As long as there's breath in my body, I don't care how fragile you and those cockamamie doctors like to think it is . . . All these years of turning over stock to Bobby and Mandy Jo . . . save my kids their precious taxes . . . Christ! My head I should have examined, not their account books! And that sneaking Adrian Miller, my protégé, I'd like to . . . You know, I think he's even out for Mark Banner's ass? *His* own protégé, Ellen, *his* own. Remember what Herb Rafkin said on the phone? 'One thing's certain, David, always will be, you are Mr. Broadcasting.' Well, maybe not 'Mr.' "—he smiled at her—"but anyway I'm damned if they're going to sneak off with it, any of them. Chairman of the Board! Hah! Chief Executive Officer! Hah! Empty goddamn titles, right?"

He's wound up now, wound up and aroused, her David of old. She knows it's wrong, knows the danger of it—her breath almost stops when he lights a cigar—but she knows too that she won't caution him again. At least, not tonight; this morning. Let him have—because he must have them—his *verboten* cigar, his excitement, his plans. Let him talk, and talk, and talk. . . .

"And that prissy McAlister, what the hell do you think he's up to? Thank God Maury Sherman called me. Looks like my baby, *my* baby, is in the hands of bandits and butchers. Well, the whole cockamamie . . . ah . . ." His pause is expansive. "I like the taste of that word in my mouth, you know? You know, Star? Cockamamie. I like it."

"I know," she says, touching his arm, his chest.

"This whole cockamamie version of the court intrigue of Louis Fourteenth—or was it Fifteenth? Sixteenth? Who the hell cares? Bobby's still writing scripts you wouldn't air at six in the morning. Almost as if his mother herself put the pen in his hand . . ."

It's dawn, very near it, when he yawns, stretches. "Yes, darling," she says, tightening her arms about his shoulders, as if her own small strength might cradle his. And then uneasy again, frightened again, for this David of hers . . . this giant . . .

TWO
The Past

32

THE UBC TELEVISION NETWORK came into being on the night of February 15, 1948—a year when David Abrams was fifty-four years old, his son Robert twenty-two, Adrian Miller twenty-four, and several hundred miles away, in a suburb of Kansas City, Missouri, Mark Banner was twelve. The premiere telecast, from the stage of the Palace Theatre in New York, was inordinately lavish, considering the fact that no more than a quarter of a million homes, serviced by only eighteen affiliated stations in the New York–New England area, could possibly have received it. The future prognosis, however, was astounding: perhaps a million and a half homes by 1950; at least fifteen major markets.

The black-tie affair was attended by, among others, Governor and Mrs. Thomas E. Dewey, Mayor and Mrs. William O'Dwyer, and Senator and Mrs. Carl Roehm of Georgia—a tribute not so much to the crude, inchoate novelty as to the stature and power of the UBC *Radio* Network. The talent, again in obeisance to the radio network's influence, counted in its roster such stellar attractions as Dick Haymes, Frances Langford, Ed Wynn, Jerry Colonna, Jerry Lester, Jack Carter, Judy Canova; Paul Winchell and Jerry Mahoney, Smith and Dale, Veloz and Yolanda; and Raymond Massey delivering the Gettysburg Address, Ellen Curry singing her famous "I Love America." Not to mention the UBC Symphony Orchestra and a full-scale Ringling Brothers elephant act, during which one of the pachyderms answered nature's call with a thudding deposit that saw the worlds of audio and video off to a resounding start.

For David Abrams, then at the height of his powers, it was a night distinct and apart, planets removed from the one back in 1926, when the UBC Radio Network had made its less than spectacular debut, nervously holding its breath. And while television as a fruitful medium was still highly questionable in the more important quarters, its snowy reality on ten- and twelve-inch screens was downright Ziegfeldian in David's large and singular vision.

This *coup d'oeil* had been with him from the beginning, from the time he and his friend Bernie Strauss had spent the better part of boyhood listening for sounds in the air from a jumble of coils and wires and a Dunwoody-Pickard crystal receiver in Bernie's bedroom in Newark, New Jersey. David had been hooked from the first, he liked to say later—a love affair that had led, inevitably as he saw it, to a nationwide hookup ten years later.

Looking back on those years, broadcasting's tenuous, then golden years—looking back, that is, from the pomp and glitter of the celebration supper he was hosting that night in the Persian Room of the Plaza Hotel, immediately following the two-hour telecast—David could feel proud, defiant even, over a triumph worthy of the sacrifices made to achieve it.

Both he and Bernie Strauss had been born into relatively poor Jewish homes on High Street in Newark, although Bernie, an only child and several years David's senior, was the more likely to expect some kind of inheritance. His family owned three of the tenement houses on High Street. Even more, Bernie, a studious learner and inveterate reader, had gone on to become a wireless communications operator in the Navy during the First World War, and from there to an engineering position at United Electric Company in Manhattan. He had brought David into the company in 1918, as a telephonic division salesman.

They had schemed from the first hour he arrived. Long before, actually. An experimental wireless operation—it had occupied their nights, their days, their thoughts, their dreams. And while their first crude effort in a converted ladies' restroom in the basement of United's meter factory in Newark had ended in farce and disaster—the flashlight powder of a local newspaper photographer had set fire not only to the make-shift studio but to half the U.E. building as well—they had gone on to establish wireless stations in Atlanta, Georgia, and Providence, Rhode Island, providence itself having sped them into the arms and eager bosom of Sackman Industries, a small manufacturer of domestic appliances and component parts, distribution of which was centered mainly in New England but whose Atlanta branch of the family had offered up Arrabella Sackman, sole heir to the fortune, whom David had courted and married in the early days of their broadcast enterprises, even while he was engaged in New York to a singer named Ellen Curry, already being hailed in those first shadowy months as the First Lady of Radio.

They had met her, he and his friend Bernie, at a speakeasy on

Twenty-third Street, on a night in 1920 when the first public "wireless" station was still in the vaguest planning stage at United Electric. She had been a pert, saucy showgirl then, fresh from Indiana (thus, New York to her toes), full of Heywood Broun and Sigmund Freud in equal measures. But her voice in song—a curious blend of Midwest innocence and Earl Carroll seductiveness—had taken her not only to the initial "broadcast" of U.E.'s wireless station in Newark, but to the bed, and eventually heart, of David Abrams.

It was while he was silencing that heart, playing the role of contented groom in Atlanta, that Ellen Curry, carrying his child (he didn't know this until some years later), had accepted a concert engagement in London, where she married her agent, a closet homosexual, thus fulfilling two tedious if eminently necessary—or so it seemed at the time—social requirements.

They had gone on seeing each other, however—lovers through most of radio's sunrise years. Years in which the timetable structure and commercial ideology (for which David himself was greatly responsible), formats that would one day carry over into television, were born. Years in which the UBC Radio Network, with its emphasis on music, comedy and shoot-'em-ups, was not only born but succeeded beyond even the most optimistic advocate's reckoning. Years in which he and Bernie Strauss had reigned as the nation's most admired broadcast team, and Ellen herself, through the top-rated *Ellen Curry Hour,* had for all practical purposes *been* UBC. Dizzying, euphoric years.

Depleting, unsettling years.

Years in which their personal lives—his half-century affair with Ellen through the with Arrabella; Ellen's marriage to Gordon Strong, then Bernie; Bernie's tortured marriage to Anna, David's sister, and her ultimate commitment to an asylum; even the births of Robert and Mandy Jo, of Joslyn, of Ellen's ill-fated son, Michael—were as inextricably bound to the fortunes of UBC as though they were some extension of it, the annex to its precarious highs and lows.

Years. Inspired, inspiring, wondrous, racking years.

It was the essence of them, these years, that David was revisiting in the manner of time-capsule daydreams on the February night in 1948, this night to which all of it had so manifestly led. Revisiting in a kind of kaleidoscopic urgency on his way back to the center table in the Persian Room of the Plaza, having just seen Ellen Curry to her car and extracted from her the promise that they would lunch together soon, dine together soon, after long, barren years, wife Arrabella or no wife Arrabella, son Robert or no son Robert. He owed himself, they owed each other that.

Above all, that.

Having seen Ellen Curry to her limousine, it was a long and satisfying walk back to the table. The Persion Room was nothing less than a verdant bouquet to UBC (still fondly remembered from the twenties, early thirties, as the Green Network), with the UBC logo seemingly everywhere you looked, its luminous silver on the baked Alaska spotlighting and complementing its overpowering subtlety on the guests' small favors—miniature television-set cigarette lighters for the men, miniature television-screen compacts for the ladies.

The center table, truly center of it all, a festive table for twenty, seated, among others, the Governor and Mrs. Dewey, the Senator and Mrs. Roehm, the Mayor and Mrs. O'Dwyer, Fulton Little, president of Hanover Mills, and Mrs. Mills, Mark Stoddard of the Federal Communications Commission, Raymond Massey, Bobby Clark, and George Jessel; and of course David's wife, Arrabella; their children, Mandy Jo and Robert; and Adrian and Joslyn Miller, who, since the death of her father, Bernie Strauss, was a major stockholder of UBC.

Seating himself, David sensed that his son Robert's remark of a few minutes earlier about tonight's premier telecast—"Abraham Lincoln and elephant shit, radio all over again"—still hung over all of them. Everyone was laughing too much, drinking too much, smoking too much, praising too much. *"Heads will be rolling at NBC and CBS." "I can just see Paley and Sarnoff, even Goldenson at ABC." "David Abrams is the best showman in America, even Goldwyn could take a lesson." "So let's face it. It's your ball game all the way now, David"*— too much. Nonetheless, David was taking careful measures of reality even as he beamed his appreciation and pride.

The woman to his right, a blonde statuesque beauty even in her middle years, was not quite so adept at this outward show. Her displeasure—contempt, fury—was etched on every inch of her well-tended Elizabeth Arden face.

"Thank you," Arrabella Abrams whispered, not so much under her breath as above it. "Thank you very, very much. Is there nothing you don't demean, debase? Walking out of here with that . . . that *person*, it's . . ."

Triumph.

Robert Abrams, from earliest childhood sensitive to his mother's every gesture, expression, could hear every word she was saying to his father. Knowing that no one else at the table could hear was in itself a kind of triumph too.

There were few enough triumphs tonight for Robert. Tonight or any night. At twenty-two, tall and imposing, handsomer even than his father, spitting image of his mother, Robert also shared with his mother an open distaste for the commercialism of nights like tonight.

"That damned telecast," he said wearily, *sotto voce,* to Adrian Miller, who was seated next to him. "Will the day ever come when quality and commerce can share the same stage? And don't tell me they do, I'll cut you to ribbons."

"Easy, kid," his friend whispered back. "This is a stage too, remember? And cynics are lucky if the audience stays with them to the final curtain. It's a time for hail-fellows, Bobby. Right?"

"Wrong. We should be on our knees blessing the cynics, or at least the skeptics. They're the ones that demand and question, the ones who eventually can force us to turn even trivia into art."

"Lord, you're full of shit, Bobby. Really full of shit."

"Oh, sure, Adrian, sure. Bring everything down to its lowest common denominator. You're good at that, Adrian, you're really an expert at that. You revel in this trash, Adrian, you actually *celebrate* it. I think I'll vomit."

"You do that, Bobby. But hold off a while, will you? The night's still young. Play your cards right, kid, and I'll get you laid."

It was the unkindest cut of all. Robert felt his face both flush and go ashen in the same instant. It had been then, hadn't it, after his first actual experience with sex, dead drunk with the Filipino girl in a nipa hut in Alabang to which Adrian Miller, quoting Milton, had led him on a dark moonless night, where he had been attacked and beaten to within an inch of his life by the barracks gang that called him a "suck-ass Jew lapping up sergeant shit"? A night that had been the start of his "trouble" with girls, which only Adrian Miller really knew or suspected. Hadn't it? Wasn't it? Unkindest cut, indeed.

"You seem to take the directing of tonight's idiocy very seriously," he said to Adrian, somewhat more loudly now; he could see both Joslyn and the senator's wife grimace. "At least no one with any brains will follow suit."

But it fell on Adrian's fixed grin. Here was this miracle of sight and sound, and the birds of prey, the *green* birds, were already circling and swooping and pecking away, the infant scarcely hours alive. The television network schedules (ABC, CBS, NBC, and DuMont, in addition to UBC), now or in planning stages, were shameless in their mass eight-year-old appeal—*Arthur Godfrey's Talent Scouts, Ted Mack and the Original Amateur Hour,* Ed Sullivan's *Toast of the Town, The Lone Ranger, Hopalong Cassidy* . . . God! And the most breathless question in the entire industry was whether UBC or NBC would get Milton Berle's *Texaco Star Theatre.* It would be just his luck, Robert thought, if his father won. Even the one halfway promising dramatic series he had managed to talk David into—*Hollywood Premiere*—now held nothing more promising than old movie scripts, mostly super-light comedy, rewritten for the New York studio's limitations. And all of Adrian Miller's assurances that he was working steadily on the Old Man for more quality programming (David had great respect for Adrian's instincts)—all these assurances were as cold as the winter that Robert was uncertain he would get through, ev.en *wanted* to get through, in the depression of his senior year at Princeton. Adrian, his friend, with his deceit, his self-indulgence . . . His friend, Adrian . . . *friend . . .*

His eyes met those of his mother across the wide festive table, and in those recesses of sympathy and love, reserved for him and him alone, he thought he found strength, a reason for being; joy. At least whatever joy there was to be had in this dreary world. Then, as he knew it would (sooner or later it always did), Adrian's arm circled his shoulders in comradely gesture, the grin eased casually into a wide, protective smile.

THE NIGHT, for Adrian Miller, was exactly as Robert had said: one he reveled in, celebrated, would never get enough of. His glow was infectious and he knew it. Even Bobby, under the magic of his arm, was for a moment transformed. Adrian had always had this quality. It was only with the Abramses that it had paid off.

Still, his life—still young life—had led as if by design to this night. Born and raised (his history wasn't the kind that ever allowed himself to think of himself as reared) in a succession of reform schools and orphanages in Cincinnati, he was the son of Nick Mazelewski, executed for murder during the Chicago gang wars of the twenties, and Marta Otescu, an illiterate Romanian cleaning woman who had died in childbirth, and had himself served a year in the Ohio state penitentiary for defrauding a book club (a nice literary touch, he thought) —altogether a background that no one in his new world had even an inkling of. Only Bernie Strauss had somehow discovered it, but the knowledge had died with him, as Adrian himself had seen to when he withheld a vial of glycerin tablets from him when he was suffering a second coronary occlusion while the two of them were alone in the new UBC television studio. All anyone else knew—or even suspected, he was certain—was that he had come from poor but honorable parents, had in spite of relative poverty developed a remarkable acquaintance with books and peripheral arts, had served as a radio announcer in Cincinnati before being drafted into the Army, had both befriended and been surrogate father to Robert at a very critical time, and in return had been rewarded by a position with UBC and the hand (and all other precious parts) of the family's reigning princess (and reigning nymphomaniac, he'd suspected it even then), Joslyn Strauss, who, on the death of her father, had come predictably into a considerable block of UBC stock.

Most rewarding of all, however, both to himself and to those around him, was his extraordinary grasp of the drama and still unexplored dimensions of television. He was, as it were, to the medium born. This night's unprecedented telecast was due largely to his talents as both writer and director. David Abrams felt—and Adrian knew he felt— that one of the few things about his son Robert that pleased him was his blind good luck in having made Adrian Miller a friend. There was so much light to bask in, in fact—so many lights, so many directions— that the only thing he feared was the possibility of stretching himself too thin.

"One doesn't condemn an infant for mewling and puking in its mother's arms, Bobby," he said now, as much a master at raising his voice to the right octave, just so, as Robert was: The whole table managed to hear him. "Give the tyke a little room to grow in. It's the Christian thing to do."

For an instant there was a slight scowl on David's face and even Arrabella's, but Robert—as always when there was some private joke between them, him and Adrian, them alone, and he'd had enough champagne—was able to be amused.

Not Joslyn.

She was still feeling the pain and humiliation to which Adrian had subjected her while they were dressing for the theatre and party.

It had begun when the maternity gown she'd planned to wear split open at the back and—tired, heavy with the baby she was carrying, frustrated from weeks of Adrian's working far into the night, scarcely aware of her when he *was* home—she'd started crying. Just sat on the end of the bed and cried. The things they'd said to each other . . .

"Oh, Christ, not again."

"I . . . I can't help it . . ."

"*The hell you can't. Wear something else, for Christ's sake.*"

"*It's the one I . . . specially . . .*"

"*Joslyn, please! The most important night of my life and you're determined to fuck it up!*"

"*No . . . no, Adrian, honest . . .*"

"*Christ! You know something, Joslyn? Bobby was right about you. 'The quintessential Jewish princess,' he called you. God, was he ever right!*"

"*When . . . when did Bobby . . . when did he say such a . . .*"

"*When? I'll tell you when. The day he told me I was a consummate asshole for even entertaining the idea of marrying you. That's when.*"

It shouldn't have been that great a shock to her; he had not very subtly hinted at it before. But it had hit her so suddenly, so crassly, that it had the impact of a body blow. Bent over with the pain of it, of everything about it, about herself, her life, she had come close, if not to panic, at least to hysteria. *"I'm the one who should have thought twice! Me! I'm the one who should have her head examined! Daddy warned me, dear God, how he warned me! And Ellen . . . She knew too. Oh, God, did she know! You and your goddamn television show! If it wasn't for me, who in hell would look at you twice?"* That's when he'd slapped her.

So much had gone through her mind with it—the sound, the sting: Bobby has never liked me, not since we were children. Is there something between them, Adrian and Bobby? No, there couldn't be. Adrian's man enough in bed for a good-sized harem. Did daddy know something I still don't? How he pleaded with me not to marry him! Ellen too. Even Ellen, who tries never to advise a soul. I wish he were here, daddy. Oh, God, how I wish he were here!

I hate it, this thing inside me. I hope it's born dead. It's the one thing I have to hold over him—he wants it so much, a boy so much. The only thing I have to . . . No, of course not. There's always my UBC stock. Oh, is there ever my UBC stock! Someday I'm going to take it all, the stock, the baby, and . . .

And what? Try living for one day, one hour, without that damn divining rod he carries so imperiously between his legs—even the *thought* of it—and see how many miles you'll put between you. Try it. Just try it. Shit.

"I'm sorry about earlier, honey. I've been so overwrought over tonight's show that I've been no better than an animal," Adrian whispered in her ear, squeezing her thigh. Everyone at the table was looking at him with such admiration; pleasure. And her thigh and all its neighbors were fit to bust. "Forgive me, baby?"

And of course she did.

Already had.

As for Arrabella . . .

She of the pitiless purse strings.

What passed now through *her* mind was the vision of herself living long enough to see her indestructible husband, David, lowered into the cold, cold ground, leaving her beloved son, Robert, to say, "Now, mother, we, you and I, mother, we—*we* are UBC."

It was the senator from Georgia who proposed the toast.

"To you, David. And the United Broadcasting Company. It's another mighty journey you've embarked upon. And although there's no way any of us here tonight can predict either its growth or its ultimate impact on our society in general, I think it safe to say that this new wonder called television will prove a strong and worthy supplement to radio, which over the past quarter of a century has not only influenced but in many ways altered our lives and our culture. To no small extent by UBC, I might add. And while this new medium may be restrictive, that is, inaccessible on any mass communications basis, it certainly holds great promise both as a theatre and as a forum for the enlightened and influential citizens of our great land. I was thinking tonight, as I saw and heard Mr. Massey's most moving rendering of Abraham Lincoln's immortal words, that the American quest and inventiveness in which he had such a profound faith have indeed been kept faith with, as tonight's extraordinary experience has borne out. Success, sir. Success."

"I'll drink to that," said Adrian.

They all did. Even Robert. However cautiously, cynically. Ambivalently.

33

ON A BRIGHT APRIL MORNING several weeks later, in the executive dining room on top of the original UBC building on Madison Avenue, the words of the senator's toast still lingered in David's ears. Across from him, radiant in a crimson wool Coco Chanel ensemble, Ellen Curry sat thoughtfully fingering her glass, an as yet untouched bourbon manhattan.

"So we got a hell of a lot to be thankful for," he was saying, sharp eyes taking in—and never tiring of it—the lovely curve of temple, brow, cheek, jaw. "We both lost part of our lives when Bernie went, but there's a fine, strong part left to live yet. Maybe Bernie's death means something bigger, I don't know. I just know he died in kind of the twilight hours of radio, not even living to see the dawn of this new rascal we got on our hands. Not that radio will ever completely die, I don't believe that for a minute. But I do believe, and every instinct I ever had for this business bears me out, I do believe television is the real future in this country. Maybe even the world. Biting off too much again, Ellen?" Tight grin he was dying to relax. "Seeing too many moonbeams again, Star?"

It was such an old ritual between them, this question-answer exchange, that Ellen's silence was response in itself. Still, he wished it
were something more than the remote wistful smile she'd been wearing since practically the hour Bernie died. "I think it's going to open
some big new worlds for you, Ellen. Hell, I don't think, I *know*. Five
years from now it's going to make radio, the theatre, movies, you name
it—everything's going to be kindergarten next to it."

When she finally did speak, it was with the same deep, catching
voice that had gone out over the air almost thirty years ago from a
tomato-can microphone in a warehouse basement in Newark. "I just
don't know whether I'm up to both a television and radio show every
week, David. I'm hardly Miss America, you know. If anything, *Madame
America's* more likely."

"Sorry, Star. I don't buy that. Your work's as much a part of your
life as Bernie was."

"Or you, David?"

"Or me."

Even the sardonic, almost playful ring of her voice did nothing to get
rid of the brooding smile. "I wish I had your enthusiasm, darling. I
know I said I'd think about a regular television show, but . . . the
radio show's almost more than I can handle right now, David. My
concert schedule is a ball breaker. And there's a new movie I'm talking
about too, with Zanuck."

David brushed it all aside like so much dust. "The ground floor,
Ellen," he said, "that's the key, that's half the battle. You of all people
should appreciate that. You were the First Lady of Radio before eighty
percent of the radio audience ever heard you. And with television . . ."

She eyed him. "Tell me, David. If I had to do one or the other,
which would you advise?"

"You mean radio or television? You mean choose?"

"If I had to, yes."

His smile tightened, but imperceptibly. "I'll tell you, Star. I think
I'd choose television. Which may sound a little crazy at first, I know.
Radio's still king and queen and crown prince put together, while television . . . well, it's barely off the ground. But two years from now,
Ellen—three, four—even the salad days of radio won't compare. But
choosing sides isn't the point here. They complement each other. It's
a tricky time right now, these next few years, Ellen. A real in-between
time. Except hardly any of these birds in the agencies and on the West
Coast can see it. That's why the extra work, whatever it'll take, is
worth it. I haven't misled you yet, have I, Star?" He paused a second,
letting his eyes dance rings. "Not professionally, anyway."

Cupping her chin in fine, slender hands, smile suddenly almost
flirtatious, she said, "Dear David. You were never more professional

than you are right now. And all the time you're positively sweating bullets, you want so desperately to be in my pants again. Right, love?"

He laughed. "You bet your ass I do," he said.

She covered a hand with her own. "Well, that too, angel, is rather like television. Maybe two years from now, three . . . Whenever. But I love your thinking it, darling, I always did. It's particularly gratifying to a little old widow lady in her fifties, when all that fresh young stuff is clamoring at the gates. But I will think about television again, I mean long and hard, I promise you. It's just that right now I . . . Who knows, love? Maybe I'm panic-stricken at the possibility of bombing again, the way I did in my last two pictures, remember? Maybe *not* being seen is what I do best, maybe . . . God, David, it's practically a Broadway production every week, the scripts, the costuming, the staging, the rehearsals. But if I *did* throw in the towel, what would we call it? I mean, would we go with the same title?"

The Ellen Curry Hour, sponsored by the Carolina Tobacco Company, premiered on the UBC Television Network in September 1948, and exactly a month to the date, David and Ellen became lovers again.

"The Main Stem and Back Street," she said. "We might even out-run *Amos 'n Andy.*"

The Fifty-second Street theatre that UBC had leased in order to have a live studio audience was the scene of the most chaotic and expensive activity in all of television that year—not excluding Milton Berle, who made his debut on NBC the same night.

The small off-Broadway auditorium, renamed the Ellen Curry Theatre, was more harassing than the legitimate stage, what with its newborn battalions of technicians, more exacting than radio because of television's emphasis on physical position and gesture. It was more uncomfortable than either, too, because of the incandescent lighting attached to grids suspended from the ceiling. But Ellen found it a rejuvenating, if maddening, experience. Even her many years of squeezing in movies between radio and concert appearances hadn't prepared her for the deadline frenzy of television. And Hedda Hopper, Louella Parsons, Jimmy Fidler, and Walter Winchell weren't half the critics that camera 1 and camera 2 and an overbearing but brilliant martinet named Casey Burns, whom Adrian Miller had engaged to direct the show, were proving to be. It was like learning to walk again, talk again, smile again, sing again, as uncertain of her unseen audience's eyes glued to eight- or ten-inch oval screens as she had been in the earliest days of radio, when frantic appeals to God had been answered in the person of David, alone her rock and her redeemer.

He was very near to being these again in this new phase of her career, history repeating itself with remarkable likeness. That the head of a broadcasting empire, for whom there could never be enough hours in the day, was spending so many of them on one program out of seven evenings of them—

It didn't faze him. He was enjoying himself too much. In many ways it was the early days of radio all over again, rough edges half the joy, the kick of it. And for long moments he was the wide-eyed young man in the hectic wings of the Mark Hellinger Theatre, waiting for the incomparable Ellen Curry to finish her mind-blowing stint in the chorus, dancing offstage into arms that would never—not in the old million—have enough of her. He savored these moments, swallowed them whole.

But there was another, less sentimental reason for his frequent presence at the show's rehearsals. He was determined to soak up as much atmosphere and technical feel for the new medium as his heavy schedule would allow. All too often in the past few months the terminology and production techniques that rolled so glibly from, say, Adrian Miller's tongue—cordioids, booms, iconoscopes, balopticons; dynodes, coaxials, scanning beams, image orthicons—had left him not only dizzy but uninformed. "That's what we pay subordinates for," Arrabella had protested (underlining the *we*), but in a process that had already cost some $8 million, without a penny returned, he was damn well going to know the name, rank, and serial number of every goddamn tube and cable in the place. Besides which, as Bernie Strauss had pointed out through the years, even familiarity with electronic sophistication paid off lovingly in lunches and dinners with the presidents of Du Pont, General Motors, and United States Steel.

There was this, too: As these first uncertain telecasts came and went, he knew the delicious pioneer feeling again, as he had in those small, crude broadcasts in 1920, '21—trailblazers to the great radio years beyond. He was as certain as he was that he was sitting there, through the long hours of trial and error, that *The Ellen Curry Hour*, with its lilt and spontaneity, its music and laughter, would be a model for television entertainment for years to come.

He was personally seeing to that. Of all the programs in the UBC lineup for this first year of operation, this single hour was his showcase, his Sunday best. Its budget was the highest of any show on any network. In return it was surpassing all expectation. The first three telecasts had become the talk of the Eastern Seaboard, responsible—so several manufacturers had informed him—for the overnight gold rush in the sales of TV sets. The fourth show, with its unprecedented roster of big-name talent, promised to be the most spectacular of them all.

It was on the morning of the dress rehearsal for this show that a comedy routine between Ellen and two of her guest stars, Edgar Bergen and Charlie McCarthy, was interrupted by the prop manager, who informed her that she had a telephone call that it was absolutely necessary she take. Puzzled, Ellen walked backstage.

"I presume my husband is there."

That it was Arrabella Abrams was obvious. The reason that she had asked to speak to her, after so many years, was not.

"May I ask why," she said, "in the middle of a dress rehearsal, you have me called to the telephone to ask me that?"

"So that you might have the honor of telling him I wish a word with him. Would you kindly?"

The voice was as she remembered it—imperiously charming, controlled; her own was taut and unwieldy by comparison.

"I haven't the vaguest idea what you're up to, Arrabella, but interrupting a rehearsal on the day of the show . . ." She was certain the backstage crew heard every word.

"Please have my husband call me. When more urgent UBC business interests him again. And please have enough decency not to address me again as Arrabella!"

Ellen hung up with a vengeance. On the set again, even the prop manager's whispered "I had no choice, Ellen," received an icy glare, and she missed cues and flubbed lines through the rest of the skit. At the midmorning break, however, when she sat beside David at the rear of the theatre, her memory was precise. She repeated the brief exchange word for word.

David's face was drawn, pale, the familiar grin several light-years from it. When he returned to his office he called his home in Darien on a private line.

"Have you lost your mind?"

Her voice was as cold and remote as he'd ever heard it. "I plant my seeds in the gardens where I know they will grow."

"During a dress rehearsal of the most important television show in the country, to call the star of that show, to deliberately try to fuck up that show . . ."

"Really, David. I'm sure your gutter language would be more appreciated in the gutters of your . . . stars."

He was certain the phone smashed to a thousand pieces. It actually stung his hand as he slammed it down.

It was a vicious day. He lunched with Harold Nast, president of Continental Can; Marshall Fraysur, UBC's first managing director of TV programming; and Al Summers, its first director of sales. The reason for their meeting was sponsorship of a television version of the radio network's popular game show *Name It*, scheduled to start in January. But David heard little, spoke even less; and even then, in brittle monosyllables, a decided embarrassment to all. He had three scotch-and-waters, which he hadn't done in the noon hour in years.

The afternoon was even worse, if that was possible. He had a 2:15 meeting with Adrian Miller and an ASCAP official. At 2:45 he saw a new sales presentation for the radio network. Three-fifteen found him surrounded by members of the National Association of Educational Broadcasters. The four-o'clock interview he granted *Broadcasting* magazine lasted until five. Between meetings he took the telephone calls of Marty Levitt, a UBC attorney; Sid Wyman, head of the radio division; Wayne Coy and Frieda Hennock of the FCC; Tom Jordan of the Midwest Alliance station group; Senator Estes Kefauver of Tennessee; a producer with Bing Crosby Enterprises; a William Morris representative; and David Selznick, Gloria Swanson, and George Brent. A range and variety of people who were probably echoing each other: What the hell was eating David Abrams today?

At 5:15 he decided not to go home to dinner, even though Arrabella's cousins from Atlanta were there. At 5:45 he was in the lobby of the Sherry Netherland Hotel, where Ellen Curry stayed on the days of her shows.

"You're mad, David. The whole world could have seen you come up here."

"I sincerely hope so."

"Small boy getting even with his mother?"

"Shut up, Star. You know damn well why I'm here."

"To give poor Louella something to write about? To give Arrabella's attorney a chance to make a killing? Or maybe to help Robert add migraine headaches to his list?"

"I love you, Ellen."

"It's the wrong day, David. Hell, the wrong decade, love. We kissed goodbye a long time ago, remember? In a hotel room in Paris when we saw how impossible it all was, when Arrabella's purse strings proved just a little too much for—"

"I need you, Star."

"Please. Please, darling. I have to be at the theatre in an hour, my hair's a public disgrace, the new makeup I'm using—"

"Us, Star. Just us."

"Goddamn you, David. Oh, goddamn your soul to hell. Oh, David . . ."

THE FOURTH EDITION of *The Ellen Curry Hour* was one of the most viewed and talked-about television programs of the year, equaled only by several of Milton Berle's. Ellen Curry, it was generally agreed by owners of television sets, surpassed even herself, her voice stronger than ever and demonstrating a flair for comedy not even guessed at on her radio shows. The guest stars—Edgar Bergen and Charlie Mc-Carthy, Marie Wilson and Faye Emerson—were at the top of their forms. And the Ellen Curry Dancers, a miniature version of the Radio City Music Hall's Rockettes (the brainchild of UBC's production head, Adrian Miller), gave even an eight- or ten-inch screen a dimension and breadth that made live theatre in the home a stunning reality. The audience applause, unsolicited, was the most prolonged ever recorded for a television program.

Among the audience that night were a Midwestern businessman and his son, the latter having been given a trip to New York as a thirteenth birthday present and the tickets to the Ellen Curry show through the courtesy of someone named Adrian Miller, whom his father had known in the Philippines during the war. It was all a new and certainly breathtaking experience for him. The lights, the bustle, the strange-looking cameras; the familiar faces, familiar voices; the images of them, as well as little armies of cigarettes marching in lifelike cadence on the little television monitors at either side of the stage—he was beside himself and made no attempt to hide it. He was a bright, handsome, and lively boy, an unusually sturdy adolescent, and his father—not unnaturally—was proud of him. Smiling over at him during what they called a commercial break, he whispered, "Enjoying it, son? Getting yourself a charge out of it?"

The boy's grin was a mile and a half wide. "You bet I am, dad," said Mark Banner. "Boy-oh-boy-oh-boy. It must be a really live-wire world these people get to live in."

34

LATE IN 1948 the Federal Communications Commission called a sudden halt to the licensing of television stations in what amounted to a moratorium or freeze. At the time there were approximately a hundred television stations either licensed or in operation within the boundaries of the continental United States. The United Broadcasting Company had affiliations with twenty-three of them.

The dimensions of this action, by which the Commission purportedly was buying time to study the "interference" problem that had plagued radio so devilishly a quarter of a century before, were more encompassing than appeared on the surface. In the virtual standstill that lasted almost three and a half years (the Korean War was the excuse for prolonging it), there was not only a soaring, shoring-up interim for commercial television; there was a welcome, if short-lived, reprieve for radio as well.

UBC took advantage of both of them. Its radio division, even if David knew in his heart that it must soon give up the ghost, at least in its present form, made a heroic rebound with such established properties as *The Barry White Show, The Big Apple, Musical Chairs,* and *Hollywood and Vine*—not to mention *The Ellen Curry Hour*— competing head-on and victoriously (in the fourth quarter of 1948 and the first quarter of 1949 UBC dominated the ratings) with such long-run successes as *Allen's Alley, The Quiz Kids, Stop the Music,* and *Take It or Leave It,* Bob Hope, Jack Benny, Eddie Cantor, and Burns and Allen, even risking a quartet of new game shows, *Talk for Twenty, Ring the Bell, Daffy Daydreams,* and *Jackpot Fever,* two of which were being prepped for television versions.

Television itself, however, was where David's heart and guts and liver were, and television's future, to his mind, was the Atlantic and Pacific oceans splashed together.

If its reality three or four years hence didn't bear him out completely, then the future itself wouldn't be worth the price of one of his dollar-and-a-half cigars. And in late 1948, early 1949, the way movie theatres and sports arenas were closing down in the major television cities was already proof of the pudding before the fire had even been fully lit.

ON NEW YEAR's DAY, 1950, in the Abrams mansion called Ravenair, in Darien, Connecticut, Robert was sitting anxiously on the edge of a Georgian love seat, especially prized by his mother, in one of her other domestic prizes, the formal music room off the garden-side terrace. Across from him, in a high-backed Windsor chair, Adrian Miller was thoughtfully reading and turning the typewritten pages of a play. In spite of his conviction that television was both sporadic and undependable, Robert was as nervous and apprehensive over his friend's opinion as he'd ever been over one of his Princeton professors'.

The silence in the musty room was almost physical, Adrian's turning of the pages practically an assault on it. Robert, who prided himself that he rarely if ever perspired, felt a mile of the Housatonic in his armpits and groin. When Adrian took forty years on the last page, he scaled the walls. When finally Adrian set the script aside and simply stared across and smiled, Robert broke the heavy spell with a despairing groan.

"You are damn exasperating, Adrian, you really are. Not only do you not tear wings off of flies like any decent bastard would, you clip the membrane fiber by fiber. You're killing me, Adrian."

"What do you want to hear, Bobby? Tell me what you want to hear, and it's yours. All yours."

"You hated it."

By the ivory baby grand that dominated the room, Adrian smiled somewhat more gently, shaking his head. "On the contrary, kid, I rather like it. I mean, it isn't every day one gets to read a modern-dress version of *The Libation Bearers*, set in Georgia, at that. No, it's good, Bobby, it really is. It has . . . style. Real style."

"Then you'll talk to father about it? About doing it?" His eyes, as happened so rarely, were practically dancing. "You'll follow up on it, Adrian?"

His friend's face now was the mask Robert remembered from the early Philippine days. He stood up slowly. "I'm not so sure, Bobby. First of all, there's not really a place for it on the network. Not as we're scheduled at the moment, I mean. Secondly, I doubt five percent of our audience has the remotest idea who Aeschylus is. It would be like sticking a round peg in a square hole. The truth is, Bobby, your script is just a little bit better than we are."

Robert now was on his feet as well. "But that's just the point, can't you see? Television—that is, commercial television—is at a crossroad before it even gets started good. We have a choice, we actually have a choice. We can create extraordinary breakthroughs right at the beginning, right at the post. We can give breadth and meaning where there's such an obvious dearth of it. We can learn from radio's history, not just perpetuate the myth of so-called mass communications. We can put the 'm' back in mass where it belongs, Adrian, not just roll along without it the way people like father have been doing, getting rich on the illiteracy they've helped to sustain. *Now*, Adrian. The time is *now*. With people like us, Adrian, people who . . . well, who know better. If being good means being neglected or just rejected out of sight, then I'll . . . I'll move to London or somewhere where 'good' is not synonymous with 'unpopular'!"

"Be honest with yourself, Bobby. You know as well as I do what the Old Man would say. This just isn't the time and place for it.

Maybe an educational channel would consider it, God knows it's superior to most of their things. But for UBC? Be realistic, Bobby. The answer's there before we've even put the question."

Bitterness in Robert's eyes, on his tongue. "Realistic. God! Every abominable creation in our history of them can be traced right to the doorstep of 'realistic.' I think I'd throw up if I weren't wearing a new vest."

Shrugging, mock smile of defeat, or resignation, or perhaps even triumph (who could ever tell with Adrian?), he squeezed Robert's shoulder and let his hand remain there. "It's also a new year, kid, a new decade. Your time's coming, Bobby. Hang in there. Now let's join the others, what do you say?"

ROBERT WOULD ALWAYS remember that afternoon and that exchange as the spark that would grow to consume him for the rest of his life. He wrote down his resolve that same night, on a piece of UBC stationery, after which he folded it and put it away in a locked drawer of the painted red and green desk he had kept in his bedroom since childhood.

> Be it resolved that I, Robert Sackman Abrams, will from this day on (1) never beg again for anything from anyone, especially Adrian Miller, who henceforth and forever shall be subservient to me, not I to him, and (2) give up all thought of teaching, or writing for the theatre, and direct all the energy and intellect I have to undoing, whenever possible, the mediocrity my father has foisted on the network, imprinting in its place the kind of style and grace that mother alone in this family seems preeminently to possess.

He was no less frustrated than before, and his love/hate relationship with his father (and Adrian, too, at the moment) was no less eased or diminished, but somehow he slept a little better that night.

NOT SO HIS COUSIN JOSLYN, who, now that she was a mother, was more determined than ever—as she phrased it to herself around four o'clock in the morning—not to take another hour's shit from Adrian either. And to underline her determination she punched him awake.

"Hunh? Whaa?"

Damn it! Half asleep and unaware of her very existence on the planet, and he could still make sounds that almost upended her resolution. But damn it again, she'd come this far—

"I won't have it! Do you understand me, Adrian? I won't have it!

You are *not* my lord and master, I don't care how your perverted mind works. I am not, I repeat *not*, going to stand another minute of it. Is that clear enough for you, goddamn God?"

"What the fuck are you talking about?"

She was knots. Several hundreds of them. He had called her every name he could think of, then slapped her silly when they'd come back from the day at David and Arrabella's, and five hours later didn't remember a word of it.

While every syllable of it burned in her throat. *"Cunt! Stupid goddamn cunt! Just my luck to be saddled with the asshole cunt of the century! Embarrass me again, will you? Mindless little mother-fucking . . ."* When all that had happened was that Uncle David had mentioned casually that the producer of the daytime radio serial *True to Life* had called him about the television version that UBC was planning for the fall, and himself casually mentioned that David's niece, Joslyn Miller, who before her marriage had acted in a number of radio soaps, had proposed to him that her career be resumed with a starring role in the television series. And that naturally being *who* she was, she would be given every possible consideration. But that he, Uncle David, would prefer that she not pursue it, not only because she was part of the family, but because her husband was one of the pivotal people in the programming and production end, and it might be somewhat uncomfortable . . . "Cunt! To even entertain such a stupid idea—"

She was crying still, the salt of tears bitter indeed. More bitter even than when she'd played Adeline Sweethaven in the UBC serial *Girl Next Door* and been cited by a *Daily News* columnist as shedding the bitterest tears in all of radio. And all because of one lousy goddamn totalitarian state in the person of . . .

"Adrian! Adrian, I'm talking to you! Now you'll goddamn well listen to me, you hear?"

"All America hears, kid. Now shut up before you wake the baby."

The baby! Adrian, Jr.! Oh, God, why did she let herself be talked into that? When all along all she'd wanted was to name him Bernard—Bernie—after her father. How could she have been so dense (so overwhelmed by him, God!) when he'd said Bernard—Bernie—was so obviously Jewish . . .

God! If she wasn't careful she'd end up hating him too, her own baby, her flesh. . . .

Sometime around five-thirty, just moments before dawn, a plan to leave him, to take the baby, had halfway hatched in her mind; not only mental but physical cruelty, the grounds were real and true and good. Someday!

No, not someday, *today*.

Tomorrow.

Then, wholly drained, knowing for the thousandth time that she was simply words, nothing more, that his sleeping body beside her was nearly as erotic to her as it was awake, she at last fell asleep at first light.

SIX MONTHS LATER, with a kind of ceremonious bow and smile, ushering him into his office, David asked Adrian Miller what he would think of the idea of being named the first vice president in charge of programming for the UBC Television Network.

35

OVER THE NEXT THREE YEARS, as the sale of television sets doubled, then tripled, then toppled even the most expansive estimates of both industry and government leaders—fifteen million sets in sixty-four cities by the start of 1952—viewers of CBS, NBC, ABC, and DuMont were served up rich and generous portions of *Texaco Star Theatre* with Milton Berle, *Toast of the Town* with Ed Sullivan, *Kukla, Fran and Ollie, Admiral Broadway Revue* (later *Your Show of Shows*) with Sid Caesar and Imogene Coca, *Arthur Godfrey's Friends* and *Talent Scouts, The Faye Emerson Show, I Love Lucy* with Lucille Ball and Desi Arnaz, *The Big Story, Big Town, Lights Out, Suspense, Danger, The Clock, The Web, The Front Page, Ethel and Albert, The Aldrich Family, The Goldbergs, Cisco Kid, Fireside Theatre, Garroway at Large, Goodyear Playhouse, Philco Playhouse, The Original Amateur Hour* with Ted Mack, *The Chesterfield Supper Club* with Perry Como, *Stop the Music!, We the People, Americana, Cavalcade of Stars, Howdy Doody,* Walter Winchell. On Broadway, *Fun for All, Winky Dink and You, Hopalong Cassidy, Studio One, The Lone Ranger, One Man's Family,* Arturo Toscanini and the NBC Symphony Orchestra, Gene Autry, *Life with Luigi, Amos 'n Andy,* and Bishop Sheen. From UBC they were dazzled by the likes of *Dreamboat, Time for Teddy, Broadway Melody, Hollywood Playhouse, The Larry Lester Show, Songs for Sale, The Trials of Tillie, Midnight Lady, Tic Tac Toe, Brute Force, The Free-for-All Game* with Barry White, *Lois and Linda, Gothic Tales, City Squad, The Spoilers, The Ghost Chaser, Ring the Bell!, Federal Men, Starstruck, The Sackman Industries Playhouse, The Bat, The Mounties, The Tubby Thomas Show, The Hero, Star-Spangled Rhythm, The Dingaling Show, The Nine O'Clock Revue* with Billy Adams and Dawn McGee, *The Crusaders, The Cowboys,* and, of course, *The Ellen Curry Hour,* the highest-rated program in the country. Not one of these time periods was unsponsored.

The years were not all roses. The licensing freeze meant that major cities like Milwaukee, Houston, Kansas City, Pittsburgh, and St. Louis had only one station each, while cities like Denver, Little Rock, Austin, Texas, Portland, Maine, and Portland, Oregon, had none at all. This in the face of eight stations each in New York and Los Angeles. On the creative side, the entertainment industry's blacklisting of persons suspected of Communist membership or sympathy, of which Adrian Miller was television's most militant adherent, had blackened the reputations of many of the country's finest talents. The so-called *Red Channels,* the industry-wide newsletter, quietly expedited the executions.

It was the scourge, in the summer of 1950, that almost destroyed *The Ellen Curry Hour* and came nearer than Arrabella ever dreamed of doing to parting Ellen and David themselves.

IT WAS on a morning in late August, a particularly hot, intemperate one, that Ellen stormed into his office without even a nod to his secretary, her eyes a stunning complement to the blue Balenciaga she wore. At the time, David was in conference with Richard Loew, president of the Association of National Manufacturers, and Lester Sackman, Arrabella's cousin and chairman of the board of Sackman Industries, once the parent company of UBC. Both men, startled, rose to leave. Ellen's blazing look and David's bewilderment did little to discourage them.

"We'll discuss it further at lunch on Friday, David."

"Thanks for your interest, David."

David's stumbling apology did nothing to ease the hasty withdrawal. The gentle closing of the door was a small explosion.

"You've flipped," he said. "That's the only reason for it, you've flipped."

The control in her voice was barely discernible. "This is one thing I won't take lying down, David. Not for you, not for UBC, not for all the rice in Chanthaburi!"

He stood up. "What the sweet sam hill are you talking about, Ellen?"

"This. This is what I'm talking about. This, David. This, this, and this!"

David took the small folded note from her hand.

PAUL T. MADDEN
EXECUTIVE PRODUCER
THE ELLEN CURRY HOUR

Ellen:

Be aware that Paul Robeson will not
appear on the October 20 show.
We'll have to substitute. Gentleman's agreement on Olympus. Shit.

PAUL

"And he's scheduled to do an excerpt from *Ballad for Americans,*" she said. "Beautiful country we break our ass entertaining, isn't it?"

He sat again. "I don't like this any more than you do, Star. But we had no choice. Adrian had no choice."

She snatched the note back. "Adrian! I'm sure he hasn't had as much fun since your son was halfway killed in a whore's shack in Alabang!"

He reddened. "That's unfair as hell, Ellen, and you know it. Like him or not, there's not a smarter programming man in the business than Adrian. This particular situation . . . well, as I said, we had no choice. We're damned if we do and damned if we don't. Adrian simply has to make sure that there's no . . . taint, I guess that's the word . . . particularly with the political climate the way it is right now. Just how much chance of surviving do you think a show even as popular as yours would have if guest stars with Robeson's leaning—admitted leaning, I remind you—were to be on it? You'd be dead in a month, Ellen, I guarantee you. The other problem is your sponsor. They said they'd drop you like a hot brick if he went on. Bill Tulley called me personally on that one."

She was shaking her head vigorously. "I've heard everything you can throw at me, David, and I'm sorry, it won't work. Somebody has to do something. Somebody has to have guts enough to—"

"Ellen. Star. Guts isn't the point. Paul Robeson is poison to ninety-nine percent of this country, and you know it. The witch-hunters have done their job pretty goddamn good. There's nothing anyone can do. Not me, not Adrian, not—"

"Me? Don't be so sure, pet. It's still *my* show, *my* hour."

"It's UBC's show, Ellen. *UBC's* hour. None of us can afford to lose sight of that."

"An artist," she said, "a great artist. A talent that comes along maybe once in a generation, and we knuckle under, we . . ."

"We're a mass medium, Star, we're a goldfish bowl. We go into people's homes, their lives. Robeson can't even get a concert engagement any more, for Christ's sake. They won't touch him. It's a pretty rotten commentary, I couldn't agree with you more, but isn't it in everybody's interest—yes, even his—to fight this thing where it *can* be fought . . . offstage? Little by little, an exchange here, one there . . . A far sight better than having no stage at all, wouldn't you say?"

Her eyes level with his, her voice softer, if still sharply edged, she said, "Now I know what you men mean when you say somebody's got you by the balls. It's not a very pleasant position to be in, darling."

"No. No, it isn't."

"Next thing you know they'll be looking into me."

"They already are."

She sagged. He came from behind the desk and brought her to him. "Time, baby, time. A word here, a word there . . . That's how it works in this business, Ellen. Star. The only way it works. Okay?"

Her voice smaller still: "Depends on how you feel about fairy tales."

It was left at that—as it was left at similar exchanges throughout the industry. Clinging to each other, they seemed to be searching, seeking. For something. Something above and outside themselves. A strength, perhaps; a largeness. Certainly neither of them had ever felt smaller.

IRONICALLY, it was Robert who, if he offered no solution, brought Ellen her most thoughtful comfort during a very bad time.

It was a miserable day on the set. Everything about the rehearsal had gone wrong from the early call: cues missed, lines blown, even familiar lyrics drawing blanks as if never heard or sung before. Plus the added burden of luminous white tape placed in strategic positions across the entire studio stage, an irritable necessity now that Ellen was being bothered with faulty eyesight. Everyone from the director down to the stagehands was testy and sullen, giving run-throughs the air of business chores. Nor were her own outspoken remarks to the press on the current witch-hunt of creative artists a particular upper. The papers were full of her, and it was hardly a secret that America's darling was no longer Washington's by any stretch of the imagination. The morning's edginess, in fact, had stretched the usual "Take five" to "Take thirty."

It was during one of these lengthy breaks, just before noon, that Ellen entered her dressing room to one of the shocks of her life. Sitting facing her, in a leather chair near her dressing table, his face as expressionless as his body was tense, Robert neither stood at her entrance nor reacted to her gasp. It took a moment, actually, for her to recognize him. She hadn't seen him since the wretched day at Fort Ord when he turned his back on her in front of thousands of servicemen, and in a private interview afterward told her he never wanted to lay eyes on her again.

He seemed taller now, more robust. More handsome too, if that was possible. There was a more knowing look about him as well, almost a worldly one. Ellen knew, from David, that he had just returned from an extended stay in Europe, following a *cum laude* sheepskin from Princeton. With what grace and charm she could muster—the sharp words of her show's director still in her ears—she said, "It's nice to see you again, Bobby . . . Robert. You should have sent word that you were here. I would have broken rehearsal sooner."

Only a slight shrug acknowledged her. "I am here, Miss Curry"—not "Ellen," not "Aunt Ellen" (she had been, after all, his uncle Bernie's wife); just "Miss Curry"—"because I feel just as outraged as you do over this Communist headhunting crap this country's engaged in, particularly among the greatest artists we have. It makes one ashamed almost to be an American. In London, Paris, Rome we're looked on with such contempt that one can only leave out of fear of actual physical reprisal. I've spoken to my friend Adrian Miller about the position the entertainment industry is taking and am advised, as I am sure you are, that under the circumstances, patience is the only possible virtue. You have done a courageous thing in failing to hold your tongue, and I wanted you to know that and to hear it from me. Which doesn't change, I'm certain I needn't add, our customary noncommunication. Except to assure you that when I am a part of this network—in an official capacity, that is—I will do all in my power to fight this thing as you have. Now, if you will excuse me . . ."

And he was gone, just like that, the echo of his voice (neither warm nor cold, no more than a monotone really) lingering after him like the shadow of an intense dream. This man, this boy, who might have been hers instead of Arrabella's—this child of David's who had hated her so much since childhood that the very act of coming here to see her, on the set of her own UBC show, must have wrenched the very heart out of him—this son, this scion, who could so grudgingly humble himself out of a sense of faith, belief . . .

Staring after him long after the room itself had dismissed him, warmed to her bones as she was chilled to her heart, not to mention stunned and confused, Ellen for the first time since the show began took "forty."

THE POLITICAL CLIMATE to which David had alluded in his conversation with Ellen was all the more pervasive in the network's coverage of news events. Even in its halcyon radio days, UBC News had never pushed for parity with the other networks. Its television departments had more or less adhered to the loosely woven fabric or structure. Unlike its radio affiliates, however, the television primary affiliates were insistent on a stronger effort. Particularly in major metropolitian areas, where news personalities like Lowell Thomas and Edward R. Murrow were drawing large and enthusiastic audiences. At the same time, the politically sensitive climate of the country at large, as well as the diversity and even polarity of its television markets, made practically all network newscasts almost reverentially informational, often bland to the point of boredom. The only controversy in all of television, in fact, was the cleavage revealed by Faye Emerson's gowns.

David knew the time had come to give priority expansion to the News and Public Affairs area, and with nudging from the Board of Directors he set about to do it. It was around this time, just days after his conversation with Ellen—with Robert returned from Europe and ready (although reluctantly) to join his father and Adrian at the network—that he began his action.

It was during a Sunday dinner in Darien, at which Adrian and Joslyn, along with Mandy Jo and Lester Sackman, were also present, that the subject was broached, unwittingly, by Arrabella's cousin from Atlanta.

"Well, Bobby, now that the grand tour's behind you, I reckon your daddy'll be puttin' your nose to the grindstone."

Robert stared one of his looks-to-kill.

"It's about time," said Mandy Jo, who was still infuriated over her brother's extended stay in France and Italy.

"I'm sure there's plenty of time later for this kind of discussion," said Arrabella, ringing the delicate crystal bell near her plate for the maid to clear the dinner dishes for dessert. "We're havin' a meringue glacé, and talk of business is downright fatal for meringue glacés." Her Georgia accent had never been more extravagant.

"Maybe it's not a bad time at all," said David. "I have a couple of ideas I'd like all of you to hear." It was clear to Robert that his father would do anything rather than confront him alone. David was as uncomfortable at that possibility as he was.

"Let me guess," said Joslyn. "Bobby will be writing Shakespearean sonnets for *The Dingaling Show?*"

"No, he'll adopt a Miltonian quatrain for *The Trials of Tillie,*" said Mandy Jo.

"Don't let 'em rile you, sport," said Adrian.

The number of mutilated bodies strewn across the landscape of Robert's mind was increasing by the minute.

As the fragile dessert was being served, David said, "I've given quite a lot of thought to this. I know you'd expected to go directly into Programming with your buddy here, Bobby, but I think—for the time being, anyway—that your talents, your writing talents in particular, could best be used in the news area. We're planning a considerable expansion, as you know. Bernie always said it was where any broadcast medium gave the best service. It makes for a good, solid foundation, too, I might add. Nothing artsy-fartsy about news."

The tone of his voice was mild, (the not so benign despot, Robert thought) and he himself almost spoken *of*, no *to*, but it didn't matter. The ruling was made. The legislation was passed.

Afterward, while David and Lester Sackman relaxed with brandy and cigars in the newly added family room, the specially built Sackman television console mesmerizing them with a segment of *The Sackman Industries Playhouse* (an adaptation of an O. Henry story), Robert managed to corner Adrian on the far side of the room in a kind of tête-à-tête ell that Arrabella had furnished with dainty Swedish imports.

"You're beautiful, Adrian, you really are, you're beautiful. Your courage under fire is most impressive. *Most* impressive."

"Come off it, Bobby. I was as much taken by surprise as you were."

" '*Don't let 'em rile you, sport.*' God! How can Joslyn take sleeping next to you every night?"

"She doesn't. Sleep next to me, I mean. She sleeps on me. On *it*."

"You're really something, Adrian. You really are. You knew all about this, you goaded father into it, I know you did, I don't care how much you deny—"

"Oh, for Christ's sake, grow up, will you, Bobby? You're not in college now, you're out here in the big bad world, and you'd damn well better get to know it. You know I'll work something out—sooner or later, I mean—but with my position still so new . . ."

"Go fuck yourself, Adrian."

His eyes moved to where his father sat so proudly, every sense of him caught up in the flashing, dancing images of the brightened screen. Not wanting to miss even the smallest gesture, the vaguest word of his towering, immortal creation. There were two bathrooms on the first floor, but to get rid of the bile practically choking him, Robert chose to climb the stairs to his own.

DAVID WAS STILL GLUED to the television set—now the one in his bedroom—as the final minutes of UBC's Sunday-night schedule played themselves out. A joyous Bonita Granville was tossing a bouquet of forget-me-nots into a milling crowd of wedding guests including Sally

Eilers and Jane Withers when Arrabella spoke from the doorway of their adjoining rooms.

"For someone who professes to love his children, I think we'd all fare a little better if you hated their guts."

"Have a seat, 'Bella," he said. "Be with you in a minute. I got to see the ending of this thing."

It took her less than three strides to reach the offending monster and snap it off. David looked up at her with his customarily patient and slightly patronizing smile. It drove her insane and he knew it; delighted in it.

She was still a stunning piece of woman, though, he thought. Age had affected her less than anyone else he knew. In anger or in grace she was a statuesque monarch—Arrabella Sackman of the Atlanta Sackmans to the end. Laying her, he'd sometimes thought, was not unlike spilling grease on the crown jewels of England, a clumsy deed for which you'd always be a little embarrassed. In satin nightdress, like tonight, she was an emerald.

Ice-green.

"It was a low, wicked, condescending thing to do, David. Why didn't you just tear his heart out with a steak knife?"

"I felt it would be the least offensive to him to several alternatives," he said. He rose and stretched and scratched, which, he knew, riled her more than any other activity of the bedroom. Once, a thousand years ago and against every fiber of her will, it had been the most exciting.

"You could have at least discussed it with me," she said. "I believe I *am* his mother." *I believe I am UBC.* He heard it, loud and clear. It was good to be able to ignore it. It might be *her* money, but it was *his* sweat—his *blood*—and he knew that she knew it, saw it cold for what it was: where the line had to be drawn, where the company's success, its solvency, depended on *his* strength, *his* philosophy; his and his alone. "I believe I am his mother." Yes, decidedly good to be able to ignore it.

The nightly ritual of chastisement wasn't over, however; prices had to be paid for everything.

"You gave him so much strength and pride when he lay dying in Manila, and then once he survived you started chipping away at him again, little by little, until . . . giving him so little, so . . ."

He began to undress, always his trump card: he at least knew she'd never stay around for the finish.

"I'd hardly call three months in Europe and a new Buick convertible so little," he said. "And if that sounds crassly materialistic, it was meant to. There's very little else of me your darling son really wants."

"He'd set his heart on working with Adrian, I know he had. It's what made his return from Paris so agreeable. And now you . . ."

There was only a word or two left him; he was down to his shorts. "Writing news will be the making of him, wait and see. There's not a better discipline in the world for a creative mind. Bernie always said that."

"God!"

And it was over for the night. Chances were pretty much in his favor that she wouldn't be stealing to his bed at one or two in the morning, wordlessly and in darkness, as she did every two or three weeks. His healthy thrusts this past Monday were good for another ten days. And so he was free to fall asleep with all the compartments of his mind in sound condition. He would sleep particularly well to-night, pleased with the way he had handled the business of Robert, and with the prospect of the next glorious week, which Arrabella would be spending with Lester Sackman and his family in French Lick, and he in the more generous arms of Ellen Curry.

36

IN MANNERVILLE, LOUISIANA, a town of about 40,000 people in the northeastern part of the state, the first week of 1953 was the most exciting and anticipatory in the memory of even its oldest inhabitants. With the license freeze lifted and the coaxial cable extended, the first television station within a 150-mile radius was airing on January 6.

Among the hundreds who were watching on that memorable first night was a seven-year-old boy named Steve Lilly. That he watched at all, and on his very own set, was itself a kind of miracle. His mother, a widow, could barely meet payments on a stove and refrigerator, much less take on an expensive and unnecessary toy.

Since her husband had been killed in a plant accident at the Green Paper Mill in West Mannerville, Doreen Lilly had made uneasy ends meet by working part time as a waitress at the downtown Burgerland Café, but even with her mother's grudging assistance, raising a child in her advanced arthritic condition was hardly a lead-pipe cinch. Her looks gone and the pain a daily, nightly nightmare, Doreen Lilly also drank a great deal. It was in that condition, whenever the boy whined too much or pestered her for a television set like the other kids were getting, that she lost patience and pinned his ears proper.

Steve was relentless in his campaign, however. He'd eat turnip greens and corn bread every day for a whole year, not ever ask for meat, not even a drumstick or a pork chop, if he could just have a picture show in the house.

"Shut up! Shut up your mouth, you hear? I'll stick a butcher knife in it, you don't shut it up, hear?" It was all he *could* hear, morning and night, for a whole month. Then when Christmas came and went with nothing but Morgan and Lindsay junk, he knew his chances of ever seeing a big Motorola or Magnavox or Zenith were pretty goddern slim.

It was about this time, however, that a strange man who worked for the Illinois Central Railroad started drinking with his mother, nearly every night, in fact, and in time started staying overnight with her too. Whatever the instinct, and wherever it came from, Steve discovered that by whining away about the television while the man was there drove his mother up the wall and the man along with her, getting meaner and boozier by the hour. Especially when they were in her room with the door closed and he staged his longsuffering act outside it. It was in this way, wearing them both down to the nub, that on the morning of KNTV's opening-day ceremonies a seventeen-inch Silvertone set from Sears Roebuck was delivered, and that the first network program he saw was *Private Secretary* with Ann Sothern, on CBS, followed immediately by *The Ellen Curry Hour* on UBC. The invention fascinated him so much that, night after night, he was its grateful prisoner, watching anything and everything, right up to sign-off time. His fascination was so all-consuming, in fact, that the night even came when he no longer listened for the squeak of his mother's bedsprings.

OF THE SAME AGE, and ages removed, Frederick Wiener, in his home in Great Neck, Long Island, was given to boasting to his classmates that *his* family, thank heaven, wouldn't be caught dead with one of those silly boob tubes in the house. *His* family, thank heaven—his mother and father, that is—valued their intellects far too highly to waste precious hours on *Mr. Peepers* and *This Is Your Life*. And as far as he himself was concerned—well, to tell you the truth, all the talk about Jackie Gleason and Red Skelton and Red Buttons and Lucy and Desi and that Ellen Whatsername was really boring to the point of nausea. Any number of his classmates threatened to knock the piss out of him, of course, but then what could you expect from boys, *Jewish* boys, who came from all too obvious *Jewish* homes, the kind his mother called *hamish* and his father called nouveau riche, and for whom the legitimate theatre and opera and symphony concerts, all of which he himself had practically cut his teeth on, were Greek or Sanskrit or Urdu. Besides, he had never liked *kids* anyway. He was much more comfortable in the company of his mother's and father's friends, who were amazed, and never hesitated to say so, at how bright and knowledgeable and *mature* he was for his age.

Then one day, a day when Steve Lilly was being mesmerized by the *Colgate Comedy Hour* in Louisiana, Fred Wiener's mother died of something called coronary thrombosis, which of course grieved and tormented him, although a disease with such a dramatic and exotic name did compensate a little for the anguish. The thing that really hurt was that his father, in despair or loneliness or mental lapse or something, had a television set, actually a *television set,* delivered to the house, which of course he came secretly to enjoy, even treasure, but which meant that he was no longer so exclusive or superior. The one good thing was that he was able to report in class on *Amahl and the Night Visitors* and Maurice Evans' *Hamlet,* with Ruth Chatterton and Joseph Schildkraut, on the *Hallmark Hall of Fame,* which he sat through doggedly and defiantly even if he didn't quite understand them, which was more than you could say for the other doltheads his age, and which did help to ease the adjustment of a confused and motherless child.

In those same weeks of 1953—for the record—Joel Griebsberg was chanting along with Buffalo Bob and Clarabell, "It's Howdy Doody time, it's Howdy Doody time" in front of the big Sackman television set in the living room of his folks' apartment on the East Side of Manhattan; Mark Banner, who would be entering college in the fall, was working Saturdays and weekends at Station WDFA-TV, the UBC affiliate in Kansas City, Missouri; Vivian Seaworth, thirteen and already a beauty, was letting one of the neighborhood boys feel her up just a little—and *just* a little, mind you—while pretending to watch *Dollar a Second* or *My Favorite Story* or *I Led Three Lives* or *Make Room for Daddy* on the television set in the family rumpus room in her home in Oklahoma City; Sharon Moore, a few years younger but somehow older than time, was singing the new Ellen Curry hit, "Just Leave Me Behind," on a Saturday-afternoon amateur hour on the local television station in Butte, Montana; and a liberal arts graduate of Princeton University, Gerald Sean McAlister, was laboring diligently in his new job as a West Coast publicity writer for United Broadcasting, grateful to his classmate Bobby Abrams (whom he occasionally yearned to embrace, though thank God Bobby'd never know it) for the splendid and rather surprising opportunity.

ROBERT HIMSELF was active and productive, if also bored. The two years' apprenticeship in the News Department as an editor on the *UBC Nightly News* had honed and broadened his writing skills, while a working knowledge of national and international affairs, particularly affairs political, proved solid grounding for the future. Grudgingly he came to admit to himself that his father had known what he was doing all along.

Meanwhile, during those first busy weeks of 1953, his life took sharp and unexpected turns. In early January he was named associate producer of UBC News Documentaries. In late February he moved into a Sutton Place apartment in the city. And in early April he became engaged to be married.

Her name was Elizabeth Ainsley. He had met her on the studio set in Washington, where they were filming a perspective of the first weeks of the Eisenhower administration. Roy Crandall, UBC's Washington correspondent, had presented her to him: a research assistant at Rowan and Reed, the outside research firm the News Department used for Washington-oriented projects. He had liked her from the beginning. Tall and slender, owning a quiet monopoly on the term "boyish," she was a bright, articulate, obviously cultured young woman, whose lawyer father was one of the social and political (Eisenhower Republican) lions of Georgetown. Not to mention the fact that everyone who saw them together (Adrian included, when she came to New York over the Washington's Birthday weekend) was impressed by the way they looked together, behaved together.

They had much in common, much as he and Adrian had, particularly in the early stage of their friendship. The Greeks, the Latin poets, the Elizabethans, the Restoration. And of course television, which she was as dedicated to upgrading as he was. She called him Robert, never Bobby. And he liked her warm, if somewhat reserved, toothy smile. She was lithe. She was a kind of nineteenth-century Romantic. He kissed her—gently—as a matter of course, but that was all. She met his family at a Sunday dinner late in February and he met hers several nights later. David was pleasant to her; Arrabella less so. Her mother and father were gracious enough to forgive Robert for being Jewish, seeing who he was and all. He touched her breasts, what there was of them, with proper reverence and what under the circumstances passed for good taste, on the second of March.

"I think you'll be happier married, I honest to Pete do," Adrian told him on the night before he asked her to marry him. "And maybe it'll happen, kid . . . the thing. I mean, these things *do* happen, you know. With time, and a little patience, and maybe the right chemistry . . ." and Robert looked uncomfortably away.

They worked hard and well together on the Eisenhower documentary, which David reluctantly (and with a not unsubtle nudging from Washington) scheduled for a prime-time slot in late April, its rating potential doubtful, to say the least. By the end of March it was still only partially sponsored.

It was while she was double-checking the Teleprompter copy in the small news studio in New York that he asked her to have dinner with him at the Forum of the Twelve Caesars that night. And there, over Chateaubriand and an imported Beaujolais, he suggested, rather vaguely, that they "get together."

"I'm not sure I know what you mean," she said. "I mean, exactly what you mean. Are you proposing that we . . . *live* together? In big bad sin? If so, then I must decline, kind sir. I may be a liberated woman but I'm still a chained and shackled daughter, I'm afraid." Her voice, clipped and throaty, was one of the more ingratiating things about her. It lingered like the tap of fine crystal. He was flushed, nonetheless, at what it suggested.

"Good lord, no," he said; actually stuttered. "That was the furthest thing from my mind. I . . . I want us to be married, Elizabeth. I want you to be my wife."

"Oh."

He was not without sympathy or intuition. He knew precisely when and how she would say that she was marvelously flattered, that she would treasure it always—the dear proposal. But did they really . . . know each other well? And had he ever really wanted her in . . . that way?

"Somehow I never thought of us as the grand passion, Robert. Somehow it's just never . . . seemed that."

"No," he said, touching her hand. "It isn't. Grand passions, as you call them, are . . . well, fantasies at best. What I have for you is more of a . . . well, sensitive regard, the kind of affection, in short, that outlasts . . . lust. It's my conceit, I suppose, but I rather imagined you had the same regard for me."

"Oh, I do, Robert, I do." Her gray eyes widened the way they did so often when she uncovered a little-known fact or idea in the documentary research at which she was so professional. "I know of no one whose mind and . . . and higher feelings . . . I admire more. It's just that—I wasn't really expecting this, you know." The wine had reached her cheeks, coloring them subtly. Clearly she was caught unawares.

"I've given a great deal of thought to this," he said. "I feel very strongly that we have much to give each other."

Her smile was thoughtful and somewhat remote. "I'm not a very pretty girl, I know. I'm rather awkward, really. Mother says I'm like a klutzy gazelle. That's a Jewish word, isn't it? Klutzy?" Clearly she was grasping at straws—used ones, at that.

"You could be of great help to me in the future of the network," he said. "Together, we have a considerable potential, with our awareness, our intellectual curiosity our pride . . . to make a large contribution, I mean. As Mrs. Robert Abrams you'd be . . . perfect."

Now it was her hand covering his. "I'll give a lot of thought to it," she said. "An awful lot of thought to it, Robert. You're really ever so much a dear, dear person."

It was exactly as he'd foreseen it—planned it, actually: a kind of Jamesian-twilight exchange. He couldn't have written the scenario better had he been able to read her mind.

She thought about it for a week, then quietly accepted. They were in his spacious new apartment, the decoration personally and relentlessly overseen by Arrabella. It reeked, as Adrian said, of good taste. Elizabeth, there was no doubt in his mind, looked at home in it. He kissed her lightly, fondly, slipping onto her finger a seventy-five-carat diamond that had belonged to Arrabella's mother, and with which Arrabella had parted with martyred nobility. The engagement lasted almost a week.

The exchanges that ended it were far from Jamesian. They were parked in his new Lincoln Continental convertible in a grove of trees near the shallow lake that ran behind the house in Darien. The evening just ended had been a strained one at best. Her parents were spending the weekend with his, ostensibly to discuss plans for an engagement party, and while Arrabella had come reluctantly to accept Elizabeth's mother (who was, after all, not only a prominent Georgetown hostess but born and bred in Virginia), David had been decidedly cool toward her father, having discovered, through several discreet inquiries, that the social and political lion of Georgetown was practically penniless; what's more, in debt over a quarter of a million dollars. "No wonder the young lady's answer was positive," Robert had overheard him telling Arrabella. "It ain't every day a girl who looks like Little Lord Fauntleroy gets herself hitched to a television network." David was making slightly complicated what had until then seemed so simple—and so clean.

It was a starless April night, and cold. Even the car's heater couldn't restrain entirely the lake's icy, remorseless wind. Robert was secretly grateful for that: The heavy sweaters and coats in which they'd bundled themselves made any serious attempt at lovemaking rather awkward.

The lady would have her pound of flesh, however. "Robert, its all right. Honestly. We *are* engaged, you know."

"Yes."

His kiss, the brush of her breasts, his hands at her waist (actually a thick Belgian fox) were, if anything, more chaste than ever. Undaunted, she pressed her mouth hard against his, her prominent teeth actually denting his flesh. "Even brains have bodies," she said, breathing a little more irregularly than before. "And you're such a handsome man, darling, did you know that? You really are. Mother thinks you look like Tyrone Power." This time her lips literally tore the inside of his own.

All he could do was press her breasts again and pray.

Which failed miserably. Within seconds her hands had found him, what there was to find, and with a strength and dedication he'd never suspected of her began a process he could compare only to kneading dough. After several torturous minutes he pulled away.

"It's all right," she said softly, kissing an ear. "It happens to men sometimes." And after an awkward silence: "I've heard."

The following night, a Monday, they met at his Sutton Place apartment for cocktails before joining Adrian and Joslyn for dinner. She was again the aggressor, this time on a delicately upholstered Empire sofa. And three daiquiris, rather than her accustomed one, hardly constituted a deterrent. Hands again, ten of them. Inside his Brooks Brothers trousers, twenty of them. "A girl has a right to know what she's getting into. Or rather, what's getting into her, as they say." She guided one of his own hands, brazenly, onto that dark, mysterious mound, from which even darker and more mysterious juices flowed. . . .

It was hopeless, he knew it. And pulling himself from her, he fell against the Tiffany lamp his mother had installed with such pride last week, its sobering crash the loudest sound of his goddamn life.

"Is something wrong, Robert?" Her voice, so small, little more than a whisper really, was now the least ingratiating thing about her. "I thought last night . . . God, I couldn't sleep, not a wink. I thought God, it must be me, I must turn you off that way. I . . . I'm hardly Rita Hayworth, but then I don't think the Visigoths would think twice about raping me. I'm . . . It's you, isn't it, Robert?"

He was standing by the tall French window-door leading onto the terrace, holding back a fine gold drape to see the cold lights of the city, the million heartless eyes, as though they were a mocking audience come to see his disgraceful performance.

"It has to be you. I mean, you breathe so hard, you're really on fire inside. I can feel it, I mean sense it, really sense it, it's as if . . . Talk to me, Robert. Please. *Please.* Say something, *Something.*"

He still couldn't face her.

"We don't need that," he said. "We have so much else without that. We're special people, you and I. We're not mindless, driven animals like ninety-nine percent of the dregs out there. We're entities, not *non*entities. We have a much finer, much richer life ahead of us, I promise you. We're going to *lead* them one day—not *be* them. We're the stuff dreams are made on, Elizabeth. Not *them.*"

Her voice was smaller still: "Have you seen a doctor, Robert?"

He whirled around, furious; all reserve in him vanished. "No! Absolutely, emphatically, unconditionally, no! How dare you even suggest it! Given the right circumstances, the right girl, I assure you I'm—" It was said before his own ears were open enough to hear it, his voice too paralyzed even to try to take it back.

At the door, a distant blur, she said, "One small piece of advice, Robert. Don't ever think of trying to adapt any of this for television. It's one thing that'll never play, certainly not in Peoria."

From a wing-tip table in the brightly lit foyer, his mother's diamond, slipped unobtrusively from her finger, winked brightly back at him.

HE THREW HIMSELF into his work. Days stretched into nights as he wrote, rewrote, rewrote again and again documentaries ranging everywhere from a daguerrotype study of John Adams and Thomas Jefferson to a comparative look at the world's leading art museums—the Metropolitan, the Tate, the Prado, the Louvre—none of which, he knew, would ever see even a bird's-eye glimpse of light. His father wouldn't have scheduled them for love or money.

Nights lumbered into days as he helped Adrian (on the sly) read the mountains of scripts from which the 1954–55 pilots would emerge. Sleeping little, he ate even less. By June he had lost twenty-seven pounds. His mother threatened to have a heart attack over it.

But it was a time of unprecedented activity for broadcasting. The coast-to-coast television boom, so long predicted, was in full and frantic swing. It was all you heard, drank, ate, breathed at the dinner table out in Darien.

"All you have to do is look at the mileage CBS got out of Lucille Ball's pregnancy. Thirty million people tuned in to watch that kid get born. And the next day—remember? It came near knocking Eisenhower's inauguration off the front page. And you worry over whether television's an art form?"

"I'm absolutely convinced that film is the real future for this business. If you think television's knocking the props out from under radio, just wait'll you see what it does to movies. It won't be three years before television owns Hollywood. Ten years and we'll own the country."

"There's no telling how far this thing will go. I told Lester last week that Sackman's got to convert to color sets right now. And don't be surprised if I'm talking floor-to-ceiling screens this time next year."

"There's no doubt in my mind that this next presidential election, the one after that for sure, will be won or lost on that crazy little screen. A hundred years from now, when they look back on this decade . . ."

David talked nothing else, thought nothing else. And against every fiber of his nature, every fabric of his intellect, but to save his life (or so he told himself), Robert did likewise. And whether David's reactions were feigned or true, Robert enjoyed for the first time in his life his father's esteem and respect, if not—God's wonders notwithstanding —his affection.

In fact, his single, most impressive contribution that year, one that he himself had no particular heart for, actually—*An Evening with the President*—secured, more than anything else, his father's newfound faith in him.

IT WAS THE TIME in the sun for Senator Joseph McCarthy. The innuendos and taints of leftist leanings that had gone before, particularly in the entertainment industry, were nothing compared to the emotional assaults and batteries of the Midwest crusader in those first months of the Eisenhower administration. From Sherwood Anderson to W. H. Auden, from Lucille Ball to Ellen Curry, nothing was sacred, no one was immune. It was against this backdrop (scenery the pinkest pink and reddest red the industry's top designers could muster) that the Anti-Defamation League of B'nai B'rith, celebrating its fortieth anniversary, inquired of President Eisenhower whether he would accept the League's Democratic Legacy Award at a banquet to be staged and televised at the Mayflower Hotel in Washington. Behind this plan, as few besides David Abrams knew, was a top-level reaffirmation of individual freedoms, inasmuch as the President himself, thus far, had done little or nothing in the cause of civil rights. With Eisenhower's acceptance, along with attendance by Chief Justice Earl Warren and five other Supreme Court justices, five cabinet members including Secretary of State John Foster Dulles and Attorney General Herbert Brownell, such assorted dignitaries as J. Edgar Hoover and Bernard Baruch, plus appearances by Richard Rodgers and Oscar Hammerstein II, who had for some time been openly critical of network blacklist practices, and Lucille Ball and Desi

Arnaz, Eddie Fisher, Jane Froman, Rex Harrison, Helen Hayes, Ethel
Merman, Jackie Robinson, William Warfield, and UBC's Larry Lester,
Barry White, and Ellen Curry, the most mammoth television spectacular in its brief but blazoned history was under way. With all television and radio networks scheduled to carry the affair, it fell to
United Broadcasting to provide the script. David, after a single night's
pondering and a five-minute conference with Adrian, assigned the
plum to his twenty-seven-year-old son. It was Robert's text and structure, virtually unchanged by the other participants, that guided *An
Evening with the President,* on November 27, to its extraordinary
airing—almost 40 million television viewers at a single sitting.

Even David himself was stunned. Using everything from vaudeville
to sophisticated revue to out-and-out sentiment and bathos, the program opened with a shot of the Statue of Liberty, which suddenly
moved and turned out to be a UBC character actress named Maud
Muller, who complained that she got pretty darn tired of holding
that heavy torch aloft: "I wonder if folks really appreciate liberty.
Sure don't act like it a lot of the time. Oh, yeah . . . welcome,
stranger. Take a left at the Battery, you can't miss it." From there
through songs and sketches in dizzying tandem—"No one tells us
how to play, no one tells us what to say"—the panorama moved to the
final moments before the President's remarks (surprisingly moving, his
prepared text discarded), when Ellen Curry, who just that week was
in the headlines again as one of McCarthy's more illustrious targets,
stood at the dais and said, "A very wise Greek philosopher said quite
a few centuries ago that a democracy, a republic, was by the very law
of nature limited to the number of people who could be reached by a
single human voice. A challenging definition—answered in the twen-
tieth century not only by the technology of television and radio, but
by the open forum of television and radio, pioneered in this democracy, this republic, by such men as . . ."

CUT TO SARNOFF

"David Sarnoff of the Radio Corporation of America . . ."

CUT TO GOLDENSON

"Leonard H. Goldenson of the American Broadcasting Company . . ."

CUT TO PALEY

"William S. Paley of the Columbia Broadcasting System . . ."

CUT TO ABRAMS

"And David Abrams, president of the United Broadcasting Company. . . ."

As David didn't hesitate to say at the White House reception afterward, "This throws down the gauntlet for all of us in broadcasting,
the gentleman from Wisconsin notwithstanding."

It was at that same reception, too, that Ellen Curry approached

Robert with a gloved hand held out. "I'm not sure I know how to thank you. Your father is a fortunate man, you know, to have a son so gifted."

Robert turned on his heels and marched away, much as he had done at Fort Ord nine years earlier. The young man who had sat in her dressing room only weeks before dissolved into an unrecognizable figment of her imagination.

TIME WAS HEAVY GOING. Aside from Adrian, he had few friends, wanted fewer. A secretive boy, man, he grew more secretive still. He dreamed a great deal, intensely. The dreams were dry.

Even with a burdensome work load, mostly self-imposed, he began drinking steadily, more often than not alone; moderately at first, then with increasing recklessness, passing out more than once in his elegant East Side apartment.

It was there, on a cold but clear noon the day after a Paramount Christmas party at the Plaza, which Adrian had insisted he attend with him, that he awoke to the sound of his bathroom shower, and to the sight on his bedside table of a Maryland marriage license, certifying that one Robert S. Abrams of New York, N.Y., and one Brenda Louise Tully of Tuscaloosa, Alabama, were by the powers invested, and so on, now man and wife.

37

Columbia, Missouri
April 7, 1954

Hi, Dad!

Sorry I haven't written for a while, but like you always say, we Banners would rather get run through a Chinese torture chamber than commit ourselves to paper.

Nothing much new since I saw you last—on the personal side, that is. I'm working hard but getting lots of rest and eating pretty good. And yes, sir, I'm still taking out Poppy, the groovy Kappa Kappa Gamma girl you met midterm, and if you're still wondering whether or not I'm getting any, then I guess the old cat has to kick over after all. I sure appreciate the last check, by the way. Bought the new overcoat like you wanted and the guys (and broads too!) say it's a smasher.

The big thing, though, is that they're letting me work around the university television station, even though I won't be eligible for Journalism School for another year. I'm getting a damn lot more experience here than I did in K.C. One day I'm writing news stories and the next day making telops and the day after that setting up camera shots for shows and the day after that— I tell you, it's what I've been wanting to be a part of all my life without ever actually knowing it. It's a real creepy feeling you get, being there day after day. I mean real creepy-good feeling, like you get sometimes when you're out fishing or something, in the early morning maybe, and everything's fresh and new, like nobody's ever been there before, even though you know it's not so and everything around you is what other people are experiencing too. Or maybe that's not the analogy I'm looking for. I guess what I'm really saying is that you feel a kind of importance in a television studio, I mean knowing that everything you do is being seen and heard by so many other people, that they're actually being influenced by it. That's an awful lot to think about, you know?

And there's a hell of a lot of fun in it, too. It's hard to put your finger on exactly, but the people in J-School who work around the studio are different from, say, the ones in Engineering or Business Administration or the others. They're more like—well, characters, I guess you'd say. They're freer and wittier and more imaginative and more all-around aware of things, and it's stimulating to be around them. I guess "theatrical" is the way you'd have to describe them, because no matter what hour of the day or night, they're "on."

This week I'm working on the set of a one-act play by Eugene O'Neill we're doing live and it's really an eye-opener to see everything that goes into a project like that, especially on the part of the producer-director. It's a lot different from Little Theatre, for example, because of the cameras. The actors have to be as aware of the cameras as they are of their lines. The cameras are all numbered and the director in the control booth is so busy going, "Take one, take two, dolly in, dolly back, pan left, pan right, tilt up, hold, roll music, set up for a lap, bring up sound, go with dissolve, fade music under, up, out"— it's a miracle things go as well as they do.

Lighting's a lot of fun too. One of the paid technicians is teaching me as we go along, stuff you couldn't get in a classroom in a million years. I've become an expert at working the boom mike.

If I sound enthusiastic, it's only because I am. I'm pretty much convinced that this or something like it is what I want to do. I'll never be able to thank you enough, dad, for making this possible for me. I promise you that you'll never have less than some kind of pride in me. I'll work my butt off to see that you do.

Well, that about wraps it up for now. I promised I'd be at the studio by four. Oh, I forgot to tell you. It looks like I'll come through the year with a B+ average. It would have been A except for that goddamn organic chemistry. I ought to have my head examined for even considering it as a science elective. Guess it's a hangover from wanting to prove I could be a doctor if I really wanted to.

I'll write again soon, dad, I promise. Hope your cold's gone, and that you feel okay again.

Love as always,
MARK

P.S. Tommy Seaforth from Oklahoma City (remember him?) had his sister visiting him last weekend. She's still in high school but he asked me to take her out. She's not bad, young as she is. Real hip, in fact. Her name's Vivian.

38

THE SUN WAS WARM, embracing; the sky blue, enchanting; it was altogether a perfect spring day. Breathing it in, swallowing it whole around the tennis court at the house in Darien, where Arrabella was matched against the Hollywood producer Sid Klimeck, were David, Adrian and Joslyn, Maury Sherman, Gerald McAlister, Dick Fullerton (UBC-TV's vice president in charge of sales) and his wife, Jeanette, Selwyn Coe (vice president, Station Relations) and his wife, Carolyn, and Robert and his bride of four months, Brenda. For the moment, whatever their thoughts, their eyes were intent upon the action on the court.

It was easy to see the shape of the match. Klimeck, a short, heavy, balding man in his early forties, was a scrambler, going after everything, returning shots it didn't seem plausible he could reach, lobbing them high enough to give him time to get back for the smash, and preventing Arrabella from coming up to the net to put them away. She was trying cross-court volleys, putting them just outside.

"I think he may take her," said Adrian.

"What is it?" said David. "Eight-seven?"

"Nine-eight," said Robert.

Klimeck had a big serve and Arrabella waited well back, moving to center court to drive his ground stroke right back at his ankles.

He aced her, however, on his next serve. Then on his next, he tried to come to the net and she made a beautiful passing shot. Her return of his next serve floated and he let it go out by about eight inches, taking advantage then on another service ace. At match point, she again tried the passing shot as he moved up quickly, but the ball slapped the tape and, to the accompaniment of a partisan groan from Robert and Adrian, fell into the court. She was smiling, of course, when she went to the net and held out her hand for a congratulatory shake, but behind the all too gracious eyes was a controlled fury that marked the man off her list from that day forward, amen, no matter what his professional standing on the Coast.

David had to admire her, though. In every move there was an economy of motion which created an authoritative kind of grace. And in her pleated white tennis skirt, her white sleeveless blouse, the narrow white band around her thick blonde hair, she was in middle age the same natural, cunning animal he had married almost thirty years before.

"Your friend's practically a professional," she said to David, racket tucked neatly under an arm. "I suggest you take him on after lunch."

"Oh?" said Klimeck, Brooklyn thick as ever on his Hollywood tongue. "I'd kind of hoped for a return match, Mrs. Abrams."

Her silence was return enough.

"We're going to be pretty occupied after lunch," said David.

"Which I can already taste," said Adrian. "Your good Geneva's doing her great New Orleans shrimp-and-rice dish again. I peeked. What's it called?"

"*Étouffé*," said Arrabella.

"Sounds divine," said Gerald McAlister.

"I'm stahved," said Brenda Abrams. "Truly and truly, I'm stahved."

David was content to let it meander on that way, even through cocktails and the stylish al fresco luncheon, prepared by the cook, Geneva, on the patio. Important discussions need unimportant warm-ups, he thought. He remembered fondly how Bernie Strauss used to say it. And he thought simultaneously, It's a far cry from the old radio days, Bernie. And it's not just the added dimension of sight to sound. It's a whole new way of thinking, of scheduling. Even in its most competitive days, in radio there was never the pivotal agony of decision that we'll be going through this afternoon, tonight. Never.

It had been an eleventh-hour hunch that had compelled him to invite Sid Klimeck to fly in from the Coast, to set up today's gathering on a Saturday, away from New York. He could trust his instinct not to misguide him. Sid Klimeck, once one of the film colony's most talked-about comers, but who in the last several years had been distinctly down on his luck, had brought in a half-hour pilot film for a

series called *Hillbilly Bill*, which—since he was an independent producer with only the scantiest working capital—would either make or
break him, the latter bringing the best odds in the trade. All of the
networks, huddled over their 1954-55 nighttime schedules, had
turned him down cold, CBS and NBC without even a modicum of
interest, UBC—following a screening for Adrian and Robert on the
West Coast—with not much more. It was only after a personal call to
David, with the most perspiring if not *inspiring* pitch David had
heard in years, that today's unprecedented rescreening (he hadn't
himself seen it) had been scheduled. The '54-'55 lineup was, after all,
pretty well set: the Public Relations people were ready to release it
to the press on Monday. It was a strained situation.

The luncheon small talk, easing from food and tennis to what
Variety was saying, what *Broadcasting* was saying, what *The Hollywood Reporter* was saying, was brave if obvious. Adrian's and Robert's
displeasure was pretty ill concealed in eyes that shot poisoned arrows
between Klimeck's ears. Particularly Adrian's, since it was his bastion
that was being stormed; his program report on the film left little
room for maneuver. David could practically read his mind, seeing the
way he ate with both savage and elegant precision. On the personal
level it was scarcely less transparent. Arrabella's graciousness was
limned with herbs and spices that even Geneva had never heard of.
Joslyn's nervous banter assured all present and gathered that she and
Adrian had had one hell of a beaut before arriving. Robert's Brenda
Louise, still the great unknown—brick shithouse unknown!—was
discomfiting all of them, and the Coes and Fullertons, obviously
honored and awed by their whiff of rarefied air, were saying as little
as social grace would allow. Only Maury Sherman, who figuratively
wore mistletoe on his coattails, and Jerry McAlister, here only because
he had been instrumental in getting Klimeck to telephone David, appeared natural and openly delighted. But then, the West Coast publicity writer was always at home in either small talk or weighty abstrac-
tions. His prissiness, which annoyed David no end, seemed not to put
off any of the others. The baba au rhum for dessert was a great success.

"Well, ladies," Arrabella said, as the last sips of coffee were swallowed, "why don't we adjourn to the east parlor? We're set up for
a few rubbers of bridge." And as a motherly afterthought: "It should
be good experience for you, Brenda—kibitzing, I mean. Bridge is one
of the few social indispensables, I think you'll find."

DAVID'S SCREENING ROOM, belowstairs, was one of the wonders of
Fairfield County. Seventy-five feet in length, forty in width, seating

a hundred persons comfortably, it was nothing less than a small auditorium. The deep wool carpeting and soft cloth-covered seats had been patterned after several Walter Reade theatres in New York. A full-stocked bar beneath the projection booth was not an afterthought.

"There's really nothing much to say at this point," said Sid Klimeck, "so why don't we just roll it?" He signaled to the projectionist that Adrian had brought in from the city.

David, for some reason, had never watched a film more intently. After five minutes he understood his son's and Adrian's, indeed the other networks', negative reaction. After ten minutes more he had reached a firm decision.

Hillbilly Bill, starring a newcomer named Eddie Morgan, was very simply ("simplemindedly," Adrian had said in his report) a situation comedy about the adventures of a back-hills Kentuckian in the luxury-hills environs of Los Angeles. Using every device from the Keystone Cops to Abbott and Costello, it was the penultimate low and campy comedy. Its leading characters were among the raunchiest ever committed to celluloid. David hated it.

"If you'll excuse us, Sid?" he said politely, at the end of the twenty-six-minute roll. Sid Klimeck, drink in hand, went sheepishly out of the room.

"Well?" said David.

Movement, if any, was barely perceptible. No one looked at him, but neither did they look at each other.

"We'll play roll call, then," he said. "As briefly as possible, Adrian?"

"My opinion hasn't changed, David. If anything, it's even lower than it was before. It's clumsily done, often downright silly, and the production values are nil. Worse, Klimeck's production company, such as it is, is the most chaotic on the Coast. Even if it were of better quality, cinematography and all that, I don't think he could swing the kind of writers and guest talent we'd need."

"I see. Robert? You're of the same mind?"

"I am. Whatever the average mentality of that big beast out there, I think even the so-called mass audience is still a notch or two above this—this drivel. It insults even five-year-olds."

He turned to Fullerton. "Dick? How do you think the street'll react?"

"Hard to say, sir. At this point, I mean. There was little enough enthusiasm for it when it was mentioned earlier in the year. It has a smell about it now—like five-day-old fish, as Tim Wheeler over at Ted Bates says. Main problems would be in the big-city markets, I think. Sophisticated buyers and all that."

"Thanks. Selwyn? The stations?"

"I think Dick's right, sir. Thing has a taint about it. I'm not so sure but there'd be a few defectors here and there. It might appeal in some of the rural areas of the South and Southwest, but that's never been our strong point, as we all know. I'd say if CBS wrote it off, it's from nowhere."

"Jerry?"

"You mean, from a press standpoint? Oh, dear. I feel so inadequate, really. I mean, I'm just a publicity writer, you know. Well, I'll make a stab, sir. As we all know, and all too well, it's positively fruitless to second-guess reviewers. Of course, on the basis of seasons past, one can extrapolate . . ."

"Thank you. Maury?"

"Well, I'll tell you, chief. It's a lousy, dirty, low-down piece of crap, and since we didn't run an ASI on it, it's impossible to put any kind of audience measurement or demographic tag on it. But if it was me pinning the tail on the donkey—even with all these sensitive intelligent gentlemen we got here—if it was me doing the pinning blindfolded and all, I'd aim straight for the goddamn asshole. And I wouldn't have much trouble finding it, neither. Pretty big hole, you ask me. Like maybe sea to shining sea. Read me, chief?"

"I read you," said David. "I also read what in the old radio days someone called my gut brain wave. And it tells me that absolutely everything you've said about this show is true, and then some. But there's one thing nobody mentioned, and it's the key to why we're here. Know what that key is? Eddie Morgan. A total unknown. The least likely man I'd like to be marooned on a desert island with I've ever seen. Kind of strange-looking. Everything a casting director ain't looking for. And the makings of one of the biggest stars in the business."

He was a master of timing and knew it. He permitted this pause to linger like a held breath. When their faces, in his mind's eye, were sufficiently blue, he said, "I'm going to follow a gut instinct. Hell, it once made UBC number one in radio. This is what I'd like to do. Since Mr. Eddie Morgan is under exclusive contract to Mr. Sidney Klimeck, we are going to have to deal with Mr. Sidney Klimeck. What's more, I believe that with priority attention we have the potential of a television series that will garner the worst goddamn reviews of any show of the new season and wind up after three or four plays with a forty percent share of audience. What's even more, I've never been comfortable with the idea of *The Frisco Kid* going up against CBS's *December Bride*. Now, I know we have a twenty-six-week commitment with Columbia for *Kid*, but not specifically—I think I'm right, Adrian?—not specifically for the '54–'55 season. So I think we can shelve the *Kid* for maybe a January start and go with this crazy hillbilly for September. A thirteen-week firm. And when Mr. Sid

Klimeck comes back in this room I trust there'll be no hesitancy about changing anything we want to change in the show. Okay?" He smiled as charmingly as ever. "Would you ask Mr. Klimeck to come back in, Maury?" He pretended not to hear his son's stage whisper to Adrian Miller: "Now, that's what I call a fucking free and open forum."

HILLBILLY BILL premiered on the UBC Television Network in September 1954 to a virtually unanimous chorus of disgusted critics, and by its fifth week was neck and neck with *The Ellen Curry Hour* for number one position in the Nielsen ratings. An estimated 48 percent share of audience, some 32 million television homes, viewed the new situation comedy every week. The corridors of UBC were paths of glory.

It was a miserable autumn for Adrian, however. And not much brighter for Robert. Their ills, while vastly different in character, had their roots in the same gray October afternoon.

IT WAS about three in the afternoon when Joslyn Miller arrived at Brenda Abrams' Sutton Place apartment. With her was five-year-old Adrian, Jr., and his nurse, a young Jamaican woman they called Didee. Little Adrian and Didee stayed at the apartment only a minute or so, just long enough for Brenda to kiss him and stuff peppermint candy in his hands and pockets and exclaim about how big and strong he was getting to be and what a spittin' image of his daddy he was. Then Didee, with repeated instructions from Joslyn—"Be sure he keeps both his sweater and jacket buttoned, you understand now, you hear me?"—was off with the child to the miniature park by the East River at Fifty-fourth Street. Though dark and dismal and damp, it was an unseasonably warm and humid day.

Ostensibly, Joslyn was there to help teach her new cousin some of the fine points of rubber bridge, but the real purpose, as it always was these past months, was to get quietly, agreeably drunk, and let Brenda "do her," as she defined it to herself, when the vodka martinis and girlish laughter had simultaneously relaxed and aroused her, enough at least to submit to a rite that she was certain she abhorred— and couldn't stop herself from indulging in to save her life.

It had begun shortly after the Saturday in late April when Arrabella had entertained at bridge following the luncheon with Sid Klimeck. Brenda Abrams had been sitting near Joslyn's chair, both behind and beside her, and from both positions there was the aura, inexplicable, of seduction. She couldn't quite name it, place it, but it was there; unmistakably. In a movement, a breath, a long silence. She of all people ought to know. It was enough, anyway, to turn her into pie itself when she'd gotten home, even though she wasn't supposed to be speaking to Adrian (she'd sworn it) for at least a week. She'd rarely held him so closely, drained him so completely, kissed him, every part of him, so long and so often through a night.

She'd thought about Brenda the next day, though; and the next, the day after. It was the strangest thing that had ever happened to her. She'd never thought that way about another girl—woman: not through all the years of camp, high school, a girls' school in New Hampshire; rooming with the cream of them, for God's sake!

But it was there; *she* was there: as clear in her mind as Adrian, or the countless other men and boys she had known. A pretty girl; not beautiful, just pretty. A face round and slightly dimpled, framed by what Arrabella called a "dirty blonde" bob, fairly tall (she came almost to Robert's forehead), certainly "stacked," as they said in the trade. The perfect opposite of Elizabeth Ainsley, that was for sure.

Green eyes. Yes, that: green eyes, ocean green.

She couldn't have told you the color of Arrabella's eyes. Or Ellen's. Or her maid's. Or her hairdresser's.

Funny. There was so little really memorable about her. Even the syrupy Southern accent, which she could turn on and off in a breath, was sort of flat, wearing thin after a while.

And they knew so little about her. That she'd been under contract to Paramount, that she'd had several bit parts, that she'd been in a couple of *Danger* episodes on UBC. Little more. Certainly the story Robert had told and Adrian had backed him on—that he'd been seeing her secretly for some time, even while he was courting Elizabeth—was the fabrication of all time, as far as she was concerned. He'd hardly known her at all, no matter how thick he'd piled it on for David and Arrabella.

Really strange. And gratifying that after a week or so she gave her little thought at all.

It was mortifying when the girl called her the following Sunday, asking her in the next afternoon for a cocktail or coffee, and her heart damn near ran away with her.

Nothing happened that Monday, or two weeks later, or even on the third afternoon visit. They'd had drinks, thrown it around a bit, mostly about the Abramses and UBC. She and Adrian had had dinner with them a time or two in between, and except for an occasional meeting of eyes, into which she read maddening tales that couldn't possibly be written—nothing. Just—nothing.

It was on the fourth of their afternoons, on the third gorgeous martini, that Brenda had taken her in her arms, so naturally and inevitably that the thing was happening before her mind was really aware of it. She had even cried out, "Adrian!" when the strange and greedy tongue had found its quarry.

It was afterward, in an almost paralyzing siege of guilt, that she had learned the truth about Brenda—and, in turn, Robert.

"I've been this way since . . . Lord, like forever, I guess. That's why Bobby happenin' along like he did was prackly the answer to a maiden's prayer. You see, we were poor—my folks, I mean—down home there. Eleven of us, if you can imagine it. I got through high school, but just barely. Then struck out as best I could. Boys were always smellin' around me, of course, and for a while I tried, I really did. But it was girls—girls like yourself, darlin'—that really sent me out of my tree. Maybe it's because, as many as we were, it was me my daddy liked the most. Me he gave presents to, even when there was barely enough food on the table. And him I got to feelin' close with, I reckon. Maybe too close, I don't know. All I do know is he was the only *man* I ever could cotton to . . . which don't exactly leave much of a field. Anyway, I was lucky—far as talk went, I mean. I mean, looking like I do and all, I was the talk of Tuscaloosa, Alabama, and for all the wrong goddern reasons, ain't it a bitch?

"Anyways, makin' fair use of a few of 'em here and there, men I mean, I managed to get an occasional Lord and Taylor on my back and a Gucci or two on my feet. And a little bit part here, little bit part there—I made it, I managed it, you could say. There's not many men can't be fooled by the right groans at the right times, I don't care what *Redbook* and *McCall's* have to say. But it couldn't go on that way. Not successful. Like, I mean, sooner or later I had to face up to things. Like I have a nice body and I know it, but the wrong bodies were wearin' it down. On top of which, for all that I looked like I was gittin' my share, I didn't have doodledy squat, not even enough to send home somethin' to daddy and mamma. And on top of that, I'd finally come to the realization that I just couldn't act, no matter how hard I tried. Those bit parts in the movies and on television—hell, it was all I could do to learn one simple line in a month. I just froze. Just stood there and froze.

"Modelin' was out, too. One look at these inner tubes and designers ran like possum in a rainstorm. So Bobby came direct from heaven, you might say.

"And this is where you got to promise not to ever open your mouth, you hear? 'Cause no one knows this except probly your own husband, and as long as he's got it to hold over poor Bobby's head, he's not about to go spoutin' off on it. You see, Bobby can't—can't get it up.

No ways and no ma'am, don't matter what you do. He's seen a doctor but not a shrink like they advised him to. And it's eatin' him up alive, I can tell you.

"Anyways, I found it out that same first time I met him. The party the studio gave here in New York, remember? You wasn't there but your hubby was. He's the one brought poor Bobby. I swear, honey, you never seen anyone pack in the booze the way he did. It was gettin' on to midnight, and he was nearin' passin'-out drunk when I got him to his car. You see, he'd formed a kind of 'tachment to me, me bein' Southern and all. This thing he's got about Southerners—real hairy, isn't it?

"So, to get on. He started makin' with the hands, and bein' who he was and all, I mean the UBC Television Network, good Lord! I made like to feel him up a little too. You never know when you'll miss your next meal. When nothin' happened, and he kept pullin' away, I figured it was on account of he was so drunk and all. But then when he looked in my eyes . . . I swear, Joslyn, you never saw such a sad, old look. He started in to cry, I mean bawlin' his heart out. And that's when the cat got out, about his problem and all, I mean.

"And that's when little Brenda found her star. Even without thinkin' it all out completely, I knew what I had to do. So I took hold of the wheel and drove us to Maryland, where I got him on his feet just long enough to belch, 'I do.' Slipped him a sleepin' pill then, one I happened to have in my purse, and drove on back to the big town a fuckin' Mrs.

"It's worked out good, too. I mean, him bein' like he is and me bein' like I am—heck, it's like a license to steal. For both of us, I mean. I've got the security and respectability to follow my own sweet unnatural desires and he's got the legal proof that he's a real by-God man, even *envied* for the first time in his life when other guys get a real good look at me.

" 'Course, it's not all beer and skittles, now. I mean, he still touches me up some, which I have to endure, and he's used one of those nasty things on me a few times, after which he's so ashamed I think he's almost ready to do away with himself. But he doesn't suspect me, that's the beauty part of it. He just thinks I married him for his money, and who he is and all, and to keep it I just put my little old animal needs in cold storage.

"He'd like to be rid of me sometimes, I know. Especially with that piss-ant mother of his havin' a heart attack every time I open my mouth. But he'd never dare. I cover up too many little old multitudes of sins. Besides, I think his old man gets a bone on every time he sees me. And pleasin' daddy is bigger'n both of us."

It had been a long recital, and one of the most revealing that Joslyn had ever heard. And when she went back a fifth time, and a sixth, she was able to tell herself that she was having an affair. No matter how much it scared her; no matter how piteously she clung to Adrian every goddamn chance she got.

"I've missed you, Brenda."

"You're in my thoughts too, Joslyn."

"Often?"

"Ever."

"Do you . . . do you ever see anyone else?"

"Bobby."

"Idiot. You know what I mean."

"And aren't supposed to ask. Keeps it cleaner that way, between us."

"I don't know how this ever started. Or keeps on. I just don't know."

"Maybe it's 'cause it tastes so good."

"Stop it! I'll bet you haven't thought of me once this week. Not once."

"Don't look at me. You're the mind-readin' expert. Besides. I don't ask you what goes on with you and Adrian, do I?"

"No. No, you don't. Sometimes I wish you did. Maybe talking about it would ease me more."

"You don't still feel guilty about this, do you? Good lord."

"Well, it is kind of . . . extramarital, isn't it? I said, isn't it? God, I love to hear you laugh."

"I love to laugh. And besides. Think how lucky you are. I don't have to keep askin' if his is bigger than mine, like some lovers."

"Lovers. It still sounds strange. It's crazy. It really is. That I love you both so much, *need* you both so much. Daddy must be shitting in his grave."

"Best be quiet about it. I might get inventive again."

"And God knows you can be that."

"Darlin'."

"It's getting on. Didee'll be back soon. With Junior."

"I wish you weren't goin'. Tonight's already miserable. I can feel Bobby and his make-believe cock comin' on—"

"Please. I can't stand even thinking about it. I think you say things like that just to upset me."

"It's good what we've got, Joslyn. Don't let anything ever make you think different."

"Oh, God . . ."

Adrian drove them home. It started to rain just as they left the city. Big, ugly drops that hit the windshield like spattered bugs. The new

Oldsmobile they'd gotten just last week registered its resentment via window wipers that wouldn't work. Adrian's sour mood, from God only knew what new crisis or calamity that had befallen the precious network this gray, foul day, was worsened considerably.

"Damn new cars! Put together with matchsticks, every last one of them!"

Adrian, Jr., on the other hand, was strangely quiet and subdued; listless by the time they'd hit the parkway.

"What's the matter, son?" Adrian asked over his shoulder, catching a glimpse of him nestled against the nurse on the back seat. "Too much popcorn and candy today?"

The child didn't answer.

"I think he got fever," said Didee.

"Fever?" said Joslyn. "From what? He was fine earlier. You didn't let him get overheated in the park, did you?"

"The park?" said Adrian; shouted Adrian, actually. "What the hell was he doing in a park?"

"Playing," said Joslyn. "What else would he be doing in a park?"

His face was red now, puffed. "You mean you let him stay outside in this . . . this soup? In the middle of October? Christ! You have about as much sense as a mongoose. Letting your own kid run around in this lousy stinking weather while you and Madame La Zonga booze it up by the fire. And don't tell me you haven't been drinking. Your eyes give you away every time."

She was choking back something—tears, something. Whatever it was, it burned her throat all the way home to Westport.

The boy's temperature was obviously high when they reached the house. He was wheezing as well, and although feverish, he was unusually pale. Joslyn teleponed their pediatrician right away. A vaguely personal friend, with whom they sometimes had a drink or two at the club, he came to the house.

It stunned them. "He's sick, really sick. Double pneumonia, almost a certainty. You'll have to get him to the hospital fast. I'll call it in and meet you there. Connecticut General."

The next hours were madness. Adrian called Robert, who in turn called his mother. Joslyn herself had called Ellen Curry, whom she still thought of as her stepmother. By nine o'clock they were all there, in a smallish waiting room on the fourth floor. Arrabella and David, Brenda and Robert, and—the last to arrive—Ellen. Her smile of concern the warmest, it served only to make Arrabella's the iciest, with Robert's a pretty close second. Had Central Casting reached for the ultimate, it couldn't have gathered together on one set a group of players more adept at avoiding each other's eyes. David avoided Ellen's, Ellen his, Arrabella avoided both, both avoided Arrabella's,

Brenda avoided Joslyn's and Adrian's, Joslyn avoided both—especially Brenda's; Robert avoided the lot of them. Only Adrian's eyes were hard and fixed, sending steel blades across the room into Joslyn.

The child died at 10:45.

"I'm sorry. The lungs had filled with fluid, his kidneys weren't functioning, his heart . . .

"It wasn't his being outside today, although it didn't help any. He was pretty sick for the last several days. . . .

"We'd like to do an autopsy."

She was in Ellen's arms, then David's. Adrian turned his head. Then they were together, just the two of them, in the boy's room, staring blankly at his small, lifeless body. The only words were Adrian's as he left her there—cold, a choked whisper: "You asshole. You stupid asshole. You'll pay, kid. You better believe it."

Alone, the child's closed eyes the mockery of all her life, she didn't hear Brenda come into the room. For a moment she didn't even feel the arms as they gently gathered her in. When she was conscious of them, however—made conscious of them by the singsong murmur that accompanied them—she pushed them from her in a fury at once so savage and so artless that it sapped what strength was left her.

"I know, my sweet, I know," Brenda was saying. "I do, I truly do. Just remember through all this, though, remember it well: that I love you, darlin', I do. I truly do." She kissed her suddenly on the mouth, unaware that Robert was in the doorway, staring. Or that Joslyn—horror now piled on grief—had seen him.

IT WAS ANOTHER BURDEN she would carry, through whatever years were left her—Robert's knowing, and so the very real possibility that Adrian would know too. And that added to Adrian, Jr.—dear God, could she bear it? Could she ever in this world bear it?

Adrian. If his hold on her had been physical, the private joke of some malevolent alchemy; if it had been this before, what, dear God, would it be tomorrow, the day after; the years and years to come?

These were her thoughts, such as they were, in those gossamer hours after seeing Robert's face in the doorway, those unreal minutes looking on her dead child for the last time. The real shock of it, however, when even a massive injection of morphine administered by one of the doctors could neither still her fear nor deaden her grief nor excise her revulsion—this would come later. She would be bedridden for days to come, her cries of "My baby, my baby" shifting gradually, and to some physicians' minds dangerously, to "Mama? Are you there, mama? Did you mean to kill me, too, mama? Why didn't you, mama? Kill me now, mama. Slash me now, mama. Do it to me, too, mama"—a recitation that broke the hearts of all who saw her or heard her; all, that is, except her husband, whose own heart had left her years ago, if ever indeed it had been hers in the first place.

On the night of little Adrian's death, Robert said nothing to Brenda on the drive back to the city, or when they got there. Nor did he touch her, not by so much as a finger, determined as he was to wipe it all from his mind. And in the late-night hours, the sleepless early-morning hours, he thought about it to the exclusion of everything else.

THE SUCCESS of *Hillbilly Bill* was followed in January by three mid-season entries—replacing two hours of nighttime programming that had failed in the October and November audience ratings—that set the industry on its ear. One was a half-hour film series depicting the courageous adventures of an orphaned sheep dog named *Laddie Boy*, which the Quince Soup Company brought to David early in October for an early-evening time slot. Another, also a half-hour, was a live game show that the Millade Company, makers of Milady beauty products, wanted for a midweek, midevening time period. Based on an old radio format, *The $50,000 Question* starred a little-known character actor named Hank August. The third new program, an hour-long anthology series of filmed comedies and dramas, featuring the internationally known star as hostess and sometime actress, was called *Ellen Curry Presents*. Together and separately, these three new entries were to set television program standards for a long time to come.

39

"BUT DAVID, you're crazy! You've flipped it for good this time. Me do a second show? Another *weekly* show? Oh, my dear, you need a sanitarium, fast. Fast, fast, fast. And I need another manhattan, quick. Quick, quick, quick!"

"Sit down, Star. Will you please sit down? You're going to damn well hear me out and that's that. The dramatics you can save for the one or two shows you actually star in, and over fifty-two weeks at that. You always wanted to sink those beautiful teeth into meatier stuff, didn't you? Well, now's your chance."

"Chance? You call a schedule like that a 'chance'? With the television variety show every week and the half-hour radio show every week, a concert schedule that would break the back of a woman half my age, and you say 'chance'? Dear God, I need a *double* manhattan."

"I said, will you please sit down? *Sit down!* Now, if you'll be a good little star and try to stop shining for five goddamn minutes, just five goddamn measly minutes, I'll lay it out for you. For the fifteenth goddamn time, if my math is right."

"All right. All right, sire. Tell it to poor little stupid Ellen one more time. One *last* time, I do assure you."

"Thank you. Now, the way this came about . . ."

They were in the playroom of her house in Mamaroneck, which he rarely if ever visited, only a few days after the death of Adrian and Joslyn's child. And no more than a half hour after one of their more vigorous performances in her bedroom two floors above. A huge fireplace both warmed and charmed the room, the fire's bright orange embers among silver ashes giving a glow to both their faces.

It had been a surprise, to say the least—the whole day. As if his actually coming to the house, her actually taking him to her room—in, dear God, broad daylight—weren't enough, there was now the sudden and preposterous notion that she host a television anthology series, even acting in one or two a year. "You can film the two-minute intros and closeouts a dozen at a time, either in New York or on the Coast, whichever you want," he'd told her. "It's a natural, Ellen, and you know it."

Did she? One thing she'd dreaded even with the weekly variety hour was the attrition of overexposure. Another was the mindless furthering of a career that, except for brief hidden hours like today's, was the only life she could properly call her own. *Ellen Curry Presents* —it was unthinkable.

The whole idea, as he explained it again, had originated with Robert, who saw it as a quality showcase for "great ladies of the theatre"—*Helen Hayes Presents, Katharine Cornell Presents, Lynn Fontanne Presents,* and so on. After Adrian, and then David, had run it through the mill, however, the producer they wanted—Craig Dallas, of Columbia—wanted to use original material rather than literary properties, and the one interested advertiser, National Motors, said it wouldn't touch a stage personality with a ten-inch piston. "Now if it was someone like Ellen Curry . . ."

". . . and that's about the size of it. Star. They're hot to get you, Carolina Cigarettes says they'll give you a contract release to do it, and the radio show's already history and we both know it. You won't have it to worry about next season. The chance of a lifetime, Star. The chance of a hundred lifetimes, Star. Have I ever steered you wrong? Professionally? Ever, Star?"

She smiled. He would do it to her again, of course—ride her on the tail of his lightning-quick comet, speed her dizzily through his star-blazoned night. As he had done from the first day she'd met him. "You're going to be the biggest goddamn storm this goddamn country ever got hit by. . . . I'm personally seeing to that." From the very first day. As she looked at him now, it was as if no years had passed at all, as if even *The Ellen Curry Hour* were still a twinkle in his eye. In the days to come, she knew, she would be as excited as a young girl, emerging for the first time from her place in the wings, hungry for lights and cheers and admiring eyes, all the puff and mist that young girls build their dreams on. Just as she had been a girl again only an hour or so ago, taking him to her with a girl's dream and blindness. How marvelous really, marvelous and frightening, that physically, mentally, emotionally, maddeningly, he still owned all the stages on which she found so much pleasure and meaning.

"I could tear your eyes out," she said, brushing her lips lightly across his hair, loving the hell out of all of him again.

WITH SO MANY CLEAR-CUT HITS, and more projects than ever in development ("*UBC Boffo at B.O.*," *Variety* headlined), the network almost doubled its personnel in the first six months of 1955. And with its expansion, inevitably, came the membranous politics of superstructure.

On a Monday in June following a weekend of reflection and several discussions with Arrabella and members of the Board, David took Adrian to lunch at 21. It was there, between cherrystone clams and *pot au feu*, that he began a series of exchanges that would drastically alter the structure, if not the character, of both the network and the company.

"I've been giving a lot of thought to what I'm about to say, Adrian. So please don't think it's a whim or because it's the thing to do this year, whatever CBS and NBC may be doing. ABC, too, for that matter. And I'm talking to you first, because, one, it concerns you directly, and two, I value your judgment."

"Jesus. Sounds ominous."

"No. But it *is* a change, you might say."

"You're hiring General Sarnoff to replace me."

"He couldn't hack it. Not in a million years. Maybe you don't realize it, lad, but you're one of the best programming sonsabitches in the business."

"I thank you, sir. At least I'll be able to digest this glorified stew. For a minute there . . ."

"You should know me better than that, Adrian. When I want to send a message I order T-bones. Well done."

"I'm all yours, sir."

"Good. You know, Adrian, this little bug called television is growing up to be a pretty big boy. A pretty big *unwieldy* boy, I might add. God knows it takes practically an army to keep it going. How many new programming people have we added since January?"

"Nineteen? Twenty?"

"Something like that. With a kind of open-end ditto in all the other areas. Not to mention the theatre and record divisions, going full gun right along with it. Oh, the radio network's cut almost in half, sure, but it's still there, it's still breathing. What I'm getting at is the whole structure now. It's . . . well, it's unwieldy, like I said. And getting more so by the day. I just have too many people, too many departments reporting to me. And I don't think it's a secret that company politics is very near to getting out of hand. God knows I don't object to a little jockeying for top hole, but it's got to be healthy to pay its way. It's getting so I'm afraid to walk down the hall, the knives are thick as thieves."

"I know. I'm getting it myself, from every end."

"It just has to have control. The one thing I won't stand for is a repeat of the Tom McCarthy episode, back in the old radio days. Before your time, of course, but McCarthy, he was head of sales at the time, actually went to Atlanta to see my wife—it's when we were separated for a while, I was in Paris with Ellen, and I don't want to go into that part of it—but he went to Atlanta, saw Arrabella, and had the *chutzpah* to try to use Bernie Strauss's Jewishness against him. Bernie was running the whole shop at the time. McCarthy actually used that anti-Semitic crap, mainly because Arrabella's a Southerner, I suppose. I guess I needn't tell you the sonofabitch was out on his ass in twenty-four hours."

"Bobby's told me a little about it."

"What I'm getting at here, Adrian, is that there are some things, a hell of a lot of things actually, that I want screened for me. I'm too involved, if you know what I mean. Something, as they say, has to give."

"I know what you mean. Bobby and I were saying just the other day that it's a goddamn miracle you keep the balance you do. Most guys would have collapsed under it."

"It's hardly that dramatic, I assure you. But it's complex, damn complex, and that's why I've decided to do something about it."

"Yes, sir?"

"I'll tell you, Adrian. For some weeks, and I think pretty quietly all things considered, I've been in discussion with the Drexler Company. They're the management consultant firm, you know."

"I know."

"They're damn good. It didn't take them two hours to see that at heart, where it really counts, I'm a dictator, a demagogue, an out-and-out czar, if you want to know. *L'état, c'est moi,* I believe you smart guys would say—however the fuck you pronounce it."

"Why not 'benevolent despot'? Who's complaining?"

"I am. I am, Adrian. Complaining like hell. Lord, I even know when Morris Russman over in Engineering takes a dose of Gelusel for his fucking ulcer."

"I know what you mean."

"It's got to stop. Not my interest, of course, not even my direct involvement, especially in the TV network's program and sales areas. They're my liver and kidneys, for God's sake. I don't think I could make it very long without 'em. No, what I'm talking about is the day-to-day operation, the administration of this cockamamie monster we seem to have spawned."

"Pierce and Lieberman aren't helping? They *are* the administrative assistants, aren't they?"

"Oh, they're all right, good men, both of them. But we know they don't have—what'll we call it?—top management quality. They're good men, but . . . No, what I have in mind is something else. Something nearer, I guess you'd say, to a station operation. The Drexler people have even carboned a couple of the group ownership operations, in fact. In their recommendation to me, that is."

"I'm afraid you've lost me."

"It's this, Adrian: I've decided to bring in a general manager for the television network, reporting directly to me, with all departments of the network, except the news operation, of course, under his direct and immediate supervision."

"You said . . . bring in?"

"Yes. A lot of thought was given to you for it, you might as well know it. In many ways you're eminently qualified. But I don't think Programming, at this point anyway, could afford to be without you. Also, you're still young, very young, and the world's your oyster over the next decade or so. Besides, with Programming at the nervous and competitive stage it is now, I don't think you'd be that happy in the ivory tower. If it *is* an ivory tower, that is. More like a lump of lead, you ask me. And of course we considered the possibility of Bobby. After all, he's my— But as fast as he's come along, I just don't think he's ready yet."

"Have you decided on someone—the new man, I mean?"

"Yes. Yes, I have. Again, with pretty good undercover activity, if I say so myself. Frankly, I'm not so sure you'll be dancing on clouds, but the decision's made."

"Yes, sir?"

"Marv Grossman at CBS."

"I see."

"And I see, too, if the color of your face is any indication, that you'd like to throw that nice heavy plate right in my teeth."

"It's no secret, of course, that Marvin Grossman is hardly the guy I'd like most to spend my summer vacation with. But he *is* a good man. Top-grade all the way. I'm sure it cost you an arm and a leg to get him."

"He's very highly qualified. He was at NBC before he joined Columbia, you know. In sales. He's also had station experience. The Corinthian group, for one. And his programming experience with CBS is . . . well, invaluable. There's no other word for it. Particularly on the administrative level. CBS runs a pretty tight shop, you know. My main concern, frankly, was what *your* reaction would be. Not only am I not about to think of losing you, Adrian, but along with Bobby, you're the goddamn future of UBC. No contract or anything like that has been signed. Grossman knows I'm talking to you. He has the highest regard for your work, by the way. As far as he's concerned, Programming is the one area he's not about to put his mark on. The one area, I might add, that I have no intention of *letting* him put his mark on. You'd report to him, of course, but it wouldn't change by a hair your working arrangement with me. That, I assure you, is completely understood from the start."

"I've never doubted anything you've ever said to me. I think you know that."

"I do know it. And I thank my stars every day that it's that way between us."

"Yes, sir."

"Now. The other thing I want to talk about for a minute, and strictly *entre nous*, is my second move."

"Second move?"

"Yes. I want to make Bobby a vice president and assistant to the general manager. To Grossman, that is. I want your opinion on it. Not your *feelings*. Your opinion."

"My opinion? Well, in this case I'd have to say that my feelings and opinion are the same. Yes. Simple as that. Hell, Bobby's in on just about everything I do anyway. I don't know what I'd do without him."

"Ah, but in the new slot it wouldn't be just Programming he'd have to deal with. There's Sales, and Affiliate Relations, and Advertising, and Promotion . . ."

"I realize. But he's going to have to get wet sooner or later, isn't he? I mean, he *is* the heir apparent, right?"

"You've answered my question. And eased my mind, I assure you. This is a major step all the way around, and the future—all our futures—are at stake."

"Yes, sir."

"Anything you want to get off your mind, while we're here?"

"Yes, sir, one thing. I think I'd like to upgrade the whole Program Development area, I mean give it a distinct stature, with a department head, the works. There's just too much confusion with everybody's hand in. I think we need to separate the Current—that is, production —and Development areas."

"A good idea. Especially with Development damn near tripled in a single year. Any thoughts on who?"

"Yes, sir. I'd like to make Steve Braderman veepee for Current, and bring Jerry McAlister in from the Coast for Development, working both coasts, of course."

"I see. We'll have to go to the Board, of course. And if you feel McAlister's the man . . ."

"I know he's not one of your favorite people, but he's a beaver, David. A bright beaver, at that. I don't think you'll be sorry."

"I don't think anything you do could ever make me sorry. If you think he can cut it, go to it. Just get a little of that fucking prissiness out of his walk, will you?"

"I'll get him laid."

"Good. And thanks for your reaction, lad. Just keep one thing in mind. I don't give a damn who comes in, and how much power he thinks he has, at UBC it's still, no matter how you pronounce it, *l'état c'est moi.*" He smiled.

On Wednesday he took Robert to lunch, same place, same table. Crabmeat Louis and leg of lamb.

"And that's about the size of it, son. Comfortable for you?"

"I wouldn't think my comfort had much bearing, one way or the other."

"Please, Bobby, can't we be alone just one time in our lives without that shit?"

"I'm all yours."

"I'm sure you are. Now, as I told you, I've already spoken with Adrian, and he's willing to go along with it. You'll be working much closer with him. It's what you've wanted, you know."

"But I report to Grossman?"

"You report to Grossman."

"A good Catholic, I presume."

"You're not getting on that kick, Bobby. Because I'm not letting you. Maybe it's good for a little tête-à-tête with your mother, but it's obnoxious as hell to me. You're not exactly Church of England yourself, you know. Now, any questions on the restructuring?"

"A couple. The thing about internal politics. I suppose it's what you say, but . . . Strange, I don't think I've noticed it. Not enough to make much impression on me, at any rate."

"You wouldn't, not over in News. But it's getting out of hand, I assure you. Fullerton in Sales doesn't miss an opportunity to throw a snider at Coe, and vice versa. And both of them sharpen their little teeth for your buddy Adrian before they've even had coffee in the morning. Adrian's not above it, either. If a show he's brought in bombs, it's not the content or format that's at fault, it's that Fullerton doesn't know the first thing about selling. Or Coe the first thing about station clearance. As for poor Maury Sherman—talk about your old-fashioned gang-ups! Anything else?"

"Yes. Is Grossman aware of my own . . . elevation?"

"He will be."

"I doubt he'll run around singing in the rain."

"Because you're my son? Well, I'm afraid that's just part of the territory, no matter who we bring in. And I feel sure that what he'll be getting, like maybe twice what he makes at CBS, is salve enough for any nepotism. Besides, I thought you didn't know him."

"Only to nod to."

"He's the best in the business. The prestige value alone is nearly worth the price. I've no doubt he'll take hold, and do it fast. We're not exactly the corner candy store, you know. Now, with all the explanations behind us, there's something I'd like to say to you, Bobby. I have every confidence in what you'll be doing because I have every confidence in you. The *Evening with the President* thing, the *Ellen Curry Presents* as it finally turned out—they convinced me you have a real feel for this business. And as long as there are people like Grossman and Adrian around to bring you down from the clouds once in a while, I think we're all on good solid ground. I'm proud of you, no matter what you want to think. Your mother, I'm sure I don't have to tell you, is damn pleased about it, and I'm sure Brenda will be equally pleased."

"I'm sure. What she's counted on, isn't it?"

Friday was Marvin Grossman day. One more of 21's napkins on his lap and David thought he'd climb their fucking walls. But it was the place to be seen, especially this week, when what he was doing would be affecting a lot of publics—stockholders, advertisers, the press, the competition. Today: Vichyssoise, Caesar salad, and prime ribs.

". . . and that about does it, Marv. I didn't tell you about Bobby because I wasn't sure of it. The timing, I mean. Now I am sure, and that's how she blows. A deal, then?"

"We'll give it all we've got, Mr. Abrams. You have my word. All we've got."

ROBERT DESPISED HIM from the first.

Those who knew him well were disposed to describe Marvin Grossman as one guy who'd gotten it pretty much together. At forty-one he had had an extraordinarily focused career, first in advertising, then in broadcasting, gathering along the way more than a small working knowledge of entire operations. His far from handsome exterior—tall, lanky, sharp-edged features, sunken cheeks, thinning hair—worked perversely in his favor, a kind of sophisticated updating of Abraham Lincoln. He spoke slowly and quietly, and almost always knowledgeably; there was no mistaking the steel authority in his sad blue eyes.

It wasn't two weeks before that authority made itself felt throughout the network. The shape-up-or-ship-out aura, never a serious presence at UBC, was suddenly part of the central heating and air conditioning. Salesmen looked sharper, moved faster. Affiliate Relations people stood straighter. Accountants and publicists, practically hourly, snapped to. Even the Program Department, which under Adrian had acquired a kind of elitist mystique, appeared actually to be part of a team.

It was in this all-important area that both Robert and Adrian had almost immediate and irreconcilable run-ins with Grossman. First, in the matter of advertiser control of most of prime-time programming, which Robert and Adrian were bent on cracking, bringing all programming under full network control, but which Grossman (with David's seeming acquiescence) was inclined to perpetuate. And second, in the matter of film as opposed to live or taped programs, Robert in particular was the champion of more live theatrical material, along the lines of *Philco Playhouse, Goodyear Playhouse, Kraft Theatre, Studio One*, while Grossman was almost 100 percent on the side of the slicker Hollywood-produced film anthologies: *Four Star Playhouse, Science Fiction Theater, Alfred Hitchcock Presents, Ellen Curry Presents*. And while Robert (not Adrian so much) wanted more news-oriented programs on the order of Edward R. Murrow's *See It Now*, Grossman, again with David's support, argued vigorously against the idea. It wasn't the UBC profile, he said. It wasn't the UBC *shtick*.

The die was cast, the days overcast. By late August, just before the new season premieres, Adrian and Robert had their heads together, designing and honing the axe that would give Marvin Grossman his.

40

Dragnet, Big Town, The Falcon, The Lineup; Official Detective, Highway Patrol, Racket Squad, The Vise; Meet McGraw, Perry Mason, Richard Diamond, M Squad; Suspicion.

Foreign Intrigue, Captain Gallant, Dangerous Assignment, Captain Midnight; A Man Called X, The Files of Jeffrey Jones, I Led Three Lives, OSS; The Silent Service, Passport to Danger, Harbor Command, Harbor Patrol; Biff Baker USA.

The $64,000 Question, Twenty-One, Treasure Hunt, Giant Step; The $64,000 Challenge, Can Do, Nothing But the Truth, The Most Beautiful Girl in the World.

Cheyenne, Sugarfoot, Colt .45, Annie Oakley; Maverick, Brave Eagle, Tales of Wells Fargo, Broken Arrow; Davy Crockett, Jim Bowie, Wyatt Earp, The Lawman; Death Valley Days, Zane Grey Theatre, Frontier, The Lone Ranger; Wild Bill Hickok, Cisco Kid, The Californians, Have Gun–Will Travel; Tombstone Territory, Restless Gun.

And on UBC: *Squad Car, Girl Cop, Crime Desk, The Sergeants; Venture, The Vulcan, Dan Daring, Precinct 90; The Spy Chief, The Kipling File, Gunrunner, Shadow Man; Hawkins, The Hellers, Paris Intrigue, Our Man in Rome; The Big Prize, The Riddle, The $50,000 Question; The Double $50,000 Challenge; The Roundup, The Lasso Kid, The Settlers, Westward Ho!; The Trail West, The Sheepman, Sam Houston, The Gun; Saddle Tramp, The Border, Union Pacific, West of the Pecos, The Luck of Roaring Camp.*

Over the next three years—1955–57—the word was Boom. Boom— a television expansion, 65 million people at a single sitting viewing Mary Martin's *Peter Pan*. Boom—rooftop antennas altered the skyline of America. Boom—for the film capital of the world, which was permitted, however deceptively, to draw a second breath. Boom—in series programming.

"Guns or money, take your choice. We're a cyclical business, not a crusading one. When the cops and cowboys and spies and jackpots have had their time in the sun, there'll be doctors and firemen and— who knows?—maybe stockbrokers and pimps. The woods never run out of dreamboys, you know," David said in an interview with a *New*

York Times reporter, whether in pride or irony no one would ever be sure, which couldn't have mattered less. Boom.

There was little doubt that what U.S. households were viewing up to six and a half hours a day per household was more often than not pioneered by the United Broadcasting Company, and more particularly by Marvin Grossman and Adrian Miller, with David Abrams' tacit encouragement. More often than not, too, the Polo Lounge of the Beverly Hills Hotel in Los Angeles was the deal center for the millions of dollars expended and taken in to captivate, it was devoutly hoped, millions more fixed and reddened eyeballs than the clowns just down the street. Like so much in this "beautiful cockamamie industry," a casual word or thought in the Polo Lounge would find its way to the twenty-one–inch screen next fall.

THE JOINT was jumping that night. Robert, waiting at the small bar for the others to arrive, recognized at least thirty familiar faces, on-screens and offs, most of which smiled generously in his direction whenever he deigned to turn around. By this time he was so settled in as the East Coast crown prince that the toadying didn't even annoy him. And for all that he was indifferent to it, or pretended to be, there was a distinct magnetism about the Lounge that kept him coming back to it time and again whenever he was on the Coast. The gracious greeting from Dino, its legendary host; the talk of books, the arts, the matters of life and death with the bright young bartender, Gary— he actually looked forward to it.

They were here this time—he and Adrian, Joslyn and Brenda in tow—to meet with producers, see rough cuts of several new pilots, and give a small cocktail reception for talent and press. It was their last night, and these were almost the first five minutes he had to himself. Their pace here was frenetic to the point of physical exhaustion. His watch showed five-thirty. He half hoped that Adrian, who was out at Metro, and the girls, who'd taken a day trip to Disneyland, would be late. Very late.

"So you're the big man's son," said the seedy, puffy, ancient man on the stool next to him, having obviously been clued by Gary or somebody else when he'd gone to the men's room. "Out here to spend a couple of million—or save 'em?"

Robert ignored him, a pose so practiced that any further encroachment was unimaginable. The man lingered uneasily for a moment, downing his martini in three swallows, signing his check so hastily that his ballpoint pen slipped twice, murmuring a weak "Nice to've talked with you" before making an exit so swift it also seemed rehearsed.

"Who's your friend?" Robert asked as Gary cleared away the man's glass and cigarette butts.

"A sad case, Mr. Abrams," said Gary, whose sentimentality was almost a virtue. There was also little or no affectation about Gary, and there was enough of it around him to make him seem twice as natural and vulnerable as he was. "I don't know that he's had work in thirty years. That straight-up martini was probably his dinner money for a whole week. But like half this phoney colony, he's still got to be seen at the Polo. The way bankers have to be seen in church. You'd never know it to look at him, but that pathetic old man was the executive producer of . . ."

Robert thought it best not to look up from his drink. "Did you enjoy the James Joyce book I sent you?" he asked. "*Finnegans Wake?*"

"But pow!" said Gary. "I'm not sure I got it all, but—well, it reads like poetry, and you know I love poetry." There was genuine intensity in the man's dark, sad, but strangely dancing eyes. "Really too bad more people don't get to know things like that. But it's not exactly your daily television show, is it? You know, there's not a night passes in this place that deals aren't started or made. Biggest talent buyers in the world, I guess. Up to their asses in *The Lone Ranger* and *Cisco Kid*, but I bet there's not one guy out of a thousand who comes through that door who's ever even heard of James Joyce, much less read him. If you didn't know who most of these clowns are, and what they do, you'd think it was the white-slave trade they're yapping about."

Robert smiled, his eyes roaming the bar's whimsical mural—Persian Art Deco, that was the nearest it came to genre. "The crime, Gary," he said, "is that people like you aren't the programmers. But like Joan of Lorraine, the world's just not quite ready for you yet. But I am, Gary. Ready for another one of those prize-winning daiquiris you whip up."

Gary smiled and set about it, while Robert thought that of the hundred or so souls in the Polo Lounge tonight, only Gary would have reason to think of him as a "nice guy."

The girls and Adrian were beside him just as Gary returned with the drink, and a look in his eyes that promised good talk for as long as he liked. With a small gesture of helplessness and regret, he followed his party to the booth Dino had reserved for them.

As their chatter got under way—Adrian's reaction to the talks he'd held in Culver City, his own to the theatrical film he'd seen at Warner's (a possible series for the '57–'58 season), Brenda's and Joslyn's to Disneyland's version of the American dream—Robert searched, as he found himself doing still, the faces of his wife and cousin for some trace of the monstrous thing between them. There wasn't the slightest clue. They behaved with each other as simply good gossipy friends; they'd made an accommodation somehow. Robert was almost certain they no longer saw each other—that way.

Certainly Joslyn's afternoon visits had stopped, and the times he touched Brenda were unlike the times before little Adrian's death. Tormenting him or not, Brenda seemed actually to relish his mouth, his hands; inventive, too, in the pervious use she made of them. Comforting him even when, spent and unsatisfied, he collapsed like a child between her breasts. But he resented her still . . . like right now, tonight, her silly rambling about the wonders of Disneyland.

". . . and the big life-size characters, from all the cartoon films, I tell you it makes you feel six years old again, no shit. Don't it, Joslyn?"

"Well, it *is* a time machine, if nothing else," said Joslyn. "I almost feel sorry for the kids today. Not to sit in a movie theatre and jump up and down just at the sight of old friends—Mickey and Minnie and Pluto and Donald Duck . . ."

"Yeah," said Brenda. "There's just nothin' you boys put on television that comes anywhere near those Disney characters. Now, you take Donald Duck . . ."

Through the next cocktail at the Polo Lounge and a five-course dinner at Chasen's, Robert could see—practically touch—the wheels grinding away in Adrian's mind. He was always inordinately quiet when he was in his creative throes. Hard to imagine, though, what grist for his creative mill he could have found in this conversation; a Disney anthology was already in the works at ABC.

It was months, in fact, before the triggering of Joslyn's and Brenda's small talk took on concrete expression. And when it did, it was big talk. Very big talk indeed.

D-O-N-A-L-D D-U-C-K Duck!
Again.
D-O-N-A-L-D D-U-C-K Duck!
Again . . .

It was like an explosion in the children's television market. A Monday-through-Friday experiment, 5:30 to 6:00, *The Donald Duck Club* was, in a matter of weeks, one of UBC's most successful day parts, a top-rated money-maker that won the critics as well. It raised Adrian's stock to the sky. Robert kept quiet in the wake of his friend's enthusiasm. It was Marvin Grossman who suffered from it. He had opposed the project from the beginning, on the grounds that it was (*a*) an overexposure, the daily strip concept by its very nature an overkill; (*b*) a marketing mishmash, promising minimum sponsor identification because of its sale on a spot basis only; and (*c*) an operation so consuming that it required a separate and extensive staff to implement it. Adrian had gotten it through only by a personal appeal to David, who came through only in an eleventh-hour go-ahead.

David's postoperative view was made known at a staff meeting some two months after the show's premiere.

"I want to compliment—and please put this in the minutes, Miss Chambers—I want to compliment Adrian Miller here for fighting all the way through on the Donald Duck thing. Which isn't to say it demonstrated nearsightedness on the part of its opponents. Just simply farsightedness on the part of its creator. Still, hindsight is hardly the equivalent of foresight in any business, especially one that moves as fast as this one."

Marvin Grossman stayed on, of course. But the honeymoon was decidedly over.

It was during the same staff meeting, at ten-thirty on a windy November morning in 1956, that Ellen passed out during a rehearsal for *The Ellen Curry Hour*. By early afternoon, when her maid was able to reach him, David learned that she was already in Lenox Hill Hospital. Arriving there around five o'clock, he found her pale and mildly sedated, but talkative as ever.

"I can't imagine what happened. One minute I was singing 'Love Walked In' . . . you know"—actually singing it, to the startled ears of a private nurse sitting sedately in a corner—" 'Love walked right in and brought my sunniest day,' and the next thing I knew I was on a goddamn stretcher with some intern or other pushing a goddamn wet rag at my face. Honestly! It's so goddamn ridiculous I'm ashamed to show my face on the set again. I'm fit as a horse, and you know it."

He smiled. "I spoke with the doctors. Extreme fatigue, they call it. They'll run a few tests anyway, though. Sure won't hurt you any. You need a few days' rest, like it or not."

"Horse shit. How long will I be here?"

"I told you. Few days at the most."

"But the show . . ."

"Screw the show. Ethel Merman or somebody'll fill in. Mary Martin, maybe. She's one of your biggest fans, you know."

Sedated or not . . . "Never! Never never never! You must be out of your tree. You're going to use the best pipes in show business, and you expect me to go back after show-stoppers like that? You know goddamn well what you can do with your Ethel Mermans and your Mary Martins."

David turned to the nurse, who needed no further encouragement to hightail it out of the room.

"You're supposed to be taking it easy," he said, turning back to her. "Like keeping your pretty little mouth shut and eating regular meals and sleeping like a baby and forgetting for a couple of weeks what a great big wonderful star you are" . . . eyes dancing . . ."*Star.*"

She found herself laughing along with him. "I suppose I have been overdoing it," she said. "Like hogging my own show like there was no tomorrow. And five starring parts in the anthology series, when two would have been more than enough. Big joke. The way I protested too much when you first suggested two new shows. Still, when you're alone so much, when there's so much time on your hands . . ." Embarrassed, she turned her eyes, her face, away. "I'm sorry, darling, I really am. But that big empty house, never knowing when I'll see you or if . . . Work's my salvation, pet, it's my life . . ."

He took her hand, brought it gently to his lips. "This won't be the first time I've said this to you, Star. And I never meant it more than I do right now. *Whatever* the cost, to UBC, me, anything, anybody, I want to divorce Arrabella. I mean it. Ellen, I want to spend every last day of my life under the same roof you spend yours. It's all I've ever wanted, you damn well know it."

Her smile was almost the same as it had been almost thirty years before, when he'd said virtually the same thing in a hotel room in Paris, just after the scandalous murder of her homosexual husband, Gordon Strong. Nor was her voice any the less playful. "At our ages, darling? Spread all over the tabloids again? It's a lovely offer, lover, a really sweet and generous offer, and you can shove it up your ass, all right? A midsummer night's dream we're not. Maybe what we started out with fell and broke into a hundred and one pieces, but let's just go on picking them up, all right? What's left of them. Now, get your ass out of here and tell Miss Prim-Priss Nurse to get hers back in, I've got to pee something awful. You always did bring out the best in me, darling."

He left, of course—the room, that is. But he remained half the night in an outside sitting room, if only to reassure himself that it was nothing serious. Which, thank God, it wasn't. This time, at least. . . .

It was after midnight when he left the hospital, and almost one-thirty when he got home, where Arrabella was waiting for him with something less than open arms.

"How could you? I mean, how *could* you? You're bound to know that everything about that—that *person* makes news. At least three people from New York have phoned me. A case of simple exhaustion and you spend half the night there! Dear God! It's unthinkable, it really is. And don't use the lame excuse that as head of UBC it was your solemn duty, I think I'll be ill. You have no right to do things like this, do you hear? No right at all. It's humiliating, it's . . . You *do* have something to say, I presume?"

"Yes. Yes, I do." He was taking his first sip of a second martini. "I do have something to say. In a pretty hectic moment today someone said something to me that I don't usually have said to me. I bring it now to you on a silver platter. I salute you with it. Shove it up your ass, Arrabella."

THROUGH THE NEXT MONTHS, her doctor's and David's lectures notwithstanding, Ellen poured herself with renewed vigor into a work schedule almost superhuman in its demands, still glad David had talked her into the additional anthology show. It meant spending more and more of her time on the West Coast, of course—for which she was also grateful. The house in Mamaroneck was lonely beyond tears, and increasingly inconvenient to her work schedule. Too, David came often to Los Angeles, and the surreptitious meetings in New York became fewer and less urgent. They were both relieved, as if the punch line of a smutty story had been heard for the last time. Eventually she bought a duplex in Bel-Air, which was blessedly free of both memory and remorse. For a time, luxuriating in it, they were both young again, feverish lovers, and truly best of friends.

Her career was at its peak. In a world where endurance was the riskiest commodity of all—neither radio nor film, even in its most halcyon days, was comparable—she endured. In a world where only a handful could even dream of abiding—Bob Hope, Bing Crosby, Perry Como, Jack Benny, Larry Lester, Lucille Ball—she abided. Already a legend and more popular than at any time in her life—more esteemed and honored now than in the early forties even, when she had belted out "I Love America" to a cheering nation at war—she was the essence of superstar, just as that composite term was coming into vogue. In a world where program cycles were as precarious as programs themselves, her old-fashioned "Good night, my dears, God bless" was as perennially symbolic for the United Broadcasting Company as the peacock was for NBC, the eye for CBS. "Let's face it," the television editor of the *Los Angeles Times* had written, "Ellen Curry isn't simply a performer, a star. She's, by God, a national treasure."

"It's still very puzzling to me," she said to David one afternoon early in 1958, as they lay on chaise longues sunning themselves on the private terrace of the house in Bel-Air, "why I'm still queen of the mountain, as it were. No false modesty, as you know. But I mean it. Lord knows there are hundreds of broads, thousands even, who sing better than I do. A hundred thousand who dance better, and you know it too. And the most beautiful girl in the world I just ain't. And enjoying it or not, my little ventures into the thespian life don't seem to have Katharine or Bette or Ingrid or even Loretta exactly shaking in their shoes. Not so's you'd notice, anyway. I may have an Emmy or two, but an Oscar's not about to grace my mantel. It's a puzzler, it really is. Here I am about to enter the dear old twilight years of life, at the very top of my form, and absolutely no idea at all what the fucking form is. A puzzler, lover, a real doozy."

"Not really," he said. "This business is busting at the seams with rhinestones. It's only the diamonds, the precious few of them, that really last. Even the naked eye knows one when it sees one. And time only increases its value. That clear it all up for you?"

"Darling, you're a goddamn poet, you know that? You're also my dearest, dearest darling. And you always scratch it right where I itch. Now, let me think a minute. I want to come up with some more crap about myself so you can play that sweet music again."

"Faker! Maybe that's the real secret. To your phenomenal longevity, I mean. Maybe people love a good crook more than they think they do."

"Devil!" But her eyes, closed against the sun, were no more aware of longevity out here than in New York. "Failure, I mean the fear of it, is so goddamn magnified out here. Everything seems so much more . . . terminal, I guess you'd say. We're the babes in Toyland, all of us. Like it'll all be over . . . the singing, the dancing, the marvelous loving . . . over bright and early tomorrow morning, when we'll be put back on our shelves, where we belong. It's just all so . . . terminal."

Some things were, anyway. For UBC and all the networks. Lying there so comfortably in the sun in those first days of the new year, David wouldn't have believed it if you'd handed it to him with a presidential seal, what would be happening in sunny, golden, untouchable television land before funky 1958 was through with it.

41

The New Yorker was scheduling a profile on David and Robert for the fall. It was in June of that year, while recounting to the New Yorker writer some of the recent on-air triumphs for which he had been personally responsible, that Robert received a phone call that shook him to his toes.

In the interview, his fifth in as many days, he'd been describing the events leading up to his coup in securing Nikita Khrushchev to appear on UBC's Sunday news-interview series Tell the Country, which Time had called "the season's most extraordinary hour of broadcasting," and of the two live 1957 specials, a television adaptation of the Broadway musical *Plain and Fancy* and a two-hour production of Maxwell Anderson's *Winterset*. He'd also begun a discussion of the medium's Western and action-adventure craze ("Personally, I think it's damned unhealthy, even though UBC is a major contributor to it") when his secretary buzzed to say that Mr. Miller, who was out of the building, needed to speak with him, and could he excuse himself from the interview for a few minutes? The reporter, leaving, said he would return in the afternoon, and Robert, not a little irritated, took the call.

"Bobby, I'm sorry I had to do this, but I had to get to you before the press does, especially with your dad still over in London. I think we have another Hiroshima on our hands. A *bastard* Hiroshima on our hands."

"What the hell . . . Where are you?"

"I'm at George Goldman's. *The Fifty-Thousand-Dollar Question* staff office. And to use an expression I know you don't find particularly palatable, the shit, good buddy, has hit the fan."

Indeed it had. A professor of Romance languages whose difficult name, Dillman Bernnhardten, was practically a household word—he was the first big-prize winner on *The $50,000 Question*—had out of the sky, a nebulous canopy that Adrian equated with things like good deeds and conscience, called a news conference at ten o'clock that morning to say that UBC's top-rated quiz program was "fixed."

For some weeks there had been hints and allegations of malpractice in the big-money shows, whose contestants—seemingly overnight—were catapulted into the world of celebrities. Most recently *Look* and *Time* had run articles speculating on the juicy proposition. The networks, UBC chief among them, had pretty much ignored the possibility, "confident," as Marvin Grossman had said in an interview with the *New York Daily News* just three weeks ago, "of the honesty and integrity, both unassailable, of George Goldman, the distinguished producer of both *The Fifty-Thousand-Dollar Question* and *The Double Fifty-Thousand-Dollar Challenge*, as well as of all other producers of the quiz programs on UBC." That, so far as UBC was concerned, was that.

The Bernnhardten statement—true or false—was a bombshell. As he detailed it for reporters:

> Before my first actual appearance on the air, George Goldman, producer of the series, asked me to come to his home. He took me into the library, where we could talk alone. It was there that he told me that Frank Sanford, the current champion, was an "unbeatable" opponent because he knew "just too damn much." He said that Sanford was very unpopular, and was knocking out opponents right and

left to the detriment of the show. He asked me if, as a personal favor, I would accede to an "arrangement" whereby I would tie Sanford and in that way increase the entertainment value of the program.

I pleaded with him to let me go on the show honestly, receiving no help from anyone. He claimed that that was impossible. He said that I wouldn't stand a Chinaman's chance—that was his expression—a Chinaman's chance to defeat Sanford because by all odds the guy was practically a genius. He also said that the show was nothing more than entertainment anyway and that giving help to quiz contestants was a common practice, and just good old-fashioned show business. I didn't believe him, of course, even though I guess I wanted to. Pretty desperately wanted to, in fact. He also emphasized the fact that by appearing on a big nationally televised program I would be doing a real service to the intellectual communities, to teachers and libraries, to higher education in general, that I would plant in the public mind a greater regard and esteem for the cerebral life, all of this through my weekly performances.

In truth, I have brought nothing but dishonor to all of them.

On the morning of the press conference, when Adrian telephoned Robert, George Goldman was "somewhere in the Caribbean, and can't be reached." Even Marvin Grossman, purportedly his best friend, said he didn't know where he was. Other quiz-show producers and celebrity-contestants, however, denied emphatically that anything had been less than "one hundred percent aboveboard," indicting Bernnhardten as someone who had fallen so in love with the limelight that, out of it for a few weeks, "he's stirring up a hornet's nest for publicity and publicity only." Robert, Marvin Grossman, and Adrian refused interviews altogether.

The impending scandal, however, was alive and well and living in New York. Three days later, Herbert Stempel, an early winner on NBC's *Twenty-One*, announced that his appearances, too, had been falsified. The next morning, the most celebrated of the *Twenty-One* winners, Charles Van Doren, who was sitting in as the summer replacement for Dave Garroway on the *Today* show, said on the air that he knew of no irregularities, certainly none as far as he himself was concerned. A New York grand jury nonetheless began to look into the allegations, and the House of Representatives' Special Subcommittee on Legislative Oversight, chaired by Representative Owen Harris, began calling witnesses. It was in one of these sessions that Van Doren, obviously shaken, began the statement that would topple a ton of houses:

> I would give almost anything I have to reverse the course of my life in the last three years. I have deceived my friends, and I had millions of them. As a child, you see, I had been good at games. . . .

That same afternoon, in Marvin Grossman's office, with only Grossman, Robert, and Adrian present, Adrian said, "Face it. It's headlines, coast to coast. And will be tomorrow, and the day after, and the day after that." His gaze, resting squarely on Grossman, was his rare nononsense one; Robert couldn't remember the last time he'd seen it. "It's hallelujah time as far as those clowns in the Press are concerned. They'll break our balls every chance they get. We're the enemy camp, we always have been, and you know it. It's mincemeat time and that's the truth."

Marvin Grossman's gaze was equally grim, and several degrees more crimson. "I don't think I like your tone. *You're* the program head, if memory serves me. If anyone on the network side has to bear responsibility—I think this is the way it goes—it's the man in the kitchen, not the one in the dining room. Which is academic anyway, as far as I'm concerned. If ever the old saw 'teamwork' meant anything, it's right now. Swim together, sink together—it's all we've got. Publicly, anyway." He turned to Robert. "When will your dad be back?"

Robert stared him down. "I haven't talked with him today. He has meetings away from London. I'm sure he'll call tonight."

"We'll have to prepare a statement for the press, with or without him," said Grossman. "It should be released under your name, Adrian. Checked out with Marty Levitt of Legal, of course."

"Oh?" Adrian had never lit a cigar more slowly. "I kind of figured you might want that honor, Marvin. You *are* Brother Goldman's old buddy-buddy, I believe. If memory serves me."

"And just what in the hell do you mean by that?"

Adrian's eyes never left him. "I just mean that I don't think anyone in the industry will ever quite believe that a producer's best friend and confidant doesn't know more than he's saying. Besides which, the quiz shows have never exactly been my favorite backyard. You're one of the heroes of them, I believe." Standing, stretching, a long deep pull on the big cigar. "If memory serves me."

Grossman, too, was on his feet. "I'd appreciate your leaving this office. And not coming back until a little simple common decency occurs to you."

And whirling toward Robert: "When your father calls, I want to speak to him. Priority, urgent, all right?"

Robert joined Adrian at the door. "Most assuredly all right. I'm sure he will be equally anxious to talk to you."

Said a major New York newspaper in its lead editorial the following morning: "*It all began three years ago when the overeager executives of the country's television networks, UBC in the driver's seat, began a ratings race that appeared all uphill. . . .*"

IN LONDON that night, in her suite at the Dorchester, Ellen Curry was more on edge than at any time since her brief hospital stay. Waiting for David's arrival with a severe and unaccustomed headache, she had been on the phone with her agent in New York for a good hour or more, and had heard that the quiz-scandal situation had reached such outlandish proportions that President Eisenhower himself, even in the midst of his own political tempest over Sherman Adams, had made a public statement to the effect that the quiz deceptions were a "terrible thing to do to the American people." Ellen was certain that by the time the Vienna steak and Grenoir that David liked so much were wheeled in, she would be serving them to a basket case.

It was coincidence, of course, that the two of them were in London at the same time; Lord knew they'd professed it enough—everywhere, both of them. She was doing a one-woman, one-night concert at the Palladium, while filming an *Ellen Curry Presents* segment with Robert Morley and Noël Coward. David was here for talks with British broadcasting interests over the country's stringent quota system. Only 14 percent of British television schedules could originate outside the British Commonwealth. David was staying at the Ritz.

For Ellen the Dorchester was as near as she'd ever get to a shrine. It was here, back in the twenties, that she'd grown heavy with David's child. It was here that she had in effect blackmailed Gordon Strong into giving it a name. It was here that she had hidden from the profoundest hurt she'd ever known. It was here that she first tasted the wine of international celebrity . . . "A distinct honor, Miss Curry"; "A real privilege, Miss Curry . . ." The suite she occupied now was five times the size and had five times the elegance of the one she'd stayed in then, but her gratitude for the refuge of the Dorchester could never again be so great as it had been in those days. If only David, on his way to its intimate delights, would come to her gay and untroubled, and a million miles from UBC.

Fat chance.

He was exactly ten times worse than even she had imagined.

"It's impossible! I tell you, impossible! How can a television network, with literally hundreds of employees, *thousands* of employees, send out over its facilities no less than five prime-time programs, three of which are among the top thirty prime-time programs in the whole goddamn country, and have no idea, not the remotest trace of an idea, that the content of those programs, presented to millions of unsuspecting viewers as the God's honest truth, is rigged right up to George Goldman's ass? How could Grossman, Marvin Grossman of all people—"

"Marvin Grossman?" she said. "Good heavens, David. Adrian's the program man, not Marvin Grossman."

"I just talked to Adrian. He's as shook as I am."

"I'm sure he is."

Still in his light raincoat, he snapped, "This is hardly the time to settle old scores, Ellen. I happen to believe Adrian Miller. And Bobby backs him up. But one mention of Grossman and they both clam up like goddamn oysters."

She had to laugh. "Your metaphors may be mixed, darling, but at least they're in the same ball park. Seems there's life in the old boy yet."

Lord, she'd never seen him so furious. "I am in no goddamn mood to play Nick and Nora. Get it, Ellen? I-am-in-no-goddamn—"

"I'll cancel the supper."

He breathed himself down a mile or two. "There's no cause to do that. Even betrayed television czars have to eat." He even managed a thin smile.

Without a word she took the raincoat from him. He sat so far out on the edge of a Windsor chair that he almost fell. It was the first time she could recall that he looked his age.

"The sponsors didn't know? Nobody knew?"

He shook his head. "I'll tell you one thing. I didn't build this company, Bernie and I didn't build this company, to see it torn down by a gang of . . . I'm flying home tomorrow. I've been asked to testify before the House subcommittee on Friday."

They were served their supper, complete with superb wine, in a kind of ironic detachment, speaking, when they spoke at all, of the wine, the food at the Dorchester compared to the food at the Ritz, the countryside he'd seen today in his drive to the British Lion studios in Devonshire, and, most incredible of all, the weather. The *weather*, for God's sake.

Her headache, if anything, was worse. He left early.

"Perhaps it's best you're going back," she said lightly—as lightly as shooting pains in the temple permitted—touching a hand to his face at the door. "Another scandal with that wanton hussy in London is just what you need right now. Smile, darling? Small smile?"

"I love you, Star," he said. "And that's the *right* goddamn answer. No quiz-show sonofabitch had to coach me."

HE THOUGHT OF HER when he stepped from his limousine to the Capitol rotunda that Friday morning. The pop of photographers' bulbs, the nascent whirr of television and newsreel cameras, the chirping chorus of newspaper and television correspondents (his own Bill Barrett of UBC's Washington bureau among them), the curious bystanders held back by police barricades—this was Ellen's world, not his. How many people even recognized him when he walked, say, down Fifth Avenue, Madison? Damn few, if any. He preferred it that way. This morning's circus, which through the years he had been instrumental in fostering, was supposed to be for Punch and Judy, not the hands that maneuvered them.

Inside the committee room there'd been nothing comparable since the heyday of Joe McCarthy. If ever the incisiveness or impact of television had to be brought into question, the verdict was here, overwhelmingly, in spades.

Marty Levitt, UBC's chief counsel for the hearings, was beside him at the witness table. Another attorney, from the company's Washington office, sat behind him.

"Mr. Chairman," David said, when the room had been brought to order, "I have a statement I want to make. I believe it's pertinent to the matter at hand."

"We'd be most obliged to hear it, sir."

"Thank you, Mr. Chairman." He leaned to the right for a moment to hear Levitt whisper a caution to smile as pleasantly as possible every so often in the direction of the dour representative from South Dakota, who it was said was out to make political hay of the whole affair. David was a damn sight more irritated with learned counsel than he would ever be with South Dakota.

"Mr. Chairman, honorable Representatives, I feel I have to say at the outset, without going into details at this time, that regardless of innocence in either the knowledge or approval of certain practices that have recently come to light, the quiz programs in question, being transmitted by the television network into millions of American homes, means unequivocally that the network itself must bear the full responsibility of program content. The United Broadcasting Company does this with chagrin and apology.

"It is in this context that I wish to announce here this morning that I have ordered the cancellation of two of the major nighttime quiz programs on the United Broadcasting Company Television Network, namely, *The Fifty-Thousand-Dollar Question* and *The Double Fifty-Thousand-Dollar Challenge*, to be replaced with suitable all-family programming, dependent on what is available to us on such short notice.

"Along with this, I have issued another directive to all UBC personnel that from now on everything seen and heard on UBC will be exactly what it says it is. For example, all canned laughter and/or applause will be so identified.

"I would only add that deception of the American people, whatever its source or intentions, cannot and will not play any role whatsoever in United Broadcasting Company presentations, on the air or off. I thank you, Mr. Chairman."

There was a noticeable stir in the press gallery. The questioning, a full morning of it, was comparatively mild and unenlightening until the ball was thrown to the representative from South Dakota. It was that exchange, brief and icy as it was, that informed the public, perhaps for the first time, of just what a television network was and how it functioned.

"That was a most generous and disarming opening statement you made, Mr. Abrams. It pretty well assures you this afternoon's headlines, doesn't it?"

"That was not my intention, Congressman. I don't need headlines to stay in office."

"Touché, sir, touché. My point, however, is that your voluntary cancellation of two of the programs in question still leaves others of the same kind intact. Isn't that so?"

"So far as their place on the network schedule is concerned, yes. We are sparing no effort, however, to see that each of these remaining series conducts itself in strict adherence to the policy I just set forth."

"Of course, of course. No one doubts for a minute your good intentions, your goodwill. But how can I help but wonder, given the machinery now operative, that things will be any different from before? If these programs are not actually originated by the networks, as you have stated in previous testimony, but are more or less in the hands of outside producers, how is it possible to have 'greater network control,' as I believe you put it? How's that, sir?"

"With greater network representation at the production level, Congressman."

"At the production level. I see. But the producer of the program, whoever he may be, is not a salaried employee of the network, is that correct?"

"Yes."

"Then what control can you exercise? A man's word? His handshake?"

"His signature on a contract, Congressman. The contract being specific on all questionable practices."

"I see. You are, then, merely the disseminating point for outside suppliers?"

"In many instances, yes."

"Can you think of any instances when you're not? When you are the producer as well as disseminator?"

"All news programs, all sports programs, all on-the-spot coverage of events, a large number of both daytime and nighttime programs. We may be called a medium, sir, but that hardly makes us a go-between."

"Yes. Then, if you are what you tell us you are, how can we be under the impression that so much of television is advertiser-controlled?"

"I don't quite follow, Congressman, or see what the question has to do with the subject at hand. For the record, however, let me repeat what I've said on any number of occasions, and that is that advertising control, which I admit was pretty widespread in the early days of television, is no longer. The network controls."

"I see. Then could you tell us why the network, rather than outside production houses, doesn't produce its own programs? Like *The Fifty-Thousand-Dollar Question*, I mean."

"Because a network has neither the facilities nor staff to produce the extraordinary range of programming that we do. That's why so many film companies, in Hollywood and New York, are back in business."

"Ah. Again, most generous of you. Almost comparable, say, to feeding a continent of starving Chinese. But to get back, sir, to your earlier ploy—"

"I resent that, Congressman! In fact, I find your whole tone damn offensive."

"I'm sure you do. Bear with me, however, for a moment longer. What I was about to say, in regard to your opening statement, is that had you not canceled the offending programs—at least, those considered offensive programs so far, I must add—either a congressional action or an action on the part of the Federal Communications Commission would have forced you to do this, is that not so?"

"Directly, you mean? Forced us directly to cancel programs? No. The television networks, whether you realize it or not, Congressman, are not subject to federal regulation of any kind. They are not a licensed entity. Only individual television stations are subject to government regulation, and control only through a license to operate or the refusal of one.

"A television *network* is only the sum of its affiliated stations, those that carry its programming, and so are indirectly at the mercy, let us say, of the courts. And even the FCC, as strong a regulatory body as it is, is not permitted direct control over a station's programming. The broadcast industry has its own self-regulatory devices, of course. Each network has a very fully staffed Standards and Practices division, which approves or disapproves what is finally aired. Then there's the NAB Code . . . that's the National Association of Broadcasters . . . the

Code being a kind of Hippocratic oath for broadcasters. A barometer of good taste, good judgment. I believe all this falls under the general heading of free enterprise."

"We do thank you for your civics lesson, Mr. Abrams, but find we must hasten to add an advisory. Free enterprise, sir, never was and never will be a license to deceive, distort, or in any way disenfranchise the ones who count most in our inquiry. And that's the American people."

"Yes, sir. *Our* viewers."

"You're a sharp man, Mr. Abrams. Very sharp, indeed. I can see quite clearly why you're in the position you're in. What I *don't* see quite clearly is what I can convey to my constituents from all this. What I can promise them for the future. No, that I don't see clearly at all."

"Then I must offer my apologies, Congressman. On the other hand, I wasn't told that my purpose here was to help score brownie points for the distinguished representative from South Dakota."

On his return to Connecticut, Arrabella, wearing that soft, submissive, transparent look of old, said, "You were magnificent, David!" And he knew that from somewhere he would have to summon up the energy (so gruelingly spent these last few days) for the dubious reward so charitably awaiting him tonight.

"UBC lives," he said dryly. He was too damn beat to tell her once more where to shove what. One more time he'd play conquering hero. He guessed he owed her that.

ON MONDAY MORNING he had Marvin Grossman in his office at nine o'clock sharp.

"I know we've been over this a hundred times, Marvin, but I also believe that just because one lives in the city he can't entirely shut his ears to the old jungle drums."

"I'm not sure I get your point, sir."

"My point, Marvin, is that, right or wrong, your long and I'm sure honorable friendship with George Goldman is a serious embarrassment in the present climate of this company. Again I want to emphasize, whether you're aware of Goldman's tactics or not, the word—among the advertisers and agencies, that is, as well as some of our key affiliates, not to mention—"

"Adrian Miller?"

". . . not to mention the Board of Directors, which leaves us all in a somewhat awkward position. My own feeling—"

"You mean Miller's? Not to mention your son's?"

"You know something, Marvin? You're really a pain in the ass."

"You can spare me the compliments, Mr. Abrams. My resignation is already written and being typed. It should be on your desk within the hour."

Long after, David stared out the window at the ambitious surrounding towers, each determined on its piece of the sky.

THAT EVENING, sometime in the darkness, from one of the twin beds they'd had installed not long after their son's death, Joslyn said, "It was you, wasn't it, Adrian? It was you who knew all along what George Goldman was doing. Wasn't it, Adrian? It's funny. I haven't one bit of evidence and I'm as sure of it as I am that I'm breathing. You maybe even hatched the whole thing yourself for all I know. For all any of us'll ever know."

"Fuck off," he said, from the twin bed some feet away, sticking a fist against a huge and satisfying yawn.

THREE WEEKS LATER, in a move as surprising as it was shocking to Robert and Adrian—indeed to the industry itself—David announced the appointment of Maury Sherman, late of Audience Research, as the new vice president and general manager of UBC.

42

IT WAS one of those perfect spring mornings that New Yorkers wish they could bottle, and that someone young, attractive, and ambitious—someone, say, like Mark Banner—doesn't mind in the least waking up to. For Mark, particularly, it was a day portentous of more pleasures than his still sleepy mind could conjure. Among them: his first day in New York as a permanent citizen; his first day on a new job, as a copy editor for UBC News; and his first glimpse in more than two years of Vivian Seaforth from Oklahoma City, in New York for Easter vacation.

He was residing, for the time being, at the Winston Hotel on Madison Avenue and Fifty-fifth Street. The room was small and depressing, but he hardly seemed to notice. Propelling himself from the brass bed, naked and cocky, he literally danced about it. A cold shower only heightened his excitement. It would take ice floes from the Arctic Ocean to dampen his enthusiasm today.

Walking along Madison, after a hasty breakfast of coffee and danish, he began sorting the breakneck events of the last few weeks.

He had been at loose ends since receiving his master's degree in journalism in January. Having been a graduate instructor in radio and television news writing laboratories for the past eighteen months, he was urged by several J-School professors to go on for his Ph.D. But teaching, as a career at least, held little interest for him. The possibility of a position with one of three television stations in Kansas City was real but remote; nothing opening through the summer, at any rate. He had been invited by television stations in small towns in Louisiana and Texas to fly down for interviews for production jobs, but the places were unappealing. He had applied for positions at two of Oklahoma City's stations (being near Vivian Seaforth was of equal priority) but nothing was open at the present. He'd taken a temporary job as a business-page space salesman—commission only—for the *Kansas City Star.*

Meanwhile his father, on one of his periodic trips to New York, had contacted his old Army buddy Adrian Miller, "now a wheel at UBC," who had made inquiries around the company and finally asked Mark to come to New York in March for interviews with the News Department.

He'd come, he'd seen, he'd conquered. Particularly Mr. Miller, who had urged him on Bill Kelly in News, even though other applicants for the job had at least two years' actual experience. Heady, he'd rushed back to Kansas City. While he was packing he received a letter from Vivian Seaforth at Smith, saying that she would be spending the spring holiday with an aunt in New York City, where she'd write him maybe from the St. Moritz Hotel, where they would be staying. New York, a national network, the sportiest chick in the whole Midwest. Was it ever his year—this sweetheart of a 1959!

He knew, of course—taking the avenue in long, purposeful strides —that it was corn itself to think you could ever conquer this amazing city; real hubris even to think it was possible. Conquering New York was like writing the Great American Novel—the impossible dreamed up by somebody who had failed even the possible. Ridiculous to think of it a minute longer. Beating your meat. Absurd.

But he did. He would.

Someday.

There were pickets outside the UBC Building. "Unfair to Television-Trained Technicians." "TV Is Theater, Not a Movie House." "All Film and No Tape Makes UBC a Dull Toy." "Operate in New York—Program in New York." "Hollywood's for the Birds." He felt almost guilty walking through them, even though he wasn't at all sure what they were picketing about.

His first stop on his first day was Adrian Miller's office. A message had been waiting for him at the hotel when he arrived the day before. He had sworn to himself that he wouldn't be overwhelmed by big offices—or by big men, with big cigars, who of course would occupy them. Or if he was overwhelmed, to be damn careful not to show it. Being shown into Adrian Miller's office with his jaw hanging open was precisely what he couldn't allow to happen. And that was precisely what Adrian Miller saw when he rose from his mile-long desk to welcome him.

"It's good to see you, Mark. Hotel all right for a while?"

"Yes, sir, fine. Really okay. Thank you."

"Let's get the 'sir' business taken care of right off the bat. I may not look it, but I'm quite a few years behind your dad. You'll call me Adrian. And if we're ever walking along a corridor or a street together, you are not—I repeat, are not—to walk the full two paces behind."

His smile was one of the most infectious Mark had ever seen. His warmth was surely the most sincere. It was his own callow youth, his Midwestern parochialism, Mark thought, that made him just a little uncomfortable with him.

"I wanted you to stop by so I could welcome you aboard, Mark. Although it's no pleasure cruise you're embarking on. You'll work your tail off, I can promise you that. Have you been to Personnel yet? For the official baptism?"

"I'm going there from here, sir," said Mark. "I mean . . . Adrian."

"Good boy."

Mark wondered if he'd ever be able to master even so small a thing as a dramatic pause. He knew he was looking at a master of it.

"I'll tell you something, Mark. And it has nothing to do with my having known your dad in the army. Has to do with just you. I have this feeling about you. That you're headed for big things. Whatever you do. I hope it's this business. There's plenty of room in this business for talent. Real talent. I think that's what you have, Mark. Real talent. But talent alone can take you only so far. The *use* of that talent . . . that's what makes the difference between competent and unbeatable. Go the unbeatable route, Mark. It's not as safe, but it's a damn sight more satisfying. In this business, particularly. A business where everything you do affects not one or two or even ten or twenty lives, but millions of lives. But remember this, too: Even though what you're doing is creative, or at least sort of edging on the creative, it's still a *business*—the meanest, roughest, most goddamn competitive business there is. Unlike a clothing manufacturer or a processed food company, or just about anything you could name, there's not a whole dais of places at the top. You can count the television networks on one hand. That means you can never go back to the starting line and try it over again. That's one luxury you have to do without.

"Good luck again, Mark. Now don't let me down, you hear? It's your sacred duty not to let Adrian Miller down. Five hundred times on the blackboard every morning. I am not to let Miller down. Give 'em hell, Mark."

It was after ten before he got to Personnel, after eleven before he got to the News Department.

IT WAS after seven before he got to the St. Moritz.

When she stepped from the elevator into the lobby at seven-fifteen, time could tick itself to hell and back.

She was a stunner. The long blonde hair, straight and waist-length; the eyes deep and dark and then wondrously flighty; the figure lithe and full, and not at all angular for someone so tall—long-legged, short-waisted; the strawberry shortcake complexion—what had been pertly suggestive at fifteen was imagination's triumph at twenty. He actually gulped.

"Mark! Mark Banner! Imagine being in New York at the same time! I almost died when I got your wire. I've been telling Aunt Gracie all about you—she's dying to meet you, by the way, she was almost as excited as I was, the very idea of meeting you in New York this way . . ."

He took her to P. J. Clarke's. The back room, not the front. An arm and a leg probably, he thought, but for this? He'd eat frankfurters from a Sabrett wagon for a month for this! He couldn't help admiring the way they looked together, even in the grimy old mirrors on the water-stained walls she called chic; or feeling both pride and resentment at the bold stares in her direction from men twice the ages of both of them. Within an hour—two—his balls ached like hell.

They talked mostly about his Big First Day.

"It's in radio news, not television, but it's a foot in the door, you can say that."

"I should say you can say that! A national network . . . and in New York yet! Mark, I'm so proud of you. I really am. I'm so proud."

"It was dad's connection, of course, but I'm damned if I'm going to lose sleep over it. *How* you get in is immaterial. *Getting* in, that's the thing. I think I'll like it, too. Being part of something that's really big and meaningful and important and . . . well, important, that just about says it, you know? I want big things out of my life, Vivian. Viv. Really damn big things of my life. . . ."

One day he would laugh, and maybe tell his son about it, when his son was old enough to take a girl of his own to Clarke's: about the time his mother, on their first date together in New York, reached over and took his hand between hers, and locked her marvelous brown eyes into a visual embrace with his, and how he couldn't get up to retrieve her purse and napkin when she knocked them to the floor because of the unconscionable swelling between his legs. *Your mother, son, now there was a lady. . . .*

"You know what I think, Mark? I think I'll make Aunt Gracie bring me right back here this summer."

They had the house's famous chili and hamburgers and washed them down with three beers each, and then had a cognac to celebrate.

They were giggling like crazy by then.

In May he moved into a Riverside Drive apartment with Joe Scherick, a UBC-TV program coordinator whom Adrian Miller had recommended. It was a full, active life, and his circle of acquaintances widened considerably. He was popular and "with it," as they said. There were girls, dozens of them, and he wasn't about to forgo his share. Within six months he was approached for other jobs, other places. One job, paying twice what he was making, was offered by a woman twice his age, an executive with a television station group in Colorado, who confessed what she liked to think of as a profound obsession with his body. But Vivian Seaforth and New York and UBC —UBC and New York and Vivian Seaforth; the order wasn't important. What was important was that he'd settled, in his own heart and mind at least, on the trinity that for him was just this side of holy.

43

"I DON'T GIVE A SHIT what those cocksuckers at Thirty Rock or anywhere else *say* they're going to do. It's what they *do* do that hangs the linen. You can talk about your *Omnibus* till the cows come home, and your *Playhouse 90,* your *Studio One,* your Henry Four, Five, and Six. Those bastards can fill the windows with all the pretties they want, you know fucking-A what the back room's stocked with. It's the numbers racket, baby, and you better not forget it. What Bob Kintner's up to at NBC, what Big Jim Aubrey's got going at CBS . . . Christ, what Ollie Treyz is up to his ass in at ABC . . . pure-dee numbers, ratings, that's what the ball game's all about. And if horses' rumps and sawed-off gats is the way to five million more fucking homes, then it's horses' rumps and sawed-off gats we're going to give 'em. Come September, UBC is going to hit pay dirt, understand? Or I'll damn well know the fucking reason why."

Thus spake Maury Sherman.

They were assembled—Adrian, Robert, Selwyn Coe, Dick Fullerton, Alan Eisner (the new Research head), Tony Parr and Steve Kerimidas (both from Programming), Gerald McAlister—in the twentieth-floor conference room. Objective: the 1960 fall prime-time schedule.

Steve Kerimidas, whom Adrian had flown in from the West Coast, had just finished making his pitch for a taped theatre-of-fact anthology series, quality dramas based on recent historical events whose several commissioned scripts compared favorably with NBC's *Omnibus,* and in which American Steel had professed a slight interest. Maury Sherman's response had been simply the hundredth or so in an unbroken series of them. Robert had reached the point where he didn't even flinch, merely racked up another X in the score against him. His father might look on Maury as some kind of diamond in the rough, but to Robert he was a cheap zircon, period. Some might respect him as a superb scheduling strategist, but to Robert he was the scourge of the medium and a source of unending embarrassment to UBC. "Hardly *our* kind of Jewish," his mother, Arrabella, had said at lunch last Sunday, and for once his father's icy stare fell on steel resolve. Without a word between them, he and Adrian had posted the banns: *Be it resolved, before all present assembled, that the execution of one Marvin Alvin Grossman will be as nothing compared with that of one Maurice Frederick Sherman.*

"Don't you think that's tilting the scales a bit?" said Adrian. "I believe it was 'balanced programming' we preached so righteously at the FCC last month. And 'programming excellence' on the press tour in February. And I don't see CBS and NBC hiding their quality dramas, few as they may be, or their lineup of quality specials, some of which they don't ever hesitate to call art, in the attic. Or do I stand corrected?"

Maury Sherman, in a high-backed leather chair at the head of the table, chomped a cigar with obvious relish between wide stained teeth. "And so what's ABC going with? I'll tell you what ABC's going with. *The Rebel, The Untouchables, The Rifleman, Hawaiian Eye, Seventy-seven Sunset Strip.* That's what so-called schlocky little ABC's going with. And you know something? Those little cocks'll be the cock of the walk. A forty share of audience buries a hell of a pile of Shakespeares. Quality? Art? Horseshit! How about some fucking honesty for a change?"

They were all exhausted. For a solid week, night and day, they had screened and rescreened, accepted or rejected the year's pilot inventory, holding scheduling sessions in the precious hours between. Working with a large all-network magnetic board, divided with cord into half-hour time periods (Monday through Sunday, 7:30–11:00 P.M.), the individual title cards of possible new *and* returning programs on all the networks—Velcro-backed cardboard—had gone every conceivable route that the biggest jackpot jigsaw puzzle in America allowed. At this particular moment, shortly before noon on a very important Friday, the latest tentative schedule version announced itself boldly from type-stamped letters on bright red and green backgrounds. *The Partners, Gun Shy, Roustabouts, Island Detective, The Californians, Highway 80, Royal Street, The Pride of San Francisco*—these were among the possible new ones. No first-rate dramatic series or anthology was listed. It was this absence that had prompted Steve Kerimidas, as Adrian put it, "to stand up there for the good guys."

Robert rubbed his eyes, closed them, slanted them, stared fixedly at the ceiling, floor—anything to avoid looking at Maury Sherman, with his perennial damn cigar, pacing either side of the long conference table.

"Pretty good schedule, right? Right?" He grinned so earnestly that Robert's teeth ached. "Right, Coe?"

Selwyn Coe, the mild-mannered Station Relations man, smiled and shrugged, obviously happy to leave the Big Things to the Big Boys.

"As programming or counterprogramming?" said Adrian. Mildly, he may have thought, but it cut.

The grin went on. "There's a difference? Ho-ho-ho. You've still got a lot to learn about this business, ain't you, boychick?" A whirl now on Fullerton of Sales. "Right, babe?"

Fullerton was less easily intimidated than Coe. "The schedule as it now reads or the furthering of Brother Miller's education?" he said dryly.

Sherman roared.

I'll shove that laugh back up his ass one day, Robert thought.

"From the street, babe, from the street."

"We're in trouble with *Roustabouts*," said Fullerton. "I had Tom Hill show it under the table to John Ryan at Grey for Hill Drugs."

"And?"

"Down, boy. Down."

"You mean one lousy agency prick and you're dressed for a funeral?"

Fullerton was dogged. "I also had Rick Shelton screen it for Chuck

Chapin over at Bowles. And for Procter and Gamble, for Liggett and Myers, for Johnson and Johnson. Deadsville."

"I see." Grin there as before, but several more wrinkles. "Where the hell do you come off screening pilots before we've got a schedule?" To all assembled: "David Abrams told a House subcommittee that this company will not, I said will not, which I interpret to mean henceforth and fucking forever, will *not* be advertiser-controlled. I interpret that to mean also that while we fucking well appreciate their business and can't fucking operate without it, we'll be damned if we'll be dictated to. I happen to know first fucking hand that both J and J and L and M are sitting on their own fucking properties, already in preproduction at Ziv, and that their strategy is at the eleventh hour to pull their little fucking rabbits out of their little fucking hats, and if the networks ain't buying, to threaten a station spot deal on a syndicated fucking basis, which where I come from is politely referred to as blackmail, or holding a knife to our fucking throats while we're choking to death. And UBC, as your papa informed me not three hours ago, Bobby, is not about to fucking break under pressure, no matter who the assassins are. *Ja wohl? Ja wohl.* Tony, pull that sheet down over the board and let's go chow."

It was while they were lunching in the executive dining room (back and forth, forth and back; if he heard *Highway 80* or *Royal Street* one more time, Robert was sure he'd scream; and David joined them for dessert and coffee to play the record all over again) that one of the building janitors, cleaning the conference room for the afternoon meetings, fell accidentally against the schedule board, sending half the title cards to the floor. Frantic, he stuck them back as best he could, relying mainly on what he considered his balanced sense of color. Upon the group's return to the room from lunch (Tony Parr uncovering their precious cargo), Maury Sherman—without so much as a pause for breath in a marathon lecture on the virtues of night-by-night programming blocks—glanced briefly at the board to reconfirm his earlier edict: "Pretty good fucking schedule, right? Right."

"Best fucking schedule you ever came up with," said Adrian, quietly lighting his own cigar. *Gun Shy, Roustabouts,* and *Highway 80* were on CBS. *The Ed Sullivan Show, The Andy Griffith Show, Gunsmoke, Bonanza, Studio One, The Play of the Week, Perry Mason, December Bride, I Love Lucy,* and *The Hallmark Hall of Fame* were all colorful new additions to UBC.

THE 1960–61 SEASON was UBC's most spectacular to date. In the reckoning of A. C. Nielsen, that is. The critics had never been so bitter or so unanimous.

David had been able to paint for the Board of Directors the rosiest profit picture ever. The stock gained seven points in three weeks.

Maury Sherman was made an executive vice president in November. Robert resigned his position in January.

CONFRONTATION with his father was the last thing on earth he'd ever wanted. If not quite peace, nor yet a truce, there had been at least an accommodation of sorts between them, and oddly, not unlike the one he had with Brenda.

Through the always hectic days of Premiere Week, and the even more anxious days of the weeks that followed, there had been an unusually rapid-fire invasion of events, beyond the confines of the network, into the ordered lives of the Abrams family itself.

First, in October, David had had a mild but nonetheless alarming attack of angina pectoris, which had confined him to Lenox Hill Hospital in the city for two weeks and the house in Darien for another three. Which, given his nature, he hadn't exactly taken lying down. He was both irritable and impatient, particularly at home, Arrabella underfoot wherever he turned. It was the first halfway serious illness he'd ever had, and he made the most of it. The familiar image of a Prometheus bound was a reality for all to see. He literally roared. Then, in mid-November, Robert himself came down with a rather painful recurrence of the kidney ailment he'd been left with from the beating he'd taken in the Philippines—the one Adrian had so patiently seen him through. He had, of course, been confined too, the ministrations of Brenda *his* hourly fate. It had been Arrabella's turn next, the discovery of a lump in her left breast demanding an immediate mastectomy, which had taken place at Doctors Hospital early in December. The malignancy, everyone was assured, had been caught in time, but any gratefulness the family might have felt was overwhelmed in the wake of rapid recovery. Her demands on Robert and Mandy Jo, and especially David, were unprecedented. A few hours out of her sight and she was implacable. In addition to the nine servants who ran the house in Darien as though it were a miniature Plaza, she had installed a pervasive and permanent nurse.

The holidays at least would be passed in relative calm. But Mandy Jo—M.J.—who, except for snide remarks directed mainly at her brother, Robert, had always been the least complicated, certainly the least troublesome of anyone in the family, had a big surprise in store for them all.

Since graduating from Bryn Mawr, Mandy Jo had done only what it was *de rigueur* to do in her mother's set, her mother's eyes. She'd played tennis, at home and at the club, gone to dances and parties in

Fairfield County, Westchester, and New York, dated infrequently and undramatically (she was almost a carbon copy of Arrabella's uncle Aaron Sackman, founder of Sackman Industries, whom *Newsweek* had once described as "rotund in face, body and philosophy"), and entertained girl friends—mostly old acquaintances—at canasta, mah-jongg, or bridge. She also read a lot, mainly best-sellers, and did crossword puzzles.

It was during the week before Christmas that she went overnight to Baltimore, ostensibly to a sorority sister's holiday dance, only to return two days later as the bride of a women's magazine editor from Great Neck, Long Island—one Arthur Wiener, almost twice her age, a widower with a fourteen-year-old son named Frederick. The family was paralyzed.

That she even knew such a man was surprise enough. As it turned out, she had known him for several years. He was the uncle on her mother's side of Carolyn Roth, who had been with her at Bryn Mawr and who lived on upper Fifth Avenue in New York. After the initial shock, when only Great Neck Jewish had made any impression on Arrabella's numbed consciousness, the Fifth Avenue connection had come in handy. In fact, both Arthur Wiener and his son were people after Arrabella's heart, eventually easing, if not erasing, the absurd difference in age between bride and groom, not to mention the scandalous way they had tied the knot. His decision to sell the house in Great Neck and take an apartment in Manhattan (and on the East Side, near Robert's) could only further his suitability. After a while, both Arrabella and David (though they would never dare say it aloud, not even to each other) came to wonder what the man ever saw in Mandy Jo.

For them all, then, that New Year's Day in 1961 was the start of a truly new year all around. And at the table that evening the new grandson-by-marriage, nephew-by-marriage, Fred Wiener, made an impression, particularly on Arrabella and Robert, who were charmed to the teeth by the boy's obvious sophistication, his strongly developed sense of discrimination, his easy disdain of the banal and mediocre. And only fourteen . . .

It was at this same dinner (scallops in ramekins, cold lobster mousse; artichokes Grecque; cushion shoulder of lamb with chicken-liver stuffing; asparagus Polonaise; Sacher torte, Moravian sugar cake; Laurent Perrier '56—a new French cook, Madame Pauline) that the March to High Noon began.

Arthur Wiener, champagne glass in hand, had just finished telling David, Robert, and Adrian about a short novel he was running in *Chic,* the magazine he edited, which he thought had series possibilities, particularly for an early-evening all-family time period. It was the story of a man-and-wife team of doctors and their intern son at a big metropolitan hospital. The parents were famous for their specialization in internal medicine, and rich as sin from it; the son was an idealist who wanted nothing more than to practice general medicine at an outpost in Lower Mongolia. Family drama. Great conflict. *Important* conflict. Heart. Notches above soaps, treated usually delicate and taboo subjects sensitively but realistically. Great thing to cast. Fred MacMurray and Irene Dunne. Maybe Melvyn Douglas and Barbara Stanwyck. Some brand-new face for the son. Handsome. Bright. Sincere to his navel. Star of tomorrow. That sort of thing. Both David and Adrian had listened. Even Robert himself, though nauseated by the whole idea, had been momentarily caught up in Arthur Wiener's engaging, knowing telling of it. David had said easily, "Maybe something to look into, Adrian. I've thought myself that doctor stories are the next big cycle." Adrian had smiled and nodded vaguely, which meant it damn well turned him off. Period.

It was inevitable, Robert thought, that his father would turn to him. And inevitable that he would stall. An idea that repelled him—but from a man like Wiener, whom he instinctively liked and respected—it was a conflict that disarmed him. "Most certainly bears looking into," he'd said finally—inadequate, but then responses to his father's habit of hot-seating him whenever he had the chance generally were.

"No, Bobby, not *bears* looking into. *Demands* looking into. And all along I thought *you* were the expert on verbs." Then, winking broadly at Arthur Wiener: "We might work up more enthusiasm from my learned son if we named the parents Dr. and Mrs. Hippocrates and the son maybe . . . what? Oedipus?"

Ordinarily Robert would simply have withdrawn, but tonight, for some reason—maybe to impress young Freddie Wiener, who clearly looked up to him?—he found himself giving it back, gun loaded for bear. "Why not make the intern a daughter, age her a little, and have her played by Ellen Curry? The lady's due for a third series about now."

Petrified forest. He couldn't imagine, much less comprehend, that he'd dared say it. His pale, handsome face was a shade green.

His mother's was similar, only blue-tinged. His father's he managed not to see. After thunderous silence unlike any he'd ever experienced in this house—how many times had his father said it to him as a child: "Go to your room!"?—it was broken by Joslyn, who asked Freddie Wiener what else he liked to do besides read Shaw and Ibsen and O'Neill, and young Wiener replied smartly, "Why, read Dion Boucicault, of course." Adrian's hand, under the tablecloth, clasping Robert's knee in reassurance, only compounded his obvious discomfort. David was nowhere in sight when he and Brenda managed to leave.

Brenda, however, kept it going on the drive back to New York.

"You really are somethin', you know that? You really are. A little good-natured teasin' and you come on like an old swamp snake. There's a meanness in you, Bobby, there really is. A plain old deep-down meanness. Just what has your daddy ever done to you, Bobby, except maybe give you too much?"

"Shut up," he said. "Just shut the hell up."

"And another thing. It's pretty obvious that you and Adrian are always plottin' against him, even if he's blind as a bat when it comes to both of you. Joslyn and I both know what was goin' back and forth between you two on the telephone when the poor man was laid up in the hospital, and you two was hopin' he'd croak. It's a wonder AT&T didn't explode in your face."

It was clearly his day for it; his night. "No more than Sappho opening her arms to you and Joslyn," he said, "on that sweet little island of Lesbos."

For all her unfamiliarity with literary allusions, Brenda not only got the message, she choked on it. Another self-proscription he'd sworn to honor had just been trampled in the dust. The rest of the night was a nightmare for both of them.

The thing in hand—something he hadn't resorted to in months—he exploited flesh as though it were earth he had to furrow; bought-and-paid-for acreage. The pungent smell of her, the low, serrated moans of pain and humiliation, stayed with him long after. Afterward her forced laugh of contempt from the other bed, in darkness, made hopeless even the shards of sleep. Large fissures, if as yet undefined, were crowding his life, and he knew it.

Over the next few weeks, even in intimate quarters, he managed to say little to either of his adversaries. Which didn't mean, of course, that he wasn't with them. The network meetings and conferences were many and frequent, David's eyes on him often—gazes he became particularly adept at avoiding. Whether he and Brenda were at home or out together, the passages between them were monosyllabic. He never touched her again. With anything.

The second clash with his father occurred during the second week in January, this time in Maury Sherman's office.

They had been called together—Adrian, Clyde Danna (UBC's News Documentary Division), George Taylor (program production co-ordinator), Gerald McAlister, himself—to review the status of a fictional documentary treatment of recent historical events for a possible 1961–62 series. A joint News and Entertainment project, it had been enthusiastically endorsed by the News people, less so by Adrian

and his new sidekick McAlister, even though the concept had originated with Robert. The remark that Clyde Danna had made earlier,
that News producers had far more expertise—*creative* expertise—than
anyone in Programming simply by the fact that they were in-house
originators rather than "buyers" of others' products, still hung heavy
in the cigar-blue air.

"Clearly, you misunderstood me," Danna was saying. "My only
point was that since we have the production facilities and you people
do not, it's only logical that both the exec and line producer come
from our shop. That's all I meant." Clyde Danna was a short, intense,
rather fussy young man, one of what Robert called "television's new
breed, accountants with the nerve to call themselves artists." Clyde
Danna sported thick hair, thick eyebrows, thick glasses. He bore an
uncanny resemblance to Bernie Strauss.

Adrian, sitting directly across from him, said, "*All* you meant? I
have two good teeth left in the bottom right. Sure you wouldn't like
to try for those?"

Only McAlister made any real sound: a high nervous giggle that
sounded twice as large as it was. George Taylor coughed, but it
sounded like a self-conscious clearing of his throat.

Maury Sherman's next outburst certainly didn't. "What the fuck
does it matter who takes credit? We're only doing this stupid thing to
please a few peacock assholes in Washington. We'll be lucky if even
Preparation H takes a stab at it." Then, to Robert: "What's the script
status?"

It was at that moment that David came in. It had become his habit
of late to walk in on meetings unannounced, and with no updating
at all to enter the exchange as if he'd been in on it from the beginning.

"I hope the second script's better than the first one," he said,
straddling a chair near Sherman's desk, his arms resting easily on its
low back: a one-of-the-boys gesture that never failed to drain what
color there was from Robert's face.

Today, more visibly than usual.

"The second script's tighter," he said, eyes fixed beyond his father's
to Maury Sherman's: the lesser, for the moment, of evils. "The motiva-
tion's not quite as thin. The dialogue still is, though. Rod Serling and
Reggie Rose he decidedly isn't."

"Hmmn," said David, his voice gentle, transparently so. Paltry peace
offering indeed compared with the new stereo equipment, the new
Buick convertible, the extended tour of Europe of days past.

Robert went on: "I think the trouble's in the point of view. It's
never clear whose POV we're actually with. Makes for a diffusion
that works against the central—"

"And who the fuck cares, hunh?" Even David turned with a look
of sharp disapproval at Maury Sherman's outburst.

"I'll tell you why I dropped by," he said, eyes taking in all of them.
"I've just made what I suppose we'll have to call a unilateral decision.
I want you to start thinking of this project on a once-a-month basis.
Rough estimates don't justify a weekly budget. Some of the sets read
like *Gone with the Wind*. Besides, Dick Fullerton's people aren't
getting a very positive reading. Seems Phil Cowles at G.E. and Newton Minow of the FCC come from different sides of the track. What
can you do? We'll just have to go into it on a preemptive basis, no
set time period." His mock disappointment was underlined by hands
spread helplessly out, palms up.

"But you can hardly expect continuity, which is absolutely essential
to a series like this," Robert said, "by such erratic scheduling. And I
might add that Gregory Peck, if we're lucky enough to get him for
host, wouldn't hold still for such hit-and-miss exposure."

"So? We can always use Barry White," said Maury Sherman. "Dress
him up in pink lounging pajamas and the fruits'll take to him like he's
a regular Bette Davis."

"Or Maria Montez," said David. "Now, there's a lady to hype the
numbers. Good for a seven share at least."

The drift, Robert saw, was obviously against him. "Under the circumstances," he said, "I've no choice except to withdraw from the
project. I never was one to come over bottom lines." Blessedly no one
added, Or over any other lines, for that matter. They didn't need to.

David was on his feet now. "I don't believe the choice *is* yours,
Bobby. You started with it, you see it through. And then fight for it,
no matter who the hell tells you different."

Deadly eyes followed his father's departure. His. *Twelve years old,*
eyes blackened by another boy, two years younger at least, David so
angry . . . "Get your butt back out there, now, now, do you hear me,
close that little bastard's eyes like they've never been closed before,"
in front of all of them, every kid in the block. In front of all of them,
all of them, Adrian, McAlister, Taylor, Clyde Danna. There was an
end to this, there had to be. . . .

Maury Sherman held him back a moment as the others were leaving
and said kindly, if sloppily, "Don't let it get to you, boychick. All
daddies are mothers, if they got an ounce of *mensch*. The thing's
called love." It was the bitterest pill of a morning of them.

That evening, after dinner and theatre with Adrian and Joslyn, he
reached out for Brenda's breasts as she was starting to undress—the
first time in months—only to feel her shudder, pull away; actually
bare her teeth like Jean Harlow in the early films. "You give me the

creeps, you know that? You give me the creeps." Her voice was like
Harlow's, too.

MORNING.

First thing.

"May I ask what the hell this means?"

David's eyes flashed their old fire.

"Precisely what it says," said Robert. "What it means to say, at any
rate."

"I see. And just what do you plan to do in this"—glancing briefly at
the note in his hand—"this 'artistically conducive absence' you're
about to 'embark' on?"

"I'm not sure, not at this point," he said. "I plan to travel a little
first, then maybe something in the theatre. I still have grandfather
Levinson's trust fund, you know. I've already had talks with Alex
Cohen and Hal Prince—"

"Real ballsy of you. Now climb down off your high horse and we'll
have lunch together, just the two of us. How does Lutèce sound?"

"I've never been more serious. I mean what I say."

"Quo Vadis? Pavillon?"

"I think I've made myself clear. Any further discussion—"

"Will you cut the crap, Bobby! We're going to have lunch together.
That's that. Late as it is in our lives—*both* our lives—we're going to sit
down together, we're going to think together. . . ."

He couldn't hear the signals of father to son. All he heard—and
responded to—were the words, which were, of course, not the point,
were beside the point. . . . "Maybe when such as Maury Sherman, and
all he *doesn't* stand for, are tar-and-feathered out of the industry . . .
well, maybe then some kind of lunch would be just fine." He added
almost slyly, "Maybe Seafare of the Aegean on Fifty-sixth Street. I
like their stuffed flounder."

David sighed. The kid just didn't know how to quit when he was
ahead. Well, he'd try again. . . . Lighting a cigar with the gold lighter
from Cartier's that Robert had given him on his last birthday, smiling
tightly, he said, "I'll tell you what. We'll just bury this memorandum
under a stack of loss statements for the radio division and leave it
there until you and Brenda get back from a good long trip, then we'll
have that stuffed flounder at Seafare and have ourselves a couple of
good laughs over the whole thing. Okay? *Okay?*"

"I'm not a child, father, and you're not a father, either. I guess
neither of us was much good at what we were supposed to be. Well,
too bad, but it's too late to start kindergarten again. For me, anyway."

"I sometimes wonder if you ever passed it, Bobby."

"I'll call mother myself."

"I'm *sure* you will."

"She'll at least understand what I'm doing . . . she's *always* understood. Me *and* you. What should I tell her when she asks what you tried to give me this time? Surely not just lunch at Lutèce. How about a yacht?"

"*You little shit.*"

Two days later Robert left for an extended vacation in Martinique. Brenda flew to Reno the day after.

44

Yours is a most honorable profession. Anyone who is in the broadcasting business has a tough row to hoe. You earn your bread by using public property. When you work in broadcasting you volunteer for public service, public pressure, and public regulation. . . .

I can think of easier ways to make a living.

I admire your courage—but that doesn't mean I would make life easier for you.

I am happy to find your health good. A 1960 gross revenue of $1,268 million has given broadcasters a profit of $243 million before taxes—a return of 19.2 percent. For your investors the price has indeed been right.

Television has had great achievements and delightful moments. *Peter Pan, Twilight Zone, Project Twenty, Victory at Sea, See It Now,* the Army-McCarthy hearings, convention and campaign broadcasts, the Great Debates, *Kraft Theatre, Studio One, Playhouse 90*—when television is good, there is nothing better. But when television is bad, nothing is worse. I invite you to sit down in front of your television set when your station goes on the air and stay there without a book, magazine, newspaper, profit and loss sheet, or rating book to distract you—and keep your eyes glued to that set until the station signs off. I can assure you that you will observe a vast wasteland.

You will see a procession of game shows, violence, audience participation shows, formula comedies about totally unbelievable families, blood and thunder, mayhem, violence, sadism, murder, western badmen, western good men, private eyes, gangsters, more violence and cartoons. And endlessly, commercials—many screaming, cajoling, and offending. And most of all, boredom. True, you will see a few things you will enjoy. But they will be very, very few. And if you think I exaggerate, try it.

Gentlemen, your trust accounting with your beneficiaries is overdue. Never have so few owed so much to so many.

Among the hundreds of broadcasters listening to Newton N. Minow, the newly appointed chairman of the Federal Communications Commission, at the annual convention of the National Association of Broadcasters in Washington that spring of 1961 was Mark Banner. He listened with particular intensity and gratitude (he was still pinching himself over his good fortune in being transferred from Radio News to Affiliate Relations for the television network—Saint Adrian again); just to be here, in this place, at this time, with the others in the UBC contingent . . . But he listened, as well, in a state of confusion: There had never, so far as he knew, been an attack on the medium either so public or so precise. Particularly after an earlier address by the new President, John F. Kennedy, who—in lofty terms and with the presence of Commander Alan B. Shephard, America's first astronaut—had praised not only the success of electronic communication but the "guardians of the most powerful and effective means of communication ever designed." But however electrifying a moment he was witness to this day, however profoundly it would affect not only UBC's but his own future—these, at the golden innocent age of twenty-five, were nonetheless overshadowed by the new importance of . . . himself.

In UBC's hospitality suite on the twenty-third floor of the Shoreham Hotel—frequented mainly by the network's affiliated station managers, program and sales execs, TV newspaper columnists—the FCC chairman's phrase-making bomb was igniting brush fires well into the early-morning hours.

"Young smart alec. What the hell does he know about broadcasting?"

"Bastard sure talks good."

"Yeah, but not about us."

"Unrealistic bureaucrat if I ever saw one."

"Mix arrogance and ignorance and what have you got?"

"Why, the well-made man, Tom, the well-made man."

"If you ask me, the clown's bucking for a bigger government job."

"What the fuck ever got into Kennedy—bringing in a prick like that?"

"Listen. You have to admit he's got guts."

"Yeah. Either that or he's world's champion innocent."

"I'll be honest with you, Clyde, I think plenty of what he said was true. He could have used a little more tact, is all."

"Bullshit. He's read all the books and never had to meet a payroll."

"Pretty sneaky kind of censorship, you ask me."

"Yes, honest to God, Pete, I can watch any TV station all day long, sign on to sign off, and enjoy every cotton-pickin' minute of it."

"Bigness is always attacked. What the hell's so special about this one?"

"I'll tell you what's so special about this one. That sneaky sonofabitch wasn't talking to broadcasters. Hell, no. He was talking directly to the press. Wait'll you see tomorrow morning's headlines."

"The sonofabitch."

"I reckon there's been nothin' like it since Jim Lawson Fly compared us to a dead mackerel in the moonlight, shinin' and stinkin'."

"The man's obviously against the whole idea of commercial television. He's all out for public broadcasting and that's that."

"Funny thing, though. I had the feeling all along that he was dumping all the sins on UBC's doorstep. Maybe a couple on ABC's. I didn't notice any CBS or NBC Adam's apples bobbing up and down from it."

"I hear Dave Abrams is real fit to be tied."

"Watch the stock in tomorrow's trading. Va-va-va-voom—but on the down side, old buddy."

"Seems to me he needs broadcasters' goodwill, not fear. Another federal despot we *don't* need."

"Big fish, though. You can't deny that."

"Yeah. Little Minow he ain't hardly likely to be."

"Christ!"

Mark, one of the network's "hosts" for the evening, was so busy listening and committing it all to memory that he got Hillary Schwartz's (KOB-TV, Denver) order of a perfect Rob Roy wrong three times running, forgot to tell Sam Hook (WLL, New Orleans) he had an important call from Zurich, dropped Harry Atherton's (KLMN, Seattle) camel's-hair coat in a puddle of water in the guest bathroom, and spilled a fresh Bloody Mary between Mrs. Wallace King's (KNOT, St. Louis) incredible breasts, and in a moment of chivalry and madness attempted to wipe it off with a monogrammed handkerchief that Vivian Seaforth had sent him for his last birthday. It was only his good looks and good nature that deterred the crowded, festive suite from declaring him a disaster area.

"You're doing fine, kid," Adrian Miller told him in a relatively empty corner along about midnight. "Just fine. Of course, we've lost nineteen affiliates in the space of three hours. But *c'est la guerre*, eh?" Winking broadly. And Maury Sherman's "Why don't you try for the broad's cunt next time around?" helped a little.

DAVID met young Banner for the first time on the last night of the convention. The hospitality suite had thinned considerably, only the talkers and drinkers remaining to the end. The network schedule board for the 1961–62 season, brightened by a hundred or so small theatrical bulbs, was scarcely more lit than the red-eyed station men who studied it. Occupying the center of the suite's main room, it was the *raison d'être* for the suite itself. Backed up by groaning boards of food and drink, plus a dozen or so of the network's stars in person, in the flesh, the generally enthusiastic station clearance men and regional managers—young men like Mark—had the overriding responsibility of seeing that as many of UBC's programs were cleared (that is, carried) on a live network-time basis as possible and that DBs (delayed broadcasts, run at the station's convenience) were held to an absolute minimum; out-and-out rejection of a program was a sound reason for fifty lashes.

David had watched Mark Banner all night. For despite his nervous initiation into the ranks of the wheels, the boy had sold more station managers on the advantages of live cable clearances than almost any beginner within memory. Adrian was right; the kid was a comer.

"You're a regular little otter, aren't you?" he said to him, in one of the calmer moments by the bar, when Station Relations smiles weren't in such breakneck, round-the-clock demand.

"Thank you for that, sir," Mark answered him, visibly weary, but his smile, though thinner, was more real.

"Thanks for what?" said David.

"For not saying eager beaver. I think that would have just about done me in."

The poise, the level eyes, the smile, though still nervous . . . David was doubly impressed. In some different but chemically related way, this young man was himself thirty-five years ago. The rest of their brief exchange was mainly surface, but easy.

"Adrian tells me you were in News."

"Yes, sir. I just transferred to Station Relations last month."

"I imagine you had a good grounding in News, though. These past few months have been ballbreakers."

"Yes, sir. Just the Kennedy-Nixon debates alone were worth the price."

"The price?"

"Of swearing off sleep, sir."

"In this business, son, you sometimes get to the point where you swear *at* sleep. Those debates you spoke of are a prime example. Bernie Strauss used to say that broadcasting was born for events like that. Television, network television, not only records history, Mark.

It makes it too. I guess no other area, Sales aside, brings the point home so clearly as Station Relations does. A network, after all, is no more nor less than the sum of its stations. Some of our people forget that sometimes. Programming people in particular."

"Yes, sir."

"Glad you made the move? To the station area?"

"Time will have to answer that, sir. When there *is* time, that is."

"I see. Where are you from, son?"

"Kansas City."

"Do you like New York?"

"Yes, sir. Overwhelming as it is sometimes . . . I guess I always felt about New York the way Robert Frost felt about New England. I missed it without ever having been there."

"Nice way to put it. Do you live in the city?"

"Riverside Drive."

"Married?"

"Come June, I hope."

"Congratulations. New York girl?"

"Oklahoma City."

"A regular Midwest invasion, eh?"

"Maybe a crusade, sir?"

And David laughed, for the first time since Newton Minow's Moses-and-Elijah act. There was no doubt about it: Mark Banner had *going places* written all over him. But even with the goodwill he whole-heartedly presented the boy, there was still that nagging, gnawing hollowness in his gut. Two sons he'd had, almost had. One never got a chance to start. The other, brilliant and austere, had learned every goddamn word there was—in three, maybe four languages—and never been able to conjugate "to love." While some obscure young kid in an overgrown cow town in *Missouri* . . .

He shook his head. Maybe a walk in the night air would clear it. Mr. Minow had certainly done his best to fuck it up.

TO FUCK THEM ALL UP.

"Did you see what that cunt Randolph said this morning?" Maury Sherman was pacing David's office three days after the NAB convention as though it were his own private cage. He was waving a fistful of newspaper clippings. "Listen to this. Quote: 'The Minow moves have a definite antimonopoly flavor to them. Network affiliation contracts have long contained clauses giving the network virtual control over blocks of time on affiliate stations. Some of the best legal minds are contending that these "network option" clauses are equivalent to the block-building process by which the major Hollywood studios once controlled theatres, and which the U.S. Supreme Court had motherfucking outlawed in 1948!' Unquote!"

"Mr. Randolph, thanks to your own creative editing, has never been in better voice," said David.

Maury Sherman wasn't amused.

"And this asshole! Washington's in-depth correspondent . . . I quote: 'It's an open secret around town that President Kennedy is giving Minow continual encouragement, telling him to keep up the good work, that a proliferation of noncommercial television is of crucial importance.' Unfucking quote."

"You read well, Maury. Very dramatically. Maybe we could revise for television, like the old La Guardia readings on radio. There's not that much difference between Bryson Randolph's columns and the Sunday comics. Besides, you're better looking. What do you say?"

Maury ignored it. "And listen to this from that creep in Chicago. You ready for this? 'Researchers are starting to amass definite evidence on the role of dramatized violence in television, specifically network television. More specifically still, the United Broadcasting Company.' Item: 'Testimony on the findings of Professor Richard H. Walters of the University of fucking Waterloo in Ontario, to the effect that male hospital attendants, after seeing a filmed knife fight, were much harsher in their handling of patients than a comparable group that had seen an innocuous film.' Item: 'Dr. Albert Bandura, professor of psychology at Stanford University, testified that children, after seeing a violent TV film, played more aggressively than comparable groups who hadn't seen it.' Item: 'The findings suggest that the filmed action, instead of purging hostile feelings, might stimulate them or at least bring them to the surface.' Item: 'Dr. Bandura has also found that children tend to copy the kinds of aggressive action they've seen, casting doubt on the value of "crime does not pay" endings stressed by the NAB Code.' Item: 'Senator Thomas J. Dodd of Connecticut, as chairman of the Senate subcommittee on juvenile delinquency, has taken up the subject that troubled Senator Kefauver so much—namely, television violence.' Item: 'The L.A. . . .'"

"Thanks, Maury, but I think I'm itemed out. I have the feeling I just might be getting the drift."

"The word's draft. Item: The piss-ant pundit from Philadelphia. And I quote: 'About the only three UBC nighttime programs currently eschewing violence are *The Ellen Curry Hour*, *Ellen Curry Presents* and *The Larry Lester Show*. This last named, however, is peripheral. For while violence per se, real physical violence, that is, is nowhere to be found, this blustering appeal to idiocy does parade a violence of sorts. A psychological violence, you might say. Certainly the specter of millions of viewers throwing up at one time is every bit the equal of gang wars in New York and Chicago.' And this from the columnist in San Francisco: 'Not since the quiz-show scandals that rocked the medium to its heels has television heard such cries for its head. As was to be expected, David Abrams and Company are taking the brunt of it. Another season or so and UBC just might have a whole new concept of situation comedy. Blood spewing forth from every conceivable wound to the cheerful accompaniment of canned laughter.' Item . . ."

"Enough, for God's sake. Now, if you'll just sit down . . ."

"Mickey Baker in *Variety*. 'The Fifty-Thousand-Dollar Question (if you'll pardon the expression) is what UBC will come up with in the way of new programming, come fall. Not only in the light of Newton Minow's far-from-veiled warning to the webs, but in the obvious differences between Programming Chief Adrian Miller and his immediate superior, Exec Veepee Maurice Sherman. Particularly with son-and-heir Robert Abrams out of the picture (for the present, at least, and quite mysteriously) and Prexy Abrams none too happy with the seemingly endless barrage of salvos. As the jungle drums have it . . .' "

"*I said for God's sake sit down!*"

He sat down.

"I'm as pissed over this as you are," said David. "But wearing holes in a new broadloom carpet isn't exactly a letters-to-the-editor column. One thing none of these jokers can ever accuse you of, Maury, and that's going soft. You chew steel, remember?"

"Horse shit's more like it. I'll tell you what I do remember" . . . pacing again. "I remember that every one of those fingers is pointed at me, whether my name is mentioned or not." Pausing for a moment. "If you'll indulge me for a second in some bitch-talk, it wouldn't surprise me if a couple of our own little sweetie-pies didn't plant a couple of those darlin' little bouquets themselves. The *Gallagher Report* item in particular." The *Gallagher Report*, a privately edited and distributed prediction pamphlet, had led off its "watch for" edition last week with the ouster of Maury Sherman and the installment of Adrian Miller practically a *fait accompli*.

"Come on, Maury," David said; half-laughed. "You know damn well how much credence Gallagher has. Or how old hat all this garbage is. You above all should remember it from the old radio days."

Maury did pause then. "I know. What the public wants we're good enough to give 'em while some horse's ass sits up there in Washington, D.C., and determines what it *ought* to like, not what it does like. Big joke, ain't it? Biggest syndicated comic strip in the country. You read me?"

"I read you," said David. "But this isn't the first or the last we'll

be under the big guns, Maury. Pea-shots, really. Still . . . something has
to be done, and quick. All the audience research in the world can't
wash away Bryson Randolph and Senator Dodd. And the truth is,
Maury—even though I know you disagree on this—it's our almost
religious attention to numbers that gets us into these binds in the
first place. I've disliked, distrusted audience measurement barometers
from the beginning, back even to the old Crossley system in the early
radio days. And been the biggest booster of them in the business. Hell,
I doubt there's another broadcaster who has as many orgasms over
favorable demographics as I do."

But the smile was far from self-reproving when he said abruptly,
"I'm going to the Coast with Adrian tomorrow morning to sit down
with every goddamn producer we've got, and if the newspapers want
to call it a tail-between-the-legs eleventh-hour ploy, they're welcome
to it. It's the public we play to, Maury—not the press. I've also asked
Sid Newton in PR to be in my office in fifteen minutes to start drafting
a policy address on the subject that I'll be giving at the IRTS dinner
next month."

Sherman started to the door, turned back. "It was because of me
that Bobby left the way he did, wasn't it?"

David shrugged, looked off. The day outside, through the murky
windows, was neither bright nor dull.

He spoke softly:

"You were only a part of it, Maury. A small part at that. More an
excuse than anything else. It was me Bobby left. And not last January. Bobby left a long time ago, Maury. Probably on his fifth birthday, when he went white as a sheet because his daddy had never
heard of Marcel Proust."

Maury's departure, for such a bear of a man, was nearly catlike.

THE BARBADOS DAY was dazzling as sin. A thousand suns, not simply
the one, seemed bent on toasting its worshipers to a crisp. Certainly
Robert, for all the discomfort it had given him, was a changed man.
That is, *looked* a changed man. One would never have guessed how
pale he had been when he arrived in the islands. "The picture of
health" was no cliché in his case. His frail good looks had given way
to manly, full-blooded ones.

It had been in a collapsible lawn chair near the oceanside pool of
the Bakoua resort hotel on the French-owned island of Martinique
that the news reached him that his mother, with young Freddie
Wiener in tow, was flying down to join him. This startling information,
coupled with a cryptic telephone call from Brenda in Reno, a strangely
supplicant one from Maury Sherman in New York, and a conspiratorial

one from Adrian in Los Angeles, had prompted his decision to move on to Barbados, particularly to the rustic elegance of Sam Lord's Castle, the bungalow-strewn resort on the northern tip of the island. Besides, the spicy creole cooking of the Bakoua, a noisy Hartford Insurance conclave, and an intellectually aggressive producer with National Educational Television from Asheville, North Carolina, named Beverly Berenson, were not exactly palliatives to a spastic colon.

It was while nursing this discomfort, on one of the chaises in the patio lounge of the Bakoua, that Robert found himself reflecting, for perhaps the hundredth time in three short days, on the assault on his sensibilities by Ma Bell.

Brenda: "I thought it best to phone you, Bobby, rather than commit anythin' to paper. My daddy always said writin' things down, specially things that got a bad smell to them, was just plain askin' for trouble. There won't be any trouble over the divorce, Bobby. Lord knows you're not about to contest it. It wouldn't really bother me any, the things that'd come out about Joslyn and me, it's been over a long time, but it sure would drive you and your buddy Adrian up a wall. Not to mention the kinky things about you, hon. I guess I just wanted to tell you that I'm takin' you for a real sweet bundle, darlin', there's just no end to what 'mental croolty' can accomplish. Besides, hon, I'll need all the chips I can get. This new sweetheart I met out here ain't exactly in the chips, and bein' as she's never seen Hawaii and places like that, it's only fair that I take her places. 'Course, bein' Miz ex-UBC won't be the same as bein' Miz UBC, but still and all . . ."

Maury Sherman: "What the hell's goin' on here, kid? You've got your old man practically climbing walls. There's nothing can't be talked out, I don't give a shit who the parties are. Especially right now with all hell breaking loose. This FCC thing's got half these old farts acting like it was the crash of '29 all over again. The thing we've got to do, Bobby . . . What the fuck? You there, Bobby? . . ."

Adrian: "For God's sake, Bobby, the one time in your life your dad would listen to you with a hundred goddam ears and you take a powder like a virgin when nothing but the head of the thing got in. 'Of schemes and storms and scores unsettled'—remember, Bobby? Now get your ass back here—now, on the double. We're at the Beverly Hills. Remember that anthology of Hemingway, Fitzgerald, Updike, O'Hara . . . the one Maury Sherman almost pissed his pants over? Laughed right in your face over? Well, buddy boy, there's every chance in the world that M-G-M . . ."

His mother: "Darling, my darling. I can't take another minute of this, I just can't. As it is, I haven't spoken to your farther in a week. No, two weeks, next Sunday. I'm drowning, darling, I'm simply drowning. I suppose if it had to be, of course, it's fortuitous to have someone like Brenda there with you. She is with you, isn't she? Bobby, I've had the most gorgeous idea. I'm going to fly down, my heart. You need me with you and you know it. Brenda, sweet a child as I know she is, just isn't fit to cope with such . . . such major crises. And since it's Easter vacation, both Arthur and M.J. have given me permission to bring Freddie Wiener along. He's such a bright child, enlivens any room he's in. Oh, I'm so looking forward to seeing you, my angel. There's so much we need to talk over. . . ."

His father: "I'm sorry, sir, Mr. Robert Abrams' suite doesn't answer."

"This happens to be the fourth time I've called today. I've left messages—"

"Yes, sir. Forgive, sir. There's a most bloody awful nor'easter heading in."

"Nor'easter? What the hell has a nor'easter got to do with telephone messages for my son?"

"The wind, you know, sir. A frightful one, really. Nothing's worth a farthing if it ain't buckled good to something, sir. Such a wind. Probably halfway to Trinidad by now. Now, if there's any way I can be of service? . . . Mr. Abrams, I said if there's any way . . ."

Robert tucked a twenty-pound note under the day clerk's ledger—the "little remembrance" that he'd always resented so much when his father did it. The clerk had had the effrontery to salute him as he made his way down the steps of the hotel and across the open patio lounge down to the catamaran waiting to ferry him across the Peninsule Trois Ilets to the little town of Fort de France for some last-minute shopping before the flight to Barbados.

There was a new Dior scent that his mother particularly liked, and he was looking for it now; a frown crossed his face at the remembrance of the same scent on Beverly Berenson, forcing him to reconsider a small vial for the new acquaintance as well.

THEY HAD MET quite naturally.

"Bobby Abrams!" The thunderous greeting (always an arena olé, no matter the time or place) could belong to no other creature than Irwin Goodman, one of the producer-directors of Filmways, the commercial production house that was breaking into telefilms with a series called The Beverly Hillbillies on CBS this fall. Robert had served on a couple of NAB and IRTS committees with him and been thoroughly put off by him.

It was nine in the morning and the Bakoua restaurant was three deep in standees, giving Robert little alternative but to ask that he join him.

"Good thing you got four chairs instead of two," boomed Goodman. "I got a first-rate piece of no-no coming to join me. Along with a very yes-yes cousin from Asheville. Girl's name is Beverly Berenson. She's here with a joint PBS–Metromedia–Filmways–Mobil Oil project —you know, one of those Goody Twoshoes presentations on public TV that has critics rushing for dictionary superlatives, and viewers, except maybe for a hand-picked suicide bunch, rushing for the nearest unoccupied toilet. But jeez, here I go again—my old mom always used to scream at me to wind down, but then never having learned the difference between up and down . . ." His outstretched palms and eyes, blue as the Caribbean, were considered endearing by those who knew and liked him, but put him in the category with Maury Sherman as far as Robert was concerned; with or without the cigar.

"Saw in *Variety* you were down here. R and R?"

"Something like that."

"Hell of a place for it, aint' it? Missus with you?"

"No." If the tall girl with the easy gait hadn't started walking toward them . . .

"Here she comes," Goodman said, "and here's all you need to know about her. Eats yogurt, carrots, digs Jenay and Camoo, whoever the fuck they are, would rather walk in a driving rain than take a bubble bath, believes passionately in television as the modern age's version of Socrates' forum, goes for guys, real sport about it, but a thirty-four-year-old virgin or I'm Fanny Brice. Also writes poetry when she's drunk." He was on his feet quickly. "Miss Berenson, may I present Mr. Robert Abrams. Of course, Mr. Abrams needs no introduction."

"Doesn't he? I should think he'd need the most detailed one in the world. The profile on him in *The New Yorker* was interesting but superficial as hell, when you come down to it. I'm not sure those boysenberry pancakes you're having for breakfast are any too kind to you, either. You do have a rather troublesome digestive tract, I believe, Mr. Abrams. Guava nectar is much better for it than orange juice. Acid stomachs are almost as distracting as acid tongues."

She sat. And every bit as gracefully as she'd stood. For one so tall— as tall as Elizabeth Ainsley, maybe taller—she had about her the least awkwardness he'd ever encountered in a girl so high and slender. Certainly nothing else about her had the faintest reminder of Elizabeth; her hair was a dark auburn, swept to and fro, to her waist, down her side—windswept when there wasn't any wind at all. As for any comparison with Brenda—"Nathan's doesn't put Chateaubriand between five-cent buns," Adrian would one day say of her.

For the moment, sitting across from him, she was the most forthcoming, wide-eyed, enthusiastic thirty-four-year-old he'd ever seen; and the most secretive, diffident, old-beyond-her-years thirty-four-year-old he'd ever talked with. It was probably this contradiction that intrigued him from the beginning. Certainly not the fact that she was both Southern and Jewish, virtues and vices that canceled themselves out. No . . . no, definitely, the rich, dissonant scale of her.

That and her voice. One minute moonstones, quick shooting stars; the next, Madame Chairman calling the idle, slothful board to order.

It was then that she donned rimless glasses and peered over them.

"You're here in Paradise to search out new locales for a series, Mr. Abrams?"

"I'm sure Mr. Goodman has told you otherwise," Robert said.

The smile—how young? how old? "Every juicy detail of it." Pause. "I was married too, once," she said. "I'll bet even Irwin the town crier doesn't know that one. It lasted all of three hours."

"Yeah," said Irwin Goodman. "Just long enough for the stay of execution."

Her laughter was so real it tickled. "If you mean saved from ineffectual penetration, Irwin, you couldn't be more right. He was a dear, sweet boy, I'm sure, but my father's choice, not mine. He was in real estate. Period. I caught sight of his private parts in an indoor swimming pool once and wrote a poem about them. Not a very good poem, but satisfying, to me. I'm really starved. Do you think those marvelous-looking stuffed creole crabs would be straining it a bit for breakfast?"

"With your stomach?" said Irwin. "I'll bet you never threw up in your life."

"Just once," she said. "When Richard Nixon made his Checkers speech in California. Now *that*, I assure you, was *television*." Smiles from the corners of her eyes. "Have you really abandoned the tube, Mr. Abrams?"

"I'm not sure," he said. "I'll look into public television when I go back. Maybe the theatre too. I've always believed the two were headed for a marriage."

Hands cupped beneath her chin, she said, "Strange. I was determined to find you offensive. Rich man's son, spoiled to the gills. Arrogant, opinionated, uncompromising, sickly. Chauvinistic, stodgy. Contentious, aesthetic. Pretty well full of shit, as your friend Irwin here might say. So far, I like you one hell of a lot, Mr. Abrams. From now, year one, it's Bev. Deal?"

In spite of himself, soft-boiled egg decorating at least three fingers, a hand went out. "Deal." So damned unlike him.

"And here comes Aunt Pittypat," said Irwin Goodman, mouth thick with buckwheat cakes and syrup. "Aunt Pittypat" was the name he'd given to Beverly's cousin Esther Amish, not only because the fluttery, butterball image fitted her to a tee, but because *Gone with the Wind* was the only book he'd ever read clear through.

Introductions, nervous acknowledgments, non sequiturs having vaguely to do with sand crabs, egrets, day yachts, blue heaven, the original bedroom fixtures of the Empress Josephine in one of the smaller cottages, the clever Island French the truly black black natives spoke, the banana daiquiris the likes of which were to be found on no other island in the Indies, the fatiguing monotony of the musical entertainment, the way the hotel's management . . . Robert's fascination was equaled only by the amused patience in Cousin Beverly's eyes.

They walked the beach together that afternoon.

"I'll not beat around the bush," she said. "The burning bush, you might say. Irwin knew you were here. At the Bakoua, that is. Opportunism was never one of Irwin's lacks. I'm not so sure I want to be a party to roping you in on this particular venture, though, Mr. Abrams . . . Robert. It's not that earth-shaking, really. Enthusiasm is hardly the same as good taste. No more than passion is real affection. What's she like—your little runaway bride out in Nevada? Taking you for the last pair of jockey shorts, the trades have it."

Robert's laugh was genuine. "Well, thank heaven I'm still old-fashioned enough to wear boxer shorts," he said. "Anything to frustrate the press."

They were barefoot, wet sand erotic between their toes. "What I really want to do," she said, "and what no one with an ounce of commercial savvy will even begin to listen to, is a series of filmed dramas based on the best literature a country has to offer. You know . . . a kind of international television theatre. *Père Goriot* . . . Kafka's *Trial* . . . *Crime and Punishment* . . . Dickens . . . Maeterlinck . . . Sigrid Undstadt . . . Alan Paton's *Cry the Beloved Country* . . . *Omoo* . . . *The Sun Also Rises* . . . You know, seven share points. With Hemingway, maybe nine. Such fantasy! I belong in somebody else's dream, Robert. Not my own."

"I do declare," said Cousin Esther-Pittypat over the candlelit service at dinner that night, "one hasn't seen hide nor hair of either one of you all day. I mean, lordy, child, there's not *that* much to do on this sticky island. I had to play 'Run for Cover' with Irwin Goodman all afternoon. It's a new card game he taught me. Kept me hiding in the most outlandish shrubbery most of the day. Exasperatin' kind of game, you ask me. I bet I lost all of five pounds. You two hook up on some television thing?"

Robert blushed; he couldn't help it. Beverly Berenson smiled. "You are a shy one, aren't you, Robert? I am, too, sometimes. Like, sometimes you have to be. Like getting enough sleep or something."

"For the next battle."

Pittypat was everywhere, persistence itself. "You're working on TV things down here, Mr. Abrams?"

"Not really, no."

"Oh. Running away from *l'affaire de coeur?*"

"No, ma'am. Nor am I preparing a recital of Negro spirituals."

"That's nice. My. It does limit us, though, doesn't it? . . . I know, you're writing a book! Why, you mouse, you. Imagine. A book! Is it a long book? I mean, is it a real fat juicy book? I tell you, there's nothin' I love more than crawlin' up in a hammock and readin' a good fat juicy book. Especially when it rains. It rains an awful lot up in Asheville. Mr. Thomas Wolfe's from there, you know. He wrote *real* fat books, I can tell you. I never went much for 'em myself. Too much dirty washin' hung around. Big fat books, though. What's your big fat book about, sir?"

"Mine?" said Robert. "Well, I'll tell you, ma'am. Mine is probably the shortest book ever written."

"Well! I . . . I'm almost afraid to ask what it's about."

"Oh, but I'm delighted to tell you. It's a history of German comedy."

Aunt Pittypat had no idea why her niece was cackling, or why she herself should be shaken so by it, but dabbing the corners of her mouth as primly as possible, she set her napkin firmly on the table and made as brave a dowager's departure as she could manage.

Beverly was still laughing. "You know," she said, finally settled down enough to say it, "you're absolutely nothing the way other people paint you. But nothing."

Smiling, he took her hand. "There's very little about these last three days that I remember ever painting about myself." He squeezed the hand sharply.

HE THOUGHT OF HER often and with unaccustomed pleasure during the long hours waiting for his mother and young Wiener to arrive on Barbados. The decor of Sam Lord's Castle, particularly the wide oak beams of the tall spacious ceilings, would have given her particular pleasure—as indeed he expected they would his mother and Freddie Wiener.

I enjoy walking these grounds, he thought, strolling the beaches alone. Nice of Phil Cash in the *Sun-Times* . . . "One of the few voices for upgrading program series at UBC is now mysteriously missing. A subpoena before a House subcommittee is a strong possibility. Robert Abrams could be the difference at UBC between an hour or two of Paddy Chayefsky and Rod Serling and a lifetime of Joan Davis, Eve Arden, and Martha Raye." And Alex Maynard in the *Ledger:* "Wherever he is, Bobby Abrams is probably in the driver's seat. The David Abrams–Maurice Sherman seats are too hot for others to sit around in." Bryson Randolph in the *Times:* "Being an I-told-you-so is cheap triumph, but in the case of UBC it just can't be helped. That give-'em-hell network may have been racking up the numbers, but the renewal licenses of some of their affiliated stations are in serious jeopardy. The big wheels like D. Abrams and M. Sherman may be the industry's foremost experts on bottom lines, but then the world's made up of some 99.9 percent who understand bottom lines, and only .01 percent or less who have an inkling of what gets you there. Quality programming *is* good business—and Robert Abrams is in my view one of the few who understands that. . . ."

The sun's fierce today, mean, he thought. Maybe it's the rum chi-chis I'm putting away. How many since noon? Four? Five? Lord knows, who cares? Those two girls at poolside, eyes taking me in like they were already under me. Under me. Hah! One more chi-chi and my balls will be coconuts, that's really what it's all about, isn't it—imagination? A strange girl, Beverly. Almost perfect girl, Beverly. Good, at least, that I left the Bakoua before the other thing happened . . . started to happen.

Rick Gutman in the *Journal:* "Odds have it that Rob't Abrams' stay-away blues (or reds, as some call it) will turn into stay-away golds and silvers and big shining rainbows. Not exactly chaos at UBC, but then nobody's feeling his oats either. Could be that . . ."

Sun's more lethal than ever. Mother should be here soon. Long walks on the beaches with young Wiener. Something to do, time to think about it. . . . "And now the best in television theatre, from the network that cares: Robert Abrams' production of *Playhouse UBC*." Hot as Caliban's little island. I'd better lie down a while, I think. . . .

"DARLING, DARLING, I can't believe it, I can't. Just to see you again, touch you. And how brown you are, a precious acorn you are. And so easy, so relaxed, when the whole trip down I was dreading it so. . . . Robert, you've been drinking."

"A touch, mother, yes. A touch. A touch of the poet, you might say. You could say, if you wanted to be generous . . ."

"Well, of course, I can understand it, only . . . you know how I feel. About alcohol, I mean. Lord knows your father . . . But oh, you darling, what does it matter? Rum you can sleep off. Heartbreak you can't. Only in *your* situation, darling, there's not even *that* to sleep off. If ever timing made the *difference* between a bomb and SRO, yours did it. David would never admit it, not in a million years, but he's in desperate need of you, sweetheart. I think it finally occurred to him that, differences and all, you're the only one he realizes he can trust."

"Hold on, mother. I didn't leave to go back—"

"That's not the point, darling. Not at all. What *is* the point is that you're needed. Wanted. How many humiliating years to come to that!"

"That's hardly the message I waited for with bated breath, mother. What gets me is that *you're* his emissary. If anyone, I'd have supposed it would be Adrian."

"But that's the irony of it, darling. You see, he hasn't the least idea I'm here. I said I was taking Freddie to Nassau, and from there we flew under assumed names."

"Well, of course, it's good of you, mother, but under the circumstances . . ."

"You mean the organization as it stands? The network pecking order? Dear heart. I have every intention in the world of interfering. I've rarely done that, you know, not even in the roughest days imaginable. Your father—and there's no one of any importance inside the industry or out of it who would contest it—your father is the most successful *strategist* in all broadcasting, my dear. This doesn't mean, of course, that I think he's some kind of Sol Hurok of television. I suppose if anybody, Billy Rose is more his shadow. And I've resented this, as you know, often and sometimes painfully. Just as certain of his other activities . . . But this is hardly the time for that. What it *is* the time for, darling, is what only you can bring the network. That . . . oh, I hate the triteness of it, the trashy people who overuse it . . . but a touch of class, my baby, a true touch of class. Lord knows there's none of us would forgo the principal bread-and-butter programming that gives us our bright little annual reports to stockholders, but the one area in which UBC has been not only weak but downright disgraceful is the creative one, where *you've* poured what you have to say on deaf ears for so long. I've every reason to believe that those ears are wide open now. Fly back with me, Bobby. In all your life . . . and has any life been more precious to me, have I ever asked you to do anything against your will? Or at least what I felt intuitively was right for you? Now, go out and talk with Freddie. He's beside himself, poor darling."

"I've missed you, Uncle Bob. I surely truly have. I *can* call you Uncle Bob, can't I?"

"I'd have it no other way, Fred."

"I'm glad if papa had to marry again it was into a family like yours. Like *you*, I mean."

"Well, thanks, young man. Now, don't miss those shells . . . see them? They make great ashtrays."

"Yes, sir. I've heard. Are you . . . are you going back to New York, Uncle Bob?"

"I haven't decided."

"The way I hear it, it's being decided for you. My dad told your sister the other night that Grandpa David would even lower his trousers for you—his Brooks Brothers trousers, at that."

He smiled. "We'll have to see, Freddie. We'll just have to see. And between us, I'm thinking of producing a play . . ."

"Wow! Me too, Uncle Bob! I'm writing a Racine-type play at Yale Drama School right now. I'm the youngest ever enrolled there. Did I tell you?"

"I think you wrote me. How's it coming?"

"Miserable. I think I'm cut out more for the sensational kinds of things . . . you know, Ibsen and Strindberg and even Eugene O'Neill. Just testing my wings, I guess you could say."

"There'll always be a place for you at UBC, you know. That goes without saying."

"Well, it's theatre I'm interested in. But it's awfully good to hear you say it, Uncle Bob. It means a—it means like a wonderful gift, or something."

"I imagine those come pretty easily for you, Freddie. Gifts, I mean. You're growing into a fine young man. The girls must notice, eh?"

"Oh, a few. I've got three gold stars so far. I think it's going to be hard to top that."

"Oh? How's that?"

"I got laid in English lit, French lit, and Italian lit. Higher education, right? Would have gotten it off in Russian lit too, but you know how squares are so quick to cry 'Pinko' these days."

"Yes, well . . . keep your eye on first things first."

"Yes, sir. There's a chance I may take Indian lit next term. I've thought a lot lately how intellectually challenging a trip up one of those saris would be." Freddy Wiener, age fourteen, going on fifteen.

"IT'S A CHARMING PLACE, darling, as of course I knew it would be. Senator Roehm's wife has been talking about this place for years. Sam Lord's Castle. You'd have thought it was one of the many mansions in His Father's house. I adore the beams. Such well-tended oak. The steel band drives me mad, though. You're terribly pensive, sweetheart. Or perhaps preoccupied's the better word. The network, or Brenda?"

"I suppose we had to get around to her sooner or later."

"Yes. Hardly one to hide her light under a bushel. That tart! Tramp!"

"I have a new Roget's *Thesaurus* upstairs if it will help any, mother."

"Such *chutzpah!* And believe me, Bobby, that's the only Yiddish word you've ever heard me utter. Unfortunately, there's not a gross enough translation for it."

"She's taking me, isn't she?"

"The letters from her attorneys to your father seem to suggest it."

"No details?"

"Mental cruelty. No more."

"Then let her have it. Whatever she wants. Within reason, of course."

"You don't want to talk about it?"

"No, Mother, I don't. Not ever."

"I see. What's that you're reading?"

"The new 1961–62 schedules. The other networks have already announced. Dad was right about the doctor cycle. *Ben Casey, Dr. Kildare,* the usual. Shirley Booth's doing *Hazel.* CBS is taking a chance with Dick Van Dyke. Ernie Kovacks and Bob Cummings, Bob Newhart and Robert Young. More cops. Or should I say copouts? *Eighty-seventh Precinct, Malibu Run, Follow the Sun, Acapulco* . . . CBS looks like it has something, though. *The Defenders.* E. G. Marshall. I saw a couple of the scripts. Above the usual. Maury Sherman turned it down. Cops and class—B.O. poison, he says. I wonder when we'll announce."

"When you get back to New York."

"Who said I'd be going back to New York?"

"Your mother, my darling. Your mother says you'll be going back to New York."

"BEVERLY, this is a surprise! I'd no idea. What a pleasant coincidence!"

"No coincidence at all, Robert. I followed you here. Of course Aunt Pittypat had a palpitation or two, but the promise of the Castle's English trifle, probably the best in the islands, won her over. This is your mother, of course. And the newfound nephew, Master Wiener? Allow me. I'm Beverly Berenson and this is my cousin, Aunt Pitty . . . I'm sorry, my cousin Esther. May we join you? I'm sure Robert can fill you in about the rest."

"I can?"

"You can."

"Well, you see . . . we just met, mother, at the Bakoua in Martinique. Miss Berenson, you see, is with . . . is it NET? That's National Educational Television. Or PSB? That's Public Service Broadcasting. It's all in such a confused state right now—public television, I mean—that I hardly know where to begin."

"Then do let me, dear heart. I do so love to talk. Even when I have absolutely nothin' on earth to say. Like dear Bevvie told you, I'm her cousin Esther from Asheville, that's in Nawth Carolina, not South like some folks think, but they all like to tease me up a little by callin' me Aunt Pittypat or some such silly thing. I don't mind, though, I truly don't.

"Anyways, as long as Bevvie had to come to the French West Indies to do a film for the NET or whatever they're callin' it, and also to be used later in schools and libraries and even the Smithsonian in Washington—ain't that grand?—I just decided on the spur of the moment to tag along with her. I'm sure you, as well as anyone, will appreciate my concern, Miz Abraham. I'm all the family this poor dear child has left her. And the very thought of all these natives runnin' around with their bare bottoms and bare ever'thingelses just put me into a real pother, I can tell you. Heaven knows I'm not a nosy parker, like they say in English mystery novels, but I do feel . . . Tell me, hon, yes, you, Miz Abraham, do you like Agatha Christie's things? I've just chunks of them in my suitcase and would be most pleased and honored if you'd . . . Stop snappin' my corselet like that, Beverly! I know very well when to talk and when not to. And I must say! They do look pretty together, don't they? My Bevvie and your Bobby . . ."

"I know I shall be ill."

"Oh, come, mother, I hardly know them. And besides. Beverly can no more help choosing her blood relations than you could your uncle Aaron Sackman you were so ashamed of."

"She's *hardly* your kind."

"Aunt Pittypat?"

"Stop playing with me, Robert. You know full well who I mean. Why, she's gangly, and socially inept, and altogether unsuitable in every—"

"She's a most unusually well-read and -traveled and talented young woman."

"*Young woman?* I'd hardly call thirty-eight a *young* woman."

"Thirty-four, mother."

"Well, she looks forty."

"And I haven't the least idea why we're having this conversation. There's nothing between Miss Berenson and me. I will say this, though. If by some chance . . . and 'if' is still the longest word in Webster's Fifth . . . *if* by some chance I should return to UBC, I'd ask that Beverly Berenson come with me. I've seen some of her work. She has a real talent at getting to the heart of a thing. Nice little special touches, too . . ."

"She makes me ill."

"I make her ill, I can tell."

"Joan of Arc would give her gastric problems."

"If only she weren't so damned attractive. I see where you get your looks, Robert."

"It could be fun, you know, Bev."

"Fun? I can't imagine how."

"Mother and Aunt Pittypat?"

"Pittypat and Pattycake . . . I see what you mean. Thank heaven Irwin Goodman didn't come over, though. I swear I think your mother would have left the table."

"No, you underestimate her, Beverly. Mother's feelings have never, not since I can remember, gotten the best of her good manners."

"You do love her, don't you, Bobby?"

"Yes, yes, I do. She's often been the only one between me and . . . Look, why don't we not talk about her right now, okay?"

"Okay."

"I THINK THIS is my favorite view in all the islands, every single one of them."

"From Cherry Tree Hill? Yes, I suppose it is. Look, Bev, there . . . Spreightstown, see? And down the eastern shore there, past Bathsheba. Ragged Point, see it?"

"Lovely. Robert, let's walk down to the Andromeda . . . you know, the gardens. There are ravines there, I hear, and caverns, with all kinds of limestone stalactites and strange trees and wild monkeys. They even claim the breadfruits are descended from seed brought ashore by Captain Bligh of the *Bounty*. And there are plantation homes, too, that . . . Not much in the mood for sight-seeing?"

"Tomorrow, maybe. I think we should be getting back to the Atlantis. Feel like it?"

"I'm not sure what I feel like. Except that I may be feeling things I shouldn't. About you, I mean. Us."

"MY GOD."

"Oh, Christ! I thought the door was locked! I wouldn't want to offend you for the world, Uncle Bob, not for anything in the world."

"Get your clothes on."

"Yes, sir. It was just a kind of . . . well, dalliance, sir—the kind that even Flaubert and Balzac used to . . ."

"Have that . . . that *disgusting* . . . Get her out of this room, *now!*"

"I just teach boy-man how use mouth and tooths and bunghole . . ."

"Out!"

"Jesus, Uncle Bob, if you knew how ashamed I am, how I'd like to slit my throat, right here and now, I just . . . Well, you really got an eyeful today, didn't you, sir?"

"Listen, you little . . . I don't give a goddamn how precocious you are. I'm not interested in your sexual show-offs. I'm not impressed, *you understand me?* I *am* disgusted . . . and do you understand *that?*"

"Yes, *sir*. It's very clear. *Sir*."

"Bridgetown's such a charming place to shop in. I almost hate leaving it. The whole island, really."

"Meetings and leave-takings—our life histories, in a way. No wonder sociologists are so full of shit when they talk about roots. That last's a direct quotation from my friend Adrian Miller, by the way. Hardly sounds like me, huh?"

"Sounds very much like you. Honestly, Bobby, St. Francis of Assisi you're not. And oh, Lord, I hate to see you go."

"But you'll be back in Washington in a month or so, Bev. And then the Coast. I'm both places, remember? *If* I'm anyplace at all, that is. A lot depends on these next two days."

"I haven't the least doubt you'll make a good accommodation. Certainly your mother seems to think so."

"Which is hardly a guarantee."

"She doesn't like me, you know."

"Don't worry. It's not *you* she dislikes. It could be anybody. Anybody I like, that is. Once when I was a child she overheard me praying to God, and I think she's hated his guts ever since."

"You've never kissed me, Bobby, you know that?"

"It's Bridgetown, Beverly. Broad daylight."

"How much I have for you, Robert . . . And don't look so startled. Or believe everything Irwin Goodman tells you. It makes him feel good to call me a thirty-four-year-old virgin. That's *his* problem. We'll meet again soon, Bobby, I know it, I feel it in my thirty-four-year-old cunt. Now don't look so *shocked.*"

"We'll be landing soon, darling. Just remember, Bobby. This *is* what we've waited for. You and I. All our hopes, our dreams . . ."

"More airborne rhetoric like that, mother, and we might very well let you co-author the first *Happy Landings* script."

"Well, son. Seafare of the Aegean, as ordered. I'm really awful glad to see you again, Bobby."

The restaurant was filled to the gills (David's small joke) as it always was on Fridays, the waiters as if choreographed for a crowd scene in *Zorba the Greek*. The aromas from surrounding tables only heightened the anticipation of their own order. When it arrived— whole Sheepshead Bay flounder stuffed with crabmeat and shrimp, accompanied by a pale, clear Metaxas—the ambiance was right for just about anything.

Which came after several long, savoring swallows.

"We've a lot ahead of us, Bobby—you and I. God knows the past can't be rubbed clean like a blackboard, but compromises *are* our most reliable inventions, kid. Even in heaven, I'm told."

"Which leads you to say to me . . . ?"

"Which leads me to say to you that I would like to implement the following changes immediately. I'm asking Maury Sherman to step down from GM to a new post we're creating—vice president in charge of Audience Research and Planning. This is the hardest thing I've ever had to do in this business, because whatever you or Adrian or Arrabella or Newton Minow may think of Maurice Sherman, he's one of the most loyal and honest men this industry's ever had. It's an affront to him, of course, but he does understand it, and since UBC's practically his whole life—goddamn *mensch* started as an errand boy for Bernie Strauss when he wasn't even out of high school—he's willing to do it. And I'll say to you, Bobby, like I'll say to everybody else at UBC, if anybody offends him because of this demotion—and let's face it, that's what it is—I'll personally kick the living shit out of him."

Robert didn't look up. "And replacing him?"

"A surprise, I'd imagine. I want to move Marty Levitt from Legal into the spot, mainly because it's designed to be mostly internal and administrative from now on. Sales, Affiliate Relations, and PR will still report to him, but Programming—*all* of Programming—will report directly to me."

Fork midway to his mouth. "Which means?"

"Which means that Adrian will continue as v.p. for Programming, with the various divisions—Daytime, Children's, Late Night, you know—under his direct supervision. And of course nighttime serial programming. You'll notice I said nighttime *serial* programming. You see, Bobby, I want to create a position that no other network has—a position for you, son—and one reporting directly and exclusively to me." He did smile now, broadly. "How does vice president in charge of Special Programming and Scheduling grab you? And with whatever staff you think necessary, here and on the Coast."

Robert cocked his head; not aggressively, merely curiously. "A free-and-clear? Like wine and roses?"

David laughed easily, politely. "Naturally you'd be expected to discuss everything you do with both Adrian and me. And with Levitt on occasion, as you see fit. He *is* one of the best legal minds in the business, you know. One of the main things about this, Bobby, aside from preemptive time periods for specials, dramatic or otherwise, is what I plan to say to the Assembly of International Communicators in Aspen two weeks from now."

"And that is?"

"That is that I've asked the television network to set aside a ninety-minute period weekly, over a full year's period, for what I'll call a *very* special evening of excellence. A special advertising and promotion budget, sold or unsold. I have Newton in PR working on it now. I'd like you to give him your ideas as soon as possible. Particularly about program types—you know, dramas, comedies, Broadway-type musicals, classics—it's your baby, baby. And high time the old man faced a little reality of his own, eh?"

Walking back along Fifty-sixth Street, still crowded seven deep with the lunchtime preweekend crowds, David said, "I got to be honest, though. I still think this whole television violence scare is for the birds. Most of it, anyway. I've never in my professional life attempted to shock or exploit, to go to sensationalism for its own sake. I'd like you to believe that." And for the first time in his life, or at least as far back as he could remember in any public room or street, his father's arm was very firm and strong around his shoulder.

". . . so that at least one evening a week will provide the discriminating viewer a program at once meaningful, provocative, and artistically satisfying—a project of such merit and excellence that not only the United Broadcasting Company, but the entire television industry, can be justly and aesthetically proud. . . ."

Robert chose as his first production in the "bold new venture" the Robinson Jeffers free-verse adaptation of *Medea*, starring Judith Anderson.

45

THE LADY *whose close-up covers the wide screen in color is household familiar. The soft, lustrous hair, the slightly impish nose; the moistened, parted lips ready to burst into song; the vague suggestion of girl-next-door, girlishly good, good-natured, freckles—who in all America hasn't seen her, hasn't at least heard her; hasn't reveled in her? Hasn't, if female, fantasized identification with her; if male, had himself some good old-fashioned dreams about her?*

The eyes, though—they're different today. Sadder, maybe; deeper. As if they're looking out on something lost, not loved. And the mouth—

that islet telling you you were home; how bitter it was now, if coura-
geous. And from it, the words no more than a whisper: "I won't cry
for you, Frank. Not tonight. It wasn't tonight you died. You died
twenty years ago, my darling—that night under a banyan tree
when . . ."

The fade-out is breathtaking. She's all colors, all hues of them—
yellow, blue, gray, violet, crimson, pink . . .

The screening-room lights began their slow, progressive ascent from
dimmest to dim to blinding bright, the entire projection area on the
UBC back lot (once the old Monogram Pictures studios in Hollywood
proper) a rather hideous amalgam of white-yellow, white-blue, and
white-silver. But to the fifteen-year-old page boy in his trim green-and-
gold uniform—the sharp UBC logo equal at least to a Scout's badge of
honor on his jacket pocket, the center of his pillbox cap—to this
teenage "gofer" it was night of nights at the Hollywood Palladium,
at Alhambra, at Grauman's Chinese.

The seven men seated at random among the first ten rows, however,
were somewhat less enchanted with the light fixtures. "Turn down the
dimmers again, you idiot!" one of them (the one named Robert, the
page boy thought) shouted to the rear, which of course meant him,
and after a nervous fumbling he brought the room back to semidarkness. Among the many things he was learning on this, his first day
on the job, was that these important, almost legendary show-business
types preferred their conference in as much darkness as possible. Must
get awful good and sick of seeing each other, he thought.

"That's better." The younger one again, son of the guy who ran
the whole shebang.

"Well?" said the head man to the man just behind him—a Mr.
Miller, head of Programming or something.

"I'll tell you this, David," the man answered him. "If Ellen Curry
doesn't take an Emmy for this one I'll pack it in and take off to an
Indian guru."

A smile was now large on the Old Man's face. "I think you're
right," he said. "I really believe this one will be compared to what Jane
Wyman did in *Johnny Belinda* and the big switch Garbo made in
Ninotchka. Or even Ed Wynn when he did *Requiem for a Heavyweight.*" He lit a cigarette slowly. "Funny, really. She swore she'd do
only comedy roles in the series. If it hadn't been for Bobby's persever-
ance, no matter what his personal feelings are, we never would have
seen what we did. First thing I want to talk about when we get back
to New York, Marty"—this to the silver-haired man two seats down
from him in the same row—"is doubling the ad budget for this particular episode. Especially the five owned-market stations and *TV
Guide*. I hear NBC's planning to put an Ethel Merman–Mary Martin

thing up against it." An important pause; at least it *looked* like an important pause. Then, turning around in his seat to address him—*him*, a nothing old country boy who couldn't afford more than two pairs of undershorts—*him!*

"Tell me, son, what do you think about what you just saw? You know who Ellen Curry is, a famous singer and comedienne . . ."

"Yes, sir, I most surely do."

"Right, and now you see her doing something very different. . . . What's your name, son?"

"Steve Lilly, sir."

"Steve Lilly. You say it like you were cutting butter. You're not from Maine, by any chance?"

The boy grinned good-naturedly. "Louisiana, sir. Mannerville, Louisiana. I'm sure you've never heard of it, sir?"

"We have station affiliates just about everywhere, son. But as I was saying, Steve, what did you think? I want your *honest* reaction, son. No bullshit—I leave that to the competition."

Steve could see that while the others were smiling—maybe fixed smiles but applied like good soldiers—the head man's son was plenty hot. Evidently the old man asked just about everybody for an opinion. Swallowing a couple of times, he said, "I had tears in my eyes, Mr. Abrams. And shivery, sort of. And I didn't even feel like that when my aunt Ferris May died last August."

"You think other young people like you will feel the same?"

"I can't see why the heck not, sir. I've always thought . . ."

"Go on," David urged, obviously loving every minute of this grass-roots research to which he was so addicted, never mind what Market Research or Bobby or anybody said. "Go on, Steve, let 'er rip."

Somehow without words for his thoughts, Steve Lilly understood what was going on.

"Well, sir, young folks are always, I think, bein' underestimated by people who make movies and TV shows. We maybe grew up on the Donald Duck Club and Pinky Lee and Buffalo Bob and all that, but we get older a lot faster than you think. Not that we don't still like to laugh it up and all, but when somethin' really gets to you . . . well, I think she's a real great actress, sir. A real great lady, too." Smooth Steve Lilly. Smooth young Steve Lilly. . . .

Bobby Abrams, it was evident to all, was very near to stamping out of the room.

"Shall we roll the Sharon Moore scene? She's the new one the William Morris people are handling." This one speaking now they called Jerry McAlister. "It's the test scene for the dramatic part of Jenny in the Siliphant script. Still rough cut, of course, and it hasn't been scored yet."

"No fades or dissolves, either," said the blond young man with glasses (Ron Homer of the network's West Coast program force; Steve Lilly had met him earlier). "Or color correction, I have to add. But she's there. That's all we're interested in anyway, isn't it? For now? Go?"

"Go," said Adrian, and Steve Lilly, in his most important responsibility to date, signaled the projectionist in the raised booth to let 'er roll.

"Me? I'll tell you what's wrong with me. Life makes pies of me. Cake. Mincemeat. Raisin. Who in his right senses ever even flirted with me? Flirted with me! Hah! Me, I wink back at a guy and my eyelid falls off. It was always Carrie got the breaks. The breaks I get? I'll tell you the breaks I get. Back breaks, heartbreaks, tooth breaks . . . Yeah, that's what I said. Tooth breaks. My sister's teeth, like everybody else's, get cavities or fall out even. Mine? They break. And not clean across, neither. No, none of that easy stuff for Jenny. Up and down, for God's sake. Up and down. Like this. See? Twice now I been down in the East River. Twice! And both times have the blind stupid luck to be rescued by sharks. Not eaten by 'em! Saved by 'em! Which is the same thing, come to think of it. I tell you, Gordie, it's a wonder I even—"

"Stop it! Jesus! Off with it, out!" Adrian Miller.

David Abrams: "How could they have the balls to show us that?"

"How right you are, sir." McAlister. "It's mortifying."

"It's a tragedy, all right—the girl, I mean." Ron Homer.

Martin Levitt: "This was on spec, wasn't it? I mean, no contract or anything?"

"Production expenses at Screen Gems, yes," said McAlister, squirming. "The agency paid the talent."

"The *talent?*" Adrian Miller looked as if he might jump across at him.

Through it all, Steve Lilly noticed that the old man's eyes were fixed on the back of Mark Banner's head, four seats in front of him. Mark Banner, as Steve had learned earlier from the projectionist, was the youngest of them all, a recruit to Programming from his position in Station Relations. The old man's gaze finally found words.

"You've been quiet enough, Mark," he said. "I got throat lozenges if you need them."

Mark, smiling, turned full around. "If you mean Miss Curry's performance, sir . . . what can anyone add? The crime is that we didn't see more of that side of her earlier. She's already given more to this medium than ten stars who pretend to be her equal. And now this." Pause. "As for this Charlotte Moore . . ."

"*Sharon* Moore," said McAlister; a little old-maidishly, Steve thought.

"Sharon Moore. Well, as to her, sir, I think that the crime in this case is not the lady herself but the jerk who saw her as some kind of Bernhardt or Duse. I may be wrong, but I think that if that same monologue were directed as an out-and-out comedy routine, you'd maybe every one of you sit up and say wow!"

The skepticism on the others' faces, particularly on young Mr. Abrams', was not to be found on his father's.

"I see," he said. "And I suppose you'd like to take it on?"

"Very much, sir. Yes."

"I'll sleep on it. And of course talk to Bobby and Adrian. Anything more before we break?"

"Yes, sir. This may be sticking my neck out worse than a tom turkey's at Thanksgiving, but I suspect this Sharon Moore might turn out to be the sort of comedy find Lucille Ball was. I really believe it."

"And I can't imagine a more appropriate moment for fond farewells." Robert Abrams stood to both his real and fancied heights. Steve Lilly felt he was finally where it was at. He intended to hang around. Sweet duty. Real sweet duty. . . .

For some reason, as they were leaving the screening room, Mark Banner smiled and winked at him. Yessir, Steve Lilly thought again. Yessireebob. He was finally where it was at.

To each his own.

Ron Homer to meet his wife and Larry Lester and *his* wife for cocktails and dinner at Scandia, to review the comic's guest-star roster for the next thirteen weeks.

Martin Levitt for an appointment with Quinn Martin, producer of ABC's highly successful *Untouchables*, for rights to a possible adventure series for UBC in '63.

Mark Banner to his room at the Beverly Hills to call his bride of two months, pining away in New York.

Gerald McAlister to his room at the Beverly Hills also, to call his invalid wife in Tarrytown, then to remove his clothes and wait for the gentle rap on the door from a bit actor in the UBC Friday night series *The West Wind*.

And David, Robert, and Adrian to the small taproom of the Bel-Air Hotel for a drink or two before dinner; David to have his with Ellen Curry in her Bel-Air mansion, Robert and Adrian theirs with the movie producer George Stevens at Chasen's.

The Bel-Air Bar, unlike the Polo Lounge or the Century Plaza's lobby pit, was small, dark, familial, and restful, frequented mainly by people who didn't give a damn about being seen. Tonight it was only half filled, and the pianist's repertoire of Porter, Rodgers, Gershwin, and Weill and unintrusive accompaniment to whatever mood one came in with.

The three of them, Adrian mainly, spent the hour or so reviewing almost impersonally a number of industry matters concerning them all: Mark Banner's surprising conviction about Sharon Moore, "who probably had to sleep with Mister Ed to get even a screen test"; the future of dramatic programs with social themes: *The Defenders, Mr. Novak, East Side/West Side,* UBC's *The Law and O'Hara;* the *Beverly Hillbillies/Green Acres* phenomenon on CBS, in the face of plunging ratings for UBC's *Hillbilly Bill;* the long-term validity of adult animated series (ABC's *The Flintstones;* one that UBC was discussing with Hanna-Barberra); the longer versions of Westerns like *The Virginian* and UBC's ninety-minute *The Dakotans,* a possibility for midseason '62; the U.S. space flights and what they would do to network schedules, fickle as they were when it came to timing; the increasing demand for prime-time television for political and government purposes, aside from conventions and elections; the advisability of someone from UBC (Marty Levitt, perhaps?) on the fifteen-man Board of Directors of COMSAT, the Communications Satellite Corporation, a prestige-power priority with the Kennedy administration; the Camelot aura that television was starting to project; the desirability of complete Olympics coverage, both day and night, fucking up schedules right and left; the notion of asking Arthur Miller to write an original two-hour play exclusively for UBC, under Robert's new Specials unit; a way to get Katharine Hepburn to television, as if everyone from Sarnoff and Paley on hadn't busted their chops trying; Adrian's determination to get Mae West to television; the rumored replacement of Jack Paar by Johnny Carson on NBC's *Tonight* show; the whoop-de-do over children's programming, particularly on Saturday and Sunday mornings, which was sure to be coming soon, making the quiz-show scandals seem like child's play.

They were just about to break for their respective dinner engagements when a call came for David from his daughter, Mandy Jo, in New York. Arrabella, while attending a performance of *La Traviata* at the Met, had collapsed and been rushed from Lincoln Center to Roosevelt Hospital.

Immediate diagnosis: brain tumor, hemorrhaged.

Operation now under way. Drs. Petrillo, Ricard, Sanderson, and Weingarten.

Chance of survival: slight.

"Paper-thin, daddy. Oh, God . . ."

. . .

"She's gone, daddy. Mother's gone. Dead.

"I said she's dead, daddy. Mother's dead. Is Bobby with you? . . .
I said is Bobby there with you? Daddy? She just died, daddy, just
like that, she just . . . She didn't even . . ."

. . .

"Daddy? Daddy?"

46

IT BEGAN AGAIN, of course—the long silences, averted eyes. The stiff
accusatory shoulders when his back was turned. *Three times you did
it. By marrying her at all, spilling yourself on her fineness. By letting a
single drop of you bring forth the likes of me, a son like me, who
hasn't for one day, one night in all his thirty-five years brought pleasure to himself or you. By murdering her where she sat, in her beloved
Diamond Horseshoe, as surely as if you'd held the gun to her head,
pulled the trigger from three thousand miles away.*

Even at the funeral in Atlanta—especially at the funeral in Atlanta
—David felt more an interloper than at any other time or place in his
life. Robert's silent accusations were only a part of it.

The site itself ("my ancestral home," she'd called it) had been speci-
fied in her will, a document remarkable for any number of fond farewells. She was to lie in state (that was her actual phrase) in an open
casket in the east drawing room of the old Sackman house on Shoreham
Drive for a period not to exceed three days nor to last less than two.
Jonquils and azaleas, whether in season or not, were to dominate both
house and temple. Rabbi Feldman, were he still B'nai Israel's spiritual
leader, was to employ Hebrew in the Kaddish and benediction only. A
paragraph from one of Mrs. Humphrey Ward's novels and a passage
from À la Recherche du Temps Perdu (in French, of course) were to
take the place of a eulogy. UBC's silver-tongued Barry White was to de-
liver the selections. Walter Houston, Raymond Massey, or Charles
Laughton would be acceptable as surrogate. And if at all possible,
Madame Renata Tibaldi was to sing "*Pace, pace, mio Dio*" from
Verdi's *La Forza del Destino*. Her own hair was to be done by Mr.
John of New York, and her burial gown was to be the black sheath

she'd worn at one of Truman Capote's little soirées at the Pierre. Her dear mother's diamond earrings and Cousin Bessie Jean Levinson's single strand of pearls were to be her sole and simple garnish. And for her first plunge into vulgarity in either life or death, her wedding ring was to be shoved up David's ass.

Even more remarkable, being, as it were, at such variance with the earlier sentiments, was that the book-length inventory of bequests and endowments, along with endless justifications for them (the domestic staffs and caretakers at both the Shoreham Road and Ravenair domiciles; the lengthy list of health and cultural remembrances, including the American Cancer Society, the Heart Association, Lincoln Center, and the Metropolitans, both opera and museum; a yearly Robert Sackman Abrams scholarship fund at Yale for the most promising new writing talent; the Atlanta house and nearby mountain retreat to Robert; remaining jewels and personal effects to Mandy Jo; several items of considerable value to Joslyn and Adrian Miller; a diamond butterfly brooch and her personal library to Frederick Wiener; and so on), had hidden among them the bequest of two-thirds of her stock in the United Broadcasting Company, both common and preferred, to David, the other third to Robert and M.J., share and share alike. Even her sop to the children in the form of her full interest in Sackman Industries did nothing to soften the visible embitterment that Robert wore like a martyr's shroud.

Even so, amid many of the Levinson and Sackman cousins and other prominent Atlantans, of the large contingents from New York, Connecticut, Los Angeles, and Washington (even the President had sent an emissary), Robert of them all was not only the most grieved, he had to be sedated at Atlanta General Hospital for the night.

It was in the weeks following, as David went through his and Arrabella's personal possessions whenever time allowed, that he found the small folded note in an unusually shaky hand (written soon after her mastectomy, he supposed) which cleared up the mystery somewhat.

David:

However heavy my heart in leaving such large controlling interest in the broadcasting operations to you, it is done in the cold knowledge that UBC's success, as it has in the past, rests almost wholly on you and your uncanny maneuvers. You, as the saying would have it, are to broadcasting born, recognizing that entertainment or enlightenment, in whatever form or context, is still first and foremost a business. My darling Bobby, I can assure you, has more creative life in a single hair of his head than your head with all its mazes put together. But running a broadcasting empire? He will be hurt, David. And God knows he's

*been hurt enough in this life. Be kind to him, David. Indulge a
dream here and there. Hard as it is—for you, anyway—give him
heart.*

As for us, David, you and me, I sometimes think

It was never finished. Maybe she'd even forgotten she'd ever begun it.

". . . a 1961 gross revenue of $2.03 billion gave broadcasters a profit
of $312.9 million before taxes. That's a return of over 20 percent. Add
to this the even more phenomenal growth pattern in '61, and you begin
to realize the very large and very real commitment that organizations
like UBC must make to its increasingly important news operations and
its special—what I like to call quality—programming. Most if not all
of you know me, of course, as the one network head who has given
its news divisions and its OTO spectaculars the lowest marks on
priority charts. I have always believed, I believe it just as firmly
today, that the week-in, week-out series . . . situation comedy, Western, cops and robbers, whatever, along with daytime serial dramas
and game shows . . . that these kinds of familiar weekly fare are what
television—commercial television—is all about. Just as it was in radio,
'way back when. But times do change, gentlemen, social structures
build and expand, and if ever News—News Documentaries and
Special Programming—if ever this kind of programming had a call
for priority attention, it's right here, now, in this new and vigorous decade."

It was David's first report to the Board since Arrabella's death, four
months earlier. A great deal of thought and preparation had gone into
it. The occasion also marked the initiation of a new Board member,
replacing Arrabella; its youngest member as well: Robert Sackman
Abrams. In a new Pierre Cardin suit and a pastel Sulka shirt and
tie, he was also its handsomest.

David was watching him, covertly, throughout his entire presentation, pleased to see that publicly, at least, he was maintaining his
cool. He hadn't even downed one of the myriad stomach pills to which
he'd become so addicted. The older hands, on either side of the
polished conference table, were keeping their cool as well, eating
right out of his hand today:

Harold Borland, chairman of the board of Silvertone Rubber; Phil
Mitchum, chairman of the board of Coastal Oil; Percy Shepherd,
president of International Steel; Roger Frye, senior vice president of
Cullum-Frye Publications; Fulton Little, president of Hanover Mills;
Jim Mortimer, president of Maritime Manhattan Bank; Joseph Warren,

vice president and general manager of KXTL in Memphis; Lester Levinson, president of Sackman Industries; and from United Broadcasting, Arthur Merck, corporate vice president and general counsel, and Fred DuBarry, vice president for all nonbroadcast activities.

It was the shortest Board meeting on record. The increased expenditures were approved without a flutter. And while David, by the very nature of his position, was the hero of record, it was Bill Kelly in News and Robert Abrams in Special Programming who came out as the lions of the moment.

The cocktail reception in the lounge area just outside the boardroom was a tradition begun by David when United Broadcasting first went public. This afternoon the affair was enlarged to accommodate a few others from Programming, News, Sports, Sales, Station Relations, Public Relations, and Audience Research, plus a guest of Robert's, a Miss Beverly Berenson from NET, and Producers Paul Madden, Sol Hurok, Lou Gordon, Herbert Brodkin, and Hubbell Robinson; and in from the Coast, Quinn Martin, Aaron Spelling, and Irwin Allen. And *crème de la crème,* Sarah Churchill, Betty Hutton, Ben Gazzara, John Raitt, Celeste Holm, Barry White, and Ellen Curry. Stuffed mushrooms, *pâté de foie gras,* crabmeat Polinière, lobster Newburg in patty shells.

"Your day, bub." Adrian Miller smiled, lifting a glass to Robert's. "A long time abornin', huh?"

Robert's own smile stretched thin. "A million years maybe?" He shrugged. "You are what your tolerance level is, I suppose."

"Wrong," said Beverly Berenson, her mouth stuffed with the lobster miniatures. "You are what you eat," and she reached enthusiastically for a couple of mushrooms from a passing tray.

"You're joining us for dinner?" said Adrian. "Joslyn and me?"

"Most definitely"—Beverly again, mouth still stuffed—"but only with your friend's solemn promise that he'll ball me to Zamboanga right after dessert."

The color of Robert's face was not discernible in the gold-tinted lighting from the walls.

"We do have to talk, you know. Soon . . . soonest." David had somehow managed an arm's-length island with Ellen.

"It's still too soon, David. We owe Arrabella that much."

"We?"

"Of course, love. Besides, she finally did make it possible for you to make an honest woman of me, didn't she . . . after a couple of hundred centuries?"

A deliberation of a different order, with a somewhat larger cast, was taking place near the floor-to-ceiling windows, whose shimmering drapery was a direct copy of the Four Seasons'.

COASTAL OIL: Like I said, I'm for the whole thing, straight down the line. Prestige is something we can all use a case or two of. Especially with that damn quiz-show fiasco. There've been times that if it hadn't been for Ellen Curry, we might have had the TV version of gamey Forty-second Street. But I have this other feeling too. Like maybe reaching for the mind could cost us our ass.

CULLUM-FRYE PUBLICATIONS: Hell, David's so persuasive he could have sold us Saudi Arabia today. And with his wife hardly cold in her grave . . .

HANOVER MILLS: I'll be frank with you fellows. I think the new budget's 'way out of line. But Rog here does have a point. Who in his right mind would have voted old Dave down today?

INTERNATIONAL STEEL: Still and all, this business of trying to look like CBS, NBC—I'm not sure that's where we should be heading. UBC's demographics have always shown a younger, less elegant skew . . .

MARITIME MANHATTAN: The News operation appeals to me, though. If I were Abrams or Kelly, I'd make one big fat beeline to either Huntley or Brinkley, grab one of them by his tail to the tune of a quarter million, break the bastards up by putting them smack up against each other.

SILVERTONE RUBBER: How about somebody like Turhan Bey for an-chor man?

COASTAL, INTERNATIONAL, SACKMAN, and KXTL: *Turhan Bey?*

SILVERTONE: Omar Sharif?

MARITIME MANHATTAN: Seriously, though, I can't remember David Abrams ever looking so well.

HANOVER MILLS: Yeah. His wife's death was sure a helluva blow. . . .

Lights dimmer now, one more drink, two at the most. Another part of the forest:

"How's it working out, Marty? Adrian and Bobby reporting directly to the Old Man? Hamstringing you?" Arthur Merck, Marty Levitt's closest friend, was the only one in the room who could get away with it.

"Too early to tell," Marty Levitt said. "No matter how you slice it, though, it's an artificial setup top to bottom."

"Like Orwell's *Animal Farm.* All animals are equal, but some animals are more equal than others."

"We'll have to watch it pretty close, Jerry"—Barry White, tight-lipped, in another corner of the room. "Adrian came within seconds of catching us in the exec washroom this morning. And for Christ's sake, don't reach for my dong that way again. It's there for you, sweetie, any time, any place. *Except* on these here cotton-pickin' premises. Okay?"

"Cockteaser," said Gerald McAlister.

From another corner still:

FULTON LITTLE: Do you really think this government business is that important? Frankly, I see it as just a lot of noise in an off-year election campaign.

ARTHUR MERCK: I wish I could believe that. But the handwriting's not measuring it quite that way. Especially from the White House. Kennedy's all for government interference or control in practically everything happening in this country, and with a philosophy like that, you know damn well who gets priority attention. Communications, baby, communications. We're the key to the kingdom, Fulton, and you'd better know it.

FRED DuBARRY: I'm inclined to agree. The potshots at program content is child's play compared to what's coming.

PAUL MADDEN: And just what *is* coming?

DICK FULLERTON: I think I can answer that. The content of television commercials. All the way down the line.

STEVE KERIMIDAS: Not to mention pay TV. It may look like a million miles away, but it's just up the street, you watch it.

WARREN MANN (Sales): And another one. This usurping of network time any time the President wants to "communicate" with his "good constituents." No small threat, I assure you.

JIM FOUNTAIN (Sales): We're not talking in small numbers, either. Revenue loss could run into the millions.

JERRY FINCH (Public Relations): And stations shaking in their boots. This license-renewal threat is intimidation of the worst kind. Thank God we've got somebody with balls like David Abrams. A weak sister could go under fast.

JIM MORTIMER: And that's what worries me.

BRIAN DORWELL (News): What worries you?

MORTIMER: That if anything were to happen to Dave . . . Well, I mean Bobby . . . Well, I certainly don't mean to imply anything, but . . . Well, one does have to think ahead. I mean, plan ahead.

SELWYN COE: Hey, did any of you guys catch Myron Cohen on Sullivan last night? I swear to God, he had one of the goddamnedest funniest bits I ever . . .

Dim; dimmer. Last call, ladies. Gentlemen.

"Ready to go, kid?" Adrian swallowed the last of his drink.

"Sure. I'll get Bev." Robert started off.

"Wait a second, Bobby."

"Yes?"

"It's pretty obvious that you haven't been anywhere near your father tonight. You're not going to go over and thank him, maybe? Something?"

"I said I'll get Bev."

The chill in his smile was not to be tampered with. Even by Adrian.

Dimmest. *Last* call, ladies. Gentlemen.

"Tell me, boychick. How's the shtupping getting on?" Maury Sherman, in front of a Koonig original, was on his fifth rye, third cigar.

"The what?" said Mark Banner.

"The shtupping. Yentzing. Humping. Fucking. You know. I been noticing how much slower you're walking lately. The first six months can cripple you for life if you don't watch it. Where is the little bride, anyway? Should of brought her along."

"She's meeting me at Gino's."

"Order yourself a big fat sirloin. And lots of milk. Keeps it up longer. Any luck and you may come in with a fifty share."

Good night, ladies. Gentlemen. And don't be surprised if you hear them saying over the next big, crucial months, "This was UBC's finest hour."

A MIRACLE. There was no other word for it. It couldn't have been the drinks. How many thousands of nights had he prayed that it would be? Or the state of his health. If anything, his lethargy—always the shadow of his days, his nights—was deeper, more worrisome than it usually was. And the very idea that it could be the death of his mother, the Oedipus thing—*that* he didn't buy for a minute. Then why?

How?

And did it matter?

All he knew was that he was inside her, full inside her, deep inside her, *hard* inside her; that he was thrusting, sliding, ramming, gliding; that he was . . . say it, say it, oh, goddamn you, say it! Fucking. Fucking. Fucking fucking fucking! Beverly. Beverly Berenson. Fucking Beverly Berenson! And coming. Coming. Inside her, through her, coming! Fucking. Coming. Miracle.

Miracle miracle miracle!

Afterward, in the gorgeously disheveled bed in his Sutton Place apartment, when she leaned gently to stroke it, kiss it, he felt gloriously like kissing it himself.

They talked quietly, easily, through the night.

He made love to her again, the real thing again, sometime around dawn. Afterward she held him as no other being on this earth had ever held him. Including his mother.

Over eggs and coffee and muffins she had made from scratch, he asked her to marry him.

IT WAS OUTRAGEOUS, of course. Perverted. But Vivian Seaforth (*Banner*, damn it; would she never get used to it?) couldn't help it to save her soul. Of all the qualities and characteristics of her new young husband —his wit, poise, sharpness, gentleness; his laughter, his seriousness, the shape of his head, his body; his depth, hardness; his whole strong blond beauty—of all of them, the thing she couldn't wait to see at night, wake up to in the morning, was the curl of his pubic hair. Even now, just after they had made love for the third time in as many hours—she was as moist and spent and lethargic as he was—the lush vegetation was as fresh, as exciting, as downright sanctifying as must surely have been Moses' burning bush.

"You touch one blade more of that swampy weed down there, and I'll chew your own apart strand by strand. Clear?" He was still half asleep.

"Oh, God, yes. Clear as air. New York air." And already half there. "Let us begin."

Awake now, laughing, he brought her to him again, making certain all parts of them touched, except depleted thighs.

"We're going to have one goddamn beautiful life together, Mark," she said; whispered, actually, into his neck.

"We will if I have anything to do with it," he said.

"Or if the UBC Television Network doesn't wind up as co-respondent."

He pulled back. "What the hell is that supposed to mean?"

"I don't know. Everything. Nothing. Sometimes I think you actually own it, secretly that is, and that everything that happens to it is either a triumph or an affront to you personally. But then that's one of the reasons I married you, I suppose. Leastways, my dad thinks so. Contrary to ladies' magazine myths, he says, any man who has an outsized passion for his work is capable of an outsized passion for his broad."

"Just *capable* of?

"So far, yes. Any man who fizzles out after only nine times a day . . ."

"Why, you . . ." Laughing, pulling her roughly astride him. Laughing more loudly, joyously. "The count is ten."

"We will not prematurely or unnecessarily risk the costs of world-wide nuclear war in which the fruits of victory would be ashes in our mouth—but neither will we shrink from that risk at any time it must be faced.

"I call upon Chairman Khrushchev to halt and eliminate this clandestine, reckless, and provocative threat to world peace and to stable relations between our nations. I call upon him further to abandon this course of world domination and to join in an historic effort to end the perilous arms race and transform the history of man. He has an opportunity now to move the world back from the abyss of destruction. . . ."

"With that ultimatum by President Kennedy on the night of October 22, 1962, over national television, and the anxious days ahead before the Cuban missile crisis was ultimately resolved—days spent largely by the American people in front of their television sets—a union was established for all time and all people," David Abrams told a meeting of the Overseas Press Club in November of that year. "And that union, of course, is the one between history and television, neither of which will ever again be independent of each other's events and the service of them."

Three nights later, Robert Abrams' production of a two-hour play written expressly for UBC by a new playwright named Samuel Gunn— *The Day No Songs Were Sung*—was televised to a relatively small audience (some twenty million viewers), but a critical reception not unlike a ticker-tape parade down Broadway.

UBC had two definite hits among its new-season premieres that fall: *Squad Car*, an hour-long police drama up against CBS's *Going My Way*, with Gene Kelly, and a half-hour situation comedy called *Lazy River*, up against NBC's *Tell It to Groucho*. Six of the ten new series were already adjudged failures, the largest number since the network's inception. None was receiving more than a 20 percent share of audience.

On November 28, Robert and Beverly Berenson were married in a small family ceremony at Ravenair in Darien.

On Christmas Day, David and Ellen were married in a civil ceremony in New York City. Robert was not in attendance.

47

NOVEMBER, 1963.

"It's a damn funny thing, memory," David said, looking out from a window of their presidential suite at the Adolphus Hotel onto a swirling but seemingly directionless body of Texans, trapped together

on a mistyped page in a mistaken volume of history in the very heart
of fashionable downtown Dallas, thirty-two stories below. It was still
only late afternoon in what was already the longest day of their lives.

"Like, say, pleasure and pain, you know? Hell, there's not one of us
can't remember pleasure by actually having it again, feeling it again,
you know? The taste of food, a good wine, even fucking. While pain
—I mean physically or emotionally rough as it might be at the time—
hell, it's never experienced again, never lived through again, you
know? In the mind, maybe, but that's all. I mean, thinking it, not
feeling it, the way you do a good steak, a good fuck. But I said that,
didn't I? I guess I don't know what I mean, who the hell could? A day
like today, you're lucky to *think* anything, much less *mean* anything.
Whole cockamamie world's falling down on our ears and I'm talking
through my asshole like Bobby."

From the chaise longue across the room, ostentatiously Victorian,
as was the rest of the suite, Ellen said vaguely, "What are you saying,
darling?" Only half of her had heard him; the other half was intent
upon the color television set nearby, its sound turned down to less
than a whisper, but the screen itself set to bursting with flashing re-
motes or playbacks from Parkland Hospital, the Dallas police station,
the motorcade route, the Texas School Book Depository, the swearing-
in ceremony aboard Air Force 1 at Love Field, the White House, the
Justice Department, the Capitol, the Johnson ranch, the studio interviews in New York, in Washington, in Dallas, around the world: UBC
in the frenetic race of its life; ABC, CBS, and NBC in the same meet.
The expanded news operation had accomplished parity in the old
steeplechase nick of time.

"I was talking about pain," he said. "Pain and pleasure. Through
my asshole." He took a chair near hers, eyes still not dried from an
afternoon's tears, riveted once more and hypnotically to the awesome
tube.

His tube.

And the stark realization that not once in all his years in broadcasting (not even in the radio reports from Nazi Germany in the thirties,
the radio coverage of the war itself) had he envisioned his life's blood
as more than just the natural flow of life, a companion of life; an
entertainer, often an enlightener, never . . . this.

"My God," he said, as much to himself as to Ellen, "this isn't just
viewing. This is getting sucked into the event, you and me, we're . . .
we're not just witnesses to an event, we're . . . Star, we *are* the event."

She reached out and touched him without moving a finger. "Say that
tonight, David. Tell that to them tonight. That's what tonight's all
about . . . now."

It was pure coincidence that they were in Dallas that day. Over
the past three years David had initiated a series of regional affiliates'

meetings at central locations throughout the country, supplementing
the national conclave in Los Angeles in May. This fall Phoenix had
been the original site for bringing together station owners and managers from the South and Southwest to see and hear UBC's multimedia
presentation for the so-called second season. It was only a week before the scheduled meet that the Phoenix hotel's presentation facilities
were destroyed in a gas explosion. The Adolphus in Dallas had been an
eleventh-hour expediency, with the added attraction of a possible
"drop in" by the President, who would be in the city to mend some
political fences.

The ironies had mounted by the minute. In line with the super superlatives and wine 'em–dine 'em philosophy that the Affiliate Relations Department had been foisting on all of them lately, a bottle of
champagne and imported cheeses had been delivered to each affiliate's
room in the early-morning hours, accompanied by a small engraved
note: "Welcome to Dallas. We'll make ourselves a little history today.
David Abrams." The "little history" had been the earth-shaking news
that AFL pro football games would become a regular Wednesday-
night feature of UBC's 1964 prime-time schedule.

"Rest a little while, David," she said. "Lie down. You didn't close
your eyes last night worrying about the presentation today, and even
with it canceled you haven't taken your eyes from this set. Let alone
been tranquil for more than thirty seconds at a time. We all know
that you *are* UBC, darling, but your being on the telephone with New
York and Washington every two minutes isn't doing any of us any
good. Bill Kelly's doing a marvelous job and you know it. And this
UBC correspondent out here is top drawer. And you still have to
speak at dinner tonight, remember? David? I said David . . ."

*"We've got the full staff at full mast, David. Morris Russman's got
the Engineering people moving at top speed. News is prepared to go
straight through the night if necessary. Which I don't think it will
be. There's only so many times you can switch from Dallas to Washington to Love Field to Andrews . . . and you can't run film retrospec-
tives all day and all night . . . and only so many times can you play
the music from* Camelot *without driving your own brains up a wall.
Adrian's idea is to just go on with the regular schedule and break in
live whenever there's something new to report. Dick Fullerton backs
him a hundred percent. The commercial loss alone, the way we're
doing things now, is staggering. Staggering. Now, the way I see it,
David . . ."*

"Is not the way I see it, Marty. Or the way Bill Kelly in News sees
it. The President of the United States has just been assassinated. Say it
to yourself, Marty. The President of the United States has just been
assassinated. Now, again: The President . . ."

"David, please, come off it. The whole country's in a state of paraly-

sis, you think I'm not aware of that? And in such a spasm of shock, a shock that great, that profound . . . Well, the more normalcy we show, the more normal the country's adjustment's going to be. It's the way things are done, David, the way America wants things to be done. America needs to get out of itself right now, David. Wants to believe, wants to see, hear, that life goes on again. Wants to be assured, re-assured that no one man, no matter who he is . . ."

"Go fuck yourself, Marty. Exactly thirty minutes ago I put Adrian and Bobby and Dick Fullerton on a plane back to New York with the following instructions. One: We stay on the air, live on the air, no matter how many days or nights are needed, until I say we go off the air. Two: Both Adrian and Bobby, as well as Dick and his people, will be working night and day to come up with compatible programming for the times between. And three: There will be no commercial messages of any kind whatsoever during the full course of this telecast. I make myself clear?"

"Clear? God Almighty, David, do you realize what the stockholders . . . the Board . . . the advertising community . . . the contract producers . . ."

"Can fuck themselves too. Say it, Marty. The President of the United States has just been assassinated. Again. The President of the United States . . ."

"David!"

". . . of America has just been . . ."

"Darling."

He turned to her slowly, red-eyed, unshaved, the musk of him strong (and terribly lovely, she thought) in the overstuffed room. "All right," he said, holding out a hand. "But only on the condition that you lie down with me."

Touching the tips of his fingers with her own: "And when wouldn't I, David? When on God's earth wouldn't I, love?"

IT WAS A STRANGELY QUIET, almost eerily solemn glide through the troubled air. Even the news reports every few minutes seemed hushed and other-worldly. It was almost as if the loudspeaker's graveyard monotony was a confirmation of their own doomed lives here in the stuffy confines of their own doomed ship.

Luckily, given the day's gravity and mystique, Adrian had been able to wrangle first-class accommodations for himself and Robert, leaving Fullerton and one of the third-string PR men to fend for themselves in the overcrowded coach section. Neither Adrian nor Robert had much use for Fullerton under the best of circumstances. Sales, while their necessary lifeblood, was always just a little beneath contempt. Today, the need to be free of him was especially felt. And not simply because a nation's tragedy was not easy to share with boors, Robert thought. But because their individual work loads had been so intense of late that he and his friend had had precious little time together. And I've missed it, Robert thought. I've really missed it.

"Well, at least we don't have to worry about missing the plane's movie," he said, passing a single-sheet playbill across to him. Adrian smiled. It was a John Wayne–Susan Hayward oater that Adrian had just this week bought in a Paramount package negotiation for two runs in 1965.

"Just as well," Adrian said, tossing the flyer aside. "Who the hell could keep his attention focused on anything today?"

"Not even on Miss Hayward's tits?"

Adrian was all smiles. "Noticing those things again, are we? Va-va-va-voom! And still making it?" Adrian asked softly.

Robert nodded. Playfully even. "Zeus has seen fit to bless once more the sacred phallus."

"I'm sure Beverly pays him pretty special homage too."

"The latest report. Dallas police have just exhibited the suspected assassin, Lee Harvey Oswald, manacled on a large platform, for reporters and cameramen. The presumed murder weapon, a rifle, has also been displayed. Meanwhile, Air Force One, carrying both the new President and the slain one, as well as his widow, is expected at Andrews Air Force Base in Washington momentarily."

"I've been thinking," said Adrian. "You know that profile Kelly started on Kennedy and never finished?"

"The 'President at Play' clips?"

"That one, yeah. I know it's still in rough form, with neither a beginning nor an ending, but with the right wrap-around I think it just might fill the bill."

"Good thought. We'll talk to Kelly first thing." He was stammering slightly, as he often did under stress, the inevitable pills not too far behind. "I've thought of something too. While the other networks are lining up their stars like crazy—and you know damn well they are; CBS wouldn't pass up Gleason, Sullivan, and Ball for all the gold at Knox. Ditto Bob Hope and Jack Benny at NBC. Anyway, while they're going after their own, why don't we make a play for all the theatre people, the ones with some real style—Alfred Drake, Cyril Ritchard, Rex Harrison, Helen Hayes, Lunt and Fontanne, Julie Harris. Maybe Merman even, Mary Martin, Bob Preston, Maurice Evans, Gwen Verdon, Freddie March. Kit Cornell. And all right, Ellen Curry. And maybe some opera stars. Maria Callas, Birgit Nilsson, Richard Tucker. Maybe tape people like Olivier in London, Chevalier in Paris . . ."

A resounding slap on his back: "Welcome to Show Business, Bobby! Welcome home!"

"Latest report. Funeral services for the slain President will be held

on Monday. Heads of states from all over the world are expected to attend. According to White House sources, special routes and functions are being planned in round-the-clock sessions. Elsewhere, reports from Texas indicate that Attorney General Katzenbach is openly censorious of what he calls the 'circus in Dallas.' Among those responding is Dallas Police Chief Jesse Curry, who contends that extraordinary events demand extraordinary measures. . . ."

"I think I'll have another drink," said Robert. "I couldn't eat if I tried."

"Same here," said Adrian, his eyes contemplative. "You know something? I'll bet you anything this coverage ends up in a network pool kind of thing. The events themselves, I mean. That's why your idea might be just what the doctor ordered. Uniqueness. A brand. A symbol, even. Because, believe me, Bobby, people will be ordering and reordering their lives on the basis of these next few days for years to come. And it won't be half bad when somebody looks back over his shoulder and says, 'Say, remember right after the funeral when UBC . . .'"

". . . while the networks continue rerunning the earlier parade, with a radiant John and Jackie Kennedy waving to crowds from their open limousine. Scenes from the Chamber of Commerce breakfast in Fort Worth this morning are also being shown, the last visual record of President Kennedy and Vice President Johnson together. Meanwhile, in Dallas . . ."

In the back of the plane, a third martini under his belt, Dick Fullerton said to the wide-eyed PR man, "Just wait, buddy. Just you wait. I don't know when I'll do it, or how I'll do it, or where I'll do it, but I'm going after Miller's ass so hot and heavy he'll wish to hell he was where John Fitzgerald Kennedy is right now."

SHOCK, LIKE COSMETIC SELECTION, has its own color chart. The next four days registered a number of variations. That Americans ever expected to see the funeral of a slain President on their favorite household toy, much less a murder committed right before their eyes—dear God! Not even the appearance of Elvis Presley on the *Ed Sullivan Show* could top it.

David never slept at all. Even in the midst of heartbreak and despair, there were decisions to be made by the hour. More often than not, by the minute.

The most immediate, and possibly the most significant, was the pooling of manpower and equipment for the coming events. After midnight Friday and again Saturday, long internetwork meetings were held, with Marty Levitt, Bill Kelly, and Morris Russman representing

UBC, but David, who arrived back in New York late Saturday morning, was in constant contact with them. It was finally agreed that the joint coverage of essential locations and routes would require a minimum of fifty television cameras, the pool on which each network could draw at any time, with CBS chosen to coordinate the entire effort. Extra equipment and personnel from each network were being flown in from Chicago, Detroit, Boston, Philadelphia, Minneapolis, Seattle, San Francisco, and Los Angeles. The only real bones of contention were ultimately buried by David's adamant insistence that each network keep cameras in reserve for special features of their own and that each also provide its own commentary. "Although at a time of such national crisis and concern," he had read at the meeting, "the American people should look on television as a single and all-pervading entity, there must be—even in the communal sense—a retention of image and enterprise uniquely one's own. I like to think that it was this kind of philosophy the late President made his own as well. . . ."

Robert's cursory suggestions to Adrian on the flight from Dallas not only took root, but in the circumscribed sequence of events blossomed and flourished. "When other networks, which will remain nameless," a New York editorial averred, "did under the guise of sanctimonious good taste create hastily put-together entertainments in tribute to President Kennedy, it was left for UBC, with little fanfare and no pretension whatever, to commemorate the death of a memorable leader with the life-affirming talents of a memorable array of artists."

"God," said Robert, over a 3:00 A.M. cup of coffee with Adrian in a back corner of Studio TV-11. "It can't be UBC he's talking about. Some wino linotype operator got it all boxed up. Had to. Memorable? Artists? United Broadcasting? God! Maybe Orson Welles's Martians landed in New Jersey again and turned the whole planet upside down. Or maybe—"

"Maybe you came through like a champ."

"And maybe you should go back to cliché school."

They both looked up to see Bill Kelly looking down, his dour expression a now familiar part of the landscape. Of all of them, Bill Kelly and David had been the most visibly affected. Kelly, in fact, had at times been so shaken that a question would be met only by a glassy stare. Cronkite at CBS had cried for a minute on-air. Kelly had cried for four days off it. He had known the President as a boy, in Boston.

"Come on, Kell," Adrian said. "It's three in the morning and we're all bushed to hell. Let the country live till breakfast, will you? Joe's Joint is sending over doughnuts."

"You really don't know, do you? You really don't see it. From this time on, for as long as this country *does* survive, there will be riots and street wars and cruelty that'll make the 1954 riots in Little Rock look like a game of tag. This isn't the end of something, *gentlemen,* as most of those stentorian voices of our brave anchor men would have us believe. Oh, no. Not on your ass. This is the *beginning* of something and I'm not sure any of us will live to see it all. Riots. Assassinations. Blacks taking to the streets. Women burning down their kitchens. I think real violence has been let loose, and I very much doubt we'll be able to come to grips with it, much less understand how it happened. Or do you prime-time assholes give a shit?"

They watched him slump off, a tired and saddened man. "He'd make a great Jesus or a great Karl Marx, I'm not certain which," said Robert, forgiving him. In truth agreeing with him.

"Ah, well," said Adrian, "we can always wrap it up with the good old saw: In the dark night of the soul it is always"—looking wickedly at his watch—"three-forty-five in the morning."

Robert could not remember ever having been so tired, or, oddly, so elated.

THE FOUR-DAY DRAMA with its improbable cast—the dead President, his wife, his children, his parents, his brothers, his sisters, his brothers-in-law, his sisters-in-law, his nephews, his nieces, his Sorenson, O'Donnell, O'Brien; his Schlesinger, Salinger, Rusk; the new President, his wife, his children, his associates, the governor of Texas; the presidents of France, Ireland, South Korea; the emperor of Ethiopia, the queen of Greece, the king of Belgium; the chancellor of West Germany, the prince of the Netherlands, the foreign minister of Israel; Lee Harvey Oswald, Jack Ruby, Jesse Curry, the cities of Dallas and Washington, the cities and towns of all America, in fact; the senators, congressmen, Supreme Court and cabinet, the most luminous stars of stage, screen, radio, and television; the most eminent historians and political scientists and philosophers and poets, psychiatrists and novelists, the most nondescript men and women of the boulevards and streets, Chet Huntley, David Brinkley, Walter Cronkite, Howard K. Smith; UBC's new anchorman, Peter Cummings—was of such height and moment to David in the long troubled hours that he ordered a small cloakroom on UBC's lobby level refurbished as a screening room seating thirty-five persons, to be called the UBC–John F. Kennedy Center, which would run on a twice-a-day schedule special films created from the footage UBC had amassed, both of the Kennedy administration years and the four torturous days that ended them. It was offered free to the public on a first-come, first-served basis.

Meanwhile, he and Ellen, along with Robert and Beverly, attended the funeral services in Washington as invited guests. It was there, while David and Robert were granted a private audience with Robert

Kennedy to discuss television coverage over the next several hours, that Ellen and Beverly, over tea in the attorney general's suite of offices, were able to discuss themselves—something Ellen had never been able to do with Brenda. She found herself liking this unique, outspoken girl from North Carolina from the first. Her feelings were not unreciprocated.

"It's unusual, to say the least, Beverly. You starting to work with Bobby on scripts and productions, I still working my behind off for David on the other side of the aisle."

"Unusual?"

"Yes. That men of such special personalities would wind up having professional wives, instead of the simple-minded clotheshorses most men in this crazy business seem to prefer."

"Yes, I suppose. I never was one to simply give a good lay and then cuddle up close for the next diamond or cottage in Southampton. You know the expression men have, 'Beating your meat'? Well, that's precisely how I've always looked on most women. The kind you're talking about, that is. *They're* really masturbators."

"We're very much alike, you know. You and I."

"Oh? Well, if a few brains and I hope some professional competence can even be mentioned in the same breath with great talent, genuine artistry really, then I can only thank you for being so muddleheaded."

Ellen laughed. "You *are* happy with him, aren't you?"

"Bobby? Why, yes, I suppose you could say that. We're such total opposites that a kind of perverse compatibility is almost inevitable. I never was one to linger very long over the word 'happy,' though. Or even one like 'content.' I don't think life's worth a shit if your bowels aren't in an uproar at least three or four times a week."

"He's kind to you, though? Thoughtful?"

"As much as he can be, I suppose. Although he's a hell of a lot more manic since his mother died. Sometimes I think that—"

"Yes?"

"Nothing. The thought eludes me completely, whatever it was."

And was with her constantly, wherever she was. For the first weeks after Arrabella's death he had been the most gloriously exhausting lover she'd ever known. And on occasions, very special occasions, since. But those times were becoming increasingly rare. Sometimes he would go for weeks without even the suggestion of an erection, no matter what she did or how she did it. But that was one compartment of her marriage that she was damned if she'd discuss with Ellen Abrams, no matter how much she liked and trusted her. Sex life, no matter whose, was not the ideal crumpet for tea, no matter where.

"You've looked preoccupied today, Ellen," she said quickly. "I mean, quite apart from this whole dreadful occasion."

Ellen smiled at her absently. "Yes," she said, "yes, I have been. You see, there's something I'm going to have to tell David and I haven't. Couldn't, that is. Not until this nightmare has settled us down a little, anyway."

Beverly grinned. "You're 'avin' a little stranger!"

Ellen's laugh this time was so raucous that a secretary had to open a door to caution quiet.

"You doll," she said, voice almost a whisper now. "I'll treasure you forever for that. Even if biology was obviously your poorest subject." She lit a cigarette. "No, it's something far more serious. As far as David's concerned, anyway."

"There are needles from one end of my butt to the other. Will you *please* get on with it!"

"You're the first one I've told, honey. It's probably the only pledge of confidence I'll ever ask of you."

"You know you have it."

Ellen walked to a window, looking out on a city already so subtly but irretrievable altered. Shrunken. "I'm going to give up *The Ellen Curry Hour*," she said. "This season will be the last."

Beverly jumped as if she'd been bitten. Her eyes widened in disbelief. "You can't be serious," she said. "Why, that's the same as the Statue of Liberty taking a powder to the Caspian Sea."

"A lovely thought, and I thank you. But my mind's so completely made up that it's only a question now of how and in what kind of language the PR people announce it."

"My God. I can just hear David saying it." Lowering her voice, swiftly raising it in mimicry. " 'Great God, Star, are you crazy? Are you mad? Are you deranged? How big a bowl of stupids did you have for breakfast?' Lord, can I hear him!"

"Well, Lord knows you sound like him, anyway. Which makes it a hell of a lot easier for me. Cuts off a lot of rehearsal time."

"I suppose you'd think I ate stupids for breakfast if I asked you why?"

"Not at all. And not that I'm sure I can say it very well, either. But . . . Well, you see, Bev, I've always believed in quitting when you're on top. Show business is a lot like a love affair, you know. It's so much nicer, so much more memorable, when you part while the passion's at its peak. The climb down—and believe me, honey, there is always a climb down—is always so degrading, so . . .ugly. I want to go before my ratings do. It's as simple as that. And, too, I'd like to do more live concerts. Around the country, I mean. Benefits. For the National Foundation for Retarded Children. For the Cancer Society, the Heart Fund. And shameful as it sounds after what we talked about earlier, I want to be home more, *there* more. When *he's* there more. I want . . . well, I want to enter my old age as a memory, a clean one. Not as some wrinkled old hag playing on the memory of what she *was*, not what she's become. Oh, I'll do a special or two maybe, something you can make a kind of event of. But as for the weekly grind . . ." Smile, shrug; out.

"And the anthology series? *Ellen Curry Presents?*"

"That's on its last legs anyway. Sixty-four–sixty-five is shaping up as the big year for escapism, or so David sees it. You know . . . spies, horror shows, more Westerns, medics. Sitcoms, fantasy things. Some hero or heroine week in, week out. Identification factor, or whatever they call it. Advertisers are leery as hell of the anthology film drama. Television's pretty biblical, you know. A time to live, a time to die . . . We're the tailor-made whatever-happened-to. And stop looking so stunned. They're burying *him* today, not me. All right, dear?"

Beverly simply shook her head. "It just seems so unreal. My God, you *are* UBC. Well, practically. We—my generation—why, we grew up on you, we cut our teeth on you. We got our behinds popped regularly for listening to you sing 'Love Walked In' and 'The Man That Got Away' when we should have been writing an English comp. And then we almost got our psyches fucked up good and proper, just fantasizing you. I remember the first time I ever touched a boy's penis. Do you know what he said? He said, "Tighter, kid, truer. Like maybe the way Ellen Curry would do it.' That's what *I* grew up on, Ellen Curry."

It was on that note—small laughter on a day so cruelly bereft of it —that David and Robert rejoined them and they walked together to the limousine that was to take them to view the bier at the Capitol.

48

New York, New York
December 4, 1963

Mr. David Abrams, President
United Broadcasting Company
New York, New York

Dear Sir:
    I am convinced that television helped kill both President Ken-
nedy and Lee Harvey Oswald, because there is almost no show
on your air that does not have guns going off. I also believe that

unless you people own up to this, and start to talk about this,
and resolve to do something about this, that the chances are good
that such terrible human things will happen again.

Sincerely yours,
Joel Griebsberg
(aged 12)

THIS WAS but one of thousands of letters that poured into UBC's New
York offices in the days and weeks following the nation's tragedy. But
it was the one David folded thoughtfully into his wallet and carried
with him wherever he went.

The truth was, this heavy outpouring of emotion was anything but
a passing post-mortem. "This is a sick society," Martin Luther King
had said, and in a time of confusion, division, and community plague,
it was the giant communicator among them—commercial television—
that bore the brunt of it. Narrowed further, it was UBC that shoul-
dered the weightiest burden.

"I think I've heard every argument there is. Psychologists, sociologists, therapists, priests. Leftists, rightists, the American Brotherhood
Movement, the WCTU, the gun clubs. The religious community, the
political community, the creative community; John Wayne, June
Allyson, Doris Day, Shirley MacLaine, and Phyllis Diller. Barry Gold-
water, John D. Rockefeller the Third, Perle Mesta, and Jane Fonda.
And there's not even the hint of agreement among any damned one
of them. How in all hell then are we—the programmers of this country—going to find definition, much less unity, among ourselves?"

The tirade was from the battle-scarred mind of UBC's new vice
president in charge of Standards and Practices, Birchall Schwartz,
who on a cold February morning in 1964 was using David's office for
both a platform and a runway, which he had traveled at least fifty
times—upside, downside—by ten o'clock in the morning. Adrian,
Marty Levitt, Arthur Merck, Dick Fullerton, Selwyn Coe, Maury
Sherman, and Jack Stroud (Advertising and Promotion) had been
asked to attend.

"Maybe Johnny Carson was right," said Adrian, when Schwartz
had slowed for a moment to a soft trot. "Maybe we really ought to
take violence off the streets and put it back in the home, where it
belongs."

"One positive note," said Arthur Merck, "if it means anything: I
doubt we'll be getting too much flak from Washington for a while. I
mean, this violence thing is Lyndon's war, too, you know. An eight-
million-dollar investment in violence research by one of the networks
just may keep a few eager-beaver subcommittees playing jacks a little
while longer."

"Besides which," said Marty Levitt, "it's an open secret that Frank Stanton at CBS has readier access to the White House than the strutting little FCC chairman ever dreamed of."

David, who up to now had simply watched and listened with his hands clasped beneath his chin, now unclasped them in an obvious windup of the morning's familiar subject all too familiarly rehashed, bringing them to his desk top like a judge's gavel. "We can talk all day, but I still want Palsky and Fischer brought in for another violence-factor study. The extremes in views are just too hairy not to give this issue priority. It may bore you to death, but I have news for you, boys. You're going to be bored for a long time to come. And now with that behind us, for the moment, let's get the hell on with getting back to business. After all the confusion and trauma of these past few months, it's high time we started in, as they say, to recoup." He stood and smiled his most deceptive smile. "I can tell you this much: The 1964–65 schedule is very likely the most crucial one this goddamn network has ever had to come up with. Last Monday at the Board of Directors meeting . . ."

On CBS: *Gomer Pyle, USMC; The Munsters; Gilligan's Island; My Favorite Martian; Mr. Broadway.*

On NBC: *The Man from U.N.C.L.E.; Flipper; The Rogues* (Charles Boyer, David Niven, Gig Young); *That Was the Week That Was.*

On ABC: *Bewitched; The Addams Family; Peyton Place; Mickey; Wendy and Me.*

And on UBC: *The Mission Men; Teenage Tina; Wonder Girl; Dancing in the Dark; Wendell Blaney, U.S.A; The Two-Timers; The UBC Wednesday Night Movie; The Sharon Moore Show.*

"Truly a season to be proud of," said Robert. "If there's a Mediocrity Room in those Archives in the Sky where all television series eventually go, then for sure UBC will be rated *número uno* this year."

"For Christ's sake, McAlister," said Adrian, "your neck is on the line, do you know that? If it weren't for Mark Banner, with the couple of development projects he personally worked on, I don't know what the devil we would have done this year."

"I tell you, boys, I've been in this business a good long time," said Dick Fullerton, "and this is the most balanced, most viable schedule we've ever come up with."

"There's no doubt about it," said Selwyn Coe, "you station guys are getting the best the creative community has to offer."

"There's range here, there's breadth. A lot of new twist in comedy. And I defy you to shout 'violence' at me from any one of the new action-adventure shows," said Marty Levitt.

"Shit," said Maury Sherman.

Clearly, the only clear-cut UBC hit of the new season was *The Sharon Moore Show,* the situation comedy about a klutzy small-town girl's adventures in the Big Apple, overseen personally by Mark Banner, competing with *Bewitched* for the top new girl-show honors. Clearly the loss of *The Ellen Curry Hour* and *Ellen Curry Presents* was the biggest program disaster in the network's history. The stock plummeted more radically than it had in a decade or so, the only stabilizing factor a healthy profit center in the company's nonbroadcast activities. The only bright lights for the television network, aside from young Banner's intuition and the Sports and Daytime strengths, were the movie packages Adrian had paid an arm and a leg for (Paramount, Columbia, Fox, and R.K.O.) and the two *UBC Theatre* specials brought in by Robert and Beverly—Ferenc Molnar's *The Guardsman* and *The Show-Off* by George Kelly—both of which were respectable if modest critical successes, and neither of which garnered more than a tight-squeeze twenty-five share. For several months David slept less and less frequently, more and more fitfully.

"POWER FAILURE AT UBC," *Variety* called it. "Abrams and Board Far from Joyful," said *Broadcasting.* "Advertiser Concern over UBC Slump Growing," wrote *Sponsor.* "UBC Management Meetings Longer, More Urgent," advised *The Wall Street Journal.* That there would be showdowns and shake-ups was inevitable, of course. But far from being flamboyant or even crisis-ridden, the alterations and crucifixions took place quietly and gradually, so that by the middle of May, 1965, when the affiliate body met with the network at the Century Plaza Hotel in Los Angeles, a whole new face was there for one and all to see, with no more than the vaguest hint at the cosmetic surgery that had been performed, profoundly and often painfully, behind closed doors.

"It's the company morale I'm concerned most about," David had said to Ellen one evening early in March. "Overall program success comes and goes too fast in this business to have coronaries over. But the people who work for us—the ones who sweat themselves silly day in, day out, year in, year out, without your even knowing their names half the goddamn time—they're the ones I'm losing sleep over. They're the ones whose faces show the sickness, the pain. And I've never seen them like they are right now. There's something wrong, Star. There's something really very seriously wrong."

"You almost make me feel guilty," Ellen had said. "Although it does seem pretty silly when one person's retirement can affect a whole season's schedule."

"Not just one person's 'retirement,'" he'd said. "Don't forget, Star.

The number two show and the number twelve show in all of television got scratched at the same damn time. Slots like that ain't so easy to fill again. But what's done's done in *that* department. It's what's happening now, where we're going now, that needs the old *Kopf*."

"And the trouble? The *real* trouble?"

"Who can say? I mean, for sure. Everybody's got his own ideas. Personally, I see it from any number of angles. First, I don't think the personnel structure's working like I hoped it would. It looked good on paper, but in the nuts and bolts . . . I also think we've gotten too . . . well, inbred I guess is the best way to put it. We go back year after year to the same old Hollywood hands, just because they've got the experience, and the equipment, and the professional know-how. Not to mention knowing the ropes when it comes to bringing in properties on budget. But that slams the door on an awful lot of good talent, an awful lot of fresh new ideas. There's no easy solution, there never is. Get yourself too many inexperienced people and I don't care how creative they are, they can put you in the red quicker than you can say—"

"Ellen Curry?"

"You dog! Squeeze a man's balls when he's just been kicked in 'em!"

In her arms, he went on: "At first I started thinking, Well, maybe it's Adrian. Maybe he's not the program man I thought he was. But then that seemed silly. My God, look at the seasons we've had hit after hit under him. And Christ knows he's far from drying up. There's just not a better man of his kind in the business. The one trouble is . . ."

"I think I know. The people he keeps around him. It's always on a kind of hit-and-miss basis."

"Right on the dime! For every one Mark Banner, he winds up with five Gerald McAlisters. But just mention getting McAlister out of the way and he goes crazy. Froths at the mouth, I mean it. Adrian has very strong loyalties—often, I admit, all to the good. . . . My God, look at the way he stood by Bobby all those months in the Philippines . . ."

"And made sure you never forgot it. Not for one single day in your life."

"All right, all right. Let's not get on that kick again. But program development's just a part of it. The selection process after the pilots come in. The right placement, the right strategy . . . I don't know. What I do know is that we've lost something, Star. And we've damn well got to get it back."

"I'M SURE there's one item you couldn't have missed," Dick Fullerton was saying, slightly nervous and confused that David had called him alone to his office. The Old Man had long since created a kind of mystique about meetings "between just the two of us." They were both rare and portentous, and more often than not involved the likes of his son or Adrian Miller or even Marty Levitt.

Dick Fullerton?

"And what item is it I couldn't have missed?" said David. His manner was pleasant enough, Fullerton thought. He hadn't once stopped smiling. Maybe it would be easier than he'd thought. God only knew how long he'd waited for such an opening.

"Well, this, sir. Even in what is now pretty generally recognized as a disaster year for us—in prime time, I mean—the sales figures are at their absolute peak. Naturally a few grumbles here and there—the P and Gs, the Colgates, they're so big they have no choice but to be s.o.b.'s when the going's rough—but on the whole the advertising community has stood by us all the way." A humble pause now, before the big enchilada. "We have only to look to Programming, sir. The prevailing achievement, and I might add climate, is shipshape down in Sales, sir. And, given a more attractive package the next time out—that is to say, the right creative team and philosophy—I'd say we're pretty well . . . well, we're pretty damned viable, sir."

There! He felt more comfortable now; larger. That he'd made a maximum impression was almost immediately discernible. The Old Man was positively beaming. Sales was always where the heart is, call it any rose you want. Damn, he felt good. Settling old scores, and with such easy subtlety, would make any man who was half a man feel good. Adrian Miller would live to regret that back-of-the-bus shit he'd pulled. Oh, man, would he ever regret it!

"Thank you," said David. "I hear you loud and clear. I'll be very happy to pass along your thoughts to Mr. Miller."

Fullerton blanched. "That was hardly my intention, sir. You wanted a broad view of the sales outlook and I think I provided it. Anything else is just . . . a misreading, sir. Or at the very least, an ill-chosen reference out of enthusiasm for my own boys. Sir."

"I see." David was leaning back expansively now, a cigar dramatically unlit between his smiling lips, so clearly *simpático* again with his vice president in charge of sales that Fullerton could again relax, cross his legs, and accept honorably the cigarette offered him from a sterling silver case initialed D. A.

"I have nothing but the profoundest respect for those guys in Programming," he said. "Hell, sir, that battleground out there don't know one army from another. The other networks might be doing better in the ratings, but I'm damned if I see much difference in either the content or look between theirs and ours. They're a hard-working bunch of guys, especially the boys on the Coast. They were just caught, like everybody else this year, with the so-called creative community's downer . . ."

A small laugh, just right. He'd never realized before just how penetratingly blue David Abrams' eyes were. Thank Christ they were as sympathetic as they were. For a minute there . . .

"As I said before, Dick, I shall certainly pass your goodwill and understanding along to Adrian. Particularly as he will be entering a kind of experiment with me in the next few days."

"Experiment, sir?"

"Yes. It's my pleasure to tell you—and you're the first to hear it—that Adrian will be named vice president in charge of Sales in a formal PR release tomorrow morning. Your own resignation will be included, of course, possibly to the effect that you have some great future plans that can't be announced at this time, and that you have all the faith in the world in UBC and its excellent management and so forth. Meanwhile, all good wishes on whatever the future happens to hold for you, or you for it, with gratitude for your good services to UBC. The severance and stock conditions will be discussed with you by Marty Levitt. I believe he's wating for you."

No one carried Dick Fullerton out of the office, of course, but he looked as though someone should have.

THE TONE AND TIMING of that meeting had been made possible by one the evening before with Adrian Miller.

"Now, I don't think you've had much doubt," David had begun that session, "that from the first time I met you—in that hospital in Manila when Bobby was so sick, remember?—that I've had plans for you in this organization, in this industry, that go all the way to the top. That assumption's still good. Even more so, if that's possible. The time will come, Adrian—not for two or three hundred years, of course, but in due course, in due course—when you and Bobby will be virtually running this place. I don't believe you ever thought otherwise, did you?"

"No, I suppose I never did, David. Not for a minute. I think Bobby and I decided a long time ago, although it's one of those things-you-don't-talk-abouts, that we more or less share the same father."

"Well, that being the case, I only hope your affections for papa are somewhat stronger than your brother's."

Adrian, of course, laughed heartily and long. Prolonging it, in fact, as long as he dared. Something was up, in the wind, going on; that much was pretty obvious. But just what—that was the old horse of another color. Whatever it was, though, it was by no means trivial. David looked too pleased with himself for that.

"Now, for a minute or two, you're going to think you've been kicked in the balls by a mule, because head of Programming, while the most vulnerable position on the charts, is also generally accepted as the most prestigious, right under the network president's."

Adrian knew he wasn't showing it—his skills were far too practiced for that—but inside his head, heart, and chest was another matter. There, the cohabitation of open curiosity and stiff resentment (even before he knew what was coming) was a pretty passionate union.

"What all this is leading to, Adrian, is an experiment I want you to share with me. A very important one, I think. For some time I've been thinking of giving Dick Fullerton the axe—you know, I hate that expression; whoever invented it deserves it—and asking you to replace him. Both for the long run and the short one. The short one because it's only an interim move. The long one because it helps prepare you for the overall management you'll be taking on one of these days.

"At first, of course, the idea seemed a little crazy, even to me. You're the best all-round programming man in the business, no matter what happened this past season. And Sales, of all areas, is the last one a smart management would think of touching. But after the thought had caught on, and the old intuition had taken over, its appeal was goddamn irresistible."

His pause was just long enough to allow Adrian the luxury (and goddamn necessity) of lighting an especially expensive cigar.

"You see, for some time I've been displeased with Fullerton. I've tried not to show it, of course, because it's just as illogical as the gut dislike I've had for Mr. Jerry McAlister. You say to yourself that personal likes and dislikes should have no place in a business or profession where competence is the only real criterion. And then you say to yourself also, Bullshit, because the very basis of any relationship is attraction, and so I find myself in the uncomfortable position of not being very attracted by Richard Fullerton.

"So why was he ever made sales chief in the first place? Well, we were smaller then, I guess. And he was just kind of there. A solid record with Kenyon and Eckhardt, and a really industrious worker all the way around. A genuine producer, as they say, everything you could ask in a man . . ."

Through smoke rings—five—Adrian smiled to hasten him on. Enough was enough.

"Still, there *are* two things greatly in his disfavor. He's not very original, not inventive. And his men aren't exactly passionate about him one way or the other. So, anyway, sound reasoning or not, there it is."

Adrian smiled on. "Which clears the way for Bobby as head of Programming."

David nodded. "It's the only sensible course, Adrian. At least for now. But with one condition. A very big one. And that's that all major programming moves be talked over with you, actually cleared with you, which in effect practically doubles your responsibilities without doubling your salary. And of course both of you will report directly to me, no one between us."

"Oh? What happens to Marty Levitt? I notice you haven't mentioned him. If you don't mind."

"I don't mind at all. He's the fly in the ointment, of course. But then, some sonofabitch always has to pay, right? Mr. Levitt, I'm afraid, is going to be placed in a pretty sensitive position. He's going to have to make a lot of decisions between tonight and tomorrow morning. You see, I'm going to dispense with the position of general manager. It's just never been a very workable structure. All right on the station level, but for a network . . ." Hands spread in that boyish way of his; when hadn't it bought him the world?

"What then?" said Adrian.

"Then," said David, "I ask Marty Levitt to take back his old post but at his current salary and with a new title. Executive vice president and general counsel for the television network."

"In other words, everybody's reporting directly to you again?"

"More or less, yes."

"But I thought . . ."

"I know, I know. You think I'm as crazy as Ellen does, taking the whole cockamamie thing on again. But until you and Bobby are ready—at least until I feel absolutely certain you and Bobby are ready, that the Board feels you're ready—that's how it's got to be. I'll need a good administrative man, though, and I'm thinking of asking Selwyn Coe to take it. Assistant to the president, some such thing. Selwyn's very good at getting things done. Organized as hell, as you know. And the station guys like him, even more they trust him, which is important as hell at a time like this. We're not exactly cock-of-the-walk these days, you know."

"You do realize how I feel about Sales, don't you? I mean, frankly, the kind of necessary evil I've always found it—"

"Of course I realize it, that's *why* I'm asking you to do it. When you're sitting in that great big wonderful overall heaven, you'll have to damn sure know how feet feel on the ground. Besides, I've every reason to believe you'll become invaluable there, as I have in every other area you've worked. It's also where I got my start, you know. Pounding the beat. I'm sorry Bobby is missing out on the experience. But dealing with advertisers, agencies, even the salesmen . . ." He looked down for a moment, to the gold-framed picture of Bobby and Mandy Jo when they were children, one of only three or four objects on his desk. "He just couldn't hack it I'm afraid."

Adrian changed the subject quickly. "Who'd head up Station Relations?" he asked.

David shrugged. "Ben Messina, I suppose. Or better yet, Pete Grimm. Another crowd pleaser with the station guys. And with George Kruger from WTAI in Tulsa practically a shoo-in for chairman of the Board of Governors next year, a shrewd move. He and Pete grew up together."

So there it was. Take it or leave it. There clearly wasn't room for very much addendum in David's eyes.

"Does Bobby know?" he asked.

"Only vaguely. Only enough to tell me that if it weren't satisfactory with you, *entirely* satisfactory with you, and that if by some crazy outside chance you were to decide to take a walk, then he'd walk with you."

Adrian smiled. "Greater friend hath no man."

"You might say, you just might say."

But there were details still; nagging ones.

Like Jerry McAlister.

"I want him moved, Adrian. Out of Programming, I mean. I know how you feel about him, but it's just not his area. He simply can't cut it there. I'd be perfectly amenable to his taking over an area like Public Relations, say, but Programming? Sorry, Adrian, but it's the one thing I'll absolutely insist that Bobby do. Besides. It just might be the perfect way to move young Banner up. Lord knows the kid's proved himself enough."

So there it was. All folded, set in the carton, wrapped with patience and care, and ready for mailing. In a way, no matter his very mixed emotions on this very mixed-up day, Adrian had to hand it to the Old Man. He was virtually revamping the personality structure of the entire television network without having to go outside for a single man.

"All things being equal," he said now, "I look forward to lunching with both you and Bobby at Twenty-one tomorrow. I think we all deserve a good three-martini lunch. Okay by you?"

"No," said Adrian, "it is not okay by me."

Just the look on David's face was worth it all.

"Four martinis," he said, thereby ushering in yet another era at UBC.

BUT WITHOUT MARK BANNER.

The one condition that Robert exacted was that Steve Kerimidas be named vice president in charge of Program Development, with

Tony Parr appointed director of the unit, directly under him. Also reporting to him would be his wife, Beverly, who as program coordinator would serve as liaison between the network and the outside programming suppliers. This left Mark to take on the title and duties of assistant manager of daytime programming or seek greener pastures somewhere else. Quietly (and bitterly, though the sonofabitch would never know it), the wonder-boy creator of *The Sharon Moore Show* submitted his letter of resignation and within a month had moved himself and Vivian, as well as his secretary, Edith Stewart, out to the West Coast, where he was made an associate producer for M-G-M Television in Culver City.

It was the first time in their professional lives together that Robert and Adrian came anywhere near an out-and-out rupture.

"Bobby, you're insane! The hottest young programming guy in the whole frigging setup and you blow it not two days after you take over your job! Bobby, I could kick the shit out of you. I really could kick the shit out of you."

They were in Adrian's old office, Robert's new one. Already the alterations were glaring. It was as if Arrabella had sneaked back in the night with her mother's *fin de siècle* furniture in tow. A Lemuel Fryer portrait of her hung on one of the off-white walls.

"I hardly need any threats from you this morning, Adrian."

"And I don't give a flying fuck what you need! Does your dad know this?"

"He does."

"And he *approves* it?"

"I didn't say that."

"Then you'd better say something, and quick!"

Robert was the color of the day outside—gray and white by turns. The blue and yellow pills being rushed to his tongue were the only real color about him. "I don't believe I owe any explanation to . . . to you or . . . anybody. . . ." Trailing off, Adrian already out the door, Robert knew he was on his way to David.

In less than ten minutes David was in the chair across from him, his quick scan of the office registering an obvious distaste for what he saw; what he had been surrounded by since the day he married Arrabella.

"You didn't exactly spell things out for me, did you, Bobby?"

Robert hesitated. "You were in such a hurry, and the other phone ringing, and it all seemed so, well, relatively unimportant, I thought . . . Well, he isn't exactly a top executive, father. One freak piece of luck with that Moore girl and everyone acts as though they'd seen the Second Coming. Certainly nothing to cause such an uproar. . . ."

"You have exactly one hour, Robert, to have Mark Banner in your office, or you in his, with the offer of director of Program Development, a vice-presidency of it promised within the year. One hour."

It was too late, of course. After Robert's failure, Adrian tried, and ultimately David himself, but Mark had seen the handwriting on the wall: *Rule 1. Have under you anyone as good as you, but never, never have anyone even the slightest bit better.*

"I'll tell you this, Mark," said Adrian, as they parted at the door to Adrian's office. "You'll be coming back here one day, and you'll be coming back in style. You can believe it."

When he got back to their apartment, Vivian—half-crying, laughing, unnerved by the events of the last few hours—informed him that in seven months or so he would be a father.

For the moment, his bitter exodus from UBC was forgotten. There was joy in him then; pride. In both of them.

49

"You DARLING BOY. I do believe you have a really exceptional staying power. A really exceptional staying power."

"It's all mental. I mean, a kind of cerebral discipline. I learned the value of that when I was five years old."

"Five years old?"

"Well, the discipline part, anyway. I mean, for just about every kind of human activity."

"Oh, my. You do have a way of expressing yourself, Freddie. A most authoritative way."

"It's really not all that much of an achievement, you know. I mean, fucking is mostly an intellectual exercise anyway."

"I wish I could buy that, dear. I really wish I could. Lord knows I've been called one of the grandest lays around, but I can't recall anyone ever suggesting the *brain* did it."

"You'd be surprised at just how sophisticated a mental aptitude you show for it, Cousin Joslyn."

"Oh, Lord! There you go again. Your lovely cock in my hand and you're still calling me Cousin Joslyn! I'll lay you ten to one it's Mandy Jo who has you calling me that, isn't it?"

"You might say she kind of suggests it. Once in a while. She says it's out of respect for your age."

"I thought as much. Hah! Poor darling would have to be given ammonia if she could see how old and cousinly I am right now. Hah?"

"It's a wonder to me your husband always looks so up-and-at-'em. If your performance with him is anything like it is with me, I'd imagine he *would* be old before his time."

"You love. But don't waste tears for Adrian. He gets his."

"So I hear. From half of UBC's secretarial pool."

"Why, you little bastard! No, bitch. You know, there *is* a lot of the bitch in you, young Freddie."

"I should hope so. A creature without venom makes a very poor lover indeed."

"Why, you know . . . you're right. You really are, you're right. Who wrote that, anyway?"

"Wrote what?"

"What you said."

"Nobody. I made it up. Just now. When you practically bit my head off. Take it easy, fair lady, that member has miles to go before it sleeps."

"You must have had an awful lot of experience for a boy your age."

"Considerable, yes."

"And so modest, too. I'm sure you'll be one of UBC's most shining assets."

"UBC? Who said anything about UBC?"

"Well, don't bite *my* head off. I simply assumed."

"Well, don't. I have much more elegant plans for *my* life. When I graduate from college, I mean. It's my intention, if it hasn't occurred to you . . . any of you . . . to go into the theatre, the home of *real* art, *real* life."

"My. We are the little uppity, aren't we? Does television really turn you off so much? One would think, given your obvious admiration of your 'Uncle Bob,' that you'd be puppying right behind him, all the way."

"So far as I'm concerned, madame, television is for the very lowest —or at least the very commonest—intellect in our society. That a man of Uncle Bob's obvious superiority and sensitivity should have had put upon him the lowliest of arts . . ."

"Hold on there, buster. I happen to have a pretty sizable stake in this 'lowliest of arts,' in case it's slipped your mind."

"It never slipped my mind at all. I'm hardly one to equate the source of one's income with his—or in this case, *her*—more superior charms."

"Sweet Jesus! You're something else. You really are. You're something else."

"A something else you obviously can't get enough of. Even though, as I'm sure you'll concede, there's really quite enough of it to go around."

"Something else! Now, tell *me* something, dear. What is it you plan to do in your superior . . . art?"

"Who knows? Produce. Direct. Right now I'm trying my hand at writing. I'm pretty well thought of at Yale Drama School."

"I'm sure you are. But just how do you plan to finance this brilliant career? Until you're earning your own keep, I mean."

"Who knows? My father . . . M.J. . . . . your uncle David . . . Uncle Bob. I kind of see myself as Pip, if you want to know."

"Pip?"

"As in Dickens' *Great Expectations.*"

"Which is exactly what I've got right now."

"Right you are!"

"ADRIAN?"

"What?"

"Do you fool around at the network? With secretaries?"

"Do I what?"

"Do you fool around at the network? With secretaries? I've been getting some rumblings here and there, and if there's one thing in this world I won't stand for, Adrian, it's a public humiliation, particularly since it's *I* who am the major stockholder in United . . ."

"Yeah. Fuck off, Joslyn."

(*So* sure of himself. . . . He must know about Brenda, her and Brenda, he must. *Must.* Bobby's sure to have told him, sure to have. Talk about somebody having somebody by the balls, dear God . . .)

"IRENE?"

"Yes, darling?"

"Have you ever mentioned our . . . our thing? I mean, to anybody? *Anybody.*"

"Of course not. I may be breaking all ten commandments at one sitting, Mr. Miller, but I dare not even entertain the notion of fracturing the eleventh."

"Okay, I bite. What's the eleventh?"

"Thou shalt not tell, should you be one of Mr. David Abrams' secretaries, that you are copping the joint of one of his most treasured executives."

"Okay, doll, just wondered."

"Why? Some particular reason?"

"My wife seems to have an inkling, that's all."

"And it would wound her most grievously should the illicit relationship be revealed?"

"Something like that."

"Because I'm David Abrams' secretary or because I'm black?"

"Come off it, Irene. You know it's never been anything like that. Not with us, babe. I mean it could be anybody . . ."

"Liar. But you're a nice hunk of meat, stinker, and I just happen to go in for pastels this season."

"Irene, please . . ."

"Hump it, honky."

". . . and it wasn't my being Mr. Abrams' secretary at all, it was my exotic coloring, the old fart."

"I still don't see what you're getting out of it, Irene. I mean, if ever there was a relationship with nowhere to go . . ."

"I might say the same thing about ours, sweetie. Mightn't I?"

"That's different. At least with me you're making a charitable contribution."

"I'm what?"

"Helping me maintain at least half a dignity. I mean, not only am I fifty-three years old come August, but as you know, I *do* swing both ways."

"Is he a nigger, too?"

"No, just thinks like one."

"You mother."

"But come to think of it, why do you keep seeing me like this?"

"Why? That's the easiest question I ever had to answer. If I drink a few too many sometimes, and feel like braggin' it around a little, it is kind of nice to be able to say I'm making it with the great Barry White. Which doesn't do you any harm either, chum. Makes all those rumors about you and Gerald McAlister that much less believable."

"My God! You *know?*"

"SHE KNOWS."

"Well, that should teach you."

"Should teach me what?"

"To stick with your own kind, precious. You *know* the trouble women can get you in."

"And do *you* know something, Jerry?"

"What, precious?"

"I may be a homosexual, or a bisexual, or whatever the world chooses to tag it these days. But you, McAlister—you're a fag. An out-and-out fag. In *every* sense of the word."

"Kiss me."

". . . and that's the *only* reason I came to you with this, Bobby. I mean, Adrian *does* mean so much to both of us that anything we can do to . . . well, nip it in the bud is the best way of saying it, I guess . . . anything we can do to serve him, protect him. I mean, if your father were ever to . . ."

"Thank you, Jerry. You were right to come to me. And I won't embarrass you by trying to find out how you learned it. It will be taken care of, I assure you. It's quite simple, actually. When couldn't a girl like . . . what did you say her name was? Irene? . . . Well, when couldn't somebody like that be bought and sold?"

". . . which settles everything sensibly, I think. And no one either the wiser or the more miserable for it."

"Except the girl. Except the poor, insulted, miserable girl. I'm sorry, Bobby. It makes me sick. It's what I've hated, despised, abhorred all my life. It's the kind of thing—"

"Honest to God, Beverly, I can't understand you. I thought you cared so much about preserving human dignity—"

"*Human dignity?* Buying that girl off? *That* is human dignity? Well, pardon me! I'm grateful for so much enlightenment, I really am. And to know that once again the honor and pride of UBC have been saved. Saved, saved, and saved."

"For all your sarcasm, Beverly, that *is* precisely what has happened."

"Gee. Gee whiz. Maybe now that you're so good at all this marvelous saving thing, you can come up with an equally brilliant solution to save our marriage."

"That was hardly necessary, Beverly."

"That was *very* necessary, Robert. While Adrian Miller's silly little to-do is being buried twenty thousand leagues under the sea, our little to-do—yours and mine, Mr. Abrams—is about to burst apart like an overripe tomato. You know it and I know it. I wonder how much bread it will take to buy *me* off."

"Beverly, *please.* This isn't the time or place—"

"Isn't it? Well, I think it is. Both the time *and* the place. Do you realize how long it's been, Bobby? Do you know how many months it's been?"

"I'm sorry. I didn't realize that . . . that *that* part of it meant so much to you."

"Meant so much to *me*? Oh, dear God. You are sick, darling, you are. You've been unable to have an erection for almost a year now, Bobby. A year. A whole goddamn year. Whatever it was before we married, whatever it is now, you had better see a shrink whether you like it or not. Because no matter how much I like you, Bobby, no matter how much I *love* you, no matter how much our work together at the network means to me, I am *not* going to spend the rest of my years in a situation so—so *unhealthy*. That I . . . I am not, I am not, I am *not*. I presume I've made myself clear."

"Very clear. Thank you."

"*Nor* should you be unmindful of the fact that others find me attractive, that others—"

"*Good night*, Beverly."

". . . my fault actually. I should have realized what was happening, what you wanted, what . . . You're a complex chick, Joslyn, you really are. You have a passion for Adrian that won't quit, the man can do anything he wants with you, talk to you the way he wouldn't talk to a dog, and I've seen you look at other men as if you could tear their clothes right off them. While all along it's *me* you've been wanting, too. *Me*. In *that* way. Sometimes, between you and Bobby, I think I'm cracking but good. Bisexual, oversexed, crazy-sexed, I really couldn't care less. Although I will be fair with you, Joslyn. I will be that."

"Fair with me, Beverly? I'm not sure I understand."

"I shall never tell anyone, not even Bobby, what you've been trying to do. God knows you've got enough inside you to take care of without the whole outside cracking up, too."

"Now, aren't you kind. Was there ever a person quite so gracious, so noble, so kind. I shall now say to you, Beverly, what Adrian says to me, every night . . ."

"AND so you're off to school again. I'll miss you loads, Freddie, I really will."

"There'll be other times, Cousin Joslyn, other days. You're really one great lay, lady, I'll say that for you. One hell of a beautiful lay."

"My. That should hold me for a few weeks, shouldn't it? And where's the harm, when you think about it? Our being together like this, I mean. As long as nobody gets hurt . . ."

"Yeah. *That* we couldn't take for a minute, could we?"

"Little devil. Now get your clothes on and get out of here. Adrian's coming home early tonight with a tax man. Something about my UBC stock. And nothing, my pet, must be allowed to get in the way of that."

"No, ma'am. Nothing. But one more lick at it? Good girl! Just think of it as a thousand shares of UBC stock."

50

THE SOUTHERN CALIFORNIA SUN is unlike sun anywhere else in the country. It is true that it's visible (even through clouds) on more days than in any other place on the mainland, Florida included. It is also true that its rays are stronger, or in any case *seem* stronger. It is true, as well, that it can be more monotonous in Southern California than anywhere else; the eye seems to tire more quickly. It's the jewel that the country's great expanse of sky has to offer—the most cursed and admired, treasured and slandered star. When it is there—day after day—it is worshiped to the point of obsession. When it is not there—day after day—it is roundly abused, as though it were the black sheep in the family. A more fickle star, a more capricious prima donna is not to be found; at least not in all Southern California, much less the rest of the continental United States.

How Vivian Banner, after a time, came to hate it! Whether logical or not, rational or not, it would represent to her (for the rest of her life, she knew) the loss of her baby, the reminder that she could never have another, and—although she didn't recognize it at the time—the beginning of her difficulty with Mark.

But how she had loved it in the beginning!

"Mark, Mark, you couldn't have pleased me more if you'd actually flown me to heaven."

They had rented a small apartment in a complex in the Hollywood Hills, so that every day of her pregnancy—well, almost every day—was spent poolside in the tenants' garden and playground area.

It had toasted her, that sun. Still deep in the days of Eden, she had taken from it what she took from Mark: a warmth, a strength, a kind of burning protection that seared away what dividers there were between night and day, making night and day one, inseparable, the lover's continuum, the sun and Mark the same gods, the same arms.

It had been good then—just to sleep, come awake. To drift lazily between sleep and wakefulness, nature's child; swell dreamily through each of them, nourishment warm for her own. There was the settling in, of course; settling down: domestic needs, chores. Food to be bought, prepared, eaten, swept off. Wine to be tasted, still sweet on each other's lips after love, after sleep. People to see, hear, dine with, laugh with; new acquaintances, friends, they both made them so easily. Clothes to be taken off, put on, run through washers, driers, smell sweet again, pure. A movie to see, a book to read. Thoughts to be had, shared; forgotten in the timeless heartbeats, the journey through time itself; the baby to kick, to laugh, to sing out its joy in coming (it did, she knew it; could feel it, hear it). Most of all there was Mark himself, the new job, adjustments to it. Then suddenly the swift, uncertain descent into darkness, whirlwind to unconsciousness; crash through acres of pain, miles of crazed screams. Days then suddenly cold, nights colder, ice. His arms reaching out to her, coldest of all. Coldest of all—the arms.

How she'd hated it then—the sun. Damn California sun.

MARK HADN'T LIKED IT from the first. The lush world on which dreams are made was tiresome and pettily competitive and devoid of stimulus. His initial assignment at Metro—associate producer on a half-hour anthology oater, *Old Trail Tales* (not a UBC project, thank God; a Universal Oil–sponsored series in national syndication)—was an unrelenting bore, the studio politics a pain in the ass. Film making had never held any particular enchantment for him; not even the weeks he had spent out here during the filming of *The Sharon Moore Show* had been particularly satisfying. But start to pull it all together, get the talk about it going, get it onto the schedule, see the publicity and promotion wheels start to turn—*there* was the nut, baby. *There* was the excitement.

Too, in the highly unionized atmosphere of studio activity, you were severely restricted. True, as an associate producer he was in on most of the production details surrounding the show, from quick-meet sessions of rewriting to the interminable dailies to the projection-room editing (slapdash indifference, most of the time) to the creation of promotion material for the stations carrying the series. But it wasn't the delicious madness of a hundred projects at once, it wasn't the diversity of network scheduling, it wasn't . . . UBC.

Which he tried not to think about. Looking at the handful of pros instead. The producer of the series, Sid Merrick, was easy to work with. The salary was good, better than the network's by a mile. His secretary from New York, Edith Stewart, was a genius at meeting crises or deadlines head on. The weather *was* more congenial: he could drive the forty or so minutes from the house to the studio, twice every day, behind the wheels of a Mercedes, his very own Mercedes, driving long into the Valley with Vivian on weekends.

Then there was Vivian herself. It was as though she were made for the place. He'd always supposed that pregnant women were pretty oblivious of place, simply ill-tempered with the growth inside them. But Vivian, riper by the day ("She carries bigger than any tall girl I ever in my life seen," an aging character actress in one of the upper level apartments said every day, twice a day), was in those first months nothing but cheer itself, sometimes amazing him with a vitality he himself could rarely match.

And then there was the "hand in," as they said. He saw the Coast's network boys as often as possible, soaking up talk of the webs, of UBC, as others soaked up the sun. And when Adrian Miller was on the Coast (which was frequently now, some 95 percent of nighttime programming churned from the Hollywood factories) he made a point always to see him, even rearranging shooting schedules or editing sessions to accommodate him.

So all in all, give some here, there, it wasn't really so bad; he was young, full of beans, he would make it clear to the top, it never crossed his mind that he wouldn't. And as long as Viv . . .

It happened so precipitately that before he could even catch his breath (or at least be aware again that he breathed) the baby was gone, Vivian was critical, and the fucking sun was strutting its stuff across the white noon sky.

It was a massive hemorrhaging, the baby was stillborn, and Vivian remained at Cedars of Lebanon for three weeks. After that it was never the same. And he was gentle with her, God knew he tried to be, but he was repulsed, repudiated, so that in time he as well fell victim to extreme melancholy, to guilt and even self-pity, and began hitting the bottle some, however casually and even unconsciously.

It was on one of these nights, when he had had three or four drinks with Jeb Lee (an administrative assistant at Universal, where there was a job opening he might be interested in) at Stefanino's on Sunset, that the new TV comedy sensation, his own personal discovery—Sharon Moore—came in.

And smiled.

And smiled.

It was enough.

VIVIAN NEVER KNEW just when her abrasive treatment of Mark began, or in truth just how or why. The loss of the baby, of course, along with the knowledge that she could never have another, was in the early postpartum days an understandable reaction, hysteria itself not exactly alien to such a condition. But as the days became weeks, the weeks months, the defection took on a kind of permanence, even the gradual return to lovemaking an awkward and (on her part) mechanical submission, the hours afterward as strained as the ones before.

She learned about Sharon Moore—and the probable others. The knowledge only added to the evils she had begun to magnify in her mind. Evils that only extreme acts of exorcism could lay to rest. The California warmth and ease she had loved so much in the beginning— they were now devils in angels' clothing. The studios, as phoney and decadent in their neo-television age as they had been in the dream-factory days of the studio czars and casting couches. The likes of overnight successes such as Sharon Moore—surely they were more seductive here, more accessible here, than they had ever been in the more solid, sensible East. And Mark himself: wanting him, not wanting him, blaming him, exonerating him—how crazy could she be? But once they were away (pray God) from this despicable place, it would all be different, be the same again, the way it was in the beginning when just the look of him would enchant—wouldn't it? Wouldn't it? Maybe back in New York, back with UBC . . . After all, she *did* miss being the wife of somebody on his way up, in the greatest competitive city in the world—didn't she? Well, didn't she?

Mark sent her home to Oklahoma City for an extended rest, where she could be spoiled little Vivian Seaforth again, but when she returned there was little, if any, discernible difference.

Still, he did love her. Wanted to love her. Life went on. Except that more and more often when she needed him, he didn't seem to be there. Even when he *was* there, she couldn't really see him. He might as well have been dead.

THE IDEA of a late-night talk show had for some time been gestating in a corner of Adrian's mind. Daring it certainly was, in the face of established and formidable competition, plus the prospect of months of research to hit on just the right format, the right personality, not to mention a financial outlay that would send management reeling. On taking over Sales he could see firsthand the extraordinary potential that such an operation held out for greater spot participations, like daytime television, in which close identification with a popular prime-time show or personality was not the goal. It was a morning in June, 1966, that he again broached the idea to Robert.

"You're insane" was Robert's initial reaction. "With prime time still in the state it's in, with the absolutely ridiculous new schedules for

the fall, with father upset as he is—no, thank you. Just the development of it alone would throw the Board into a panic. Your timing,
Adrian—my God."

The "absolutely ridiculous" 1966–67 schedules boasted such titles as
*Mission: Impossible, The Monkees, The Dating Game, The Newlywed
Game, The Green Hornet, T.H.E. Cat, The Girl from U.N.C.L.E.*, *Run
Buddy Run, The Secret Life of Henry Phyffe*, Phyllis Diller, Milton
Berle, Tammy Grimes, and *Batman*. Not to mention the ones on UBC
—*The Blue Bat, The Old Ghost, The P. T. Scarum Horror Show,
Silverdust, Graveyard George, Monster Spy*, and *Godzilla II*. Only the
three-hour revival of Cole Porter's 1940s musical *Mexican Hayride* and
the two-hour taped dramas like Tennessee Williams' *A Streetcar
Named Desire*, Chekhov's *The Three Sisters*, and Eugene O'Neill's *The
Hairy Ape* had kept him from either resigning or going the head-in-
oven route. Even the O'Neill project had its irony. "It's a cinch for a
forty share in this kind of season," Adrian had said. "How many millions do you think will tune in expecting the same crap as *T.H.E. Cat*
and *The Blue Bat* and *Godzilla*? . . . By the way, Bobby, I take it as a
sign of your growing maturity, not to mention corruption, that you not
only don't reach for a pill, you don't even bat an eye. Seriously, it's
the perfect time, Bobby. A literate talk show is the ideal antidote to
the whole prime-time mess. Think now. Just think. Don't sleep tonight, not a wink. Just let it all go through your mind, and we'll have
breakfast together at the Brasserie. Okay?"

At eight-thirty the next morning, over *café au lait* and fresh crois-
sants, Robert said, "Just what did you mean by 'literate'?"

It was the question he had expected. "Afraid you'd never ask," he
said. "Because that, old buddy, is the key to the whole thing. What do
all of the current laties have in common? I'll tell you what. They have
guests that are the same old show-business faces you could throw up
from you've seen them so much. As if a big movie or a hit TV series
or a smash Broadway play suddenly makes them overnight the Kants
and Schopenhauers and Santayanas of our time. You with me?"

"So far. Go on."

"Now, who's missing? I'll tell you who's missing. Lewis Mumford
is missing. Saul Bellow is missing. Will and Ariel Durant are missing.
Mark Van Doren and Alfred Kazin are missing. Philip Johnson is missing. Jonas Salk is missing. Aaron Copeland is missing. George Oppen-
heimer is missing. Arthur Miller is missing. Archibald MacLeish is
missing. Stephen Spender, Jimmy Baldwin, Norman Cousins, Mary
McCarthy . . ."

"All right! All right! If I'd known you were going to sit up with an
intellectual *Who's Who* all night while I was busy *thinking* . . ."

Adrian hadn't seen a smile quite so spontaneous on Robert's increasingly dour features in the old coon's age. He said softly, "In-trigued?"

Robert nodded. "I was just wondering what father would say if he heard all those names. 'Six percent share, if you're lucky.' I can just hear him." He cupped his hands under his chin. "I wonder where in the world we'd find a host who's charming, erudite, witty, photogenic, and identifiable with, all in one unlikely package."

It was such an honest-to-God problem that they shared another homemade croissant. . . .

A week later, at dinner with David, Ellen, and Beverly at La Cara-velle, before seeing a new Albee play, Robert brought up the idea.

"I have to be honest," he said. "Anything resembling a carbon of the kind of thing we have now would be a disgrace. Not to mention financial disaster. This has to be the real thing, the genuine article, or we're wasting our breath."

David, mouth loaded with *coq au vin*, said, "Tell me. Does Adrian really think advertisers would take to a show like this? Bette Davis, Shelley Winters, Buddy Hackett, Sammy Davis—these I can see. These people sell products. But Saul Bellow?"

"That's just the *point*. There are any number of quality products that are primed for selective audiences. If they just had somewhere to go—"

"And the host? An intellectual Johnny Carson you think you'll find?"

"There was Jack Paar, of course," said Ellen. "But I doubt that's quite what you have in mind. And you have to be so careful, in this area particularly. There are so many phoneys . . ."

"And if there's one thing Big Long climbs the walls over it's a phoney." David laughed. "He spots them before they open their mouths." He paused thoughtfully. "It would still have to be someone with huge appeal," he said. "And all eggheads for guests is death before you start. You'd have to have your Phyllis Dillers and Myron Cohens, no matter what literary lion you throw in the cage."

"A kind of sneaky sneak-in, hmn?" said Beverly.

David nodded. "It's a rough time for the whole idea," he said. "All these street riots, campus upheavals, bombings, flag burnings. Draft dodgers. Most people blame the eggheads and Communists, and you know it. Good idea. Bad timing."

"And tough shit." Beverly had come around to saying pretty much anything she wanted when she was with them. Ellen ate it up, she knew. She was never quite sure of David.

"I'd say that just about sums it up," said David. Smiling, though.

"Has anything changed?" said Ellen. "Ever? How many times in my career was I on the most-wanted-pinko lists, and somehow I managed to go on being fairly popular, you should pardon my immodesty."

David put down his knife and fork. "I don't get the point. What does what happened in the forties and fifties have to do with a late-night talk show?"

"Everything," she said. "When you think about it. And that's the least you can do, you know. Think about it. Personally, I think it would be a little fresh air that the business pretty desperately needs."

It was almost as if she had cast the deciding vote. The next weeks, months, were times of unusual marketing and audience research, which was of course as far as David would go for the moment. But at least some machinery had been put in motion, an idea given light. Compromise, when and if it came, was still a year or so off. Meanwhile Robert knew that he owed a great deal to Ellen Curry; knew that she knew it too. Another of those thin-edged ironies that crept in and out of his life like hungry leeches. Had it been Arrabella who'd said the very same words, the project more than likely would never have been heard from again. And it had been Arrabella who'd owned the controlling stock in UBC. Maybe the difference was that Ellen owned it in David Abrams.

IT WAS DURING premiere week in September, 1966, that Robert learned that Beverly was having what he himself was still old-fashioned enough to refer to as an "affair."

Steve Kerimidas, UBC's vice president in charge of program development, was younger, of course, and passionately attached to the United Broadcasting Company, but these hadn't deterred him. He had even taught her how to say "It's bigger than both of us" in Greek.

One of the projects Beverly had become particularly interested in over the previous several months was a projected 1967–68 series called *Carrie*. This was an hour-long comedy-drama with music about a young black woman and her small son and mother-in-law, musical-variety performers who were finding it tough going in show business, which, like most other established orders of the time, was subject to the white boss man's consciousness and largesse. It was to star the popular nightclub singer Diana Jones, a young newcomer named Billy Joe Hill, and the veteran actress-singer Sister Rae, to whom David had given her first break in broadcasting in the 1920s, and Ellen Curry a recurring guest spot in her radio shows of the thirties and forties. Beverly had extolled its virtues to Robert until he was "black in the face" (one of his rare stabs at humor), and subsequently Steve Kerimidas had been given the substantial budget to bring in a pilot film. Beverly had been on the Coast with him several times during the preproduction and production stages of the project.

Robert would have liked to think that he learned about them accidentally, but given the present climate of the Program Department in New York, this was obviously unlikely. And since it was Tony Parr from whom he'd learned it (Parr openly and actively seeking to discredit Kerimidas at the drop of a rating point), it was more unlikely still. The executive dining rooms, separated from each other by walls as fragile as Japanese partitions, were hardly places where you'd be saying to an outside producer in a voice several octaves above your usual, "And that pretty-boy Greek is pumping the broad right under poor Abrams' nose," when you knew perfectly well that the man was lunching with Bryson Randolph in the dining room directly on your left.

It was a week before Robert confronted her with it.

"The jig's up, huh?" she said, seeing his mirrored image as she let down her hair. They were in the bedroom of a new and larger apartment that they had taken during the summer, less than a block from the old one on Sutton Place. It was well after midnight.

"I might have known you'd have some wonderful bright riposte," he said. "Is nothing beyond you, Beverly?"

The look on her face in the slow turn she made in her dressing-table chair was incredulous. "Dear God," she said, "am I hearing right? A man who hasn't been able to fuck his wife for almost two years, and he has the audacity to act the outraged husband? What did you expect I was doing all that time, angel? Finger—"

"*Shut up!*"

It was another week before he spoke of it again.

"You're still seeing him?"

"Yes, Bobby, I'm still seeing him. *All* of him."

"And you expect me to sit here and do nothing."

"That's what you've been doing, isn't it? For two years?"

He was drinking heavily again lately. It showed in his walk, in his eyes.

"I fired Kerimidas this morning," he said. "You can think what you want about it. Do what you want about it. I'd hoped . . . I'd hoped that the things we have in common . . . the work . . ."

Toward three in the morning, four, hearing her slight breathing, knowing she was awake, he said, knowing even as he said it how ridiculous he sounded, "Damn you, Beverly, oh, God damn you. Not for screwing that creep. I can understand *that*, I'm not entirely a fool, but to be so obvious about it, rub my face in it. By God, Beverly, you are one cruel woman, and I hope to God you someday—" and bit back the rest, feeling as humiliated by his outburst as by what had caused it.

Beverly and Steve left the network's employ early in October. She instituted divorce proceedings the same week. Mental cruelty. She moved in with Steve Kerimidas in his small apartment in the Village. Some people said they deserved each other.

Tony Parr remained at the network but was passed over for the Program Development post for which he was in line. Instead a thirty-one-year-old media director from the J. Walter Thompson advertising agency, Clifford Gold, was brought in to fill the vacancy. Parr walked out in a fit of rage. David said little and was unusually tight-lipped through the whole thing.

STEVE LILLY was twenty-one years old on February 8, 1967. To celebrate, he got married.

He had come to New York via Chicago from the UBC studios in Los Angeles, where he'd gotten his first job as a page while taking business administration courses at UCLA. He'd continued his studies in Chicago, where he had served for two years in the radio network's publicity department. With him to New York, where he was made a salesman for the radio network, he brought a degree in business administration from the University of Chicago and a 4F draft card detailing an inner-ear ailment that had plagued him since childhood. Vietnam was seven thousand miles away and UBC just forty-three blocks from his brownstone walk-up apartment on West Eighty-first Street. Life was a pretty fair sonofabitch all around.

Steve's mother had always bragged that he was one for the girls, and if Los Angeles and Chicago had been open season, New York was without a gun law to its name. Thursday's, Friday's, Maxwell's Plum —the New York woods were full of them.

He met Beth Jennings at Friday's. She was probably the prettiest girl he had met on any of his nightly excursions. Her creamy complexion; red-tinted auburn hair; moist, slightly open mouth; brown-gold eyes—he was in love with her before she ever spoke a word.

Their first meeting was in the crowded winter quarters for the circus-followers of the Hampshires, Fire Island, the Jersey coast, and Lauderdale, even in the din and packed so tightly against the bar that their diaphragms struck up a speaking acquaintance as well.

"You like places like this?"

"I can't abide them."

"Why do you come, then?"

"Who knows? It's the thing to do, I suppose. My girlfriends come and I just seem to float along with them. That's what I am, I guess. A floater."

"You work in the city?"

"Korvette's."

"A clerk?"

"Secretary."

"Sounds . . ."

"Dismal. I know. But then why should it be different from everything else in life?"

"Jesus. You sound like a case for the East River."

"Not at all. I'm just stoical about everything. Which isn't a bad way to be, really. It gets you through an awful lot of bad times."

"I suppose. But then, knockout that you are, I guess you're pretty much in the driver's seat in places like this. Just this minute I see six, no, seven, nine, twelve, I've lost count, eyes runnin' all over you. All up and down you."

"I know. And it pleases me, I guess. But that's as far as it goes. I've never gone out with anybody I've met here. I probably never will. I'm really awful with strangers."

"The hell you say."

"Really."

"You could knock me over with a feather. Care for a drink?"

"No, thank you. I don't drink."

"Then why a place like this?"

"I told you. My girlfriends . . ."

"Okay. I dig you. Weed?"

"That neither. Pretty rough to get to know, aren't I?"

"I'm in there. Sweatin' bullets, but I'm in there."

"What do you do?"

"Jobwise?"

"Yes."

"Account executive."

"With an advertising agency?"

"A radio network. UBC."

"Oh. What exactly does an account executive do?"

"Sells. You know. Time. Sells time."

"Oh. I thought people like that were called salesmen."

"Account executive sounds better."

"More important, you mean."

"Somethin' like that. Takes some of the rat out of rat race. Mind if I have another?"

"Not at all. I like seeing men drink. They look more joyful when they drink. Are you a good salesman . . . account executive?"

"The best."

"I wouldn't doubt it. You're from the South, aren't you?"

"How'd you guess?"

"The way you say everything so crisplike. If I weren't pretty good at accents, I could have sworn you were from Boston."

"Hey! A sense of humor too."

"Sometimes."

"Reads great on you. You from New York?"

"Idaho."

"Sun Valley?"

"Near it. Idaho Falls."

"How the hell'd you get here?"

"I flew."

"Come on. You know what I mean."

"I don't know. I just up and came, I guess. Big cities excite me. I mean, really turn me on. I just wished I liked them more."

"Well, I'll tell you somethin'. They like you. Scotch on the rocks. Make it a double. Thanks. The way these guys get around to you every two hours you've got to like plan ahead."

"I know. Where are you from in the South?"

"Louisiana. Mannerville. You ever heard of it?"

"I think so. Somewhere. Do you miss it?"

"I'll never go back."

"Are you always this happy? I mean, you kind of radiate it, you know? I imagine people like being around you."

"Thank you. That's a nice thing to say."

"I said it because I meant it."

"That's why it's so nice. What's your name, anyway?"

"Beth. Beth Jennings. What's yours?"

"Lilly. Steve. Steve Lilly, that is. Well, here's to."

"Yes, here's to."

"Damn, it's a madhouse in here. Want to go over to Maxwell's?"

"No, thank you. I'm going home early. But thank you all the same."

"Okay. Some other time maybe."

"Yes. Some other time."

"Sure hot in here. You'd think it was August."

"Yes. Very warm."

"Very warm. Well . . . here's to."

He didn't take her home, of course. He went home instead with a stacked blonde, whose name by the time he met her he was too drunk to remember—or care.

He next saw Beth Jennings at Maxwell's Plum. And this time he did take her home. A large old brownstone apartment on West Seventy-second Street, which she shared with two other girls. And in front of which he kissed her good night, but that was all. It was the first night he'd gone without it for two months.

Why he married her he really wasn't certain. Except perhaps that she gave him something no other person had ever given him before, something he thought he'd never needed before. He told himself it was a kind of self-respect, but he knew it was somehow more complicated than that.

Anyway, they were married on his birthday and he had the honor and pleasure of teaching her to love, for she really was one of those 1960s freaks, a real-life, walking, talking virgin. They moved into an apartment on the Upper East Side, which he felt was essential to his position and ambition. She couldn't have cared less. UBC, with all its bigness and social aggression and life style that he reveled in, didn't cut any ice with her. But Steve . . . well, he'd already made it as far as she was concerned.

51

THE 1968–69 SEASON, like the 1967–68 season before it, was long on promotion, short on innovation. David called it a period of "shoring up." Sharper critics found words like "bland" and "mediocre" more descriptive. There were some (hell, many) who thought the commercials were more inventive than the programs.

There were milestones, of course: ABC's full-evening study of Africa. NBC's *Laugh-In*. UBC's *Carrie*, as well as its entry into the late-night field with *The Don Spinnet Show*, which the *New York Times* called "the most literate and sophisticated show ever introduced into the intelligent home," and for which Robert had had to compromise less than he'd expected, mainly because Spinnet himself, a remarkably polished and insightful young performer, called most of the shots. The ninety-minute program, although fully sponsored, had yet to make much of a dent in the Nielsens and was undoubtedly doomed to a thirteen-week fate, but the love affair with the press had brought the network more attention and commendation than anyone had even begun to anticipate.

In other areas, principally the networks' coverage of the Vietnam War, the networks themselves were a fierce battleground. The convention and election coverage, though more elaborate than ever, was "neither new nor reflective," as one critic commented, but then, as David remarked at one of the Sunday-night dinners (a tradition Ellen had upheld when David moved into her home in Mamaroneck), "So when were carnivals ever so new or provocative? The people never had it so good. When was the political process ever served by such coverage like we give it? And a goddamn money-loser at that. I'd like to see the *Times* and *Post* and *Chicago Tribune* say that!" Perhaps the most distinctive characteristic of the two "bidin' time" years (Steve Lilly's description of them later) was that there were theatrical-release movies on one or the other of the networks every night of the week.

In the spring of '68, Ellen made a return to television for the first time since she'd left it, in a ninety-minute special that UBC called *Ellen Returns.*

"David, I'm scared to death. You'd think I was doing five minutes on Ed Sullivan in 1949. I know I'll just stand there like a statue. Are you sure there's enough video tape in New York—just in case?"

They were at home, a week before the taping.

"You have a short memory, Star." He laughed. "I can't recall ever seeing you before a show when you didn't work up a sweat to kill a horse."

"Oh?" The coquettishness of her—that, too, after all the years. "Funny. I don't recall your being with me all those years."

He looked around, carefully, his eyes lighting here and there on particular items, on the coffered ceiling. "No, it's your house, all right," he said. "For a minute I thought it might be Arrabella's. Christ knows you sounded enough like her."

They both laughed.

Then she, seriously: "There's one very positive thing before going in. And that's the attention Bobby's giving the show. I know he'll never like me, never even accept me really, but he's a pro. You can't take that away from him. He's become a real pro."

"Yes, I guess he is. It's just that sometimes—"

"Sometimes?"

"Nothing. I suppose I'll never understand him, that's all. Anyway, I have no intention of getting into an analysis of my *verkochter* son and heir at this late date. Do the 'Blues in the Night' number for me again."

Ellen Returns took seven Emmy awards the following year, including Best Musical Variety Special and Best Performer in a Musical Variety Special. Ellen agreed tentatively to do another in the fall of '69.

THEY WERE long days for Robert. The network, although it hadn't recovered entirely from its disastrous '64–'65 showing, had at least managed a level of competence and respectability. Sales were good. The stock was far from depressed. There were several development pilots for the 1969–70 season that looked promising if not exactly breakthroughs. Clifford Gold was proving adequate, nothing more. It had become something of a truism in the industry that its "creative" people couldn't make it without a business administration degree.

The most conspicuous successes were the made-for-TV movies Robert had played such a large part in developing—ninety-minute films to fit a rigid schedule, but feature pictures of some originality in direction if not in content. They were already being called mini-movies, but it was a misnomer. Many of the films in theatrical packages were at least as short, some shorter. "They're the future of television," he had told his father, and he believed it.

There were other breadwinners in the current schedule, of course. *The Larry Lester Show,* and more recently *The Sharon Moore Show,* made much-needed copy for the company's annual reports.

Carrie, with its many black players, appeared to be the forerunner of other black-oriented projects. Certainly it had opened a number of closed doors.

Still, there was something missing, something lacking. Bryson Randolph had called it "event dynamism."

> *Remember when the principal topic of conversation in the morning was what you saw on television last night? Now it's what you didn't see, or didn't want to see.* Lucy, Ed Sullivan, Sid Caesar, Ellen Curry. *You couldn't wait to share a particular moment, a side-splitting bit. Or* Studio One, Philco Playhouse, Playhouse 90. *You could talk about them all day. Even the big quiz shows: they lasted at least until noon. But* The Man from U.N.C.L.E., The Flying Nun, Monster Spy? *A sense of excitement, a sense of involvement, a kind of event dynamism —these are what have been lost in TV's slick little journey to technical skill. Gloss covers up a multitude.*

"We're all in the same boat," Robert had told Adrian. "Movies, the theatre, all of us. Maybe the times are just too uncertain for the creative.

"I don't believe that for a minute," Adrian had said. "I think the trouble is right here, right with us. Not to cast shadows on our own waters, old buddy, but it's talent like Mark Banner we're passing by. Professional perfectionists who may not be able to write a decent piece of grafitti on a men's-room wall, or direct one hour's shooting of a series film, but who know the people who do, or who at least have the potential for doing, and most important of all can bring out talents in people who didn't even know they had them. Who, in short, can get blood from a turnip."

But other things kept Robert low-spirited, mean-spirited, as well. Deep, unspoken, shamefully personal things. The apartment he had taken when he thought Beverly would be there forever—it had its bumps in the night, it was so large. But he couldn't bring himself to leave it; the city in late night, early morning. In some inexplicable way he had come to need it, rely on it.

He walked it often, alone. It was on one of these postmidnight treks that he spotted Beverly and Steve Kerimidas, arm in arm, strolling on an East Sixties street between Second and Third. There was between them (or so he imagined) an experience at once so real and so profound that for a moment he had the strangest need to run after them, take them both in his arms, wish them well. And in the next moment to curse them to hell and back. It was then he realized how really drunk he was, and so he staggered home, had two more large and gripping ones, and fell across his bed in, he hoped, a memoryless stupor.

HE WAS PARTICULARLY HUNG OVER on a morning in January—the morning of the day, as luck would have it, of the start of UBC's "second season"—when a call came from one of his father's secretaries requesting that he and Mr. Miller join him for lunch in the executive dining room, twelve sharp. Nervously, and throughout the morning, Robert tossed pills into himself. He was hardly even tense by eleven-thirty.

David permitted only one cocktail before lunch; in the company's dining areas, that is. Robert politely declined. David and Adrian each ordered a screwdriver. The meeting itself, at least the calling of it, was not unusual; David often had his key people for lunch. What *was* unusual was the elaborateness of it. One of the imported Belgian table linen sets, for example; fresh flowers on the table; two waiters instead of one. The main course was one of the most noble sirloins Robert had ever seen.

"Well, gentlemen," said David, raising his glass, "the time has come..."

" 'The Walrus said,' " said Adrian, handing it with his eyes to Robert.

" 'To talk of many things: of shoes and ships and sealing wax ...' "

"You may not be too far off the mark," said David.

He's wearing a new suit today, too, Robert noted. And as charming as I think I've ever seen him. He's wearing one of his "personal" ties again too. The soft-dotted, non-rep. His eyes are bright and inquisitive. I wish to hell I were a thousand miles from here.

"There are fifty million television sets in this country," said David. "That's roughly one hundred and eighty-five million people."

Their looks—Robert's and Adrian's—showed they were obviously puzzled. All this for a television Information Office boxcar number? "I see you're puzzled," said David. "Well, let me unpuzzle you."

He looked at both directly. "Fifty-eight million television homes—one hundred and eighty-five million viewers. This means that our responsibility is so awesome that every move we make, every step we take, has to be weighed like it was filet mignon. . . ."

Dear God, what's he doing? thought Robert. Another damn blue-sky Minow speech to the IRTS? Not his style . . .

" 'A lot of bread,' the Walrus said, 'is what we chiefly need: Pepper and vinegar besides are very good indeed. Now if you're ready, Oysters dear, we can begin to feed.' "

This time he had their mouths agape, literally.

"Thought I wouldn't have any idea how the rest of it went, eh?" Laughing. "Well, ordinarily I wouldn't. It just happens to be one of the things Ellen used to recite. Anyway, I ended up learning it by heart. 'I sometimes dig for buttered rolls, or set limed twigs for crabs. I sometimes search' . . . But never mind. What the walrus said about a lot of bread, though—now, that *does* hold a certain relevance for us."

So that's it, Robert thought. Money again. Up-front money, probably. Which one of the day parts is he unhappy with now?

"But not necessarily in revenue," he went on. "At least, not *entirely* in revenue. It's just that I've been doing some very serious thinking. And you know what happens when I do some very serious thinking. I don't sleep for a week. I'm sure my eyes show it."

They had never looked more alert.

"A lot of this heavy thinking," he went on, "was started up by what's going on over at ABC. I think Elton Rule, as president of their television network, is going to have quite an influence on every area—Programming and Sales especially. And with Jim Duffy probably the best sales v.p. in the business—in other words, tougher competition calls for a response. Certainly it was the organization strengths of CBS and NBC that pushed Leonard Goldenson to make the move he did. . . . Say, this steak is something else, isn't it?"

There was something here not like the times before, when a command appearance in the executive dining room could mean anything from a renewed concern over children's programs to misleading advertising to another political number with the FCC. Today's they had neither of them figured out, and their exchange of glances confirmed their continued puzzlement.

"Yes, a great steak," said Adrian.

"Great," said Robert.

"And I'm further along with *it* than I am with the subject. Right?" The Picasso Harlequin on the wall behind him seemed to smile.

"The subject: a major reorganization of UBC." Harlequin's smile itself.

His father was intuitively masterful at dramatic suspense—this Robert remembered even from the earliest days—the abrupt pauses between bites at the dinner table, the searching looks before some following bombshell.

David put his knife and fork aside and folded his arms, an unlit cigar in one of his hands. His tone was as flat as Robert had ever heard it.

"Gentlemen, I propose to go before the Board on the first of February with the recommendation that effective March 1, I be elevated to the position of chairman of the Board and chief executive officer; that you, Robert, be appointed president and chief operating officer; and you, Adrian, president of the UBC Television Network and a member of the Board of Directors. Inasmuch as I've already discussed these moves with most of the Board—you excepted, of course, Bobby—I expect them to be passed by unanimous consent."

It was one of those moments when God *does* come down and walk the earth like a natural man. Neither Robert nor Adrian could speak for several minutes. When they finally could, they said exactly what was expected of them: "I don't know what to say."

"This has been in the works for some time," David said. "The reasoning behind it was that of course I'm not getting any younger. And also that I think you're both ready now for that room at the top. Well, *near* the top, anyway. I've also had the feeling that we need new and younger blood around this place. Now, with both the Programming and Sales positions open, that's precisely what we're going to get. . . .

"I'll make no secret of the fact that I want Mark Banner back here to head up Programming. No matter what it takes to get him. As for Sales"—here he shrugged—"it's hard to say. I'm sure you'll have some ideas there, Adrian. I just want somebody from outside and somebody who's with it. We're going to cut further into ABC's and Jim Duffy's territory if it's the last thing we do. Nothing would give me greater pleasure than to see Mr. Nice Guy out on his ass. He's taken more business from us in the past two years than the other networks combined."

"That still leaves Selwyn Coe," Robert said. "How does he fit into this thing?"

David shrugged again. "He has to stay with the television network, of course. I don't see a place for him in the corporate structure. I think the best thing for now is to let him stay on as assistant to the president of the television network—you, Adrian. I think you'll find him as indispensable as I have. Anything else?"

Adrian shook his head incredulously. "Anything else? My God, on a day when we're all pill-popping like crazy with ten new shows going into a new season, to hear this . . . that is, if we *did* hear it . . . well, 'anything else' seems just a little bit gratuitous, wouldn't you say, sir?"

"Yes, Adrian, I would say, sir. Oh, one other thing. My move up-stairs changes in no way my full and active participation in all phases of the company generally and the television network particularly. And when I say 'no way,' I mean 'no way.' You remember, Adrian, some years back at Lutèce—it was Lutèce, wasn't it?—when I told you *l'état c'est moi?* Well, it still goes."

Had anyone thought it didn't?

IT WAS THE TALK of the industry.

"Has David Abrams lost his mind? Bobby Abrams up top—just like that? *Bobby?*"—you heard it everywhere. Robert was certain he saw it on the lips of half the diners at 21 that night. This was where David and Ellen had brought them—him, Adrian and Joslyn—to celebrate the promotions.

"Caught everybody by surprise," said Adrian. "I can just see *Variety* on Wednesday."

"It's best not to pussyfoot around with these things," David said. "Since it's just rubber stamp with the Board, I asked Jerry McAlister to draw up a press release for tomorrow morning and Affiliate Relations to prepare a teletype to stations."

"Thank you," said Robert. "I agree with you about the spec."

"It's certainly a headline-grabber," Joslyn said—actually and demurely pretty tonight in a new Lord & Taylor knit. "A wonder to me either of you can keep your cool. I'd be dancing cartwheels on the table."

"I'm sure you would," said Adrian. "Now get down, you might *hurt* yourself."

After a moment—"I put in a call to Mark Banner today," Adrian said.

"And?"

"I'm meeting him on the Coast Thursday."

"Tell him much?" asked Adrian.

"Pretty vague."

"I only hope that way of his that *some* people might mistake for overconfidence has gone through basic training out there," Robert said.

Nobody said anything.

"It's a lovely move," Ellen said. "It can only mean uphill."

"My God," said Joslyn. "You're sounding like *them*. Next thing you know, you'll be talking about up-front money and bottom line and input and game plans and cost-per-thousand and reach and frequency and—"

"Shut up," said Adrian.

"Tell me," said David, trying to ignore the familiar yet still un-comfortable-making, "any thought yet on the Sales job?"

"A couple," said Adrian. "Vague mostly at this point. I do think a guy like Hitch Cummings over at J. Walter is what we're looking for."

"No doubt about it," said David. "Course, that's a pretty hefty number he's pulling down over there."

"I know, but he's always had a yen for the network side. More prestige, he thinks. More accessibility to Mia Farrow and Diahann Carroll and Sharon Moore and—"

"That's prestige?" said Joslyn. "Daydreaming about getting it off with the stars?"

"Eat your lizard legs. Or whatever the hell they are," Adrian told her.

"Maury Sherman and Marty Levitt . . ." began Robert.

"They won't like it, of course," said David. "But then, what the hell, they're the ones got least to worry about. They'll never get the axe. Not from UBC. Not while I'm around. And seventy-five on me is more like fifty. Right?"

"Forty," said Ellen. "I'm still a wreck from last night."

Adrian smiled. "I have hopes for Banner. I heard Don Durgin at NBC has been after him. Not for Programming v.p., though. I have hopes."

"I have more than hopes," said David. "For the whole restructuring. I think it's the way Bernie would have wanted it. I hope it is."

"I was thinking about him last night," Joslyn said. "When Adrian told me the news. How *proud* he would have been." She leaned on the word as she looked away from him.

"Jesus," said Adrian. Meaning more than she could imagine. Trying not to remember.

"Dessert?" said Ellen.

ADRIAN AND JOSLYN had decided to stay in the city. The Pierre. She was upstairs sleeping (he hoped) while he kept Robert company in the downstairs bar.

"Well, kid. A long day, huh? Long-assed day."

"I never thought he'd do it," said Robert. "Not so soon, anyway."

"Soon?" said Adrian. "My Christ, your father's seventy-five years old, Bobby."

"A baby. You heard him tonight. He wasn't kidding."

"Oh, come on, will you? The biggest day of your life and you act like life's come to an end. Forty-five years old and you're one of a handful of major communications guys in this country. Talk about never being pleased. Jesus!"

"He'll be into everything," Robert said. "The way he is right now. I know him. A title won't change things—for me, anyway. Don't forget, the television network will be only a part of my bailiwick. There's radio, don't forget, and the theatre division, records . . ."

"So? You have my counterparts in those areas. You'll still be up to your ass in the television network. Watch."

"It's different with you." He was getting drunk again; he could feel it. "Your appointment *means* something. There's . . . there's authority in it. You're . . . visible."

"Jesus! Don't tell me you're jealous of *me*."

"Hardly. What I was trying to say . . . trying to say . . . Oh, forget it. You're right. It *has* been a long day. Very damn long day. You're set on Banner, aren't you?"

"Your dad's set on Banner."

"He's your boy, though. Isn't he? Isn't he your boy?"

"He's nobody's 'boy.' He's a very talented, persuasive young man. Get to like him, Bobby. He'll be around a long time."

"You're pretty sure about getting him. He wasn't exactly crazy about me when he left. Remember?"

"He'll come," said Adrian. "He'll come back."

"I wonder what Beverly will say when she hears it. Brenda, too, for that matter."

"They'll be sorry as hell they ever left, old buddy. No stiff cock on earth can compare to Mrs. President of United Broadcasting Companies, Incorporated, and Chief Executive Officer."

"You're very goddamn cruel, Adrian. You're one very cruel man. . . ."

MARK was many things.

He was delighted. He was overwhelmed. He was surprised. He was euphoric. He was suspicious. He was eager. He was reluctant. He was the luckiest sonofabitch who ever lived.

"But with my own guys?" he said, for the tenth time perhaps since meeting Adrian in the Beverly Hills garden restaurant.

"Your own guys," said Adrian. "Of course your own guys. Subject to my approval. But no problem there. Now, finish your drink. I want another."

"I'm really excited about this, Adrian. You've done one hell of a lot for me, from the very beginning."

"You're a good man."

"You know, I've felt like one of those fancy Park Avenue poodles the last few months. An awful lot of sniffing around my ass."

"Why not? Other people are as smart in smelling out talent as we are. Even more sometimes, from the look of things."

"I have a hundred ideas, you know, Adrian? All this time at Metro,

I think I've spent half of it planning for this day. As though it was bound to happen. You know?"

"Maybe it was. This is your meat, Mark. Broadcasting. You have a wide range, you know. You're not parochial. You're not too New York or Los Angeles. Which is what our station people are always screaming about. There *is* an Atlanta, you know. There *is* a Philadelphia. And a Peoria and a Sioux Falls and a Denver. Can't blame them. Sometimes you'd think love, sex, murder, manslaughter, living, dying doesn't happen anywhere else but New York and Los Angeles. It's one of our biggest problems, I think."

"I know. There *is* a Kansas City."

"Welcome back, Mark."

"IT'LL BE GOOD to get back, Mark," Edith Stewart said. "Being born in New York, I suppose I'd miss it wherever I was. Thank heaven Allen can get his old job back. Thank heaven for Allen, period. You ever hear of a husband who goes where his wife goes because of *her* job? Especially when she's just a secretary. And one who hasn't even been invited to her boss's bed, at that. It'll be good being back in dirty, slushy old New York. I never was much for the sun. That is, my body in bikinis was never much for the sun. We'll kill 'em, Mark." . . .

"I'm glad, Mark, I really am," said Vivian, still physically distant from him as she had been ever since the baby, as though touching his flesh were too painful a reminder of the other she'd never touch . . . had never touched. . . . "Anything to get away from this awful place. God! How you could vegetate here; never have another thought in your life. Only let's bypass the city if we can. All right? Maybe something in Westchester . . . Fairfield County. Where you can feel the seasons again. Smell them. It'll be good being back, Mark. I promise you that."

They arrived in New York on February 20 and on the twenty-first he was shown his new office at UBC. It was two and one-half times larger than his last one.

VIVIAN celebrated the return to life in a number of ways. Once she'd found the house she wanted in Westport and talked Mark into taking it, she began accepting—graciously—the invitations of Ellen, Joslyn, and others for lunch, dinner parties, coffee hours, and home screenings of the latest unreleased theatrical movies. She even gave a luncheon for the wives of the Programming executives who reported to Mark, a particular success talked about for weeks. She and Mark joined the Fairfield County Hunt Club. They became an addition to Fairfield County society, as well as to the more notable Manhattan affairs, she herself winding up on most lists of New York's best-dressed women.

As for Mark himself and the long hours he was away from her, particularly during the first few months of his new position—these she accepted with what everyone agreed was a remarkable degree of equanimity. On those occasions when they were together—alone, that is—her arms were open to him, her insides stifling the eternal cry for her lost child, her babe, the one glory Mark had brought her and that had been so cruelly taken from her, the one glory he could never bring her again. She never mentioned it again, however, nor would she even begin to entertain the idea of adoption. And as their times of getting together became fewer and fewer, their relationship more as it had been before they moved back, she marked the change up to his almost superhuman schedule (as she was certain he did, too), camouflaging her need of him as adroitly as she did her resentment of him, becoming increasingly, ironically more beautiful, more polished, more desirable by the day. Words—harsh words—rarely if ever passed between them.

They were the perfect couple, adjusted to the perfect life. Always and everywhere in demand. A sterling showpiece for the growing charm, sophistication, and solidity of United Broadcasting Companies, Inc.

THE OFFICIAL STAMP, or image, of the new regime, however, was provided by none other than Robert Abrams. Within days of the announcement of his succession and the company's reorganization, Robert—to the bewilderment, surprise, and pleasure of both David and Adrian—arranged in quick succession for a luncheon meeting of all division heads, where he laid down a number of ground rules for his administration; a continental breakfast meeting of all UBC personnel (for which he leased the Ziegfeld Theatre on Sixth Avenue), at which he gave a short address outlining some of his goals and projects and asking hands to the helm and noses to the grindstone and that sort of thing in a surprisingly, for him, ingratiating manner; followed by a cocktail reception for advertising and agency executives in New York and Chicago and a similar one for the creative community and station management (both radio and television) in New York and Los Angeles.

David and Adrian kept their fingers crossed, especially when Robert, so unobtrusively that his actions went almost undetected, gradually withdrew from all but the most seemingly urgent face-to-face confrontations, leaving Adrian to carry the burden of the day-to-day television network operation, with Marty Levitt and Gerald McAlister attending to other divisional and corporate matters.

Smart executive maneuvering? Or Robert reverting to Bobby . . . rising up with his admitted talents for a brief display, only to subside again, as with others at other times, in the shadow of the inevitable nonpareil, the great god David?

52

Somewhere in South Vietnam
July 30, 1969

Dear Sylvan:

How's the eldest? The youngest, as you can see, is still in action. To tell what tales I'm not exactly sure, but then imagining grandchildren on my knee listening to them is so far removed from my present reality that to dwell on it would be foolish indeed. I can tell you, however, that I am well, relatively sane, more in hate than love with all wars and men who start them, that I am deeply tanned or yellow, according to imagination, that we are near water, that coastal towns with names like Phan Rang and Phan Thiet have a very lovely sound, if nothing else, that the time or two I've been in Saigon brought to mind so many things about my trip to Paris with you and mama, exactly as they say, it must truly have been the Paris of the Orient before this CENSORED.

I know it must have been as thrilling to all of you as it was to us here to see the first moon landing, which we received by tele-satellite. I say "thrilling" because up until now a few of us here thought maybe we were the ones walking on the moon. As for the rest—over here, I mean—I'm sure you see a great deal of it on television every night, so anything I might say would be gratuitous, not to mention censored. Suffice it to say, I lead a really swinging social life.

I'm still at work on my novel, although it's painfully slow. I keep having these fantasies of rich famous writers sitting in their book-lined studies, pipe in mouth, looking out on vast expanses of wood or lawn. See what illusions we grow up with? Like all this "suffering" is supposed to make me a better writer. Not that it matters, but I tore up the last fifty pages. Maybe I wasn't meant to be a writer anyway. A halfway decent one, that is. Who knows? My best buddy here will be going into the advertising agency business when we get home. His father is media director for Masters and Young, and he spends a lot of time trying to persuade me to give up this artsy CENSORED attitude and come in with him. Working mostly on the television end of it. We'll see. One thing good may come out of this. That I was such a screwed-up kid that I entered college at 15½, and with a degree already in my pocket—at least those wonderful days are behind me.

All love as always to you and Esther and the kids, and of course all the others and mama. It still seems strange signing myself as I will, when it was Griebsberg for so many CENSORED *centuries.*

Hang in there.

Your loving brother,
JOEL GREER

Bronxville, New York
October 8, 1969

Hi, Mom!

Sorry I haven't written for a while, but it's been really impossible. Just in the time since I wrote you last, Beth has given birth to yet another—another girl, too, can you believe it? We've named her Marietta. (Naughty Marietta, remember? With Jeanette MacDonald and Nelson Eddy? It was your favorite movie.) It's so tuneful a name that now little Andrea won't speak to either of us. She hardly talks well yet, but just enough so we can make out "I want pooty name too." Isn't that cute? A snapshot of both kids is enclosed. And, again, just since I wrote you last, I've been given the transfer to the television sales area that I've wanted so badly for so long. The v.p. for sales is a guy named Harold (Hitch) Cummings who I get along with really great. Television is really the place to be these days. You get to meet everybody. Like right now I'm working in Daytime Sales and the big advertisers in the country are part of it. I tell you, mom, you'd go crazy, this talk of millions and millions of dollars, from the time we get in in the morning till we leave at night. I love it, though. It's my meat, mom.

Well, that's about all for now. How's everything in Mannerville? Good, I hope. Beth and Andrea send love.

Your son,
STEVE

P.S. It's a go-getting world up here, mom. You've got to be alive, act alive, every minute you're in it. But I was like that as a kid, if I remember. You're always what you were, as the fellow says. Reckon that's why I like sex so much. It just seemed like it was naturally around the house all the time. Sort of like part of the family, mom.

New York, New York
December 8, 1969

Dear Dad and M.J.:

It's raining like hell here, an icy kind of rain, and there you two are —in the middle of that glorious Caribbean. I did appreciate your card and envy hell out of you.

I've been giving considerable thought to what you want for me, M.J., and certainly Uncle Bob hasn't let up on me a minute. But I'm just not ready to chuck it all for television right now. Although UBC is on top again, I hear. A couple of really hit shows. But until I get rid of the greasepaint bug once and for all, I'm afraid you'll just have to put up with me. I do have faith in this new musical I'm producing off-Broadway, though. Thanks to you, M.J., and Uncle Bob. A really lot of faith, I might add. The idea of Antigone *being done in a pop-rock style is intriguing. When you see it performed I think you'll flip. Critics and fickle audiences aside, it should run even through your Mediterranean cruise next year (joke).*

Well, that's the most and least of it for now. Keep soaking up the sun. Know you'll both be the envy of the Old Man's and Ellen's Sunday-night dinners. Oh, I almost forgot. I got married yesterday. Her name's Darlene and I was drunk.

Best,

FREDERICK WIENER *(your son, remember?)*

Westport, Connecticut
March 26, 1970

Dear Dad:

It's only at a relatively quiet moment like this, late at night, when the telephone isn't ringing its fool head off with network business that seems never to be smooth, that I can come down here in the study and share some thoughts with you.

The "second season," as you know, is now under way, and it does appear that the things we did right in September will pay off even more the rest of the season.

As I've told you, I thought this whole "relevancy" thing was artificial from the beginning, a "socially conscious" series having a peculiarly academic smell about it. Either a show's a good show or a bad show, and all the psychological or sociological labels you lay on aren't going to make one damn one of them smell sweeter.

Sure, times are changing. Drug scene, riot scene, sure—all the rest. But in any entertainment it seems to me it's really theatre that counts.

Anyway, it's all you hear in the studios on the Coast. If I told you how many pilots are loaded down with higher consciousness and community action right now—for all the networks—you wouldn't believe it. The fall schedules (1970–71 season) are going to be so weighted down with them that the good old-fashioned laugh or moment of truth will be as hard to find as an honest producer.

I won't lie to you. We have a pretty good share of them in development at UBC. But I think I've prevailed enough that when our schedule is announced next week it will have a little better balance than the others. Whichever way it goes, though, it's going to be the most competitive season we've ever had. I think I spend as much time in Los Angeles as I do here.

But it's one hell of a job, dad. I know it's not exactly the same as being a scientist or writer or statesman, but I tell you the truth, some-

times I say to myself on those nights when I can't sleep, "There are only four network vice presidents for programming in this whole country and you're one of them." Then after that, I couldn't sleep if I wanted to. It's a little silly when you say it out loud, but it means I love what I do. I figure that makes up for a lot.

I owe a very great deal to your friend Adrian Miller. There's a lot of truth in that "right time, right place" idea. Even more in the old "luck" saw. Through you I got to them, and I'm grateful every day of my life.

Of course there are days when you'd have to be mad or a masochist, or both, to even think you're enjoying this crazy party. But then along come the others, days when you know that you couldn't possibly be anywhere else. One thing does bother me, though. Robert Abrams still doesn't like me very much, or apparently have that much faith in my competence, for that matter. Oh, he's polite enough, correct enough, but . . . what the hell, it's after one and I have to be up for a breakfast date with Harold Prince—we're talking with him about a series of theatrical specials—and I'll be damned if I'm going to sit here and analyze the whys and wherefores of Robert (Bobby) Abrams.

Vivian joins me in regards, wants to know when you're coming up again. Her folks were in from Oklahoma City last week. 'Nuff said. Except that they did try their best to persuade Viv to at least think about adoption, but she's adamant about it and that's that. She hasn't been feeling well lately.

Thanks for the barrel of pecans. We'll make good use of them. Pecan pies all year. Mother's old recipe, of course. I'll never forget how we loved her pies! Good night, dad. I love you.

MARK

53

IT WAS A COLD APRIL DAY in New York, the kind tulips almost curse out loud. A gray, driving snow had been intermittently persistent since early morning, damned if it would be that easily gotten rid of. Flecks of blue had tried, you could give them that. But the slush of winter was with them for a spell to come. The sidewalk trees seemed humiliatingly bare, dismal in their protracted trial.

Sharon Moore, from her suite at the Waldorf, looked out on them with a poutish distaste. She always liked coming to New York; she always loved leaving it. As for staying in the large commercial hotels, she didn't care how chic it was to stay at the Gotham or the Carlyle, or very particularly the Regency. She wanted to be seen, made over. It had taken too many years of not being seen, not being made over, not to love every sweet fucking minute of it.

It was just after five, and she was waiting for Mark Banner. It would be a close one this time. A real quickie because both of them had to be at the Pierre by seven-thirty—separately. The International Radio and Television Society was honoring David Abrams tonight with its "1970 Man of the Year" gold emblem. Vivian was driving in from Westport.

Moving from the window, she turned to a mirror—the most natural act on earth for her these days. She had always to be not just pretty, not just radiant, but magnificent. That was the reason her cosmetic schedule was such an exacting one. She had to plan to within split seconds when one of her unscheduled fucks came along. She'd practically written the "business before pleasure" injunction.

But damn it, she did look gorgeous tonight. The fatty (baby-fatty) look she'd always had, and in many ways been catapulted to fame by, was less pronounced tonight, more suggestively lush, hair upswept and sparkling, the kind of natural tiara you didn't see very often these days.

From the mirror she turned to one of the twin beds, across which lay a tight-fitting sequined gown. When Mark was gone, Minnie, her maid, would come in to help her squeeze herself into it. The thought of it, the image of herself in it, was just too much. She had to have a drink if it killed her.

She should never have taken up with Mark Banner, she thought, pouring the clear brown liquid over an ice cube. Not that it was anything serious: she'd never had a more casual lay in her life. But he was beginning to act very fudgy about it, a bourgeois hangup you'd hardly expect from somebody *Time* had called "one of the most sophisticated executives in network television." And she'd really had no intention of ever starting up with him in the first place, grateful as she was for the part he'd played in her success. But that night at Stefanino's in Beverly Hills, the way he'd looked at her, smiled kind of drunkenly at her . . . Depressed as he'd been over his wife or something . . .

Damn, he should be here! The most important UBC star since Ellen Curry and he treated her like . . .

This was silly really. She wasn't nearly as furious as she made herself out to be. Not even that impatient, when you came down to it. She poured herself another anyway. "Better safe than sorry" was another of her trusted gems.

"Welcome to *The Sharon Moore Show*," she said—sarcastically, she hoped—when he finally showed up at five-thirty. He fell into an arm-chair.

He did look tired. The day had obviously been impossible. She knew exactly what he would say.

"Not today, huh, Sharon? I'm just too whipped not to take it slow and easy."

She almost mouthed the words along with him. But if he thought he was getting off that easy, he had a real goddamn other think com-ing. He didn't put out often, but when he did, it was the best. The grade-A number one best. It was going to be too boring and pompous an evening not to have that hour she so richly deserved.

"Some chump you are," she said. "I'm standing here in a negligee that would give half America a bone on and you say 'Not today, huh, Sharon.' You don't deserve to come, in more ways than one."

He smiled.

She smoldered. "What do we do, then? Sit around and talk shop till it's time to leave?"

"Something like that."

She poured him a drink, which he declined. She drank it herself, knowing full well she was headed for disaster.

"Okay then," she said, sitting across from him, making certain, through a slight adjustment of the sheer fabric, that he could see every pubic hair on her, so close he could count 'em one by one. "If it's rap you want, it's rap you get. Beginning with this: Why the fuck is my show already in rerun?"

"Sharon," he said—that damn direct glance of his that could drive you to drink—"all arrangements on the number of original episodes and the number of reruns, and when and where, and the economics thereof, are between your agent and the studio and between the studio and the network, just so you can be left free to act your beautiful little heart out and give the people of this great country the kind of fresh, inventive comedy it so desperately needs in these uncertain, despairing times."

"Why, you—" She had risen, leaped across to him, tried to slap his face (and for real this time). His hands locked around her wrists, their bodies had touched and not drawn back, and the breathing of each had the rapidity and tone of a single magnified heartbeat. The soft carpeting on the floor among the baroque-framed mirrors and Venetian sconces was infinitely preferable (for this particular moment, anyway) to the most luxurious bed. It was hard and mean, and when finally he withdrew, it was to lie flat on top of her, the thick moistness of their bodies the lovers' glue. She knew she would play hell getting washed and toweled and into the gown, then getting herself together in some reasonable facsimile of the princess she had envisioned earlier, but it had been worth it. Every goddamn second of it.

They said little while he was getting dressed, and at the door when he was leaving, only "See you at the blowout" and "Yeah."

AND BLOWOUT it was. The IRTS had honored only two men with its "Man of the Year" medal—Stanton of CBS and Newton Minow of the FCC—and neither of these had drawn such an elaborate and enthusiastic turnout. David Abrams was not only one of broadcasting's most legendary figures, he was also one of its most loved. "To miss this bash," as one of UBC's station managers had put it, "would not only be treason—in this business it would mean you were dead."

It was at this fashionable melee that Fred Wiener announced that he was divorcing his wife on grounds of adultery (hers for a change); that Mark Banner came up with the concept of a "magazine of the air," which would gestate some five years before it was born; that Gerald McAlister fell out of love with Barry White; that Robert Abrams met a divorcée from Sea Island, Georgia, named Jean Marie Bright; and that Ellen Curry, at the age of seventy-four, sang *As Time Goes By* in honor of the honored guest.

David had just finished his acceptance speech to a standing ovation, the final ghost-written words still ringing through the ballroom, when the room went suddenly dark, and with no introductions a single blue-and-white spotlight fell on Ellen Curry in front of a small orchestra to one side of the dais, singing to and through the seemingly limitless applause,

> *You must remember this:*
> *A kiss is just a kiss,*
> *A sigh is just a sigh.*
> *The fundamental things*
> *apply . . .*

As time goes by. It was almost one o'clock, but nobody (who was anybody) was leaving. It was a night of such nostalgia, such out-and-out sentiment, that even cynic eggheads couldn't hatch themselves loose. A quiet nightcap was served to an invited few in a small room just off the big one. There another burst of spring flowers (pink and yellow tulips, carnations, pink and yellow roses, irises and jonquils) met the already dazzled eye. But "quiet" cocktail indeed! In the coterie surrounding David and Ellen—

"Such a dream, such a night to remember."

"Such a good title for a film."

"How proud you must be! Of each other, my dears, of each other."

"The acceptance speech was great, David. Just great. Just right for the occasion. You didn't say much, thank God, but occasions like this are hardly the time for bombshells."

"*Or* bombs. Most others I've been to, inside the industry and out, not only lay eggs, they throw them."

"I'd no idea you were that age, of course. Lord give me half the energy and drive when I . . ."

"And that song, Miss Curry, that song! I'll swear I cried as much in there as I did when Dooley Wilson sang it in *Casablanca.*"

"Things as gung-ho as you paint them, David?"

"Think you'll hit CBS's stride this season, David?"

"Big dog-and-pony show for the affiliates in L.A. next month, David?"

"Proud of the showing tonight, David?"

"Good Lord, who wouldn't be? Every important star, director, producer in New York was here."

"And the ones who flew in from the Coast! It's a wonder that vest is still on you, David."

"And the others. Paley, Stanton, Bobby Sarnoff, Goldenson. Must have been little-green-man time for at least three of them. Stanton's had his . . ."

"Hear some publisher is thinking of bringing out your bio, David. Expanding the *New Yorker* profile. True?"

"What did you think about the President's telegram, David? I know it's not fashionable these days, but I got goose pimples hearing it. I really did."

"New structure working out okay, David? Putting Miller in charge of the network, Bobby of the company in general? Lord knows Mark Banner's calling some damn fine shots these days."

"Hear you're into everything from office to janitor supplies, David. More active than ever, I hear. Keep it that way. You'll die at a hundred and fifty—that is, if you die at all."

"Expect this big a turnout, David? Ellen?"

" 'You must remember this, a kiss is just a kiss.' Your voice hasn't changed in fifty years, my dear."

"Kind of an irony to it, isn't it? Having no place else to go. Having seen it all, done it all. You're the top, as Cole Porter put it."

"Hear they're offering you an ambassadorship, David. True?"

"Must be enormously gratifying, David. To see the culmination of a life's work—"

"Who the hell is talking about culmination?" said David. "I've hardly begun, thank you."

"And does he mean it!" said Ellen, taking his arm.

A FEW FEET from them, in a much smaller, more concentric circle, Mark Banner was holding his own subcourt on programming views, with Adrian and Joslyn Miller just to the side. This sort of thing, this center of attention, was still new to Mark, on top of which he had had to explain at least a hundred times that Vivian's aunt in Stamford was ill.

Which was a lie, of course. She had been dressed to come in and was calling him just as he returned to his office to change after the explosion with Sharon Moore. Another kind of explosion awaited him on the phone. A semihysterical outburst in which he could make out only a few things—a new dress that didn't fit and that no pins could camouflage; a new hairdo absolutely ruined by the weather; a terrible argument with Thelma, their day maid and cook, who had walked out cold; an exasperation with the drugstore . . . hard time explaining. Especially when he himself hadn't the least notion why.

(That is, he tried to tell himself he hadn't the least notion why. God knew her periodic cases of "nerves" had grown increasingly more frequent these past months. One minute laying it on him with a near-to-strangling sympathy: "You give too much to that network, Mark, they've no idea what a treasure they have"; the next minute depressed by some fancied persecution: "They're holding you back deliberately. You should have been president of the network by now. It's that snake Adrian Miller, the one you call your friend. Hah! I can see him now, scheming with Bobby Abrams right under your very nose, planning ways to get you out. . . ." She talked in her sleep: "Don't leave me, Mark, I need you, Mark . . . love you, Mark . . ." and "Hate you, Mark, hate you, hurt my baby . . . killed my baby . . ." Not to mention the lightning-quick changes of mood, particularly, for some reason, when it came to her clothes, and bordering on the paranoid: "It's exciting as hell, isn't it? Hattie Carnegie really outdid herself for me. What's she doing to me, that bitch? I'll be the laughingstock of the party. I'll never set my foot inside her place again, never, goddamn you!")

He was more comfortable now, even though the attention he was getting, while it seemed to amuse Adrian Miller, brought forth only an icy smile from Robert, who was part of still another circle a few feet away.

It was during an exchange of the usual show-business banter that he was maneuvered to a side of the group, rather artfully, by Seymour

Kranz, the editor of *Living Today*. The conversation, though cursory, not only was worth the price of admission tonight but was more provocative than anything that had happened to him since seeing Sharon Moore on a projection-room screen, thinking she was doing melodrama when all along the comedienne in her was screaming to get out.

"A crazy idea's been running around in my head, Mark. I know it's the thing to keep the media as fragmented as possible—you do your thing, I'll do mine—but a bright young fellow I've just recently brought into the editorial department was sort of idea-doodling one morning, formating a kind of television magazine, I suppose you'd say. Now I know the idea is hardly a new one—it's been around, I suppose, since the early days of radio, when every hour called for something new. And newspapers and magazines were the only thing around for format-building."

"True," said Mark, "but in a sense a night's television *is* a kind of magazine, isn't it? News, entertainment series, specials sometimes, more news, talk shows. I'm just not quite sure I get your point."

"Which proves, as I've always said it does, that I'm a hell of a better writer and editor than I'd ever be as a salesman. The idea here, Mark, is that there would only be interruptions for station identification, the whole thing would be a single unit . . ."

"But a *Living Today* on television?" Mark smiled.

"You might think of it that way."

"Tell you what, Seymour. Why don't we lunch soon? The one thing about it that appeals to me, at this point anyway, is an opportunity for greater experimentation. Not to mention that almost *anything* new in television is highly promotable. The thing about it that worries me is that it flies in the face of block programming, which, as you know, the whole damn thing's built on. But lunch soon, all right?"

"I'll look forward to it."

It was at that moment that Sharon, stunning on the arm of her escort for the evening, Barry White, approached, and the thin exchange was all but forgotten. There *was* an aura about this animal, he thought. Something that seemed to carry an unusual set of batteries around with it, lighting here and there for a fast recharge. An absolutely unmistakable—and pretty much irresistible—amorality that through some alchemy translated itself before the camera into a winningly inept, if still sexually healthy, comedienne. Maybe it was a kind of built-in safety device; taken straight, that battery of hers would have blown out the tube. Humor, unself-conscious as it was, cut the voltage to easier tolerance levels. Whatever, it drew millions to her— millions who prided themselves on their ability to recognize the real thing when they saw it.

Remarkable too, he thought, the near-magical transformation of her, the poised (if vaguely boozy) cream pastry of her, when only hours ago . . .

"I see dear Vivian isn't with you tonight. Baby-sitting problem?"

"We have no children." *As if you didn't know, you . . .*

"I'm sorry. Do give her my best, though, whatever it is." And in a voice loud enough for all to hear, as she pretended it was for his ears alone: "Believe me, darling, I wouldn't be here either if it weren't for darling David Abrams. Community banquets aren't exactly my style." And then the voice lowered to scarcely a murmur, this time genuinely for him alone: "Gives us till dawn or so, doesn't it?"

He smiled politely, said, "Good seeing you, Sharon, you look marvelous," and with an arm about Kranz's shoulder moved off, saying, "My secretary will call when I get back from the Coast," and then easily lost Kranz in the crowd. He could feel eyes penetrating his back, though—across the room and for the rest of the party.

Meanwhile, Gerald McAlister had joined Sharon and Barry White. Casually, and with the usual light pleasantry. If there was one secret in all of broadcasting, all of UBC, that had been marvelously kept, McAlister thought, it was the thing between him and Barry White. But when White, whether to make him jealous or simply to infuriate him, began playing up so transparently to the vanilla-soda star, it came very near to being an open secret. And when McAlister was able finally to get his lover aside through the simple stratagem of a PR problem that couldn't wait, the situation was, if anything, worse.

"Are you out of your mind?" White said through his teeth. "Calling me out in the middle of a conversation with one of UBC's biggest stars? You're outrageous, Jerry."

"Why? Because the PR chief of UBC wants a moment with one of *its* most important stars?"

"Thanks for the flattery," said White (gorgeous tonight, thought McAlister, in a new royal-blue dinner jacket), "but you're still behaving unprofessional as hell. I'm dead certain Sharon Moore is seeing right through you. By the way you're looking at me, if nothing else."

"Barry, I'm warning you, I won't put up with this. Even if you are an important property."

The laugh was low but unmistakable. "It's really time to call a halt anyway, Jerry. My *macho* side is the one in fashion this week. I'll miss you, though, Jerry. You really give the best blow job in town."

Open-mouthed, McAlister watched him walk away, knowing that with him went another in a long string of hopeless humiliations, an evanescent but nonetheless scarring pain.

FRED WIENER HAD HAD TOO MUCH to drink. Deliberately. Good drama, to be spontaneous, demanded it. While the aftermath of good drama (and he fully intended it to be that) required a fairly decent explanation, such as, say, the innocence of youth getting smashed.

The problem, and the reason for such an elaborate solution, had begun the instant he'd opened his eyes on the morning of December 8. Beside him, in a ridiculously narrow bed in a crow's-nest apartment, vaguely familiar, had been a tousled brunette who in deep and naked slumber both snored and hissed at the same time. After an hour or so of wrestling with a usually faultless memory, it had begun coming back to him in a series of kaleidoscopic visions, sort of like an Ingmar Bergman film he'd seen a few weeks back.

A party. Bob Hickham's party. Big Bob's. The Village. Party. Way out. December 7. Pearl Harbor party. Come as your favorite Japanese lady or gentleman. He, Hirohito. Two dozen Hirohitos. She, a geisha. A hundred geishas. Midnight, thereabouts. Giggly toasting of marshmallows in a crackling fireplace. Marshmallows attached to little flags. Flags into fire when the confection toasted. Laughter. Chanting. Remember Pearl Harbor. Chanting. Laughing. Remember Korea. Dancing. Shouting. Remember Nam. Laughing. Kissing. Singing. Nam.

Stars and stripes into fire again, laughing. Girls. Many. Girls. Darlene. Darlene saying it was time to go. Go.

Car. His. Being driven. Her. Laughing. Singing. Feeling each other up to the point where they almost had a wreck. Something teasing his mind. Yes. Yes. Mitzi Green. Saying. A saying. It's all right to have affection, but not when you drive. Something else. Somewhere else. Maryland. Uncle. Bob, Maryland, Maryland. Uncle Bob. Old people, strangers. Car again. Laughing. Singing. Singing.

"Morning, sweets. May I introduce myself? I'm Mrs. Fred Wiener. *The* Fred Wiener. Care for an egg? The only way I know to fix them is scrambled."

He had met her several weeks ago when she'd auditioned for the role of Antigone. She'd missed out on the lead, but a certain quality about her—remarkably poised for such a kind of street girl—had landed her a role as one of the handmaidens. Her voice had been good, nothing spectacular. He'd slept with her that same night.

And most nights since. But marriage!

"You look like you still don't believe it. Well, here, feast your eyes." The document undoubtedly was legal. Just as Uncle Bob's had been (or so it was told about) when his first wife worked virtually the same deal.

"All you've got to do is pick out a nice ring today, honey. And won't it be something! Not the ring, sweets. The looks on the faces of the cast and crew when they come face to face with the producer's new wife!"

He'd sought an annulment immediately. And was refused it, of course. If ever a marriage had been consummated, it was this one.

He'd asked her politely, hourly, to let him be, but she'd simply pirouetted as she did in the show and looked lovingly at the ring she'd been forced to buy herself (Cartier's, of course) and his stepmother, M.J., had been forced to pay for. Meanwhile he'd put a good face on it. As good as it was possible to put on anything, given the circumstances. He'd been on his knees—literally—begging her; taken to biting his fingernails, something he hadn't done since he was a child.

"It'll be a good life for us together, you and me, sweets. I promise you. I was born to make men happy, my daddy always used to say that. Born to make men happy."

She had moved into his apartment, and it was there that the solution, at least a vague idea of it, had come to him. He refused to sleep with her.

"Don't go getting no cute ideas now, sweets. I don't know what you're trying to do, but it won't work. There's a dozen witnesses to you asking me to be your wife, that night of Big Bob's party. All ready to testify to it in court if need be."

It was all out now—the war he was determined to win. And after a while the sex stratagem he'd counted on had begun to work. She'd begun looking pale, suspicious. Her work at rehearsals had become sloppy, stale. Finally, a week before opening, she quit. "It just ain't dignified—the producer's wife and all, I mean." And whether in consequence or not, *Antigone* as a rock-pop musical had opened to nearly unanimous praise and was within days a modest but established off-Broadway hit. For Fred Wiener it was little more than a heady footnote by now. The woman was driving him senseless.

"I just thought I ought to tell you again, after consulting some pretty smart people in this town, that I got everything on my side, everything. You better start leaving me some household and other necessities-of-living money too. I'm warning you, sweets. You got to start fucking me too. It says so in the Bible."

He'd moved out of his apartment into a downtown hotel. Consulted both his father's and Mandy Jo's lawyers. To no avail. She could sue him for desertion if she'd a mind to. He'd sworn off sex for six weeks.

"I only come by here to tell you that it won't work, buster. You got your ass in a sling and that's that."

Finally, in desperation, he'd hired a private detective, and it was this simple device that had at last paid off (and why in hell he hadn't thought of it earlier he couldn't imagine; knowing her sex habits—real nympho—she'd have somebody's tool around, no matter what any attorney or friend might advise).

"I'm glad I run into you this way. You know? I've been doing an awful lot of thinking, honest to pete, hon. It's just not natural your staying away like this, I don't care how rich and snooty your folks are. I mean, we did have fun together, didn't we? I mean, we did come at the same time, didn't we?"

The detective had come up with photographs of no fewer than three men (one of them Big Bob Hickham) in varying degrees of *delicto* with his precious wife. By this time, however, his bitterness had reached such vendetta proportions that he didn't dare confront her privately at all. Instead he had shocked her out of her tree by inviting her to make her public debut on his arm at the IRTS dinner for David Abrams. Whatever misgivings she might have had ("You up to something sneaking, sweets?), the idea of attendance at one of the big social and professional events of the year as Mrs. Frederick Wiener was just too much to pass up.

She didn't look so bad tonight, either. Sort of a Pygmalion conversion, if you let your imagination run free. From the kind of blowzy (if pretty) piece she was to this well-groomed, well-behaved woman who spoke little, but when she did speak sounded as crisp and as prideful as Eliza herself. Fred was forced to take three or four more drinks than he'd planned on.

The truth was that by the time they were in the small anteroom, he was smashed. He only vaguely remembered, as they were going through the tall open doors, Darlene hissing under her breath at him, "Jesus Lord, Freddie, you're shit-faced!" The rest, like the night of the Pearl Harbor party, he would have to piece together out of fragments tomorrow.

As it happened, they were in a group that by this time included Adrian and Joslyn Miller, Mark Banner, Sharon Moore and Barry White, and his father and Mandy Jo.

"You were disgusting," his father was to tell him the next morning. "Standing there in front of everybody—*staggering* there in front of everybody, I should say—having some crazy fit of adolescent giggles, then taking a stance like some outraged Hamlet, pointing a finger at that pathetic girl and citing chapter and verse the details of her love life since she became your 'better half.' Which, much as the girl repels me, were the only words of your little speech I could agree with."

"But you will be rid of her," Mandy Jo was to say. "Which was the object of your little performance, wasn't it? And do call Mark Banner, will you, dear? Mark's the one who saw you home."

ROBERT HAD TRIED to smile his way through the evening, but with only partial success. The tranquilizer he'd taken earlier hadn't cohabited too well with the drinks, so that while his hands were no longer shaking, his head was.

It was a new wrinkle, this head-shaking. A manifestation, probably, of long-ago fears of his father, present-day ambivalence toward him still. Whatever, it occurred only in his father's presence, and then mainly at some public function or another. Tonight it had been particularly disturbing, since it happened involuntarily during his father's acceptance speech. He had been certain that people at the dinner tables could detect it, especially the ones nearest the dais, where he sat at one of the ends. If so, he could just see next week's Gallagher Report: "What network VIP and heir apparent appeared to disagree with everything his honored father was saying the other night in an acceptance speech at . . ." He had breathed more easily when the remarks and standing ovation were finished and the room was darkened for Ellen's nostalgic performance—grateful his mother at least wasn't there to see what to him was an embarrassing reminder of his father's years of deceit.

He was easier even at the small reception afterward, where he was presently engaged in conversation with Hugo Wertmuller, president of one of the public broadcasting operations in New York.

"See this?" Wertmuller asked, bringing a folded newspaper page from an inside pocket. "Bryson Randolph's column for today's editions. Only take a minute. There's better light over there near the piano."

Robert reluctantly agreed.

With the new fall season schedules of the major networks now announced, it is easier to assess the strategy behind them. With all four in the "relevancy" sweepstakes, at the same time holding steadily, whenever possible, to situation comedy or musical-variety successes, viewers will be seeing (among the new programs, that is) a surfeit of both formats. Thus titles such as *The Young Lawyers, Storefront Lawyers, Dan August, The Immortal, The Senator* (on *The Bold Ones*), *Matt Lincoln, Headmaster, The Shamus, Congressman Dewey Brown, The Potboilers,* and *Sam Gross, L.L.D.*—the latter four UBC's entries, that network having to fill twice as many hours as the others—will be living side by side with *The Flip Wilson Show,* Mary Tyler Moore, *The Partridge Family, The Odd Couple, Nancy,* Tim Conway, Don Knotts, Danny Thomas's *Make Room for Granddaddy,* and, on UBC, *The Sedgwick Family, The Beach Party, Boys and Girls, Firehouse Five, Lillian* (spin-off of *The Sharon Moore Show*), and *Any Thursday,* with an all-black cast.

It's pretty well an open secret by now that wonder-boy Mark Banner, v.p. for programming at UBC, decided months ago not to put all of that network's eggs in a single basket. He appears to be going along with some of the so-called relevance programming, but has in development dramas that contain what he calls "social significance," without the plodding labels or the messages that bowl you over with their portentousness.

However the fall season turns out, it's obviously the Year of Relevance and nastier competition than ever. Whether Mr. Banner's go-easy strategy will succeed or fail will be interesting to watch.

"New girl on the block," said Robert, wry twist of the mouth his only expression. "And you know how the boys always sniff around a new girl. It's older than sin, Hugo. But after the honeymoon . . ." His imitation of Larry Lester slitting his throat (a Lester staple by this time) was oddly humorless.

"It wasn't Banner I was talking about," said Wertmuller. "It was the extraordinary budget you boys came up with for a drift against the tide. What rationale is there, Bobby?"

He was about to answer, attempt to answer, when Randolph himself came strolling over, a still young-looking and attractive woman on his arm. "Ah, Bobby . . . Hugo . . . I'd like you to meet Miss Jean Marie Bright, from Sea Island, Georgia, whose accent will positively destroy you. I'll not bother introducing the two of you. She knows exactly who you are and what you do. May I?"—pulling his arm loose. "I'm sure you'll find her utterly charming."

Robert certainly did. Of all the women he had known and been attracted to, this one—with her coal-black hair limning a patrician face, nose a little too prominent and sharp but still leading one's glance to the deep purple eyes above it, the full complement of a mouth beneath—this one was not only the loveliest but the most feminine; the most coquettish. And still carried herself like a duchess.

"Miss Bright," Randolph continued, "is here as a guest of the Haleys." Ronald Haley was a group vice president at Collier and Collier, the advertising agency that handled the UBC account. "She's Sara Haley's sister. The only other statistics I'm going to supply is that she's a divorcée and writes the society page for the *Sea Island Eagle*. The remainder of the dossier you will have to discover for yourselves."

And he was off, a hand airily over his shoulder in fond farewell.

"He's something else, isn't he?" said Jean Marie Bright.

"Kind to us at NET, though, I must say," said Wertmuller. "One of the reasons we continue to receive public funding the way we do is because of men like Bryson Randolph."

"Perhaps it's just anything commercial he has it in for," said Robert. "Still, all in all, he is a serious critic, and unlike most of them, he's taken the trouble to learn something about our medium. That alone makes him an asset."

"Even when he's knocking your network?" the young woman asked (coquettishly?) as her eyes took both of them in.

"*Especially* when he's knocking my network," said Robert. "Keeps us looking at ourselves. The public we deal with. Self-examination—

it's the only responsible way an influential operation like a television network can—should—stay in business."

Jean Marie Bright smiled. A nice smile, Robert thought; softened even her nose. "You must have a marvelous PR man, Mr. Abrams," she said.

With a laugh and a brush of Robert's shoulder, Hugo Wertmuller excused himself, noticing a friend across the way.

"He must have a real headache, the job he has," the young woman said seriously. "Educational and public television aren't even powerful enough in this country to rate as stepchildren. They're like Oliver Twist holding out his little porridge bowl—'More, sir. Please, sir. More, sir.' And Washington and the foundations and all but a handful of the general public looking down their noses and screaming, 'More? More? Did you say more?'"

"Nicely put," he said. "I hadn't realized anybody but those of us in the business—"

"Oh, a few things cross the border, even all the way down to Sea Island, Mr. Abrams. And it's television that's mostly responsible, which is why noncommercial television's so essential in this country. And I hope I won't shock or offend you, but I believe fervently that much of the funding should come from the commercial networks. You *are* rather fat cats, aren't you? Why wouldn't it be saner—anyway, healthier—to be fat pussycats for a change?"

He smiled, looked off for a moment. It was pretty obvious she'd been rehearsed. Her little speech had been at such perfect pitch and cadence. It was no secret that Ron Haley was a vociferous patron of NET, and the fact that it was Bryson Randolph who'd brought her over simply accentuated the ploy.

But did it matter? Anything would sound fresh, even appetizing, in that mouth. He offered to see her back to the Haleys' on Ninety-second Street, and she accepted.

"Our rebels now are . . . rebels now . . . rebels, revels . . . Our revels now are ended. These our actors, as I foretold you . . ." Fred Wiener had somehow worked his way back to the hotel after being put firmly into a taxi by Mark Banner. And with a burst of apologetic eloquence, went on: "Leave not a rack behind. We are such stuff as dreams are made on, and our little life . . ."

His words fell, however, on an empty room.

Vivian was still up when Mark got home.

"What in the world happened to you?" he asked. "I couldn't make much sense of it over the phone."

"What *didn't* happen," she said. "That goddamn dress practically tore to pieces getting it on, Thelma as much as admitted she'd been taking money from the petty-cash fund in the kitchen, the goddamn drugstore refused to renew my prescription for Valium without a call from my doctor, who naturally is out of town . . . The way you sounded on the phone, like you didn't care one way or the other whether I came into the city or not . . ."

"Vivian, that's not true and you know it. All *I* knew was that you were all in little pieces over something, and that I had to be at the dinner for David Abrams, come hell or high. You're all right now?"

She nodded. "Better, anyway. I got hold of a standby, a Dr. Malinsky, who was very obliging. I tell you without them, those pills, I'd . . . What time is it, anyway?"

"About two-thirty, I think."

"Two-thirty? Aren't you home pretty early?"

"Vivian, please," he said, starting to undress. "It was just a bad day all around and tomorrow's got to be a decided improvement, okay?"

She thought a moment, pouted perhaps, then reached out for him in the room's dim light. "Mark. Mark, please. Help me. Mark, help me. I need you. Oh, God, I need you. Even when I hate it to have to need you, I need you. I didn't come in tonight because I wanted to punish you. I'm not certain for what. Maybe for being so wrapped up in that damned network, hardly ever seeing you, missing you. Mark, missing . . . love."

And he was kind.

"WELL, another milestone, eh, Star?"

"In its way, dear, yes."

"Was I really all right?"

"Haven't I told you you were? More than all right. You were excellent."

"You hated the speech."

"Who said so?"

"You didn't have to say so. I know when you like or dislike something. My God, after all these years . . . You didn't like it."

"It was all right. I suppose any speech that starts off 'One of the more interesting challenges in the life of a broadcaster is that each day you wake up to new problems' has to be all downhill."

"Damn! I had the thing written five times."

"You should have done it yourself, David. Or, better yet, asked Bobby to do it. It's *his* forte, you know. But don't fret over it. There'll be others, darling. I daresay there's not an honor in the industry, or out of it for that matter, that you won't get. Someplace. Sometime."

"Maybe. Who knows? What I do know is that I gave a second-rate performance tonight while my wife gave a first-rate one. That's what I know."

"Male chauvinism, David? At this late date? At our advanced ages? Or did you imagine you were competing with Mr. Sarnoff?"

"Don't be funny. And you can cut it with that 'advanced ages' crap. Tell me another woman your age, or a man mine for that matter, who enjoys things more. Even gets more. Just you tell me *that*."

"I have no intention of telling you anything except to get some sleep."

"I can't."

"You'd better."

"I won't."

"You will."

"You were great tonight, Star, you know that? You were really great. 'The Great Lady of Television.' That's the title of the *Ladies' Home Journal* story, you know. I like it. It says it all."

"Maybe. But wouldn't 'Grand Old Lady' be more appropriate?"

"Stuff it, Star."

"If you'll go to sleep. All right?"

"You know something? I think Bobby liked that house guest of the Haleys'."

"How could you know?"

"A hunch."

"I hope it's a lucky one. I haven't the least idea who she is, but it would be a relief to see him . . . settled again."

"Settled? Again? Bobby'll never be settled. Not all the 'agains' in the world will do that. But she is a looker, I'll admit that."

"I like your Mark Banner. He's . . . oh, I don't know, the real goods, I suppose you'd say. Why is it so many people in television are so unreal?"

"Who knows? Maybe it's because we work twenty-four hours a day cooking up reality for the rest of the country. The killer never returns to the scene of the crime, right?"

"Go to sleep."

"I was thinking up there tonight, Star. About Bernie. About how far we've come. I doubt either of us ever dreamed, back in that make-shift old studio in the Newark warehouse, ever dreamed we'd be . . . this."

"Perhaps not consciously, darling. But you were always a kind of dreamer, David. I'm certain of that. In a way the whole world's been a big jar of candy just out of reach, and you've been the little boy who's bound and determined to find some way to get his little hands in it. You still are. It's always been candy you're after, David. One kind or another."

"Candy? Whatever you say, Star."

"I don't like Gerald McAlister."

"Go to sleep, Star."

"There's something about him that's so . . . I don't know. I never cared for Adrian much either, and look how far he's come in the business. I used to be intuitive, David. I wonder if I am anymore."

"Sleep well, Ellen."

"I think Adrian hit her again. Joslyn, I mean. I'm certain of it. She had on pancake makeup an inch thick. And of course there's one performance tonight we've avoided mentioning altogether. . . ."

"Good. Now get some sleep."

"I can't imagine what got into him. The girl's no bargain, I'll admit, but to get drunk and marry her and then drunk and calling her a slut, in front of at least a hundred people in that room. Oh, I've no doubt he'll get his divorce, and be humble and shamed for weeks and weeks to come, but why on earth he—"

" 'Night, Star."

"He's doing another play, did you know? Broadway this time. Bobby's backing some of it. Something about a chain-letter disaster in Australia. I think it's called *The Cockatoo*. I imagine he'll be coming to you—"

"Won't touch it. Now, sleep."

"You never cared much for Fred, did you?"

"Sleep well, Star."

"Funny. I've never been so undecided about a person in my life. I'm sure he'll end up at UBC, though. Mandy Jo says it's just a matter of time. Oh, well, why think of it? Now especially. It was a grand night, darling, and you were grander still, and I love you very, very much, now *that* I do."

"Mmn-hmn. Stuff it, Star."

54

"It's the biggest mistake we ever made, not fighting more decisively the ban on cigarette advertising on radio and television. Oh, we'll make it up—advertisers like Sears are already coming into the fold—but I think it's a bad omen, any way you look at it. We let ourselves and everybody else down by being cowed, the same way we caved in on the beer issue, letting the beer be displayed but not drunk. It's really so ludicrous. I get angry every time I think about it. The truth is, I'm sick and tired of jumping every time Washington snaps its fingers. We're a major communications force, for God's sake. *The* major communications force, when you get down to it. And more than almost any other industry or business we're highly visible. Goes with the territory. But being bound and fettered by a bunch of Lilliputians who don't know quite what to make of this still relatively new giant . . . well, we have to draw the line somewhere and I say draw it now. Give every affiliate in this country a good dressing down. They're the licensees, you might remind them—therefore *their* senators and congressmen are more accessible to them personally. As to the whole moral or ethical set of values in this thing, we have to remember that millions haven't even begun to think about giving up smoking. If you ask me, the moral and ethical principle is on our side. Nobody's benefited from this unilateral action except the newspapers and magazines. Who in turn pop our butts every chance they get. It's discrimination, pure and simple. It should have gone all the way to the Supreme Court. Anyway, Adrian, that's the tone I think we ought to take with those guys. Time somebody around here got tough." Martin Levitt was finishing his report on likely discussion areas when the regional representatives on the Network-Affiliate Board of Governors would meet with network management at Dorado Beach in Puerto Rico in early December, 1970. It was now the second week in November.

Adrian looked thoughtfully around the room. In addition to Levitt, there were Selwyn Coe, Clifford Gold of Program Development, Mark Banner, Hitch Cummings, Maury Sherman, Gerald McAlister, Jack Stroud (head of Advertising and Promotion), Dutch Cottingham (head of Sports), Bill Kelly of News, and Pete Grimm, new head of Station Relations.

For some reason it had been a meeting freer from tension than just about any Adrian could remember. Also the least cautious, most cocky. One reason, of course, was the way Maury Sherman had expressed it: "Shit! What's all the fuss about pampering nine old farts or having to blow up our rationales? We're going into these meetings in the best position we've been in in years, thanks to Banner here. So to make up this big dog-and-pony act for a fistful of shitheads, no, thanks."

Shermaneze aside, there was more than a kernel of truth in what he'd said. UBC was going into the Network-Affiliate Board of Governors meetings with more definite hits than the other networks could boast about, mainly because of Mark Banner's feelings that the "relevancy" series was a fad, nothing more. On the other hand, the other networks were taking nothing lying down, and next season, the next, could be CBS's again, NBC's, ABC's. Probably would be. All of them had stuck their necks out on the relevancy shows; UBC had extended only half a neck.

Still, it was no time to eat crow. The menu this year called for caviar.

"The one thing I want to see this year—and don't think for a minute that these nine station men aren't important—the thing I want this year is a very positive feeling, upbeat as all hell. Sherman's right. We *do* have a lot going for us. Prime time, sports, the big improvement in news, the late-night talk show . . . Maybe not daytime so much, or children's programming yet, but we're ahead of the game. Way ahead of the game. There's something genuine and positive about every god-damn day part we have. If after Stroud here has gotten us through a super audio-visual presentation there are questions, then of course we'll answer them. Honestly when possible. Dishonestly when not."

Adrian waited for the recurring laughter to settle down, then went on: "In other words, I don't want to muddy any waters this year. We've had an enviable season to date, and for the first time in two or three years we can walk into those meeting rooms ten feet tall."

In the silence that followed, Adrian moved his eyes slowly toward Mark Banner and Cliff Gold. "One of the real stiff ones," he said, "is how far a stewardship report should take us into Program Development. There are enough dikes with holes in them, you should forgive me, enough jungle drums in this industry as it is. Program Development is probably the least-kept secret we have. Still, we don't want to stir things up by going too deeply into what we're doing for next year. At the same time, these fellows get awfully pissed when we hold everything back. Makes them feel like distant relatives when they figure without them we wouldn't even have a family." Broad smile now. "I suppose I am playing devil's advocate, but it's just so important that we go in on top and leave on top. Important as hell. Right, Pete?"

The new vice president in charge of Station Relations was a comer: the kind so easily recognized and often catered to in the industry. Blond, good height, good looks, thoroughly masculine, thoroughly at home on the tennis courts; reasonably bright but not terribly inventive. Somehow they managed, this breed, to go through life thinking it theirs and theirs alone. Grimm was unusual in one respect, though. He was a thoroughly devoted husband and father (two years younger than Mark and eight of 'em, eight kids, count 'em) who limited his nights out with the boys to a few rounds of drinks and that was that. Adrian had recruited him from a Midwest station group.

"I feel basically the same," Grimm said. "I've talked with a hell of a lot of the guys there, two or three times—Tim Ickes, the new chairman, a half-dozen times at least. And it's simply got to be a smooth-as-glass kind of meeting. Only two or three areas where they'll try to rattle us a bit. News. The plans for expansion we keep snowing them with every year. But I'm sure Bill has that one under control. Station compensation's another sticky one. As when hasn't it been? But program success and higher rate cards . . . Well, you can't blame them for wanting a slice of the pie. But we'll have a separate meeting on that." A quick glance at Adrian, who smiled him on. "And, of course, another perennial, the sex-violence issue, which Mark and Birchall Schwartz from Standards and Practices will have to face up to at one point or other. Other than that . . ." Shrug, smile, and out.

"Anything else?" asked Adrian. The answer was a sweeping silence. It was already seven-fifteen and they'd been at it since three in the afternoon. Adrian had a passion for meetings, the later the better. Going home to his wife must be rough, they thought.

The meeting dismissed, Adrian walked back to his suite of offices with Mark Banner.

"Do you really think these series with social themes are out, Mark? Or is it just a bad year for them? I mean, all of them—ours included—look like they were put together with paste. Which of course they were. But even given the failures, do you really think socially relevant themes are dead? Before we've even started?"

"Not necessarily," Mark said. "It's just that when a program puts a neon sign on itself—'Hey, mom, looka me! I'm a relevant!'—the jig's up. Social consciousness, moral consciousness—these happen because they're inherent in a show, not because out on the Coast Aaron or Quinn or Harry or Doug sit down one day over lunch at the Brown Derby and say, 'Look, we need another relevant theme. Can you think of one?' "

"I suppose," said Adrian. "I just hope we're not pronouncing the death sentence before we've had a decent trial."

"That's just the point. It's the promotion of these programs, not the programs themselves, that we should give the axe to. There's always a place for a *Defenders* on anybody's schedule, Adrian."

"Of course. Who's disagreeing? I do think, though, that in two or three years at the latest a whole new area will open up to us."

"I couldn't agree more. Ten, fifteen years and you'll see two fags kissing. In a bathtub. But we won't be labeling it, Adrian, that's the point. We'll be pleasing or provoking the people—not Washington. That's what Marty was getting at in there, I think. Give half an inch and you've given away the ball field. You know damn well children's programming is the next big act. And after that—who knows? Programs too bland, a repeat performance of Minow's day? Or too permissive? Who knows?"

"Meanwhile, they'll come after us one way or another?"

"Yes'm."

"Well, as long as we have programming men like you around, I don't think old Gabe'll be blowing his horn very soon."

"Why, thank you, Adrian, I . . . That was a damned nice thing to say."

"And all of it meant. Now get your ass out of here so I can get to this paper work—which translates 'so I can use my private line for a quickie.' And I'll see you tomorrow."

"Yes, *sir*." He smiled when he said it.

Mark wondered all the way home if Vivian would be sober. A lady drunk he decidedly didn't need tonight.

And he was in luck. She'd had only one or two.

"All packed?" he asked.

"For Dorado? Hardly, pet. I haven't even finished all my shopping. Lord! I don't think either of us can get into our bathing suits. The good life goes to fat, Mark. Or hadn't you heard?"

He hadn't heard. . . . He was trying, God knew he was trying. It was just that he never knew what he'd come home to.

Tonight was far and away the most serene he'd had in weeks. A cocktail (one only), a lovely New England boiled dinner, the coming over of neighbors, Rick and Dorothy Sayres, to watch the latest Hitchcock film, still unreleased, which he'd brought home for a private screening.

Then later, in bed, holding her close, very close, whispering to her as he might to a child . . . but nothing else. Not even the suggestion of anything else.

Maybe in Dorado, he thought. Maybe that marvelous hotel, that perfect beach, maybe they'll be good for her, restore her. . . .

THEY MAY BE MISLEADING, the travel posters, about other vacation spots in the world. But on Dorado Beach and the Dorado Beach Hotel, they have been miserly.

From its lush green lawns and gardens to its wide expanse of clean white sand; from its open lobby, tiled in soft colors, to its luxuriant suites of rooms; from its great circular driveway to its narrow shrub-lined walkways; from its golf courses and tennis courts to its small but well-equipped casino; from its *al fresco* oceanside area for breakfast and lunch to its elegantly appointed dining room; from its self-contained isolation (San Juan is over an hour's drive in) to its service, its pleasantry, its Continental food; from an exotic fruit here to an exquisite flower there, the Dorado Beach is the ultimate in gracious holiday living. . . .

So they say, and they are right.

And Mark hated every inch of it.

He couldn't say exactly why. It wasn't really the great walking distances (two-story bungalows stretch from the main building almost as far as you can see) or that dress for the dining room and casino were *de rigueur*. Not really.

Perhaps it was because Vivian, in one of her abrupt changes of mood, had instantly fallen in love with it, much as she had fallen in love with California in another time. Could anything be more foreboding than that? Or, for practical purposes, matter less, considering that it was Robert Abrams himself who had insisted on the site?

The meetings, particularly the staged multimedia presentation under Jack Stroud's supervision, were a smashing success. Which meant, in translation, a controlled hostility. It was in the nature of station managers to hold their gigantic brother in almost continual suspicion; and in the nature of network executives not directly concerned with individual markets (programmers, for example; sales managers to a lesser degree) to lord it over the "boys from the sticks."

Two pilot films for series scheduled to start out the second season were shown: a half-hour comedy, *The Bleekers and the Blues*, about a white family and a black family who live next door to each other, and which was certain to be one of the most controversial and talked-about programs in years; and *Dead Heat*, a police drama starring a newcomer named Will Barnett, all six feet three of whom would be flying over for the final banquet on Thursday night.

With the meetings scheduled for the mornings, the afternoons were generally free. But during golf, at the courts, on the beaches, in the blue-green waters, the shop talk, in one way or another, went on. "We're twenty-four-hourers," Adrian Miller had once declared when getting drunk, and it was true. Somehow they found it easy to talk about the marvelous staying power of Lucille Ball; the bewilderment over violence and just what constituted it (Efrem Zimbalist, Jr., star of *The FBI*, had said recently to the press, "They tell me we're going to do the show nonviolently. How they expect to do a show about violence without violence seems idiotic to me, and the best way to drive the audience away"); the brilliance (and controversy) of Tennessee Williams' *The Milk Train Doesn't Stop Here Anymore*, which UBC had done over the Thanksgiving holidays; the luck in running across Sharon Moore when they did—when Mark Banner did; the whole Washington scene: the possibility of television commercials' suggestibility coming under closer government scrutiny ("*Mama mia*, that's-a some spicy meat-a-ball!"; "Take it off—take it all off"—a shaving cream commercial, you learn, but only at the tag end); the increasing need for more newscasts, more in-depth news documentaries; the so-called sweep periods when individual stations had their own local market ratings; the outlook for next season; the *New York Times* article just yesterday in which John Kenneth Galbraith said that the American industrial system "is profoundly dependent on commercial television and could not exist in its present form without it"; the new pilots they'd seen, the brief discussion of development projects; Bob Hope, Jack Benny, Jerry Lewis, Mary Tyler Moore; the future of public television, CATV; Johnny Carson, Doris Day, Flip Wilson, Tim Conway; the big sports packages the network was coming up with; Diahann Carroll, Raymond Burr (whom UBC was trying to lure); Barry White; and Dave, Aaron Spelling, Len, Quinn Martin—the Hollywood television royalty. Somehow it was always easy to talk about this and these, around the clock if necessary. You found it easy to talk about, for hours on end, because no matter where you hailed from—Chicago or Dallas or Idaho Falls—you owned a share in, had a stake in, that mysterious turn-on called show business. You also got to drop names . . . feel like you made and owned them. Big deal. Heady stuff.

Mark was fascinated by the differences in men and ideas at the station level. On the one hand, men whose sophistication in the business was as keen as the network's; on the other, men—veterans, at that—who appeared as naive and wide-eyed at the sight of Ellen Curry as a Kansas hayseed might reasonably be (and more often than not hailed from St. Louis or Milwaukee).

He was fascinated, too—no, flabbergasted—at the elaborateness of the week's social calendar. The Roman emperors, the czars, the kings of England, France—none could possibly have been served so richly, so lavishly, so *frequently*. The social planning was in the hands of one Hamlin J. Hirschmyer, whose one function and purpose in life was to see that UBC management was kept happy. This kept Hirschmyer happy—to the tune of a half-million at the least. The other networks had tried to woo the indefatigable Hirschmyer with the same dedication they might the current hotshot in Programming or Sales, but somehow UBC managed to keep their unique bird content on his perch.

Seven kinds of lobster, five shrimp dishes, prime rib roast, fried chicken, *coq au vin*, veal Parmesan, loin of pork, lamb shish kebab—for lunch. "To give the ladies something to remember and talk about the whole year," Hamlin Hirschmyer had told Mark, broad wink as much a trademark of his as his choice between *béarnaise* and *béchamel*.

Set up also, in one of the hotel's large suites of offices, was a communications system linking UBC management and Board members with the mainland that not even the President of the United States could carry with him. Almost fifty telephones to all major network markets, a crew of at least a dozen people to man them. A complete office complex. Someone or something at your beck and call every half hour. "A luxury," as Vivian saw it, "you could get used to mighty quickly."

"Hamlin's probably the most accomplished one of all of you," Ellen Curry Abrams had said at the second night's dinner. "He's certainly the most endearing."

Mark looked around him, at the great dining hall's altered decor: everywhere flowers, the ones on tables fashioned into the letters UBC; the centerpiece of the buffet (itself approximately as long as a crow's flight from New York to Philadelphia) was a carved-ice swan atop another block of ice, from which the UBC logo had been hollowed out. Around it *boeuf Bourguignon, fricandeaux à la Niçoise, suprêmes de volaille à blanc, quenelles de saumon, poulet en gelée à l'estragon, gigot ou épaule de présalé farci, court-bouillon, pompano amandine,* and more were enticingly, sacrificially displayed.

"Hardly like the old days," Mark said to Adrian across their table, shaking his head still in disbelief.

"What is?" said Adrian.

"And just think," Joslyn broke in, "it wasn't thirty years ago that dad and Uncle David had to ponder a trip to Pittsburgh for a week."

"A trip to Pittsburgh would *still* be pondered for a week," Adrian said.

"Really marvelous feast, though," said Carolyn Coe. "Not much to take issue with tonight."

"Oh, I ain't so sure," Burl Hollander, a station manager from Texas, drawled. "Kind of stuff we feed the hawgs back home."

You took the bitter with the sweet, thought Mark. This—Burl Hollander—this was this business, too. An important part of it, at that.

"Don't let him pull y'all's legs none," his wife, Mission Hollander, said, laughing. "Old Burl here's got fancies would squeeze the boundaries of the whole state of Texas."

"Where we got more to offer than a hound's got fleas," her husband rejoined.

"Like what?" said Vivian. "Assassinations?"

Through the almost audible gasps, Hollander said slowly, "My, my. And I heard you hailed from Oklahoma, too. I wouldn't say that's bein' very neighborly. All due respects to your husband's position."

It was the darkest moment of the evening, lightened only by Ellen Curry's bell-like laugh. "I was just remembering the first time I was here. Right after it was built, I think. I was in San Juan for a concert series and several of us . . ."

David, as if one or another of her words were a code signal for

"Help us for heaven's sake, it's your party, remember?" softly disen-
gaged himself from the head-to-head conversation he'd been having
with Tim Ickes since they'd sat down at this table for twelve. Now, his
voice leveled what he hoped was just that right pitch between casual-
ness and confidence, said, "Burl . . . Tim . . . I was on the Coast last
week looking at a couple of rough cuts of pilots we already have in
production for the '71–'72 season. A few projects like this and we'll
have that lead time we're always talking about. And that's something,
when you realize the kind of assembly-line programming we have
to do."

"Any chance of learning what they are?" said Tim Ickes.

David's eyes ranged the circle of faces, coming slowly back to
Mark's in a kind of "I'm helpless, what else can I do?" apology. He
said, "Well, as you know, we didn't want to get into development so
early, but what the hell. You're family, right? Well, one of them is a
new made-for-television movie that's just about as professional a job
as you've ever seen, on television or in a theatre. It could be the kickoff show for the UBC world premiere series we're talking about. It's
about a National League ballplayer who's dying of cancer, and I swear
I cried half the way through it. And you know *me*. I cry only at fu-
nerals and bank statements. Anyway, it's a beauty.

"The other—pretty rough cut here, no color separation yet, un-
scored—is an hour version of *To Kill a Mockingbird*, which we're
projecting for a series possibility. Project has a lot going for it, you
know. The Pulitzer book, the fine movie—Gregory Peck—the kind of
warmth and appeal it has. The main point here, though, is that Banner
here—and I don't want by any means to embarrass him—but he *has*
gotten us on an advance planning track that I think will really pay off.

"And these are high-quality films. You see it in every frame. I think
the secret to the new hits we have this fall, as well as so many in
development, is that Mark has an uncanny knack for smelling out
quality work that has mass appeal. Enough, Mark?"

Humble grin, his best. "No, sir, not nearly enough. You could tell
them about my plans for bringing over the Taj Mahal for this Indian
love story we're doing. . . ."

Dinner passed smoothly then, Hollander even addressing him as
Marco ("You got yourself a big old job there, Marco"), which may
have meant "All's forgiven" but ran the length of his spine all night.

At the end of dessert, David's eyes swept them all again. "Well, ladies? Gentlemen? It's nine-thirty. I do believe the gaming tables are
open. Join me?"

As they were walking out, stopping at tables for chat, Hollander's
arm somehow found its way around his shoulder, and he was saying,

low enough for half the island to hear, "That mockin'bird thing's got possibilities, by gar. Think we could get old Greg Peck back to do it for us, Marco?"

Jesus!

THE CASINO was in full swing. Most of the UBC and station people had already arrived, the roulette and blackjack tables attracting most of them. Only a handful were at the more hazardous crap tables. Vivian went quickly for roulette, prolonging as long as possible the dressing down from Mark that was sure to come.

Mark himself shot craps, as David and Adrian did: small stakes. With Burl Hollander literally breathing down his neck, it was lucky he ever came out even. Hollander was throwing fifty-dollar bills around like ones.

The surprise of the evening, though, was Robert. To Mark, at any rate. He seemed crazed, demoniacal.

He was a big loser tonight, a bad loser any night. The way he elbowed away people around him, as though he couldn't stand to have them touch him . . . The way he handled and blew on the dice, as if such mystical rites were for him alone. The suspicious looks he would direct at the croupier. The muttering to himself, seemingly unaware of anyone else around him. Not Adrian or even his father. Certainly not him, Mark, directly across the table from him.

It was a pretty ugly display, no getting away from it. And it was something else even more frightening, more revealing. It was there, naked to behold, and Mark couldn't have failed to take note of it. Robert Abrams, heir apparent, was, pure and not so simple, scared shitless.

With Cliff Gold of Program Development in tow, Mark made his way now to the cocktail lounge, where at least half the group was living it up with after-dinner drinks, much to the annoyance of three other couples in a darkened corner. The singing lasted into the morning hours. All the old ones—"Margie," "My Gal Sal," "Row, Row, Row Your Boat," "Strawberry Blonde," "The Sidewalks of New York," "Don't Sit Under the Apple Tree," "Million-Dollar Baby," "Harrigan," "Hold Tight," "Mary," "Bicycle Built for Two," "Shine On, Harvest Moon," "Blue Moon," "Me and My Shadow," "Paper Moon," "Broadway Lullaby." Among the last of the revelers was Vivian, who, excusing herself boozily from the station manager in Seattle (whose hands were just about to forget themselves), joined her husband at the door.

The walk back to their rooms was a silent one. He said nothing as they got ready for bed. Once in them (twins, thank God), an argument followed by a cold rump to his inflamed thigh was more than he was ready to cope with tonight, this morning. Besides, it was *his* presentation that would be given tomorrow, and he wanted to be up early to check out the slides and film clips he planned to use. From the other bed she said, "All *right*, I drink too much. So toss me in the Caribbean. It's icy cold at night. Easier way to die, freeze to death before you do. Joke. Sorry...."

"I don't recall saying anything to you, Viv. And you've avoided me like crazy tonight. What did you think I was going to do? Ream your ass out in front of everybody? Good Lord, Viv, grow up. But if it had to be anybody you let have it, I can't imagine a more likely candidate than good ol' boy Burl Hollandaise."

"Hollander, and you're a darling! Oh, Mark, Mark, thank you." She was into his bed, onto him before he could think, which suited him just fine. The hell, for once, with questions, with wondering.

THE SURPRISE of the meetings occurred on the last day. Jean Marie Bright flew in from Atlanta, and five minutes later was known by all to be Jean Marie Abrams. Ring, thing, everything. She and Robert had been married just two days before the trip to Puerto Rico. She had had several matters to attend to in Georgia, and they'd decided to give a coronary to anyone who needed one.

David came near to one.

"What in all hell are you doing? You hardly know this girl . . . woman. My God, Bobby, this is your third time out. Whose record are you after? Tommy Manville's?"

They were in an arbor on the south grounds. Ellen was off helping the new bride unpack. David's face was gray, despite the beginning of a tan. Robert's was paler still.

"You'll learn to love her, I know it," he said, not too enthusiastically. It might be a source of rich humor and gossip among all the others (it was), but to his father it was yet another detour, the sort of deviation that seemed always to come when his son was on the verge of making an important contribution to the network, the industry, the corporation.

"It's not a question of whether *I* love her, Bobby. It's a question of whether *you* love her. Wouldn't you think so?"

The arbor was thick with sweet-smelling hyacinth, the light air carrying its scent like the spreading of pollen. The green-blue waters, stretching forever, were as tranquil as dreams. All dreams except his, that is.

"Father," he said, "we have never in the forty-three years of my lifetime discussed the girls I saw, the girls I kissed, the women I see, or the women I marry. It's pretty late for that, wouldn't you think?"

"I think you sound so goddamn like your mother . . . even *look* like her when you're talking . . . I could choke you, Bobby."

"I'm sure of it. There's no point in all this talk. She's my wife, she's from mother's beloved Georgia"—he couldn't leave that out—"she's here, she's now, and that's that."

"But what the hell do you know about her? What do *I* know about her? You may not realize it, son, but even at the advanced age of forty-three you're what's known as a catch. They called them gold diggers in my day. God knows what they call them now. But it's only the name that's changed, I assure you."

"Father, Jean Marie happens to have a damn fine background. She's Sara Haley's sister, for God's sake. She's from one of the oldest and most respected families in Georgia."

"And up to their magnolia-scented asses in debt. When I knew you were seeing her I had a little research done on her. Not a copper cent. Bobby—you and I—we can't afford to be reckless . . . crazy. You've already had two disastrous marriages. . . ."

Robert was already on his way back to his bungalow and his newly arrived wife. David stood for a moment, watching him, then turned and slowly walked off in the opposite direction.

IT'S A CRYIN' SHAME REALLY, Jean Marie was thinking as she watched him striding up the walk from the main building. She was sure—well, *pretty* sure—she wouldn't have married him if she'd known. But then she wasn't so sure either, because the Abrams fortune, the Abrams name, the power and prestige of the United Broadcasting Company— these beat the piggy little act every time. Somehow they'd just have to overcome it. For a while, anyway. Vaguely, intuitively, she could visualize a day when all the trump cards would be in her hands. Her well-kept, soft, and slender hands.

David's dossier was right, of course. She hadn't the proverbial sou to her name. And it would take one hell of a basket of sous to keep herself in the shape she'd sunk so much pride and energy into. Outside appearances and acquaintances (rarely close friends) were far more significant and purifying than any intimate, usually possessive relationship. That she'd already had, and no thanks. Johnny Bright had been enough relationship for a lifetime. Give her Mrs. Robert Abrams any time. Yessir, any old time.

Of course, the sex thing wasn't going to be easy. . . .

He had come from behind while she was so reflecting, and was kissing the nape of her neck. From below there was the softness straining into her buttocks, softness meeting softness, nothing more.

Pulling herself away, she said, "You were talking with your father?"

"Yes."
"He's upset."
"Confused."
"He'll like me."
"I told him that."
"Thanks. I'll make sure he does."
"What makes you so confident?"
"Instinct, Bobby. I've fed on it all my life."
"Like I'll feed on you."
"I know it. But we'll have to learn the right formula for it, won't we, darlin'? What's the dress tonight?"
"Long dress."
"Help me choose, darlin'?"

IN THEIR BUNGALOW just a few doors down, Joslyn Miller was in the process of choosing an outfit too. It wasn't very easy when she'd spent the better part of an afternoon trying desperately to find in herself some kind of shame, guilt, self-disgust, something. And couldn't. But it had exhausted her so that another dinner with the same faces she'd seen for a week cast quite a pall over even the selection of a blue silk or a white-and-yellow perforated cotton.

She showered, half-listening for the turn of a key—Adrian's. Returning from his several matches, double or single, or eighteen holes on one of the finest courses in the world. He'd have something hateful to say when he did show up, of course. Something mean and crude, and then when her face with all its makeup was streaked just enough with tears, he'd most likely throw her on one of the beds and pound out his hard day between her legs. Which she would welcome with open everything, as she'd done a thousand times before, regardless of the way the late morning of this particular day had been spent.

The way the late morning had been spent, after an early-morning tennis match with Janie Levitt and two of the affiliates' wives, was . . .

"My name Nita. I your own person maid rest time you here. Hokay?" Small, dark, lighter still than most, pretty in a sullen, poutish way. Small eyes following Joslyn wherever she went in the suite, always within stepping distance from her. Watching solemnly as she took off her tennis skirt to take a shower. She was startled when she turned the water off to have the shower curtain pulled open to reveal the girl standing there with a towel, a smile on her face. Then, not handing her the towel, or holding it out for her to wrap herself in, but starting to dry her herself, so gentle and loving, everywhere, that she thought perhaps she'd cry. Scream. It had been so long . . . with a girl . . . so long . . . with a woman . . . so long . . . "I know. I see thing. Know

thing. Nita smart. You like kissy? Pussy? You like Nita?" She like Nita: maddening, maddeningly marvelous—devilish, devilishly divine, comparable only with the early days with Adrian; not even Brenda was as good. She was just about ready to take another shower when a quiet rap on the door startled her. Large man. Muscled man. Behind him another, tiny, dwarflike, you might say, swallowed up in the big man's shadow. Shades were drawn. Big man inside door, in sitting room, small man outside, sitting on porch, whittling on a monkey pod. "He be look-in," said the big man. "Case nobody he come." For the first time she was frightened, staring at both their fine polished faces, unable to scream (not wanting to scream?), listening as though in a trance to Nita, her eyes knowing again. Everything. "You like see Nita, Big Paw-Paw do for you? Give show you? Fifty pesos?" By this time she was so mesmerized she could manage only a nod as the big man started to take off his faded chinos, khaki shirt. Nothing on underneath. And God! Jesus God! Not even a satyr could be hung so monstrously. Marvelously monstrously. Then they were on the bed, the man and Nita, linked, not linked, every known (some probably unknown) position of superman shows on practically every tourist island in the world. They were good performers: their movements permitted her to view the performance from the front, from the rear, from the side, always the giant growth pushing quickly to climax—"Got watch time, time"—finally managing it by transferring from girl's vagina to girl's mouth. Joslyn saw finally the last suction, heard finally the last moan. She was reaching shakily for her purse when she heard Nita's small dainty voice: "You like now all three? Four? Two hundred pesos?" The big man went to the door and beckoned the dwarf inside. The dwarf's place was taken by a thin man, older, dull-eyed, indifferent. The faces of them locked, unlocked, breathy, breathless. She inhaled suddenly an elixir so exhilarating that she wanted all of them, all, even the dwarf, inside her, mouth, vagina, all, a thousand pesos, ten! Just to hold in hand, in mind, in breasts, in dream the crazy dreamlike mosaic they made in the mirrored door to the sitting room. Whose sperm, where, did it matter, could it count? Sticky bodies, hair, faces, three hundred pesos, five . . . I am Joslyn Miller, I am a wife, also a former mother. Oh, my God, my hair—how will I ever get it right? Joslyn Miller, insatiable Joslyn Miller, pig . . .

She heard the sound of a door opening, a large sigh. Quickly she turned off the shower and in a striped terry-cloth robe worked frantically for a moment to do something with her hair. She called out, "Honey? Adrian? That you?"

"No," the reply came flatly through, "it's Joan of Arc. Who else were you expecting?"

"A clerk from one of the shops. I need a turquoise scarf for my ensemble."

"I'm sure you do. If one day of your life passed without buying something or other, I really think you'd just lie down and expire."

"Happy thought." She came into the room with a towel wrapped turban-like around her hair.

"And what the hell have you been up to? Smells like an incense factory in here."

"Doesn't it? These natives have the strangest ideas of keeping house, keeping clean. . . ."

"No editorial, okay? We'll have to get dressed early. Bobby's having a few of us for cocktails at his place before dinner. So hop to it."

Well, at least, she thought, the acid was fairly diluted tonight. And from his preoccupied look, his already worked-over body would be spared anything more. . . .

They met Gerald McAlister coming from a bungalow across the way, and walked with him to Robert's place. "Did you have a nice day?" she asked casually, unaware that his own early afternoon had been uncommonly similar to hers, except that the roles of the dwarf and Nita had been taken by two husky local youths. Seven hundred pesos.

ROBERT'S VERY RESTRICTED RECEPTION was perhaps the quietest gathering of the week. Certainly it was the most subdued. When you've been with the same people in such confining quarters for an entire week, you get a little starved for strangers. This was a void that Barry White, who was to be tonight's speaker, and Robert's stunning bride did more than a little to fill.

Particularly Jean Marie.

Of all his wives, she was bound to make the best impression. She won hands down in terms of actual beauty. She hadn't Brenda's lush spread or Beverly's tall muscular slenderness, which was just as well. She was just perfectly put together for a woman her size and age. Certainly she was the most gracious in the social sense, with a tactfulness that neither of the previous wives had been particularly adept at. The way she greeted the few guests, you might have thought she was the wife of a senator or governor, just that subtle blend of politics and breeding that marked her at once, and favorably. Adrian hadn't the least idea how Robert had sold himself to this one—what it was in her nature that allowed her to give secondary consideration to sex—but he had done himself proud. Who in all the world could look at *this* and doubt for a moment her husband's manhood?

David, from his vantage point—and against all the instincts and cynicism that had led him to remonstrate as he had with Robert earlier —found himself equally enthralled. Bite your tongue, he told himself. *This* girl was something else indeed.

Ellen, beside him on one of the Mediterranean-style sofas in the comfortable suite, was less dazzled. Hardly a thing one could put one's finger on, but too-perfect specimens had always put her off. She'd see.

Besides, there was something else on her mind right now, something that had been irritating her for several minutes. "Have you played count-the-noses yet, darling?" she whispered in David's ear.

"Count-the-noses?" he said. "What the hell are you talking about, Star?"

"The Who's Who of Who's Here, my darling. And who isn't. It's pretty obvious."

"Will you please to hell, darling, sweetheart, love, crazy lady, get to what the hell you're trying to tell me?"

"I would have thought you'd figure this one out for yourself. Just glance around and notice that every president or vice president of a division is here, Mark Banner included, which I'm sure sent Bobby's gall to his throat. But *that* one he daren't pass up. You don't play games with wonder boys."

"So?" said David. "So they're all here. The way it should be. For the life of me, Star, I don't get you. If there's someone—"

"Maury Sherman?"

David's blood pressure rose before the name was all the way out. "Goddamn!" He had Robert aside before he could catch his breath.

"I'm aware of his position, father, and I'm sure you're aware of the . . . impression he makes. I at least wanted Jean Marie's first impression of us—network management, I mean—to be a good one. I admit Maury Sherman has a razor-sharp mind, especially for the numbers, but he just doesn't fit. Not to mention his wife. Shirley . . . well, if there ever was such a thing as Brooklyn Jewish . . ."

David could have hit him then and there. "Middle age you reach," he said, "and you're still sounding like your mother word for word. Now you hear me, Bobby, I want you to get on that phone and apologize to Mr. Sherman. Tell him it was a typist's error and for him and Shirley to get over here like an hour ago. *All right?*"

The gall was doubly bitter when Maury Sherman said, "Don't you worry about it, kid. Good typists are as hard to come by as virgins these days. Shirley and me'll haul ass over there right now."

A scream never left Robert's throat, of course, although for a minute there he wasn't too sure it wouldn't. He told Adrian about it in a quiet corner in the suite's foyer.

"Hell, Bobby, you knew it was wrong. The man's a v.p., for Christ's sake. And it's not as if anyone didn't know him. Hell, he was general manager once, remember? There's not a station man here who hasn't had business of one kind or another with Maury Sherman. He's a goddamn legend in this business, and he's here for the duration. You'd better believe it."

Easier said . . .

". . . think they can get away with anything. And truth to tell, they just about can. Because *we* let them. I've said it before, I'll say it again. The day those motherfuckers in Washington . . ."

The mortal anguish on Shirley Sherman's face (large and thick and plagued even at her age with acne, only the light-green eyes, intelligent eyes, as signs that a woman of valor might live inside) was a terrible thing to see. That she felt uncomfortable with most of the people there, the wives especially, was an obvious and daily chore to be got through. That her burden had to be doubled by language he'd dare not use at home—and so deliberately loud—it was almost the last straw. It was only when David rushed to the rescue (literally, from his place beside Ellen) and tapped Maury lightly on the shoulder, calling him aside from his small group for a private conversation about the "feasibility of another demographic study," that the room settled back to its studied politeness.

Ellen motioned Shirley to sit beside her.

"Thank you," Shirley said, taking up most of the rest of the sofa. "For a minute there I was hoping for a forty-five in the head or maybe at least the ceiling falling in."

"I know exactly the feeling," said Ellen. "For a lot of my life, my dear, every day and every night brought that kind of feeling."

"Oh, sure. But you're . . . well, you're *the*."

"My dear, a *the*, as you call it, is also an *a*."

"I'm so mortified."

"But why? A slip of the tongue? Good heavens. I'd like a penny for everything that's come out of my mouth all these years."

"That's different. You're . . . you're Ellen Curry. But what you said a second ago . . . a slip of the tongue. Don't you believe it. It's no slip of the tongue, not by a long shot. It's a trademark of the tongue, as far as Maury's concerned. He's expected to play the tough little Jewish bantam with the nasty little tongue. Even among strangers. And at home . . . we've got five children, Miss Curry . . . Mrs. Abrams. Five children, and not one of them has ever heard a curse word in his life. Not in my home, they don't."

"You're very religious, Shirley?"

She shrugged. "*Comme çi, comme ça*. I do keep a kosher home, though. Like my mama and her mama before her. I'm afraid I've never been very inventive, Miss C—Mrs. Abrams."

"Make it Ellen. Please."

"Yes . . . Ellen. Anyway, what I mean to say is that the worse he feels, well, the worse that tongue of his gets. I don't say he's some diamond in the rough or anything like that, but Maury isn't what you all think he is. Not really."

Ellen smiled, beckoning a waiter. "Why don't you and I have ourselves a planter's punch? They're really terrific here."

"I tasted one of Maury's yesterday. Yes, I'd like that . . . Ellen."

The waiter nodded, was off and lost, the few guests having turned into practically the whole hotel.

"It's not an easy thing to say, Ellen," Shirley went on. "I mean, hardly knowing you and all, but there're two kinds of Jewish—and not Ashkenazi and Sephardic, either. I mean Jew like, say, your husband and his son, and Jew like Marty and Jane Levitt over there. They're the ones who made it, and not just financially either. You know what I mean. We may have identical backgrounds with the others, the white Jews, but there we part company. It just didn't take or something."

"What didn't take?"

"The Wasp Jew injection. That's what Maury calls it, anyway. But he's a good man, Maurice. He wouldn't look at another woman. And the children think he's God. Really God."

"Well, I will say this, Shirley: He's certainly a legend in broadcasting. And there aren't many legends who live to see it. You both should be very proud."

"Please"—Shirley Sherman shook her head—"don't try to make me feel good about it. It was awful and you know it."

"I'm not so sure. There's something so innocent . . . so harmless . . . when Maury throws the book away. And for the good things, well, I'd bet you're a damn good wife and mother—it shows all over you. As for Maury . . . as my husband has said, 'I'd give up ten slick-and-polished men for one-half of a Maury Sherman. That's how important he is.' Unquote. That's not such a bad thing to have said about you. Not a bad thing at all."

Shirley Sherman rose. "Thank you, Ellen. That means a lot to me. Thank you again. I . . ."

Within seconds Maury Sherman was back with his group, chuckling to himself, voice lowered for confidence but really raised for the world to hear. "Can you imagine what the Old Man wanted? He wants me to stop using raw language so much. Can you imagine? I mean, what else is there to call those pricks in Washington but cocksuckers?"

A presentation such as we have just experienced makes all of us realize, even for the thousandth time, that a network is indeed the sum of many diverse parts.

A word? A phrase? No. We couldn't begin to do justice to it. What

I think instead must be mentioned in these closing minutes of the presentation is the variety, the independence, the singularity—and at the same time the extraordinary teamwork—of the people *behind* the schedule: the many you have seen and heard these past two days, the others who work with such dedication to making a network, *your* network, what it is. When you have people power such as this, crises seem to lose their force.

And it is that same marvelous chemistry of individualism and collectivism that makes this affiliate body the strong and supple and lively and serious force it is in the communities of this country.

In my opening remarks I said that all of us in this room—the network, its affiliate family—that all of us are bound together by the same interests, and that our primary interest, together, is the American people. I would like to reestablish that thought now, before our business meeting this afternoon, because even there—in the intimate and detailed dialogue between us—this must be our pervading thought. Because now, more than ever before in the history of any nation's communications, the responsibility—and I prefer to call it "privilege" —is on us. And the way we manage our house affects every house in this nation we serve.

We have brought you our best. We are fortunate that we had the best to give to it. And I must say that the golden days of television, so often referred to in speeches and articles, were *not* twenty years ago, as so many would have us believe. They are now . . . today, tomorrow . . . and with the spirit of cooperation and enterprise among all of us here, they can be golden for a long time to come.

I thank you, and God bless.

With this peroration from David, and a coaxing of Ellen Curry to sing a song or two, the formal meetings at Dorado drew to a close. Ellen, suspecting they'd ask her to sing, had rehearsed "Happy Days" and "Side by Side" with the island orchestra most of the morning.

The social affairs, as always, were elaborate beyond conception. Hamlin J. Hirschmyer had outdone even himself. The business meetings had been the smoothest ever. Even violence in children's programs, station rivalry, hyping up the news programs, the perennial hostility of station managers toward network program departments, a deep-rooted resentment of the mystique and silent intrigue, real or imagined, under which the programmers seemed to operate, thorns in the stations' sides—even these were submerged. In other words, the network was pleased as punch with its stations, and its stations held the network in great esteem. They had all arrived on a good note, were leaving on a good note: communications executives of America at work, at play. Not a good headache among them.

The headaches were back in New York, where over the next three years the television networks would be as bullish, bearish, bullish again, and bearish, as the roller-coaster New York Stock Exchange. It would be some time before the network and its affiliates would again meet for such a love feast.

NOT TO MENTION some of its most prominent movers and shakers, including their wives, old and new.

55

FEBRUARY, 1973. Late afternoon.
Hollywood, California.
Adrian Miller:
"I'd like to make this brief, and suspect you would, too. A general observation first. Three recent phenoms have come our way of late, and I doubt we can overestimate their impact. First is CBS's guts in putting on *All in the Family*, which may have been obvious for the British viewing public, but for America . . . no one could see it. Except somebody *did*. Second—and don't laugh—is Howard Cosell. He's made pro football a national prime-time attraction. He's someone they can love to hate. Irritation, in the right package, we're amazed to find, can be endearing as mother love. Mark here and Dutch Cottingham have tried to get him, but he's apparently ABC's body and soul, at least for now.

"You ready for the third? I thought you'd never ask. Well, it's the made-for-TV movie; ninety minutes, two hours. It's meant that movies are no longer placed into movie-night spots, just another program in the endless stream of them. No. Thanks particularly to Mark here, the TV original movie is what we now build our schedules around.

"So much for the prime-time wisdom, except to tell all of you that all of us believe the 1973–74 season can be the turning point for *all* our fortunes. We'll toss it around awhile now, if you like. Okay?"

A meeting of all the West Coast program and promotion people in UBC's new quarters on Sunset Boulevard. The conference room alone was nearly twice the size of the New York editions. Adrian, at the head of the table, sat back now.

"Care to tell us, Adrian, what you think of the development product you've seen?" Digger Green, one of the new men. Always the first.

"Well, let's put it this way. I refuse to answer on the grounds . . ."

"I mean it *seriously*, sir."

In just about two minutes he was going to pin that little shit's ears back for him.

"There is never a time when I am *not* serious, Mr. Green. But questions like 'How did you like Italy?' 'Did you dig France?' 'How was Madrid?'—questions that leave no room for one hotel better than another, one restaurant better than another, one *program* better than another—frankly, they annoy me."

Green said nothing, lowered his eyes to the pad and pencils in front of him. Mark jumped in.

"There is a point I think we ought to make clear, Adrian. A success like *All in the Family*—still number one in the ratings—can mislead us badly. We all run the risk of jumping on bandwagons and not looking where we're going. A meteorically successful live-audience comedy about a Brooklyn bigot is not a mandate for anything goes. We've already been through the violence thing, and we'll go through it again, no doubt. From some of those birds in Washington you'd think television was nothing but a Commie-inspired Walter Cronkite and a vast rerun of *Bonnie and Clyde*.

"After violence, after the startling frankness of a Bunker family, what's the coming cry—sex! I can already hear them. It's not alarm time yet, but it *is* time we kept strict rein on series content as well as specials. There's no doubt that a year from now, two, we'll be deluged with stuff ranging from prostitution to rape, from homosexuality to incest. So I suggest that in reading scripts we try especially to evaluate for good taste. And not just by L.A. and New York standards, either. Right now we *can* do a show like *That Certain Summer*—you know, ABC's movie about a homosexual marriage. It was handled in such good taste and with such sensibility that it put us maybe two or three years ahead of the game. Well, on UBC we want nothing less than that kind of quality approach.

"Again, this isn't to say that someday the home screens won't be lighting up with the likes of *I Am Curious (Yellow)* or *Last Tango in Paris*, but that day's one *hell* of a long time off. And while we're at it, what we say or suggest in our on-air and print advertising is equally important to the judgment of the program involved.

"I guess we just have to remind ourselves morning, noon, and night that this really is a family medium, supported *by* the family—through its purchase of products as well as our numbers watching—and it's going to be that for a long while to come. . . . I didn't mean to go on so long, but—like our esteemed leader here—I felt there were a few things that maybe needed saying."

*And maybe you're getting a little too smart for your own good,
Mark. Like they say, I made you, I can break you. "Esteemed leader,"
my ass! Just watch it there, boy. Just watch it.*

"Something else?" said Adrian. "Rod?"

Rod Kellerman, in charge of programming for the Los Angeles
offices, had been handpicked by Adrian, even though Robert at the
time had found him "too lackadaisical, too good-natured; doesn't
know how to cat-and-mouse it with producers. And that's what a
Coast job calls for—cat-and-mouse." He'd recently been named the
most popular programmer in the industry by a *TV Times* poll. He was
balding blond, pleasant if not especially good-looking, often under-
rated because he spoke softly and seldom.

"One thing," he said now. "How does it look to Levitt and Merck
and the others on a reversal of the access rule?" The so-called prime-
time access rule, to which the FCC had ordered stations to adhere,
effective October 1, 1971, returned to local stations for local programming thirty minutes of prime time for which the networks had pre-
viously always provided programming. That meant that the networks
had had to relinquish seven half-hours a week, which at the time had
appeared to be a financial stunner. The obvious purpose of the ruling,
of course, was to provide stations with a part of those precious evening
hours of maximum viewership for programs of their own origin, a
"community effort of a quality nature." Most stations throughout the
country, however, had gleefully gobbled up the most popular in
syndicated game shows, outdoor adventure shows, and second- and
third-rate dramas of doctors and cops—a marketable bonanza for station ownership, since the revenues from full local or regional or even
national sponsorship didn't have to be shared with the networks. It
was the 7:30–8:00 P.M. EST time period that was eventually returned
to the stations, and it soon became clear that there would be no really
meaningful "access" to prime time for independent quality producers,
as the FCC had hoped. A hand-delivered letter from the FCC to all
the networks had read, "It seems to the Commission that the particular
hours of network occupancy of prime time may well have a significant
effect in demonstrating the efficacy of the rule. Specifically, the Commission believes that the selection of an 8–11 P.M. time period would
better serve the public interest as a general matter." As the months
passed, the so-called blow to the networks was proving to be over-
rated. In meeting the accommodations, the networks had been able to
concentrate more of their time on a few fractions less of a backbreaking national programming scheduling.

Or, as Adrian now answered Rod Kellerman's query, "Why don't
we put it this way, Rod: None of us is ready to take the pipe over it.
Truth is that, at UBC anyway, we never wanted to start prime time

at seven-thirty. You boys out here must be as well aware of that as we are in New York. Seven-thirty has always been one bitch of a time to fill. A time period—nationally, at any rate—that's not very successful whatever you do. And I think it's pretty much an open secret that the demographic makeup at that early-evening hour is poor; they're either too young or too old, as the song goes. So we see no change in status in the near future. Since the specific half-hour time period a network has to relinquish to an affiliate is not spelled out, I wouldn't be surprised to see the other networks play musical chairs, using the seven-thirty time period when it seems competitively advantageous, giving the ten-thirty–to–eleven period back to the station when that's more congenial. A back-and-forth kind of thing. At UBC, however, I think I can safely say it's eight to eleven across the board.

"Question? Yes, Carl?"

Carl Klempner was a relatively new program executive, hired personally by Mark after a single hour's interview. Like Mark, he had been with Metro.

"Does it look like we'll add another movie night in the near future?"

"Care to take that one, Mark?"

"Depends. First, on product availability. Secondly, on the competition. Of course, most if not all of you know my own personal feeling about this. If we let ourselves become merely the motion picture projector through which theatrical film is run, then I wonder about our reason for existence."

Adrian: "Another? Sure, Price. What's eating at that legal-eagle brain this afternoon?"

Cavett Price was notorious around the studios for his attention to every item in small print, no matter how many hours or days it took him.

"Hope this isn't a bomb or something," he said, eyes directly on Mark, "but the question's for Mark. Is the magazine concept still viable or is it out? And if my timing in asking is lousy, am *I* out?"

Mark laughed with the others. "You're saved by the bell, Cav. A bell that rang just this morning, in fact. The Board has approved additional funds for researching the project, so we're alive and well. As of this moment, at least."

"And living in the bottomless brain of Mark Banner," said Adrian; jocularly, he thought, intended. . . . He was sorry the moment it was out, but there was nothing he could do. There being no further questions . . .

"I can't imagine why I said that," he said afterward to Mark as the chauffeured limousine took them back to the Bel-Air Hotel, where they were staying.

"Doesn't matter, Adrian. Doesn't matter at all"—grinning so openly, good-naturedly.

I could tear that damn grin off your face, thought Adrian. And what the hell's the matter with me, anyway?

SEVERAL THINGS.

First, they'd brought their wives, which they rarely did on business trips. But Robert had insisted, so they were here.

Second, the one night out with the boys—last night—had left his head one hell of a mess.

Third, David and Ellen, for reasons beyond comprehension, were flying to Los Angeles tomorrow.

It must have been on Mark's mind, too, because he asked as they rounded the steep curves of Sunset as the car neared the Bel-Air enclave, "Pretty unusual for the Old Man to be doing this, isn't it? I thought they were taking off for the Greek Islands tomorrow."

"Yes," said Adrian. "Well . . . I haven't the foggiest."

"Maybe he wants to see rough cuts," Mark said.

Adrian didn't answer. The rest of the drive was silent.

Robert and Jean Marie, Joslyn and Vivian were dressed and waiting in the cocktail lounge when they arrived. His precious mate, Adrian could see, was already on her third or fourth. What the hell manner of guilt was she exorcizing this time? Mark's newly beloved, he noticed too, was likewise feeling no pain.

He and Mark hurried through their showers to join them. Adrian could have anticipated most of the scenario over drinks. It went like this:

ROBERT: The staff meeting went well, I presume?

ADRIAN: Fine.

ROBERT: No disturbing questions?

ADRIAN: All questions are disturbing.

ROBERT: Please, Adrian. I'm hardly in the mood for wit tonight. Much less half-wit.

JEAN MARIE: What in the world? Why in creation do ya'll go at each other that way? Every time you meet, seems to me.

JOSLYN: It's called long-standing mutual admiration and affection.

JEAN MARIE: Well, no thank you. I'll take mine in different bottles, I assure you.

ROBERT: You screened the two new ones?

ADRIAN: *The Sunsetters* and *Fung Yu?*

JEAN MARIE: Well, pardon me! But you all aren't about to put a show with a name like *that* on. Are you?

ROBERT: A working title.

JOSLYN: It's working, all right. For everybody but me.

ROBERT: So?

ADRIAN: I think Mark feels better about *Sunsetters* than I do. It's just too . . . slick. I suppose that's the word. Too pretty-pretty to believe. The lead's a stiff.

ROBERT: Who cast him? The studio? Us?

ADRIAN: Digger Green was hot on him for some reason.

MARK: That's not quite true, Adrian. He's a contract player at the studio. Tell you the truth, I think we got took. Anyway, he'd have to go, under any circumstances.

JOSLYN: What's his name?

MARK: Dick Dixon.

JOSLYN: I like him already.

ADRIAN: Another? Bobby? Mark?

ROBERT: One, perhaps. We'll have more at the Zanuck's. What time are we due?

JEAN MARIE: Sevenish.

ROBERT: How were the *Fung* dailies?

ADRIAN: Floor's yours, Mark.

MARK: I think you know my feeling. From the first script.

ROBERT: I still can't imagine what father saw in it. From the scripts, I mean.

ADRIAN: Something different, I suppose. Half-Chinese, half-American private eye. Actually, with a lighter touch it just might have worked. Lippman's so heavy-handed at direction.

ROBERT: Altogether, an encouraging day. What's on for tomorrow?

MARK: Universal. Ed O'Leary has enough of *Time for Simba* to take up the morning. They're pretty high on it.

JOSLYN: They're right. Big cats spell sex, this or any year.

ADRIAN: I kind of dread the lunch with Jimmy Black. Poor bastard. Nothing's worked for him in ten years.

ROBERT: You're relieved of that, anyway.

ADRIAN: Oh?

ROBERT: Father. He wants the three of us for lunch at the Brown Derby. Ellen's taking the girls to Scandia.

ADRIAN: When are they due in?

ROBERT: Early. Before noon.

ADRIAN: I admit I'm Alice's shadow right now. Getting curiouser and couriouser.

ROBERT: You're hardly alone.

MARK: You're sure he wants me too?

ROBERT: I would hardly have bothered you, Mark, if I weren't certain, now would I?

JEAN MARIE: My *lord*, Joslyn, what's wrong with you tonight, hon?

There's oodles of room, darlin'. I'd be obliged if you wouldn't keep bumpin' up against me.

MARK: That's a beautiful dress, Viv. I don't remember it. New?

VIVIAN: I've worn it to at least five dinner parties with you.

JEAN MARIE: Men! Aren't they maddenin'?

MARK: We haven't had time to go over the Lincoln special, Adrian. Bill Covey wants to see us while we're here.

ADRIAN: You see him. He gives me hives.

MARK: Whatever you say.

VIVIAN: I hate this place. It's all sun, and it's all so goddamn cold. I hate this goddamn place.

JEAN MARIE: We'll go shoppin' tomorrow, honey. At Bullock's. I'll have you goin' away lovin' it! You'll come too, Joslyn, darlin'? If you'll promise to stop bumpin' against everybody all the time.

ADRIAN: Curiouser and curiouser. Is there something you're holding back, Bobby?

ROBERT: Well, nothing to cause father to change plans so abruptly and come out here.

ADRIAN: And that's?

ROBERT: Hitch Cummings had a heart attack this afternoon.

MARK: Hitch? My God, what kind?

ROBERT: Coronary.

ADRIAN: Jesus! Where?

ROBERT: In his office.

MARK: God! Where is he? Doctors? Lenox Hill?

ROBERT: He died on the way to Bellevue.

"WHAT'S THIS DRINKING all of a sudden?" Mark asked her when they'd returned to the bungalow from the dinner party.

"I know," Vivian said. "It is too much. This place, Mark. This terrible awful place."

"You're not exactly a teetotaler in New York or Westport."

She frowned, went on removing her gown. Then smiled, shyly, slyly. "Mark, fix me a nightcap? Please?"

Would it ever be right again? Ever? Would she?

"WHAT'S ALL THIS BUSINESS of you bumping into people? Brushing up against people?" Adrian asked, taking off his slacks.

"I drink," Joslyn said, her heart in her throat. Was he going to tell her finally that he knew about her, as she suspected?

"Well, do it on your own time."

"My own time? What the *hell* are you talking about?"

"When you're with me, you're Mrs. Adrian Miller, wife of the president of the UBC Television Network. Dig? When you are away from me—far away from me—you can be Miss Joslyn Cunt Strauss to your heart's content. Dig?"

He popped her once across the bottom but otherwise didn't touch her again all night.

Not even when she cried.

And she cried partly in relief that he really didn't know what Robert, for all his meanness, apparently had never told him. But for how long . . . ?

"WHY DO YOU PICK on Joslyn like that?" Robert asked her through half-closed doors as they prepared for bed.

"I didn't know I did."

"All that ridiculous chatter about bumping into people, brushing against people . . . really, Jeanie, it *does* get somewhat, well, suggestive at times."

"It's meant to, hon."

"Well, I'd appreciate it if you'd allow that irrepressible charm to take a breather once in a while."

"You mean bite my tongue?"

"I mean that an occasional low profile is not a mortal sin."

"All right, I'm hip," she said, but not really understanding his irritation. "I'll try to do better by you, darlin', I promise. Now turn the lights out and go play with yourself like a good boy."

"So WE WONDER again, eh? What's the old fart up to this time?"

David was dipping generously into his Cobb salad, his favorite at the Derby since his first visit in the early thirties. With him in the soft leather booth were Robert, Adrian, and Mark Banner. Whatever it was David Abrams had chosen to impart to three of his top executives, he couldn't have chosen a more conspicuous spot. They were dead center in the main room, *Daily Variety* a few booths south, *The Hollywood Reporter* a few feet north. And from the opening line they had not found a more agreeable ambiance than the hundreds of show-business caricatures fighting for space on the walls.

"So I won't be smart-ass and do the preamble to the Constitution. I'll do the first line of the Constitution itself. Mark Banner, how would you feel about being named president of the United Broadcasting Company Television Network?"

Daily Variety starts scribbling furiously. The Hollywood Reporter runs like sixty for a foyer phone. The paid executive secretary of the

Hollywood Radio and Television Society starts writing on a napkin.
Three booths down an excited voice is raised: "Get Stanton at his
hotel in Washington! Now!" Several booths up, another voice is heard
to command, "Go get Elton Rule in New York." In the booth con-
nected with it no fewer than six pieces of silverware and three pieces
of good china clatter to the floor.

Which wasn't what happened, of course, but to Mark Banner it was
as real as his own grasp of what David Abrams had just finished
saying. And if Robert Abrams and Adrian Miller had been omitted
from the fantasy, it was only because their faces had achieved a color
unrelated to any known or describable ones.

Hollywood, California
February 18, 1973
. . . and I had to get this down on paper, and in your hands, dad, be-
fore the shock wears off. Pronto! And the reality of it hits like a pile of
bricks.

The whole thing happened, as I try to piece it together, with a
special Board meeting in New York, the only members absent being
Adrian Miller and Robert Abrams, who have been with me on the
Coast, looking at dailies, rough cuts, etc., of the materials we'll be
creating next year's schedule from.

The basic idea of restructuring now had to come from the Old Man
himself, and that he caught his own son by surprise is the most sur-
prising thing of all. If Robert Abrams had any inkling at all, he at
least never revealed it out here.

It seems UBC is expanding in all directions: more theatre complexes,
reshaping of the Record Division with three new labels, broad acquisi-
tion program that takes in more trade publications, national spot-sales
representation agency, expansion of owned-stations operations in New
York, Chicago, Los Angeles, San Francisco, and Boston; and millions
invested in theatrical enterprises (mostly concert and popular operatic,
obviously some kind of sop to Robert Abrams), increased leisure-time
activities, including UBC parks and zoos, and a special corporate Bi-
centennial operation for the years beyond 1976. All this, plus a con-
centration on news and news documentaries, which Robert Abrams has
been pushing for so long, and a complete overhauling of the radio
network and the seven owned-and-operated radio stations.

As I get it, the thinking went this way: a top-heavy program but the
company found itself far too light at the top—the Old Man and Robert
Abrams the only real visible heavyweights, the rest competent and
bright, etc., but not of "substantial public weight," as the Old Man
put it. So—your old buddy Adrian Miller moves up to senior vice
president in charge of all UBC corporate activities, directly under
Robert Abrams, who continues in his presidency but now on a much-

enlarged scale. And of course he's still on the Board of Directors. I go into Adrian's spot as president of the Television Network (reporting still to Adrian), which leaves v.p. for Programming and v.p. for Sales (poor old Hitch Cummings checked out, as you know) again up for grabs. My own hunch is that Robert Abrams' "nephew," Fred Wiener —he's produced an off-Broadway hit and a Broadway bomb, with Abrams money—is practically a sure shot for programming v.p., never mind what I might think about it. And to balance that out, the sales position will more or less be left to my discretion, with Adrian Miller advising. I lean at the moment toward Steve Lilly, the Southern boy I think I once wrote you about when he and his wife had dinner with Vivian and me one weekend.

The main event for you, I realize—and yours truly as well, I admit it—is that your son Mark has finally bagged some very choice real estate in that room at the top, but while you're busting buttons, pop, leave some room for the backbreaking responsibility and ass-breaking work I've got ahead of me. Which I quickly add I look forward to. By the way, my appointment was by unanimous consent of the Board.

There are a few flies in the ointment, though. Vivian's pleased, I guess. In a way it's what she's wanted from the beginning, but she's not exactly turning cartwheels. Says it also means seeing even less of me than she does now. I've been doing everything I can think of to get her to start adoption proceedings, but the strike out is full and complete. I've even confidentially looked into the possibility of adopting a Vietnamese orphan, something I feel deeply about. But if and when the opportunity comes, unless Viv is a hell of a long way from where she is now . . .

Maybe you can do something, say something, when you come up in May, dad. God knows she needs something—friend, psychiatrist, minister, something. Or maybe I do. Maybe it's all me, as she so often seems to be saying with her eyes if never even by the least slip of the tongue. I don't know, dad. I honest to God don't know.

The other one or two less than three cheers is from, of all people, Adrian Miller himself. Not that anything has been said, at least not to me directly. Just your son's damn intuition again. But for a time or two here—well, it's been as if some grand design of his, some planned split-second timing almost—as if he'd been caught off balance by all this and suspects I personally have done something underhanded to make it come out so in my favor. I don't know, God only knows what really goes through that one's mind. Anyway, it's done, I had nothing to do with its doing except being there and being good (and damn it, dad, I am, I know that in my guts and I'll be damned if I'll plead false modesty). Still, as you can gather, there promise to be some interesting times ahead. Edith, with her sure-shot talent for deflating in advance the well-stuffed shirt, intoned, "Now he belongs to the ages," which opened it up for a few minutes of unrestrained needling by the whole Programming Department.

I'll be back in New York next week and will call you as soon as I can. We look forward to seeing you in May, dad, and if Aunt Jennie wants to come with you, you know she's more than welcome. Take care now, and try to stay with that diet Dr. Temple put you on. He dropped me a note that the weight loss is the best thing that ever happened to you.

Till soon, then, dad. Love from both of us,

MARK

David and Robert's reception on the Coast to honor Adrian, Mark, Fred Wiener, and Steve Lilly (both of whom, as Mark had anticipated, had received their own appointments within the week) was held at the Bel-Air Hotel, with Hamlin J. Hirschmyer flown in from New York to oversee—to *produce* it. In a specially erected tent in one of the lush front gardens.

In attendance, paying court, were eight hundred people. Nine? A thousand? The long and the short and the tall.

The music had started. . . .

Heaven. I'm in heaven. And I'm so thrilled that I can hardly speak . . .

"HAVE YOU EVER?"

"I've never."

"Hasn't been a wingding like this since the bad good old days when Louis Mayer threw one just to get laid."

"No DOUBT in my mind. David Abrams wouldn't be putting on this kind of deal if he wasn't making a very special point—name of Mark Banner."

"I agree he's the key—"

"Key? The Miller move looks like the old kick upstairs, whatever the hell they try to make of it. Banner is what this was all about. Question is, can he hack it?"

"SHE's one lucky woman, right?"

"Who?"

"Vivian Banner. Having *that*."

"He can, as the old saying goes, put his shoes under my bed any old time he wants. I just may send a message."

"Couldn't agree more."

"Congratulations, Mark."
"Thanks, Sharon. A million."
"Thanks for calling, Mark."
"You know I couldn't."
"Up your ass, Mark. Up Vivian's too, for good measure."

"Ava Gardner do a TV series? Are you crazy?"
"If anyone can pull it off, it's Mark Banner."
"You really believe that?"
"Wait and see, chum. Chump. Wait and see."

"Imagine! Lana here! Ingrid! Bette!"
"So?"
"Well, I mean . . . imagine!"
"Because it's only TV, you mean?"
"Well, it's just that—"
"Come off it, kid. It's a new scene out there. The lions and tigers aren't named Mayer or Thalberg any more. Or Daryl or C.B. either. It's David now, as in David Abrams. And Frank and Bill and Leonard and Bob, as in money."
"Please, honey. No sad songs, I'm having too good a time."

"Never would have thought Abrams would make such a move this fast. Doesn't sit too well with the heir apparent, you can bet on that."
"You mean Bobby?"
"I mean Bobby."
"I don't get it. Robert Abrams has as much power as any man can have. At least while his old man's still around."
"You think so? David Abrams was, is, and will be UBC, as long as there's a breath in him."
"But there's never been that much politics at UBC. The others, yes, but UBC?"
"UBC invented it."

"Now that he's prexy, do you think he'll really push this magazine concept?"
"Wouldn't surprise me."
"He'd be crazy as hell to move before he's really in."
"I take it you're not with it. The magazine thing, I mean."

"Oh, I'm with it, all right. All the way. It has an unmistakable aroma."

"SHE's GOOD-LOOKING actually."
"Banner's wife?"
"Her."
"Not particularly friendly, I must say."
"One of two reasons, hard to say which."
"Oh?"
"Either she takes being Mrs. President seriously or she drinks."
"You can say that again."
"What?"
"She drinks."

"How WELL do you think he'll work with Bobby?"
"Mark? Hard to say. Mark's a pretty rare bird, you know? A dreamer and a realist."
"Jesus. Finish your drink."

"SAY, WHAT'S with the Miller broad?"
"Joslyn?"
"Josh-lyn."
"I don't get it."
"You will. Just get in line. She's even feeling up the waiters. First bash I've ever been to where champagne was served by a battalion of hard-ons."

"STOCK jumped almost two points today, I see."
"Banner's reputation's no secret to the Street, you know."
"Old man looks like he's swallowed canaries."
"Pigeons, darling."

"BIG JUMP for you, Steve. Congrats."
"Thanks, pal. Need all the congrats I can get."
"Still a dream, eh?"
"Don't pinch me. I bleed."

"YOU MUST BE a very happy woman tonight, Mrs. Miller."
"Shut the fuck up."

"THINK Wiener'll make it?"

"If Banner makes it."

"Wiener's Banner's boy? That what you mean?"

"The opposite. Wiener's a kind of Abrams in-law."

"Then what the hell are you getting at?"

"Simple. Banner's as much a one-man show as old David Abrams himself. He could kill himself with success . . . leaving room for young Freddie."

"Crazy business."

"Believe it."

"PRETTY LITTLE THING, isn't she?"

"Steve Lilly's wife?"

"The same."

"Mousy little thing, you mean. Right?"

"Right on."

"Great material for a soap. Real twist. This time out the cat *marries* the mouse."

"I GUESS I'll just have to get used to it, Jean Marie. It's not easy, a person like myself. It's like having to come up every few minutes or so for another don't-fail-Steve pill or something."

"You're doin' fine, Beth. Fine. Don't keep underestimating yourself. It's worse than drink. Absolutely destroys the liver."

"I'VE LOOKED FORWARD so to meeting you, Mr. Wiener."

"Fred. Freddie."

"Well, Fred, Freddie. Your reputation precedes you."

"Thanks. A couple of things precede you too, Miss Moore."

"MARK, I have a terrible headache. I'm going back to the room."

"Viv, please, I'm a guest of honor. . . ."

"*I said I'm going back to the room!*"

"Vivian, look. Viv . . ."

"I SEE Cosell's here. Think he'd really leave ABC?"

"Doubt it. Just gets a charge out of scaring 'em to death."

"Freddie interested in the *Northwest Passage* thing you want to do?"
"Mark Banner is. That's all that matters. Freddie's just warming the
seat—a family courtesy. Or haven't you heard?"
"Tell me more."

"So you're his wife."
"I beg your pardon?"
"Mark Banner's. You're his wife."
"Yes. Occasionally."
"Ma'am?"
"Nothing."

"Think they'll drop *The Larry Lester Show*?"
"You mean since Mark's been upped?"
"Something like that. He's never been happy with it, you know."
"In Lester's case it doesn't signify."
"Oh? Why not?"
"UBC dropping silly-ass Lester would be like India giving up
people."

"Congratulations, Adrian. Must be pretty rarefied air up there."
"Thanks. On a clear day I can see it coming from above and below."

"They tell me Banner's going ass to elbows on the movies-made-for-
television kick. Could be great for us chickens."
"Already is. I can't think of more than a half-dozen or so holdouts.
Brando, Newman, Redford, Peck . . . not a good fistful when you think
about it. And I doubt that even those guys will hold out much longer.
Hardly a man alive doesn't need a quickie or two in between."

"I hear she's doing a pilot for them."
"That has-been?"
"She's an actress. And a real actress isn't that easy to come by these
days. Not out here, anyway."
"She'll bomb."
"But at least she'll have *worked*. Two weeks maybe, but at least
she'll have . . ."

———————

"You SHOULD never have retired, Miss Curry. If ever the industry needed you, it's now. All that unpalatable junk—it's downright demoralizing."

"It's lovely of you to say it, my dear, but I can't imagine a more demoralizing situation than a hundred-and-ten-year-old broad singing 'Baby, It's Cold Outside.' Can you?"

"You KNOW, the big money's going on a walloping UBC season this fall. You've got your job cut out for you to top that, Mark."

"It's top or the bottom, Joe."

"I HEAR David Abrams has promised to keep a low profile, now that the restructuring's been done."

"Yeah. Try holding your breath."

"MR. ABRAMS? David Abrams?"

"Yes?"

"My name is Greer, sir. Joel Greer. I happened to be out here from New York on agency business and was invited tonight. I wanted to say—"

"Which agency is that?"

"BBD&O. I'm in media."

"And your name again?"

"Greer, sir. Joel Greer. Once upon a time it was Griebsberg. Anyway, when I was eleven or twelve, somewhere in there, that was the name when I wrote you a letter, something about violence on television. And you were nice enough to write me back a personal note. I just wanted to say that—"

"Would it be this letter?" Taking it from his wallet.

"My God! You mean you've kept that letter all these years? I can't believe—"

"You can believe, Mr. Greer. I found your letter so impressive that I've just carried it around with me all these years. As a reminder of who and what we are, as responsible broadcasters, I mean. Hell, I still read it at staff meetings. A few people may want your scalp when they find out you wrote the letter I use as the text of my sermons so often. . . . Of course, its effect was based on the fact that it was written by a bright and sensitive child. And you're obviously no longer a child. . . . In media, you say? Ad agency? Television?"

"Mainly, sir, yes. For all house accounts. I worked often, of course, with Hitch before he died, and I know Steve Lilly. But this . . . after all these years . . ."

"Let's find a quieter corner somewhere, shall we, Joel? I'd like to talk to you. You know, I've often wondered what kind of man the boy who wrote that letter would turn out to be."

"HE's A SNOB, I think. In every sense of the word. Socially, intellectually, sexually . . ."

"Wiener? Yes, so I hear. Well, at least with snobs you know where you stand. It's the just-folks guys you want to worry about. The honest ones too. Like Banner over there. Nice and honest, and a sonofabitch to deal with, I tell you."

"WONDER why Bob Abrams always looks like he's sucking on an onion. Christ, with a wife like he's got I'd be sucking on. . . ."

"TWENTY SHARE. That's all I'll give it. The doctor shows have had it, man."

"Okay, wise-ass, so what's the next cycle?"

"Sanitation workers?"

"WELL. Big evening, Steve?"

"The biggest, Mark. For me, I mean. Thanks to you. I'll never forget this, Mark. Not ever."

"Just keep us in the black, Steve, which should keep me in the pink— you should forgive the new president's turn of phrase."

"I JUST HEARD Barbra Streisand's coming here."

"So what? Isn't everybody?"

"But my God, what'll I do?"

"What'll you do?"

"Oh, come off it, Stella. You know I look exactly like her."

"WHAT'D YOU THINK of the Hooray for Hilda thing?"

"Back to the drawing board."

"But Mark, that pilot's already cost twice as much as a feature film."

"Back to the drawing board."

"I wish a real-life writer would walk in."

"Writer? We got hundreds of them here."

"I mean honest-to-God writers. Like Koszinsky, Heller, Capote, Taylor Caldwell, Victoria Holt, Harold Robbins, Nabokov, Frank Slaughter . . ."

"Your discrimination, Ethel, is something else."

"Word has it that the reason Miller was kicked upstairs is his involvement in too much day-to-day stuff."

"You kidding? David Abrams knows it every time they change a roll of toilet paper in the fourth-floor men's room. Look again." . . . looking at Mark.

"I hear Larry Lester's on his way out. And Barry White's just about had it too."

"Don't be too sure. UBC may change the chairs at the top, but the one thing it's never had enough of is star value. Don't forget, Ellen Curry pulled 'em through more than one shaky season."

"That's Bob Abrams' third wife, isn't it? Jean something, I think?"

"Jean Marie, real southernlike. He's partial to the area—his mother was from there, you know."

"No, I didn't, but I do know this one is tits and tail, and a real smart head as well. Wonder how much she'll take him for?"

"Don't be such a cynic. Maybe this one will make it. You know, even the high and mighty are entitled to a break once in a while."

"This one's son of David. That's starting out with a pretty good break right there . . ."

"I wonder why father's spending so much time with that Greer fellow. Almost half the night."

"Whatever it is, it isn't good, so relax and enjoy it, Bobby."

"This whole new setup, Adrian. I know, of course, it's more than it seems, but exactly *what* . . ."

"What's the matter?"

"I left my pills in the room."

"You mean that's Ellen Curry?"

"None other."

"My God, she doesn't look a day over forty. If that."
"Same old deal, kid. Them that's got . . ."

"PAUL, TELL ME SOMETHING. There's a rumor making the rounds that ICP is prepped to make a takeover bid of UBC. Anything to it?"
"With the Washington troubles ICP has? I wouldn't put much faith in it."
"Still, if ever a communications outfit was ripe for the picking . . ."

"THE NETWORKS are like the Tournament of Roses. Break your ass all year and half the pretties are dead or dying by nightfall."
"So?"
"I need a refill."

"THINK HE'LL SWEEP OUT the Coast?"
"Who? Wiener? It's still Banner's ball game. With Miller behind him. Head your nose in *that* direction." Said with straight face.

"DAVID?"
"Yes, Star?"
"Can we call it a night?"
"Still oversexed?"
"Exhausted."
"Save a little, huh?"
"Is there no limit to you, darling?"
"To neither of us, Star. To neither of us."

56

THE SUN rose slowly in the early morning hours, the red-brown hills awakening patchily to meet it. Few of the night's revelers were on hand to see it, however.

An exception was Joel Greer. He'd hardly slept at all.

"Baby?"

The yawning intimacy of his wife Janet beside him told him that while she may have dozed once or twice, it had been a fitful night for her as well. Her snuggling closeness was reassuring.

"Baby?" she murmured again.

"Mmn?"

"Tell it to me again. Word for word. One more time."

"Mmn. Soon. Soon. First things first."

"Before I even go to the bathroom?"

"Before you even go to the bathroom."

And love. Lingering, languorous love. Lasting, or so it seemed, a honeyed decade or two; honey-scent in every pore, every stretch length of her; honey-hair in every part of him. They came together, lay together in tangled moisture for minutes afterward.

And held to each other in still another amazed retelling. "And what Banner's and Wiener's reactions were, it's pretty hard to say. I mean, what could it be when the old man as good as says, 'I want you to meet your new vice president in charge of Program Development,' right in the middle of a Barnum and Bailey celebration? And that's the storeee!"

"It's lovely. I mean, he must be a lovely man. A really very lovely man."

"An in-charge man, with a reputation for instant decisions."

She stretched against the length of him. "A letter written by a twelve-year-old boy, carried with him in his wallet all these years . . . I'm going to feel silly even telling our friends . . . I mean, these things don't happen, I mean, they just don't—"

"You mean, they just did." He pulled her closer. "Mama's going to blow her cork," he said.

Some minutes later, allowing for the three-hour time difference, he had told his mother in New York the bare bones of the story. The sign-off (to Janet) was classic.

"Yes, mama. Yes, all your boys, mama. All big five successes, mama. All papa could have hoped for, mama. All your babies, mama. All taken care of by Jehovah Himself, mama. Ask Aunt Sophie to come over, mama. Aunt Sophie loves to cry, mama. No . . . no, you got it right the first time, mama. The United Broadcasting Company, mama. I'll tell you all about it when we come to dinner Monday. Yes, Janet's here, mama. She's pleased as . . . yes, mama, talk to you soon, mama . . ."

"I'm not so sure," said Janet.

"Not so sure of what?" he said, some minutes after the phone call and a warm shower.

"Of any of it," she said. "I don't know." She was leaning on an elbow, the honey-colored hair still matted. "We always promised each other that a job, *any* job, would be just in between. The novel was the thing, what it was all—"

"Janet!"

She shook her face free of hair. "I know. We also promised ourselves not to mention the novel. I guess it's your lovemaking, lover. You rattle everything up inside me."

Getting into his undershorts, he said, "A half-assed, half-finished, sophomoric fiction and you lie there and treat it like 'Madame Bovary.' This, as they say, is the opportunity of a lifetime, Janet, and you know it. A v.p. at UBC . . . in Programming yet . . . Honey, the Lawd done sent down manna, bless de Lawd, bless de Lawd. Now get up off that beautiful behind and let's go have breakfast."

Her smile was remote. "Don't lose it altogether, Joel. Don't forget *you*, Joel, no matter how glittering it all seems, don't lose sight—"

"Of the Griesbergs? I know. Only it's Greer now, Janet. Greer. Now get a move on, huh? I'm meeting with my new boss, Fred Wiener, at nine."

It was Wiener's third cup.

"Well, at least we're going into this thing at the same time. I have to be frank with you, though. With Cliff Gold moving over to CBS, I was planning on bringing in the director of my last play, Hugh Bennett. But the old man is known for jumping the gun. Particularly when it's loaded."

In the now-emptying Bel-Air dining room Joel made a quick assessment of his position. He didn't like Fred Wiener in this, their first real meeting. He wasn't certain he even respected him. Still, he was equally certain that he could work with the man; even for the man. Particularly with Mark Banner in charge.

Fred Wiener, for his part, was still smarting. As was his Uncle Bob, he'd noted—and filed away for future use. Uncle Bob's entire anatomy was on his face, as Adrian Miller had once pointed out, and there was no missing the stiff, resistant look that had greeted David Abrams' impulsive gesture toward Joel Greer last night. As for Miller—it was hard to say; he wore too many faces at too many times. But Banner— the golden boy seemed in some kind of silent collaboration, if he'd read the man right. He wondered if the son of a bitch knew he'd banged his wife in a Southport woods a few months back.

"I'm sure we'll make it just fine together, Joe . . . or is it Joel? . . . Which do you prefer? . . ."

"It's Joel."

". . . just fine together, Joel. We have our work cut out for us, as they say."

"Yes," said Joel. "I'd say we do."

"Now, before we get down to any particulars, I'd think as a general principle that we'd stay here on the Coast for a week or so, getting the lay of the land and laying whatever the land happens to offer."

You smile, say nothing—which is to say the right thing.

MARK JOINED THEM for the fourth cup, the fifth; who was keeping count on this luscious spring-in-winter morning? Steve Lilly arrived only seconds later.

"Well," Mark said, smiling at each in turn, "the new regime appears to be open for business." And with his chilled orange juice, "Here's to."

"Hell of a deal," said Steve Lilly, in the process of ordering eggs Benedict and coffee, "one fair hell of a deal. When the old man moves, he *moves*. Still seems like some kind of dream or something."

"A hastily written first act," said Fred Wiener, but Mark, beside him, was already making notes on a single sheet of bond paper.

"I'll tell you what I'd like to do today and the early part of next week," he said. "I'd like to set up meetings with all the major suppliers for Fred, Joel, and myself to reassess what's already on the boards and as a first step toward '74-'75 development." Turning to Steve: "I think you ought to work for a day or two with Lance Lombardi [Los Angeles sales representative] on some of the heavy accounts, then get back to New York. I imagine the Sales Department's in some confusion since Hitch's death . . ." To Wiener and Greer again: "We'll start with Harry Ackerman and Bill Ashley at Screen Gems. They're pros, and it never hurts while you're doing business to learn something. Quinn Martin or Lee Rich next. And we don't want to pass up Chuck Jones this trip. I was talking to him last night. He has some damn good ideas for animated children's specials that could be what we're looking for. And in addition to the regulars—Frank Price at Universal, Bill Self at Fox, Dave Gerber, Norman Lear, Jack Webb—I want feelers put out to the independents. We're an open shop from today on." The unmistakable authority (Joel Greer found it near hypnotic) in the new president's voice, and their attention riveted to it, kept them from noticing Robert and Adrian enter and make their way to a frond-hidden table near the back, where their heads were immediately together over the morning's edition of the Los Angeles *Times*.

Just as well they didn't see them. Neither Robert nor Adrian was in much of a mood for chitchat this morning.

Adrian scanned the offending column again.

> . . . *leaves little doubt that for all the hierarchical changes, David Abrams, as before, remains in command, right down to the page boys' shoes. He'll have a good assist from Adrian Miller, known for his attention to detail, no doubt one of the reasons behind all the shifts.*

Chief beneficiary of it all, of course, is Mark Banner, who's being given a freer hand than any of his predecessors. The big question is how son and heir Robert Abrams fits in. His title is clear enough— President of United Broadcasting Companies and Chief Operating Officer—but with so many heavyweight egos at the top, all work- horses as well, it's difficult to define overall the real place of Robert S. Abrams. . . .

No doubt about it, it was an offending piece or perhaps just good reportage of an offending situation—offending especially to Robert Abrams. Adrian trusted that the smile inside him would remain just there. It had better.

"A gnat on an elephant's ass, to use one of your favorites," he told Bobby.

"Nonetheless, a good kick in the ass is pointedly due Gerald McAlister. What the hell's a PR man for if not to be aware of trash like this *before* it breaks? . . ."

Neither of them knew it, nor did Mark and his party, but several tables away David, behind a convenient post, was quietly breakfasting with Ellen. It was the way he wanted it. He never made breakfast dates anymore.

Ellen was saying, "You seem to have made quite a stir, my friend. Sometimes you remind me of my Aunt Stella. Lord, I haven't thought of that woman in years."

"Your Aunt Stella." He frowned, which meant he was smiling. "I suppose I'm supposed to bite."

"You are. And did. You see, every March and October my Aunt Stella would move all the furniture around—I mean completely out of kilter with the way it ever was before, or ever should have been for that matter. And then she'd slipcover it, every piece of it, in a different material and pattern from last time. Anyway, she'd invite the whole family over for lunch, which meant tuna fish sandwiches and potato chips, no matter what month it was, what day it was, and watch while we tried to locate the chair or divan we felt most comfortable in—I mean, the one we remembered and liked from all the years back. At first it was a kind of game, really innocent and childlike. Then as she got older—as we all got older, I should say—it got kind of somber, really serious. And then, then as we got older still, it sort of reversed itself. It was a game again, it was playful. But there was still something a little malicious about it too."

"And I remind you of that? Your old Aunt Sophie in her dotage, changing chairs around because she was malicious?"

"That's not really what I meant and you know it. But if you'll think about it, darling, there is a little something mean when people protected . . . by age, by position . . . start to rearrange things . . . like people's lives?"

"So call me Aunt Sophie," he said, setting his knife and fork aside, jabbing the corners of his mouth with his napkin, folding it then into a perfect square.

"Idiot. What I was saying, I guess, is that *we* are older persons, too, dear heart."

"Hmmn." He finished the last of his coffee, poured himself another cup. "I wouldn't have called us 'older persons' at about five o'clock this morning—"

At which she laughed. "You always manage to come back to that, don't you? You always *did* manage to come back to that."

"Damn right," he said. "A piece like you comes along only once in a lifetime, Star. If that. You're the only broad I ever knew who was as good in fact as she was in memory."

Her eyes sparkling, she said, "All right, enough . . . for now, that is. Let's get to the serious stuff. You've been on tenterhooks all night to talk about it. Whatever *it* is."

"Yes. Yes, I have."

The waitress, clearing away the dishes, seemed unusually nervous, her eyes darting from Ellen to him and back again. Even in a town where "celebrity" was as common as coconut palms, Ellen Curry, never mind her age, was still a special attraction. She gave the waitress her very best famous smile, feeling pleased, if just a little foolish. She always had in the face of "celebrity watching"—she always would.

"It's Bobby," David said, to which Ellen replied, "I know."

"I seem to step on his heart, everything I do." He sighed. "I go to the bathroom, he resents it. There's only one thing that would put a smile on that face. Me stepping down. Out."

"Which you're not about to do."

"Which I'm not about to do."

Her look was thoughtful, sympathetic even. But not indulgent. "Has there ever been a time, really a time, when it wasn't that way?"

He stared her down. "No. And maybe that's the trouble."

"The trouble?"

"Most of it. I think I'm going to say something, Star, that I try not even to think, much less say. He has a good many talents, Bobby. He has education and taste and ideas I wouldn't recognize if I smacked up against them in broad daylight. He can also, when he's a mind to, be a pretty effective executive . . . when he has a mind to or the stomach for . . . I don't know, but I do know that if anything happens to me . . . *when* it happens to me . . . I already have nightmares about it."

"David, really," she said, touching his hand, "it's not nearly as bad as

you're trying to make it. After a while an organization like UBC kind
of runs itself, anyway. Sure, you need managers, but . . . an overlord?
I'm not so sure, darling. All those jokes about computers—they're
truer than we'd like to think. . . ."

"I know," he said, "except I don't for a minute believe it. This shop
has run *under* me, that's the way I've done it, for better or worse. I've
never believed anything really goes without a top banana, as you old
grease painters used to say. So I pay . . . so now *my* heart breaks while
I'm breaking his. I do wonder if he can cut it, I mean, sustain it. . . .
I think Adrian can, even if it's gotten so I don't trust him out of my
sight. I think a fellow like Mark Banner over there can, except it
doesn't really belong to Mark Banner, it's not his—sorry, I'm old-
fashioned—by birthright. I don't know, Star. I really *don't* know."
Sigh longer and deeper than she remembered. "Some joke on us, ain't
it? Mortality. Crummiest joke they ever thought up."

As they were preparing to leave, she said *sotto voce*, deadpan
seriously, "You'd best go up and change, lover. I'm afraid you have egg
on your fly."

SEVERAL WEEKS LATER, in New York, David spoke before the annual
luncheon meeting of the Society of Security Analysts, at which time
he revealed that in the first quarter of 1973 the United Broadcasting
Company had enjoyed, for the first time, a gross revenue of one billion
dollars. UBC stock rose three points within the hour.

Internally, however, the outlook for the television network in the
1973–74 season was somewhat bleaker. The development program un-
der Clifford Gold wasn't promising. Mark Banner and Company *did*
have their work cut out for them. With such established or new hits
on the other networks as *All in the Family, Sanford and Son, The
Waltons, M*A*S*H*, Columbo, McCloud, Medical Center, Marcus
Welby, M.D., Hawaii Five-O, Movie of the Week, Adam 12, The FBI,
The Odd Couple, The Streets of San Francisco, Mannix, Cannon, The
Rookies, Maude, Gunsmoke, Carol Burnett, Bob Newhart, Mary Tyler
Moore*—such as these, quality or not, were formidable to counter-
program. Mark called staff meetings three times a week. It was at one
of these that the *UBC Magazine of the Air* began to be born.

"I'VE HAD AN IDEA for some time," Mark began it. "Although actually,
it's as old as our business. It's the magazine format you've all cut your
first teeth on. I'm thinking of a version that's formalized, a three-hour
segmented program on a single night, every week, utilizing live, tape,
film, the works . . . a single host for the entire evening—either the

same one every week or maybe three or four on a rotating basis, or a different one for each edition. Which is what each showing would be —an edition, including, say, a short story, a feature or two on current affairs, a comedy routine, a musical segment, one or two hard news reports, another play, comedy or drama, an editorial, a 'people in the news' . . . hell, just about anything and everything that goes between printed covers, so that by the end of an evening a viewer will feel he's been through an entire issue of something, cover to cover.

"Now I realize there are disadvantages to such a format. The viewer wouldn't have the hour or half-hour format he's used to—viewing habits would undergo a mild shock. Keeping a three-hour segmented program alive and kicking for every minute of those three hours would demand terrific input. The kind of bridging we're accustomed to in counterprogramming would be out . . . it wouldn't be tune in, tune out because the lengths of segments as well as their placement would be different each time. And there's the staff and talent for such an ambitious enterprise . . .

"Given some luck, though, we'd have something so different we'd make press damn near every time out, and, Steve, I think we'd have one hell of a sales story to hit the agencies with—a flexible format would allow commercials to seem more a part of the show instead of alien to it.

"Maury, I'd like you to start a research program on the format. Freddie and Joel, start thinking up ways we could best use talent and start talking with Bill Kelly on the news angle. Dutch, think on how we can bring sports and sports events into the thing. And Steve—of course as subtly as possible—start getting a feel of the marketplace.

"We're taking a risk, letting the idea out, but there's no other way. The only thing we can do is go about our business as quietly as possible, particularly Jerry, where press is concerned. The less written before it's further along, the better. A kind of Project X for now. Hell, who knows, we just might be on to a good thing. Anyway, give it a full shot, okay? And let's get on with the serious business of the day— *Hooray for Hilda?*"

"Yeah," said Freddie Wiener. "Hooray."

"HE'S CRAZY."

"Never work."

"Time-wasting."

"Just a publicity number, never mind the warning to McAlister."

"Ego trip plus."

"Staffing would be a ballbreaker."

"Damned if I'll bust *my* chops over it. Project X my ass."

"Bob Abrams will need fifteen new kinds of pills."

"Think Miller'll buy it?"

"Hard to say, hard to say *anything* about where those two stand with each other."

"An in-house production, and you know three studios couldn't handle it."

"Think advertisers'll go for it?"

"Hard to say. He has a point about closer identification. But they'd never get the precise timing they're used to."

"How do you think stations will react?"

"Like a swarm of bees. Especially those carrying us on delayed basis. Fucks up a whole night for them."

"It just doesn't make sense . . ."

WHEN HE TRIED to tell Vivian about it, he was met with polite interest —and a remoteness that had become even more evident these past months. At the end of his brief description of the kind of program he wanted (by this time already dulled by her lack of burning interest), he paused for moments, waiting for her to speak, move, *something*. The polite smile frozen to her face, she only sat. Waiting, too.

"I've some work to do," he said finally, reaching for his attaché case. They were in his study-den, finishing an after-dinner coffee, and by habit, if nothing else, she got up to leave.

Gathering up his cup and saucer as well as her own, she said, "I hope it's successful, darling . . . your idea . . . your program."

He went to her then, took the dishes from her hands, held her to him for a moment, but it wasn't *their* moment. The sudden stiffness of her shoulders, the held breath that pulled in her abdomen, the turn of her face, offering him a remote cheek—no, definitely not theirs.

Still, as she was leaving, he said, "You're a particularly beautiful woman, Viv, did I ever tell you that?"

She spoke quietly from the doorway. "I think so, Mark. In ways. In lots of ways, I suppose." And then went out.

He knew he would work late, into the morning hours actually. And that she would be sleeping when he finished. . . .

Sleeping, her ass! When was the last time she'd been asleep when he knocked off a night's work, crept like a thief into his own bed? And how many times did you curse yourself, *hear* yourself curse yourself, when he made no move toward yours—nor you toward his? Thank God for the pills and the tears to wash them down with.

And God, dear God! Everything she'd ever dreamed of, and more. Wife of the president of the network, the envy of every woman . . . a man whose body had once given meaning, given a *purpose* to her own

—still could, except no more purpose . . . that went with the baby . . . what job for *that*? Tell her *that*, dear God. . . . Tomorrow would be easier, different. Perhaps tomorrow . . .

Sleep . . . try again tomorrow. . . .

MARK BANNER'S PROJECT-X was topic-A at Robert and Jean Marie's table in their Scarsdale home that evening, Adrian and Joslyn breaking bread with them, their first guests. It was a handsome house, as near to Arrabella's family manse in Atlanta as it was possible to be, right down to the antebellum sideboard in the dining room. On top of which the silver service that had belonged to Arrabella's great grandmother—so lovingly preserved through the decades—was symbolic of the time and place this house and at least one of its inhabitants were unquestionably pledged to. Adrian, were he more romantically inclined, might have sworn he was dining with Timothy O'Hara and family at Tara. Even big, buxom Titania (yet!), who served them baked ham and fried chicken, was not out of place in this memorial to a long-ago world. (The yams and butter beans had actually been grown on the Atlanta land which Robert had never sold.)

It was Joslyn who brought up the subject of Mark's *Magazine*. ". . . and Vivian says he's really hooked on the idea, works at it till all hours of the night."

"Which I'd say says a bundle for Vivian's sex appeal," said Jean Marie.

"It is nearly an obsession with him," said Adrian. "In a way I can see why—it's so all inclusive, *too* all-inclusive, maybe that's the trouble . . ."

Robert, seated at the head of the table like ol' massa himself (Jean Marie called him that in her unfailingly authentic tongue), said, "I don't need to tell any of you that Banner rubs me the wrong way, always has. But credit where it's due . . . there are more chances for moments of real quality in a protean format like this. I certainly have no intention of discouraging it."

Which was pretty ironic, Adrian thought. David, like himself, was Mark's sponsor, more his benefactor, and yet was opposed to the show's idea, finding it impractical for the day-to-day routine of broadcasting (which was, at least partly, why son Robert was for it?).

"Well, I'm with you," Adrian said. "I think the more we expose your father to the practicalities of the idea, the closer to home we'll get. Mark and I have an appointment with him tomorrow, in fact."

"Practical, practical, practical." Robert chewed on the words as if they were pieces of ham or chicken. "When will he learn?"

"Learn what?" Joslyn said. "Seems to me he's done pretty right by himself, by all of us in fact, by being just that. Practical."

"You miss my point," Robert said. "As usual." Almost a smile. "Something really exciting could come of it—"

"Like what?" said Joslyn.

"Like a scene from, say, Arthur Miller's *The Crucible* following one from *No No Nanette*. In other words, the viewer, caught up in segment after segment, is being served caviar right along with hash. At least a more balanced diet than he's *been* getting. I really think it can work. . . ."

They were still talking about *Magazine* when the evening ended.

"Let me know how the meeting with father goes, immediately after it's over," Robert said, helping Adrian into his topcoat.

"Why don't you sit in?"

"And kill it right off? No thanks. A mention of *The Crucible* by me and father would have me in one."

ROBERT, putting on his pajamas, said, "It was a decent evening. In fact, a very nice evening."

"Which you can't say for all of them," she said, turning down the covers of both beds.

"What do you mean by that?"

"Just what I said. That you can't say that for all of them."

"I don't much like your tone."

He was at the small bar in his dressing room, mixing his sixth drink of the evening, washing three colorful capsules down with it. "You have a back-door way of saying things," he said, watching her undress from his post between the dressing room and bedroom. She made a small, seemingly unself-conscious ceremony of it. About as unconscious of it as she was of being Mrs. Robert Abrams of United Broadcasting. The removal of her pantyhose was porn in slow motion. She knew it drove him up walls.

"What do you mean?" she said. "What's a back-door way of saying things?"

A long, chest-burning swallow. "A damn sneaky way," he said. "Not straightforward, like for a change knocking at the front door."

A sly, lascivious grin met his stare. "Get yourself another drinkie-poo and pilly-poo to get you ready to knock on *this* door," she said. Her bare lower half was luminous, pubic hair lush and dark—tease of a sweet summer night. Swallowing hard, he found it hard to swallow.

"Which pills tonight? The blue ones? The pink? The magenta?" When he'd downed two more stiff ones, another capsule, he was ready. His whiskey-flavored mouth could already taste her. Back home again down South. . . .

. . . IT's DAWN, *very near it, when he stretches beside her, winded and worn.*

"What happened, Star?" he asks quietly, his breathing labored and raw. "How did I let it happen, Star? That it's come to this . . ."

"It was always this, darling," she says, bringing his aged head to her breasts as she might a child's.

"But different," he says. "Different as hell. We had dreams then. There was room for dreams then. We were smaller of course—it was all smaller then. Not so damn sophisticated. But, by God, we were giants then, Star. . . ."

"Yes, darling," she says, tightening her arms about his shoulders as if her own small strength might cradle his. And then uneasy again, frightened again, for this David of hers . . . this giant. . . .

Three
A Day in the Present
Wednesday

57

THE FIRST THING David does on waking is to reach for a cigar. Lifting his weight to an elbow, coughing, he squeezes the fat Corona into a silver holder, lights it greedily, and as its strong, sweet aroma lures him full awake, coughs again until the room, almost in focus, becomes again the kaleidoscope of reds, greens, yellows, and ambers of which Ellen is so fond.

"Oh, Lord," she says, protesting, indulging, leaning forward to slap him vigorously on the back.

It happens this way most mornings now. He wakes early, five-thirty, six, and after the coughing spell (which lasted longer than usual this morning) gets up, washes in one of the two baths adjoining the miles of bedroom, and then, apparently full of his old gingersnap, goes downstairs to the kitchen (nearly as long and wide as the bedroom), where Ellen in a light cotton robe has already arrived and is boiling water for coffee. Seven tend the Mamaroneck estate, three in-house, but Ellen reserves for herself her husband's morning coffee. Or better, morning Sanka, since the last attack of angina and viral pneumonia. Svelte and stylish still, even at this insane hour and in the unpretentious robe, she moves about the kitchen with an early-morning lightness that David finds deeply reassuring at the start of a day.

"Do you want the newspapers before or after your coffee?" she asks, as she asks every morning of a week of premieres.

"After," he replies gently (as gently as the racking cough will let him), sliding into an alcove at the far end of the room.

"That's a switch, anyway," she says.

"*Outcasts* and *Science Fiction Theatre* will make it," he says. "I promised the Board they would. Didn't I?"

"Yes, love. You want a piece of dry toast?"

347

"Buttered."

"Dry."

"Forget it."

He starts coughing again, this time almost uncontrollably, his face puffed, the fluid from his eyes streaming to his large strained neck. Ellen practically leaps the length of the room, seizes the oversized cigar from his fingers, and crushes it in an ashtray. "Enough's enough," she says. "You know what Dr. Rosenberg told you. Now *I'm* telling you. You'd look ridiculous in a casket. You're too much overweight. You know how unappealing fat people are in caskets."

As soon as he's able he smiles. "So I cough and all of a sudden you start acting like you're my wife. Pour the coffee and I'll try not to hold it against you."

"Well, if I do get a little wifey now and then, it's all your fault," she says, returning to the giant built-in range, where she pours the boiling water into the same battered pot she's been using for at least twenty years. Stirring vigorously. "And another thing, empire builder," she says over her shoulder, "you can just cut out all that brandy at night."

He has already taken another cigar from the pocket of his robe and is lighting it. Her mouth is pursed and her eyes are fierce, but instinctively she pursues it no further. She pours the steaming liquid and starts away.

"Sit with me," he says. "While yours is making." She had earlier plugged in an electric percolator for her own brew, a mixture of New Orleans chicory and Chock Full o' Nuts. She moves in beside him, covering a hand with one of her own. She sits very close. He thinks that of all the moments of his day, these few at the alcove table with Ellen, in the quiet early morning, are surely the most complete. When he's away from New York, in Washington or on the West Coast or even in Europe, it is always this hour or so after waking, without her near him, that seem so empty.

"Finish what you were telling me last night," he says, biting down on the cigar with obvious relish. "I think I fell asleep."

"You know damn well you fell alseep."

"So resume."

"It's not very important. It's really gossip, now that I think about it. And you know how I feel about gossip." She takes a handkerchief from her robe and brushes it across his cheeks, where the involuntary tears have started to dry.

"Like you feel about fur coats." He laughs. "And besides, nothing that concerns my top people can be called gossip. You know that. Now spill it."

She sighs a small sigh. It's an artifice, to be sure, one that always precedes such a moment. David can usually gauge the significance of what she's about to impart by the length and volume of it. "Well," she says, pausing only to swallow, "it's as I told you before you decided sleep was more important. Vivian Banner gave a luncheon at her house a week ago Thursday . . . or was it Thursday? No, Friday. And I realized something I'd never realized before. They have separate bedrooms. Adjoining, but separate. I had the oddest feeling. . . . Now it does sound flimsy when I say it out loud like that. Your sleep *was* the better choice."

"I guess." He smiles.

"And yet . . . a young couple like that . . ."

"Maybe she's not as sexy as you are."

"David, really."

"It's true. You're still a good piece. Everybody says so."

She laughs. "It *is* a silly piece of gossip, isn't it? But still, to be serious . . ."

He shrugs. "Can't see very much to be serious about. I'd say you picked yourself a real molehill this trip, Star. Real molehill."

She moves slightly away from him. "I suppose so," she says. "I guess I was looking for things. It was such a terrible luncheon, David. They can call her chic all they want to, but tuna-fish salad, a boiled egg, a snip of carrot . . ."

"Mark Banner's almost the only man I trust in the whole army," he says. "Him and Maury Sherman."

"I know."

"Over fifty years in this cockamamie business and just two men . . . men that could be my children . . ."

"Darling . . ."

"Your coffee's ready."

Drinking slowly, they don't speak for three or four minutes. Then, as though no words have passed earlier between them, they begin again, as though the morning has just begun; easily, from long and trusting years. They talk about the party the network will be giving at the Waldorf on Saturday; about the way UBC common stock closed on the Exchange yesterday (down one-eighth); about the surprisingly good showing United Records (a UBC division) has made in the third quarter; about having Mandy Jo and her husband, Arthur, and his son, Fred, and Arthur's sister Bella from Pittsburgh for dinner next Sunday; about a speech David will be making to a communications seminar in San Francisco in November; about his upcoming trip to Washington with Robert, Marty Levitt, and Bill Kelly to support a bill to knock out of the Communications Act the equal-time requirements for presidential and vice-presidential political campaigns; about a Mediterranean cruise they've been planning, once the UBC season is under way.

After his second cup, David pushes himself up, lights another cigar, and prepares to go to the library on the second floor, where he always spends an hour (no more, no less) before dressing for the day. "Now for *Outcasts*," he says.

Ellen nods. "I hope it had a great tune-in," she says. "Mark deserves it."

He gives her an affectionate pat on the buttocks. "Our precious Mark doesn't half realize what support he has around here," he says.

She pours herself another half cup of coffee. "He worked hard to get it scheduled. You said so yourself. And please don't light another cigar the second you finish this one."

David draws his breath in uncomfortably, takes the morning papers from one of the work counters, and folds them under an arm. He feels suddenly leaden, too full, but it passes.

HE PRIZES his desk in the second-floor library even more than the two Picassos and the recently acquired Modigliani that hang in the elaborate entrance hall downstairs. Art he has never understood; it's just something he's supposed to have, like trips to Europe. But the desk—this is the treasure, the jewel of his house. It once belonged to an impoverished Alsatian duke, and the coat of arms, including a bold brandishing of swords, is embedded in the side of its ancient yellow wood. Massive and angular, it appears at first glance to be graceless, but it has what Ellen likes to call an "inner grace." Its profusion of drawers, hollows, recesses, and secret shelves, bounded and traversed by surfaces of deep black inlay, are a source of never-ending pleasure, a maze of almost daily discovery. He can never understand how Arrabella could have called it "hideous."

Sitting in the black leather chair behind it (sold as a rebuilt relic from parliamentary chambers in London), he pulls out several drawers, toying here and there with a sliding shelf or hidden cranny. This is a morning ritual to which he allots perhaps a minute, minute and a half —an explorer. Sometimes he actually discovers a new compartment, a drawer behind a drawer, or even beneath one he'd been certain couldn't hide another. All the while he's looking with pleasure about the room, his favorite in the house, paneled and book-lined and interspersed with plaques that bear witness to his life. He keeps them here rather than in his New York offices mainly because Ellen (whose honors admittedly are more impressive than his) has for years influenced his public tastes, if not his private ones. He'd once thought success would mean a world where a man could pick his nose or scratch his balls in the presence even of kings. The plaques, in some way, are material reminders of the frailty and waste of illusion. They're from everywhere—the National Association of Broadcasters, the International Radio and Television Society, the Academy of Television Arts and Sciences, Communications Workers of America, Broadcast Pioneers, the Association of Advertising Agencies of America, the United States Chamber of Commerce, the United States Junior Chamber of Commerce, the AFL–CIO, the Red Cross; Heart, Cancer, Cerebral Palsy, Mental Health; the Anti-Defamation League of B'nai B'rith—and in the privacy of the library, which few eyes but his and Ellen's ever view, they are daily discourses on how little a man can reveal of himself to others while seeming to remain above them. They are also accusers this morning, censuring him for consciously delaying the next step in the premiere-week ritual. With a grunt he opens the newspapers to their respective television sections.

Bryson Randolph's column, while not the first to catch his eye, is the first he reads, attacking his cigar with every line.

> *It's called "Outcasts," and it happened on the UBC Television Network last night. It isn't really a bad show; it just isn't a very good one. One has the feeling he's seen it too many times before—and I'm not talking about "The Three Musketeers," which in a clumsy way it sometimes attempts to parody. I'm talking about all the precinct melodramas that have preceded it. What may at first have appeared original, or at least unusual, is simply a diversionary tactic to palm off the same old wares. . . .*

In the other paper the headline is OUTCASTS JUST SO-SO, the signature a prissy H.L.T., and the copy between them a two-column blur.

Reviews, he knows from long experience, mean next to nothing in television, Jerry McAlister and image notwithstanding. The most honored series often dies after thirteen weeks. Bryson Randolph, in particular, is a sullen neurotic (that sick review of *Hooray for Hilda* day before yesterday; granted the particular episode Mark had chosen for kickoff might be questioned, but goddamnit, it *is* a funny format, and his intuition, call it whatever you like, tells him it can't be that far off). And in the end, what Maury Sherman in Research will tell him when he calls at seven (every morning during premieres) will be a helluva lot more to the point. Still . . . He wishes to hell newspaper notices didn't get to him the way they do. It goes back a long way . . . he has always (secretly) regarded print as the real gospel, even while fighting print media to the death.

Grunting again, he scans the ads for UBC's Wednesday-night schedule, full pages in both papers. The headline, NEW AND BIG TO-NIGHT ON UBC, is bold, almost carney, an approach Mark had insisted on in this year's advertising campaign. Most of the space is devoted to the full evening, 8 to 11, *UBC Magazine of the Air,* "the newest, biggest, boldest adventure in television viewing ever presented to the American people." NEW AND BIG . . . In a minute the thick black type will be spelling MARK BANNER. Eyes closed, he prays for its success.

In the few minutes still left before seven, to get the taste of the reviews out of his mouth, he lights another cigar, scans a few papers for corporate matters he'll be facing this morning.

The phone rings promptly at seven. He doesn't have to wait to hear a voice.

"Morning, Maury."

"It's that, all right. Va-va-va-voom!"

"Impressive?"

"Fifty-seven share."

"Impressive. Very."

"We can't miss in the Nielsen nationals."

"Have you called Mark yet?"

"Soon as I hang up."

"Good. Anything else?"

"Yeah. Fuck Bryson Randolph."

"Thank you for calling, Maury."

As soon as he hangs up, it rings again. This time, too, he has no doubt whom he'll hear. But Gerald McAlister calls him every morning, just as he does Robert and Adrian, and not just during premieres.

"Have you seen the reviews, sir?"

"Yes. And Maury just expressed my own sentiments about Randolph —since the show happened to get a fifty-seven share."

"Fifty-seven. Well. Excellent. Excellent. Steve Lilly for sure has tidings for the sponsors this morning."

Pause. "Mark was personally responsible for the *Outcasts* sale, Jerry."

"Yes. Well, what's in a name, right, sir? I mean, the result's the thing."

"I'll see you in a while, Jerry."

"Yes. Several things I need to go over with you this morning, sir. Ten all right?"

"I suppose. Anything pressing?"

"Not exactly. The NAACP thing, mainly. Mark's reaction yesterday was . . . interesting."

"I see. Make it ten-thirty, Jerry."

It's pressing in, he thinks, returning the receiver to its cradle. Pressing in. From every direction. Everywhere at once. Jean Marie's leaving Robert. Robert's and Adrian's manipulations to get him off the Board. Mark Banner.

Banner.

Strange.

Strange how a man like Mark Banner can have accumulated so many who want him out—and before the new season is even under way. Strange how he, David Abrams, can have been edged into the position of defending him, when he's supposed to be Adrian Miller's boy. Strange that . . . Too goddamn much to think about.

And now isn't the time. The television network—the gut maybe, but it's still just a division of the company; there's the radio network, too—plenty of problems there also. Seems as if only United Records now is even halfway free and clear. He shakes his head, goes back for a few minutes to the papers he was studying earlier, and when the hour is up (the clock inside him is remarkably accurate), gets up to go to his room to dress for the day. Before he leaves he reads the review again, thinks of how he should be building Fred Wiener's image in the others' eyes—hell, he's the son of his daughter's husband . . . family—and just can't bring himself to do it. And of how curiously alike Fred and Mark Banner are. Curiously. He makes a mental note, too, to ask Big Long what he thought of *Outcasts*. No use trying to break old habits—no way.

He touches the desk almost as affectionately as he had his wife's buttocks and starts out. The heaviness comes again, as suddenly as before, but again it passes. He supposes he'll have to see Simon Rosenberg again and be lectured on the virtues of slowing down. He tosses his half-finished cigar into an ash stand near the door and defiantly lights a new one.

58

ROBERT'S WAKING.

The difference between sleeping and waking is so thin, so fine, that only the movement of an eyelid gives an inkling of one or the other. Even as the day, the thoughts of a day, bring him fully out of slumber, he lies as still, as lifeless, as before.

He knows he's alone; it's the first thing that penetrates. That it's a clear, even beautiful day, slipping opaquely, teasingly through the blinds, is the second. The rest come one by one and in procession.

1. Adrian will be calling soon with last night's ratings, the New York and Los Angeles overnights. Could run from fair to good for both shows. He hopes not. Fervently hopes not. Triumphs for Mark Banner —any triumphs—he decidedly doesn't need right now.

2. As of last night, midnight last night, the Board of Directors is about evenly divided on the question of his father's going or staying. That includes his and Adrian's votes.

3. His head hurts, for some reason. A genuinely real, if mild, headache. Must take pills first thing.

4. Jean Marie is somewhere—county, city, state, country, planet. He wonders where. All else aside, where.

5. The meeting with division heads scheduled for eleven. He'll cancel it. Simply not up to it. Not today.

6. The servants. They know now. For a certainty. He will have to decide whether to retain them all or let several go. He can't decide, not today. Definitely not today.

7. Bermuda. As soon as the Board decision is over, the television network's position made clear, Mark Banner's fate decided, he must plan on Bermuda. An extended stay.

8. The *Early Evening News*. He'll have to get Adrian and Bill Kelly together—something has to be done. It's starting to slip—ratings, content. A new producer? Format's getting stale. Format of all television news programs is getting stale. Television news can't be the *New York Times*, the *Washington Post*—the *Daily News* either. But news judgment is off, story selection and balance are off. A priority. He must talk to Adrian today.

9. Today is the night. *The UBC Magazine of the Air*. Banner's baby. The maker or breaker.

10. There is no ten. He is very tired. Bone-tired. He wishes he could sleep again. Knows he can't. Won't.

Adrian's call: ". . . a fifty-seven share for *Outcasts* and forty-one for *Sci-Fi Theatre* in New York. Best sampling night we've ever had."

"No doubt," says Robert. "I'm sure your Mark Banner is beaming; his cup runneth over."

"Come on, Bobby, cut it. This is getting to be an obsession with you. And you know what happens when you start blowing things up."

"I do? Well, I don't. Why don't you tell me what happens when I start blowing things up?"

"You start on another pill. And I'm afraid we've about run out of colors."

"You were put on this earth for one purpose, Adrian," he says. "To make life miserable for everyone around you."

"Time enough for the compliments later," says Adrian. "Wait'll you see what Brother Bryson's up to this time."

"Later."

He has a difficult time getting going this morning. And he knows why. No Jean Marie and her cockteasing routine while he shaves and showers.

HANGING UP after talking with Robert, Adrian twists himself under the covers, pulling himself up and out of the bed. His eyes are fixed on the half-sleeping form of his wife, in a lotus position.

"Get your fat ass up, will you?" he says, starting for the bathroom. "Emma's not coming until ten today, remember? And I'm starved."

Actually Joslyn is the farthest thing from his mind this morning. This morning there is in his mind, his soul, in fact, the distinct possibility that he's had his money on the wrong horse all along. Since eleven o'clock last night, when he had his usual nightly telephone conversation with Robert, he's known it's there, is growing: the doubt, the certainty of doubt. *So, the way it stacks up, Adrian, it's a tie. Board's split down the middle. I think it's Walters and Ziegen we have to work on. They're the ones with the least personal relationship with father. With them, at least, we have a fighting chance.* He slept hardly at all, and it shows in the bathroom mirror. He looks ten years older this morning. It takes him nearly that much longer to dress.

Surprisingly, Joslyn has prepared an exceptional breakfast. It cuts his water a bit. She's always the perfect cushion for his spleen. So he's silent for the most part, simply wolfing the food. She says little or nothing herself, except—just as he's preparing to leave the house— "Isn't tonight the big one?"

"The big one?"

"Banner's thing. You know. The newspaper."

"Magazine."

"That one, yes. If you're not home in time I'll watch. The really big one, huh?"

"Yes," he says. "The really big one huh."

But he doesn't like the look on her face. Contemptuous, suspicious, knowing—he isn't certain which. He just knows he doesn't like it.

59

STEVE LILLY's waking this morning is prophetic. It signals what surely will be another spectacular day. As much as he had to drink last night (first with Barbara Ermeling, then with some of the boys at Toots Shor's), with as little sleep as he's had, he is surprisingly intact. Both his stomach and his head, if for a second or two undecided, are as quiet as thieves by the time he opens his eyes.

Actually, it's *how* he opens his eyes that seals the day. Slowly, lazily, he seems to be drifting from warm sleep into warmer sleep, from one warm moistness into another. It takes him a moment to realize why he's waking in darkness. Beth's mouth is full on his, and her hair covers both his eyes. Her breasts are bare on his neck and shoulder.

"Lord," he manages to get out, "you balmy, Beth?" He can count on one hand the times she's wanted him like this. There had never been a time she'd refused him, of course, but it usually took one hell of a warming up.

"I suppose I am," she whispers, closing his lips with her tongue. She lisps a little, especially when she whispers, and the soft "thuhpoth" is hugely exciting. The rest of her body, round and solid, moves to touch him. Nipples as fresh and sweet as giant mushroom caps meet the rise and fall of his surprised chest.

"I have to go to the bathroom first," he whispers back. "You know."

"I'm . . . protected," she murmurs. "While you were sleeping."

"I mean, to take a leak." He forgets from time to time how much she hates that word.

"No . . ."

"Beth, I gotta *urinate*."

"No . . ."

"Honey, I've got to go so bad I—"

"Not now."

"Beth!"

She has covered him wholly (itself a revelation), and he's dipping to meet her, hard now and demanding, his arms encircling her buttocks, his own straining toward depths—or heights—it seems like both. In unison they're rolling, and now it's she beneath him (he's never seen her so abandoned—she's like a worm in hot ashes), and when he slips from her, as he does once or twice, she claims him again like a suction cup.

"Whoa," he says, "hold on, baby, huh? I don't want to come yet." He rolls from her, kissing her breasts, attempting to mollify her with his hands. But within seconds he has penetrated her again, and her legs are locked across his back. "Lord," he moans, knotting his stomach to hold back (trying urgently to think of something, the network, anything), but it's too late. His spasm is quick, unsparing, and full.

He breathes into her neck. "You all right?"

"I'm all right."

"Jesus, I tried . . ."

"I'm all right."

"Maybe in a minute . . ." Still astride her, he glances over at the

clock on the night table. Six-fifty. Mark's Wednesday-morning plans
meeting is at eight-thirty. He is out of her, out of the bed.

"Get breakfast goin'," he says. "It's Wednesday."

"I know."

Showering, he thinks about his wife. When he married her, of
course, she was a shy, unambitious girl, respectable enough, but small-
town Georgia to her toes—aspiring to little, so far as he could see, beyond a comfortable house in a lake-view section of Westchester or
overlooking the Sound in Fairfield County, and maybe, just maybe, the
good Lord willing, an invitation to join the Junior League.

He's had a doubt or two as to whether she can ever properly keep
pace with him (if he's doubted her, he's never doubted himself), but
now here she is, eleven years later, running their $95,000 house as sweet
as you please, and making it home for him and their four children.
And she loves him (this he's never doubted), even if she isn't always
the hotshot she was this morning. And even if she does shy away from
network functions. He feels very good about her, in fact—family-man
good. It's comforting to know she's there. And early-morning sex is
the greatest. He almost hates to wash away the odor of her.

He does, though, as quickly as he can, for there's a day to be got on
with. Not only the plans meeting this morning, but his own Sales
Department meeting in the afternoon, and Lord only knows how many
meetings in between. Next year's first-quarter sales are still considerably lower than they were last year at this time. Thanks to a piss-ant
policy of having to clear practically every pitch with Mark Banner!
Which thought leads naturally enough to other thoughts, not the least
of which is the brief exchange he had with the president of the network after the *Home Town* screening Monday. He was so hopped up
on Scotch and martinis that he really didn't think much about what
was said or not said. And the dinner with McAlister wiped everything
else clean away. It hits him now, though—two whole days later—
that he wasn't even allowed to report the Continental Tires sale himself; that that agency sonofabitch had to call Daddy Bigshit right off;
that he, Lilly, Steven Garrison Lilly, stood there grinning like a kid, a
kid who's just been patted on the head for going to the head of the
class, and said, "You're beautiful, Mark." *You're beautiful, Mark!*—and
he slams the bar of soap into his armpits. He brings himself up short,
though, muttering, "Whoa there, boy, hold on, you got too much
goin' for you," and in a minute he's right as rain again and drying
himself with good-natured vigor.

In the bedroom, dressing, a new gray pinstripe ("I'm a Bloomin'dale
man myself"), he glances at the clock again, sees that he's spent far too
long in the shower, and grins. He does hurry himself along, though. In
less than five minutes he's taking the walk he never fails to enjoy—

across the softly carpeted bedroom out into the softly carpeted hallway, down the softly carpeted stairs into the softly carpeted dining room. Delighting in the fact that sheer salesman magnetism has paid for every beautiful goddamn inch of it.

Beth is waiting for him in the dining room. They always have their breakfast here alone, while the children, before school, eat in the dinette just off the kitchen. Except, of course, on Saturdays and Sundays, when they sleep late. He prefers it that way. He finds kids much more satisfying at dinner than at breakfast.

Their Jamaican cook brings in their plates. He smiles at her, as he does every morning, but as usual no more than a brief "Thank you" passes between them. He has never really gotten used to the woman. She's too aloof and independent as far as he's concerned. Not warm and joshing, like domestic nigras are supposed to be, North or no North. But Beth likes her, and Lord knows she's efficient as hell.

When she's gone, and he's swallowed half an egg, he looks across at his wife—tall and auburn-haired, clear-skinned; mouth too large, nose too sharp to call her pretty; only her eyes, ocher and deep, really beautiful. In a flowered morning coat she wears to drive the children to school, drinking her coffee, she is anything but the excited animal she was upstairs. Still, he says, small-boyishly, "You were great, Beth, thanks. I don't know what you've been taking, but buy some more of it, will you?"

She blushes and doesn't look up, but he can tell she's pleased. Almost immediately she starts talking, in that slow, occasionally lisping way she has, about things alien to the bedroom, as alien as she can find: domestic things, the children, school, a party Sunday night at the Broadhursts', friends down the block. He listens absently, then tells her between mouthfuls about the confirmed Continental Tires sale yesterday. "That's very nice," she says. "They must be pleased as punch." She's really a very ordinary woman, but he forgives her. And he decides definitely not to tell her about the dinner with McAlister. Definitely.

He's just finishing his coffee when the phone rings. The cook answers it in the kitchen. In a moment she comes in, handing him an extension phone from the sideboard. "For you, sir," she says stiffly.

"Thank you."

It's Gerald McAlister, calling from his home in White Plains. He is abrupt and as straight-to-the-point as Maury Sherman.

"I don't know what you're doing for lunch today, Steve, but I think we'd better have another chat. In the open. So that nobody—I mean nobody—gets the idea we're conspiring behind their backs. Gallagher's at twelve-thirty? Did you have a lunch date?"

"Nothin' I can't get out of."

"Good. Twelve-thirty. We're off to the races, as they say."

"Betcha ass."

His ear-to-ear grin is uncontrollable when he hangs up. "There's a great big world out there, honey," he says. "A great big gorgeous old world."

She smiles. "It always will be for you, Steve," she says. "You make it gorgeous."

He could walk the ceiling.

"You'd better hurry," she says. "You'll miss the seven-fifty."

He kisses her largely, holding her lips longer than usual; then, reaching for his briefcase (which she's placed on the sideboard), he goes through the kitchen to the dinette, where he pauses just long enough to tousle the heads of his children—all blond, or near it—before dashing downstairs to the carport, where he gets into a red Thunderbird (leaving a blue Plymouth station wagon for Beth), and at considerable speed drives to the Bronxville station. Parking, grabbing a newspaper, he barely makes it.

The train isn't too crowded. None of the men he usually rides with are ever with him on Wednesday mornings, and this morning he finds the isolation particularly welcome. He scans the paper—the entertainment section, sports, the financial section—before turning to the Bryson Randolph review of *Outcasts*, which he reads twice, once with a half frown, once with an unconcealed grin. Then he sits back and lets his hundred and one thoughts possess him, concluding almost wistfully, by the time the train pulls into Grand Central, that it's really a shame old Mark isn't a Jew; Lord knows there are few enough top-level Christian boys at UBC. . . .

He's ten minutes late for the meeting in the fortieth-floor conference room and is somewhat taken aback when Mark Banner, at the head of the long teakwood table, says, "We've just been shooting the breeze until you got here, Steve. Couldn't very well start without the hero of the day."

60

MARK SMILES when he says it, or means to. Few others in the room are smiling. Or mean to. Despite Maury Sherman's crowing over the results of last night's twenty-four–market index (even *Love and Kisses* and *Mr. Magic*, both returning shows, have held their own, giving UBC an average for the evening at least two rating points ahead of the nearest competition), there is only mild enthusiasm. UBC's eggs are in the Wednesday *Magazine* basket, and until that's safely behind them, there will be a tension that a dozen *Outcasts* won't offset.

Mark looks around him. The Television Plans Board consists of what David Abrams, describing it last spring at an FCC hearing in Washington, called "the top administrative and creative and, by God, integrity-oriented minds in the industry." Their combined annual salaries, he had more than once lamented (that is, boasted), could practically finance a small war in Southeast Asia. In addition to Mark, Fred Wiener, Selwyn Coe, Steve Lilly, Marty Levitt, Pete Grimm, Dutch Cottingham, Bill Kelly, Joel Greer, and Maury Sherman, the Board includes not only representatives from their particular departments but from Advertising and Promotion, Marketing Services, Press Information, Station Coordination, Daytime Operations, Finance and Planning, Sales Services, Sales Planning, and Engineering. Although others, such as Gerald McAlister and Conrad Hirschman in Legal, sit in from time to time, they do so only on a corporate level. They are not present this morning.

As soon as Steve Lilly has poured himself a cup of coffee from the side table and taken his accustomed seat to Mark's left, Mark looks down the conference table to Maury Sherman. "You have any more to add on last night's ratings, Maury?"

"Nope," Sherman replies, wetting a finger in pursuit of a new coffee stain on his tie (the same one he wore yesterday). "It's a clear-cut case of rape, your honor. Looks like we got Tuesday night sewed up again this year. Still our best night. And that's no shit."

Mark can see several around the table in varying degrees of contempt (especially Jack Stroud in Advertising, whom Maury once described as a man who probably fucks with his clothes on), but he nods approvingly toward his research director. "We'll get started, then. While it's on my mind, though, Marv"—this last directed to Marvin Goldberg at the other end of the table, who doubles as secretary of the Board meeting—"have somebody in your department get out a one-pager on last night's performance. I want it sent to the full agency-advertiser list. No, make it a jumbo card. All right? I want it in tonight's mail."

Goldberg nods.

"Let's get on with the *Home Town* pilot, then," Mark continues. "Sorry more of you didn't get to see it Monday. Those who did . . . any thoughts?" He lights a cigarette slowly, casually. "Fred? Steve?"

He knows he's caught them off guard. First of all, decisions on pilots —particularly preliminary program approval—are rarely made at Plans Board meetings. They're made privately, and by him, with routine approval from Adrian Miller and Robert Abrams and—still—the Old

Man. That's one of several assurances he was given (privately, and by David Abrams himself) when they elevated him to the presidency. But he announced Monday at the screening that they'd discuss it this morning. Second, and more unnerving, he's put them in the position of having to give an opinion *before* he indicates his, something he almost never does.

Fred Wiener's smile is easy enough, but his eyes are hard. "It has its points," he says. "Frankly, I was disappointed in the way Gil Rawlins directed the girl. Too many pauses. But the camera work's great, and with tighter scripts, the thing's got a fighting chance."

"To sell?" drawls Steve Lilly.

"Of course not," Wiener snaps. "As a program. We *do* consider programs as programs occasionally, I believe. Even if the majority of minds in this industry look on television as solely an advertising medium."

"Just askin'," says Steve. Mark waits a moment, but it's obvious Lilly isn't volunteering an opinion if he can avoid it.

"You, Steve?" Mark persists.

Lilly grins, but shifts uncomfortably. "Well, hell," he says, "you plan on showing it to Wilson's Drugs, don't you? They encouraged it, didn't they?"

"For a possible half. What about the other half?"

"Well . . . it's sure not *Gone with the Wind,* as the feller says, but I think it'll sell. Community Brands is lookin' for a new property in January. They lean to sob-sister stuff, you know."

"You'd like to show it to them?"

"Sure. Why not?"

Mark eyes him impassively. Then, directing his gaze to Joel Greer, who sits next to Wiener, he says, "Joel? Anything?"

"It's no better than the rushes indicated it would be," Joel says. "Personally, I find it all wrong. Gil played it for soap opera. The script was melodrama, naturally, but at least it was a few notches above soap. That was mistake number one and the others just pale beside it."

In a blink of an eye Mark sees the reactions. Fred Wiener controls his annoyance, but it's there. Steve Lilly simply looks puzzled. Mark addresses himself to the group at large: "We're shelving the whole project," he says. "I spoke with Adrian earlier. Wilson's can see it if they want, but it's out."

The head of Programming and head of Sales stiffen. Billy Boulder, as Mark has expected, breaks the silence with the question he unvaryingly asks when even five dollars are lost: "Down the drain?"

"Not in this instance. They did a ninety-minute version, so we have the overseas film market."

"Smart thinking," says Fred Heller, who's seated midway down the table between Garrett Dix and Jerry Rothman, and who at least once during every Plans Board meeting says "Smart thinking" or "Good idea" or "Nice touch" or "Right direction," and then falls primly silent for the rest of the meeting, unless called on for an on-air promotion report, which is infrequent, or an opinion, which is unlikely. There are echoes of him, here and there—the kind of communal sound, essentially wordless, that registers not approbation or even agreement so much as awkwardness or uncertainty or the unease of men who sense, rather than know, that something has happened that probably concerns them but whose long experience in impotence has conditioned them to keep their distance. Mark, in fact, has the peculiar sensation of being the pilot of a plane, the long polished table its aisle, the men on either side its passengers; of having just informed them that there may be a time bomb on board, and that its hiding place, if any, is as yet undiscovered, its perpetrator as yet undetermined; of watching them endure not only him but each other in that strange nervous silence that often passes for courage and almost always dampens their foreheads and their stiff upper lips with the resigned acceptance that the rest is up to God.

The moment passes—not quickly, but seductively—and the meeting goes on. It is a long, precise, and uncommonly orderly one. Few speak out of turn, few talk too loudly. Even Maury Sherman, making a half-hearted pretense of cleaning his fingernails, forgoes interrupting it. Wiener and Joel Greer report on pilots under development for next season, progress on scripts and possible casting, the target date of April 1 for at least the bulk of the pilots ready for internal and client screening. Steve Lilly makes his sales report, precipitating a general discussion on the Rod Marshall specials, details of which Daniel Lyons, head of Production, has been assigned to get under way. Marvin Goldberg reports on last-minute arrangements for the Waldorf party Saturday night, which Sales Planning, with the inimitable aid of Hamlin J. Hirschmyer, is overseeing. John Abelman, an assistant to Bill Kelly, summarizes the progress of UBC News in the development of a series of documentary specials based on the lives of the world's great lawgivers. Douglas Shipp makes one of his interminable analyses of the highly competitive state of top-drawer sports franchises, looking for approval, every other word, from Dutch Cottingham. Jerry Rothman and Terry Goodall discuss affiliate reaction to the first of the week's closed-circuit telecasts Monday, reading several telegrams. Jack Stroud makes a brief and formal statement about follow-up plans to implement the season's initial advertising campaign, which he has already gone over with Mark in private. Garrett Dix talks about the newspaper and magazine coverage they can anticipate in the coming weeks from such as *Time, Newsweek, Playboy,* and *Cosmopolitan.*

It's a long meeting, with not a word said about the big question mark—*the* program premiering tonight—that monopolizes their unspoken thoughts.

61

FRED WIENER wasn't called on once, not once. Not even for an opinion when Joel Greer made his development report.

It just cannot go on this way. No dignity left to any of them—particularly himself. Success tonight can only make the man more intolerable. Adrian . . . Uncle Bob . . . they *have* to be made aware of the urgency of the situation, the immediacy of it . . . the *crisis*.

No time left now. A virtual dictator, a czar . . .

Has to be stopped, has to be—

You're a dead man, Mark Banner. You are a dead, dead man.

And if he is overdramatizing it, the hell with it. Hell is what it has been around here, and hell is where Fred Wiener will see Mark Banner, interloper, before he's through. After all, he, Freddie Wiener, *is* family, isn't he? Well, then let it be all in the family. He only hopes the heads of the family, *père* and *fils*, will appreciate his sentiments. . . .

His eyes roam his office, his very commodious office, with some attempt to calm himself. A resentment smoldering too long, just below the surface, can lead to mindless action—he knows that. A confrontation without guns, the big guns, can bring only disaster—he knows that too. Angrily, he buzzes Joel Greer.

"Yes, Fred?"

"Anything on the matter we discussed Monday?"

"Not yet, Fred."

"I see. Well, there's something you should know, Joel. The milk train doesn't stop here anymore. They use diesel engines now, Joel."

He hangs up with a vengeance. Taps his fingers on his knees. Stands. Stretches. Paces the office—twice, three times, four. Clears his throat so he won't scream, because that's exactly what he feels like doing. Switches on all four of his television sets, soundlessly: two daytime serials, a game show, a women's interview show—ABC, CBS, NBC, UBC dream in radiant color.

They match his mood. The fury of a woman scorned, devastating without sound. The terror-stricken face of a teenage girl when she learns she may have syphilis. The dour expression of a middle-aged man when he learns he hasn't given the right answer. The forced expression of tranquillity on an existentialist guru, the morning's guest on UBC's *Sally Shelton Show*. Fred stares at each in turn, is rewarded by each in turn. He switches them off fitfully.

"Linda!" he calls sharply, irritated even further when she opens the door with her attention focused entirely on her nails, evidently just polished again by the way she breathes on them. Her mass of red hair drives him ape.

"Are you certain I've had no calls?"

"Certain. No calls."

"Even when you were away from the desk?"

"I haven't been away from the desk."

"Oh, come on, who're you kidding? I consider myself privileged to find you at your desk right now."

"No calls."

He blanches. "Finish typing the status reports," he snaps, turning his back to her as she shrugs (secretly smiling) her way out. He is contemplating a heart attack, a seizure of sorts, when his private line rings.

"Yes?"

"Fred?"

"Yes?"

"Fred, it's Vivian."

"Oh. Yes. How are you?"

"I need to see you."

"Well, of course, but you caught me at such—"

"Today? The apartment?"

"You're crazy."

"I know. I have to see you."

"I have a lunch date. Business. A producer."

"Break it. Please."

"Suppose I'd said it was with your husband?"

"Be as cruel as you want. Only be there. Twelve-thirty?"

"Look, Vivian, all kidding aside, this is really—"

"Twelve-thirty."

"You're not serious . . ."

"I'm dead serious. Twelve-thirty."

No sooner has he hung up than the private number rings again.

"Sweetie?"

"Sharon? You're still here?"

"Reluctantly. I'm doing the *Sally Shelton Show* tomorrow. Barry Gray tonight."

"Well. I hadn't expected to talk to you again until I'm on the Coast."

"Your lucky day."

"You might say that. Everything all right with you?"

"Depends on how you feel about phoney small talk."

"A needle?"

"Oh, cut the shit and tell me when I'll see you."

"Lousy day. I'm up to here."

"Not quite. But you will be. By the time I get through with you, pet. You will be."

"I believe it. Nice of you to call, Sharon. Luck on the Gray show."

"Not so fast, chum. I think I'm going to feel desperately raunchy around about noon."

"I'm taken. Important producer bit—you know the drill. Sorry, babe."

"I'll be raunchy as hell about six, six-thirty."

"You win. Six-thirty it is. The Oak Room bar, though. I'll need fortifying, the day I'm in for."

"You got it."

That does it. The two he plans to use. Has already used. From here on in, though, the stakes are so much higher, and the timing is now.

62

HANGING UP from his boss Fred Wiener, still shaking his head in disbelief at the corny "milk train" crack, Joel Greer resumes his reading of a pilot script, *The Surgeons*, just arrived by courier from the Coast.

ACT TWO

FADE IN:

EXT. LOS ANGELES HOTEL—DAY

A cab pulls up. DR. JOHN ADAMS gets out. A bellboy takes his bags, moves briskly inside. Dr. Adams pays the cab and follows after.

INT. HOTEL LOBBY—LONGSHOT—DAY

Busy lobby, much going on. Dr. Adams checks in at desk. Bellboy starts to pick up luggage again when

MARY JOHNSON (v.o.)

I thought you'd come.

INTERCUT with Mary Johnson

MARY

I *knew* it. Oh, Jack . . .

ANOTHER ANGLE

as Dr. Adams stares lovingly into Mary's eyes.

INT. HOTEL LOBBY

CAMERA TRUCKING with Dr. Adams and Mary as they walk toward

Walk toward, talk toward, who gives a damn? Good, bad, or in-different—any script has to play second banana to the heavy drama going on right under his nose. Wiener's tone of voice—so transparent, God! Still, after Mark Banner's game of entrapment, what could you expect? One thing, though: the battle lines—however shifting—are being drawn. And he—Joel Greer Schmier Griebsburg Greer—is still laughing inside at the memory of Wiener's embarrassment. Even if it does affect him, too—the whole Program Development Department, in fact. You just can't help admiring Banner's play—ploy. He knows more about surgery—and survival—than a hundred middling scripts like this one.

He sighs. He still doesn't feel good. His mother's Monday night is lasting a hell of a lot longer than usual. Even the baking soda hasn't helped. *There's nothing like plain old baking soda, I don't care what the doctors tell you.* His mother's remedy since the dawn of time.

Nnnnnng.

The phone again. Ron Hughes at Warner's. Yes, the script has arrived. No, no readings yet. Soon as possible, yes. Lunch soon? Fine.

Nnnnnng.

Seth Siebert at Wolfstone Productions. Yes, a preliminary discussion but nothing new. Let you know a.s.a.p. Yes. No. Thanks. Lunch soon, then. Good.

Nnnnnng.

Art Noble at William Morris . . .

Tom Dodson at Universal . . .

Wes Huntley at BBD&O . . .

Nnnnnng.

"Hi."

"Oh. Janet. Hi, darling."

"Busy?"

"The usual."

"I thought I'd break up the routine."

"You do. You did. And thanks."

"Joel?"

"Mmn?"

"I love you."

"Thanks, Janet. I know that. It's my rod and my staff."
"You know something?"
"What?"
"I've been reading the novel again."
"The novel?"
"*Your* novel. Don't play so dumb."
"And?"
"It's good, Joel. It's still good. A younger you, maybe a more naive
you. But a *you*, Joel. A *you*."
"We'll talk tonight."
"Stomach still bothering you?"
"A little."
"We'll talk a lot tonight."
"Okay. A lot tonight."
"Promise?"
"Promise."
"Joel, you're still young, your life is still—"
"Are you sure you've been reading the novel? Or *True Confessions?*"
"Ricky says to tell you hewoh. He sends wove."
"Wove back."
"Bye."
"Bye."
Back to the damn thing, no matter who, what . . .

    INT. HOTEL ROOM—LONGSHOT—DAY
    Dr. Adams and Mary enter, bellboy just behind them with bags. Mary

Nnnnnnng.
"Joel?"
His secretary.
"Yeah?"
"It's Mr. Banner's secretary. Wants to know if you can lunch with
him. Out of the building. Across town, in fact. Christ Cella."
"Yes. I'd be most pleased."
"Twelve-forty-five okay?"
"Twelve-forty-five is . . . okay."

walks to the windows, looks out, smiles.

               MARY
You brought the sun, darling. Along with your scalpel.

CUT TO:
             DR. ADAMS
I'm still not sure it's the right thing. If only Phil

Nnnnnnng.
"Joel, darling?"
"Oh. Hello, mother."
"How are you, precious?"
"All right, mother. You?"
"Any reason I shouldn't be?"
"No. No, of course not."
"I haven't heard from you. *Or* your wife. I just wanted to know if you enjoyed yourselves the other night. Just that, darling. Nothing else."
"Yes. Yes, of course we did. We always do, mother."
"Good. Good. Only I don't think you looked so good, darling. Stomach again?"
"Slightly."
"You work too hard."
"I suppose. And I'm swamped with it right now, mother."
"Well, I won't keep you. Only to tell you that we're very proud of you, Joel. All of us. Everyone in the family. You've gone very far for a boy still in his twenties. It's such a comfort to me. To all of us. Take a little baking soda, darling. There's nothing like it, I don't care what the doctors say. I was talking just now to Corinne Loeb—you know, the one who can't walk? Anyway, she was telling me . . ."

had asked me to come. Of course, with the best surgeons in the world right here in Los Angeles, you

". . . so remember the baking soda, darling, and take good, good care of yourself . . ."
Mark Banner. Christ Cella. Twelve-forty-five.
Jesus!
Nnnnnnng.

63

ONE OF THE THINGS David Abrams appreciates in Gerald McAlister (there isn't too much) is his dedication to time. Ten-thirty doesn't mean ten-thirty-five to the vice president in charge of public relations. Sitting across from him now, in his elegant stage set of an office, David chomps firmly on his cigar and studies him. He has a way of doing this without appearing to be anything more than an amiable listener. His mind, however, is what he likes to call two-for-one—that is, two separate and functioning compartments, one hearing, responding, the other observing, perceiving. Each of them thinking, but rarely the same thought. A little like being at the foot and peak of Olympus at the same time, Ellen had once kidded him when he tried, too solemnly, to describe it to her.

". . . so I thought we ought to discuss this, David. I knew you'd want to." McAlister's manner, on the surface, is smooth as ever, but there is an unmistakable pump of adrenalin beneath it.

"I'm not sure I know what you're getting at," David says.

"Yes, I can understand," McAlister agrees, his eyes fastened on a gold clock-and-fountain-pen unit on the acre of desk. "These things are never comfortable."

"Make it uncomfortable, then." David smiles. "For a minute there it sounded like you were getting ready to fire *me*."

McAlister smiles, of course, but the smile is brief and obligatory, and perhaps just the least bit indulgent. Like an old-fashioned nanny's. His PR chief's special attribute, David long ago decided, is that once he assumes a loyalty, it is unshakable. Whatever his intrigues, they at least are always somewhere down in the court, never at the throne. And the throne, so far as it is possible to identify, is the Abramses, father and son, and Adrian Miller. And regardless of his own feelings about the man (repugnance is close to it), he does recognize the superior job he has done, is doing. There are those, of course, who consider him little more than a eunuch (Mark Banner, for one), but without him, David thinks, a communications system as large and far-flung as UBC would require several more pairs of eyes.

"Go on, Jerry," he says. "Don't mind my foolishness. Ellen's coffee was strong as hell this morning."

McAlister nods. "What I meant, David, was that I asked him, quite deliberately I admit, if Lilly or anyone else had influenced him in the film's selection, simply to see if for once he'd admit being influenced by *somebody*, and his answer, if you can call it that, was . . . well, indignation, I suppose you'd call it. With Mark Banner you're never certain."

Through gray-blue pillars of smoke, David sighs. Coughs. And feels a slight twinge of pain, a kind of pushing and pulling inside his chest. It will pass. It has all morning.

"Naturally," he says, "and how else could he answer? Mark Banner has an innate sense of responsibility, my friend—whether it's his or not. He takes on responsibility like some men take on women. And as Maury Sherman would say, give a real man a sniff of tail . . ."

"Yes, well . . ." There are many colors in the opulent room and McAlister turns a few of them. Clearing his throat (damn, it's fun, watching him harumph like this—even an allusion to heterosex flusters him . . . and I ought to be ashamed at the cheap shot, David thinks), he continues: "It's not just yesterday, David, or the day before, or last week. It's every minute, every working minute. It's reached a point where he apparently doesn't believe anyone—Wiener, Lilly, Bill Kelly, *anyone*—is capable of even a routine decision. And when he does. want something done, he . . . Does he even know *how* to ask? It's worse, David, I mean visibly worse. It's reflected on every floor in this building. It reaches clear across a continent—I'm not exaggerating. They resent him, David. They deeply resent him."

The smoke is circular now. His chest is easier. "Maybe it's good they do," he says. "Maybe it's a blessing in disguise that they do. Resent him, I mean. Hell, hate him, why not? Hate of a general can bring an army together, you know? Drive them closer, give them a common ground. Make them fight, give them a few balls. Love and kisses in business can be boring, Jerry. Also dangerous."

"You don't mean that," says McAlister.

"Don't be so sure."

There are delicate gold threads in the great brown draperies behind the desk, and McAlister, out of long habit, is contemplating them. Like the combination clock and fountain pen, they seem to give him some private satisfaction. David has noticed for years that whenever he sits across from him, McAlister will invariably seek refuge in objects. Well, to be frank if ungenerous, that seems only appropriate. McAlister is an object too. Sweets to the sweet.

"You were saying, Jerry?" he prods.

"I think I've said it."

"I'm not so sure." He holds the cigar at arm's length and, closing an eye, isolates it. "You mentioned Bill Kelly a minute ago. How does Kelly figure in this thing?"

"How?" McAlister says readily, like a witness who's been carefully coached. "It's an open secret, David, that Banner runs roughshod over News. Which isn't really in his province, all things considered."

"Technically, it isn't," David says, adding, "but all things considered . . ."

"Well, it should be autonomous," McAlister continues doggedly. "That's the only way News really functions."

"We agree. But I'm not quite ready to have a president of UBC News who's out there on cloud nine on his own. Not quite." The cigar comes back to his mouth like an act of love.

McAlister is intractable, however. "The other networks have it," he says. David has never seen him so determined.

"UBC may be competitive, Jerry," he says, "but competitive don't mean carbon copy. I learned that when I didn't know where the next meal was coming from."

There is detour in McAlister's voice now, though it's far from retreat. "I'm only doing my duty as I see it, David," he says. "I feel that one man is abusing a structure. He's getting an impossible press, I might add. It was you, if you remember, who first expressed fear of this, over a year ago. You *wanted* me to be watchful. I believe that was your word, David. Watchful."

David smiles. "I know," he says, almost gently. "I know." Then, running a hand across his forehead (he's perspiring so; still, the pain has gone), he affects a thoughtful scowl. "The timing's wrong, Jerry," he says. "We're in the middle of premieres. We're also . . . obligated to Mark Banner. In more ways than we like to think. He's given us a record few years. He's given this network excitement. Not many are capable of that. Excitement. He may have been fumbling some during the past couple of years, but any man—" He breaks off abruptly. "But then it's his method we're talking about, isn't it?"

"Both," says McAlister. "The ads this morning for tonight's big show. Really, David. Those seem the work of a desperate man. You don't switch from taste to carnival overnight. Jack Stroud in Advertising . . . the agency . . . even our whole PR staff . . . we were all beaten down on this one. Oh, I know you and Bobby and Adrian had to go along with him on it, but—" He, too, breaks off abruptly. It's obvious that he's mouthing everything Bobby has been telling the Old Man all along. It's always like this, as if he's talking to himself.

The silence, in the cool spaciousness, is cavernous. Echoes, in near-rhythmic succession, crowd the room. It is into them, rather startlingly, that one of his secretaries (stout, stern, and not easily ruffled) makes an unusually excited entry, and with no more than a hasty rap on the door.

"I hate interrupting, Mr. Abrams, but . . ." dramatically: "The President's calling, sir."

David's eyes are sharply teasing. "My son, Sarah?" he asks.

The woman's own eyes are indignant. "The President of the United States," she says.

"Oh?"

"On four."

With a gesture of puzzlement to McAlister, he pushes four and picks up the receiver. Hearing the familiar nasal voice in a none-too-satisfactory connection, he is not quite as calm and natural as he may have hoped.

". . . Yes, Mr. President. . . . Yes, of course. . . . Sunday? Sure, certainly. I'm both honored and delighted, sir. . . . Yes, yes, of course. . . .

It was good of you to call me personally, sir. . . . Thank you. . . . Yes. . . . Until Sunday, then. . . . I look forward to it, too, Mr. President."

His expression is not exactly stunned when he replaces the receiver, but it isn't exactly ordinary either. "The man himself, all right," he says, after a lapse. "Lunch at the White House on Sunday. I wonder what's up. He's having all the broadcasting heads."

McAlister says quickly, too quickly, "Does that mean Mark, too?"

David's tone is somewhat chiding. "No, it doesn't mean Mark too. But don't make too much of that, Jerry. No network presidents are involved." He leans back expansively. "I'm damn glad I'm wearing a three-hundred-dollar suit today." He chuckles.

He enjoys the luxury of his delight for a few seconds more, then brings himself matter-of-factly back to the desk. He notices on his appointment pad that Carl Gottlieb, president of the O&O's (UBC's owned-and-operated television stations in five cities), is dropping in at eleven. There's also a reminder to have one of the girls call Si Rosenberg for an appointment, but he feels fine now, the chest is sleeping like a baby, not a trace of the early-morning heaviness. He reaches over and scratches the notation out.

"Mark Banner," he says softly, relighting the diminishing cigar. "Tell me something, Jerry. Does Bobby know you've come to me with this?"

"Yes . . . yes, he knows."

"Hmmn. Mark Banner." He blows a perfect smoke ring. "I'll tell you, Jerry. I'm not going to speak with him about any of this. I'm not going to tell him at all."

McAlister doesn't say anything, nor does his dour expression change. Nor is he particularly heartened, as he's leaving, by an intercom buzz to which David responds, "That's very thoughtful of you, Adrian. As it happens I am free for lunch. Mike Manuche's? Why not? Dr. Rosenberg doesn't approve of most of my living habits anyway."

64

MARK, coming out of Adrian Miller's office on forty-two (he's been giving his immediate superior a quick rundown of the Plans Board meeting), sees McAlister entering the sacred suite of offices, but it doesn't occur to him to wonder at it. If there is anything conceivably common to the fortieth floor it is Gerald McAlister pussyfooting it to the Old Man's or Robert's or Adrian's door. Besides, at the moment he himself is far too immersed in his own thoughts even to begin to speculate on the devious activity of somebody else.

He's done it, that much is certain. In the Plans Board meeting he did it. Without so much as a raised voice he nailed his ninety-five theses to the door. He knows, they know he knows, and if it takes more than open humiliation, then he's prepared for that route too. You don't sit back and watch cancers grow. At least he doesn't. He thinks of Vivian. Well, at least not if he can help it. The battle is damn well joined. His walk back to his office is crisper than it has been in weeks.

"I won't be having coffee this morning, Barbara," he says, taking the outer office in long, brisk strides. "I had a cup or two in Plans." He's somewhat surprised at how visibly relieved she seems.

"Dictation?" Edith asks.

"Yes, please."

"You're in rare form today," she says, pulling a chair to the desk. "Dare I say it? I'd say your teeth are bared."

"And sharp." He smiles. "Many calls this morning?"

"A round dozen."

"I'll look at them after these letters. First one, Bill Hatfield at U.A. Copies to the usual. Dear Bill: I was hoping we'd see something on the *Sky Spy* project before this. I must impress on you the meaning of time right now. Tempus, as they say, fugits." He looks at Edith. "Well, damn it, he went to Haavad, didn't he? A little Latin might go a long way." She smiles her okay. "Next one to Ted Bosley at International Steel in Pittsburgh. Copies, the agency and . . . Lilly. Dear Ted: I've decided to make the multiprogram presentation to International myself, early next month if that's convenient for you. Meanwhile, if you're—"

"I thought Lilly was doing this one," Edith interrupts.

He says impatiently, "I'll be doing it," then, seeing the small hurt on her face (it always settles so incongruously on her broad cheeks), he says more gently, "Change of plans, Edith. Now let's see. Meanwhile, if you're in New York . . ."

It is in the middle of a letter to Dillman Ernst, head of a new syndicated film company, that Barbara buzzes on the intercom to tell him that Hal Berlin of *Variety* is "here for the interview."

"Damn," he says, "I'd completely forgotten." Shrugging, he nods to Edith while telling Barbara to show him in.

HAL BERLIN is a quiet, diffident, gentle, peaceable sort of man, which may or may not account for his pugnacity as a newspaper reporter. His look of sympathy, of *understanding*, is so clear and present that only the most callous soul can fail to respond. But, as Mark has pointed out on a number of occasions, "you give him your heart and he takes your ass along with it."

Today Berlin is even more hangdog than usual. His ten-year-old suit, which was probably carefully ill fitted when new, hangs on his bony frame like a museum's cover on a prehistoric skeleton. His whole being is skeletal, actually. The melancholy eyes in a face all angles and points are so poignant you could cry. He takes the proffered chair across from Mark's desk as though he has been taken in from a cold, dark, bleak, and stormy night. The subject of the prescheduled interview is the so-called new permissiveness in prime-time programming.

"It's a big bore to you by this time, I know," Hal Berlin says. "But aside from perhaps one other substantive question, Mark, the sex-and-violence issue is uppermost in almost everybody's mind these days. As I need hardly tell you, of course." Gently.

Mark smiles. "The 'perhaps one other substantive question' being whether we're able to bring off tonight's magazine format?"

"How devilishly clever of you!" Without, incredibly, a trace of malice. "Now, I feel it only fair to tell you, Mark, that we're also talking to Bob Wood at CBS and Jim Duffy at ABC, and the whole kit and kaboodle at NBC. You see, it's probably the major industry issue right now. A preliminary survey shows that all the networks are receiving the largest amount of audience mail ever—some ninety-five percent of it critical of the sex, the violence, the whole permissiveness nut."

Mark nods indulgently. "We prefer to call it 'progressive programming,'" he says.

Hal Berlin smiles. "This time it's not just that big faceless them out there. And not just the FCC either. It's Congress, it's the press, it's your own station managers, for heaven's sake. You should hear Dick Beesemyer at ABC on the subject. And even advertisers—that last refuge of stomaching practically anything."

"I'm aware of it."

"Gosh. It seems so gratuitous in a way, what with the new NAB Code guidelines and all. But it's a 'Banner said this,' 'Banner said that' kind of piece. As I know you understand."

Mark, who rarely leans back in the classic executive pose, leans back—far back—in the classic executive pose. "Well, Hal, I'll tell you," he says. Which he does for some twenty to twenty-five minutes. In what he hopes is neither offense nor defense he briefly traces the history of television program content related to social and cultural change. He brings up to date UBC's supporting adoption of the NAB TV Code Board's provisions for implementing a "family viewing hour" policy (8–9 P.M. EST). As for UBC's policy in portraying violence or adult themes, "We're very much aware of current public concerns, and for that reason have stepped up our advisory announcements, when appropriate, in certain entertainment programs, affording parents the opportunity to exercise discretion in regard to younger viewers.

"It's the most we can do," he says. "After all, we are—and have always been—aware of our obligation to select our programs with awareness of the possible effect that violence and adult themes may have on an audience."

He leans forward again. "It's such a complex subject, Hal. What's bold and enlightening in Boston or New Haven is a sin against God in Memphis and Little Rock. I know I've said it before, but we do try for a balanced schedule.

"You know how we feel about violence. That the use of it for its own sake is out. The same holds for so-called adult subject matter."

Gentle Hal nods gently.

"You like previews, Hal. Here's one that won't thrill you. It's from a talk I plan to make on film properties for television. . . . 'In the event a film that we propose to air was originally rated R, we require that it be resubmitted to the Motion Picture Association of America for reclassification on the basis of our editing. If the MPAA feels that the edits would have made the picture presentable theatrically with a higher rating than R—PG or G, for example—we will then accept it for telecast.' Does anything I've said say anything to you?"

Hal Berlin smiles. "Well, I *am* pretty familiar with your sentiments," he says, "but so far, frankly, I haven't heard much that's new. Like" —the sweet-tempered way he says it!—"how does all this apply to the first hour of your *Magazine* show tonight, which I'm given to understand treats gonorrhea as if it were the common cold?"

Mark shakes his head and smiles pleasantly. "Until you see it, Hal, I don't think we can properly discuss it."

Finally the bitch in him rears its head. "The press wasn't allowed to see this particular night's program matter in advance. As you, of course, know."

"Of course. I'm the one who said, 'Hell, no.' "

"Of course." Sadly. Smiling. "We're really on the same wavelength, you know. I mean, I feel you'll always . . . level with me. When you can, that is."

"When I can, Hal? I'm not sure I like that."

"I was merely referring to certain . . . shall we say corporate injunctions?"

"Don't make it harder for me than it is, will you, pal? It's a rough day."

They welcome the moment's silence, the sound of breathing. "I still have to do my job, Mark. You know that. No matter whose rear end is on the line."

Mark manages a frail laugh. "I'll have to get you together with Maury Sherman more," he says. "Both your vocabularies could benefit. Meanwhile, may I say it's a question of whose ass is on the line? And in this case that's not much of a question—now is it, Hal?"

Hal smiles. "But seriously, now . . ."

Seriously now. Here it comes.

"All the usual public statements aside, Mark, what really caused UBC to slip these past two years? In prime time, I mean."

Mark shrugs. He's used to this one. "A lot of factors," he says. "We really haven't made the scene, no matter what your view. We've deserved a little of the comeuppance, I suppose. Riding the crest for as long as we have. But I do think it's been blown out of all proportion. What happened? Mediocre performances, I suppose. We've certainly fallen behind in the adult comedy field. Which of course we're working like hell to turn around this season. And we've done an extraordinary number of quality classic specials. I needn't tell you what the three-hour *Troilus and Cressida* did"—it received a 6 percent share of audience, the lowest recorded in network history—"but we felt we owed it to the public . . . to ourselves . . . to undertake the project."

"*We*, Mark? Or Mr. Bobby?"

"Stay on the line, kid, or I'll bust your ass proper."

They both laugh. Mark goes on: "We all know that UBC's prime-time schedule is designed to appeal mainly to the inner city or urban areas. The young adults, the middle-aged adults. We're rooted in that tradition, all the way back to radio. But some of what we've come up with"—spreading his arms wide—"we just forget who our people are, I guess. Last season's schedule, for example. It would have had a forty share across the board on CBS."

"Which brings me to a key question, Mark. Why in such a crazy competitive season did you decide to stick your necks out with something so radically different as *Magazine*?"

"Pure guts," says Mark.

For the most part, it's over. Mark does manage to tell him that he's planning an industry-wide open forum on children's programming as part of the network's ongoing plans. And that the network, just this morning, has completed negotiations for a twelve-hour mini-series of Thomas B. Costain's *The Tontine*. But the grilling—call it finally what it really is—is over.

While the *real* issue, so far as he's concerned, hasn't been touched on at all, and isn't likely to be. Not where the president of the television network is concerned, anyway. And that is that the audience measurement system that makes or breaks television programs, no matter how worthy or unworthy they happen to be, is in the hands of all 1,200 Nielsen families—comprising some 0.000018 percent of the national television audience. A condemnation of which, by him especially, would be considered high—also low—treason. Thousands of letters a day on sex and violence, and how many or how much is the American viewer being cheated—every hour of his viewing day? But that's for another time, another place, Mark knows. For now—God knows, for tonight—he's as involved a collaborator in the system as Nielsen himself.

At the door Hal Berlin holds out his hand, limp as it is, wishing Mark the very best on *Magazine*, "even though I haven't the *faintest* idea what it's all about."

"Then go thou and do what you're always telling us to do—use your imagination," Mark suggests. Smiles. Goodbyes. Exit Prince Hal.

"So?" says Edith.

"So, as usual. If that sneaky little Milquetoast had his way, the headline in the radio-TV section next week would read Banner Waves Banner—Horseshit."

"And the sex and violence?"

"I guess that's mine too. Like original sin." Shaking his head clear, he says, "The lunch date with Greer set up?"

"All set," she says.

"Then get out the jungle drums, will you? I want to make certain that our Mr. Frederick Wiener is fully apprised of this particular engagement."

"I have an engagement, Bobby," says Adrian. "I'm sorry. If you'd said something sooner—"

"Forget it."

Robert replaces the receiver with the most overt feeling—in this case anger—he's shown in some time, even when alone.

Alone.

The long and the short of it, as always.

When he learns by accident (and of course not by accident at all, executive secretaries being the most congenial communicators of them all) that Adrian is lunching with his father, nausea hits him so that he just makes it back to his suite of offices and private bathroom. Afterward he sits at his desk, and with a sheet of his engraved stationery and pen in hand begins writing a letter, even though he hasn't the least idea where to send it.

Dear Jean Marie:
   I don't make a habit of humbling myself to anyone, including my humbling father, as I think you know. I am humbling myself now, to you. I love you, however I've forced myself to show it, however you've forced me to. I am sick of being alone. I don't want to walk into that house again without you. I know how frustrating, how humiliating it's been for you—and for me. I know how it's made you cruel until you couldn't stand it. Until I couldn't. I tell you I've never stopped hoping (honestly didn't) that my "problem" would work itself out—in time, somehow. I even hoped that you, being the desirable woman you are . . .

Then, just as passionately as his pen has ravaged the paper, he takes the fine bond sheet in both his fists, rips it into shreds, watches them fall into a teakwood wastepaper basket.

66

WHILE GERALD MCALISTER and Steve Lilly lunch at Gallagher's on top sirloin and Caesar salad, and David and Adrian lunch at Mike Manuche's on calves' liver and onions, and Mark Banner and Joel Greer lunch on lamb chops and potatoes au gratin at Christ Cella, and Robert Abrams lunches alone on turkey broth in his office, Fred Wiener feasts once again on Vivian Banner at the Park Avenue apartment of her friend Marian Graham.

But what seemed the icing on the cake on Monday is a stale loaf on Wednesday.

Ever since word has filtered down to him—or up to him, as the case may be—on the who's-doing-what-to-whom luncheon engagements of the day, he has been in a state of barely controlled fury. And while it heightens, ironically, his passion as a lover, it makes his mood foul indeed. Once relieved, lying beside her, he would be pleased to strangle her.

"You know," she says, "this was my idea, and I still feel as though I was raped."

"Maybe you were." He turns his head away from her.

The room (dowdier each time he sees it) presses in on him; he feels the need to be out of it. Out of it, and out of her.

He pushes himself up, reaches across to a chair for his clothes.

"No seconds?"

He doesn't answer.

"I won't call you again," she says. "At the office, anyway."

"Thanks."

She turns on her stomach. "I'm a fool. You're a good lover, Fred. You also don't give a damn. Nothing but a quick clean fuck for you. That's good. That's very good. People like me . . . like Mark . . ."

"Look, Vivian. Please. I'm in no mood."

As he's leaving he starts to say, then doesn't, that he wishes for her husband's three-hour brainchild tonight the same that she had for five minutes this afternoon.

YOU LIE THERE. *I'm leaving you, Mark. I've left you, Mark. I'm coming, Fred. I need you, Fred, I need . . . At least no memories, no past with Fred.*

You try to move, to rise. You mean to rise. You don't. Can't.

Won't.

Strange, she thinks. How unhealthily attracted she is to Fred Wiener. And how much she despises herself for it, him for it, Mark for it. Mark most of all for it.

Did she say that to him this morning? *I'm leaving you, Mark. I've left you, Mark.* She has the oddest sensation that she did, sometime in the early morning, while he slept, pretended to sleep. It's hard to tell. Everything's hard to tell these days. Like her being here now, so newly fucked, recalling every rough, brutal minute of it, but not anything of how or when she came to be here, or why. She'd called him, of course, said something. Must have said something. But for the life of her she can't remember. Even as she conjures her own voice, the timbre of it through the mouthpiece, there are no words.

She's losing her hold on reality—has lost it. Somewhere. At some point, on some day, but they run together so—time, people. Herself. Images of herself.

Like now. Like right this very minute. She's sitting at the dressing table, seeing herself full in the small oval mirror, and yet still there on the bed, sweaty and naked as he left her, not an inch of her moved;

moving. There's a cry in her throat (from the dressing table? the bed?).

Help me, Mark. Take me back, Mark. Tell me I never left you, darling, tell me I never was here, never held him.

She's dressed. Strange. She is, isn't she? Fully dressed? The plaid suit she came in with?

Has she bathed? When did she bathe? She knows she did, there's the too-sweet odor of Marian's perfumed soap. But how . . . ?

It returns, a little. A little at a time. The two martinis she had at some cocktail lounge around the corner before coming here. She *did* come here. That much was certain. She *is* here. . . .

Somehow it comes to her in mist. Mark. Wednesday. *The UBC Magazine of the Air.* Mark. Wednesday. *The UBC* . . .

"You needed me. You need me. It's your day. Your night. It's beginnings or endings, and you've needed me and I'm not . . . haven't . . ."

Haven't . . .

Another drink in her hand too? How many?

"Edith? Hello, dear. Is he in?"

She's on the phone, talking. It's Edith. She knows that, at least. *Something.*

67

"No, NOT BACK from lunch yet. Do you want him to call you? At home? In a couple of hours or so—all right. I'll tell him. Bye, dear."

Edith replaces the receiver, rather gingerly; something about Vivian's voice wasn't quite right. Drinking again, probably. No doubt she does a lot of it these days.

But Vivian Banner is the least of her problems right now. Barbara Ermeling, for some reason, out of a clear sky, said she didn't feel well and went home for the day. And the work is piled practically to the ceiling. Something strange about that girl. Something funny-strange about that girl.

Mark is in high spirits when he returns. He's actually whistling. After a lunch with Joel Greer? Ridiculous day. An absolutely ridiculous day.

Mark returns the first of his calls. Adrian Miller.

"Mark? How goes it?"

"Fine, Adrian. You?"

"Great. Just great. Had lunch with the Old Man today."

"Oh?"

"Good lunch. Very good lunch. We spoke of you quite a bit."

". . ."

"Well, you know, of course. He continues to think very highly of you. Very highly indeed."

". . ."

"I think he'd even be inclined to name you president of the television network. If that position weren't already taken."

"Adrian, you're a messenger of peace that passeth understanding. Anything else on your mind?"

"Nothing particularly. Just dividing the goodies."

"My thanks. See you later."

"Right."

"WHAT THE HELL is going on around here? Just what the hell . . ."

Edith asks the question of herself as she replaces the phone's earpiece, and in the otherwise empty outer office she hears too many answers.

68

STEVE LILLY feels a little cruddy, as he always does when he's been with McAlister, but outside of that—Lord! How much sweeter could the old world be?

It's already three, so the lobby isn't too crowded. He stops at the clinically clean tobacco counter near the elevators, buys a package of cigarettes and a Binaca spray (he's got to watch it, the smell of drinks on his breath; Mark's obviously been noticing it) and a roll of Life-Savers, stepping into the first twenty-to-forty-two car to light up. It's his alone and he whistles "Love Is a Many Splendored Thing" all the way to his floor.

His office (much like Mark's, though smaller) is quiet and cool, and

Laura, his secretary, is ugly as sin—thank the Lord. He has enough cunt running around in his life these days. He has her return a couple of calls (Dick Patten at McCann-Erickson, Marv Goldberg in Sales Planning), and on his private wire calls Tully Tipper at *Variety*, an old drinking buddy from his early New York days, to see what's up (*who's* up). He then dictates three memorandums to the salesmen and, alone again, buzzes Mark on the intercom to remind him of the sales meeting at four. Mark insists on sitting in on them, usually ends up running them. But today . . . hell, let him have his fireworks, least a fellow can do for a dying man. When he finds the line busy, he asks Laura to ring the extension. Edith answers.

"No, he won't be attending the meeting today, Mr. Lilly. He's tied up."

"I see," he says. "Well, okay, thanks."

"And Barbara's not here. She went home. Said she wasn't feeling well. Goodbye, Mr. Lilly."

The phone is a firecracker in his hands. Damn broad! Where does she get off pulling a stunt like that? How dare she throw Barbara Ermeling in his face! Where does a frumpy middle-aged cunt come off speaking to him that way?

It takes him a good ten minutes to calm down. Mainly because he knows that Laura, on her earpiece, heard the whole goddamn thing. Of all the stupid goddamn . . .

He does think about her, though: Barbara. He knows damn well she's sitting by her phone in that pretty-pretty apartment just waiting for him to call. Lord! Give a broad your cock and she wants your balls. He's got to do something about the kid, that's for sure. She's just about served her time. Things are secure enough now with McAlister (and bless his heart, Tully Tipper: there'll be a nice fat rumor piece in next week's *Variety*), and it does seem pretty silly having a private game preserve like this. Not to mention costly. The girl shouldn't be that hard to get rid of, anyway. He'll play it easy, though.

He rings her number on his private line.

"Hello?"

"Hi, there. What's wrong?"

"I don't know. I just didn't feel like being at the desk there all afternoon, I guess. I just felt like . . . coming home, I guess. Will I . . . will I see you, Steve?"

"Sure. Sure you will, kid. Christy's? Same time?"

"Yes, Steve. Yes."

"Good girl."

Play it right, nice and gentle. He calls home to tell Beth he'll be detained again tonight ("This dern premiere time, you know how it is, sweetheart"), then leans back to ponder. Damned if their voices, both of them, haven't given him an erection. He'll be some fucking tiger at his sales meeting.

69

THE SALES MEETING is held in the conference room on the fifteenth floor, where Sales and Sales Services are located. Maury Sherman (whose offices are with Research, Sales Planning, and a branch of Continuity Acceptance on seventeen always attends the Wednesday-afternoon meetings, along with Jack Stroud, Marv Goldberg, Paul Hughes, and Ted Lancaster, all of whose areas, like his, provide the network with its most important sales and promotion tools. The meetings usually bore the Jockeys off him, except when Mark's in attendance; then they're sharp and alive. Mark not only keeps them moving along; there's always a direction, a point of view with Mark. Steve's own meetings tend to flounder. But the thirty-odd New York salesmen (you'll pardon the expression, he says to himself: I mean fucking *account executives*), half of whom are Jewish and half of whom are lazy, and none of whom takes home less than forty grand a year, outright worship him.

Most of them are there when he arrives, and Maury takes a chair at the far end, away from the conference table. As usual, he observes, Lilly is the good guy charming the balls off them, taking the few minutes before actually starting the meeting to recall an incident from his early radio days that has some vague analogy to network scatter-buy plans. Wolf Glover, at his boss's right, is chuckling so transparently it's an embarrassment to look at him. Maury makes it a point not to strain himself listening.

Today he's disturbed. It started with the way Mark double-fisted his way through the Plans Board meeting this morning, which, if he doesn't exactly approve, he knows the man has his reasons for. Mark Banner never acts out of impulse or petulance. The real *menschen* never do. They may wield a cleaver, but it's a cinch their hands are guided by their heads. At any rate, the meeting has had its effect, it has agitated the day, and the ballsy brightness that Steve Lilly's displaying in his own meeting does nothing to temper it.

Talk about water off a duck's back! The swamp bastard is acting like he has a private stethoscope up Robert Abrams' . . . Which is really what has been bugging him all day. He hasn't been a numbers man all his life for nothing. Two and two always added up to "something smells." Lilly's humping that piece in Mark's office (he suspected and then saw them staggering into her apartment house one night while he was driving down Ninth to avoid heavy midtown traffic), the too-sudden-buddy way he's seen McAlister stop to speak with him in the hall a couple of times; then dinner together at Sweet's. Lunch today at Gallagher's. All *very* open. Nothing you can put your finger on. Just your whole frigging hand!

He hadn't intended to let it get to him, but it has. "I think there's going to be what the writers call a power play," he kidded Shirley not long ago, "but I'm not going to get involved in it, so don't beg me." They've come and gone—how many years now?—and he isn't about to start playing back-alley politics now. Not again. He's had his time in the sun. And it's dark out. But he respects Mark Banner, and he can count on one hand the men he's genuinely respected through the years. Mark . . . sure, he uses too many vice presidents more for leg-work than for headwork; sure, he makes mistakes. But does that bantamweight shit up there in Sales think he's even a tenth of the man Mark Banner is? Or that make-believe stud, family once removed, in Programming? Give those tricky bastards a week, one week, and they'll have wheeled and dealed the network off the air. How can Robert Abrams . . .

"Maury?"

He raises his eyes. He hasn't realized how long they've been sitting here. Lilly's grinning at him. "Sorry to disturb your rev'ry, old buddy, but we've finished our rundown of first-quarter budgets we're goin' after this week. You were plannin' on enlightenin' us on the *Broadway Round the World* special, I believe."

Maury nods. They'd spoken earlier about his trying to come up with a better audience-estimate story for this one-shot commitment Mark has made with a new independent production company. It's a costly film tour of theatre districts in both European and Oriental cities and has gone unsold. Mark is willing to preempt *Outcasts* for it, in late fall, if the right taker comes along. An elaborate sales presentation has already been shown extensively. Research has now revised its audience and cost-efficiency estimates in light of last night's pay dirt with *Outcasts*. "Gene Springer from the department's been working on it," he says. "I told him to be outside here."

When he opens the door a young black man in his late twenties walks in. Maury glances at Lilly. Springer, a former agency researcher, has only recently been hired (by Mark) and Lilly has never seen him. He's now the highest-salaried black in the network. If the vice president in charge of sales reacts, however, it isn't visible.

Springer's report is brief, factual, and well organized. When he's finished he passes out mimeographed copies of the revised estimates and leaves.

"If you want my personal opinion," Maury says, "this thing's a prestige show and has to be sold that way. The numbers don't mean crap."

"You could have given the report yourself," Lilly says, still grinning.

"I could have," says Maury.

He knows he did it on purpose and it shames him that he did. He didn't realize how far he'd gone in the baiting game.

The rest of the meeting is devoted to a proposed change in rate structures. When it's over, and the room is emptying, Maury lingers behind. Lilly is speaking in a low voice with Wolf Glover. When Glover, too, has gone, Lilly says, "I gather you wanted to see me, Maury?"

"Not my choice of verb, but then, who the fuck's grading English papers, huh?" He wonders if he's finally overdoing it, and decides he doesn't care.

"What's on your mind?"

"Statistics." He feels the small, comfortable hole in his right pocket. "Tell me something, kid. How's it going with you and your new buddy?"

"My new who?"

"Your new asshole buddy."

Lilly lights a cigarette. "What the hell are you talkin' about, Maury?"

"What else?" Maury widens his eyes considerably. "Jerry baby, of course."

If it hadn't been there on the big face before, it's there now. Lilly's jaw is tight, and he isn't grinning. "I don't know what the hell you're talkin' about or what you're up to, Sherman, but I got better ways to spend my time than wastin' it heah."

It's Maury now who grins. "I just bet you have." He kind of rocks on his heels, the way he's always admired Jimmy Cagney doing (gives a small guy a curious advantage over a big one). "You know something, Lilly?" he goes on. "You're a prick. That's right, a prick. A real A-number-one first-class prick. If it wasn't for Mark Banner you wouldn't be sitting where you are right now. He made you, whether you know it or not. I'll tell you something else. It won't work, prick. Take some real old fatherly advice from Maurice Sherman. Sit right where you are and count your blessings. You're lucky you got this far.

Oh . . . one other thing, schmuck." He starts to open the door. "Smart boys don't do their schtupping with well-placed ladies from the for-tieth floor."

It is almost five-thirty.

THE AFTERNOON has passed slowly, full of slow, uncertain thoughts. For Joel Greer it has been an exhausting experience. By five-thirty he is limp.

And from nothing. That is, he's been in the office all day (except for lunch with Mark Banner, which was friendly enough but imper-sonal—a discussion of program development they'd often had), more or less closeted with his scripts and his thoughts (illusions?), an island in an ominously calm sea. No reason for such exhaustion except . . .

Except for Fred Wiener?

Weiner *did* come in around noon, didn't he? He *did* stand there by the Utrillo print, supercilious even in a hurry, didn't he? He *did* say (surely this no stretch of the imagination could make imaginary), "You can forget about what I asked you to do, Joel. A competitive pilot report is academic at this point. And your lapse in judgment at the Plans Board meeting won't be held against you. Just have a little more faith in me, will you? You're quite a valuable program man, Joel. For once Mr. Banner and I have an area of agreement. Who knows? You might be Programming v.p. one of these days. Yessireebob—as Steve Lilly, who by then should be out on his Alabama ass, would say—yessireebob, you just might." He *did* say it, didn't he?

Damn right he did. Enough to make a man . . .

Make a man what?

Throw up? Play ball? Wonder in the rush of expectation just how much difference there really was between them? Come on, Joel, how much difference? Revulsion one minute, willingness to join up for the power and the glory the next . . . well, damn tempted, anyway. Mother would be proud. Cut the novelist-manqué shit, Joel. . . . Strange, he thinks. The qualities that offend us in others somehow take on light and reason in ourselves. Or seem to. We like to think they do. How else can we talk of *our* intellectual honesty, superiority? *Our* shit, by God, smells like a rose. Or is he really as bad as all that? Self-indul-gence can cut both ways.

He stands, stretches. He's known for over an hour what he's going to do. He has to talk to Mark Banner. *Really* talk. Somehow, involve-ment—the simplest level of it; a gesture to a man he respects; call it what you will—seems kinder (not only to Mark—to himself) than staying aloof. It also feels as if his own preservation is at stake.

Edith Stewart had told him earlier that Mark would be unavailable

until late in the day. He decides to chance it. On his way to the fortieth floor it occurs to him that what he is doing is probably as foolish
and naive as anything he's ever done; that Wiener's sudden "in" (well,
intimation of "in") is at this point probably as much an exaggeration
of fact as it is of fantasy. But—what was it Janet said once?—"Im-
pulses are sometimes nice to give in to, Joel. Sometimes they're more
serviceable than laxatives."

Edith and the other one, the pale Barbara, have left, but Mark's
door is open. He's at his desk, and it's obvious he's finishing up for
the day: his hands are moving over the familiar terrain like a blind
man's cane. Looking in, Joel says, "I know you're in a bind today,
Mark, but could I . . . Do you have a minute?"

"Of course. Come in. Want the door closed?"

"If you don't mind."

In, seated, Joel again feels absurd, regardless of whose soul stands
to profit. "Mark, I wanted to say . . ." he says, and smiling sheepishly,
trails off. "I'm not really sure what the hell I wanted to say."

Mark returns his smile, but otherwise waits him out.

Joel hasn't the least idea what he'll be saying next, but somehow
the words pour out. "Look, I'll just talk, even if half of it doesn't make
sense. All right? Maybe I should have said all this at lunch, but I just
. . . I think on my way up here it was in the back of my mind to start
off with something real profound like 'Something's not exactly right,'
which on a day like this rates right up there with 'Thou shalt not
covet thy neighbor's wife.' Or even 'Something's rotten in . . .' which
God knows isn't what I came up here to say. I came up here to say"—
his arms feel peculiarly like barbells, dead weights on his knees— ". . .
to say . . . I'm not sure I've broken it down into so many words, Mark,
even to myself . . . but to say that I think the real reason I wanted to
come to UBC in the beginning was that I'd be able to work with you.
Yes, I think that's it. No matter how affectionately I'm regarded as"—
the words crawl from his throat—"Wiener's boy."

Mark sits back, studying him. "I appreciate your saying that, Joel,"
he says. "Although I can't say I ever really thought of you as 'Wiener's
boy.' Of all of us you're probably more your own man than even you
realize. As for what precipitated all this . . ." He lights a cigarette and
smiles again, a rather withdrawn smile. "I suppose speculation is rife,
as they say, in the corridors. How could it not be? But nothing has
changed, Joel, I assure you. We're not overnight people, even in an
overnight business. Besides, your course is pretty well set—you must
know that. You're certain to take over Programming one day, someplace, sometime, no matter what happens anywhere else. Even without seniority you're a cinch. I'm sure I'm not telling you anything you
haven't already figured out."

"No," Joel admits. "But you're the second one who's said it today." Mark's tone is sharper. "Wiener?"

Joel nods. "He was in earlier. There was just something about the way he . . . I don't know, Mark. I guess I'm in the right job—melodrama's my style—but I thought it was evil."

Mark's laugh is low, a little indulgent. "That's a mouthful of a word, Joel—evil. A little stuffy, too, if you don't mind my saying. None of us in this business—yes, and nothing we do—has quite the depth or the consciousness required for evil. We're too busy being desperate to be evil. This is a desperate industry, Joel. Straddling a fence between quality and quantity is inherently desperate, I suppose. And when the fence is colored green, look out. Besides, so much sitting irritates the crotch. And you know how desperate a raw crotch can make you."

Joel starts to say something like "I'm not exactly a child," then realizes how childish it would be to say it. As if sensing it, Mark adds, "I'm oversimplifying, of course, but that's television for you. Black and white. Or living color—take your pick."

When Joel barely smiles, he goes on: "Look, I'm not sure I'm leading up to any more than you were, Joel. There's no 'he did it, she did it, we did it.' Nothing really concrete to talk out. If there were, I would have initiated it at lunch. I'm sure you know what I mean."

Joel searches the floor. "I knew when I came up here," he says. "Or thought I knew. It was just . . . Mark, I've been thinking of leaving. For a while, anyway. If only to . . ." To what? he thinks. To think about things? To write? Pretty starry-eyed, for a man with a wife, a child, a going thing. He feels more sophomoric than when he walked in. His face is flushed with it.

"To write?" Mark asks—almost echoes, in fact.

Joel is startled. "How did you know that?" His voice is half accusing, half defensive (a little shameful), as once it had been with his mother, those years ago, when he was a dreamy child with secrets.

"I didn't," Mark said. "But it's not too wild a guess. A mind as alive as yours couldn't help but want to break the corporate chains once in a while."

"I guess it's this crazy week," Joel says. "The day. I'd blame it on the heat, except I haven't been out of this goddamn air conditioning long enough."

"It's more than that," Mark says. "I can see that. And I won't let myself be put in the position of trying either to block you or encourage you. But . . . remember what I said about fence-straddling a minute ago, Joel? Well, you come nearer to knocking those fences down than most I've seen. I'm not sure the industry can afford to lose too many like you. Network television—and I mean *commercial* television—has hardly started, I don't care what the pay-TVers and the other doomsayers tell you. Fundamentally, it's sound, it always has been. I think that's what I'm trying to say with *Magazine*. That, given some breadth, scope . . ." He leans forward wearily, as if in midsentence he suddenly remembered something. "Shame Maury Sherman's not here," he says. "Perfect cue for 'Shit.' " He rises—cue itself, of course—saying, "Joel, whatever it is, hang in a while, huh? We'll talk again. When it's open season. Thanks for coming up. I mean that. Sorry I have to end this, but I have an appointment."

Waiting for an elevator, Joel thinks how uneven, how unsatisfactory the exchange was. Not only for himself. From the beginning, Mark was vaguely preoccupied, which isn't his style, not even in a crisis— especially not in a crisis. And not only preoccupied. Withdrawn. Oh, not from him, but from the network, business at hand . . . No, not withdrawn either. Hard to say exactly. Except that the old strength of ten wasn't there. Barely the strength of one. He seemed—even with his frail reassurances—almost without authority, without control.

Even . . . defeated?

70

THE REASON for Mark's withdrawal, or the sense of it, the reason even for Joel Greer's feeling that he has just left a man defeated, is that he is doing something—that is, he is about to do something—he swore to himself he would never do. Again, that is. He is meeting Sharon Moore for a drink.

"*Sharon, I thought we'd settled this. You know I—*"

"*Don't stretch it, pet. I think you'll find what I have to say particularly fruitful, even for such a straight arrow as yourself.*"

"*You're talking in riddles.*"

"*I'm talking in rhyme. Mark Banner had better make a pass. If Mark Banner knows what's good for his ass. Not bad for off the top of the head, right, angel?*"

"*You never say quit, do you, Sharon?*"

"*Never. And I have only the profoundest contempt for those who do. My hotel? Sixish?*"

"*You win. What's the room number?*"

"*Not so fast, buster. I want to be seen. With you preferably, but in any case seen. Like the Oak Room bar? I should think it would do your morale a bit of the old good too. Sitting around lushing it up with the great Hollywood tramp, cool and nonchalant as you please, and with his great big life-or-death showcase deal premiering this very night! Earl Wilson can have fits with it, love.*"

"*This had better be good.*"

"*When wasn't it, buster?*"

But would he have gone, he wonders—even considered going—if not for the telephone call just before hers? After all, he has to pack, leave for the Coast tomorrow. Was it the phone call that did it?

"*Vivian? You called?*"

"*Earlier, yes. I can't exactly remember why.*"

"*I've tried to get you several times.*"

"*No need. Some silly domestic something, I suppose. I can't remember, really.*"

"*Can't remember? That's strange. Edith said you seemed to need to . . . talk to me.*"

"*Edith can be mistaken.*"

"*Vivian, are you all right?*"

"*Of course I'm all right. I've just had so many things to do today, that's all.*"

"*Oh? What?*"

"*Things. Things women—wives—have to do. Don't be so worried, Mark. I'm really all right. Fine. Really. Should I have Emma make dinner? I wasn't sure.*"

"*Better not. It's an . . . uncertain day, you know.*"

"*Yes. Uncertain.*"

"*I'll call you when to expect me.*"

"*It's all right. Don't bother. There's a new novel I want to start tonight anyway.*"

"*Oh? Not watching television?*"

"*Oh. Yes, it's the big night, isn't it? I'm glad you reminded me. Eight?*"

"*Eight.*"

"*Thank you. Later then?*"

"*Yes. Later.*"

HE LOOKS at his watch. Almost six. Foolish, the feeling that he's hanging back here in the office to delay an execution as long as possible, not to stay one. Foolish.

And almost six.

71

SIX

The end of a day.

The UBC Building, at any rate, is mainly emptied of its charges, their individual identities merged now with the greater stream of New York's humanity, particularly the swell that fills the pavements along Broadcasters Row. And on from there, the teeming hundreds burgeoning into thousands, the thousands somewhere into millions, hurrying home in this bright September dusk to have their dinners or suppers or whatever, thereafter to settle down (it is devoutly to be wished) to watch the highly advertised and presumably major event of the television season, the premiere of *The UBC Magazine of the Air.*

The UBC lobby has thinned to a trickle as the drivers, the security guards, Carl, Lena Lightfoot bid their good nights to the few honestly overworked, but more the lingerers who have so well clocked the comings and goings of the big brass that they rarely fail to make a down elevator with Robert Abrams or Adrian Miller or Marty Levitt or Gerald McAlister or Mark Banner or Fred Wiener or Steve Lilly or Selwyn Coe or Pete Grimm or Dutch Cottingham or Bill Kelly or Jack Stroud (or, by God, maybe the Old Man himself) or whomever one wishes to be seen with, or near, or whose backside is of particular interest at a given time. The big boys, always the first to arrive in the morning, are almost certainly the last to leave at night, their departures, if only in the imaginations of either themselves or their admirers, accompanied invariably by the audible strains of martial music.

"Good night, Mr. Wiener."

"Mr. Lilly."

"Mr. Levitt."

"Mr. McAlister."

"Have a good evening, Mr. Stroud."

"Mr. Banner."

"Mr. Grimm."

"Nice night, sir, Mr. Kelly."

"Mr. Cottingham."

"Mr. Coe."

" 'Night, sir."

"... sir ..."

"Sir ..."

"Good night, Mr. Miller."

"Mr. Abrams! Sir!"

Six on the dot.

WHILE WAITING on the loading ramp at the side of the building, each for his car and driver, Robert and Adrian are strangely ill at ease with one another.

It's Robert who breaks the silence: "I haven't been able to catch you today."

"Yes," says Adrian. "It was a heavy day, wasn't it?"

"Depends on one's definition of 'heavy.' If it means doing things behind someone's back, then yes, I think you could call it a heavy day."

The smile on Adrian's face is all flint. "It's times like this, Bobby, when I could wholeheartedly kick the shit out of you."

Robert's face, even in the gathering dusk, is a beacon of crimson light. "Really great, lunching alone with father when there's so much at stake, when we need to be *together* in everything we do, say. . . ."

"Easy, Bobby. Things in their stride. All in good time, Bobby, all in good time."

"What in hell are you talking about? The Board meeting is Monday!"

"Bobby!"

Robert gets hold of himself, and just in time. Selwyn Coe and Dutch Cottingham are passing right behind them. After the perfunctory nods, Robert says stiffly, "We will speak later, on the phone. I am in no mood for it now."

His car and driver, from the underground garage, are, fortunately, at his side at this percise moment.

Adrian watches the car move down and out, into the crosstown traffic. And on his own drive home to Westport begins a long series of thoughts, and rethinking, about the once and future fortunes of Adrian Miller and UBC, and the place in them, if any, of long-ago friend Bobby Abrams.

72

IT IS LONG AFTER SIX when Steve Lilly bounds into Christy's, where Barbara Ermeling awaits him in their familiar booth. She is pale tonight, more lethargic than usual, but her adoration at the sight of him is not unchanged. If anything, it brings a momentary spot of color to her cheeks, like a magical rouge applied before a sweeping entrance. He slides in easily beside her, touches her hand.

"Hi there," he says.

"Hi there."

The waitress, catching his eyes, simply acknowledges it by an order to the bartender.

When he's served he says, "What happened today? Period?"

She blushes, looks away. "No. I just felt . . . I don't know. Kind of funny sitting there. Kind of wrong. Like maybe I wasn't meant to be there or something. I just know I couldn't sit there another minute."

"Better now?"

She smiles—wanly, but smiles. "What's better? I just sat around counting cracks in the walls all afternoon. I don't think I even got up for a Coke."

"You need a vacation or somethin'," he says. "You know . . . a trip somewhere. A holiday."

She seems to brighten. "Could we, Steve? Could we go somewhere? For a few days maybe? Even a weekend. It would be so neat. Could we?"

He removes his hand. "Hell, honey, you forget. I'm not only a workin' stiff, I got a wife and little old brood packed away out there in the country."

Forced smile now: "It's okay. I understand. I guess I've just got the downs a little. They pass. I'll be myself again tomorrow. I always am. A person can manage if he tried hard enough, right? Tries. I think. That's what you're supposed to think, anyway." Then, trying her damnedest: "Tell me about your day. Busy? Boy, I'll bet you are, all the excitement and all with the premieres. I'm going to watch the big one tonight. When you've left, I mean. I know it'll be super. Just super."

He doesn't answer. Just signals the waitress for another round.

Thinking: Damn! She really is sweet, but I've got to get this hump off my back if it's the last thing I do. The time's come and that's that. It was great while it lasted, baby, but . . .

"I thought about going shopping today," she says. "Since I had the time. But I just honestly couldn't seem to get going. You know?"

"Yeah. Yeah, sure." He swallows the new drink practically whole, makes eyes for still another.

"I have the funniest feeling," she says. "It's hard to explain really. I mean, nothing's ever said or even intimated, for that matter. But it's like . . . well, like everybody knows. Like everybody knows everything there is to know and won't say anything. I mean, like Edith. Sitting there all day, and then when your name comes up, a kind of . . . Oh, I don't know, a look, a movement of some kind, something. And Mr. Banner. I know it's silly, but I have this tingly feeling inside that even him, Mr. Banner I mean, that even him . . ."

One good long swallow, that'll do it. That'll *have* to do it. Yessireebob.

"Look, doll," he says, "Barb'ra. I have a feelin' that maybe your feelin' is . . . well, *real*, you know? Like maybe we ought to cool it a while. You know?"

Her eyes are on her still-virgin drink; she holds them there. "No, Steve, I don't know. Maybe you'd better tell me. I'm not the brightest kid on the block, you know. I was never very good at spelling. Maybe you'd better give me a spelling lesson. You know, Steve? Like 'D-O-N-A-L-D D-O-C-K *Duck*.' The kind I grew up on. Sitting there hour after hour in front of the television set. Saying it over and over, 'D-O-N . . .'"

"All right! All right, stop it. Okay? I get the point. Okay?"

". . . 'D-O-C-K *Duck*.' Never very good at it. Not at all. Mama used to say she couldn't for the world imagine what I'd grow up like . . ."

And all the time stroking the inside of his thigh, the trace of a small weary smile crinkling the corners of her mouth when she knows she has him, when her hand around its swell starts to knead, massage, to squeeze, her voice in knowing rhythm with it.

". . . and then to grow up and find myself actually at a television network, right in the middle of all the glamour and excitement and truly like, well, a treasure-trove of people . . ."

It isn't easy, but he pushes her hand away, his breathing (now, especially, with the drinks under his belt) actually heavy and labored, as if he's actually been a participant in the act itself. He manages some control again only when another drink is set before him.

"My old granddaddy used to have a favorite sayin'," he says. "'There hath no temptation taken you but such as is common to man: but God is faithful, who will not suffer you to be tempted above that ye are able; but will with the temptation also make a way of escape, that ye

may be able to bear it.' From the Bible, of course. First Corinthians,
I think. It's the only thing from the Bible I ever learned by heart. My
granddaddy, who I can hardly even remember now, was a really mean
old bastard who went around spoutin' the Holy Writ while he kicked
the bejesus out of somebody or other. I sure don't aim to be like him,
Barb. I don't think I am—as any guy can see himself, that is. But sometimes what seems cruel is really to the good, you know? I mean, somethin' like me, somebody like me, can't bring you nothin' but lousy tidin',
you know? And you don't have to worry any about the rent and all.
Leastways for a while yet. Till you get settled somewhere else or
somethin'—whatever you want. You're a great gal, Barbie, you really
are. If things were different . . ."

She is already pushing at him, tears welling so you can hardly see
her eyes. "Let me out . . . please . . . move out, Steve . . . let me . . .
out . . ."

"Look, Barb'ra. This isn't a partin' of the ways, for Christ sake. It's
just a kind of coolin'-off time, a stretchin' time, you might say. For both
of us."

"Move! Goddamn you, Steve, move! Please!"

Sadly (or so it seems . . . hell, he even feels it as he stands to make
way for her), and then she is away, gone beyond his life, he expects.
Now and forever. Amen.

He signals the waitress for the compulsory one for the road, and
breathes still a little heavily, but more at ease now—free. One down.
How many more to go? The paths are rough and rocky, but he's the
man for them, that's for sure. If ever a man on this earth had it all by
the balls . . .

For an instant he remembers Maury Sherman and what the little
kike bastard laid on him today. But the new drink drowns that one,
too, and he's got it made, man, clear track ahead.

Bet your boots.

Bet your ass.

DARKNESS is such a good, a private, thing. Oh, she thinks about a note,
of course, a word of some kind. If only for her family, the few friends
she may have made. But it doesn't matter really, wouldn't matter even
if she did leave a note. Notes like that are just like people in their
caskets, all embalmed. They say as much about a person's life as em-
balmers and people like that, working so hard to make death look
like life. Just somebody else's hand dressing you up for proper showing,
as if a few little words could tell a lifetime—what it was.

What it is.

Drowsiness is a sweet thing, too, as private and dear as the darkness.

The two together strengthen a person's will. They leave no room for regret because they're friends, the last she'll know. Which is oddly comforting, too, because they were the first she ever knew.

She's glad she chose the oven; it's so much quieter, easier. She suddenly remembers having read about a lady writer named Sylvia something, Sylvia Plath—yes, that was it—who had done the very same thing, done it the very same way. She'd never read a poem or anything by the lady, but she hoped she would meet her sometime so they could maybe compare notes or something. Not that a famous writer would have much to do with the likes of her, but then you never know until you get there, do you now?

It's comforting to know that your last thought is not about how anyone will act when they find you. Nor even of him. How far away he's come to be—he has no face, no part at all. And funny, it really is, that the last thing you're conscious of is how you take the morning coffee into that very nice Mr. Banner, making sure his shoulder rubs against your breast, a time or two anyway—that or something of you—some part of you. And that maybe you should have waited an hour or two at least, until at least you'd seen the big show they're all talking about, the one that makes or breaks, or so they

Say

73

". . . AND if you don't think I eat it up, you're out of your mind. There's not an eye in this room that's not popping out of its socket. 'Is it her? It's really her!' I eat it up. Damn right I do. I eat it up."

"And the other eye popping from *its* socket? What's it saying? 'Who the hell is he?'"

"No. Who the *fuck* is he. After all, pet, the affairs of the heart of one Sharon Moore, celebrity, are a matter of legend, if not record. Just being seen with me is like a dry martini in the bathtub. Like you've finally made it, kid, you're really there."

The Oak Room bar of the Plaza is, as always at this hour, both lively and chatty, a place to see, be seen, above all be heard. Their table is by the windows, overlooking the park, but with a direct view of the door. Mark is certain she planned it that way; whoever entered

would from that very first step be aware that he was in the presence
of a Star. And be self-conscious and discomfited accordingly. Just as
he himself most certainly is. Being with Sharon in private is beating
enough. Publicly it is out-and-out flagellation.

He scans the room (for the fifth or so time; no reason except to avoid
looking so continuously at her. She not only drinks you in, she sits
there and eats you), looks again at his watch. Twenty-five minutes or
so after six. In another hour and a half . . . But he's promised himself
to think about that one as little as possible. He is, after all, a pretty
conditioned general. Large or small, the *UBC Magazine* is still just
another battle.

"Another round?"

He nods for the waiter. Ordering, he can't help being impressed by
the extraordinary way she has of handling her various publics. The
dumbstruck waiter is made to feel all the more a man by the way she
beams at him with all the innocence of a Circe. He also notices that
she looks more vibrant than ever tonight. Sea green is just her color,
and milieu.

"I really hate doing the Barry Gray thing tonight," she says. "I feel
so naked on radio. I never was one to project with just my voice,
you know."

"I know," he says. "You need a couple of other things to precede
you."

She smiles, looks poignantly (her interpretation of it, anyway) at his
fine, strong hands, one around his glass, the other resting casually on
the table. It's this one she covers with one of her cool, much-cared-for
own.

"Darling Mark. You *are* an angel coming over here like this. On
such an important night for you, too. I mean, everyone knows that
Magazine is all your own invention, whatever label it carries. I suppose
one could say you're already a really important part of history—TV's
history, that is—you're already set, no matter what happens from here
on in. Not that anything—"

The act may be obvious but he isn't immune. "Sharon, sweetheart.
What exactly the hell is it that's so mind-blowing in the first act that
this little preamble is taking so long?"

She withdraws her hand but not her eyes. Nor are her slightly moist
lips in the least disturbed.

(Disturbing though, yes. In addition to—in fact, far and above—all
the other conflicting emotions she induces is the primary one of wanting to devour her then and there.)

"Well, we'll just first-act it, then," she says. "From the moment the
script reads 'Enter Sharon.' All right?"

"Your show."

"Your luck. That I stayed up half the night thinking about this, I mean. After hot-and-heavy Freddie departed the premises."

He does look at her. "Wiener?"

"The same. He of the gargantuan appetites, or something or other. Anyway, he chews the scenery, or certainly plans to. I believe he departed with the notion that UBC's number one star would be his chewing partner."

"Oh? To what end?"

"To the dead end of the network's distinguished president, whom I wish I had between my legs this very minute."

He isn't surprised. Exactly how and to what purpose Wiener has planned on using Sharon Moore is secondary. That he's playing his hand so openly is the thing. He must feel pretty secure. . . . "Uncle Bob," most probably. Which makes Adrian's odd call to him this afternoon that much odder. It's an open secret that Robert Abrams and Adrian Miller are out to cut the Old Man's water with the Board. But Sharon Moore? What? How? Turn her against him? Have her threaten to move to CBS, NBC, if Mark Banner isn't moved out?

"It's really not surprising," he says. "I'm kind of the object of a lot of affections these days. You know. The king is dead. Long live the king."

She pouts but smiles. "And here I thought I was laying before you the wines of Arabia. Anyway, angel, he's out for your ass and little Sharon thought you ought to know. Just exactly what devious means he's using or planning to use—well, that's for somebody else to figure. Of course, you could ask him outright. He's standing right over there with his mouth hanging open."

And so he is, his eyes as wide, as uncertain, as taken by surprise as eyes can get. Then, within fractions of a second, hard and self-protecting. He turns and ambles out. Casual as all hell.

Mark shakes his head. "I don't get it," he says. "You set this up deliberately, didn't you?"

"I did."

"But why? What on earth could you hope to—"

"I'm really much simpler than you make me out to be, angel. And more selfish than you would dare to think me. You're a much nicer lay than he is. It's as simple as that."

"Oh? Well, flattery, they say, will get you nowhere. . . ."

But of course he doesn't mean it, and of course he pays the check knowing full well where they're headed. He doesn't think twice, or once, when they get there.

She's really a sensational piece.

74

VIVIAN lies in semidarkness, her eyes wide open. Her thoughts, while occasionally real and specific, are for the most part fleeting and abstract. The few times that the phone has rung, Emma has answered it downstairs; all the calls have been for Mark, three from New York, a couple from the Coast. She's hardly noticed them. She remembers, now and then, that there is something she has to do tonight—oh, yes, the three-hour *Magazine*—but as quickly as she remembers, she forgets. A half-empty bottle of Chivas Regal rests comfortably on the night table beside her. She's settled in and quite content. Quite. The dried tears across her cheeks, chin, aren't tears at all. They're simply the lingering remnant of a morning dew, a lapse in freshness soon to be washed away by another, more sparkling moisture; moisture of another, sweeter morning. A morning of a new and joyous waking.

As any fool can see.

JOSLYN, TOO, is in her bed. About her are boxes of chocolates and bonbons—sticky-sweet pacifiers to accompany the slick-smooth draughts of John D. McDonald paperbacks, as well as copies of *Newsweek*, *Ladies' Home Journal*, and pirated copies of *Porno*, whose illustrations go well with chocolate-covered cherries. Adrian is downstairs in his study, on the telephone as usual, talking to some member of the Board or other—she can't keep up with them. He's playing so many ends against ends, and middles against middles, it's not only difficult but really tiresome keeping up with them. In fact, her attention has been diverted from all the court intrigues for some weeks now. Except insofar as Mark Banner is concerned, because here at least she is silently pulling for someone, waiting herself to see his much-talked-about *Magazine*, wishing only the very best for it. No matter what they're trying to do to him or why.

"But it's *my* stock," she says to no one in particular, the empty room in general. "And don't you ever forget that, mister." It just sounds good to her, is reassuring in a way, and—spoken through large-size bites of the delicious confections—somehow brings a sense of basic if undefined comfort.

It is Robert with whom Adrian is talking. And for the first time within memory being vague and almost impersonal in his reassurances. Robert hangs up in a state of anxiety as pervasive as the one he drove home with.

Beside his hand, on the cluttered desk in his study, is a note from Jean Marie, posted air mail special delivery from the Royal Orleans in New Orleans—only two lines in her lazy crawl visible under the hotel envelope: *"Will be in touch with your lawyer very shortly and I'm sure you won't make trouble, no matter how."* He pushes even that back out of sight, thankful, though, that he tore up that letter to her.

Something is getting very politically and very personally distorted in what has seemed, at least until now, a rather promising and uncomplicated course of action—himself with Adrian deposing his father from the Board; Mark Banner diminished or out after defeat by his own hand. He decides not to think further on it now—to try not to— but to wait until after Mark Banner's impending three-hour disaster (which he himself supported, at least in the beginning). To wait until after the thud to put the question squarely and openly to Adrian.

Meanwhile, with brandy and pills to keep him company, he girds himself for the night's ordeal.

Alone.

75

For all that the vague discomfort has returned off and on to his chest, David has enjoyed the drive home to Mamaroneck. Big Long has been particularly expansive and communicative, filling him in on advance reaction to tonight's premiere.

The "big bombshell," as Big Long describes it, is destined for a pretty hearty sampling. . . . "You hear about a guy gettin' lynched long enough, you got to be there for the head-snap." Mrs. Big, in fact, has invited her brother and sister-in-law over to watch it with them, "makin' a friggin' supper party out of it, can you beat that?"

"I suspect Bob Sarnoff and Arthur Taylor and Leonard Goldenson are doing the exact same thing," David had said, confident of Big

Long's familiarity with both the names and their associations after so many years of hearing them.

"Yeah, took balls and then some to go out on that kind of limb, chief. Mr. Banner's and yours, if you don't mind my sayin' so."

Dinner, too, was particularly pleasurable tonight, just he and Ellen and a prime rib of beef, and talk that soothed rather than stimulated— a welcome relief. His day, hers. Hers: usual household chores; lunch at the club with Julia Newcombe from down the street. His: meetings, phone calls, and so on; lunch at Mike Manuche's with Adrian, unusual in itself but mostly an arm's-length, determinedly friendly exchange about company matters. Robert's name did not come up. The dessert that Ellen made herself, the cinnamon *rogelach* his mother used to make, was inspired.

Now, settled into the den, waiting for eight o'clock and the pre- miere of *Magazine*—Ellen not even complaining when he lights his after-dinner cigar, sips at a brandy—they continue their easy banter, mainly about the company; the company that has fed them, clothed them, warmed and sustained them a full half century—even more.

"I have a feeling about tonight's show," she says. "Hard to explain, David, but a real true feeling."

"That it could make it?"

"More than that. We're due for some new forms, new ways. . . . My God, I sound like one of your speeches. But when you think about it, so many of our taboos are still hangovers from the radio days. As if they were divine commandments or something. When actually every day of our lives then—day? hour!—we were only improvising. Making up tradition when all we wanted to do was get through and get out."

"You've got a point," he says. "I haven't thought much about it. Mark has, though. The time thing, for instance. Station break on the hour and fifteen-minute segments, half-hour segments . . . foolish, when you think about it."

"And that's why I think tonight's show—*feel* tonight's show—will make it," she says. "Even if it isn't totally *successful*. After all, with so many parts to it . . . so many bits and pieces . . ."

"Good Lord, you haven't seen the first thing of it and already you're reviewing. Hold your ponies there, Star."

"I don't need to see it for what I'm talking about: its concept, its *feel*. Besides, something so radically different—I don't think you'd have let it in the door if it didn't have something . . ."

"Something? That's a good one. I don't like a lot of it, you know."

"I know. But you like Mark Banner. At least, you like what Mark Banner stands for."

"His guts. Yeah, I suppose. I guess any creative effort like this tells something about the man."

"The man? Not the *men*?"

"You know what I mean. I'm not talking about the outsiders, the 'talent,' in quotes. I'm talking about *our* people. *My* people. Of which creative ones, real creative ones, we ain't got such a lot of. Funny."

"What, dear, what's funny?"

"Times. The times. They really do change, don't they? Right under your nose, right while you're part of them—they really change. Even while you're looking right at 'em and don't even see it, they change, all right."

"And we don't? Is that what you're trying to say?"

"I don't know, Star. Something like that, I guess. Maybe it's like plants or something. That African violet over there. Maybe from the first, from the time our roots are covered with dirt, maybe it's all predetermined . . . how we'll grow, how we'll flower—straight up or bent—white or pink or blue or yellow . . ."

He's talking a little more quickly now, as though to deny the chest pains that have moved up through his arms to his shoulder, his back. He'll have to give Simon Rosenberg a call tomorrow.

She looks at him. "Are you all right, David?"

"Damn right," he says. "Well, maybe getting soft in the head with all this heavy talk."

She smiles. "You know something, David?"

"Hmmn?"

"I think I'm actually starting to believe in God again. Oh, not in some way that the Holy Spirit suddenly overwhelms you and you go shrieking down the aisle. But—well, quietly. Gradually. I suppose it's age. The sense of mortality. Who knows?"

"Not me, Star. Not me. I just get older and know less. Like everybody else. There's a leveling-off process, I guess. I do know this, though: I wouldn't want to have been in any other business in the world than the one I've been in. *We've* been in. And we'll be damned if we take our fingers out of the pie, right? Not till we're six feet under, by God."

"Six feet? For you, my darling, it'll be ten feet. I don't think there's a mound of dirt or concrete or anything else that can ever hold you under anyway."

"Star, that's my Star. *The Ellen Curry Hour*. Has there ever been anything equal to it? In all these years?"

"Lord, it's almost eight."

She goes to one of the massive television sets, switches it on. The previous program, a local syndicated game show called *Higher*, is just ending. The credits are rolling over a big-band finale.

She sits again. "I do hope the first hour is strong enough to hold people for the rest. That's so important in a show like this, isn't it?"

She looks over at him when he doesn't answer. He looks a little pale, but then he always does at this time of day. It's only when she peers more closely that she sees the cigar on the floor.

"David?" she says. "David, you've dropped your . . ."

She's at his side before the words are fully out. And it takes only that long for her to realize that he's gone. While in a burst of color and sound the words sweep across the thirty-inch television screen:

THE UBC MAGAZINE OF THE AIR

Four

A Day in the Present
Friday

76

It's a warm September morning, perhaps the warmest of the month. Waking to it, swallowing it, Janet Greer wishes for a moment she hadn't talked Joel out of air-conditioning units, fickle weather or not. But after a few breaths she's again glad that she did, for her light perspiration, blended with his on the sheet, is reaffirming, like warm milk and the taste of lips after love. She turns on her side.

Joel, in sleep, is almost beautiful, she thinks. The severity—the seriousness that sits like so many schoolmasters on his face—some at the corners of his mouth, some on his forehead, some guarding his eyes —sleeps quietly (invisibly), leaving an expression so innocent, so vulnerable, it almost breaks her heart. Rewardingly, though. There is nothing she enjoys more than waking early, turning on her side, and watching him sleep. It amazes her sometimes that she can love another human being as she loves this man.

She lies still, hardly breathing, simply looking at him. After a few minutes, however—his nose and damp upper lip grossly magnified in the fixed line of her vision—she turns her eyes away and remembers. Not that it is ever really out of her mind—not for very long, anyway. She touches her stomach and sighs.

She should have told him Monday, she supposes, when she'd arrived late at the High Life, the thing glorious inside her, the doctor's affirmation like the Song of Solomon in her breasts. But something in his face, a depression; the network; another Monday night at his mother's—oh, more than that; who is she fooling? How can she tell him they're having another baby when nothing else is more important right now than that he leave UBC, at least the executive ranks of it; the Wiener, Lilly, yes, even the Mark Banner of it; even the sudden passing of David Abrams of it; if only to know himself again, whether he finishes the novel or not; whether he ever writes another word. They can manage it, too—even with the new baby. Impractical as it seems, they can make it, she knows it. So what if their AT&T, their Standard Oil, their General Motors, their UBC—so what if they go down? she thinks. So what if the economy is at its recession-inflation depth, peak? There's Joel, isn't there? *Joel*, that's what matters; Joel Griebsberg, *Griebsberg* —that's what screams for release. And just when he himself is hearing it again (it has been mute so long, but even mute, tearing him apart) —now when he's hearing it, wants to hear it—the news of another child . . .

The hand on her stomach is a fist. No, she's right, she decides. This wonder inside her will remain a wonder even if she's silent about it just a little while longer. Joel with his pride, his great-provider complex (thanks to that impossible family he's shackled to, but then she's promised herself not to think about *them*), his tendency (these past few years anyway) to think-before-you-leap, weigh-before-you-buy— to tell him now would silence the wonder in him, perhaps forever. . . .

"Muv."

It's all so mixed up. Joel (well, basically) is the romantic of them, yet this last year or so at UBC you'd think he'd invented reality (it might be unfashionable to call it a rat race, but what else is it really?); while she—since she can remember, Miss Practical One herself—is suddenly ready to throw caution (even this Sutton Place South apartment she admittedly adores) to the wind.

"Muv. You 'wake yet, Muv?"

He's a blond, fair (and face it, gorgeous) five-year-old, and his eyes are just inches from hers. "Richard!" she shushes, brushing her lips across his cheeks; whispering, "I've told you not to come in here like this. Daddy's still asleep. Go in the kitchen, love, I'll be right there."

As he sits at the dinette table in his striped pajamas, his chin cupped in his hands, she could swallow him whole. "You mess," she says, nuzzling his neck. "Here, drink this orange juice before I eat you up."

"Muv! You wouldn't do *that!*"

"Oh, wouldn't I!" She laughs. It's a ritual with them, as inseparable from a day as watching Joel sleep. That is, when Joel is here. The months leading up to premiere time are definitely the exception, not the rule. He's on the Coast practically every other week, developing other people's properties while his own goes begging. "Drink it all," she says, probably more brusquely than she should, for the boy's eyes are slightly unbelieving. She smooths his hair.

Sighing (he has a way of doing this that is heartbreakingly beautiful), he asks, "Why is daddy sleeping so late? Because old Mr. Abrams got died?"

"He isn't sleeping late at all," she says, starting the coffee. "It's still early. Besides, daddy was up very late last night."

"Doing what?"

"On the phone with people about Mr. Abrams. About the new *Magazine* show. And reading his book."

"What book?"

"*His* book. Richard, I've told you several times about daddy's book. Do you want some more juice?"

"What did you do?"

"When?"

"Last night. Muv, are you hard of hearing?"

She sits across from him. "When we came home from the funeral parlor and dinner I watched daddy's network's new program," she says. "The last half of it, anyway. Now anything else, Mr. Inquisitor?"

"Miz Kirschman and I watched it before I went to bed." He nods, obviously in his glory in this grown-up early-morning exchange with his mother. "I didn't understand it. Some of it. Most of it." He gamely smiles. "Any of it."

"Dear, it isn't a child's program," she says.

"I don't care. I still didn't like it."

Smiling, she remembers. The New York reviews. Habit this week, if nothing else. The *Magazine* notices are held over until today because of Mark Banner's insistence on no preshowings to the press. She goes to the front door, where the papers lie folded on the corridor carpet. There's more than the usual apprehension when she turns to the radio and television sections this morning, as if the show and Joel's involvement (and for months he has been involved in the myriad details of *Magazine*) are somehow the juncture toward which they have both been driving.

"Muv, I was talking about bullfights with Miz Kirschman last night," Richard says, but she shushes him again, a hand gently covering his.

The Bryson Randolph column is compressed between two rival network ads, its sedate heading, THE BIG ONE DEBUTS, supported by a subhead declaring *UBC Magazine of the Air a Three-Hour Mixed Bag.* And reading:

> The experiment awaited with more than passing curiosity has had its night in court, so to speak. Wednesday's UBC "Magazine of the Air," as it calls itself, is a something-for-everybody that runs from 8:00 to 11:00 P.M. (EST). It is big, and it is uneven. Parts of it in the premiere showing were really quite good, parts of it at least respectable, and parts of it woefully inadequate.
>
> Briefly, the "UBC Magazine" (they even simulate the turning of pages) is a departmentalized collection, under one roof, of many of television's most cherished staples. The premiere, for example, included an animated adult satire on suburban living, an original film drama about a mental institution, a documentary about the war on crime in the larger cities, an abridged version of the old Broadway

musical comedy "Anything Goes," an interview with some theatre luminaries, and a brief tribute to the U.S. Congress in the manner of "Mr. Smith Goes to Washington" of a generation ago.

Taken in order: The cartoon (that's all it was) was a dismal failure. Neither child nor adult could have stomached it. The mental hospital drama, on the other hand (which starred Celia Scott as a retiring nurse), if standard, was at times provocative. A cast of unusual force and quality made it appear more significant than it was. The public affairs concession following it was often brilliant, particularly in its expanded use of the subjective camera technique. John Abelman of UBC's News Department was personally responsible for this one. As for the inclusion of "Anything Goes" on video tape, one can only wonder at the decision to reproduce it. Not even such first-rate performers as Sandra Kelly and Rick LeFevre could overcome such uninspired nonsense. Only the familiar Cole Porter music saved it. The interview that followed, in which Bill Collins (host for the entire premiere show) discussed musicals of the twenties and thirties with Ethel Merman, star of the original stage production of "Anything Goes," and such old-time luminaries as George Burns and Larry Lester, was generally rather diverting. These are professionals. It's unfortunate they had to follow something as amateurish as this version of "Anything Goes." It must have made Merman wince. The last item in this marathon entertainment was a comedy-drama called "Your Country and Mine," which starred Martin O'Neal. "Let's have a real bang-up patriotic finale—you know, funny and heartwarming and upbeat." Obviously somebody at UBC said this (Mark Banner? It's his baby), and the result was a wrap-up drenched in saccharin.

That's it. What can you say? It's a magazine, all right, but how many magazines can you read cover to cover? Perhaps in the coming weeks . . .

She forgoes the rest of it, gets milk and eggs from the refrigerator and cooking oil from the cupboard, and is deep-frying three slices of French toast when a warm hand touches her neck. "Darling," she says, reaching to take it, "I didn't hear you come in."

"I did," said Richard. "I even saw him. Didn't I, daddy? I didn't say anything either. Did I? I let you surprise her, didn't I?"

"That you did," says Joel, kissing him on the forehead. The boy beams.

"The coffee," says Janet. "I almost forgot it. It ought to be ready. But I was so damned pissed off by Bryson Randolph—if you'll forgive the language—"

"I'm not sure I'll read it," says Joel, tightening the sash on his robe.

"I guess it's fair, though," she says, pouring the coffee. "I mean, no show like that can be *My Fair Lady* every minute." She smiles. "Have some coffee while I finish the French toast. How about that?"

"Goddamn, that's beautiful," says Richard.

"Now who did you get that from, me or your daddy?" She laughs. "Here, drink this milk."

"I got it from me. I happen to be a indivijul, that's what Miz Kirschman told me, and indivijuls think up things all by themselves, especially when they're child progidies."

She smiles, shakes her head, turns to Joel. "How late did you read?"

His answer is slow in coming. "I not only read," he said. "I even wrote a page or two."

Her heart leaps. It *will* work out, she thinks; it has to. The baby smiles inside her.

"A page or two of what?" says Richard.

"A page or two of daddy's Divine Comedy, and that's milk in front of you, my gorgeous progidy, so drink already."

Joel watches her face intently. She's barely able to conceal her joy. He's relieved, though—wordlessly thanks her—that she doesn't pursue it, that she returns to combat with the French toast in a silence they both need and can share. He had no intention of mentioning it when he walked in; a page or two, what do they mean? But somehow knowing it would please her . . .

He looks across to Richard, who is running a finger around the rim of his milk glass. Even Richard is silent, which is hardly his natural state. Does he sense something too? A commitment? Joel frowns, pours another cup of coffee. How can there be commitment in no more than a simple, casual . . .

There is. To Janet, anyway. And in some unclear way to himself as well. He reaches for the morning papers. Is he out of his mind? he wonders. When will there be time to write a novel? How could he even think of giving up everything with which he long ago made his accommodations? It's too late. It's just too damn late. He has a wife, a child . . . It's this crazy, nerve-racking week.

On all the front pages, of course, the funeral today of David Abrams is prominently displayed, tributes pouring in by the thousands. "*And as the President said by telegram from Washington . . .*" Joel's own almost storybook beginnings at UBC directly through David make the Old Man's passing especially poignant for him, as he thinks back to that barely remembered time when he wrote his child's letter to David, and of course to the very well-remembered chance meeting in California that led directly to his being hired and his present job. Actually he didn't see that much of David after he was hired, but the man's passing is surely a kind of milestone in his life too. He spot-reads the stories, then moves on to the radio–television sections. To Bryson Randolph. Some wake-up tonic. He reads the review quickly, then opens another paper to a review not unlike it, raves for parts rather than the whole. "From unrelieved black to shades of gray," Joel sums up. "Well, we're coming up in the world."

The sound of the sizzling French toast is comfortable, like the restoration of sanity. "Hardly anything surprising about that," Janet says over her shoulder. "After all, with so many unrelated elements—"

"That's not the real point," he says. "Sure, it's fair game and traditional to examine the elements on their own merits. We never expected otherwise, although some of these self-righteous assholes—"

"Joel!"

"What's a self-rightchus . . ." begins Richard.

"Nothing. An absolute nothing." Janet pauses, turning the toast. "Richard, daddy was talking."

"I know it. He said 'some of these self-rightchus—' "

"They really missed the thing entirely," Joel says. "It's the format, the *concept*, that's unique . . ."

She brings the toast and a pitcher of syrup to the table. "You sound like one of Marvin Goldberg's Sales Promotion pieces. Besides, Jack Stroud managed to have the format—all right, *concept*—anyway, he managed to get it talked about in practically every magazine and newspaper column in the country, didn't he? Why, *TV Guide* gave practically a whole issue to it. They've been writing about it for months. I'll bet more people know what a magazine concept is than a balanced diet. . . . Here, eat it while it's nice and warm. And Lord knows the ratings bear me out. What was it? A forty-seven share in New York? Nearly fifty percent of the whole pie? What's so bad . . ."

It's a relaxed breakfast—chatty. Janet is now like a little girl playing house. Delicious secrets are everywhere. Conversation is a camouflage (and painlessly easy, as though UBC were China and prognostication interesting but impersonal). Richard has never been livelier.

Joel keeps away the temptations of stocktaking, tries his best to banish all heavy thoughts. He, too, is playing house.

Before he leaves she says, "I know it won't be an easy day. Everybody going by the funeral home or to the hotel . . . Take it easy, huh, darling?"

He gets a cab at the corner. He's early this morning, but it's just as well. There are a thousand and one things to do today and tomorrow, what with the funeral and his own departure for the Coast again Sunday. Away from the apartment (the lovely fantasy), it springs to life, takes hold of him—the discipline of a network program executive. *Bring Marvin Goldberg and his Sales Planning writers up to date on the status of pilots; look over their sales brochure ideas to be sure program concepts are being followed; meet with Collie Levy of Samson Pictures (in from the Coast) at the Essex House about where the "Rome Adventure" script is going before the later meetings with Wiener and*

of course Mark; see Con Hirschman's people in Legal on several series
title conflicts; check with Wiener—with Mark—on whether they want
to go through with the negotiations on the Milt Duncan comedy series;
get with Bill Kelly's people on the three-part Dillinger documentary
for Magazine, before discussing it with Wiener or Mark; give a run-
down of the "Napoleon" problems to Mark before he too leaves for the
Coast, if he does decide to go. Talk to Hal Diller at GAC on the "Jam-
boree" pilot taping. . . .

And all the time wondering just what effect the Old Man's death
will have on the whole setup. On Robert Abrams and Adrian Miller.
On Mark. Wiener. Steve Lilly. On himself.

He is apparently the first to make the scene on the thirty-sixth floor.
Not even a lone secretary is visible. The sepulchral quiet, which some
mornings is a blessing, is this morning an annoyance, as though being
alone with his thoughts is in some way a duplicity—made so by the
very real presence of several characters in his novel who keep pushing
aside John Abelman and Milt Duncan and Hal Diller and Collie Levy
as if they were so many mechanical toys and his own mind a counter
at F. A. O. Schwartz. He is actually pleased when Sam Koblenzer,
whom he's never particularly liked, sticks his head through the doorway and says, "Hi, the worms worth it?" Koblenzer laughs. "Early bird
and all that." He sits down and faces Joel across the desk. "Well, I see
you've survived the last two days, anyway."

"I've survived," says Joel, "as I see you have. Not exactly headline
stuff, Sam."

Koblenzer ignores it. "Any word on the overnight ratings?"

"For the other networks? I haven't spoken with anyone this morning."

"I'm interested in what happened when our documentary came on.
I realize it bridged the other nets' nine-thirty shows, but I still think
it should have followed *The Brave Men*."

Through the open door Joel can see his secretary setting her handbag on her desk, opening it for a cigarette, disappearing for a minute.
Scattered sounds of activity have begun. Koblenzer is rambling on
about *Magazine* and tonight's single premiere, *Missy*, a situation comedy about Manhattan newlyweds, and since, even if tuned out, he's
looking at Koblenzer, he at first isn't aware that Marvin Goldberg has
been standing in the doorway for some seconds. He looks at his watch.
It's only nine-ten and the conference with Goldberg isn't until nine-
forty-five.

"You're early, Marv," he says. "I hadn't planned—"

Something in the Sales Planning director's manner stops him. Marv's
face is tight, paler than usual. His weight is on his heels, a bad sign.
"Word just came down," Marvin Goldberg says. "The Entertainment

Division, along with News, is supposed to produce a two-hour retrospective on the Old Man and his contribution to the industry and the country. In three days, count 'em, three."

"You're crazy," says Joel. "Who in hell ordered that? Not Mark?"

"Adrian Miller. Through Bob Abrams. Ding-dong. Drop everything else. Every player on the team. Oh . . . prime time and unsponsored. God bless."

77

THE MASTER BEDROOM of Fred Wiener's apartment on East Seventy-third Street, like the rest of the five-room duplex, is a monument to past elegances while unmistakably a room of its time. Accenting its tobacco-green grass-cloth walls, light melon ceiling, and cornflower blue carpeting is antique French and English furniture highlighted by a massive mahogany blanket chest and a tall Georgian linen press that houses a twenty-four-inch color television set. The paintings—there are three—are contemporary. The drapes, ranging two half walls of windows, are English linen printed in a floral, tobacco-leaf design—gold, white-gray, green, and blue. The adjoining dressing room and bath are of white Vermont marble with gold-plated fixtures. But the focal point of the room is a handsomely wrought, huge eighteenth-century English tester four-poster bed. Lying wide awake in this treasure, at about seven-forty-five this morning, are Fred Wiener and Sally Leeds, an actress anxious for the role of Hester Prynne in a new two-hour film version of *The Scarlet Letter* which UBC is producing in conjunction with Dearborn Films in London.

They have just finished making love, so to speak. Earlier, when he awoke, she was sitting in a chair by the windows, her face freshly made up, her dark hair loose but brushed—and with her legs curled under her she looked no more than a girl in her late teens, early twenties; and the sight of her, coupled with a merry-go-round recall of her amazing virtuosity during the night (she's apparently been in some exotic places in the two years since he's seen her), had him primed to go again. But now, limp from their most strenuous go-round yet, she is incontestably her age (thirty? thirty-one?), and much as it grieves him to have to agree with Mark Banner, she really is too pretty and dimply for the part. But what Mark Banner won't understand (wouldn't if it were shoved in his face) is that parts can be tailored, certain people can be accommodated (hell, in view of his precocious exploits with Joslyn Miller, age is obviously in the eye of the beholder anyway), and it's the performance that counts. You just have to be flexible in this business. How different, basically, is television from films? He wishes he could help her. She pleases him. But when Mark hasn't even brought him into the thing . . . Well, no point in ruining her day.

"You're in," he says.

Exhausted as she is, she bursts out laughing. "Freddie, you kill me," she says, "you really do. What would you have said if you hadn't liked it?"

"You're not in," he says, and laughs, reaching for her again.

"Lover, you're marvelous," she says. "A regular hard-core voluptuary. Did you know that?"

It's coming, he thinks. The one thing about her that annoys him. She talks too much afterward.

"You don't know, Fred"—she sighs—"you just don't know. Living the way I do. I mean, if I wasn't a name it would be understandable. But I *am* a name. So why do I still wind up in bed? Goodness knows I don't *have* to any longer. Not that I ever *had* to, you know. At least I can act—that's more than you can say for these impossible little things coming up in television today. Don't you think, Freddie? My analyst calls it overidentification. Over*simp*lification, if you ask me. Fred, I have two Tonys, an Obie, and two Emmy nominations. You don't win those between sheets. I suppose I should have married again. But twice burned, well . . . Freddie, I need this part, I mean seriously, Freddie. Guest spots are harder and harder to come by, and films . . . Fred, I haven't had a film in two years. Of course, I'm in the process of changing agents. Fred, what are you like? I mean, *really* like? You know, I can't say I know you. I mean, *know* you. You can be a charming man . . ."

He listens; half listens. She's good for a half hour at least. He thinks vaguely about a cup of coffee. Mostly his thoughts—if the elusive little snipers can be called thoughts at all—center on the Old Man's passing and what it will mean in the maneuvering for the top (won't *family* count more—more than some others, anyway, some *one* other named Hotshot Banner, not to mention Very Big Shot Miller?); on the mixed blessings of *Magazine,* the impossibility of reading its success or failure so soon (the fat rating share, though, for sure doesn't hurt Mark Banner); on the sight of Sharon Moore and Mark Banner together (from which his stomach still hasn't recovered; he'd been counting on Sharon). Also on what the hell he's doing screwing around with Sally Leeds anyway, except it's a relief from figuring every angle,

how every act fits or doesn't fit into his plans. No question there—Sally
Leeds doesn't fit anything except his cock. The phone rings at eight-
fifteen. His stepmother, M.J., is calling from her apartment four blocks
away to remind him to be at Ellen's suite at the Waldorf. He's a pallbearer. The funeral services are to be held at Temple Emanu-El on
Fifth Avenue. And when he has hung up, naked and for the moment
vulnerable by the side of the bed, the world seems alien, as though he's
never set foot to it, as though everything in it is the enemy, hostile and
carnivorous. But the sight of Sally Leeds, naked herself under a thin
blue sheet, reconstitutes him. It's her natural habitat, and she fills it
with life. He snaps out of his mood, ready to go forward into the
jungle world, chock-full of lively plans to appropriate its treasures.

"I have to get cracking. Funeral's today, you know," he says.

Instantly she's beside him. "Lord, that dear man."

"I'm a pallbearer."

How cold it sounds. Even to him.

"A great man gone," she says. "And still so active. Oh, it's really
unfair, don't you agree, Freddie?" Her hand on his arm, meant to be
comforting, is a spur to activity. He begins dashing about the room,
showering, shaving, dressing with urgency.

There's urgency in his voice, too. "I'm going to their suite at the
Waldorf. Let yourself out, will you? Use this way." He points to a
special door that opens only from the inside onto the fifteenth-floor
corridor (his apartment door is on fourteen), and which from the outside seems merely part of the wall. "My maid comes at noon," he adds.

When he emerges from the dressing room, attired handsomely in
a dark blue worsted, she says, "You have to ask yourself why such a
fine man, and a statesman of our business, they're calling him . . ." and
even in his agitated state it's funny to see her, pontificating so solemnly
while slipping hastily into panties, the familiar breasts, still uncovered,
looking at him across the room that still smells of their lovemaking. He
sneezes. "Bless you," she says, and that, too, tragically.

He reads the *Magazine* notices on the short cab ride to the hotel.
But he is already light-years beyond *Magazine*.

There seems to be an unaccustomed quiet on Park, on Forty-ninth.
The Waldorf lobby, too—that royal labyrinth of a hall—also seems
strangely hushed for the hour, as though in low voices the presence
of death might be banished. It's obvious the news is now broadcast,
he thinks; even in a hotel as vast and of as many worlds as the Waldorf, the presence on its premises of the widow of an important man
like David Abrams becomes an event. He's pretty sure he isn't just
imagining it—employees and guests with "Abrams" and "Youbeecee"
unmistakably on their lips. Near the elevators, one woman to another:
". . . but I believe Mark Banner's the name of the other president, I
never did know which was which. . . . I guess he'll be running the

whole thing now. He's Jewish, too, you know." She shrugs. "At least I think . . . no, I'm sure he is. They all are." In the elevator now, the operator snaps to when he asks for the eighteenth floor.

There are already two dozen or so people in the suite's living room: Robert, Adrian and Joslyn, M.J. and his father. The mayor, New York's lieutenant governor, the FCC chairman, both U.S. senators from New York, the U.S. ambassador to the U.N., the British ambassador to the United States, several members of the Board of Directors. The presidents of Xerox, Mobil, U.S. Steel. The heads of J. Walter Thompson, McCann, BBD&O. A clutch of Broadway producers. Sharon Moore (the bitch) and Larry Lester, still in town. Arthur Merck. Gerald McAlister. Maury Sherman. Marty Levitt. Lester Levinson from Atlanta. Two or three cousins from Brooklyn. Some of the Mamaroneck domestic staff. The room is large, and they are in small groups, or sitting, standing alone. Some show grief. All seem rather bewildered. Not only McAlister and Sherman; the VIPs too; and Big Long, the chauffeur. David Abrams was the center. What happens to circles without centers?

"Fred, I'm glad you're here." Gerald McAlister touches his arm. "There are so few relatives, you know."

"Such a day," one of the cousins mutters, touching him too. "Such a terrible day, Fred."

"Yes," he replies, head bowed and solemn.

The bedroom, too, is large, and like the living room pervasively gray. Ellen rests on one of the three-quarter beds, her eyes fixed on the high ceiling. Only Joslyn and her personal maid are with her. They sit like stones on either side of a dressing table.

"Fred," she says, lifting her pale damp face to receive him. Stricken, no doubt, but hardly undone. Far from it, and Fred has little doubt that now that the Old Man is gone, the gentle, gracious Ellen Curry will prove to be a much tougher old bird than even the wariest of them has even begun to suspect.

78

How now, brown cow?

Even in stunned sorrow (and David Abrams had been a sure, if not intimate, friend), Maury Sherman is thinking ahead. Nor has Gerald McAlister, and now Fred Wiener, triggered him. When he came to the hotel at eight to see if everything was in order, the foremost thought in his head was Ellen. The show is Ellen's. Whole thing is Ellen's. Regardless of what Bobby Boy may think. And that first thought was the rallying point for all the others.

Smiling wryly (though it appears less smile than scowl), he glances over at Gerald McAlister, a few feet away by one of the radiators under a thickly draped window. The vice president in charge of bewilderment is simply staring into space, the measure of his disbelief compounded by slumped shoulders and homeless hands. But sensing the attention, McAlister glances back, and straightening himself he walks heavily toward him.

"I do wish Fred Wiener would come out." He sighs. "There are so many arrangements and things to discuss, things one can't possibly bother Bobby or Adrian with."

Maury looks to the closed door. "So now it's Wiener," he says. "Because he's a pallbearer? I see you haven't neglected your homework, Jerry. Still, he *is* Jewish, and you know how Bobby and Adrian feel about that. For the top slots, that is. Right? So maybe your boy Lilly's in the running after all."

McAlister's indignity is sharp even in his tired, glazed eyes. "What are you talking about?" he snaps, but in a guardedly low voice. "You know, you have a way of being very insulting, Sherman. This is hardly the time or place, and the least you can do . . . This is a very difficult moment for all of us who cared for him. *Cared* for him, Sherman." He turns away. "Because of David Abrams we've put up with a great deal from you, Maury, but I'm warning you . . ." In his excitement he knocks over an ashtray from the table between them, and its dull thump on the carpet is like a gunshot. All eyes in the room are on him accusingly, and McAlister slumps again under the weight of them. He looks incredibly like a child whose disobedience has been made scornfully public. Maury can hardly believe it is Gerald McAlister. He's sorry he baited him; the man has gone to pieces.

Time passes like . . . time—time when you're very conscious of it.

In the respectful quiet, echolike fragments of soft conversations (mainly the relatives') fill the room.

"But he wasn't that old, Claire—mama said he was younger than Cousin Siggy, and Siggy was, let's see, how old was Siggy when he died?"

". . . has to be today, they can't bury him on Saturday, not on the sabbath."

". . . just sitting there, I hear, waiting to see the big new show on his television, and boom . . ."

". . . poor thing, they were so close."

". . . and brave. They didn't even have to give her sedation."

"Yes, I'm sure of it, every big star you can name will be there."

". . . has to be. Ellen wouldn't consider any place but Temple Emanu-El."

"The one over there, he was his right hand, they say."

"Such a good man, decent, never so much as looked at another . . ."

". . . Wiener. I'm sure Ellen . . ."

". . . live for, so much to live for. . . ."

Maury looks up. Two more men have come in and are talking with the mayor, their gray heads together like old grads calling signals at a playing field reunion. The two senators have left. Serving trays of coffee and danish have been rolled in and a uniformed waiter, directed by Hamlin Hirschmyer, is passing them around. Maury takes a half cup, drinks it in two swallows, and in the course of one of them spills some coffee down his tie. He looks around for McAlister but he's no longer in the room. If Fred Wiener has come out of the bedroom he isn't aware of it. He looks at his watch. It's nearing nine. Where's Mark? he wonders. It's hard to understand. He personally called him at his own suite here at the Waldorf, where Mark and his wife had stayed the night, just after he got here. It's unlike Mark; he's probably been up for hours. And if ever in his life Mark Banner needed to be somewhere . . .

79

YOU SAY NOTHING. You lie there and listen, and after a while she says, "I'm leaving you, Mark," and you're not dreaming, you're awake, except that maybe you're not, because the phone's ringing and Maury Sherman is saying, "I'm here at the hotel. In their suite. Wanted to see if everything's all right. UBC got a thirty-seven share for the night, which ain't bad considering we had no shows premiering. . . . Oh, don't bother reading Brother Bryson—he'll only make you throw up." And then finally, grudgingly, it's morning. Before, it was night.

Night. Mark shakes his head. He's having coffee in the living room of their suite on the seventh floor, the morning newspapers (folded with compulsive neatness at the television sections) beside him. It's nine o'clock, he's dressed, but he hasn't budged for an hour. Vivian still sleeps in the bedroom to his left. The coffee is hot, he's ordered it twice. He's endured five cups. The sixth is tasteless.

Mark Banner sits in a hotel suite at nine o'clock on a Friday morning of a premiere week, drinking a sixth cup of coffee. The thought dismays him but he makes no move to get up. In sorting the night from the morning (and this odd exercise has preoccupied him since the phone call from Maury Sherman), he considers David Abrams' death in the unnatural order of things begun with Sharon Moore on Wednesday night and continued through last night.

What possessed him, anyway, wanting Vivian so suddenly—*needing* her? Because she was there in a hotel room with him and not in the too familiar chill of their own home? Because of Sharon Moore? Because of . . . ? The memory, try to lose it all you like, is vivid.

Taking rooms in the city, as Ellen has done.

Weary, depleted from the night with Sharon; the anxiety over *Magazine,* the whole war of nerves, the pecking order; the shock and grief of David Abrams' death. The disturbing and mystifying suicide of Barbara Ermeling. The parts, the sum.

A quiet dinner, the two of them, steaks and a salad in the suite.

A nearness. A need.

"Marvelous steak."

"Great."

"Unusual for a hotel."

"Very."

"Should we order more coffee?"

"Why don't we?"

"Brandy too?"

"Why not?"

"Glad the show's premiered? That it's over?"

"I suppose. Yes."

"David's death will make a difference."

"Yes."

"A large one."

"Yes."

Not the most intimate sort of talk. And nothing afterward really, not even the usually liberating warmth of the cognac, the rush of memory . . .

And aside from that one allusion, not a word about *Magazine.* The crossroads of a career, and not a further word, not a glance. Only the briefest of words when the meal was over: "I'm terribly tired tonight, Mark," and then alone. Alone. And thinking (or had he actually thought it then? Was he thinking it only now?): I haven't really been fair to Vivian. She still needs me. It's not too late. . . . An hour or so more, making notes on people to see, things to do on his trip to the Coast; shutting from his mind the death, *Magazine;* himself alone again.

Alone.

One bedroom in the suite, but a large one, spacious. He undresses in it, in the dark, but sees in shadows the curve of her back in one of the wide twin beds. Strange. All his life he has wanted, never said needed. Like two opposing ideologies, they have been separate for him—wanting and needing—in everything he thought, everything he did, to the point of almost religious certainty. Needing: it is evil, devilishly threatening. In wanting you are safe—your head clear, your stomach hard. In needing you lose control, surrender the truth too easily. Now, in one lifetime of a week, his cosmogony has come unstuck and he is awash in the dreaded gray. Even Vivian—perhaps most of all Vivian—as if in desire (undeniably present) were embedded the stranger he thought he'd shaken, at least through the hours of a crucial week. Tenderness, too; there was tenderness, too.

Observing years; memory. Moving to her bed.

Touching her.

Gently.

Easing his hand along her hip, ignoring the muscular contraction as she stiffened.

Sitting beside her, leaning into the curve of her back; stroking her shoulder, kissing her neck.

Confused when she lay without moving (she who always seized like a cat); saying, "Vivian, we'll make it right, this time we'll make it right. . . ." Lifting her gown, caressing her thighs, asking for the softness between them with fingers unused to asking, feeling her twist from his hand, from all of him.

Not drowsily; meaning it.

Angered, gripping her wrist until it hurt, until he knew it hurt, edging her hand to his own thigh, to himself . . .

"Vivian. Vivian, please."

Hearing her short "No!" and, unless his ears failed him altogether, "Isn't one dead one enough for you?" Finding his own bed, grateful only for what the darkness left him.

Left him listening, for what seemed hours, to silence. Not thinking (unless thirty-nine years, stuck like hard glue to the roof of his mind, could be called thoughts). Not even feeling. Just lying there, listening, and after a while she says, "I'm leaving you, Mark," and you're not dreaming, you're awake, except that maybe you're not. . . .

Again he shakes his head, this time as much in rejection of the acrid coffee as to clear his head. And it is in this motion, this *physical* movement, that David Abrams' death really hits him. For a moment he thinks his own insides have stopped, like the too tightly wound mainspring of a clock. His hand actually shakes when he sets his cup on the coffee table. Fortunately, that sight alone is enough to bring him back to his senses, and if when he adjusts his tie, brushes lint from his jacket, his motions lack last year's cool, or even last week's, they at least offer a facsimile of it. He has much to do: Go to the Abrams suite, call Edith, check on arrangements, cancel the trip to the Coast . . . .

He's rising to leave when Vivian comes in. She's wearing a green dressing gown, carelessly, even untidily, and her hair is matted, her eyes puffed from sleep. And he thinks he has never seen her quite so beautiful.

"Oh," she says, "I didn't know you were still here. It's already after nine, you know."

"I know."

She yawns. "Coffee," she says. "Good. It *is* warm, isn't it?"

"Enough."

She pours a cup, takes a lump of sugar, and sits across from him. "Didn't the phone ring?" she asks. "I thought I heard it."

"Yes."

"It wasn't anything more on the girl's suicide?"

"No." He's standing now, and staring. "It was Maury Sherman. He's in Ellen's suite."

"Oh." She says nothing more. Her eyes are fixed on her cup.

He reaches for his attaché case, folds the newspapers in it, and starts toward the door. "I'm going to Ellen's suite," he says. "I think maybe we ought to stay over again tonight . . . So much going on, after the funeral . . ."

"I'll call Emma." She doesn't look up.

He pauses, half-facing her. "You meant it, didn't you?"

"I meant it," she says.

"I don't want that, you know."

"It doesn't matter."

He reaches in his shirt pocket for a cigarette. And lighting it, half-smiles. "I suppose I've always thought that at least the habit in a marriage could offset some—"

"I'm sorry, Mark. The habit's . . ." She too reaches for a cigarette, a single wrinkled one in a crumpled pack on the table. "I'll get dressed and come up in a few minutes. I won't embarrass you. I'll wait a few days."

He leaves without looking back.

STARING AFTER HIM, Vivian lights the cigarette that has been standing guard between her fingers, wizened as it is. Inhaling deeply, she sits back.

Well, it's done, she thinks. She's done it. She's hurt him, she knows she has. She hadn't thought it possible. It wasn't a planned thing, not a stratagem. More a . . . knowing. A clearing, a sudden clearing as in a forest. And done—simply said and done—easy as that. For once being able to seize a moment, not being prisoner to it. Doing, not being done to. *She*, for a change, taking. Taking, by God. Fred . . .

For the next hour or so, bathing and dressing—attending to her flesh as though she were both princess and handmaiden—she thinks almost exclusively of Fred Wiener. Her thoughts are round, grooved, repetitive; the center of her mind is hollow and dark. It's all perfectly clear: He's rotten, he's unprincipled, he's deadly, he's skin-deep. And she herself—she's practically a parody of Lena Horne singing "My Man." With every image of him there's a gnawing sickness in her stomach. And she wants him. At least her body is alive with him. She's going to have him. Come hell or high water she's going to have him.

Besides, she'll think the way he does too, the way they all do—he's on his way up, Mark's on his way down. Isn't he? With David Abrams, his biggest supporter, gone? Well, isn't he?

At ten-thirty-five, elegant in white linen (in her expansive mood she can accommodate Mark up to a point, but she looks lousy in black), she is in Ellen's suite on the eighteenth floor.

In its miniature way it seems an extension of every cocktail party she's ever been to. No one's laughing, of course, and coffee and orange juice are sober reminders of the occasion's solemnity, but the same faces are there (practically every department of the network, every division of UBC, Incorporated, is represented, along with enough industry VIPs to make a broadcasters' convention—enough government, business, and show-business stars to sink an Earl Wilson column), and if in the crush, overflowing into the corridor, the password now is "death" (the victim a mere eighty-one years) instead of *Magazine* (a respectable 47 percent share of audience), the common bond is still numbers, the common good still the size of them. Missing only is the man with the big cigar, whose ghostly presence in a fashionable hotel suite makes the fate of a television program suddenly a relatively small matter in the wake of this morning's speculation over the fate of an empire.

Vivian can hardly make her way through. When at last she is inside the suite, she goes directly to the bedroom, where Ellen Abrams receives her with an outstretched hand, not a cheek to peck—a measure of the distance between them? Robert and M.J. receive her almost as coolly. She's introduced to several government people and within moments is back in the maelstrom. She speaks to some people, reserved exchanges, and looks around for Fred Wiener. She finally spies him in a corner, talking intently with Gerald McAlister and another man she doesn't know, his head bobbing as if he were dictating steps one through twenty in a memorandum. A few feet away, Mark stands in quiet conversation with some agency head (she's met him before but can't remember his name), and she supposes she should join him, as long as she's here. It's only right. She inches her way across to Mark and bears as best she can Frederick Chappel's (that's the man's name) involved account of how more than once David Abrams was able to soften the FCC's attitude toward broadcasters, of how he always was able to strike that delicate balance between service to the public and service to advertisers, of how sorely the industry would miss him. After several minutes of this (really an eternity in her state of mind), she sees Fred Wiener heading for the door with the man he's been talking with.

"I think I'll go on, Mark," she interrupts casually. "I have a few things to do before I meet Marian and Jenny Masters for lunch. I'll see you at the temple."

"Fine, dear." He barely looks at her.

"Nice to see you again," Chappel says absently, assuming a now-where-was-I expression, holding Mark practically prisoner in the crowded room.

In the corridor, mercifully, Fred has walked the man all the way to the elevators, one of which is just taking him from sight when she approaches them.

"Down?" Fred asks, starting to press the button for her.

"In just a minute," she says, looking back to make certain no one is coming.

"I have to get back," he says, annoyance visible when her gloved hand detains him.

"Fred, we have to talk."

"This isn't the time."

"I said I have to see you!" Her tone is controlled, but commanding. "Today. This afternoon. After the funeral. Just a few minutes. I need to talk to you. I'll be back in our suite—it's on seven, we're staying over—about four. I'm sure Mark won't be there. Ten minutes won't kill you."

"Look, Vivian . . ."

"You're not the only one in the cockpit, Fred. There are, I believe, two seats." She's surprised at how evenly she says it.

His eyes narrow, but he smiles. "All right, a few minutes. I'll call after the funeral."

She touches his fingers with her own and whispers, "Thank you, darling," unable to see what reaction, if any, comes to his already turned face.

Outside, in the midmorning heat, she feels almost giddy, almost a girl again—eager, made of softness and giving, full of splendor and secrets. There are troubles ahead, of course. Divorce is messy, any way you look at it—long months, legalities, the settlement. But oh, the release, the relief . . . She'll call her sister in Oklahoma City—yes, that's first. They'll take a cruise, a long one, the Mediterranean. Yes, the Mediterranean, lovely, and Fred can fly over—oh, some pretense or other—until the divorce is official, a foreign locale series, something—and she can join him somewhere, somewhere lovely, perhaps the Greek islands, Capri . . .

There are some shoes she wants to look at in I. Miller's before meeting Marian Graham and Jenny Masters at Mercurio's. Which will nicely take care of the morning.

And by then she'll be ready for a martini. A good, long, strong one. Two.

Three . . .

80

Joslyn Miller is standing by one of the windows in the bedroom of the eighteenth-floor suite. In a new black Pierre Cardin, so tight that she literally can't sit, she is hardly a figure one neglects in the grand parade. But between greetings and expressions of sorrow (she was, after all, David's niece), her mind is more alive than it has been in months. Like most of the people filing in and out of the spacious bedrooms, she tends to agree with the general refrain ("The end of an era . . . the beginning of a new one"), but for her it has a special meaning. Whereas the banality being tossed about so carelessly has something vaguely to do with a business, an industry—all right, maybe a creative enterprise—for her there is something intensely personal about it. The center of their world may have gone, but the world itself will go spinning on. What's changed is not so much the cast of characters as the billing.

But for herself—herself and Adrian—in some way her uncle David's death has signaled not only the end of a life but the start of new one—her own. Her very own.

This morning, for instance, in the company suite at the Gotham:

"Joslyn, will you for Christ's sake get a move on! We have to be there first. With Bobby. Jesus! What kind of idiot are you?"

"There's plenty of time. It's hardly light out, you know. Besides, Ellen needs her sleep. No one ever loved him like she did, you know."

"So what the hell does that have to do with being there?"

"Appearances. That's what it has to do with. Appearances."

"What the fuck are you trying to say?"

"What your whole life is. Appearances. Nothing but. That's what I'm saying. What a person's feeling, what he's thinking . . . pfft! Nothing. But let Mr. Right seem one eensy-weensy bit wrong and the whole sky falls down. Chicken Little shit with it."

"Now look, lady, I want no trouble from you today, you understand? There's enough already . . ."

"At stake, you mean? Enough at stake? Don't get that oh-this-stupid-broad-I'm-stuck-with expression on your face with me, mister. I've got your number, even if no one else has. Even if Uncle David went to his grave not knowing, which I doubt."

"Not knowing what?"

"That's for me to know and you to find out."

"Are you crazy?"

"You'll see. Oh, you'll see, mister. Oh, will you ever see."

She was not certain, perhaps, exactly what she meant, but she knew a thing or two, without question, nonetheless. One thing she knew was that he wouldn't lay a hand on her this time, he'd better not, and he didn't. And she knew too that she couldn't care less now what he and his precious Bobby might know about her terrible sometime need . . . lack . . . which Bobby had once been witness to, all those years ago. Even if Bobby finally tells him, or threatens to, she can handle it now. After all, she's the only surviving niece of the late David Abrams, the daughter of the late Bernard Strauss, his founding partner. Add that to the reality of her stock . . . oh, yes, damn right she can handle it. Because it's changed now. She can sense it, confirm it in the way Adrian looks at her, and Robert too—when he's not shaking his head, that is—in that mournful expression he bought somewhere, passing as it does for one whale of a deep-seated grief. And the strange thing Ellen said to her, even in the midst of a real, a terrible grief—"We're going to need each other, dear. We're doing to need each other very, very much."

"YOU HAVE our deepest sympathy, my dear."

"You'll be of great comfort to dear Ellen in the weeks to come, I know."

"Such a man. So . . . vital. We won't see the likes of him again."

"Well, at least he's with your own dear father now. The two of them, Bernie and David, together again, dreaming and doing the way they did in the beginning, all those years ago. . . ."

Even in the midst of the crush and the crud, she knows it. She's
something now. She's really something now.

IT DEPENDS ENTIRELY on the will.

That, at any rate, is what Adrian keeps telling himself. With the
Old Man's death so sudden and disruptive ("I'll live to be a hundred"—
how many times had they heard it at one of the Sunday suppers? And
been conditioned to take it as gospel?), the whole scene is radically
altered. Ellen Curry, always so quietly outside any talk of stock and
finances—now what? Where? Even with the "gifts" of stock the Old
Man has made over the years to Robert and M.J., the great bulk, the
nut, he kept intact. For Ellen. And together with Joslyn's . . .

He isn't certain when or how the thought occurred to him, but it is
now full force in his design, his strategy. The chess board is still there,
solid and intact. But the kings, the knights, the bishops, the rooks . . .
It's hard to know which way to move, which piece to move. Move up
to . . . Even to himself he has to smile scornfully and touch his nose:
pretty soon he'll be running out of behinds.

It's from the corner of an eye that he sees Robert in apparently
serious conversation with (of all people) Mark Banner, and Bill Kelly
in a corner of the bedroom where great bouquets of flowers almost
set it apart as a room of its own. Casually, he wanders over.

". . . but a program, a retrospective that does justice not to just the
man, but to our whole industry . . . that in such a relatively short time
we have come so far that a whole society . . . Oh, Adrian, I'm glad
you're here, I was just passing along some of my notions about the
program honoring father to Mark and Bill here. Perhaps you can en-
large on them." Robert is more animated, more articulate than Adrian
has seen or heard him in weeks. As if the father's passing brings the
rebirth of the son. . . . Old wives' tale, maybe, but seemingly true
here. His eyes (when they're not registering grief for an army of
sympathizers), the movement of his hands, the gestures of his shoulders, his head—there's a kind of excitement in him. An authority. And
a dozen or so pills? Adrian wonders.

"I'm sure you've covered it," he says. "I'd only suggest that on such
a tight schedule we ought to have three or four writers take a stab at
it, each independently of the other. I suspect it'll make it easier for us
to come up with a final draft. If ever there was a program by committee, this is it. One other thing, though. And this is where you come
in, Bill." He's not doing badly himself, he thinks. Their eyes are riveted
on him. "I do feel that it should have some perspective on the times
themselves. I mean, David Abrams' life spanned not only all of this

century, but the end years of the last. Which means that broadcasting, so to speak, has been the mirror of most of them, and the Old Man the living spirit of that."

"I think you should write it." Bill Kelly smiles.

"He already has," says Mark. "It's a good idea, though. Bill, I think we should get together first thing tomorrow. I've canceled my trip to the Coast."

"The show on the old man?" A new voice, grating. It can be none other than Maury Sherman's. "A seven share is what I bet the old man would say. But I agree we have to do it. If you need me, I'm available. After all, I lived through it, right along with David. . . . It's a good way to blow our own horn a little, too. Christ knows we blow everybody else's. They make our paydays, but we've got General Foods, General Motors, P&G, the oil companies up to our ass. Time we started taking advantage of our own facilities to talk about ourselves a little. I think the Old Man would have liked that. He always felt that most of the flak was over a misunderstanding of just what a television network is, what it does, what it contributes on its own. A show like this can go a long way in saying it. Especially when its star is the greatest goddamn broadcaster that ever lived. General Sarnoff or no General Sarnoff. Right, Mark?"

We really have to rid ourselves of this monstrosity, Adrian thinks. Now that his Great Protector is no longer around . . .

The talk goes on. Adrian listens, half-listens. Is more on edge even than Bobby.

If only he knew the terms and conditions of the will. If he only knew that.

81

THE TIME, for Robert, is not an easy one. When his mother died it was different. Then a part of him died too—a large part. His grief then was whole, his marrow sick with it. The last sight of her burned its way into his pores, his blood. She was there forever.

But this—today, yesterday, the night before. Not so uncomplicated, this. So many conflicts, in fact, have deposited themselves on his mind, his stomach, that finding peace with a dead father seems a distant reckoning indeed.

Last night at Campbell's Funeral Home (where the body has been on view for the family and close friends only) he had his moment alone with the cosmeticized, all-too-lifelike corpse. His moment alone, and not a single thought, not even a voluntary utterance to take away with him as some kind of solace, some comfort—some fury even, something. The ambiguity that marked their lives together from the very beginning is no less marked in the presence of death. *I feel nothing. I think nothing. I see nothing. I ask nothing. The awe, the fear, the need to please, displease—all these that shaped, misshaped our times together, our times apart—where? Isn't death the great divider, the time of temperance, of truth? "The other, let it sleep with death." But not mine, not ours. I see you now as I always saw you. You see me no more, no less than you ever did. You love me no more, no less than you ever did. You still laugh at me—no more, no less. You still berate me— no more, no less. I am neither freer nor more bound. Whatever death may be, tonight it says nothing. Gives nothing. Neither heat nor cold, love nor hate. Nothing. Not even a final word for me, farther? One I can take with me now, from this room, a greater hate, a greater love, a greater contempt, a greater awe? . . . They front-paged you in the* New York Times *today, father. They said a giant has passed this way. They really did. A giant of a man. Giant of a father . . .*

A curious energy in him today, though. He not only senses it himself, he senses its effect on others. Adrian, Mark Banner, Bill Kelly—they haven't stopped looking at him since they arrived. And Ellen too. Her eyes are seemingly on him every chance they get, as if somewhere in his liveliness she sees the secret compartment, the magic storehouse where all the answers they'll all be seeking are cunningly stored away, a tiny darkness where all the answers dwell. It's all he can do not to smile.

". . . and this other thing, the host. Father always admired Jimmy Stewart. Do you think it possible we might get him on such short notice?" He's in command today, he'll say that for himself. Never felt surer, more direct.

"No trouble there," Mark Banner says. "In a way, from an actor's viewpoint, it's the plum of the year."

"Nothing maudlin now, remember that. A tribute, a portrait, yes. But sit down hard on the rhetoric. That, I know I needn't tell you, father would raise hell over."

I am him now—at least that. Like it or not, approve it or not, it's a thing you'll have to live with, as I will. I am him now. How long. . . ?

82

SHE HAS WEPT her last, prayed her last. This now, this march of the emperor's subjects—these public hours, they're simply times to be got through, like the continuance of pain after the baby's been delivered. For Ellen Curry Abrams, the door is closed, the day past. The best is not yet to be. She's had her dream, her life. The rest is a living on, a living to.

Quietly, while some congressman or other is patting her hand, she whispers to Joslyn to ask Maury Sherman to come over to her. He's there in a moment, smiling. She beckons him to sit beside her on a small divan.

"I know," he says. "You got tired of all this pomp and wanted to talk dirty."

She takes his hand, squeezes it. "Stay a moment with me. Till this new group's gone, anyway."

They must be ten deep out there, she thinks. Not that it's really that tiring to see them all. She's often wondered what it would be like if all the people that have touched her life, whose lives she's touched, were to pass in procession before her, one by one.

"Ethel, how lovely . . ."

". . . and Frank, so kind . . ."

"Dear Lakey, you remembered. The old Blumhearst Theatre, what was the show?"

"And Tom. Sammy, dear. Those marvelous times, remember? When radio was forever and that silly upstart television . . ."

"Miriam. The war bond show. Of course!"

"Cal. Sister Rae. How David adored you! From that very first night in the Cotton Club, when was it . . . 1923? Twenty-four?"

"Mr. Davidson, how kind. David always spoke so well . . ."

". . . the night of the Shubert show, of course."

"The old Romanoff's, how I remember . . ."

"John."

"Martin."

"Addie."

"Julia."

"Sarah."

"Adam."

"Jim Bosworth . . ."

"Paul . . ."

Hamlin Hirschmyer presides over juice and coffee and sandwiches and French pastry. A small bar has been set up in the other room. The hellos and goodbyes are coming faster. Perhaps she'll have a bit of something herself in a moment. A glass of sherry. She leans across Maury to ask Fred Wiener if he'll bring her one. She notes the bloom of anticipation on his face. That, as they say (and if they don't, she does), is show business.

It is during a momentary lull that she says quietly to Maury Sherman, "In a few minutes a Mr. Richard Cohen, one of David's outside attorneys, will be here. He'll want to see Bobby, M.J., and myself for a little while. When I nod to you, I'd appreciate your helping Joslyn clear the room. You might actually start now, that's a dear. It's almost time."

She squeezes his hand again. There's no reason on earth, she knows, why she should be asking Maury Sherman to do such a menial thing, except to let him know, in some tangible way, how very fond of him David was and how much she herself appreciates him. She has long ago learned that asking small tasks of people can be a show of endearment that all the silver from Tiffany and all the crystal from Steuben could never convey.

Mr. Cohen and company arrive within seconds.

83

STEVE LILLY doesn't arrive until shortly before noon. Mainly because he's been thinking. He's had some two days, all right.

It began yesterday with fantasy, a vision of himself as president of the UBC Television Network. Waking (Beth's still-warm place empty beside him), he was at his executive best, blending authority with the knowing delegation of it, surely the quality that caught Gerald McAlister's eye in the first place. It was a luxurious waking, a proud one.

But the punctures started early. Right after showering he'd called Buzz Boland, one of Maury Sherman's assistants and the initial contact on overnight ratings, to learn the disastrous fate of Mark's crazy *Magazine*. Boland's excited report of a healthy forty-seven share, punctuated with lip-smacking predictions of how the overall Nielsen nationals were certain to be as good, maybe better (*Magazine's* strength, for example, has always seemed more likely in the one- and two-channel markets, more doubtful in the majors), had its sting. Too early to tell —a sampling week, after all—but the momentum was there, which meant Mark's flag would be high—well, higher, anyway—especially where it counted, in Westport and Mamaroneck. Of course, there *was* the untarnished other side of the coin: with *Magazine* well in the running, advertiser interest was bound to perk up, which meant that a few fast killings—hell, maybe even S.R.O.—would have Bobby Abrams singing "Lilly" in his sleep. So Thursday's first blow was handled, overcome with his usual resiliency, however naggingly it pursued him through breakfast.

The second annoyance (and it was no more than that) had occurred when he was leaving the house. Beth, kissing him absently—itself unusual—had said, "Steve, that secretary of Mark Banner's who killed herself. Wasn't she the pale blonde girl who acted so funny toward me at the Sales cocktail party last week?" He responded as though she had been seeing things that weren't there, but it rankled nonetheless. Like the reviews of the competition's new Wednesday-night shows. However, the first five minutes of his train ride into Manhattan helped counterbalance that one some. So again—for the moment, anyway—he was nearly even.

But he was hardly prepared for the big one. He was staring out the window, half-smiling to himself. (The reflection this time: Mark Banner was an eventual loser even if *Magazine* wasn't, hadn't McAlister assured him? And as for Barbara Ermeling—well, hell, who knew how many crazy problems that one had? He was sorry, sure. Sorry as hell. But he sure as hell wasn't fool enough to think he was the whole ball of wax. She'd have done it over something or somebody else sooner or later, wouldn't she?) Don Meadow, an NBC executive he knew only slightly but who sat with him occasionally on the morning trips in, had gone from an adjoining car, and, seeing him, called out loudly, "Lilly! I was wondring if you were on this train or if you'd taken an earlier one. I heard it on the radio just before I left. God, so sudden!"

"What's so sudden?" he said.

"Why, Abrams' dying like that. *Your* Abrams. You didn't know? Hell, Lilly, I'm sorry. . . ."

He had gone directly to the office, where the secretaries' faces were practically death masks, and for an hour or more refused to see a soul. Later, Wolf Glover and two or three of the other divisional sales managers had dropped in to chew the fat, and with each visit, each speculation, the day had grown darker, especially since Ellen Abrams, who now obviously held the reins, was Unknown Quantity Z, and it had been all he could do to drawl his assurances that nobody's job, for cryin' out loud, was in jeopardy. As for his private thoughts:

1. Ellen Abrams (or so McAlister hinted) has never really liked Mark Banner all that much for all the old man's crap. Wishful thinking? . . .
2. Fred Wiener is pretty close to all of them—"family," you know.
3. Fred Wiener holds the trumps now.
4. Wiener is a Jew.
5. That takes care of Wiener. As far as Bobby and Adrian Miller are concerned, anyway. Which is pretty far country.
6. Hell, nothing has changed.
7. If anything, he is in a better position than ever. Ellen Abrams is now a grief-stricken woman, isn't she? She needs the aid and comfort of a real son. . . .

And with that, an hour or two of that (wedged between phone calls, sales reports, memorandums, the morning mail, rescheduling of appointments), he'd been sufficiently cheered—well, enough anyway to be his familiar good-natured self, modified appropriately for the funereal occasion.

Until he'd gone up to Mark Banner's office, that is. For even with Mark out (over at the funeral home before going to the Waldorf, where the family was receiving people), his hawkeyed secretary Edith was very much in.

So quietly she'd said it. Almost a sigh. "Marvelous country, this. More people should know about it. Murderers get to walk the streets just like everybody else."

He'd waited to burn until he got back to his office. But even that had seemed the wrong place to be. To have to be. He'd closed out the day and gone home, saying as little as possible to Beth and the kids, taking a few necessary calls from clients on the Old Man's passing, what it might mean to the network, watching a Knicks game on television, turning in early.

Sleeping late. Waking uneasily.

Forgetting to kiss Beth goodbye.

THE CROWDS in the suite have thinned considerably by the time he arrives. Mark and Fred Wiener are nowhere in sight, and Gerald McAlister, if he saw him come in (and Steve is certain he did), makes no acknowledgment of his presence. Pausing here and there to shake hands with men he knows from UBC or elsewhere ("Lord, this is somethin', isn't it? Isn't this somethin'?"—shaking his head sadly, moving on to the next one), Steve is admitted to the bedroom by an old man he doesn't know, an old man whose cadaverous flesh only heightens his sharp Semitic features, and after a word or two of condolence to Queen Ellen (who sits graciously, even regally, in a corner chair), is introduced by her—to relatives mostly, some show-business people—as "Sam" Lilly, which at the moment is equivalent to cutting his heart out with a machete. *Grief-stricken widow . . . aid and comfort*—who was he kidding?)

Though properly boiling, he's himself—*Steve* Lilly—when he comes out. Looking about, he sees that McAlister, who before had appeared to be giving instructions to Sarah whatever-her-name-was, Abrams' ice-assed secretary, is alone near the door, staring out into the corridor as if he's pining for someone. Steve is beside him in an instant. "Anything I can do, Jerry?" he asks quietly, which he knows sounds absurd, except that it is the Southern Christian thing to say.

McAlister shakes his head without looking at him and, almost imperceptibly, backs away.

There is suddenly nothing else to say. Steve can't recall ever having felt so awkward. Shifting from one foot to the other, he senses immediately that the man is frost itself; that there is more than just shock and grief in his downcast eyes; that there is something hard—deliberate—that goddamnit he is actually being cold-goddamn-shouldered.

Fred Wiener, emerging suddenly from the corridor, brushes busily past them, heading for the telephone on a corner table. It would be obvious even to a stranger that the pivot has just walked in. Lifting the phone, speaking softly into it, he is unmistakably the man of the moment. Every eye in the room seems to confirm his ascendance.

"You'll have to excuse me," McAlister says abruptly. "Fred's in charge of arrangements, of course, and he'll be needing me." The last view Steve has of him is with his face close to Wiener's, awaiting assignment, and it is an image not likely to leave him for some hours to come.

Nor is the image of Maury Sherman, directly across from him in a group of strangers, the look of contempt on his face the most open Steve has ever seen on any man, anywhere. That damn kike Maury Sherman. Now why? Why? The Ermeling broad, probably. Sure, the girl's suicide, had to be. And that's all he needs today. Edith and Sherman and all their shit on a day when it looks like his whole world is coming unscrewed. . . .

Well, this is clearly no place for him today, nosireebob. No place for Doreen Lilly's boy Steve.

When he leaves the suite, five minutes or so later, he knows he can't go to the office, not for a while anyway. He's canceled his lunch date, thank God; he isn't ready for food just yet. He thinks about playing

golf, but doesn't want to see anybody—or be seen. Besides, the funeral.
Still, he has to think. That's all—just be alone and think. That stinkin'
friggin' McAlister . . . He has to think. Just be somewhere and think.
There are some great thinking bars on Lexington.

84

TEMPLE EMANU-EL on Fifth Avenue is one of the largest temples
in the world. Today it seems like one of the smallest. They're everywhere—the people. The most famous faces in the country are surrounded by a crowd of nameless, faceless beings, most of them there,
of course, because of Ellen's still legendary fame. Traffic has been dis-
rupted for fifteen blocks.

The service itself is short, concise, as Ellen had ordered it. The brief
eulogy is spoken in the familiarly orotund tones of UBC's Barry White.
Mark hears only fragments of it. Even the few Hebrew passages go
nearly unnoticed, the more sonorous readings like "Praised be Thou,
O Lord, God of our fathers, God of Abraham, Isaac and Jacob, great,
mighty, and exalted. Thou bestowest loving kindness upon all thy
children. Thou rememberest the devotion of the faithful. In Thy love
Thou bringest redemption to their descendents for the sake of Thy
name. Thou art our King and Helper"—these too go mostly unheard.
Perhaps a number of these people are professional funeral-goers, Mark
thinks. He's heard of such people all his life, never knowingly seen
them. He has never seen so many tears, heard so many laments in a
single place of worship in all his life. He finds himself strangely but
deeply moved. He wonders if Vivian, beside him, feels anything. Her
face is almost totally expressionless, except for an occasional half-
strangled hiccough that completely disarranges it—the result, he's sure,
of one martini too many at lunch.

The service at graveside, at Mount Sinai Cemetery, in a plot that has
been set aside for a David Abrams chapel, is shorter still, and suddenly,
as though without notice, the man himself is gone, taken from them.
He will not be there when one returns to the hotel. He will not be
there when one goes to the office on Monday. That quick. That sudden. That final. Unbelievable.

BACK in Ellen's suite at the Waldorf, Vivian says, "I'll just say a word to her and to Bobby, and then go back to our rooms and lie down. Will you be here?"

"For a while, yes."

"And then?"

"Would you like dinner sent up or would you like to eat out?"

"I don't know. I'll have to see. I'll just have to *see.*"

He's seen her nervous before, but never like this. He should talk to her about the drinking. Then he remembers it's not for him to talk to her about anything anymore.

The suite is filling up again. There are even more people here now than there were this morning. For a few moments Ellen is again closeted with M.J. and Robert and three men Mark has never seen before, presumably attorneys. When the door to the bedroom does open, a tight-lipped Robert emerges first, followed by a slightly bewildered-looking Mandy Jo and the poker-faced strangers. Only Ellen remains behind, waiting again to receive, and in the depths of her sadness, so telling in eyes that tell all there is, a very small smile.

"Mark," she leans to whisper, "I'll want a few words alone with you in an hour or so. Help play host in the meantime, would you?"

He nods.

"I'm going back to our suite," says Vivian. And seems in a considerable hurry to get there.

SHE FEELS LIKE LAUGHING. No reason really, except that her head is swimming with plans, she's still somewhat exhilarated by the three martinis she had at Mercurio's, and now she's waiting for Fred Wiener.

She's been back in the suite a half hour, long enough to bathe again, dress—an elegant orchid dressing gown she picked up at Bonwit's just after lunch. She's decided to wear a slip underneath it. She can afford the touch of restraint. She looks glorious. She's sure of it.

He arrives at three-forty-five. Opening the door for him (his rap is cautious), she wonders for a moment if perhaps the exposed cleavage of her breasts—the gown's front is V'd to her navel—doesn't render her almost a caricature of seduction, a worry swiftly confirmed by Fred's narrowing eyes and the way in which he says, "Unlike Antony, madam, *I* came to talk." But laughing softly, making light of what God knows she hasn't intended to make light of, she pulls him into the room.

"I can't stay," he says shortly. "This is a rough day, Vivian. Ellen and Uncle Bob, and of course M.J., need me. I only came because you seemed so . . ."

"Insistent? Very. Sit down, Fred." She'll be damned if he'll play wham-bam-thank-you-ma'am with her today. Not today. The hotel caterers aren't due with cocktails until six (Mark had told her that just before she left Ellen's suite), and with all of Ellen Curry's old friends, there's no reason . . .

"Just what is so urgent, Vivian?"

She holds out a package of cigarettes.

"No, thank you," he says, sitting impatiently on the edge of a chair.

She sits across from him. When she's lit a cigarette, inhaled, released the smoke (good! He hasn't taken his eyes from her), she leans forward and smiles. "I'm leaving Mark," she says.

"Oh?" Not a muscle in his face moves.

"I told him this morning."

Slivers of light, thieving through the blinds of a window where the drapes are only partially drawn, lie on one section of the carpet like dead speckled fish. Two three-way lamps, one in a far corner, the other near Fred, are both on low, desperately dim. The room is dark, darker than she'd intended.

"Well, that's your affair," he says. "I don't see what it has to do with me." (He doesn't add that, on the contrary, she's finally washed them up . . . that she was of use to him only so long as she and Mark were solidly married. If Mark doesn't care, can't be threatened with exposure as a cuckold . . . well, goodbye, Vivian.)

She cocks her head—saucily, she hopes. She'd fully expected his initial reaction would be like this. Men like Fred Wiener have to be backed into corners (or under rocks). "Sooner or later it probably would have happened," she says, "with or without you. But you were around, darling, you were the catalyst. You're the lucky Johnny-on-the-spot, darling. Now don't be difficult. I'm no what's-her-name . . . you know, the poor little girl I hear Steve Lilly drove to her—"

He laughs. "My God, Vivian, stop the Theda Bara act. Come on, you honestly believe that a couple of lays . . . ? Hell, you just said it yourself—you were in the market for a beachboy, with or without the beach." He shakes his head. "You kill me, lady, you really do. Tell me: just exactly what leading role am I supposed to be playing in your little farce? Pardon me . . . *drama*. Sometimes it's according to who's in the audience, isn't it?"

She neither moves nor changes expression. "You're running scared, of course," she says, "but then I expected that. And don't look so sure of yourself. You're not fooling me. I know you a little too well, Freddie. You haven't exactly been suffering with me. You're *here*, aren't you? You want me too. I excite you and you know it."

"So? So what does any of that have to do with running off hand in hand into the sunset?"

"Oh, Freddie, stop it. Why do we always have to . . . ?" She mashes her cigarette into an ashtray, stalking embers with it until a wide circle of black relieves her fingers of a sorely needed function. "Let's start all over again," she says. "You just came in, all right? You just sat down." She sits up straight, lights another cigarette, inhales and says, "Fred, I'm leaving Mark."

"Congratulations."

She smiles slightly but says, "Freddie, I'm not playing games. Please."

He makes a mock gesture of concession. "All right, you're not playing games. Your way, then. My first reaction? You picked a lovely goddamn time. And now I have to get back to Ellen. Much to do. You see, Vivian, there happens to be—"

"Fred!"

"Oh, cut it out, Vivian. I'm not even slightly involved in what you do about Mark, whether you leave him or go to Vladivostok with him, so cover up those ridiculous melons and better luck next time. Okay?" He stands up.

She starts to rise too, but she isn't sure she can stand. "Fred, this is all so silly. We ... I'm not leaving him *today*, if that's what's annoying you. I plan to wait a few days, of course, and then ... Fred, it really can work out. You could meet me somewhere in Europe—no one need know. You could go over for program ideas or something. ... Freddie, my God, what do I have to do?"

"Get another writer," he says.

"Oh, Jesus, Freddie ..." And then, with effort, straightens. "I'm warning you, Freddie—"

"Look, let's get one thing straight. If you're about to threaten to use my name with Mark, you go right ahead. Just remember who undressed who."

"But you're *involved* with me. You can't just have it any way you want without even the smallest responsibility."

"Responsibility? Oh-ho, so that's it? I'm supposed to be your way out. Off the sinking ship ... You're crazy, you know that? You didn't seriously think ..."

"You're the one who isn't thinking! *You* work for Mark, remember? Mark's not *your* messenger boy. Not just yet." (And saying it, she knows how hollow it sounds, how hollow it *is*.)

He starts to answer her, is stopped by the desperate look of her. He moves toward the door, but before he can take two steps she's in front of him, blocking him. "Fred, don't leave. I don't know what got into me, it'll be the way you want it, anyway it doesn't matter, just please don't leave ..." almost pushing him off balance.

"Jesus!" He removes her like a raincoat. "You're in a bad way, you know it? You're a beautiful woman, Vivian. Why do you have to make yourself so ugly?"

"Fred, don't. All I want—"

"I'm quite aware of what you want."

"Fred . . . Freddie . . . I don't understand you. On Monday . . . Wednesday . . ."

"Monday and Wednesday were the Middle Ages," he says. "This is Friday."

"But you—"

"Christ, let it go, Vivian. Do yourself a favor. Go to Rome. I hear the Italians are all studs, walk around with all-day hard ons."

She slaps him—hard—she at least does that. But tears are pouring from her eyes, she's shaking, her throat screams. "What is it? What's wrong with me? What in *God's* name is wrong with me?"

"Maybe you just piss him off, too" he says. "God, that is." And he finally makes it out the door.

85

THEIR MOMENT ALONE comes around five-thirty.

"Mark," she says, smiling briefly at him, then starting to pace: the Ellen Curry of all those thousands of *Ellen Curry Hours,* all those hundreds of *Ellen Curry Presents*—the star herself at stage center and never forget it. "It's much too early to say all this, there's so much to be thought out, talked over, who knows what else. But there's something I felt you should know, and after talking it over with Joslyn I've decided to tell you. Besides, there's Bobby and M.J. . . . . Fred, too . . . had to be told."

He hears a beating, but it can't be him—his heart has stopped.

"David, without any of us knowing, added a codicil to his will about two weeks ago." She stops pacing, sits on the bed beside him. "He said in it that he felt it was his duty, even from the grave, to advise on the corporate structure of the company he'd built from those two little wireless stations in Providence and Atlanta over a half-century ago. What he hoped for, Mark, was of course that Bobby would be named chairman of the Board and chief executive officer, and, directly under him, you. As president of United Broadcasting Companies, Inc." She stops abruptly. "Excuse me, dear. Are you all right?"

He *is* something to see. Shock has frozen itself to his face. It is only by slow degrees that his consciousness is again focused on her.

"The reason I can say this to you now is that my inherited stock, combined with Joslyn's, gives us a voting power not merely equal to but actually greater than the combination of Robert's and Mandy Jo's. The Board members have already been told of all this. Of course they're not bound to follow David's wishes, but a straw vote has shown they're in favor."

She stands again, again paces.

"I wanted you to hear this from me, Mark, because we both know that Bobby would have moved heaven and earth to be free of you. So we have to start from that rather unpleasant premise. Which means that, if you accept the position, you'll have no easy time of it. Quite the opposite. Bobby will have to work with you, of course. And vice versa. Quite closely. There's no other way."

She stops in front of him, touches his face lightly. "I know you're wondering where Adrian comes into all this. We're all wondering. I won't go into the reasons why Joslyn decided to block her stock with mine, except that it's a firm decision of hers. She's like a changed person. I can also tell you that, as a member of the Board, I plan to be active. I believe it's what David would have wanted.

"One other thing you should know. In the codicil David said that while your ideas may not always have worked out, and while your means to an end may have been different, there never was any doubt in his mind that, like him, you tried to put the audience, the viewer, above any other consideration. This meant a great deal to him. A very great deal, I can tell you. His last words in the codicil were that 'even in a tough competitive climate Mark Banner remains a man of moral intelligence.' Pretty grand for my David, wouldn't you say? And for you, Mark. I'll see that in time you receive a copy of that part of it."

When the numbness finally passes from him, when he at least feels himself move, feels touch again, he says, "Adrian . . . I don't understand, I just . . . don't understand. And the television network . . . especially now. It's such a crucial time for it."

She nods, sits again. "I agree. As for Adrian . . . well, I'd say he's as much on the limb as off it. He's status quo. Which means, of course, reporting to Robert as he does now, and in an advisory capacity, I suppose. It's such a confusing time. In the end . . . Oh. One other thing. David mentioned Maury Sherman too. As a very good, very loyal and decent man. It wouldn't surprise me at all to see you put him in your present chair as an interim move, senior vice president or something. You boys are good at coming up with titles." She smiles. "But something, Mark. Until you can name a network president to replace you, that is."

She stands. It's almost over.

"We'll talk again later, tomorrow. Meanwhile, we all just go on.

He was a big man, Mark, my David. I hope . . . I *know* that we'll be able to say that about you one of these days."

He leaves her, dazed, and almost immediately collides with Robert, who says, more stiff-necked than ever, "We shall speak together over the weekend. I'm sure there is much we have to say to each other."

Adrian is nowhere around. Nor is Steve Lilly. Only Fred Wiener and Gerald McAlister, their heads more closely together than ever, their desultory faces almost comical in what can only be assumed is their bitter frustration. In a near trance still, Mark leaves them to their pickings, moving swiftly into the corridor and an elevator that takes him down to the seventh floor.

VIVIAN, IN TEARS, is several martinis ahead of him. "Sinking ship," Freddie had said. Hers? Or Mark's?

"Mark! Oh, Mark, thank heaven you're here. Oh, my dear, my poor dear, I'd no idea you were in such straits. None at all. God, I'd never have added to your burden at a time like this . . ."

It takes him several minutes to calm her, if not bring her precisely to coherence. "Who the hell have you been talking to?"

"Freddie. Fred Wiener. He said that you—"

Mark's laughter (how long since she's heard it?) fills the room. "Fred Wiener," he says. "Sonofabitch'll be lucky if he still has a job Monday."

She mixes herself another drink, stares quizzically at him. "Then you're not . . . ?"

"Not exactly," he says, reaching across a chair for a briefcase.

"You're going somewhere?" she says. "At this hour?"

"To the office for a few minutes. Just something I want to do."

She comes from around the small bar to stand beside him. "Mark. Mark, forgive me, please. I don't know what I was talking about, saying I was leaving you. I . . . I don't think I've been well lately. Perhaps a cruise with my sister . . . You could join us somewhere, Mark. Anywhere you like. And we'd be together, just the two of us, like we—"

"Go to bed, Vivian," he says. "Just can it and go on to bed."

"But what about dinner?"

"Order up if you want. I don't know when I'll be back."

"Mark," she says, falling across a sofa, "Mark, don't. Don't be cold like this. I need you, darling. I do, Mark. I swear to God. Mark, what would I *do* . . . ?"

At the door to the hall, as he puts his hand on the knob, it's too much to resist. "Well," he says, "with all this great playacting, we might as well go whole hog, as Steve Lilly'd say." He pauses and looks her right in the eye. "As a well-known character says at the end of a very well-known film—which by the way CBS beat us out for the television rights to by half a million, if memory serves—anyway, as this well-known character says as he goes out the door, 'Frankly, my dear, I don't give a damn.'"

IT'S ALMOST SEVEN. The UBC Building is of course all but deserted. Mark nods to one of the three security guards in the lobby, signs himself in, and waits while one of the guards prepares to take him to his floor.

Where he is surprised to see Edith.

"I just couldn't get myself to move," she says. "I suppose it's everything happening at once the way it has. Mr. Abrams . . . poor Barbara . . ." She takes a deep breath and looks up. "And how fare you, fearless leader?"

Quietly, he tells her.

When he's finished she says, "Maybe that's why I didn't go home. Maybe some sixth sense was holding me here. I'll be goddamned."

He laughs.

"You're the first one I've told all this to Edith. I wasn't asked not to, but under the circumstances I'm taking it on myself to roll over and play dumb for a while."

"And say, 'Wow!'"

"Yes," he says, "and say, 'Wow!'"

"Have you spoken to Mr. Abrams yet?"

"Briefly."

"Rough weather ahead, huh?"

"Pretty rough."

"Well, I don't want to make it any rougher, but there's one thing I have to get off my mind."

"What's that?"

"Steve Lilly. He's murder. I mean it. Ask me no questions, I'll . . ."

"Barbara," he says. "I thought so. Okay. No questions asked. . . . So. Here we are."

She smiles. "I'll tell you one thing. I'm going to make my darling husband take me out for a good thick steak tonight. Not only to celebrate. I think I'll need the energy. All I can get."

"That you will, babe. That you will."

"Well. I'm glad I hung around. And there is one good thing I see coming out of it."

"Oh?"

"The mail boys will henceforth and forever call me *Mrs.* Stewart."

"Have a good weekend, Edith. Next week sometime Vivian and I . . . that is, *I* want to take you out for a drink on this. A deal?"

"A deal. All marvelous things to you, Mark. All marvelous things to UBC because of you."

> Who is this and what is here?
> And in the lighted palace near
> Died the sound of royal cheer;
> And they crossed themselves for fear,
>   All the knights at Camelot.

Why he should remember this (Tennyson, isn't it? "The Lady of Shalott"?) in a quiet private moment of putting a few pieces back together is beyond him. He'd been sitting at his desk, doodling on a pad, trying to draw a bead on the television network generally, the presidency and program and sales heads particularly, when the old memorized verse had marched itself onto the stage of his thinking, tossing aside everything and everybody in its path. Fred Wiener, Steve Lilly, and Gerald McAlister in particular had been pretty well knocked about, with Wolf Glover as a possible replacement for Lilly and Maury Sherman hanking tough, shouting a number of choice epithets for the record.

"And they crossed themselves for fear, all the knights . . ." He's very tired, he knows it. It still hasn't hit him, not really; not in any sudden-jolt kind of way.

President of United Broadcasting Companies, Incorporated.

Vivian. He's not so proud of that exit line, no matter how justified it may have been. Will he ever sleep tonight? Where? In the suite with Vivian?

He looks up just in time to catch Joel Greer standing in the doorway.

"Hey," he says, "you want to give a guy a coronary? You know what time it is? What the hell are you doing here?"

Joel shrugs. "I don't know. I got involved in a script, I guess, and . . . No, no, that's bullshit. I think I was trying to clean out my mind the way you clean out your desk, and it just got worse and worse as I went along. Like the crap in my desk, I guess I couldn't bring myself to throw anything away."

"Join the club."

"Everything all right at the hotel?"

"Big crowd. I imagine Ellen's out on her feet. She's a marvel, though. A real wonder."

"I'll stop over tomorrow. Janet wants to go with me."

"You should."

Joel has taken a chair across from him, easily, not even questioningly, and on impulse (one he has long since learned to trust) he says, "Joel, what would you think of doing *Magazine* on a twice-weekly basis next year? Assuming it's successful this season, that is. You know, the way we do movies now. *The Wednesday Magazine of the Air, The Friday Magazine of the Air,* that kind of thing."

"I've thought about it," says Joel. "I really have. One big advantage in it, you open yourself up for that many more new writers, producers, directors."

"Hey, I like that. I'll talk to Jack Stroud about it. Has a good promotional feel to it, too. And a format flexible enough for news breaks, convention and election coverage, presidential or other newsmaking interviews, for sports events too, like the Olympics. For . . . anything. The way I think television was meant to be used, meant to be opened up. Hell, you could have short plays, long plays, symphonies, rock concerts. Opera segments, ballet; even, don't drop dead, an occasional poetry reading, for Christ's sake. And by God, no more of that crap about what's commercial and what's not. With so many different and entertaining elements it could be the advertiser's dream come true. I believe it"—a quick smile—"but keep it under your hat for a while, okay? I'd like to keep this job for the weekend, anyway."

"And as much live as possible too," Joel says, caught up in Mark's enthusiasm. "We rely pretty heavily on film and tape."

Mark is damn near beaming. "And as long as we do, we'll just be a Xerox of the real thing. I couldn't agree more, Joel. With live cameras, with that good old moment-to-moment excitement we seem to have sacrificed for the expediency and professionalism of film . . . with that again we'll be back doing our own thing. Which may compensate a little even for taking you away from that novel for a while."

"Something to sleep on," says Joel, dazzled. "If sleep's still on the schedule, that is."

"It's on. I decree it." Smiling tiredly. "Joel, have you by any chance read Tom Wicker's *A Time to Die?*"

"No, no, I haven't."

"Well, among other things, he says you can't make a revolution with rosewater, and you have to be realistic even when you *are* a revolutionary. I buy those."

Joel nods. "I thought the party line was evolution, not revolution."

"Sometimes," says Mark, "the party line manages to get disconnected. . . . Joel, does this novel you've taken up again mean that much to you? Be honest, now."

"I wish I could answer that," he says. "It's a hell of a thing, Mark. Almost as if I'm two different people. There's also the sneaking suspicion that all this novel talk again comes out of some uneasiness here, which we've already talked about. And then there's Janet. She's in her make-a-Balzac-out-of-him phase again. Maybe she's pregnant again. She decided I was the American Flaubert when she was carrying Richie."

Mark's staring at him hard, through the latticework of fingers cover-ing his face. "Tell me this," he says. "If on Monday or Tuesday next week you were offered the job of vice president in charge of Program-ming, what would you say?"

Joel understands that the question is a serious one. "Right now? Right now, I'd say yes, Mark. Provided Fred Wiener had nothing to do with me. And provided I could work with you."

Mark knows he's taking a risk, decides he has to do it. "I accept that answer, Joel, and will speak with you again on Monday at"—he looks briefly at his calendar—"at three-thirty Monday afternoon. Now, if you'll excuse me, I have a couple of things to wrap up here."

Joel Greer, departing, shares the state of shock more than a few others have discovered during the last few hours.

> Out flew the web and floated wide:
> The mirror cracked from side to side:
> "The curse is come upon me," cried
>
> • • •

Call it the curiosity in him, the ego of him, a way to get those damn verses out of his mind once and for all, call it what the hell you will— he is suddenly and compulsively on the forty-second floor—the place of kings and czars.

His place?

At first he finds the darkness warm and reassuring, shadows of so many shades and depths that the variations themselves are playful, almost flirtatious. The sanctum he has always found so forbidding is strangely seductive when its lights are out, its occupants departed. He is tempted to laugh out loud, sing—something. He's glad he doesn't. From a far corner a vague light shows, for a moment only, then a figure emerges, swallowed by the shadows for one of their own. As he nears the double doors leading to the elevators Mark makes it out. Adrian.

Who sees him in practically the same instant.

"Well. Look who's here. The newly anointed come to the altar. Welcome."

"Caught in the act," Mark says, starting toward the doors.

"Wait. It's a good time for a word. We need that, you know."

Mark waits impatiently.

Adrian comes nearer. "Have you seen Bobby?" he says.

"Yes. At the hotel. For a moment."

"I presume you noticed he's somewhat, so to say, fit to be tied."

"Yes."

"Tell me, Mark. How did you react when she told you? Ellen, I mean. I *presume* she told you."

"Yes," says Mark. "A few minutes ago, in fact. I'm still trying to absorb it."

"I see. Yes, it *is* something that needs a bit of getting accustomed to. Did you talk to my wife, by any chance?"

"Joslyn? No."

"You must make it a point to talk to her. For the first time in all these years, you know, she acted independently of my judgment. She went it alone, you might say. She was—is—the deciding factor, you know. You owe her a great deal. As do I," he adds. "I suppose you could call it getting back at me after all these years. For letting her live, I mean." Pause. "Ah, well, the deed is done. I'm sure you realize what a . . . shall we say tenuous position I'm in? Neither fish nor fowl nor billy goat, as they used to say at the orphanage. But then, coming from an orphanage, I'm confident we'll find a home for me. The *right* home. Somehow it always manages to work itself out. . . . You know, Mark, there may be starts and stops in this business, but there are no beginnings and ends. I'm sure I needn't tell *you* that. None of my protégés has ever worked out so satisfactorily. You're a credit to my judgment, Mark. A quality in which I have never been found wanting."

It's not so much the words, the sense of them. It's the tone. It's all the phoney actors that have passed across his horizon in his years in the business. Mark is glad he can barely make out his face. It makes it easier.

"It's odd," the voice drones on. "I really don't feel anything's different. As on many nights when I've been the last to leave, it's a simple look in either direction, to make sure Robert's lights are off. And the Old Man's." He's nearer now, the breath is felt. "Lord . . . Wiener, Lilly, McAlister . . . Must be many a shoe doing a St. Vitus dance tonight."

An arm—so comradely an arm—is on his shoulder. "Let's complete the journey you're on, what do you say? Come on."

Mark warily follows him, knowing it's to Robert Abrams' suite of offices. Adrian unlocks the outer door leading to the enormous secretarial and reception area, then just as deftly turns the key to the gargantuan office itself. "It's my assumption that Bobby will take the Old Man's suite, leaving this for you. I'm rather certain of it, in fact. It's what's called ineluctable logic."

One whack, Mark thinks, across that handsome expanse of face. One whack . . .

"The fair Arrabella's possessions will fit so much better in the other offices."

Suddenly Mark finds himself bathed in light, overpowered by it. The great antiques are like haunts in a nightmare.

"Turn it off!" Mark says. Commands.

The darkness again, blessed darkness; a moment or two to readjust to it.

"So." The voice, much to his chagrin, has undergone no change. It drones, unstoppably on. "Here we are. Why don't you just stay on here a moment? Alone. There's just enough light from the city out there to give you a rare view of your new home. Your new aerie. Just make sure you lock the doors from the inside when you leave."

Mark, staring at the draped windows through which slivers of light from surrounding skyscrapers edge cautiously in, hears the voice lowering, softening; retreating.

"A long trip from Monday to Friday . . ."

"Yes," he says, momentarily caught up in Adrian's mood despite himself, "it was."

"Longer to come. Rougher, too."

"I'm sure."

"The fickle old bitch herself." That pause, how lovingly he uses it. "Clichéd as hell, but right for the business we're in. Like it or not. What do you think?"

"I think you'll find it more to Bobby Abrams' liking than mine."

"Well. We *are* the command post, aren't we? And to think, Adrian, old man, you raised him from a pup. Your greatest discovery, old fellow, you'll have to admit. But then, like so much in this business, it gets so you can't tell up from down without a compass. . . . You should count your blessings, old man, that I'm around to get you off on the right track with Bobby."

"It'll all work out, Adrian," he says. "I'll see to that."

"I'm sure you will. The irony of uncompromising directives from the grave is the compromise they generally impose upon the living. Or something like that. Well. Again, congratulations, Mark. Now, if you'll excuse me? I can restrain myself no longer from getting my beloved helpmeet home and—"

"Good night, Adrian. Have a pleasant weekend."

"Thanks. After all, it was, when all's said and done, one really dandy, one really hell of a week. In one hell of a business. Wouldn't you say?"

"I would," says Mark.

FOR LONG MOMENTS (they seem like long moments) he stands at the windows of the formidable office, looking down, across, up—no direction. His thoughts are uncertain, only David Abrams large and comfortable in them. Somewhere in them, too, is the back-to-reality recollection of what just about everybody has forgotten—the new half-hour comedy series *The Winston Family* is premiering tonight, a series important to the whole Friday-night comedy line-up on UBC. . . . But it doesn't stay with him. How can it? Win or lose, it will all go on. Friday night. Saturday night, Sunday night. Monday . . .

ABC, CBS, NBC . . .

UBC.

AFTER A WHILE he leaves the office, not forgetting, even in the trance he's made for himself, to close and lock all the doors. As he's making his way from them, though—through the multishadowed darkness—he finds himself stopped, frozen in his tracks. He realizes he is standing just outside the Old Man's suite of offices, and that from inside them, in a way more real and alive than anything else about this night, there comes the infectious laugh that has always distinguished this particular corner from the other offices on the floor, accompanied by the sweet, strong smell of a Corona-Corona, the smoke filtering through doors and walls, until he's completely enclosed by it. . . .

He makes his way on. But the smoke and the laughter follow him all the way to the elevators, even down to his own office on the fortieth floor.

His *old* office on the fortieth floor.

Where he sits down, breathes easier. It will take a while.

ANSELL
GIANTS

51896
78

9.95

DISCARDED

OSSINING PUBLIC LIBRARY

WILson 1-2416

HOURS

M. T. W. TH.   10 - 9
F.   10 - 5:30
S.   9 - 5:30
Closed Sun. & Holidays

DO NOT REMOVE CARDS

MAY 21 1976

DEMCO